Praise for the Merch

'A marvelous romp through this
master of the imaginative thrill-r... ...ese books will remain
on my shelf for many years to come'
Karl Schroeder

'Inventive, irreverent, and delightful . . . an alternate world
where business is simultaneously low and high tech, and where
romance, murder, marriage, and business are hopelessly
intertwined – and deadly.
L. E. Modesitt, Jr.

'Shocks, surprises, reversals, and elaborations keep tumbling from
Stross's nimble fingers . . . These books are immense fun'
Locus

'Fantasies with this much invention, wit and gusto don't
come along every day'
SFX

'Fans of the author's previous work will recognize his trademark
skill at world building – you can almost see the filth on the streets of
New England, feel the closeted oppression of the Clan hierarchy,
and experience Miriam's terror at the horrifying circumstances
she finds herself in'
SciFiNow

'Fast-moving action with a number of interesting characters . . .
Stross's ability to combine interesting ideas with solid plotting
is one of his great strengths'
Asimov's Science Fiction

THE REVOLUTION TRADE

Charles Stross was born in Leeds, England, in 1964. He has worked as a pharmacist, software engineer and freelance journalist, but now writes full-time. To date, Stross has won two Hugo awards and been nominated twelve times. He has also won the Locus Award for Best Novel, the Locus Award for Best Novella and has been shortlisted for the Arthur C. Clarke and Nebula Awards. In addition, his fiction has been translated into around a dozen languages.

Stross lives in Edinburgh, Scotland, with his wife Feòrag, a couple of cats, several thousand books, and an ever-changing herd of obsolescent computers.

By Charles Stross

The Merchant Princes series

The Bloodline Feud

(Originally published as *The Family Trade* and *The Hidden Family*)

The Traders' War

(Originally published as *The Clan Corporate* and *The Merchants' War*)

The Revolution Trade

(Originally published as *The Revolution Business* and *The Trade of Queens*)

THE

REVOLUTION
TRADE

Originally published as

THE REVOLUTION BUSINESS and THE TRADE OF QUEENS

Charles Stross

TOR

The Revolution Business first published 2009 by Tor, Tom Doherty Associates, NY
The Trade of Queens first published 2010 by Tor, Tom Doherty Associates, NY

This revised and updated edition is published 2013 by Tor
an imprint of Pan Macmillan
20 New Wharf Road, London N1 9RR
Associated companies throughout the world
www.panmacmillan.com

ISBN 978-1-4472-3764-8

5 7 9 8 6 4

A CIP catalogue record for this book is available from the British Library.

Typeset by Ellipsis Digital Limited, Glasgow
Printed and bound in Great Britain by CPI Group (UK) Ltd, Croydon, CR0 4YY

For Gav: better read than dead

Acknowledgments

This is the third omnibus collecting an ongoing series of six novels – and the final one in this story line. It wouldn't exist without help from a multitude of people; no novelist works in a creative vacuum, and whatever we do, we owe a debt both to the giants upon whose shoulders we stand, and to our test readers and editors. Giants first: This book – indeed, this whole series – would not have happened if I hadn't read the works of H. Beam Piper and Roger Zelazny.

But literary giants aren't the only folks I want to thank. This series wouldn't have been written without the intervention of several other people. My agent, Caitlin Blaisdell, nudged me to make a radical change of direction from my previous novels. David Hartwell and Tom Doherty of Tor encouraged me further, and the editorial process benefited from the valuable assistance of Moshe Feder and Stacy Hague-Hill, not to mention Tor's outside copy editors. My wife, Feòrag, lent me her own inimitable support while I worked on the series. Other friends and critics helped me in one way or another. I'd like to single out for their contributions: my father; also Steve Glover, Andrew Wilson, Robert 'Nojay' Sneddon, Cory Doctorow, Sydney Webb, and James Nicoll. Thank you all. And then there is my army of test readers, who went over early drafts of the manuscript, asking awkward questions: Soon Lee, Charles Petit, Hugh Hancock, Martin Page, Emmet O'Brien, Dan Ritter, Erik Olson, Stephen Harris, Larry Schoen, Fragano Ledgister, Luna Black, Cat Faber, Lakeland Dawn, Harry Payne, Marcus Rowland, Carlos Wu, Doug Muir, Tom Womack, Zane Bruce, Jeff Wilson, and others – so many I've lost track of them, for which I can only apologize. Thank you all!

Finally, I'd like to thank the Office of the Under-Secretary of Defense for inviting me to talk at the Highlands Forum in Washington, D.C., thereby giving me the opportunity to do my reconnaissance.

PROLOGUE: EMPTY QUIVER

The inspectors arrived before dawn.

A convoy of six gray government cars pulling up at the east gate to the complex was the first warning anyone on site was permitted – and the two security police officers in the gate booth took it. 'Call Ops,' the older cop grunted, narrowing his eyes as the cars dimmed their headlights and queued up between the concrete barriers for inspection. 'Tell them we've got visitors.'

'Protesters?' The younger officer straightened up as he reached for the secure handset that tied the booth to the Operations Center. They'd had a problem with the peacenik protesters earlier in the year, some new folks from outside who'd tried to block traffic outside the perimeter: mostly the protesters stuck to the Peace Farm round the far side of the site.

'Not likely.' He opened the door and stepped out into the twilight. After dark it cooled off – the open-oven-door temperatures of summer in Carson County had subsided to an arid stillness. Five hundred hours was dead time; the other eight officers who worked the entrance during the morning rush would still be signing in and getting their kit. His hand went to his two-way radio. 'Sergeant Brady on east gate two, requesting backup. Over.' He walked towards the first car. A silver-gray Town Car with a minivan behind it. As he approached, the driver's door opened. Some instinct tipped him off. He straightened his back: 'Let me see your badge, sir!'

The driver stepped out and held up a badge. Blue, for Q-level access, Brady saw. 'I need to touch that, sir.'

'Of course.'

The driver was in his early thirties, with a certain look to him that gave Brady unpleasant flashbacks. The passenger seats were occupied, too. 'Everyone out.' Brady peered at the badge, and at the other federal ID the driver was holding. His handheld scanner said the badge was the real deal, so . . . 'There y'are, Agent Cruz.' He handed the badge back. *Let someone in Ops deal with this.* 'I need to check everyone in person.'

That meant checking three cars and three minivans, and by the end of it Brady was in a cold sweat – not because of the work, but because of what it implied. Six FBI agents and four federal agents from the NNSA's Office of Secure Transportation was one thing, but there were another five close-faced men and women who didn't have any ID for him other than their Q-level site badges, and they seemed to be running this circus. *Not my job to ask,* Brady reminded himself dubiously, *but someone's about to get a nasty shock.* 'Welcome to Pantex, sir,' he said, walking back to Agent Cruz's car. 'Do you know who your assigned escort is? You're not on my roster.'

Cruz didn't smile. 'I think it'll be whoever that is, over there.' Brady glanced round. A car was coming from the direction of Ops, clearly in a hurry. 'Meanwhile, our business is in Area Twelve and we will be requiring security to secure a particular building. You and Officer Nelson are due to be relieved in half an·hour – sooner, now.'

Brady's two-way crackled: 'Brady to secure line, over.'

'So you're coming with us.'

Rich Wall hung as far back as he could behind the NNSA muscle and the local Agency staffers, doing his best to people-watch without attracting the attention of the local officers, who were clearly unhappy about their shift being extended without warning. *Fascinating,* he decided. *They're* all *acting out.* Nothing surprising there, of course – everyone from the NNSA agents to the site security commander would be on tenterhooks and trying to look as professional as possible – but if the colonel's tip-off panned out, it would make his job somewhat harder. He fingered his Q-level badge again, and waited for the RWI staffer to work her way along the line outside Access Control, pinning dosimeters to the visitors' jackets.

'Y'all been cleared for this visit already,' the staffer announced, her voice flat. 'Ah'm therefore assuming y'all have read and signed the radiological training test books. Ah just want to remind y'all to keep your hands to yourselves. Ah *mean* that. The things we store in this building are not toys. Sergeant.' She nodded at the older, grumpier security cop – who in his forage cap and desert camo looked a lot more like a soldier than a police officer. Wall noted the M16 on his shoulder. *Definitely* a soldier.

Maybe the colonel's wrong. Maybe it's just a bookkeeping error.

Having been thus admonished, it came as a minor anticlimax to be told to climb back in the car. 'Where now?' Rich asked as Lisa Chavez pulled on her seat belt.

'Now we play follow the leader.' She stared at the people mover full of serious-minded FBI agents from Utah. 'Hope someone in this clusterfuck knows what they're doing. Hope somebody's wrong.'

'Why isn't Rand on this case?'

Chavez stared at him. 'You ask too many questions.'

Rich leaned back as she started the car's engine. 'Asking questions is my job.'

The convoy moved off slowly, hugging the shoulder of the narrow road in the thin dawn light. They drove for some minutes before stopping for another checkpoint in a chain-link fence. *Sixteen thousand acres*, thought Rich. More cops dressed as soldiers, armed like soldiers, checking badges and waving vehicles through, one at a time. *Looks like Fort Meade, without the office blocks.*

A big barn of a building loomed up on one side. Chavez followed the convoy into a wide doorway, then into an enclosed ramp – a corridor about five meters wide, lined with pipes and branch routes leading off to other buildings. Walls rolled past at walking pace. Air monitoring units at head height glowed steady green, like traffic lights: no tritium release, no alpha radiation. The Pantex plant sprawled across the Texas landscape north of Amarillo, almost the size of a city in its own right. But the inhabitants weren't anything you'd want for a neighbor.

After a half-hour-long eternity they rolled back out onto a strip of blacktop road, past a clump of low earth berms, and halted again outside another chain-link fence. This, too, was guarded: 'Everyone out,' crackled the radio on the dash.

'You heard the man.' Chavez opened her door. 'Come on.'

They queued up at a gate in the fence to be individually checked

3

by officers with metal detectors backed by more heavily-armed guards. For a moment, Rich's spirits rose. *Real security?* But no. *The colonel's right. They'd be totally unprepared.*

There was a brief argument over some of the monitoring equipment, but in the end the NNSA specialists said something – Rich was too far away to hear – and one of the guards headed for a windowless hut at the double, and when he came back they were allowed to proceed after opening the heavy cases for inspection. *It's not as if we're taking anything* out *of here, after all.*

'Welcome to Area Twelve,' said one of the NNRT staffers. He gestured at the low earth berms around them. 'Doesn't look like much, does it?'

'Cut it out,' said Cruz. 'Which is Building Sixteen?'

'You're standing on its roof.' Cruz looked down as the staffer gestured at a windowless bunker. 'This way.'

Rich glanced back beyond the fence. 'Are we expecting visitors?' he murmured to Chavez.

'I don't think so.' She followed his gaze. 'Huh. Someone in Operations has finally woken up.'

Rich shook his head. 'Let's catch the floor show. This should be good.'

The secure storage vault was a concrete-lined tomb with two rows of six coffin-sized trapdoors in the floor separated by aisles a meter wide. A small forklift truck waited patiently under the ceiling, ready to lift the lids and raise their contents. Yellow guidelines painted on the concrete promised dire consequences for anyone who crossed them without due caution; more air filters and warning lamps hung from the walls, quiet sentinels keeping a graveyard watch.

With this many people this close to their charges, the guards were clearly edgy. 'If you all could stay behind that red line, this will go much easier,' the sergeant from the gatehouse announced. 'Three at a time. Who's first on the list?'

'Agent Moran, Major Alvarez, and Captain Hu,' said one of the NNSA staffers, reading from the checklist. 'Step forward and present your credentials.' Everything, Rich noted, was scripted as closely as the protocol surrounding an execution. With the gate cops and the

4

regular guards and now a group of officials from Control who included the site administrator – looking distinctly unhappy about having his usual morning routine upset like this – the vault was getting crowded. 'Sergeant, your turn.' The to-ing and fro-ing over identity verification went on for almost half an hour as checklists were exchanged and a bulky procedures manual – one of the NNSA agents had brought along a rolling flight case crammed with files – was thumbed through.

Finally: 'Open storage cell number one, please.' Someone in the back row coughed; Rich nearly jumped out of his skin. The duty technician drove his truck into position, skillfully threading its forks through the rings in the top of the lid before lifting the heavy trapdoor off the storage cell. Rich leaned forward to get a view of the narrow crypt below, taking care to stay behind the red line on the floor: the signs warned that lethal force would be used if anyone crossed it without authorization, and the guards were clearly twitchy.

The contents of the crypt didn't look like much: a pair of olive-drab containers, one briefcase-sized and the other more like a dwarfish oil drum, swathed in canvas straps, with a pair of grab-handles on top. 'Major Alvarez, Captain Hu, please step forward and identify the items.'

The two army officers placed their equipment case on the floor, knelt by the side of the crypt, and peered at the objects within. 'Storage cell one appears to contain an H-912 transport container and a D-902 detonation sequencer,' Alvarez reported. 'Released for active inventory under special executive privilege as per Executive Order 13223, secret codicil A.'

'I concur,' agreed Hu.

Hang on, Rich thought, *'Released for active inventory'? What the hell . . . ?*

'Please determine whether the H-912 is active.'

'We'll need to enter the storage cell.' Alvarez's tone was matter-of-fact, almost bored.

'You may enter when ready,' said the lead NNSA inspector.

One of the guards tensed.

'You may enter,' repeated the inspector; the chief administrator cleared his throat.

'Sergeant Jackson? If these inspectors' authorization isn't good enough for you, then put it on *my* tab.'

'Sir, I – ' The guard subsided, clearly unhappy.

'Thank you, Mr. Ellis.' The NNSA inspector raised an eyebrow at the chief administrator.

'We've all got our jobs to do,' Ellis grunted. 'And unauthorized access *is* an issue here.' He fell silent as Alvarez and Hu climbed down into the crypt and bent over the cylinder, their heads nearly touching.

As with all nuclear weapons procedures, two commissioned officers were called for. There was a small inspection window on the top of the cylinder; if an actual core was installed, a colored reflector would be positioned right behind it. 'I can confirm that the H-912 inspection window is showing code orange,' said Alvarez. 'Captain?'

Hu echoed him: 'I concur with the major.'

The minder of the checklists ticked off another box.

'Next, uh, if you could verify that your instrument is working using the test sample, we can proceed to step six – '

More to-ing and fro-ing as Alvarez and Hu proceeded to calibrate their portable detector. 'It's working all right,' Alvarez confirmed. 'We're going to check the H-912 now.' More to-ing and fro-ing as he fastened a stubby cylinder to the top of the olive-drab container and pushed buttons. A minute passed. 'I'm not getting anything.'

'Agreed. Something isn't right here . . .'

Someone swore. 'Agent Moran, if you'd like to try your instrument now?'

Rich felt an unpleasant numbness creep over him, a resignation to the unfolding process of discovery and the horrors that it promised to reveal. Everything that had happened to bring them to this situation had taken place weeks, months, or even years ago; nor was he implicated in it. Other people would have to defend their actions, possibly in court – not Rich. But that didn't make things better. *Nothing* made things better, not when they were the kind of things that were the bread and butter of his occupation. Agent Moran unpacked his detector as carefully as a forensic tech attending a particularly gruesome murder scene. 'Nothing,' he announced.

'Right.' The NNSA inspector sounded as unhappy as Rich felt. 'Mr. Ellis, with your permission, I think we ought to proceed to open the H-912 and see what's really in there.'

'You're sure those detectors' – Ellis nudged forward – 'let me see that. McDonnell, if you could check this reference sample – '

More to-ing and fro-ing as Ellis and his staff confirmed (not to anyone's relief) that the reference samples the inspectors were using were, indeed, the real deal – 'All right, on my authority, Willis? Unseal this carrier for internal visual inspection.'

'Sir.' The senior guard made it sound like a cough. 'Opening a device on inactive inventory is a security – '

'Sergeant, I am very much afraid that this is not, in fact, a device on inactive inventory. It's something else. In which case, the regulation you're about to quote at me doesn't apply, does it?'

'Right.' The guard looked unhappy. 'Will you put that in writing, sir? Because if not, I'll have to . . .'

Ellis took a deep breath. 'Yes, I will put it in writing for you. Witnessed by everybody here.' He jerked a thumb over his shoulder. 'Now, are we going to keep these people waiting?'

Rich felt an elbow in his ribs. 'Have to *what?*' whispered Chavez.

'Shoot somebody,' Rich grunted. 'Probably us.'

'Captain Hu . . .'

'I'm on it.'

The audience in the storage room fell silent as Captain Hu set to work, unfastening catches and then going to work with a torque wrench under Alvarez's gaze. He took barely five minutes, but to Rich it felt closer to five hours. Finally, the lid of the carrier came free.

'Well?' asked Ellis.

Hu held the carrier open as Alvarez reached down and pulled. 'We've got an empty quiver,' he said laconically, and held up his catch: an object which, from the way he held it, had to be unusually heavy. 'Unless we've taken to storing lead bricks in nuclear weapon carriers . . .'

*

The transportation of cell phones – let alone camera phones – into the secure areas of Pantex was more than slightly discouraged. Rich stayed with the crowd scene for the next two hours, as the inspectors ripped through the other eleven storage cells in the facility with increasing desperation. Then, with the final tally – six H-912s filled with the sleeping FADM lightweight nukes, six H-912s empty but for lead bricks and a slip of red paper taped inside the inspection window – he slipped outside.

Chavez followed him. 'The colonel will want to know,' she said as the door closed behind them.

'Yeah,' he agreed. He nodded to the guard on duty outside, then presented his badge. 'We have to make a call. Where can I find a phone?'

The cop looked at him with barely concealed suspicion. 'You don't get to go anywhere until I confirm you're free to leave the area, sir.'

Chavez snorted. 'You have no legal authority over us, soldier.' She held up her warrant card. 'C'mon, Rich, we're – '

The guard tensed. 'You're not leaving!' he repeated, louder.

Rich spread his hands. 'Whoa! We don't need an argument and we don't need to leave the area, we just need to make a phone call. Is there a voice terminal we can use nearby? Preferably secure?'

'You want an outside line?' The guard looked aghast.

'No, just one that can put me through to Operations Control. Operations Control? Come on, there must be one – '

'Internal phone's over there.' The cop pointed at a box on the wall. 'Just don't try to leave the area until you've been cleared, sir, ma'am. I don't know what's going on in there, but nobody's to leave. And I don't care what your badges say, I've got my orders and I'm sticking to 'em. Don't put me in a position where I've gotta do something we'll all regret.'

'I don't intend to.' Rich tried to look as unthreatening as possible. 'I just need to talk to someone in Operations Control. We're not going to be any trouble.'

He could feel Chavez's eyes drilling a hole in his back. He glanced round. 'You want to make this one?'

'No, you go first. I'll just watch your back.'

'Right.' Rich picked up the handset and dialed a four-digit number. 'Ops? This is a call for SERENE AMBLER. Yeah, that's SERENE AMBLER. They're expecting you to connect me immediately . . . good. Colonel? Rich here.'

'What's the news?' Colonel Smith sounded bone-tired: two time zones east, he'd probably been awake all night waiting for this call.

'Our FADM inventory is fucked, and it's worse than we feared. We're out by another five, in addition to the one we found in Boston. That one was on forward deployment when it went walkabout, but the ones we're missing here were supposed to be in secure storage. Turns out they've been tampered with – someone has gotten inside the storage cells. I slipped out while they were declaring an official Pinnacle Empty Quiver so I could warn you; the missing items are all from the covert resource allocated to SECDEF and VPOTUS back in 2001, so somebody needs to brief Mr. Cheney urgently to head it off at the pass before the shitstorm hits the National Command Authority and confuses the president.'

'I see.' The colonel fell uncharacteristically silent for a few seconds. 'And what does the scene look like to you, right now?'

Rich paused, glancing at the guard, who was pointedly not listening – too pointedly, he thought. 'The area's secured against normal threats, so your guess is as good as mine as to how they got in.' Which was to say, not a guess at all – they both knew perfectly well how these particular bad guys might sneak into a secure area. 'The building's surrounded by a – the usual kind of security you'd expect – but it's AGL. The guards seem alert enough to' – yes, the guard was *very pointedly* not listening – 'intruders. I'm not making any guesses how they managed to make the substitution, but the H-912 cases were full of ballast. Which suggests whoever took them knows exactly what they're doing with the contents.'

Another pause. 'Can you confirm six missing, and no more?'

That was an easy one to answer: 'No, sir. I can confirm six empty quivers and six full ones, but I can *not* rule out the possibility that there are more missing.' He licked his dry lips. 'I would be astonished if the site authority doesn't order a full lockdown immediately and commence an audit within the next hour or two, in anticipation of

9

NCA's likely orders. Meanwhile, it looks like we'll be stuck here for a few hours, if not days. What do you want us to do?'

Silence. 'Leave it to the NNSA,' the colonel finally said. 'I'll escalate it for WARBUCKS's attention immediately. Meanwhile, as soon as you can disengage I want you back in Boston. There's a problem with COLDPLAY . . .'

HEIR APPARENT

I am not hearing this, Miriam Beckstein told herself. The temptation to giggle, to laugh it all off as a bizarre joke, was enormous. *Pretend it isn't happening; yeah, right. Story of my life.* She tightened her grip on the valise holding her notebook PC and its precious CD-ROMs. Except that for the past six months, the mad stuff had made a habit of punching her in the guts whenever she least expected it. 'Run that by me again,' she said.

'It's quite simple,' said the hard-eyed young debutante with the machine pistol. 'Your mother wants to use you to consolidate power.' She kept her eyes focused on Miriam as she twisted the magazine free of the gun, worked a slide to eject a cartridge, and swapped another magazine into place. 'The duke agrees with her. And *we*' – the eloquent roll of her shoulder took in their companions, a cohort of young and alarmingly heavily armed Clan world-walkers – 'intend to make sure you're not just there for show.'

They look like students, thought Miriam. Students outfitted by The North Face for a weekend hike; accessories by Fabrique Nationale and Heckler & Koch. Of course they were nothing of the kind. Young aristocrats of the Clan nobility – born in the curious quasi-medieval kingdom of Gruinmarkt, and able to travel to other worlds at will – they might look like ordinary American undergrads, but the mindset behind those fresh young faces was very different.

'Oh, really?' she managed. The idea of her mother – and the duke – plotting to put her on the throne of the Gruinmarkt was pretty preposterous, on the face of it – but then, so were so many of the other intrigues the Clan seemed to generate. Then another thought struck her: *You said 'we', didn't you?* So Brill had an agenda of her own, over and above her loyalty to the duke – or Miriam, for that matter? Time to probe . . .

11

'Was this' – she pointed at her belly, quiet anger in her voice – 'part of their plan?'

'Milady' Brill – Lady Brilliana d'Ost, a mere twenty-something – furrowed her brow. 'With all due respect, if you think *that*, you're paranoid. Do you really think the duke – or your mother – know you so poorly as to think you a suitable mother for the heir to the throne? Much less, under duress? Henryk and your – his backer – were fools for thinking they could manipulate you that way, and now they are dead fools. The rest of us are just trying to make the best of a bad deal. And if you want to talk politics, would you mind leaving it until later? I've got a splitting headache and it's about to get worse.'

Miriam winced in unconscious sympathy. World-walking took it out of a member of the Clan's inner families, those with the ability: Doing it more than once in a day risked migrainelike symptoms and a blood pressure spike. There were other symptoms, too: pregnancy, she'd learned the hard way, made world-walking under your own power impossible. But they'd come here from New Britain, escaping after the abortive ambush at a provincial railway station in that world's version of California, immediately after picking her up.

One of the young men pacing the perimeter of the clearing raised a hand, twirled it in a warning circle. 'One hour to go.'

'Yah.' Brill glanced round again. The forest clearing was peaceful, unoccupied but for Miriam, Brill, and her three young bloods, but she never stopped scanning.

'Are we in any immediate danger?' Miriam asked, shifting her balance on the fallen tree trunk.

'Probably not right now.' Brill paused to continue her inspection. 'The Kao's patrols don't usually sweep this far northeast. Better not linger, though. We'll be ready to move in another hour.'

'The Kao?'

'The Favored of Heaven's border troops. Most of the local tribes give them a wide berth. We should, too.' A warning look in her eyes gave Miriam a cold shiver; if Brill was scared of them, that was enough for her.

'What are you planning on doing once we cross over?'

'We've got a hotel suite in San Jose. I plan to get us over there,

12

then make contact with the duke and ask for further instructions. I imagine he'll want us back on the east coast immediately – we've got a bizjet standing by. Otherwise, we'll do what Security tells us to do. Unless you have other plans?' Brill raised a carefully shaped eyebrow. Even though she'd started the day with a brisk firefight, then a forced crossing into wilderness, she'd taken pains with her makeup.

Miriam shrugged. 'I thought I did.' Her hands were restless; trying to keep them still, she thrust them deep in the pockets of her overly heavy coat. 'The political situation in New Britain is going to hell in a handbasket. Erasmus was on his way to meet a big wheel in the, uh, resistance.' In point of fact, the *biggest* wheel in the underground, returning from exile after a generation – to whom he had once been a personal assistant. 'It's much too hot for comfort. I was only going along because I couldn't think of anything else to do; when I fetched up in London all I had was the clothes on my back.'

'Well, at least you got away from the mess at the Summer Palace with your skin intact. And thank whatever gods you believe in for that.'

She fell silent for a few minutes. But finally Miriam's curiosity got the better of her. 'I can guess how you tracked me down. But what about Huw? And the other two? Who are they? You said something about a job I'd suggested, but I don't recall . . . and they don't look like Uncle Angbard's little helpers to me.'

'They're not.' Brilliana's eyes narrowed. 'I just called in help and head office sent them along. Hey! Sir Huw? Have you a minute?'

Huw nodded. 'Bro, cover for me,' he told the tall, heavily built guy with the semiauto shotgun as he walked towards them. Huw was anything but husky: skinny and intense. 'Has something come up?'

'Huw.' Brill smiled, oddly cheerful. 'We've got a couple of hours to kill. Why don't you tell her grace what you found?'

Her grace? But I'm not a duchess. Miriam blinked. Suddenly bits of the big picture were falling into place. *Heir to the throne – what exactly does that entail?* 'What you found, where?'

'We're calling it world four right now, but I think a better name for it would be Transition A–B,' Huw said as he sat down at the far end of the fallen trunk. 'It's where you go if you use the Hidden Family's knotwork as a focus in your world, uh, the United States.' He looked twitchily pleased with himself. 'Nobody was able to cross over in New England because, well, it's probably under an ice sheet – the weather there's definitely a lot colder than in any of the other time lines we know about.'

Hang on, time lines – Miriam held up a hand. 'What were you doing?'

'The duke tasked me with setting up a systematic exploration program,' Huw explained. 'So I started by taking the second known knotwork design and seeing where it'd take you if you used it in world two, in the USA, which the Hidden Family had no access to. The initial tests in Massachusetts and New York failed, so I guessed there might be a really large obstacle in the way. There's some kind of exclusion effect . . . but anyway, we found a new world. A fourth one.'

Miriam narrowly resisted the urge to grab him and start yelling questions. 'Go on.'

'World four is cold, about ten degrees celsius below datum for the other worlds we've found. That's about the climate difference you'd expect if it's in an ice age right now. We didn't have time to do much exploring, but we found evidence that there were people there, once. We didn't see any signs of current habitation but we found relics. High tech, *very* high tech – perfect dentistry, gantries made out of titanium, and other stuff. We're still trying to figure out the other stuff, but it's a whole different ball game. The building we found looked like it had been struck from above by some kind of directed energy weapon – '

'Some kind of – ' Miriam stopped. On the opposite side of the clearing, the young blond woman who'd come with Huw was kneeling, her weapon trained on something invisible through the trees.

Brill was already moving. 'Get ready to go.'

'But it's too early.'

'What's Elena spotted?' Huw rose to his feet. The big guy at the far side of the clearing – the one Huw had called 'bro' – was crouching behind the blonde, his shotgun raised: A moment later she turned and scrambled towards them, staying low.

'Riders,' she said quietly, addressing Brill. 'At least three, maybe more. They're trying to stay quiet. Milady, we await your instructions.'

'I think' – Brill's eyes narrowed – 'we'd better cross over. Right now. Huw, can you carry her grace?'

'I think so.' Huw knelt down. 'Miriam, if you could climb on my shoulders?'

Miriam swallowed. 'Is this necessary? It's too early – '

Brill cut her off. 'It is necessary to move as fast as possible, unless you want another shoot-out. I generally try to limit them to no more than one before lunch on any given day. Huw, get her across. We'll be along momentarily.'

Miriam stood up, wrapped her arms around Huw's shoulders, and tried to haul her legs up. Huw rose into a half-crouch. She strained to clamp her knees around his waist. 'Are you all right?' she asked anxiously.

'Just a second,' he gasped. 'All right. Three. Two.' Something flickered in the palm of his hand, just in the corner of her vision: a fiery knot that tried to turn her eyes and her stomach inside out. 'One.'

The world around them flickered and Huw collapsed under her, dry-retching. Miriam fell sideways, landing heavily on one hip.

They were in scrubland, and alone. Someone's untended back lot, by the look of it: a few stunted trees straggling across a nearby hillside like hairs across a balding man's pate, a fence meandering drunkenly to one side. A windowless barn that had clearly seen better days slumped nearby.

Miriam rose to her feet and dusted herself off. Her traveling clothes, unremarkable in New Britain, would look distinctly odd to American eyes: a dark woolen coat of unusual cut over the mutant offspring of a shalwar kameez. It was a disguise that had outlived its usefulness, along with her temporarily blond, permed hair. 'Where are you parked?' she asked Huw as his retching subsided.

'Front of. Barn.' He staggered to a crouch. 'Need. Painkillers . . .'

Something moved in the corner of her sight. Miriam's head whipped round as she thrust a hand in her coat pocket, reaching for the small pistol Erasmus had given her before she recognized Elena. A few seconds later Huw's brother Hulius popped into view, followed almost immediately by Brilliana. 'Come on, people!' Brill sounded more annoyed than nauseous. 'Cover! Check!'

'Check,' Huw echoed. 'I think we're still alone.'

'Check!' trilled Elena. 'Did they see you, Yul? Ooh, you don't look so good!'

'*Guuuh* . . . Check. I don't think so. Going. Be sick.'

Brill clapped her hands. 'Let's get *going*, people.' She was almost tapping her feet with impatience. 'We've got a safe house to get to. You can throw up all you like once we report in, but first we've got a job to do.' She nodded at Miriam. 'After you, milady.'

*

In a soot-stained industrial city nestling in the Appalachians, beneath a sky stained amber by the fires of half a million coal-burning stoves, there was a noble house defended by the illusion of poverty.

The Lee family and their clients did not like to draw attention to themselves. The long habit of secrecy was deeply ingrained in their insular souls; they'd lived alone among enemies for almost ten generations, abandoned by the eastern Clan that had once – so they had thought until recently, and so some still thought – cast them out and betrayed them. Here in the industrial heartland of Irongate there was little love for rich foreigners, much less wealthy Chinese merchants, at the best of times. And the times were anything but good: With the empire locked in a bewildering and expensive overseas war (to say nothing of multiple consecutive crop failures and a bare treasury, freak weather disasters, deflation, and high unemployment), the city was as inflammable as a powder keg.

Consequently, the Lees did not flaunt their wealth and power openly. Nor did their home resemble a palatial mansion. Rather, it resembled a tenement block fronted by the dusty window displays of failing shops (for only the pawnbroker's business remained good). Between two such shops there stood a blank-faced door, a row of bellpulls discreetly off to one side. It might have been a stairwell leading to the cramped flats of shopkeepers and factory foremen. But the reality was very different.

'Be seated, nephew,' said the old man with the long, wispy beard. 'And tell me what brings you here?'

James Lee bowed his head, concealing his unease for a few more moments. As was right, he went to his knees and then sat cross-legged before the low platform on which his great uncle, the eldest of days – and his companions, the eldest's younger sibling, Great-Uncle Huan, and his first wife – perched.

'The Clan has gone too far,' he began, then paused.

'Tea for my favorite nephew,' the eldest commented, and one of the servants who had been standing behind James bowed and slipped out through a side door. 'You may continue.'

James took a deep breath. 'They resumed their scheme to capture the royal house. My understanding is that the chosen bride, the long-lost daughter of the western alliance, was not an enthusiastic participant: The architect of the marriage, her grandmother, allied with the conservative faction at court to coerce her.'

He paused for a moment as the servant, returning, placed a tray bearing a steaming cup before him. 'I considered the merits of direct action, but concluded the cost would far outweigh any benefit. It would be interpreted as base treachery, and I did not feel able to take such measures without your approval.'

'Just so.' His great-uncle nodded. 'What happened next?'

James chose his next words very carefully, aware of the tension in the room: There was no whispering in corners, and none of the usual cross-play between the ancients that was normal when the eldest held court. 'The baroness and her coconspirators made a fundamental error of judgment when they arranged the betrothal of the heir Miriam to the youngest son of the King. They failed to see how this would be received by his elder brother. Prince Egon is not of the blood and therefore they ignored him; Creon, though damaged, was thought by them to be an occulted carrier' – one who carried the recessive trait for the world-walking ability, but was not able himself to world-walk – 'and so they planned to breed from him a king who would be one of their own. Egon took as dim a view of this marriage as you would expect, and the result was bound to be messy. Although I did not realize how drastically he would react at the time.'

He reached out and picked up the cup of tea, then took a sip before continuing.

'I intervened at the betrothal by presenting the eastern heir – Helge, as they call her, Miriam, in her own tongue – with a locket containing our house sigil. She had made it clear that she felt no filial piety, and wished to escape. I therefore concluded that there was no reason to kill her if it was her heart's desire to do what we wanted: I merely gave her the means. I confess that I did not anticipate Egon's attempt to massacre everybody at the ceremony – but by now either she's dead or in exile, so our goal is achieved without her blood on our hands.'

'About the massacre.' Great-Uncle Huan leaned forward. 'You were present, were you not?'

James nodded.

'How did you escape?'

Another sip of tea: 'The situation was confused. When Egon's men detonated a petard beneath the palace and then attacked, the royal life guards fought back. While this was going on, those of the Clan's leaders who were present made themselves scarce. They left their dead behind. I hid under a table until I could get out, using my spare sigil.' With one hand, James reached into the sleeve of his robe. *Now or never.* He pulled out a small gilded locket on a fine chain. 'Before I left, I removed this from the body of a dead baron. It's the authentic sigil of the eastern Clan. I have tested it myself.' He laid it on the dais before the eldest. 'I brought it here directly.'

He sat back to wait, straining to reveal no sign of his inner tension. *It's like trying not to think of invisible elephants*, Helge's mother Patricia had told him with a twinkle in her eyes. *All you have to do is learn to ignore the elephant in the room.* Which was perfectly true, but when the elephant in question was the huge lie you'd just told the patriarch of your family, that was easier said than done. The background was true enough, if one chose to overlook some judicious omissions. But his escape – that was another matter. Yes, he'd hidden under a table, shivering and concussed. But it had been one of the eastern Clan's soldiers who'd carried him across to that strange doppelgänger city of New York, and it had been a very much alive

18

Lady Olga Thorold who had gifted him with the locket, in return for certain undertakings. Because, when you got down to it, sometimes treachery was a two-way street.

The elders stared at the locket greedily but with trepidation, as if it might bite. 'This is definitely the sigil of the eastern Clan?' the eldest asked, in a tone of almost superstitious disbelief. 'Have you compared it to our own?'

James stifled a gasp of relief. 'Not directly, uncle,' he admitted. 'It allowed me to travel, and its bite is the same – I think it subtly different, but I thought it best to leave the comparison to someone who knows nothing of our ways.'

The eldest nodded thoughtfully, then looked up. 'Leave us,' he said, encompassing everyone in the room but his brother, his brother's wife, and James. There was a mass exodus towards the doors at the back of the day room as various servants and no few guards bowed themselves out, but presently the shuffling and whispering died down. Finally, his great-uncle spoke again. 'Do they know you live, nephew?'

The implied claim on his familial loyalty nearly made James overlook the implicit threat in the question. 'I don't believe so, uncle, but I may be mistaken,' he said politely. 'I stand ready to return to them if you so order it.' He might have said more, but instead bit his lower lip, waiting. He'd spent more than six months living among the eastern families as a hostage: His disappearance might be taken as a sign of treachery. *Might*. Except the events of that fateful night a week ago would make a perfect excuse for absence – one that would be accepted, unquestioned, if Olga was in a position to hold her patron to his side of their bargain. On the other hand, if he returned to the Clan too soon he'd be unable to make good his side of their pact. It was, all in all, a delicate situation.

'You broke their parole.' Great-Uncle Huan's eyes narrowed accusingly.

'He had good reason,' Number One Wife remonstrated.

'Humph.' Huan slouched sideways on his cushion. 'Still looks bad.'

'Appearances are everything,' the eldest agreed. 'Nephew, we will think on this. I believe, however, it would be for the best if you wrote a letter to the eastern Clan's elders, perhaps to the white duke himself, explaining your absence. Apologize, remind him of the circumstances that caused you to flee, and ask whether their security will be able to guarantee your safety upon your return.' He smiled, evidently amused. 'Shame them for forcing you into an act of cowardice.'

James bowed his head. 'I'll do that.' He paused. 'Do you expect me to return?'

'Only if they can guarantee your safety.' Eldest's smile widened. He picked up the locket. 'You've done excellent work already, my nephew. I wish we'd been able to persuade them to provide bed, board, and bodyguards for our spies back in my father's day. It would have made things so much more entertaining!'

*

The sun had long since set behind the battlements of the Hjalmar Palace, and the besieging forces had settled down to intermittent sniping, seemingly intent on making the defenders keep their heads down. Which might be good news or bad news, Lady Olga thought, depending on whether they were doing so to conserve ammunition for an attack, or simply planning on keeping the Clan security force bottled up indefinitely. The former seemed likely: The usurper had demonstrated a dismaying talent for keeping the Clan on the defensive.

Not that a prolonged siege was in any way preferable. The usurper's army had taken the castle by stealth, planted explosives, and nearly succeeded in mousetrapping the Clan's inevitable counterattack. Only the extreme paranoia of Clan security's leadership (who had prepared a secret way in, against the possibility of treachery) and the professionalism of their assault team (who had found and defused the explosive charges) had stopped them massacring the counterattack. But the situation was far from resolved. Egon's men had an unpleasant additional surprise for the Clan forces, in the shape of a handful of machine guns – presumably looted from a Clan arms dump earlier in the war – emplaced on top of the castle's gatehouse. The enemy were still clinging on to the gatehouse – largely because Clan security didn't have enough spare troops to mount a frontal attack on what was effectively a small castle in its own right – and so they were forced to keep their heads down and stay away from the front windows of the inner keep.

What the enemy didn't know was that the Clan's main mobile strength was bottled up in the castle: The doppelgänger site in the United States was knee-deep in Special Forces troops, for the secret cross-agency task force set up to track down the Clan had spotted their hastily prepared operation and brought the hammer down *hard*.

And that was the *good* news.

Olga turned and paced back across the width of the stone-flagged hall, past the map-strewn table and the improvised command and control station where hollow-eyed radio technicians tried to pull useful information together from the walkie-talkie equipped guards on the outer hard-points, to the cluster of men standing around the foot of the table. 'Baron Hjorth. Earl Wu. Lieutenant Anders.' She nodded agreeably, trying to maintain a facade of confidence. *Angbard's valkyrie*, they called her behind her back; a nickname freighted with significance, and one she'd have to work doubly hard to live up to when they learned the truth. 'What word from Riordan?' she asked.

'Nothing in the past ten minutes.' Carl, Earl of Wu by Hjorth, and captain of the Clan's security service, rubbed his mustache. A blunt, bulky fellow, his usually ruddy features showed signs of sagging under the burden of responsibility that had landed on his shoulders. 'Riordan tells me the plane's not equipped for night flying and they're running short of fuel – we're at the extremity of its flight radius, and they didn't have much stockpiled. It's not a real airborne detachment: We wouldn't have it at all except that Rudi pursued his hobby despite official discouragement . . . Well, that's a question for another time. Right now, we're not getting anything in or out tonight. I've got guards with infrared sights on all four bastions and the gatehouse, with con- tinuous radio coverage and M249 sections to cover the approaches, but the enemy have got the sally ports pinned down, and they brought down the riverside culvert so we can't sneak anyone out that way. All the early warning we've got is what we can see from the walls.'

'That's going to do us a lot of good if the pretender shows up with an army in the middle of the night,' Oliver, Baron Hjorth, said sharply.

'I don't think that's very likely,' pointed out Sir Helmut Anders, a portly figure in the camouflage surcoat he wore over his body armor. 'He can't be closer than Wergatsfurt and it'll take him a day to move a large force from there to here. Small forces we can deal with, yes? The real threat will arrive on the morrow. So it seems to me that we need to locate the usurper's main force, and then trap him between Riordan's mobile force and this stronghold.' It all sounded so reasonable, until she reminded herself that Riordan's mobility owed itself to his ability to move his troops across to the other world, and that the United States was not hospitable territory for Clan security detachments right now. And the other complications . . .

'How is his grace?' Helmut asked, in a misplaced attempt to divert Baron Hjorth. Olga tensed, hunting for an excuse, but then Oliver nodded emphatically.

'Yes, damn it, how is he?' They were staring at her, expecting an answer.

'He's hanging on.' Olga glanced away from the table as she extemporized. 'Ivar and Morgaine are tending to him in the baron's bedroom. If we weren't mewed up in here I'd have him in a hospital as soon as look at him – the apoplexy has taken his left side and left him sleepy.' Which was a major understatement, but they didn't need to hear the unvarnished truth right now. Duke Angbard Lofstrom, the foundation stone on which Clan Security was built – the one professionally organized institution to which all five member families deferred – had managed to gargle a few words after his collapse, following the disastrous forced world-walk out of their assembly area near Concord. He was enfeebled and incoherent, and it was well past the magic first hour in which advanced medical care might reap rewards. He wasn't exactly dead, but the likelihood of him ever making a recovery was very poor – especially if they couldn't get him to a stroke center. But the last thing they needed right now was to be leaderless, so . . . 'He gave me instructions to resolve this situation,

22

but it's going to take a little while to set up.' She shrugged. 'I don't suppose we could fly him out tomorrow morning?'

It was a faint hope, and Carl's shaken head told her all she needed to know. 'The ultralight's not equipped to carry a passenger who's incapacitated. If we had a real airplane, maybe things would be different. I already asked. When this is over – '

She could finish the thought herself: *When this is over, we will have ultralight helicopters and jeeps with mortars and two-way radio systems in every stronghold. Even if it takes us a decade to carry them across.* And, of course, a chicken in every world-walker's pot. *But for now –*

'What are we going to do?' asked Baron Hjorth. To his credit, there was no quaver in his voice. 'What *are* these special orders of yours?'

'Sir Anders mentioned trapping the usurper's army, didn't he? We have certain weapons that aren't public knowledge. I'd rather not disclose the precise details, my lord, until we're ready to deploy them, but if we can locate the usurper I am certain they will make the job of ending his rampage easier. But for that, we need to know where the pretender *is*. And we need to get out of this mousetrap.' She smiled happily. 'None of which should be particularly hard.'

'But we're doppelgängered – '

'Not in New Britain.' She tried not to laugh at his expression. 'And that's where we're all going, just as soon as the mail arrives.'

*

It was late in the day: The sun had already set, and the evening rush of homebound commuters was well under way. Business was beginning to slacken off, which was fine by Jason. The sooner they all went home, the sooner the boss would shut up shop and *he* could go home. But for now . . .

The store was mostly empty: a couple of tired guys with handbaskets down by the discount stationery, a harried suburban mom riding herd on two preteens round the aisle of toy musical instruments; nothing much to do. Jason waited by the cash register, trying to look attentive. It'd be just like Bill to hang out in back and watch him on the CCTV, then jump on anything he did wrong. That was the trouble

23

with this job – with a busybody like Bill minding the floor, you just couldn't fart without him noticing. One of the fluorescents overhead was flickering, its strobing glow reflecting off the glass cabinets. He shifted from foot to foot – sore as usual, after a day of pacing the aisles.

The doors opened. A few seconds later Jason glanced up, registered the two weirdly dressed men. 'Can I help you?' he mumbled, taken aback.

'Yes.' The younger of the two grinned. 'We've got a shopping list. And we're in a real hurry.' He held up a sheet of paper in one gloved hand.

That's armor, isn't it? Jason blinked. The glove was made out of ringlets of metal, knitted together as if by machine – dull gray metal, hundreds of ringlets. Both men were wearing chain-mail suits under loose tunics. The tunics were speckled with camouflage dye, like army fatigues. The older man had a full beard and a livid scar drew an emphatic frownline across his brow. 'Uh, I can't leave the register, sir – '

The old guy – middle-aged, by the gray hairs speckling his beard – shook his head. 'Call your manager, son. We do not have much time.' His voice was heavily accented.

'Uh, I can't – '

'What seems to be the problem?'

Jason gritted his teeth as Bill materialized somewhere behind him. 'These folks need a personal shopper.'

'Well, you'd better look after them.' He could practically *hear* Bill's shit-eating grin. 'I'll mind the register for you.'

'Let me see that list.'

The young guy handed it over. Jason squinted. 'A Hewlett-Packard 4550N? I don't know if we've got one of those in stock – '

'Please check.' The young guy shrugged. 'If you've got one, we want it *right now*. And the other items. If you do not have that precise model, we'll discuss alternatives. Whatever you've got in the way of heavy-duty color laser printers.'

'Okay, let me have a look.'

Jason scanned the list. A laptop, an office-grade laser printer, a scanner, software – all big-ticket items. Some cheaper stuff: a badge laminator, paper, spare toner cartridges, a paper cutter. And some stuff that didn't make sense: an uninterruptible power supply and a gas-fueled generator? He didn't bother to glance at his watch, he already knew the time: three minutes to closing. *Shit. I'll be here all evening.* But the stuff on this list was worth close to ten big ones; the commission on it was close to a day's wages. Bill would have his guts if he let these fish go. *Jesus.* 'I'll get the big stuff out of the stockroom if we've got it, sir. Do you want to pick up the software? It's over on that aisle – '

'Hurry up, we don't have all night.' That was Bill, grinning at him from behind the register.

Jason shoved through the doors into the stockroom, grabbed a cart, and went hunting. Yet another fucked-up job to add to his list of eccentrics and weirdos who passed through the shop on a daily basis: *Did you hear the one about the two guys in chain mail and camo who came in to buy a DTP system at three minutes to closing?* They *did* have the printer in stock, and just his luck, it weighed more than a hundred pounds. No scanner, so he picked the next model up. Laptop, ditto.

It took him just five minutes to rush round the stockroom and grab the big ticket stuff on the list. Finally, impatient to get them the hell out of the shop and cash up and go home, Jason shoved the hand truck back out onto the floor. Bill slouched behind the cash register, evidently chatting with the older customer. As he followed the cart out, Bill glared at him. 'I wanna take this sale,' he said.

'No you don't.' Bill laid one hand on the truck as the younger guy appeared round the end of an aisle, carrying a full basket. 'You want to go home, kid, that's the only reason you were so fast. Go on, shove off.'

'But I – ' Now he got it: Bill would log himself in and process the sale and claim the commission, while Jason did all the heavy lifting.

'Think I'm stupid? Think I don't see you watching the clock? Shove off, Jason.' Bill leaned towards him, menacing. 'Unless you want me to notice your timekeeping.'

The younger of the two customers glanced at Bill. 'What is your problem?' he asked, placing his basket on the counter.

25

'We get a commission on each sale,' mumbled Jason. 'He's my supervisor.'

'I see.' The older customer looked at Jason, then at the laden hand truck, then back at Jason. 'Well, thank you for your fast work.' He held out his hand, a couple of notes rolled between his fingers; Jason took them. He turned back to Bill. 'Put the purchases on this card. We will need help loading them.'

Jason nodded and headed for the back room to grab his coat. *Fucking Bill*, he thought disgustedly, then glanced at the banknotes before he slid them into his pocket.

There were five of them, and they were all hundreds.

*

'I'm sorry, but that's impossible, sir.'

Rudi paused to buy himself time to find the words he needed. Standing up in front of the CO to brief him on a tool they'd never used before was hard work: How to explain? 'The Saber 16 is an *ultralight*. It has to be – that's the only way I could carry it over here on my own. The wing weighs about a hundred pounds, and the trike weighs close to two hundred and fifty; maximum takeoff weight is nine hundred pounds, including fifty gallons of fuel and a pilot. You – I mean whoever's flying the thing – steer it with your body. It's a sport trike, not a general aviation vehicle. It's like a motorbike, and what you want is a truck.'

Earl Riordan raised an eyebrow. 'I thought you could carry a passenger, or cargo?'

The question, paradoxically, made it easier to keep going. 'It's true I can lift a passenger or maybe a hundred pounds of cargo, sir, but dropping stuff – anything I drop means taking a hand off the controls and changing the center of gravity, and that's just asking for trouble. I can dump a well-packaged box of paper off the passenger seat and hit a courtyard, sure, but a two-hundred-pound bomb? That's a different matter. Even if I could figure out a way to rig it so I could drop it without tearing the wing off or stalling, I'd have to be flying high enough up that the shrapnel doesn't reach me, and fast enough to clear the blast radius, and the Saber's got a top speed of only fifty-five, so I'd have to drop it from high up, so I'd need some kind of bombsight – and they don't sell them down at Wal-Mart. I can drop grenades or flares, and given a tool shop and some help we might even be able to bolt an M249 to the trike, but that's all. In terms of military aviation we're state of the art for 1913, unless you've got something squirreled away somewhere that I don't know about.'

Earl Riordan stared at him for a few seconds, then shook his head. 'No such luck,' he grunted. 'Damn their eyes.' The CO wasn't swearing about him, for which Rudi was grateful.

'So what *are* you good for?' demanded Vincenze, loudly.

Rudi shrugged. The cornet had maybe had a drop too much rum in his coffee. Not terribly clever when you'd been summoned into the CO's office for a quiet chat, but then again nobody ever accused Vince of being long on brains: they weren't much of an asset in a cavalry-man.

'Fair-weather observation. Dropping small packets, accurate to within a hundred feet or so. If you can find me somewhere to land that isn't under the usurper's guns I can carry a single passenger in and out, or up to a hundred and fifty pounds of luggage.'

'A single passenger.' Hmm. The earl looked distracted. 'Hold that thought. Out of curiosity, is it possible to parachute from the passenger seat?'

'It'd be very dangerous.' Rudi didn't need to search for words anymore: they were coming naturally. 'It's a pusher prop so you couldn't use a static line. It'd have to be free fall, which would mean close to maximum altitude – I can only reach five thousand feet with a passenger – and if their primary chute didn't open they wouldn't have time to try a secondary, and I'd have fun keeping control, too.'

'So scratch that idea.' Riordan raised his mug and took a mouthful of coffee. 'Okay. Suppose you need to land somewhere, pick up a passenger, and fly out. What do you need?'

'A runway.' Rudi glanced into his own coffee mug: It was still empty, dammit. 'With a passenger it depends on the weather, but a minimum thousand feet to be safe. I can probably get airborne in significantly less than that, but if anything goes wrong you need the extra room to slow down again. Ideally it needs to be clear-cut for the same again, past the end of the runway – most engine problems show up once you're just airborne because that's when you're climbing at maximum throttle and maximum weight.'

'A thousand feet?' Vincenze looked surprised. 'But you took off from the courtyard!'

'That was me, without a passenger,' Rudi pointed out. 'At two-thirds maximum takeoff weight you get in the air faster and you can stop a lot faster, too, if something goes wrong. If you want to take off with less than five hundred feet of runway, you really need an ultra-light helicopter or preferably a gyrocopter – ultralight choppers are dangerous. Oh, and a pilot who knows how to fly them. It was on my to-do list.'

'Noted.' Riordan jotted a note on his pad. 'Assume bad people with guns are shooting at you when you take off. How vulnerable would you be?'

Rudi shivered. He'd been shot at before, in his previous flight. 'Very. The Saber 16 can only climb at about six hundred feet per minute. Takeoff is about thirty miles per hour. Handguns or musketry I could risk, but if they've got rifles? Or M60s? I'm toast. I'd be in their sights and within range for at least two minutes.'

'So we won't ask you to do that, then,' Riordan muttered to himself. Louder: 'Right. So, if we asked you to deliver a cargo weighing about a hundred and fifty pounds into the Hjalmar Palace you could land in the courtyard – as long as we've got the usurper's men out of that gatehouse – and you could probably fly out of it on your own, but if you had a problem on takeoff you'd hit the wall, and again, the usurper's men would have you in rifle range for a minute or two. You can't fly at night, and you can't fly low enough to drop anything useful on the enemy without them riddling you with bullets. Am I missing anything? Is that a fair summary of your limitations?'

Rudi nodded. 'Yes, sir, I think so. Uh, that and, we need more gas. Sorry.' He shrugged. 'I think we've got about five gallons left. Avgas, not regular.'

'Damn.' Riordan glanced round. 'Steward? More coffee.' He turned back to the table. 'Have Joachim and Stefan reported in yet?'

Vincenze looked thoughtful. 'Not unless they've come in since we started in here.'

'Go and chase them up, then.'

Dismissed, Vincenze rose. He nodded at Rudi. 'Good luck, cuz.'

Startled, Rudi watched him leave.

'The cornet has no need to know what I'm about to tell you,' Riordan said quietly. He paused while the steward placed fresh mugs of coffee in front of them. 'That will be all.'

'Sir.' The steward bowed then left the room.

Rudi waited until the door was shut. 'Sir, you obviously have something in mind?'

'Yes.' Riordan fell silent. Then: 'I sent Joachim and Stefan out to buy some office equipment. Most of a print shop, in fact – a laptop, graphics software, a printer, a scanner, and equipment for making badges.'

'Badges?'

'You know of our long lost cousins, I take it?'

Rudi nodded cautiously. 'I've never met any of them.'

'Hmm. You will, soon enough.' Riordan picked up his coffee mug and blew on it. 'When Joachim gets back he's to run off two hundred laminated color cards with our lost cousins' knotwork seal on it.'

'Their – ' Rudi stopped. 'It's not the same as ours, is it?' he asked.

'No.' Riordan put his mug down. 'According to the duke, they became lost two centuries ago when – you know the story about how the seventh brother went west, to make a home for himself in the outer kingdom, what the Americans call California? He fell on hard times, and lost his sigil. Later, he tried to recreate it from memory, and got it subtly wrong. That's why neither he nor his descendants could visit the United States; they found themselves in another world, only slightly different at that time. Anyway, we have a copy of the lost family's sigil, and we are going to make enough duplicates of it to equip every world-walker in the Hjalmar Palace. As its doppelgänger site in Massachusetts is crawling with federal agents, and we have not accurately surveyed the terrain in the other world, you're going to fly the badges in.'

Rudi's thoughts spun. 'So I won't need to fly out . . . ?'

'No. The duke's men will help you dismantle your aircraft and carry it with them when they leave. Lady Olga is developing the evacuation plan and will organize your logistics. The larger goal is to present the usurper with a tempting target, and then give him a nasty surprise when he tries to take it. Do you understand?'

'Yes, I think so. But I thought he knew about our talent? And is clearly taking pains to avoid situations where we can use it?'

'Indeed.' The earl nodded. 'I'm counting on it. Egon knows about world-walking, and plans his moves accordingly. Which makes his behavior predictable . . . and I'm going to use it to kill him.'

*

Mike Fleming was trapped in the basement of his apartment, trying to figure out how to get out, when the phone rang.

He was there because of the colonel. 'Son, I'm relying on you to stay home and convalesce,' he'd said sternly, after handing over a brown paper bag containing an anonymous cell phone and a semiautomatic pistol. 'I want you back in the saddle as soon as you're fit for duty. But you're not going to be any use to me if you overdo it. So relax, take it easy, and try to remember your job is to get well, and maybe see to the other thing.' (The *other thing* being his mission if the Mad Grandmother or the Ice Princess made contact – but Mike had an uneasy feeling that this latter duty was more than slightly deniable.) But there was only so much sitting on his ass that he could do, and after a few days frittered away watching *Friends* reruns and reading pop-history books about the Middle East, he was ready to climb the walls.

Hence, the basement.

Most apartments don't have basements, but the one Mike rented in a converted brownstone was the exception to the rule: A steep staircase opening off one wall of the kitchen led down into the low-ceilinged cellar. With perfect hindsight, Mike had to admit, deciding to clean house while recovering from a broken leg and a nasty little infection was not one of his most sensible moves. But once he'd gotten down those steps, it turned out that filling garbage sacks and trying to figure out how to dismantle the dead drier that had been stranded down here for years was a whole lot easier than trying to figure out how to get back up the stairs. Especially because he wasn't sure he'd be able to make it around the tight bend at the top, and having to phone for help to dig him out of his own cellar would do his self-image no good at all. *(You're a special agent working for a secret government organization and you had to call in help to* climb a staircase? *What is this, the CIA?)*

So naturally the phone rang while he was stuck in the basement.

Mike swore. The bell rang twice more as he disentangled himself from the cable of the defunct drier and hopped around the workbench, trying to find the extension handset behind the pile of rusting paint cans and the overflowing toolbox. 'Yes?' he barked, making a one-handed grab for the phone and simultaneously putting too much weight on his bad leg.

'Is that Mr Fleming?' It was a woman's voice, a noisy office providing unwelcome background context. *If this is a junk call . . .* Mike felt a hot flash of anger, echoing the pain in his right ankle. About a week and a half ago he'd trodden on a mantrap – a medieval antipersonnel mine, as Sergeant Hastert had put it – and with the cracked bone, torn ligaments, and nice little infection he'd picked up, he'd been lucky to keep the leg.

'Who is this?' Mike demanded.

'I'm Letitia, from Family Home Services. Can I speak to Mr. Fleming, please?'

The spark of helpless anger passed rapidly. 'Yeah, that's me.' He glanced round instinctively. 'Free to talk.' No, *not* a telesales call; the background office noise was a recording and the company name a cover. 'It's Tuesday today, isn't it?'

'No, it's Wednesday,' said the woman at the other end of the line, who wasn't called Letitia any more than it was any day other than Monday. 'You're late for your CAT scan. Dr. James wants to see you as soon as possible, and as it happens we've got a slot free right now – are you free now?'

Mike glanced round at the dusty basement again, his pulse quickening. 'I believe I can fit you in.'

'Good. An ambulance will collect you in fifteen minutes, if that's convenient?'

'I'll be waiting.' The usual pleasantries, and Mike hung up the handset, staring at it in surprise. So the colonel's boss wanted to talk to him? But the colonel knew damn well what shape his leg was in, and the boss man was in the loop, so what could he want . . . ?

Mike began to smile, for the first time in days.

The ambulance that pulled up outside his front door twenty minutes later looked just like any other, and the two paramedics made short work of wheeling Mike – sitting up, chatting, no need to alarm the neighbors unduly – into the back of their vehicle. The door shut, and there the resemblance stopped: Normal ambulances didn't have door gunners in black fatigues riding behind the one-way glass windows. They didn't roll like a foundering ship beneath the weight of armor, either; and they especially didn't come with passengers like Dr. James, whose specialty was distinctly nonmedical.

Dr. Andrew James scared the crap out of Mike Fleming, with his Ph.D. from Harvard and the flag pin that had lately replaced the tiny crucifix on his lapel. Gaunt and skinny and utterly dedicated, James attended to the ills of the body politic with all the care you could expect of an apprentice engineer of human souls; and if an amputation was required, he could get a consent form any time he liked, signed by the office of the vice president. 'How's your leg?' he asked as the ambulance moved off.

'Still bad, but I can get about indoors. Last time I asked they said I'd be able to get the cast off in another six weeks, be back to normal in three or four months.' *Why is he asking me this stuff?* Mike stared at him sidelong. *It's not like he can't pull my medical records any time he wants . . .*

'Not good enough.' James frowned, his lips forming a bloodless crease. 'There's a change of plan.'

Mike shivered under the thin thermal blanket the 'paramedics' had draped over him. He could see what was coming next, like a freight locomotive glimpsed through the side window of his crossing-stalled car. *He's cutting around the chain of command. Which means I'm in trouble.* James was political, and even in the flattened wartime hierarchy of the Family Trade Organization he was several levels above Mike. If he was descending from on high to give Mike orders in person, it meant that either Mike's boss, Colonel Smith, was on the out – or that Mike was being snipped out of the org chart. Spoiled goods, a deniable asset, disposable on demand. 'What do you want me to do?' he asked, keeping his face as still as possible.

The ambulance turned a corner and began to accelerate, swaying from side to side as it shoved across two lanes of traffic. 'We've made a breakthrough in the past week, and it's led us to review our existing programs.' James was looking at him, but not meeting his eyes. 'You speak the bad guys' language, as much as anyone does. We need you as an interpreter.'

'But – ' Mike shook his head, confused. 'What about the negotiations?' Miriam's crazy mother and her sidekick, the blond sniper who looked like a Russian princess: They were supposed to be making contact, negotiating over the stolen nuke. 'Don't you want – '

'Son, don't be naïve.' Dr. James smiled, and this time he looked Mike in the eyes. Mike tried not to shiver; he'd seen a warmer smile on the pet alligator he'd once tripped over during a raid on a drug dealer's pad. 'The missing gadget has been retrieved so the negotiations are over. We don't need them anymore. Our job is now to hit these people so hard they won't ever mess with the USA again.' The ambulance bounced hard across a pothole and Mike's stomach lurched as he felt it accelerate down a steep gradient. 'I don't think your contacts will be back, but if they are, it's kill-or-capture time.'

'The phone . . . ?' Colonel Smith had given him an untraceable cell phone to pass on to the ice princess if the Clan wanted to negotiate.

'It's a Kidon special.' Made by Mossad's – the Israeli secret service's – assassination cell. 'It works fine, but there's ten grams of C4 in the earpiece. If one of them tries to call us, that's one less bad guy to worry about.'

'Oh.' For a moment a vision of Olga's blond head flashed through Mike's mind, bloodied and slack-jawed. He bit down on his reaction: *That's assassination!* He swallowed, queasy. 'If that's the way you're playing it.' *(You're a cop, he's a spook. You knew these things happened. So why's he telling you now?)* 'You said you want an interpreter, but you're not talking to the Clan. So what's going on?'

'There's been a breakthrough.' Dr. James leaned back against the side of the ambulance, his death's-head grin fading. 'Pretty soon we're not going to need the freaks for transport anymore, so we're winding up to restart CLEANSWEEP. This time we've got the logistic support to set up a full-scale expeditionary force on the other side. You'll be going over in about three months as a civilian advisor. But in the meantime, I've got a little extra job for you as soon as you're cleared for duty again. You've already got a clearance; you're going to need a higher one for this job. Unless you think there's something that might disqualify you . . . ?'

Mike swallowed again. 'Uh, what do you mean?'

James gestured irritably: 'I can't tell you what you're needed for until you've been cleared. Additional background checks will be required. So this is your chance to come clean about anything you wouldn't want to disclose during a polygraph interrogation.'

'You're offering me an amnesty?' Mike raised an eyebrow.

'Son, I don't care if you're f– . . . sleeping with the Russian ambassador's grandson; all I care is that you're not keeping secrets from *me*, you're not going to embarrass me in front of an internal affairs polygraph, and you're up to, to listening in on a bunch of conversations in gook-speak and translating them into English for me. And keeping a lid on it. So. Is there anything you really *don't* want to be quizzed about during your clearance interview?'

'I – ' The penny dropped. 'It's not CLEANSWEEP that's so damn secret, is it?' he said without thinking. 'It's the content, isn't it? You've got some kind of source – '

'Mr. Fleming.' Dr. James's stare was leaden. 'What do we pay you for?'

Mike winced. 'Sorry. Forget I asked.' He took a deep breath. 'As for your question, I'm not blackmailable. Nothing to hide here.' He tapped his chest. 'So. When do I begin?'

'Soon as you go back to the office, son. You'll be scheduled for a full security re-cert within a couple of days, then I'll have some extra work for you. Which will go on your worksheet as routine admin, incidentally. That should keep you busy right up until the invasion.'

'Invasion?' Mike echoed incredulously. 'You're going to invade the Gruinmarkt?'

'We're going to have to sooner or later. Unless you've got any better ideas for how we ought to handle the existence of such a major security threat to American soil . . . ?'

'But how?'

James cast Mike a knowing look. 'Ask me again when you're cleared.'

RECEPTION COMMITTEE

Baron Otto Neuhalle was afraid of very few things; the wrath of gods, the scorn of women, and the guns of his enemies were not among them. He was, however, utterly terrified of one man – Egon the First, former crown prince and now self-proclaimed monarch of Gruinmarkt. Egon was a handsome-faced, graceful, hale, and charismatic young man who had all the pity of a rattlesnake for those who failed him. Even if Otto hadn't failed yet, failure nevertheless looked disturbingly possible in light of the witch-clan's continuing occupation of the Hjalmar Palace. And the cloud of dust he could see from his vantage point near the brow of the hill was almost certainly the vanguard of Egon's army.

'Another hour, sir,' said Anders, who had materialized at his elbow while he peered through the witch-bought 'binoculars'.

'Nonsense, they'll be three at least – ' He blinked. 'Wait. *What* will be another hour?'

'The ammunition, my lord.'

'*Scheisse . . .*' Otto turned back to the castle, barely visible behind its banked ramparts on the other side of the moat and the sloped killing apron. Bodies littered the ground before it, and clouds of smoke still billowed from the gatehouse his men had latterly abandoned. He'd gotten two of the witch-clan's machine guns out of the gatehouse to cover his soldiers' retreat, but things hadn't gone well: The enemy forces had laid down a stupefying volume of fire, and they'd brought some kind of artillery with them, not honest cannon but an arquebus-sized tube that belched fingers of flame that exploded on impact. And his gunners, undertrained, had burned through their ammunition too fast. *They weren't supposed to counterattack for at least a day. If it hadn't been for that flying spy . . .* He shook his head. The buzzing witch-bird would cut less ice with his majesty than the heat-warped machine gun barrels and prematurely expended stockpiles of valuable, irreplaceable cartridges. 'What word is there from Hern?'

'The waterway holds so far, my lord. That's recent.'

Otto nodded thoughtfully. The castle's dependence for fresh water on a buried culvert leading to the nearby river was a weakness. If the new defenders were foolish enough to rely on the well, or the casks in the cellar . . . *No, they're not inexperienced.* He glanced at a nearby soldier. 'You, March. Bring me paper. And pen. I have a report to write.'

'My lord.' March bowed and scurried back towards the hastily established headquarters tent.

And if I write well, will it save my neck? Otto suppressed a shudder. All told, it had been a *good* plan, and the witches had been on the defensive for the past several weeks as the king's forces harried their homesteads and burned their crops – the plan to force them to counterattack in a place of his choosing, where they could be chopped up by the king's stealthily stolen machine guns and mines, was a good one. But the upstart clan of witches-turned-nobles had struck back viciously fast, and shown a good few surprises of their own, from the flying spy down. *And they can walk through the shadow world,* Otto reminded himself. Evidence of witchcraft, but he'd also seen a couple of them vanish in front of his own eyes: Otto was a believer. *What could I do with an army like that?* He raised his glasses again and peered at the castle. 'Sir Anders,' he said quietly. 'A general order. Be on watch for the dog that fails to bark in the night. If any man notices that the enemy have fallen silent for more than a quarter of a bell, they are to send word to me immediately, regardless of the hour of day or night.'

'Sir?' Anders raised a craggy brow.

'Remember who we are fighting.' Otto watched as dawning understanding – and fear – crept across his hetman's face.

The dust cast up by the royal army crept closer over the next half hour as Otto scratched an abbreviated report, then sealed it in a hide tube and sent a messenger careening towards the vanguard. Occasionally he had one or another of his troops' preprepared positions light up the walls, or take careful aimed shots at the windows of the castle: The returning spasms of automatic fire were reassuringly solid, evidence that the enemy was not yet melting into shadows and mist that could reappear in his rear at any moment. Otto didn't waste his reprieve. His men were beginning to grumble about the amount of ditch-work he was making them dig, but his periodic rounds of the trenches and foxholes they were preparing kept the muttering under control. With a high, fine overcast to keep the sun off their necks, and no rain to bog them down, the weather wasn't giving them much to complain about – but if the witch-clan staged a breakout, or the king arrived to find the works incomplete, they'd have something to moan about for the rest of their lives, however short.

The shadows were beginning to lengthen across the apron in front of the castle (putting his snipers at a considerable disadvantage) when the first column of riders thundered up the valley floor and came to a stop by the guards. They didn't pause for long: After no small amount of shouting, half a dozen of them walked on, mounts breathing heavily, towards the headquarters tent. Otto, who had been checking the second gun emplacement, steeled himself as he walked back downhill towards the group. He'd been expecting this moment, trying not to allow it to get in the way of his urgent defensive preparations for most of the day.

'Your Majesty.' He bowed deeply, but without flourish.

'Otto.' The golden boy's face was calm, but his eyes were stony. 'Your tent, please. We will have words.' The guards behind him sported strange black weapons, machine-pistols looted or stolen from the Clan's dead.

'Yes, sire.' He gestured towards the tent. 'If you would follow me?'

'Certainly,' Egon said, easily enough, but Otto had a hard time pretending to ignore the two guards who preceded them, or the two who took up stations beside the tent.

Inside the tent, the young king turned to face Otto. 'What happened?' he asked. 'In your own words.'

'They counterattacked too early.' Otto frowned. 'We took the castle as planned. But we'd only been there for half a day when a witch – flying beneath a wing like a bat's – flew overhead. My men shot at him, but he got away. High up, high as an eagle. I redoubled my efforts to prepare the grounds, but only two hours later there was an explosion, then witch-troops everywhere. They came from inside the palace, as your majesty predicted, but they arrived before we were ready for them. Seven hours, I reckon, from our entry to their arrival.'

'Seven hours . . .' Egon stared at Otto measuringly, although Otto couldn't guess whether it might be for a medal or a noose. 'This flying witch. Describe what you saw.'

Otto felt himself burst into chilly perspiration. 'It made a buzzing noise, as of bees, only louder . . .' He described the ultralight haltingly, its arrival from the southwest and subsequent departure after overflying the castle.

'And two hours later they arrived in force,' Egon said musingly. 'What of your force did you recover?'

The next ten minutes were the hardest examination of Otto's life, as he explained the precise disposition of his withdrawal. 'In the end, we lost two of the machine guns, and we have but four gun barrels left. We have also expended all but four belts of ammunition,' he finished. 'Of men, eighteen dead and twenty-three wounded. The defensive positions are nearly complete, although I do not propose to defend them past dawn tomorrow – too much risk of the witches infiltrating our lines. My men are at your disposal, sire.'

Egon glanced at the rough map of the surrounding area on Otto's camp chair. 'Flying spies. Some sort of artillery – that's a new twist.' He nodded to himself. 'They are still bottled up in there?'

'Yes, sire.' Otto nodded back, reflexively. 'I've detailed my men to tell me at once if the witches stop replying to our probing fire. But so far they're sitting tight. It's almost as if they can't simply walk away.'

For the first time, the young king's poker face relaxed. 'Well.' His lips quirked. 'You've done no worse than aught of our commanders might. And that flying witch – yes.' He nodded briskly. 'Bravely done, Baron Neuhalle.' Then he smiled, and Otto's blood ran cold at the look in the royal eyes. 'Something you might not know about the witches is that they have to use their magic sparingly – should they walk through the paths of the dead too frequently, they fall ill and die. By your own word it is barely a day since they retook the palace. Normally that would be enough time to allow them to escape, but I have

39

intelligence that suggests to me a new possibility. Your men *did* succeed in dropping the culvert and poisoning the well, I trust?' Unsure where this was leading, Otto nodded. 'Good.' The king clapped his hands. 'Krentz. Fetch Sir Geraunt and Baron Rolfuss.'

'Sire.' One of the bodyguards bowed, then ducked through the tent door; the other visibly tensed, watching Otto alertly.

'Your Majesty?' Otto tried not to let his own tension show.

'We're going to take them.' Egon's eyes twinkled. 'Because, you see, they are not only under siege *here*. They may be able to walk through the realm of the dead, but the dead, I am informed, have taken a dislike to them. They won't be able to escape this time. All that remains to be established is how we may dig them out of that castle. And my other intelligence suggests a solution.'

*

The house squatting behind the densely tree-clad hillside had seen better years, that much was clear: its wooden decking needed a fresh coat of paint, the shingled roof was silver and cracked behind the eaves, and the chain-link fence that surrounded the acre lot was rusted. But the padlock holding the gate closed was well-oiled, and as she followed Brill and her team of bright young adventurers up the front steps, Miriam spotted the discreet black dome of a CCTV camera lurking in the shadows of the verandah. That, at least, looked to be new and well-maintained.

'It's a safe house,' Brill explained as she pushed buttons on an alarm system that was far fancier – and newer – than the building it was attached to. 'We own a bunch of them, lease them out for short stays via a local agent, so there's a lot of turnover. There's always one free when we need it, and it doesn't look suspicious. We actually make money on the deal: We can buy the properties with spare capital and they're mostly going up.'

Miriam glanced around as they entered the front hall. Dust tickled her nostrils; the husk of a dead beetle lay, legs upturned, in the middle of the floor. She wrinkled her nose. 'What's the plan?'

'Oh, I just phoned the agent and told them I was a friend of the owner and we were taking it for two weeks.' She held up a key. 'There's some emergency gear stashed in the cellar, behind a false wall. Other than that, it's clean – the emergency gear's the kind of stuff a survival nut would have, nothing to attract special attention. The only real trouble we've ever had with these safe houses was when one of them was accidentally let to a meth dealer. We cleared them out good. The Sheriff's department *like* us.' She said it with such evident satisfaction that Miriam shivered. For a meth dealer, setting up a clandestine lab in a Clan safe house was a bit like a fox setting up house in a grizzly's den. 'You may want to take the front bedroom, milady. I'll get the air and hot water working and everyone else settled in, then we can talk.'

Three hours later, Miriam felt a lot more human. Air conditioning! Proper showers! Toilets with lids and a handle you turned to flush, rather than yanking on a chain! It was almost like being home again. Brill had even, somehow, managed to find the time to scare up some clothes that fit her, so she didn't look totally weird. Well, Brill had been her lady-in-waiting for some months, as one of the jobs she did for the thin white duke – Miriam's uncle – so knowing her measurements wasn't that odd. It was a shame she'd bleached her hair blond while she'd been on the run, Miriam told herself; the colors Brill had picked didn't match her new look, and besides, her roots were starting to show.

But I'm home. So, what now?

She sat on the edge of the bed, one leg of a very new pair of jeans dangling, and stared at the window. It was utterly unlike the stony castle casement she'd spent weeks staring at in a state of desperation, under house arrest and facing a forced political marriage as a lesser evil to paying the price of her earlier mistakes, but it was still a window in a house guarded by the Clan's traditions and rules. The formal betrothal had gone adrift in a sea of flame and gunfire, as Crown Prince Egon took exception to the idea of a Clan heiress marrying his younger (and retarded) brother; then she'd been on the run in the confusing political underworld of New Britain, moving too fast to think. But now –

It all depends on what else has been going on since I left. She sighed and began to work her other foot down the pants leg. *Is Mom okay?* She paused again. *Brill said something about being under attack over here. Is* Paulie *okay?* Paulette, her sometime PA, was an outsider to all this – but if the Clan was being attacked from outside, she could be in big trouble, stuck in Cambridge. Guilt by association: Some within the Clan would see her as a tool tainted by Miriam's low stock, while whatever agency was going after the Clan would assume the worst. *I've got to find out,* Miriam decided, and stood up just as there was a tentative knock at the door.

'Come in,' she called, hastily buttoning up.

The door opened and Brilliana looked in. 'Milady?'

'I'm nearly done here.' Miriam glanced around. 'Where did I put my shoes?' Handmade leather ankle boots from New Britain wouldn't look too out of place, and shoes were the one thing Brill hadn't been able to buy for her. 'Eh.' They were hiding under the dressing table.

'I think we need to talk.'

'Yes.' Miriam bent over and began working on her left foot. 'What exactly has been going on since the, the banquet?' Her brain began to catch up with her earlier thoughts: 'My mother – is she all right? What about the duke? My grandmother – '

'It's a mess,' said Brill. She perched on the stool by the table. 'We're not sure exactly how long Egon had been planning it for, but he used Henryk's scheme' – the plan to forcibly marry Miriam into the Gruinmarkt's royal dynasty – 'as leverage to get a bunch of the backwood peers behind him. He's declared the entire Clan outlaw and placed a price on our heads, and is promising half our estates to those nobles who back him. It's turned into a messy civil war and Angbard's hands were tied trying to defend individual holdings instead of going after the pretender's army. While all that was going on, we've had some disturbing – well, a couple of couriers have gone missing over the past six months. Missing with no explanation, no hint of trouble. Not only did that bastard Matthias rat us out to the Drug Enforcement Agency, now there's some sort of secret government cross-agency committee trying to hunt us down. Everyone on this side has had to activate their emergency cover plans. And the really bad news is that this agency managed to sneak a couple of agents into the Gruinmarkt, which means it's serious.'

'Yes, I know.' Miriam sat up and took a deep breath. 'I told you about meeting Mike, didn't I?' She'd once had a thing going with Mike Fleming. Odd, it seemed an awfully long time ago. 'He got me out of the palace alive.' She shrugged. 'He was unexpectedly honest.' Another deep breath. 'Told me that if I wanted to join the federal witness protection program . . .'

The words hung in the air for a few seconds. Finally, Brilliana nodded. 'We know. And it will count for much when it comes to the Council's attention, I think,' she said slowly. A longer pause. 'Olga and your mother have been talking to him. Trying to negotiate a, a temporary ceasefire. But things are really bad. They believe we've stolen a nuclear weapon, and they want it back.'

'Jesus.' Miriam shook her head. 'Why would they think *that*?' She looked at Brill, aghast. 'Hang on. They *believe* the Clan has stolen a *nuke*? *Why*? Why would they believe that? Has Angbard – ? He'd have to be mad! Tell me he hasn't?'

Brill looked uncomfortable. '*Angbard* hasn't stolen a nuke. But they leave them in undoppelgängered bunkers; is that not a temptation?'

'Oh, *shit*.' Miriam shoved her hair back from her face. 'Has someone in the Clan actually gone and stolen a nuclear weapon? How? I mean, I thought they were too big to carry – '

'Not one,' Brill said, then bit her lip. 'Six, we think. Maybe more. They're backpack devices, part of the inactive inventory – the CIA asked for them, originally.'

Aghast, Miriam stared at her. 'Is that why they're all over us?'

Brill nodded.

'Then who – '

'Oliver, Baron Hjorth, is the key-holder designated by the Clan committee.'

'Jesus, why *him*?' The thought of what might happen if the feds discovered the Clan had haunted Miriam ever since she'd learned about her own ancestry; what they might do if they thought the extradimensional narcoterrorists had nuclear weapons didn't bear thinking about. And Baron Oliver was about the worst person she could think of to be holding them – an unregenerate backwoodsman and dyed-in-the-wool conservative faction member. 'And they can get their own people into the Gruinmarkt, can't they.'

'There's more bad news,' Brill added after a moment. 'Why don't you come downstairs? Then Huw can deliver it himself.'

*

Elena sprawled across the sofa in the living room, pulling an oiled cleaning cloth through the breech of her P90. 'Find another channel, minion,' she drawled without looking up. 'I can't *stand Friends.*'

'As you wish, my princess.' Yul, hulking and fair-haired as any Viking warrior, carefully squeezed the remote. Advertisements and sitcoms strobed across the eviscerated guts of the machine pistol on the coffee table until he arrived at MTV. 'Ah, that is better.' Marilyn Manson strutted and howled through 'The Last Day on Earth'; Elena pulled a face. 'Manly music for martial – ' an oily rag landed on his head.

'Children.'

Elena glanced round, pulled a face. '*He* started it!'

'Sure.' Huw stood in the doorway, trying not to smile. 'Did you get the Internet working?'

'Something's wrong with it,' Yul said apologetically.

'Ah, well.' Huw shrugged and walked over to the armchair, where a laptop trailed bits of many-colored spaghetti towards the wall. 'I'll sort it out. Got to report in.' Expecting Yul or Elena to do anything technical had been a forlorn hope. *Am I the only competent person around here?* he wondered. Dumb question: While he'd been studying in schools and colleges in the United States under a false identity, Yul had been bringing joy to their backwoods father's heart, riding and hunting and being a traditional son on their country estate in the western marches of the Gruinmarkt; and Elena had been under the stifling constraints of a noble daughter, although she'd kicked up enough of a fuss that her parents had allowed her to escape into Clan Security, leaving them with one less dowry to worry about. Which left Huw as the guy who knew one end of an Internet router and a secure voice-over IP connection from another, and Yul and Elena as the armed muscle to watch over him when they weren't engaging in risky post-adolescent high jinks – risky because the older generation weren't many years past fighting blood feuds over that sort of thing.

It took him a few minutes, some scrabbling with cables, and a reboot to get everything working properly. Huw was setting up the encrypted link to the ClanSec e-mail hub and looking forward to checking in when he heard footsteps.

'Yes?' He glanced round. It was Miriam. She looked – not tired, exactly, but careworn. And something else.

'Brill tells me we need to talk,' she said, then glanced across the room at the sofa.

'She said – ' Huw's larynx froze for a few seconds as he stared at her. The first time he'd met her, gowned and bejeweled at a royal reception, she'd been turned out in the very mode of Gruinmarkt nobility; then earlier, when Lady Brilliana had so rudely yanked him (and Yul, and Elena) away from his survey, she'd been wearing an outlandish getup. Now she looked – *at ease*, he decided. *This is her. She isn't acting a part. How* interesting. 'Ah. Well, she did, did she?'

'She said.' Miriam leaned on the back of his chair. 'You've been exploring. Whatever that means.' She sounded bored, but there was a glint in her eye.

'Uh, yeah.' Huw leaned forward and shut the laptop's lid. 'Why don't we go fix something to drink?' He glanced sidelong at Yul and Elena, who were sitting on the sofa, bickering amiably over the gun, their heads leaning together. 'Somewhere quieter.' The TV howled mournfully, recycling the sound track of a guitar in torment.

The kitchen was bland, basic, and undersupplied – they'd traveled light and hadn't had time to buy much more than a bunch of frozen pizzas – but there was coffee, a carton of half-and-half, and a coffee maker. Huw busied himself filling it while Miriam searched the cupboards for mugs. 'How did you go about it?' she asked, finally.

Huw took a deep breath. 'Systematically. We haven't started deconvoluting the knotwork' – the two worlds to which the Clan's members could walk were distinguished by the use of a different knot that the world-walker had to concentrate on – 'but I'm pretty sure we'll start finding others once we do. The fourth world we found – it's accessed from this one, if you use the Lees' knot. We couldn't get through to it in New England, but it worked down south; I think it may be in the middle of an ice age.'

'Did you find anyone? People, I mean?'

'Yes.' Huw paused as the coffee maker coughed and grumbled to itself. 'Their bones. A big dome, made out of something like, like a very odd kind of concrete. Residual radioactivity. A skull with perfect dentistry, bits of damaged metalwork, fire escapes or gantries or something, that I'll swear are made out of titanium. It's clearly been there decades or centuries. And then there's the door.'

'Door?'

'Yul hit it with an axe. Nearly killed us – there was hard vacuum on the other side.'

'Whoops.' Miriam pulled out a stool and sat down at the breakfast bar. 'Too fast. *Vacuum?* You think you found a *door* onto another world?'

'We didn't stick around to make sure. But it didn't stop sucking after a couple of minutes. Last time we saw the dome, it was surrounded by fog.'

'Oh my.' Her shoulders were shaking. 'God.'

Huw watched her, not unsympathetically. He'd had more than a day to get used to the idea: If Lady Brilliana was right – and his own judgement was right – and Miriam was fit to lead them . . .

'That changes a lot of things,' she said, looking straight at him. 'If it *is* a door to another world . . . how do you think it works?'

Huw shrugged again. 'We are cursed by our total ignorance of our family talent's origins,' he pointed out. 'But what we seem to have is a trait that can be externally controlled – that's what the knot's for – and I figure if it turns out that other knots take us to other worlds, then it's no huge leap to conclude that it was engineered. I don't think anyone's looked inside us – I figure the mechanism, if there is one, has got to be something intracellular – but the fact that it's controllable, that we don't world-walk at random when we look at a maze or a fractal generator on a PC, screams design. This door? There's more stuff in that dome, lots more, and it looks like wreckage left behind by a civilization more advanced than this one.' He pointed at the coffee maker. 'Think what a peasant back home would make of that? You know, and I know, what it is and how it works, because we went to school and college in this country.' He pulled the jug out and poured two mugs of coffee. 'Electricity. But to a peasant . . .'

'Magic.' The word hung in the air as Miriam poured milk into both mugs.

'So.' He chose his words carefully. 'What do you think it means?'

'Oh boy.' Miriam stared at her coffee mug, then blew on it and took a first sip. 'Where do you want me to start? If nothing else, it makes all the Clan's defensive structures obsolete overnight. One extra universe is useful, two is embarrassing, three extra universes implies . . . lots. Which means, assuming there are more, that doppelgängered houses stop being effectively defended.' Doppelgängering – the practice of building defenses in the other worlds, physically collocated with the space occupied by the defended structure, in order to stop hostile world-walkers gaining access – was a key element in all the Clan families' buildings. But you could build an earth berm or a safe house in one parallel universe – how could you hope to do it if there were millions? 'And then . . . well. I tried telling the Council their business model was broken, but I didn't realize *how* broken it was.'

'Really?'

'Really.' She put her mug down. 'The – hell, I'm doing it again. Distancing. *We* got rich in the Gruinmarkt by exploiting superior technology – being able to move messages around fast, make markets, that kind of thing. And we got rich in *this* world' – she glanced at the window, which opened out onto an unkempt yard – 'by smuggling. But what they were *really* doing was exploiting a development imbalance. Making money through a monopoly on superior technology – okay, call it a family talent, and it may be something you can selectively breed for, but if you're right and it's a technology, then *it's not a monopoly anymore.*'

'Uh.' Huw took a mouthful of coffee. 'What's your reasoning?'

'Well, you're the one who just told me you thought our ability was artificial? And we've established that someone else – let's take your door into a vacuum realm as a given – has a way of moving stuff between time lines – yes, I'm going to take the idea that we're in a bunch of parallel universes that branch off each other as a given. New

Britain really rubs your nose in it – and I think if they can just *open a door* then we have to admit that – what the Clan can do? The postal corvée? Is a joke.'

Miriam closed her eyes for a moment. 'The Council are *so* not going to want to hear this. And it's not the worst of it.'

'What else do you figure we're looking at?' Huw stared at her, fascinated. *Have you figured out the other thing . . . ?*

'Okay, let's speculate wildly. There are other people out there who can travel between parallel worlds. They're better at it than us, and they know what they're doing. That's really bad, right there, but not necessarily fatal. However . . . we've been pointedly ignoring, all along, the fact that what we do isn't magical. It's not unique. It's like, after 1945, the government pretended for a few years that making nuclear weapons was some kind of big secret. Then the Russians got the bomb, and the Brits, and the Chinese, and before you can blink we're worrying about the North Koreans, or the Iranians. What the Clan Council needs to worry about is the US government – who they've spent the past few decades systematically provoking – and who now know we exist. What do *you* think they'll do?'

'But we don't know how the world-walking mechanism works. It's got to take them time – '

Miriam took another mouthful of coffee. 'They've had *seven or eight months*, Huw. That's how long it's been since Matthias went over the wall. And there's' – she paused, as if considering her words – 'stuff that's happened, stuff that will turn hunting us down into a screaming crash priority, higher than al-Qaeda, higher than the Iraq occupation. They've got to be throwing money at it like the Manhattan project . . .' She trailed off.

'I don't think they'll have got anywhere yet.' Huw reached for the coffee pot again, emptying the dregs into their mugs. 'It takes time to organize a research project and they'll be doing it under conditions of complete secrecy.'

'Yes, but they've already got the big national laboratories. And if they've got captive Clan members, they're *starting* from where the Clan stood, as of forty-eight hours ago. And they could have started months ago! It all depends on whether the problem they're trying to crack is a hard one or an easy one. If we've got some kind of mechanism that lets us do this, then it's designed to replicate, and there's got to be some sort of control system wired into our brains – are you telling me nobody has put bits of a Clan member under an electron microscope before to look for anomalies?'

'You've met enough of your cousins by now. How many brain surgeons did you spot?' Huw looked defensive. 'It wasn't a high priority.'

'Well it is, *now*. Because if they can figure out what makes us world-walk, they're probably halfway to mass-producing it. Given they've got scouts in the Gruinmarkt – '

'They've got *what?*' Huw sat bolt upright.

'Eh.' Miriam cocked her head to one side. 'Forget I said that?'

'Sure . . . but can I finish your sentence for you before I forget?'

'Um . . .'

'Right now, any scouts they can send our way are going to be riding piggyback. Lightning Child knows how they're making the couriers cooperate, but nothing would surprise me: The current administration are so Machiavellian they make Prince Egon look like a White House intern. But what you're speculating about is how long we've got until there's a large-scale incursion.' Her expression made him look for other words. '*Invasion*. Is that what you're thinking?'

Miriam nodded. 'I – no, *we* – have got to talk to Angbard, and fast. Whatever the prince has been up to back, uh, home' – he spotted the moment's deliberation before she chose the word – 'it's a sideshow compared to what's coming. I don't know how long we've got, but I'd guess it's going to be weeks to months, not months to years.' She pushed her empty mug away. 'Do you have Google on that laptop of yours?'

'What are you thinking of trawling for?'

'News items. Foreign stuff, not more shit about Paris Hilton's funeral; I want to hear about anything that suggests that State is planning a hasty exit from Iraq. They're not going to try and occupy Iraq and Afghanistan *and* invade the Gruinmarkt simultaneously, are they?' She slid off her bar stool, visibly jittery. *Iraq* had been a ghastly object lesson in what the current administration could do to people they didn't like: the increasingly desperate pleas of the coup plotters after they deposed Saddam, the cringing threats of gas attacks in event of invasion – and in response, the huge B52 raids on Baghdad. All of it had been calculated to send a message: *This is what you get if you mess with us.*

'Depends.' Huw reached over and switched off the coffee maker. 'Don't they have some kind of doctrine about being able to fight two wars simultaneously, anywhere on the planet? And the supply lines to the Gruinmarkt are *real* short, if they can build a world-walking machine. Much less some kind of gate.'

'And mostly they'd be up against irregulars with muskets. They could roll over in their sleep and crush us, if – '

A door slammed in the passage. Moments later, Brill darted into the kitchen. 'Oh. There you are!' Visibly agitated, she focused on the coffee pot. 'Ah, you emptied it. Huw, have you brought the e-mail service to life?'

'Not yet, I was going to – '

'*Scheisse.*' Brill glanced aside. 'I'm sorry, milady. The news is bad. I *must* get in touch right away. Huw, if you would be so good – '

'What's happened?' demanded Miriam.

'My pager ordered me to call in, in the clear – maximum urgency. It's the duke, my lady. I'm afraid there's been an accident.'

*

There was a room on one of the upper floors of the Hjalmar Palace with a huge canopied bed in it, and the bed stank of death and uncontrolled bowels. Lady Olga sat on the edge of the bed and spoke to its occupant, as a medic cleaned him and a soldier stood by, waiting to replace the fouled sheets.

He'd been strong once, and clever and ruthless, a bulwark for his allies and a terror to his faction's foes, during the years of madness when the Clan's member families had engaged in a bloody succession of mortal feuds. Then, as the madness receded, he'd helped broker a series of treaties – some on paper, others cemented by blood in marriage – to disarm the worst of the remaining hostilities. He'd risen to dominate the Clan's external security apparat, modernizing it and turning it into the glue that bound the new settlement together. The hammer of the council, his combination of force and guile had cowed the hotheads and brought the wily to his table. But he was just one man – now paralyzed on one side and barely conscious, lonely and adrift in what might be his deathbed.

'We're holding out,' she said quietly, touching his immobile left hand, hoping against hope for a reaction. 'Earl Fredryck's observers report that the federal presence at the doppelgänger site is continuing, but all our people made it across ahead of the siege. We have plenty of ammunition. The monarchists dropped the culvert from the river, and attempted to poison the well, but the osmotic purifier is working. Earl Riordan reports that the pretender's army is encamped athwart the valley just downriver of the bend, 'tween here and Wergatsfurt. The scouts are already preparing a route for us through New Britain, once Riordan's men have manufactured a sufficiency of knotwork badges.'

The duke made an odd noise in the back of his throat, something between a cluck and a gurgle. Olga leaned close, trying to discern words. His eyes rolled, agitated: 'Guh-uh . . .'

'Fear not, we have prepared for you.' A fireman's carry and a hike in the dark – then, if he survived the one-kilometer haul, a stealthy transit back to the American side, land of neurological wards and intensive care facilities, where a private ambulance would be waiting to whisk him to a hospital bed. 'The body of the force will return, taking the Pervert's army in the rear if he's still encamped. And should he occupy the palace, we have a warm welcome prepared for him.'

Olga was of the opinion that it was better to beg forgiveness than to ask permission; and in any event, the warm welcome in question was one with a short expiry date – shorter than ever, now that she'd learned what that thrice-cursed bastard idiot Matthias had told the DEA, or whoever they were. And what Otto had been doing was the icing on a very unpalatable cake. To his credit, he'd actually *volunteered* the information. 'Baron Henryk never put his faith in intangibles,' he'd explained. 'He wanted to *see* these mythical nuclear weapons. He wanted to *own* them. He argued about it with the duke, but then the duke changed his mind – one suspects Matthias forged his signature on the letter – and so the baron set me to oversee

Matthias on organizing the theft. It was meant to be a harmless shell game, and additional leverage in council. Nobody had looked at them for more than eight years! How were we to know Matthias would sell his story to the outlanders?'

'Guh. Uh. Pa. Pat. Uh.' He was clearly trying to say something. Alerted, Olga leaned closer.

'Please, I ask you, try to speak slowly. Is it a person?'

'Uh!'

'Patricia?' It was the obvious name: his half sister, mother of Helge, the wayward wildcat orphan and loose cannon who called herself Miriam.

'Yuh.'

'Oh! Good. Do you want to see her?' *That could be difficult.* Like most of the Clan's elders who were familiar with American culture, she'd vanished into a deep cover identity when the shit hit the fan, and trying to bring her over could draw attention to her.

'Nuh.'

'All right.' Olga racked her mind for options. 'Do you have a message for her? Or about her? Hang on, if it's a message for her, blink once? About her, twice?'

One blink.

Olga sat up, heart hammering. *He's still inside there.* A hot flush of relief washed over her: The idea that Angbard, Duke Lofstrom, had lost his mind had been too terrible to voice, or even think. Paralyzed, deathly sick, but still the will to control went on . . . 'Can you spell it out? One for no, two for yes?'

Blink-blink.

'Milady, he looks very weak to me – ' The first-aider sounded worried.

'He's the best judge of his condition,' she said sharply. 'And if he has a message of such import, he must give it. Have you pen and paper?'

'Uh, yes, milady.'

'Then take a note.'

It took half an hour, but they extracted two sentences from the duke before the corpsman's entreaties began to sway Olga. False starts and mistakes made it a frustrating process – but his words dispelled any remaining fear she had for his mind. Finally, she sighed and stood up. 'I'll see it gets to her,' she reassured the duke. 'Tomorrow, we'll get you to a proper hospital bed. I must go now.' She bowed and stepped back, then took the sheet of paper from the corpsman's pad. 'You heard nothing,' she warned him. 'This must go no further. And the duke needs to rest now.'

'Milady.' He bowed as she left the room and hurried towards the improvised communications center downstairs.

Carl, Earl of Wu by Hjorth – and the commander of the small army currently encamped in the castle – looked up as she entered. By a miracle, Oliver, Baron Hjorth, was absent. 'What news?'

'Nothing bad.' She hurried to his side at the map table. 'He's sleeping now,' she continued quietly, 'but he's very weak. The good news is, he has his senses. He gave me a message to relay to Patricia Thorold-Hjorth by any means necessary.'

'He's talking . . . ?' Carl's fist clenched.

'Do not hope for too much. It took much work to say this much.' She passed him the note. 'Please, send this by way of Earl Riordan. There is no way of knowing how long it will take to reach her, and I fear it may be urgent. I'd advise keeping it from Baron Oliver.'

'All right.' Carl took the piece of paper and stared at it. 'What does it mean?'

'You'll find out,' Olga assured him. 'In good time.'

TELL PATRICIA GIVE CLINIC RECORDS TO HELGE. GET HELGE IN FRONT OF COUNCIL. MY WORD, HER PLAN B ONLY WAY FORWARD NOW.

WET WORK

Downtown Boston: humid and warm and smelly with truck exhaust fumes in summer, rumbling and roaring from the nearby turnpike. A well-dressed woman in late middle age drove an electric wheelchair along the sidewalk, chatting to a young woman walking alongside her – a daughter, perhaps, or carer. The security guard glanced away from his screen, disinterested. He didn't notice them stop and turn abruptly to enter the lobby of the office suite he was monitoring. Not that it would have made any difference if he had. They didn't look like the sort of people he was supposed to keep out, and their faces didn't feature on any watch list of undesirables. Not that he'd have been able to keep them out, even if they did.

The woman in the wheelchair hummed towards the receptionist's station. 'Iris Beckstein, to see Dr. Darling. He's expecting me.' She smiled at the secretary: the self-assured smile of the financially secure.

'Sure, sign in here . . .'

The receptionist's lack of interest was convenient, Iris noted; possibly the doctor had encouraged it, although, if so, his overreliance on other security precautions was risky. Iris signed, and nodded, and waited while her companion signed. False names, one and all, but the false name she was using would be a red flag to the people who would, in due course, check the visitor book.

'This way, dear,' Iris told her companion, then scooted towards the elevators. Mhara nodded and followed obediently, keeping her mouth shut. Despite having a good understanding of the tongue, she'd spent little enough time in America that her accent was still heavy. Most folks would mistake her for an Eastern European immigrant, but Iris didn't feel like taking risks around this office – especially in view of the contents of her bag. As the doors slid shut,

Iris reached for the fourth floor button. 'On my word – but not a moment sooner,' she said in Hochsprache, the underused words heavy in her mouth.

'Yes, milady.'

'You are about to be exposed to some of our most perilous secrets. If they confuse or dismay you, you may ask me – or the duke – about them in private. But they must go no further.'

They ascended the rest of the way in silence. The lift was unusually slow, and Iris spent the time trying to relax. *Adrenaline makes fools of us all*, she reminded herself, then blinked irritably as the elevator doors opened. *Ah, well.*

The office suite was surprisingly quiet for this time of day, a few people moving between card-key-locked doors clutching mugs and papers. Iris rolled along the corridor, following memorized directions, until she found the correct door. She reached up with a card, swiped it, and pushed through as the lock clicked open.

'Hey, you can't come in – '

'Cover him,' she said in Hochsprache. 'Hello, Griben. Sit down, please.' The door clicked shut behind Mhara as she felt the weight of an empty leather shoulder bag land on one of her chair's handles.

Griben ven Hjalmar, plump and goateed, in a brown three-piece suit, sat down slowly, keeping his hands clearly visible. His face was expressionless. The other man sitting in the swivel chair behind the desk was frozen in surprise. 'And Dr. Darling. What a pleasant surprise.'

'Mrs. Beckstein? What's the' – Darling swallowed convulsively – 'what's going on?'

Iris smiled crookedly. 'Griben, what a coincidence. I was just thinking about looking you up. What brings you here? Thinking about cleaning up some loose ends?'

Dr. Darling – lean, middle-aged, the picture of a successful gynecologist – was looking between ven Hjalmar, Iris, and the suppressor on the end of Mhara's Glock in slack-jawed surmise. 'You – you – '

'I'd like to thank you both for the little number you played on my daughter. It wasn't *quite* what I had in mind when I suggested the arrangement.'

Ven Hjalmar flushed beneath the force of her glare. 'What did you *expect* us to do?' he demanded. 'She was under house arrest! With an execution warrant on her head! You wanted the leverage – '

'Nevertheless.' Iris shifted uncomfortably in her wheelchair. 'This is neither the time nor the place for this discussion.'

'Excuse me?' Three heads turned to stare at Dr. Darling. 'What are you – '

'Griben, do you mind?' Iris asked casually, speaking Hochsprache.

'If you absolutely must. I'd finished with him, anyway.'

'Did you get the disks from him?' she added.

'Of course.'

'What do you *want*?' demanded Darling.

In Hochsprache: 'Mhara, *now.*'

Outside the office, the two muffled shots would be mistaken for a door banging. Darling dropped forward across his desk, spilling blood and fatty tissue onto the keyboard of his PC.

Griben sighed. 'Was that strictly necessary?'

'Yes,' Iris said shortly. She glanced round. Mhara was standing, frozen, her pistol angled slightly upwards and a confused look in her eyes. 'Mhara? Child?'

The young woman shook her head. 'I'm sorry.' She picked up the shoulder bag and carefully stowed her pistol inside, using hook-and-eye strips to secure it. 'I've never done that before.'

'You've attended executions, surely . . .'

'Yes, milady. But it's *different* when you do it yourself.'

'You'll get used to it,' Iris reassured her. 'Griben, he knew too much. This Family Trade Organization is on our tail and he's not Outer Family or personal retainer. He had to go. You've got the disks. Mhara, the other device, please.'

'Other – oh.' Ven Hjalmar looked at the PC in distaste. 'You don't expect me to – '

'I surely do.' Iris held up a pair of latex gloves. 'You'll want these.'

None of them were particularly experienced at black-bag jobs; it took them nearly ten minutes to unscrew the casing of the PC and position the bulk eraser's electromagnet above the hard disk drive. Finally, Iris hit the power switch. 'Ah, good,' she said, as the disk error warning came up on the blood-specked screen. 'Mhara, you see the filing cabinets yonder? You take the right one, Griben can take the middle, and I shall take the left. Start at the top and work down. You are looking for anything pertaining to Applied Genomics Corporation, the W-316 clinical trial, Angbard Lofstrom, Griben ven Hjalmar here, or adoption papers relating to children.'

'*Adoption* papers?' Mhara sounded confused.

'Legal documents,' Iris said blandly.

'Iris.' Griben looked worried. 'This is going to take some time. What if someone – '

'You have your locket, yes? I had the site prepared.'

'But we're on the fourth floor!'

'There's a net. Try not to break your nose with your kneecaps. It'll be harder for me if we have to take it, so let us start searching right away, no?' She levered herself out of her wheelchair and shuffled cautiously towards the wall of cabinets.

The office was overheated, and the smells of burned powder and spilled blood hung over them as they pored over the file drawers. After ten minutes Griben finally hit pay dirt. 'He had a file on Applied Genomics,' he announced.

'Ah, excellent.' Iris gestured at her wheelchair. 'Put it in there.'

'Milady.' Mhara gestured politely at another drawer. 'Is this important?'

Iris leaned over to look. 'My, my, how interesting.' She lifted the fat, spiral-bound document out of its hanger. 'Names and addresses. It seems you're not the only doctor who doesn't trust computers to remember everything for you, Griben.'

'Dash it! We specifically instructed him *not* to do that!'

'I ordered someone to black-bag his house this morning. His divorce came through nine months ago, so I think there is no need to trouble his ex-wife and children.' She frowned, pensive. 'What have I forgotten?'

Griben nodded across the room. 'I should check the bookcase. And the desk drawers. Just to be sure.'

'An excellent idea. Perhaps you'd like to see me out, afterwards?'

Ven Hjalmar raised an eyebrow. 'Why – '

Iris nodded at Mhara. 'She has other tasks.'

'Ah, jolly good.' He nodded. Mhara picked up the files and waited attentively as he scoured the bookcases and finally the desk drawers – working carefully around Dr. Darling's body – then nodded again. 'That's all,' he announced. Darling's desk was mostly for show; beyond the usual collection of stationery items, the pedestal unit was empty.

Iris shuffled back to her wheelchair. 'Good. Mhara?'

'Milady.' She bobbed her head, holding the files two-handed.

'I want these files burned immediately. Afterwards, make your way back to the house when you are ready.'

'Yes, milady.' Mhara smiled, a brief flash of expression crossing her face. Then she tilted her left wrist to expose the face of a wristwatch, and vanished.

'You're sure about the net,' Griben said reflectively.

'*She's* sure about it, and that's what matters.' Iris lowered herself carefully into the wheelchair. 'Mind you, she was there when I ordered its construction.'

A thoughtful pause, then: 'I think I can see where your daughter gets it from.'

'I'm not *that* ruthless.' Iris whirred towards the door, then glanced over her shoulder with a fey expression. 'Come *on*, Griben! We have a conspiracy to conceal and if you keep thinking about it we'll be here until suppertime.'

They left the room with the conviction of a job well done, and no inkling of the significance of the encrypted memory stick attached to the key ring in the corpse's coat pocket.

*

In a muddy field outside Concord, behind a sign declaring it to be a HISTORY FAIRE, the circus-sized tent was swarming with spooks.

Colonel Smith's driver stopped outside the gate. A pair of police cars, their lights strobing, blocked the entrance; beyond the uniformed officers Smith could see parked buses and the tents of the forensic crews. Serious-looking officers in black windbreakers bearing the letters DEA paced around under the watchful eyes of guards in body armor and helmets. Casual rubberneckers might mistake them for a police SWAT team, but Smith was under no such illusion.

'Give me that badge.' Smith waited as the cop checked his name against a clipboard, carefully compared his face to the photograph, then nodded. 'Go ahead, sir. HQ is the third tent on the left.'

'You heard him.' Smith leaned back and closed his eyes for a minute as his driver crept across the rutted ground. Too many vehicles had come this way too recently. A familiar drumming noise prompted him to open his eyes. Sure enough, a big helicopter was thuttering across the sky, descending towards the field. *It's not black; just very, very, dark gray*. Smith suppressed a grin: what had happened at this site was no laughing matter. *How the* hell *did they manage it?* he asked himself as he opened the door and climbed out of the back of the car.

The mood in the headquarters tent was gray, too, as he discovered the moment he walked through the door. 'Sir? How up to date are you?' Judith Herz, latterly of the FBI but currently answering to Smith, had been on-site when the shit hit the fan. Now she looked drained, hollows under her eyes from close to twenty-four hours supervising the site cleanup.

'I've been too busy fighting brushfires and keeping the press off your neck to track everything. Have you got time to give me a guided tour?'

Herz rubbed the side of her face then glanced at one of the men sitting in front of a rack of radios and laptop computers. 'John, you want to take over for an hour? I need to bring the colonel up to speed.'

'Okay, I'll do that.' John – heavily built, wearing one of the ubiquitous DEA windbreakers – nodded briefly before turning back to his screen.

'This way, Colonel.' Herz gestured back to the front awning of the tent. 'Let me show you what we found.'

Forensics had already finished with the big top before Herz beckoned Smith past the incident tape and into the open space within. Smith glanced around curiously. Like any big top, the tent was held up by a pair of huge posts. But the resemblance stopped at that point;

there were no seats, no trapezes or safety nets, and nothing in this particular ring could be described as a laughing matter.

'It's a regular headquarters setup, we think,' Herz commented as she walked towards a row of tables at one side of the space. 'Look.' The tables showed every sign of having been abandoned in a hurry: folding chairs tipped over, equipment crates lying on their sides. One of the tables was covered completely by a large relief map, various implements strewn across it – notepads, pens, protractors, and folded pieces of card.

'Pay dirt,' breathed Smith. He paused momentarily. 'Has it been checked out?'

'Everything's been photographed in situ. I think they even dusted for fingerprints, just in case.'

'Gotcha.' Smith leaned over the map. It didn't take much to recognize the foothills, and the river valley forking downstream. But there was something odd about the map. He frowned. 'Concord should be here, shouldn't it?'

Herz followed the direction of his finger. 'I guess so.'

'Hmm. Look.' The moving finger trailed south. A much smaller clump of buildings perched beside the river, surrounded by a sharply incised wall. 'This is printed. It's even got grid coordinates. Betcha they bought the map data from someone over here, in our world, then added their own survey points. Saves time, assuming the geography's the same, and I guess they would know about any major features like landslides.'

'You mean this is a map of, of fairyland.'

'It's not fairyland,' Smith said sharply. 'It's real enough that they can make a map of it like this, and plan . . .'

He paused, then peered back at the map. Hunting upstream of the small town, at the fork in the river, he found what he was looking for. 'Go get one of *our* maps. I want to confirm that *this* is where we are,' he said, moving one of the cardboard markers to sit atop the heptagonal feature he'd noticed. 'They were here for a reason, and I want to know what they were doing that needed nearly two hundred of the bastards.'

He straightened up and looked around. There were more tables dotted around, and a stack of empty kit bags, but the center of the tent was dominated by a two-story-high aluminum scaffold with ramps and ladders leading up to platforms on both upper floors. Surveyor's posts and reflector disks fastened to the uprights, and a pair of theodolites at opposite sides of the tent, made it clear that whoever had built the scaffold had taken pains over its exact location. Smith frowned, thoughtful. *Nearly two hundred of them and they vanished into thin air in less than three minutes. How did they avoid falling over each other?* A precision operation, like paratroops jumping in quick succession from the back of a plane. *And why did they do it out in public, risking detection?* It had to be something to do with this location, and whatever it was collocated with in the other time line.

Herz was muttering into a walkie-talkie. 'I need geographic input. Is Amanda – yes, I'll hold, over.'

Smith walked partway round the scaffold. A faint memory began to surface, grade school on an Air Force base somewhere in Germany: knights in armor, huge creaking wooden contraptions grinding their way across a field of battle towards a walled castle. The whole medieval thing. *It's a siege tower.* A siege tower without wheels, because you could build it in a parallel universe, butting right up against wherever you were going to go in. A siege tower without armor, and made of aluminum scaffolding components because they were easier to use than logs.

Voices pulled him back to the present. He glanced round, annoyed, then frowned. It was his political supervisor, Dr. James, he of the cadaverous face and the connections to the current occupant of Number One Observatory Circle, plotting and scheming inside the beltway. A couple of flunkies – administrative assistants, pasty-skinned managerial types from Crypto city, even a discreet Secret Service bodyguard doing the men-in-black thing – followed him. 'Ah, Eric! Excellent. Martin, you can stop trying to reach him now. What's your analysis?'

Smith took a deep breath, held it for a moment. The smells of crushed grass and gun oil and desperate men filled his nostrils. 'It's a siege tower. They weren't running away from us, they were breaking *into* something.' He gestured at the theodolites and the scaffolding.

'That's positioned with extreme care. I think it's a siege tower – they had a target in their own world and this took them to a precise location. The map' – Herz was waving at him – 'excuse me.' He walked over to the table. 'Yes?'

'You were right,' she said. 'We're here.' Her finger stabbed at the heptagonal structure. 'This thing is about five hundred feet across, look, concentric rings – does that remind you of anything?'

Smith nodded and turned to Dr. James. 'If their map's telling the truth, that structure is some kind of fortification. And we already know from CLEANSWEEP that some kind of internal struggle was going down fourteen to sixteen days ago. We could do a lot worse than send a couple of scouts across in the next valley over.' He cracked his knuckles, first the right hand then his left. 'It's a shame we don't have anything that can touch them, because they're probably still bottled up in there, in strength.'

James grinned like a skull. 'Well, I have an update for you. Let's take a walk.'

BEGIN TELEPHONE TRANSCRIPT

(*A telephone buzzes for attention.*)

'Hello?'

'Ah, is that the Lee residence?'

(*Pause.*) 'Who is this?'

'I'd like to speak to James Lee, please. It is *dringen* – urgent.'

(*Pause.*) 'Please wait.'

(*Two minutes later.*)

'Hello? Hello?'

'Who is this? Is – James? James, is that you?'

'Ah, yes – Who, um – '

'Poul, Poul ven Wu. You may remember me, from my cousin Raph's wedding to Kara ven – '

'Ah, yes! I remember now! Yes, indeed. How good to hear from you. But surely this isn't just a social call?'

'I wish it were. Unfortunately a somewhat delicate situation has arisen at short notice, and I hoped you might be able to advise me on how it might be resolved without undue difficulty.'

(*Pause.*) 'Ah. I see, I think.' (*Pause.*) 'Would this situation have anything to do with the events at the Thorold Palace earlier this month?'

'Mm . . . in a manner of speaking, yes. It's a delicate matter, as I said, and we're anxious to resolve it without violating the terms of the settlement between our families, but it's quite urgent and it appears to be becoming time-critical.'

'Hmm. Can you be more specific? I think I can safely say that we would also like to remain within the conditions of the truce, but I cannot commit to anything without my elders' approval, and I am quite anxious to know what I shall be putting before them.'

(*Pause.*) 'We would like to arrange for the safe passage of a substantial group of our people, from a location near Irongate – near Wergatsfurt – across a distance of some three miles, on foot, at night.'

'Passage. You mean, from Wergatsfurt, in Gruinmarkt, to somewhere about three miles away, also in Gruinmarkt, but through our world, I take it?'

'Precisely.' (*Pause.*) 'In addition, the group is armed. Not civilian.'

(*Long pause.*) 'You're asking us to give safe passage to a small army.'

(*Hastily.*) 'Only for about three hours, at night! And there are only two hundred and eighteen of them. Eleven walking wounded, six stretcher cases. We don't want to attract attention – we want to keep it out of sight of the Polis, and everybody else. Can you – is it possible – to arrange this? I can supply details of the end-points of the sortie, and precise numbers – but what we would like, if it is possible, is not simply a dispensation within our agreement but active help. If you can organize covered trucks, and secure the destination, for example . . .'

'I can't agree to that, Poul. I don't have the authority to make agreements like that. I *can* tell you that my father can make such a decision, but it would be better to petition him yourself – '

(*Urgently*) 'It has to be done tonight!'

'I'm sure it does. And I can arrange for my father to see you within the hour – but the request must come directly from your lips to his ears.' (*Pause.*) 'You understand that he will expect some reward for this inconvenience.'

'Of course.' (*Pause.*) 'We expect to pay for any assistance, and I am authorized to negotiate with you – or your father. Only understand that it is a matter of some urgency, and while we are prepared to be generous, we would take a very poor view of any attempt to exploit the situation to our detriment.'

'Oh, that's understood. Give me an hour to prepare things and you will be welcome at my father's house. Do you need directions?'

END TRANSCRIPT

Erasmus Burgeson arrived in Fort Petrograd four days late, footsore and weary and out-of-pocket – but a free man, thanks to those extraordinary friends of Miriam Beckstein who had arrived just in time to stop the secret police from collaring the two of them.

After the shoot-out at the one-cow railroad station in the middle of nowhere, he'd taken up Miriam's invitation to help himself to the political officer's no-longer-needed steamer, and topped off both its tanks before cracking open the throttle and bumping across dirt tracks and paved military roads in the general direction of the south-west and the Bay Area. But the car had run out of steam ten miles before he reached Miwoc City, and he'd had second (and third) thoughts about the wisdom of paying a mechanic to come out and get her rolling again, in light of the car's bloodstained provenance. (Not to mention the bullet hole in the left, passenger side, door.)

So he'd walked into Miwoc, dusty and sore-footed, and taken a room in a working men's hostel, and spent the night lying awake listening to the fights and the begging and the runners clubbing indigents outside the thin wall of his dive – and set off for Fort Petrograd the next morning, whistling and doubtless mangling a ditty he'd picked up from Miriam, about a hotel in California.

It was a hundred miles to the big city, where the guns of Fort Petrograd loomed out across the headland of the bay, aiming south towards San Mateo. It shouldn't have taken three days, but Erasmus decided to avoid the railways – one close shave with the law was more than enough – and not risk buying an automobile: A solitary man driving alone was as good as a green flag to a certain kind of highwayman, and it would swallow all his remaining funds besides. The buses and streetcars that connected the grids of these western townships were more than adequate, if one made allowances for delayed connections . . . and the increasing number of checkpoints where nervous thief takers and magistrate's men stood guard with shotguns while the transport Polis examined internal passports and work permits. These, at least, Erasmus was equipped to deceive, thanks to the package Edward had given him in New London.

This worked until the third day, when the bus he was riding from Abadon reached Patwin (which Miriam would have pointed to on a map and called 'Vallejo'), and ran into a general strike, and barricades, and grim-faced men beneath a blue flag slashed diagonally with a cross of St. Andrew beneath the glaring face of a wild turkey. 'Ye can gae nae farthur,' said the leader of the band blocking the high street, 'wi'out any in calling ye strikebreaker.' He stood in front of the bus with arms crossed in front of him and the stolid self-confidence born of having two brothers-in-arms standing behind him with hunting rifles and an elderly and unreliable-looking carronade – probably looted from the town hall's front steps – to back *them* up.

'I'm no' arguing wi' t'artillery,' said the driver, turning to address his passengers. 'End of t'road!'

An hour later, by means of various secret handshakes and circumlocutions, Erasmus was talking to the leader of the strike force, a lean, rat-faced man called Dunstable. 'I was on my way to Fort Petrograd on Party business when I was forced off the train and only just escaped with my life. I need to get there immediately.'

'Let me see what I can do,' said Dunstable, then vanished into the back of the Town Aldermen's office, doubtless to cable for directions. The two hard-faced men with pistols sat with Erasmus in silence; he made himself comfortable until Dunstable returned. 'Aye, well, your story checks out.' Dunstable nodded at the two men. 'Joe, go and get the mayor's runabout. Frank, you stay with Mister Burgeson here. You and Joe will drive Mister Burgeson straight to Fort Petrograd, to the Crimea Barracks – you know how to find it? Good. Our people hold it. When you get there, do as Mister Burgeson says.'

Erasmus stood. 'I'll send them back as soon as possible,' he promised. 'Good luck here.'

'Luck?' Dunstable snorted. 'Luck's got now't to do with it: People are starving and the frogs are trying to retake New France!'

'They're *what?*' Erasmus stared at him.

'Oh, the king's got it nailed down quiet like, but we know the score. Furrin troops in Red Club, a dauphin looking to set foot in New Orleans next week.' Dunstable tapped the side of his nose. 'Got to look oot fer our selves in times of unrest, 'aven't we?'

It took eight hours to drive the fifty miles from Patwin, overlooking the inner shore of the great bay, to Fort Petrograd and the downtown strip of barracks and museums and great houses that defined the core of western society on the edge of the Pacific. The roads were good, but the two ferries they required ran only infrequently at present, and they had to stop every five to ten miles to convince another roadblock, revolutionary caucus, civil defense brigade, emergency committee, republican guard, and ladies' union that they were not, in fact, agents of the secret political police, the French dauphin (who had simultaneously invaded New France, or Louisiana as the French called it, and Alaska, and the Brazilian Directorate, not to mention New London), or even the Black Fist Freedom Guard (which last was worryingly close to the truth). Luckily the situation was so confused, the news so hazy, that Erasmus discovered that sounding vague and asking lots of questions quickly convinced most of them that he was what he said he was – an innocent business traveler trapped on the road with his driver and bodyguard. A couple of the local militias made halfhearted attempts to shake him down, but his invincible self-righteousness, combined with a pious appeal to the forces of order and justice once the emergency resolved itself, scared them off. The British were, it seemed, still half-convinced that it was all a bad dream, and the breakdown of government – it seemed the exchequer had run out of money two days ago, and the king had reconvened parliament, then told parliament to resign again when he didn't like what they had to say, and parliament had refused, and the unpaid dragoons had refused to clear the benches – was not quite real.

It was, in short, exactly the sort of confused pre-revolutionary situation that Erasmus had spent most of his life not praying, but hoping for. And he was in very nearly exactly the wrong place, if not for having had the good luck to run into Dunstable and his fellow travelers.

The broad boulevards and steel-framed stone buildings of metropolitan Fort Petrograd were awash with excited strikers from the munitions factories and – not entirely to Erasmus's surprise – sailors from the vast naval base sprawling across the southwestern rim of the bay. Erasmus made a snap decision. 'Forget the Crimea Barracks, take me to City Hall,' he told Joe.

City Hall, a neoclassical lump of concrete reinforced with steel – and, curiously, featuring no windows less than eighteen feet above ground level, and clear lines of fire in all directions – was the logical place to go. And so, when they were stopped two blocks from the place by a barricade manned by marines who had torn their insignia of rank from their uniforms, Erasmus climbed out of the car. 'I'm here to see Adam,' he said. 'Take me to him.'

It took a while, but half an hour later Erasmus slid to the front of a queue of supplicants. They were queuing to see the man in the mayor's office, but the man behind the mayor's desk was not the mayor, and he wasn't doing ordinary civic business as usual. When Erasmus entered the room he was holding forth animatedly with a group of hard-looking types who he recognized instantly as party cadres. Sir Adam Burroughs had aged in the nearly twenty years since Erasmus had last seen him: His hair was thin and straggling, and his high forehead was deeply grooved with worry lines. But the magnetic charm and hyperactive temperament remained –

'Hello? Who's this?' Burroughs looked at him for a few seconds. Then his eyes widened. 'Joshua? Is that you?'

'It is indeed.' Erasmus bowed low – not a flourishing courtier's bow, but a salute born of deep respect. 'Lady Margaret sends her regards, and her hopes for your success in this venture.' He smiled. 'Though it seems to me that you've made a good start already!'

'Joshua, man – ' Burroughs stood up and flew from behind his desk, then gripped Erasmus by the shoulders. 'It's been too long!' He turned to face his half-dozen assistants. 'This man is Joshua Cooke! During the eighty-six he was my secretary and correspondent, he ran the *People's Voice* in New York. Since then he's been a mainstay of the movement out east.' Eyes were staring, lips mumbling silently. 'You've come to join us, I take it.'

'Oh yes.' Erasmus nodded. 'And to plug you into what's been happening out east. I go by the name of Erasmus Burgeson these days, and it's gotten to be something of a habit. I was delayed, I'm afraid, by the Polis – got away, but it was a near thing. And everywhere I went, rumor was chasing falsehood's tail for truth's bone. I take it loyalists are thin on the ground around here?'

'Vanished like rats from a sinking ship,' grumped one of Burroughs's new assistants, a heavy-set fellow with a nautical beard. 'We'll root 'em out.'

'Organization first,' Burroughs said mildly. 'Josh – Erasmus, is it? – you've arrived at exactly the right time. We've got to get the word out, now that the Hanoverian has emptied his treasury, get control – I want you to take a flying picket down to the *Petrograd Times* and get the presses rolling again. And the telautograph senders on the east bay mount. I need a solid hand running the propaganda ministry. Can you do that?'

Erasmus cracked his knuckles, grinning cadaverously. 'It'll be a good start.'

*

'An accident.' Miriam stared at Brill across the width of the safe house's kitchen. *She looks like someone told her the family dog's got cancer.* 'What kind of accident?'

'The duke – ' Brill swallowed.

Huw sidestepped towards the sink, making an adroit grab for a water glass.

'Yes?' Miriam said encouragingly, her heart sinking.

'He's had a stroke, they say. World-walking.'

'But why would he – ' Huw fell silent, seeing Miriam's expression.

'The pretender's army took the Hjalmar Palace by treachery. His grace was organizing a force to take it back when . . . something happened, something bad. Near Concord. Everyone had to cross over in a hurry. They retook the fortifications, but the duke – '

Brilliana swallowed.

'Well *shit*,' Huw said.

Miriam raised a finger. 'Is he still alive?' she asked. 'Is he conscious? Because – '

'Wait.' Brill took the water glass from Huw's fingers. 'Anything. To put in this?'

'There's a bottle of brandy in the luggage.' Huw headed for the door. 'Don't go away. Be right back.'

Miriam pulled a stool out and steered it behind Brilliana, who sat, gratefully.

'He's in a bad way,' she said eventually, visibly gathering her wits. 'Paralyzed on one side. They need to get him to a neurology ward but they're trapped in the Hjalmar Palace – a big castle near Concord, in this world – by some Winter Crone-cursed police or paramilitary force that tried to raid them just as they were mounting the counter-attack on the pretender's forces.'

Huw reappeared with a dark green bottle. 'Here.' He splashed amber fluid into Brill's glass, then fetched down another and offered it to Miriam. 'Yourself?'

'No thanks.' She glanced at him dubiously as he poured two fingers for himself. 'What if you need to drive somewhere?'

'Firstly, I delegate to Yul, and secondly, there's a difference between having a shot and getting drunk. Are you sure . . . ?'

'Oh hell, go ahead.' Miriam snorted. Sometimes it was the little things about her relatives who'd grown up in the Gruinmarkt that tripped her up the hardest, like their extremely un-American attitude to alcohol. 'Can they get him to a hospital?'

Brill lowered her glass. 'It's in train, I think. I mean, Olga's there, she's working something out with Earl Riordan. They couldn't tell me more – need to know. But – it's spooky. The feds swooped on ClanSec just as they concentrated to go across to relieve the Hjalmar Palace. It's almost as if someone told them exactly when – '

'Matthias is dead,' Miriam interrupted.

'Matthias?' Huw looked fascinated. 'Wasn't he the duke's personal secretary? I knew he disappeared, but – '

Miriam looked at Brill, who silently shook her head. 'Later, Huw,' she promised. 'Brill, we need to get back to, to – ' She stopped, the words *to wherever we need to be* piling up like a car crash on her tongue.

Brill took a sip of brandy. 'By the time we could get back to the east coast it'd all be over,' she said huskily. 'The important thing is what happens after that.'

I can't believe how fast it's all falling apart. Miriam shook her head. 'Something about this doesn't make sense,' she said. 'Things fell to pieces in Niejwein when Egon decided Henryk's little power play was a personal threat to him, that's clear. But this new stuff, the feds – it's one coincidence too many.' She paused. 'Could they be connected? Beyond the obvious, beyond Matthias defecting and spilling his guts?'

Brill gave her an odd look. 'You might think that. I couldn't possibly comment.'

'Oh for – ' Miriam forced herself to stop. 'Okay, let me tell you what I think is probably happening, Brill. *You're* in Angbard's chain of command, *you* deal with it.'

'You'd better wait outside, Huw,' Brill said sharply.

He shrugged and walked over to the door. 'Call me when you've finished politicking,' he called, then closed it.

Miriam took a deep breath and tried to gather the unraveling threads of her concentration. *Too much, too fast.* 'I think that we figured out Matthias had defected seven, eight months ago, when it first happened. And what followed was a factional race to get into the best position to come out on top when the US government figured out what was going on and brought the hammer down on the trade network. I stood up and told them their business model was flawed, and they didn't do anything – but they weren't all ignoring me. The conservative faction, led by Baron Henryk, decided to shut me up, but they had to be subtle about it. Angbard didn't block him because he hoped they'd fail and discredit themselves in the process. Meanwhile, some other groups were looking into the possibilities dragged up by my stumbling over the hidden family and New Britain. That'd be where Huw comes in, yes? Angbard's sitting at the center of a web, like a spider, holding everything together – trying to keep business running as usual, but trying to hedge everybody's bets.'

She swallowed, then took a sip of brandy. 'Trouble is, everybody's doing different things. There have been sub rosa attempts to modernize the Clan going on for decades; I just didn't recognize them. That's what I got wrong – I took you all at face value, didn't look below the surface. Everyone pays lip service to the status quo, but not everyone goes along with it. There's the breeding program that was intended to rebuild the population base eroded by the civil war over the past fifty years, and crack the manpower monopoly effectively controlled by the marriage-brokering old grannies' – she watched Brilliana for signs of surprise, but didn't see any – 'and that debating society and talking shop Huw's into. There's even Clan Security, for heaven's sake! Which is more like the, the Russian KGB, than something you'd expect in a post-feudal society like the Gruinmarkt. Am I right?'

She waited for Brill to say something, but the silence dragged out. After a few seconds, she cleared her throat and continued. 'So, I upset a bunch of applecarts, and the fallout included Matthias going over the wall. I expect someone's been trying to negotiate with the feds, buying time, patching things up. And I expect everyone's been scrambling to secure a workable Plan B for their particular faction. I'm not going to ask what the hell ClanSec or the Council or whoever thought they were doing, messing around with stolen nukes, it's immaterial; I just want to note that it was a *really* bad idea, because from the feds' point of view it turned the Clan from a minor nuisance into a deadly threat. You can negotiate with a nuisance, but you shoot threats – isn't that right?' She put her glass down and looked at Brill. After a minute she asked, 'Well?'

Brilliana looked uncomfortable. 'I can't talk about . . . certain . . . matters without getting permission first. But broadly speaking' – she looked at Miriam appraisingly – 'you are speculating along the right lines.' She coughed. 'But please, refrain from airing your speculation in public? Lest other factions conclude that you know more than you do, and attempt to silence you.'

Miriam's left eyelid twitched. 'I've had enough of that, thank you. Since even my dear mother is prone to, to . . .' It was too painful to continue. She rested one hand on her lap. 'And what that bastard ven Hjalmar tried to do. Did.' A long pause. 'It's only been about six weeks. I could get an abortion. *If* I'm pregnant.'

Brill looked at her oddly. 'If you did that, you'd be throwing away your best lever.' She took another sip of brandy. 'Because it's Creon's get, and you've got a fistful of witnesses to the betrothal, including the conservative faction and – by implication – the pretender. That's the throne to the Gruinmarkt, Miriam.'

'And it's my body.' Miriam looked at her half-empty glass and twitched, then she picked it up again and swallowed it in a single mouthful. 'Not that that seems to mean much to you people.'

Brilliana reached out and grabbed her hand. 'Helge!'

'What?' Miriam glared at her across the breakfast bar.

'This world is not fair or just. But I swore I would look after you – '

' – Who to?'

'To you, and to your uncle: but that is not important. I swore an oath to protect you. I must tell you that as long as you carry the heir to the throne of Niejwein, nobody in the six families will *dare* to lift a finger against you. And if, if we are still alive in eight months, things will be different. The pretender will be dead and Angbard will need a regent's council and at a minimum you will be on it. He told me, if necessary' – her voice cracked – 'tell her that if she does this thing, all debts are canceled.'

'And if I don't?' Miriam made as if to pull her arm back, but paused. 'You know there are no guarantees. I'm old for this. Miscarriages aren't that unusual in older pregnancies. And there's only a fifty-fifty chance it's a boy, anyway. What if it doesn't work?'

'Then at least you tried.' Brill moderated her voice. 'You came back willingly: That weighs in your favor. The more you do for us, the harder it becomes for your enemies to belittle or ignore you. Thus has it ever been.'

'You make it sound as if the Clan runs on honor.'

'But it does!' Brill's expression of surprise took her aback. 'How else do you control an aristocracy?'

'I don't think I'll ever understand you guys.' Miriam watched while Brill refilled both their glasses. 'Hey, I'm probably pregnant? You want to go easy with that.'

'What's that got to do with it?' She looked perplexed.

'The Surgeon General's – no, *fuck* it.' Miriam picked up the glass. 'Next time you send someone out for a pizza, try and get them to buy me a pregnancy test kit . . . hell, make that two of them, just in case.' She sipped at her brandy defiantly. 'So anyway, I kicked over an anthill. And Henryk's faction try to tie me down, to control the damage, and it backfired spectacularly and set Egon off. Is that how I'm reading it? While at the same time, I set Matthias off, which set the feds on us. Right?'

'Wrong.' Brill raised her glass and stared at it. 'It was a powder keg, Helge. Even before you returned, it was balanced on a sword's edge. You unleashed chaos, but without you – you strengthened Angbard's hand immensely, did you not notice that? And you have unleashed Huw. Don't underestimate him. He has connections. You can be at the center of things if you play the hand you have been dealt.'

'There won't be any center to be at, if the feds figure out a way of getting over here in force,' Miriam said darkly.

'They won't.'

'Huh. But anyway. Is it all right to bring him back in?'

'What? You've finished spilling our innermost secrets?'

'Innermost secrets, feh: It's just uninformed speculation. No, I need to talk to Huw. *We* need to talk, that is.'

'Oh. All right.' Brill stood up and walked to the door. 'Huw!'

A moment's silence, then feet pounded down the staircase. 'Yes? What's – oh.'

'Come in, sit down,' Miriam called over. 'We've got to head back to Boston tomorrow, or as soon as possible.'

'But – ' Brill stopped. 'Why?'

'No politics, remember?' Miriam twitched. 'If Angbard's ill, we can't risk being too far away. But what's really important – Huw, I

73

want you to tell me all about how you went about probing that new world. Because I think once everyone gets past running around and being worried about the pretender, we are really going to need to work out how to open up new worlds.'

'Eh?' Brilliana stared at her. 'I don't see why that's a priority right now.'

Miriam sighed heavily and pushed her glass away. 'It wouldn't be, if we were just up against another bunch of upstart aristocrats, or if the US government were entirely reliant on captured couriers. Huw, why don't you tell her about what we were discussing earlier?'

'The, uh, wild speculation?'

'Yes, that. I'm tired, I don't want to repeat myself, and I think she needs to know.' She stood up and stretched. 'I'm going to catch a nap. Call me if anything happens.'

*

Despite the summer heat, the sky was overcast and gray; it was threatening to rain as Dr. James led Colonel Smith around the side of the big top. Two minders followed at a discreet distance. 'How certain are you that the bad guys are on the other side of that siege tower?'

Eric gave it scant seconds of consideration. 'Very. They wouldn't have come out here and stuck a couple of hundred assets in a field under our nose without an extremely urgent motivation. These people aren't into cat-and-mouse games – they've been staying under cover very carefully until now. This has got all the signs of an emergency operation, and we disturbed them in the middle of it. That map alone, that's dynamite. And it checks out: The scaffolding is right in the middle of what looks like a major fortification in their world.'

Dr. James halted – so fast that Eric nearly stumbled. 'Good!' A curious half-smile played around his lips. 'Then I've got a solution for you, son.'

'A – ' Eric did a double take. 'Excuse me?'

'It's a political problem.' James began walking again, more slowly this time. 'We want to send them a *message*. They think they can play with us. They stole six nukes from the inactive inventory. The message we have been instructed to send is, "If you play with us we will mess you up." If I wasn't a man of faith I'd be using the f-word, Colonel. We want to send them a message and we want to underline *don't f– with us* in blood.'

'In my experience,' Eric commented, feeling light-headed, 'messages signed in blood ought to be delivered in a way that ensures the recipients don't live long enough to read them. Anything else is asking for trouble.'

'Spoken like a flyboy at heart. You're absolutely right. Nuke 'em 'til they glow, then shoot 'em in the dark.' Eric stared at him until he nodded. 'That's a direct quote from the vice president, son. Although *he* probably lifted it from someone else.'

'That puts an interesting light on things,' Eric agreed, slightly aghast. The Secret Service's code name for Mr. Cheney, DADDY WAR-BUCKS, was also a comment on his neoconservative leanings, but such bloodthirsty words coming from the executive branch were somewhat surprising, even post-9/11.

'So he's getting you a piece of paper on the White House blotter,' Dr. James continued blandly, 'ordering you to take control of the gadget retrieved from Government Center and to, ah, *return* it to the person or persons who so carelessly left it under the Blue Line platform with *extreme* prejudice.'

But! Smith's tongue froze. 'But!' He tried again. It came out as almost a squeak. 'We don't have nuclear release authority, we're not in the chain of command, you can't *do* that – '

'Son.' James's smile turned icy. 'They stole *six* of them. The United States *does not give in to nuclear blackmail.* Never mind that it would be *embarrassing* to return it to inventory, admitting on the record that it went walkies on our watch; they stole it, so you are going to shove it up their, their behind, so hard they can *taste* it. It's the perfect solution. It's completely deniable: They stole it, it went off in their hands. And it sends the right message. Mess with us and we will hurt you. And besides – ' He slid his spectacles down his nose and pulled out a cleaning cloth. 'Mr. Cheney is *real keen* to make sure the FADMs work as designed. We haven't had a chance to test these gadgets since the Test Ban Treaty came in – but as the Attorney General notes, it only bans us from testing nuclear devices in *this* universe. And Major

Alvarez knows how to use them. He *is* part of the chain, and he's seconded to us. He knows what the score is. Why do you think we've been recruiting so widely . . . and selectively?'

'Okay,' Eric said thoughtfully. 'I follow the logic.' He paused. 'But how are we going to deliver it? We've only got two mules.' He left unspoken the corollary: *Are you willing to let me strap an atomic device on a timer to a captured Clan courier who hates our guts?* It would violate so many protocols that the stack of charges would be higher than the Washington Monument.

'Well now.' James stopped smiling. 'You remember your little visit out west? They got Preparation Fifteen working. I'm having one of them flown out here right now – this will be its first deployment.'

'Wait.' Eric raised a hand. 'Preparation Fifteen? I only saw number twelve. The, the disappearing tissue.' Tissue harvested from the brain of a captured Clan member – God only knew what had happened to the donor because Eric certainly didn't want to. 'Is Fifteen what I think it is?'

'Yes. Push the button, watch the black box vanish. Along with whatever it's bolted to, as long as it's in a conductive sack and is isolated from earth. It's single-use, unfortunately; it has to be assembled by hand and lasts for about sixteen hours. But during that time – '

'Have you tried bolting one to an airframe?' Eric asked. 'Sorry.'

'Good question. We'd need two – one for the return trip – and they're not that reliable yet, but it's on the road map. You can test fly the helicopter if you want.' James noticed Eric's expression. 'That was a joke, son, you're not expendable.'

'I'm not licensed for choppers,' Smith muttered, under his breath. *Just in case you get any crazy ideas.* 'So how are we going to deliver the, the physics package?'

'The usual way.' James started walking again; they were almost round the circumference of the big top, the awning just in view around the curve of its flank. 'Written orders are coming down from the White House; it's WARBUCK's toy, but he's gotten the President to sign off on it, and we're – well, certain of the Joint Chiefs have been briefed about the PINNACLE BROKEN ARROW and it's been made clear to them that this is necessary. I gather they've even gotten Chief

Justice Bork on board. You'll use your man Rand and his crew to prepare the gadget, they're already cleared. They'll hand it and the timer controller to Major Alvarez and Captain Hu, who have orders to put a timer controller on it, set to detonate sixty seconds after activation. It's tamperproof; any attempt to disarm it other than by using the code-wheel to enter the locking key will make it detonate, but they'll have the key to hand just in case. *You* will bolt the Preparation Fifteen unit to the detonation sequencer and put the gadget on top of the, the siege tower. You and the major will start the sequencer, push the button on the transport unit to send it across. If the transport unit fails, you can enter the disarm code and try again later. If it succeeds . . . it's *their* problem. May they burn in hell for making us do this,' he added quietly.

COVERED WAGON

To a soldier in an army dependent on muscle power, there are few sights as grim as a fortress occupied by an enemy force standing squarely in the line of advance.

The Hjalmar Palace was palatial only on the inside: Squatting behind ominous earthworks at the fork of a major river, the face it presented to the world at large was eyeless and intimidating, scarred by cannon and fire. The merchant clan barons who had reinforced and extended the revetments around the central keep over the past fifty years had not been as parochial as their backwoodsman cousins. They'd scoured the historical archives of the Boston Public Library, keeping a wary eye on the royal army's ironworks and the forging of their great siege bombards. Behind the outer wet moat and its fortified gatehouse, beyond the flat killing ground of the apron, the stone walls of the castle sank below ground level; backed by rammed earth to absorb the blows of any cannon balls that might make it over the rim, the glacis rose harsh and steep, fronted by a deep dry moat.

It had taken treachery to get Otto's men into the palace the first time round, using a shortcut revealed under duress by one of the residents. He'd been in the process of installing defenses against the inevitable world-walking attempt to retake the complex, but the Clan had struck back with astonishing speed and terrifying force – a far cry from their dilatory defensiveness when outlying estates and villages were picked off. *They weren't really exerting themselves until we threatened their fortresses instead of their farms,* Otto mused. It was an unpleasant realization. His defenses hadn't been ready; they'd driven him out and he still didn't know for sure precisely where they'd flooded back into the building from. But if nothing else, at least now he had a map of the internal layout. In principle that should make things easier. In practice –

He lowered his binoculars, then looked back. The fortress was still there, looming in the east, mocking him. *Your bones at my feet*, it was saying. *Your blood: my mortar.*

A loud *crack!* caught his attention. Behind the line, the royal artillery's light cannon began to fire, deep-throated coughs that spat clouds of smoke and sparks as they threw cold iron at the gatehouse. Stone chips flew, but the gatehouse was, itself, a castle in miniature, and beyond it the drawbridge across the wet moat and the sunken road allowed the defenders to reinforce it at need. The range was almost half a mile: The bombardment wouldn't do much save to make the defenders keep their heads down. But that was better than nothing, Otto supposed. That, and the king's plan – if it worked – might get them close enough to the defenses to at least have a chance. And if the king's plan didn't work . . . *At least we've got an entire army*, he told himself. Scant comfort, looking up at those ramparts.

Otto turned back to the clump of men waiting behind him. 'Tomorrow the king's going to reduce the gatehouse,' he announced. 'Then it's right on to the castle. But we've got an easy job to do. Once Raeder's men finish moving the ammunition up, we're to advance behind the vanguard and keep the witches' heads down.' He looked his men in their eyes. 'There will be *no* indiscriminate firing.' Not like the day before yesterday, when his undertrained men had burned through crates of priceless ammunition and wrecked a pair of irreplaceable M60 barrels. 'There will be no damaged guns. If any man wrecks a witch-gun barrel by firing too fast, I'll forge it to red-heat and beat him to death with it. And there will be no casualties, if I have any say in the matter.' He assayed a thin smile. His hetmen had been quietly gloomy, a minute ago; now they visibly cheered up. 'The other side's to do the dying today. We'll just stay nice and safe in the rear, and rain on the enemy battlements with lead.'

'Aye!' Shutz knew his cue, and put his leathery lungs into it. The sergeants and hetmen, not to mention the sprinkling of hedge-knights who'd joined his banner out of hope of self-enrichment, joined in enthusiastically.

'To your men, then, and let them know,' Otto said, allowing

himself to relax slightly. 'I will make an inspection round in the next hour, and give you your disposition before we advance, an hour before sunset.'

*

Night fell heavy on the castle walls, illuminated by the slow lightning of the field cannon and the thunder that echoed in reply, and the moans of the victims, growing weaker now. Olga stared from a darkened window casement, following the action around the base of the gatehouse, picked out in the livid green of night-vision goggles. 'The stupid, *stupid* bastards,' she hissed.

Behind her, Baron Oliver cleared his throat. The distant sounds of preparations, banging and scraping and swearing, carried through the door from the grand hall. 'As long as the Pervert's troops think we're heavily invested, and unable to move . . .'

'But the waste! Lightning Child strike him blind.' Olga was not prone to fits of unreasoning rage. Bright, hot anger was no stranger; but it passed rapidly, and she knew better than to let it rule her. But what the king had done outside the barred gate of the moat house was something else. *It's a deliberate provocation*, she told herself. *He doesn't want or expect our surrender, so he thinks to unhinge us.* And he was certainly trying hard. No one sane would have wasted noble prisoners as he had done, crucifying them outside the gatehouse, forgoing all hope of ransom and calling down eternal blood feud from their surviving relatives.

'Carl will deal with him tomorrow, I am sure,' Oliver declared, although whether he was being patronizing towards her age and status, or merely ironically detached, Olga was unsure. 'Tonight we have other work.'

'Indeed.' Olga lowered her goggles and switched them off, blinking at the twilight.

'Meanwhile, Earl Riordan sent his compliments, and would like to know what additional resources you need to move the duke, and when you'll be ready.'

Since when is he employing you *as a messenger boy?* Olga stepped aside from the window and turned to face him. 'I've got a corpsman and two soldiers, one to do the portage and one secondary body-guard; between them they're a stretcher team. That's plenty until we get to the crossover point. What I then need is for Grieffen or who-ever's in Central Ops to arrange to have a secure ambulance waiting for us in Concord at zero four hundred hours, and I need their cell number so I can guide them in when we cross over.' She patted her belt. 'I've got a GPS unit and a phone. We'll travel with everyone else as far as the drop zone then continue on a little further before we go back to the United States.' It wasn't the entire truth – and not just because she didn't trust the Baron. Oliver was trustworthy after his own fashion; but his loyalty was to his conception of the Clan, not to Olga's faction. He didn't have any need to know the details, and Olga wasn't inclined to take even the remotest of risks with the duke's per-sonal security.

'Do you want me to arrange the ambulance?' he asked attentively.

That did it: He *was* questioning her competence. 'No!' she snapped. 'I'll do it myself. The sooner I see him in a hospital bed the happier I'll be.' Moving an acute stroke patient was risky enough without trying to do it in the dark, under fire, and without benefit of any specialized medication more sophisticated than a couple of aspirin; the only reason even to consider it was out there in the dark and the chaos before the gatehouse.

'So will we all,' he said piously, turning to leave.

*

The hours passed quickly, in a frenzy of preparations for the evacu-ation. Not everyone was to leave; someone had to light the keep, fill the helmets visibly watching over it, and fire the occasional volley to convince the besieging forces that the palace wasn't an empty prize. But nine in every ten men and women would be world-walking out of the Hjalmar Palace before dawn, stealing away like thieves in the night once the hastily printed and laminated knotwork cards arrived. Almost everyone – Olga, the duke, and the wounded excepted – would return, with the early morning sun at their backs, half a mile behind the pretender's encampment. Trapped between the machine guns on the battlements and the rifles and recoilless rockets of the mobile force, the royalists would have scant time to regret their misplaced allegiance; their best strategy ought to be to melt back into the trees again. But from the lack of movement in the enemy camp it looked as if they'd swallowed the bait: While they clearly knew of the world-walker's ability, it seemed that they had not fully understood its tactical significance. That, or their commander was getting greedy.

Olga took a couple of hours to catch a nap, on a cot at the end of Angbard's bed. She awakened in near-darkness as a hand touched her shoulder. She grasped a wrist almost before she opened her eyes. 'What time . . . ?'

'Midnight plus four minutes, milady.' The soldier – a stocky woman called Irma, one of Helmut's lance and the daughter of an earl, if Olga remembered her rightly – straightened up. 'Martyn and I are your detail, along with Gerd' – the corpsman – 'to take his grace to safety, is that right?'

'Yes,' Olga said tersely. She rubbed her eyes and sat up, shook her head to clear the cobwebs, and yawned. 'You have a stretcher, yes? And suitable clothes.'

'A stretcher, aye,' Gerd called softly from the far side of the four-poster bed. 'He still sleeps, milady,' he added, forestalling her next question.

Irma grimaced. 'I hate stretchers.' She stepped back, to leave Olga some space. 'On the subject of suitable clothes – we are going to America, to meet an ambulance, at dead of night, I was told? But this other world, I've never been there before. So I don't know what's a suitable disguise for sneaking around there . . .'

'Don't worry about that aspect of things, we've got covered transport.' *I hope.* Olga sat up creakily. 'Here's the plan. We're going to cross over with everyone else. Have the cards arrived yet?' Irma shook her head. 'Well. When they arrive – it's a new world. This site is undeveloped farmland. Our agents have laid on trucks, and they'll drive Captain Hjorth and his force to the drop-off point for the counterattack. We'll be taking a car into Irongate, which is near as makes no difference sitting on the south side of Concord, and where there's a doppelgängered building in this world. Then we make two more transfers, crossing back at zero five hundred, and I'll phone for an

82

ambulance. I've got GPS, so we should be picked up within half an hour. Our main challenges are: keeping his grace comfortable, avoiding attention from the locals, and not killing ourselves by world-walking too much. Is that clear?'

'Yes, milady. Makes things easier.' Irma shook her head. 'Three crossings in four hours – that's harsh.'

'Yes. That's why for the first crossing we'll all be going piggyback on whichever members of your lance draw the short straws. And for the second crossing, Gerd will carry his grace and Martyn will carry you. On the third crossing, you can take the duke. This will be the hardest, but that way, only one of us risks breaking our head.'

'Do you think we should ditch our field gear?'

Olga thought for a moment. 'If it's not too much to carry, I think we should hang onto it until we're ready to make the final transit. But once we hit Concord' – she paused – 'we can't be wearing armor or carrying long arms. What clothing did you find for us?'

'Nothing for sure, milady, we must see if it fits – but the baron's family maintained a wardrobe with some American clothing, and it has not been looted yet. I hope,' she added under her breath.

'Let's go see, shall we,' Olga suggested, stretching as she stood up. Her own state she passed over: She and Angbard had never expected to wind up here, and her neat trouser suit would be fine. 'We need clothing that will pass at a distance for Gerd, Martyn, and you.'

'This way, then.' Irma led her from the master bedroom into an adjacent room, its rich paneling splintered and holed by small arms fire. Chests of drawers and a huge wooden chest dominated half a wall. 'I think this is what you're looking for.'

*

Late afternoon.

Miriam segued into wakefulness to the rattle and jabber of day-time television fuzzed into incoherence through a thin stud wall. Gathering her wits, she rolled over. *The bed isn't moving*, she realized. She'd found it difficult to rest, her worries chasing their tails through her mind, but she'd spent the last few nights on a transcontinental express train and the novelty of a bed that didn't sway side-to-side and periodically bump across railroad points had eventually drawn her down into a deep abyss of dreamless sleep. Yawning, she sat up and rolled off the comforter. *What time is it . . . ?* She glanced at the dressing table. Her notebook PC sat there, its LEDs winking as it charged. Whether it would start up was a moot point – it had spent six months in a hidden compartment in a disused office – but it had a clock; maybe it would still be working. She reached over and pressed the power button, then started gathering her clothes.

The regular startup chord and busy clicking of a hard disk provided welcome background noise as she dressed; but as the computer seemed to want to twiddle its thumbs instead of talking to her, she locked the screen and headed for the bathroom, and then the stairs, rather than waiting. To think that only four days ago she'd risked arrest and imprisonment to retake the thing, seeing it as central to her hopes for survival and prosperity . . .! Her understanding of her circumstances was changing almost from hour to hour, leaving her unable to rely on plans she'd made only the day before. It gave her an anxious sense of insecurity, rising to the level of nervous dread whenever her thoughts circled back to the pregnancy question.

The television noise was coming from the living room, along with other sounds. As Miriam pushed the door open she caught a burst of conversation: '. . . she's right, then what are we going to do? We won't be able to go back! Had you thought of' – a blond head turned – 'Oh, hi!'

Miriam paused. 'I hope I'm not interrupting anything . . .'

'Not really.' Huw was slouched in a recliner, propping up a laptop, while the two younger ones, Yul and Elena, had been either watching TV or arguing about something while sharing a large pizza of uncertain parentage. 'Feel free to join us.'

'Yah,' agreed Yul, chewing rhythmically.

Elena thumped him. 'Don't talk with your mouth full!'

'Yuh.' He took her punch on one shoulder, looking amused rather than hurt.

Miriam turned to address Huw. 'Where's Brill?'

'Oh, she went out.' He sounded disinterested. 'Hmm, that's interesting.'

Miriam glanced at the window. It was clearly getting late, and the shadows of the trees out front were lengthening. 'Is there anything to eat around here?' Her gaze was drawn to Elena and Yul's pizza, almost against her will.

'Uh?' Huw looked up at her, and visibly did a double take. 'Food? Um . . . yeah, food! Just a minute.' A rattle of hastily struck keys later, he closed the laptop's lid and stood up. 'Let's see what's in the kitchen?'

The kitchen was as sparsely equipped as it had been earlier in the afternoon. Huw headed straight for the freezer and the microwave, but Miriam stopped him. 'Let me.' While she rooted around in the cupboards, she asked, 'Any idea where Brill went? Did she ask you to get me a pregnancy test kit?'

'A what?' He walked over to the kitchen door and closed it carefully. 'No, that's women's stuff. If you asked for such a thing, she wouldn't trust a man to procure it.'

'Oh.' Miriam froze for a couple of seconds, disappointed. Then she opened the next cupboard. 'So where did she go?'

'If not to attend to your request, I'd guess she has a private call to make. She was getting extremely itchy about being on the wrong coast, and even itchier about how we're going to get back out east without attracting attention.'

'Attention' – Miriam paused to pull out a can of tomatoes and a bag of pasta – 'what kind of attention?'

'She came out here in the company biz-jet, but . . . someone tipped the feds off about where ClanSec were concentrating? Somewhere near Concord, apparently. We've had hints' – Miriam rattled past him, rifling a drawer in search of utensils – 'they're getting serious about tracking us down. So I don't think there's a biz-jet ride home in our immediate future.' Miriam slammed the cupboard door. 'What?'

'This is useless!' She pointed at her haul. 'What did they think we were going to do, eat at Mickey D's every day?'

'Freezer. Microwave. If you were stocking a house for a bunch of kids who're not used to living away from home without servants, what would you do?'

'Leave a cookbook!'

'We-ell, okay.' Huw made for the freezer again. 'Memo to Duke Angbard Lofstrom, Office of Clan Security. Re: Training program for armed couriers. Classification: Clan Confidential. All couriers must attend mandatory *Cooking with Rachael Ray* video screening and Culinary Skills 101 course prior to commencing overnight missions. Malnutrition a threat to morale, combat-readiness, and operational security.' He straightened up, a pizza box in each hand. 'Meat lover's feast or four cheese, my lady?'

'Oh hell, I'll take the cheese.' She smiled to take the sting out of her words. 'Sorry. It just bugs me.'

'It'd be good to have a staff, or use a hotel or something,' Huw agreed. 'But this is less conspicuous, and less conspicuous is good right now.'

'What do you mean?' She pulled out a chair and sat down.

'Well.' He slid the first pizza onto a plate and put it in the microwave. 'I have a nasty suspicion that in the interests of looking inconspicuous we're going to end up driving back to Massachusetts. Or driving part of the way, to avoid tracking. If we just fly point-to-point and they're paying attention, we'd show up. And then there's the communication discipline. All Internet traffic is monitored by the NSA. *All* of it. So we fall back on 1930s tech – old-fashioned letters written in runic Hochsprache, flash memory cards sealed under postage stamps instead of microdots, that kind of thing. It works well, but it's slow: that's probably why my lady Brilliana is taking so long.'

'Oh.' Miriam stared at the second pizza, feeling a stab of acute déjà vu. It was just like Erasmus's problems in New Britain, seen through a high-tech looking glass. 'I think I'm getting a headache.'

The oven pinged for attention. Huw opened it, sniffed, then slid the steaming microwave-limp pizza in front of her. 'Sorry – '

'Don't be, it's not your fault.' She picked up a knife and began to cut as he put the second pizza in. 'What do you want, Huw?'

'Huh?'

'What do you *want*?' She put down her knife. 'Here, help yourself to a slice.'

'Uh, you mean, what do I want, as in, what is my heart's desire, or what do I want, as in, what am I trying to achieve right now?' He reached over and took a piece, holding it twitchily on his fingertips.

'The former.' Miriam picked up a wedge of hot pizza and nibbled at it. 'Because I'd say, right now you're trying not to burn your fingers.'

'Ouch, yes! Um, life's little ambitions. I want to finish my master's, and I wanted to do a Ph.D., obviously. Only the duke more or less handed me a doctoral subject a couple of weeks ago! Hell, not even a doctorate: it's a life's work. The implications are *enormous*. As for the other stuff . . . I'm a younger son. Clan shareholder, but at least I'm not going to get roped in and tied down into running a backwoods estate. There's more to life than the Gruinmarkt, and if I must do the getting married and raising a family thing, I want to do it somewhere civilized, with electricity and running water, and a partner of my own choosing.'

'Got anyone in mind?'

'Oh, I think so.' His expression turned inward for a moment. 'Although it's too early to ask . . .' He shook his head. The microwave dinged again. 'Is that what you wanted to know?'

'It'll do for a start.' Miriam watched as he stood up and pulled the second pizza out of the oven. 'How many – of your generation – do you think see eye-to-eye with you on the last bit? Electricity and running water and marrying for love rather than because your parents say so?'

Huw reached for the knife. 'It's funny . . . there are a bunch of foreign students at MIT? You can't go there and not know a couple of them. We had a lot in common. It's like, we all got used to the amenities and advantages of living over here, but it's not *home*. The Chinese and Middle-Eastern and developing-nation students all wanted to spend time over here, earning a stake, maybe settle down. It's a deprivation thing. I didn't see it with the European students – there weren't as many of them, either – but then, you wouldn't. The difference in standards of living isn't so pronounced. But you want to know about my generation? There are those who've never spent much time over here – a minority, these days – and they don't know any better, but there's an outright majority who'd be over the wall in an instant if they could keep visitation rights. And if you promised to install electricity and running water and start Niejwein developing, they'd elect you pope-emperor. Shame that's not going to happen, of course. I'd have liked to have seen you on the throne in the Summer Palace, taking names and kicking butt. I think you'd have been good at it.'

'In your dreams.' Miriam gnawed at a fresh chunk of pizza. 'Well, we've got a bigger problem now.'

'Yes, I was just thinking that . . .' Huw slid another portion onto her plate. 'Here, have a chunk of mine. Um. So what's *your* life's ambition?'

'Uh?' Miriam stared at him, a chunk of pizza crust held in one hand. 'Excuse me?'

'Go on.' Huw grinned. 'There must be something, right? Or someone?'

'I – uh.' She lowered the piece of crust very carefully, as if it had suddenly been replaced by high explosive. 'You know,' she continued, in a thoughtful tone of voice, 'I really have absolutely no idea.' She cleared her throat. 'Is there anything to drink?'

'Wine, or Diet Coke?'

'Ugh. Wine, I think, just not too much of it . . .'

'Okay.' Huw fetched a pair of glasses and a bottle.

'I used to think I had the normal kinds of ambition,' she said thoughtfully. 'Married, kids, the family thing. Finish college, get a job. Except it didn't quite work out right, whatever I did. I did everything the wrong way round, the kid came too soon and I gave her up for adoption because things were . . . fucked up right then? Yes, that's about the size of it. Mom suggested it, I think.' Her face froze for a moment. 'I wonder why,' she said softly.

Huw slid a glass in front of her. 'I didn't know you had a child?'

'Most people don't.' She sipped briefly, then took a mouthful of wine. 'I married him. The father. Afterwards, I mean. And it didn't work out and we got divorced.' She stifled an unhappy laugh. 'That's what I mean about doing things in the wrong order. And before you ask, no, I'm not in contact with the adoptive parents. Mom might know how to trace them, but I bet' – she looked thoughtful – 'she won't have made it easy. For blackmail, you see. So anyway, after my marriage fell apart I had a career for a decade until some slime in a vice president's office flushed it down the toilet. And I'd still *have* a career, a freelance one, except I discovered I had a family, and they wanted me to get married and have a baby, preferably in the right order, thanks, electricity and running water strictly optional. Oh, and my mother is an alien in both senses of the word; the first man I met in ten years who I thought I'd be willing to risk the marriage thing with was shot dead in front of me; the boyfriend before *that*, who I dropped because of the thousand-yard stare, turns out to be a government spy who's got my number; I'm probably pregnant with a different dead man's baby; and the whole world's turned to shit.' She was gripping the glass much too tightly, she realized. 'I just want it to *stop.*'

Huw was staring at her as if she'd grown a second head. *Poor kid,* she thought. *Still at the mooning after girlfriends stage, not sure what he wants – why did I dump all that on him?* Now she knew what to look for – now she knew the pressure that had broken Roland – she could see what was looming in his future, the inevitable collision between youthful optimism and brutal realpolitik. *Did I really just say all that?*

While she was trying to work it out, Huw reached across the breakfast bar and laid a finger on the back of her hand. 'You've been bottling that up for a long time, haven't you?'

'How old are you?' she asked.

'I'm twenty-seven,' he said calmly, taking her by surprise: He had five years on her estimate. 'And I hear what you're not saying. You're what, thirty? Thirty-one? And – '

'Thirty-four,' she heard herself saying.

' – Thirty-four is a hard age to be finding out about the Clan for the first time, and even harder if you're a woman. It's a shame you're not ten or fifteen years older,' he continued, tilting his head to one side as he stared at her, 'because they understand old maids; they wouldn't bother trying to marry you off.' He shook his head abruptly. 'I'm sorry, I'm treating your life like a puzzle, but it's . . .'

'No, that's okay.'

'Ah, thank you.' He paused for a few seconds. 'I shall forget whatever you want me to, of course.'

'Um?' Miriam blinked.

'I assume you don't want your confidences written up and mailed to every gossip and scandalmonger in the Gruinmarkt?' He raised an eyebrow.

'Of course not!' Catching the gleam in his eye: 'You wouldn't. Right?'

'I'm not suicidal.' He calmly reached out and took the final wedge of her pizza. 'I bribe easily.'

'Here's to wine and pizza!' She raised her glass, trying to cover her rattled nerves with a veneer of flippancy. *Damn, he's not that unsophisticated at all. Why do I keep getting these people wrong?*

'Wine and pizza.' Huw let her off the hook gracefully.

'You wanted to know what my life's ambitions were,' she said. 'May I ask why?'

Huw stopped chewing, then swallowed. 'I'd like to know what motivates the leader I'm betting my life on.' He looked at her quizzically. 'That heavy enough for you?'

'Whoa!' She put her glass down slightly too hard. 'I'm not leading anyone!' But Brill's words, earlier, returned to her memory. *Your mother intends to put you on the throne; and we intend to make sure you're not just there for show.* 'I'm – ' She stopped, at a loss for words.

'You're going to end up leading us whether you like it or not,' Huw said mildly. 'I'm not going to shove you into it, or anything like that. You're just in the right position at the right time, and if you *don't*, we'll all hang. Or worse.'

'What do you mean?'

Huw turned his head and looked at the window, his expression opaque. 'The duke has been holding the Clan together, through ClanSec, for a generation. He's, he's a modernizer, in his own way. But there aren't enough of us, and he's aging. He's also a fascist.' Huw held up a finger: 'I say that in the strict technical sense of the word – he's what you get when you take the principle of aristocratic exceptionalism and push it down a level onto the bourgeoisie, and throw in a big dose of the subordination of the will of the individual to the needs of the collective. Ahem.'

He took a sip of wine. 'Sorry, Political Econ 301, back before I ended up in MIT. The Clan is only five generations removed from folks who remember being itinerant tinkers in a late medieval marcher kingdom. We are the nearest thing that the Gruinmarkt has thrown up to a middle class, and it's the lack of any effective alternative that had our great-grandparents buying titles of nobility and living it up. Anyway, the duke took a bunch of warring, feuding extended families and gave them a security organization that guards them all. He's kicked butt and taken names, and secured a truce, and virtually everyone now agrees it's a good thing. But he's a single point of failure. When he goes, who's going to be the next generalissimo? *Your* trouble is that you're his niece, by his wildcat stepsister. More importantly, you're the only surviving one in the direct line of succession – the attrition rate forty years ago was fearsome. So if you decide not to play your cards you'd better be ready to run like hell. Whichever of the conservative hard-liners comes out on top will figure you're a mortal threat.'

'Hang on, whichever? Conservatives? Aren't you jumping the gun – '

'No, because *we're not ready*. Give us another few years and maybe Earl Riordan could do it. Or Olga, Baroness Thorold, although she's even younger. There are others: Kennard Heilbrunner ven Arnesen, Albericht Hjalmar-Hjorth. But they're not in position. You're in an unusual spot: You're young but not too young, you've got *different* experience, you demonstrated a remarkable ability to innovate under pressure, and – the icing on the cake – assuming you're pregnant, you're carrying a legitimate heir to the throne. Or at least one who everyone who survived the betrothal will swear is legitimate, and that's what counts. And they'll swear to it because, while the old nobility wouldn't know a DNA paternity test from a hole in the ground, the *Clan* nobility have heard of it, and even the old folks have a near-superstitious respect for the products of science.'

'But I'm not –' Miriam stopped. She picked up her glass again, rolling it between her palms. 'Did Brill tell you the details of Dr. ven

Hjalmar's creepy plan?' Huw nodded. 'Good. But you know some-thing? I'm old, and not all pregnancies come to term, and I am really *not fucking happy* about being turned into a brood mare. And I com-pleted enough of pre-med that if – that's an *if* – I decide to lose it, you – that's a collective *you* – are going to have to keep me in a straitjacket for the next nine months if you want your precious heir. Assuming it exists and it's a boy. And I haven't made my mind up yet. And as for what ven Hjalmar's got coming, if he isn't dead, if I ever see him again . . .'

Silence. Then Huw spoke, in a low voice, as if talking to himself: 'Miriam, if you are pregnant and you decide you don't want to go through with it, I would consider it a matter of my personal honor to help you end it. Just as long as you keep it quiet . . . the old folks, they wouldn't understand. But I won't be party to keeping you in a strait-jacket.'

'Uh. I. Er.' Miriam drained her wineglass, trying to cover her con-fusion. 'What you just offered. You know what you just said?'

'Yes.' Huw nodded. 'I will either get you the appropriate medica-tion, or, if it's too late for that, help you get to an abortion clinic.' He paused. 'It wouldn't be the first time I've helped a girl out that way.'

'Uh.' Miriam stared at him. *Just when I think I'm getting to under-stand them . . .* 'No offense, but you made it sound like organizing a shopping trip . . .'

'I may be an MIT graduate student, but I'm from *the Gruinmarkt.*' Huw visibly searched for words. 'We don't place much stock in a babe 'til it's born. Which is perhaps a good thing. You wouldn't want it to be born if it would trigger a blood feud that would claim its own – and its parents' – lives, would you?'

'But – you said it was leverage – '

'Yes, I did.' He looked back at her. 'But it's not the only lever you've got. The duke's accident elevates your rank in the game. You might still have a chance, even if you throw it away.' He slid off his bar stool and picked up the dirty plates. 'Just try to give the rest of us some warning when you make your mind up, huh?'

'I know what this looks like.' She was still gripping the wineglass tightly, she realized, tightly enough to stop her hands shaking. 'I am not going to flip. I've been here before, a long time ago.'

'But' – Huw peered at her – 'you're doing fine, so far.'

'It's a control thing.' Miriam forced herself to let go of the glass. 'You never know, I might *not* be pregnant. I need a test kit. And then I need some space to think, to get my head around this.' She paused. 'Were you serious about that offer?'

Huw hesitated for a few seconds before answering. 'All the plans anyone's making – they all rely on your active participation. We need you to trust us. Therefore' – he shrugged uncomfortably – 'having made that offer I'm bound by it; if I forswear myself you'll never trust me ever again. And we, my faction, need you to show us what to do. That's more important than any crazy plan Henryk hatched to manipulate the succession. We need your trust. And that's something that can only be bought with our own.'

*

Three o'clock in the morning.

The occasional crack of heavy-caliber gunfire, punctuated by the boom of a black-powder cannon, split the nighttime quiet outside the castle walls. Nobody was getting much sleep, least of all the guards who hunkered down in the courtyard around the central keep, night-vision goggles active, waiting for a sign.

The sign, when it came, was a mere flickering in the shadows near the dynamited well house. Two of the guards spotted it at once, lowered their guns, and darted out across the open ground towards it. Their target bent over, emptying his stomach on the hard-packed cobblestones. 'This way, sir! We need to get under cover.'

The traveler nodded weakly, straightening up. 'Take. This.' He held out a shoulder bag. 'I'll mark the spot. It's crowded around there.' His clothing was unfamiliar, but not his face; the sergeant nodded and took his bag.

'You sit down and wait, then. We'll be along presently.' He glanced at the sky: So far the enemy forces hadn't tried lobbing shells into the courtyard at random, but it was only a matter of time before they got bored with sniping at window casements. 'Try to stay close to the wall.'

He dashed back towards the keep, not bothering to jink – they held the walls so far, Lightning Child be praised – going flat-out with the shoulder bag clenched in both hands.

Carl was waiting in the grand hall with his staff. By lamplight, his face was heavily lined. He seemed, to the sergeant's eye, to have aged a decade in the past two days. 'Let's see that,' he suggested.

'Sir.'

The guard upended the bag's contents in the middle of the table with a thin clatter of plastic. Carl picked one of the cards up and carefully angled it for a glance. He drew breath sharply. 'What do you think?'

Oliver Hjorth took the card and squinted at it. 'Yes, this looks like the right thing.' He glanced at the guard. 'You recognized the courier.'

'It's Morgan du Hjalmar, somewhat the worse for wear.'

The baron thought for a moment. 'He'll be wanting a ride back over, won't he.'

Carl nodded. 'See to it,' he told the sergeant, then glanced sideways at Helmut Anders, his lieutenant. 'Get everyone moving out. The recon lance first, as planned, then if the insertion site is cold the, the casualty and his party' – he couldn't bring himself to refer to the duke by name – 'followed by everyone else. My lord Hjorth, if you'd care to accompany my headquarters staff . . . Let's get a move on, people!'

The crowd gathered around the table scattered, except for the core of officers and Helmut, who carefully removed his helmet and scooped the laminated plastic cards into it, averting his eyes as he did so. He moved to stand by the door, waiting for the clatter and clump of boots as the recon lance descended the grand staircase, weapons ready.

'Take a card, move on out, Morgan over by the well house will show you the transit spot,' he told them, holding the helmet before him. 'You know what to do.'

'Secure the area!' Erik grinned at Helmut, his enthusiasm evidently barely dampened by the disaster on the rooftop two days ago.

'They're supposed to be friendly,' Helmut chided him. 'So use your discretion.'

'Aye!' Erik took a card and stepped forward. 'Come on, you guys. Party's this way.'

Olga watched from the back of the hall as the recon lance marched towards the well house and an appointment with an uncertain world. *Better them than me*, she told herself. There were any number of things that could go wrong. They might have the wrong knotwork, a subtle flaw in the design, and go . . . somewhere. Or the long-lost cousins of the hidden family might decide to use this opportunity to settle their old score against the eastern families. Any number of nasty little possibilities lay in that particular direction. Morgan's appearance suggested otherwise, but Olga had no great faith in his abilities, especially after what Helge – Miriam – had told her about the way he'd run her works in New Britain into the ground. *Whatever can go wrong, probably has* already *gone wrong, and there's no point worrying about it.* She tried the thought for size and decided it was an ill-fit for her anxiety. There's nothing to be done but wait and see . . .

Minutes passed, then there was another flicker in the shadows, out in the courtyard. A brief pause, then a figure trotted back towards the great hall.

'Sir! The area was as described, and Cornet du Thorold sends word that he has secured the perimeter.' The soldier looked slightly pale, but otherwise in good shape – he'd made his first transit on a comrade's back, specifically so he'd be able to make a quick return dash. 'To my eye it's looking good. There are four covered trucks waiting, and eight men, not obviously armed, with your cousin Leonhard.'

'Good.' Captain Wu nodded. Then he glanced Olga's way. 'Your cue, milady.'

'Indeed.' Olga turned back to the side chamber where her small team was waiting. They'd brought the duke downstairs earlier. Now he lay on a stretcher, eyes closed, breathing so slowly that she had to watch him closely to be sure he was still alive. 'Come on,' she told Irma, Gerd, Martyn, and the four soldiers she'd roped in. 'Let's get him to safety.'

The slow march out to the moonlit well house, matching her pace to the stretcher beside her, the smooth touch of the laminated card between her fingers: Olga felt herself winding tight as a watch spring. The gun slung across her shoulder was a familiar presence, but for once it was oppressive: If she found herself using it in the next few minutes, then the duke's life – and by extension, the stable governance of the Clan – would be in mortal jeopardy. *This has to work. Because if it doesn't . . .*

Seconds spun down into focused moments. Olga found herself crouching astride a heavily built trooper. 'Are we ready?' she asked, as the soldiers raised their cards and shone pocket flashlights on them. 'Because – '

The world lurched –

'Oh,' she said, and slid down her porter's back as he staggered.

There were *floodlights*. And walls of wood, and between the walls, four large trucks of unfamiliar design, and soldiers. *Familiar* soldiers, thank Sky Father, in defensive positions near the gates to the compound. 'What *is* this place?' she demanded.

'Lumberyard,' said Leonhard Wu, beside her shoulder.

Olga suppressed an unladylike urge to punch him. Leonhard always left her feeling slightly dirty: something about the way his gaze always lingered for just a few seconds too long. 'Nice to see you, too,' she replied. *Whose lumberyard*? she left unasked. The security implications were likely to prove disquieting, and right now she had a single task to focus on –

'How is he?' she asked Gerd, who crouched beside the duke, holding his wrist.

'As good as can – '

' – Is that the *duke*?' Leonhard's voice cracked into a squawk.

'Hsst.' Olga leaned towards him. 'This is not Angbard Lofstrom, he wasn't here, and you haven't seen him. Not now, not here, not in this state. Do you understand?' She glared at him.

'No need for that!' He nearly collapsed in his haste to back away. 'Ah, no, I haven't seen anything. But, uh, don't you think you ought to get your nothing-to-see-here out of sight, Olga? Before the cousins – '

'That's the idea.' She nodded at the trucks. 'Which of them is designated for officers?'

'That one – '

'Good. You can help Gerd here carry John Doe over to the load bed and make him comfortable. Hmm. Irma, why don't you go with Leonhard here and make sure everyone works together splendidly? I have another job to do before we leave.'

She left Leonhard looking over his shoulder at her in fear and strode towards the gate, where Erik, the cornet in charge of the recon lance, stood with a couple of unfamiliar men in strange, drab clothing.

'Cornet, gentlemen.' She nodded. 'I believe you have a tactical plan.'

One of the men looked vaguely familiar. 'Lady, ah, Thorold-Hjorth? You are a friend of, of Helge?'

She blinked. 'Yes. You are . . . ah, Sir James.' She bobbed her head. 'I see you made it back home.'

'Indeed.' He smiled faintly. 'And how may I serve you?'

'Let's walk.'

'Certainly.'

James Lee had been dangerously smooth, she remembered, so smooth you could almost forget that his uncle and ancestors had waged a quiet war of assassination against her parents and grandparents, almost as soon as they'd concluded – erroneously – that their patriarch had been abandoned by his eastern brothers. James was friendly, affable, polished, and a much better diplomat than anyone had expected when, as part of the settlement between the families, he'd been sent to stay in Niejwein as a guest – or hostage. *Which only makes him more dangerous*, she reminded herself. 'I have a little problem,' she said quietly.

'A problem?' He raised an eyebrow as they neared the rear of the truck where Irma and Gerd, with Leonhard's unwilling help, were lifting the duke into the covered load bed.

'A passenger who is somewhat . . . sick. We need dropping off elsewhere from the rest of Carl's men, to make a crossing to the United States where he can receive urgent medical care.'

'If he's so sick, why – ' James paused. 'Oh. Who is he?'

'I don't think you want to know. Officially.'

James paused in midstride. 'There have been signals,' he said. 'Huge disturbances, civil strife in Gruinmarkt. We have eyes and ears; we cannot help but notice that things are not going according to your plans.'

Olga nodded politely, trying not to give anything away. 'Your point, sir?'

'You are imposing on us for a big favor,' he pointed out. 'Six months ago our elders were at daggers drawn. Some of them are still not sure that sheathing them was a good idea. We have our own external security problems, especially here, and escorting your soldiers through our territory is bound to attract unwanted attention. I'm sorry to have to say this so bluntly, but I need something to give my elders, lest they conclude that you have nothing to offer them.'

'I see.' Olga kept her smile bland as she frantically considered and discarded options. *Shoot his men and steal their vehicles* was, regrettably, not viable; without native guides to the roads of Irongate they'd risk getting hopelessly lost, and in any case the hidden family's elders wouldn't have sent James without an insurance policy. *Offer him something later* would send entirely the wrong signal, make her look as weak as the debtor turning out his purse before a loan shark's collection agents. Her every instinct screamed *no* at the idea of showing him the duke in his current state, but on the other hand . . .

'Let me put it to you that your elders' interests are served by the continued stability of our existing leadership,' she pointed out. 'If one of our . . . leaders . . . had experienced an unfortunate mishap, perhaps in the course of world-walking, it would hardly enhance your security to keep him from reaching medical treatment.'

'Of course not.' James nodded. 'And if I thought for a second that one of your leaders was so stricken, I would of course offer them the hospitality of our house – at least, for as long as they lingered.' He raised an eyebrow quizzically.

Olga sighed. 'You know we travel to another world, not like New Britain.' Well, of course he did. 'Their doctors can work miracles, often – at least, they are better than anything I've ever seen here, or anything available back home. It does not reflect on your honor that I must decline your offer of hospitality; it is merely the fact that the casualty might survive if we can get him into the hospital that is waiting for him, but he will probably die if we linger here.' She looked James Lee in the eye. 'And if he dies without a designated successor, all hell will break loose.'

James' pupils dilated. The violent amber flare of the floodlights made it hard to be sure, but it seemed to her that he looked paler than normal. 'If it's the duke – ' He began to turn towards the truck, and Olga grabbed him by one elbow.

'Don't!' she said urgently. 'Don't get involved. Forget your speculation. It's not the duke; the duke cannot possibly be seen to be less than hale, lest a struggle to inherit his seat break out in the middle of a civil war with the Pervert's faction. Let Ang – Let our sick officer pass, and if he recovers he will remember; and if he dies, you can remind his successors that you acted in good faith. But if you delay us and he dies . . . you wouldn't want that to happen.'

She felt him tense under her hand, and clenched her teeth. James was taller than she, and significantly stronger: If he chose not to be restrained, if he insisted on looking in the truck –

He relaxed infinitesimally, and nodded. 'You'd better go, my lady.' Shadows flickered behind them – another lance of Wu's soldiers coming through. 'Right now. Your men Leonhard or Morgan, one of them can guide you. Take this truck; I will arrange a replacement for your soldiers.' Olga released his elbow. He rubbed it with his other hand. 'I hope you are right about your dream-world's doctors. Losing the thin white duke at this point would indeed not be in our interests.'

'I'm pleased you agree.' Olga glanced round, spotted Leonhard walking towards the driver's cabin. 'I'd better go.'

'One thing,' James said hastily. 'Is there any news of the lady Helge?'

'Helge?' Olga looked back at him. 'She passed through New London a week ago. One of my peers is following her.'

'Oh,' James said quietly. 'Well, good luck to her.' He turned and walked back towards the gate.

Olga watched him speculatively for a few seconds. *Now what was that about?* she wondered. But there was no time to be lost, not with the duke stricken and semiconscious on the back. She climbed into the cab of the truck behind Leonhard and a close-lipped driver. 'Let's go,' she told them.

'There's no time to lose.'

THE EXECUTION PROTOCOL

Governments run on order and process. There was probably a protocol for everything, thought agent Judith Herz – formerly of the FBI, now attached semipermanently to the Family Trade Organization – short of launching a nuclear attack on your own territory. Unfortunately that was exactly what she'd been tasked with doing, and probably nobody since the more psychotic members of the Joint Chiefs of Staff tasked with planning Operation Northwood during the 1960s had even imagined it. And even though a checklist had come down from on high, and the colonel and Major Alvarez had confirmed it looked good, just thinking about it gave her a headache.

(1) *Secure the package at all times.* She glanced up from her clipboard, across the muddy field, at the white armored truck with the rectangular box body. The floodlights they'd hastily rigged that afternoon showed that it was having some difficulty reversing towards the big top; the rear axle would periodically spin, the engine roaring like an angry tiger as the driver grappled with its overweight frame. *Maybe we ought to have just used a minivan,* she thought. *With a suitable escort, it would have been less conspicuous* . . . On the other hand, the armed guards in the back, watching each other as well as the physics package, would probably disagree.

(2) *Do not deploy the package until arrival of ARMBAND.* ARMBAND, whatever it was – some kind of magic box that did whatever it was the world-walking freaks from fairyland did in their heads – had landed at MacArthur Airport; she'd sent Rich Hall and Amanda Cruz to escort it in. *Check.*

(3) *PAL codes – call WARBUCKS for release authorization. That* was the bit that brought her out in a cold sweat, because along with the half-dozen unsmiling federal agents from the NNSA, call sign *WARBUCKS* meant that this was the real deal, that the permissive action

lock code to activate the nuclear device would be issued by vice president Cheney himself, as explained in the signed Presidential Order she'd been allowed to read – but not to hold – by the corpse-faced bastard from the West Wing who Colonel Smith answered to. *Since when does the President give the VP backpack nukes to play with, anyway?* she asked herself; but it *looked* official enough, and the folder full of top secret code words that had landed on her desk with a palpable thud yesterday suggested that this might be a cowboy operation, but if so, it was being led by the number one rancher himself. At least, that was what the signatures of half the National Command Authority and a couple of Supreme Court justices implied.

(4) *FADM/ARMBAND final assembly and PAL programming to be carried out on launch scaffold.* The thing in the tent gave her the creeps; Smith called it a transdimensional siege tower, but it looked too close to a field-expedient gallows for her liking. She was going to go up there with Dr. Rand and a posse of inspectors from NNSA and a couple of army officers, and when they came down from the platform, some person or persons unknown would be dead. Not that she was anti-death-penalty or anything, but she'd started out as an FBI agent: The anonymous military way of killing felt profoundly wrong, like a gap in a row of teeth, or a death in the family.

(5) *ARMBAND failure contingency plan. That* was the worst bit of all, because if ARMBAND failed to work as advertised, she and Lucius Rand and everyone else would be standing on a scaffold with a ticking bomb on a sixty-second countdown, and they'd get precisely two chances to enter the eight-digit abort code.

It was a good thing that she'd taken the time for holy communion and attended confession that morning, she thought, as she walked towards the tent. It had been a long day, and she had a feeling that the night was going to be even longer.

Her earbud crackled: 'Herz, speak to me.' It was the colonel.

'Stage one is in hand, I'm waiting on news of ARMBAND.' Out of one corner of her eye she saw moving headlights, another of the undercover patrol cars circling the block slowly, looking for rubber-neckers. 'Everything seems to be on track so far.'

'Please hold.' She walked on, briefly looking round to check on the armored car. (It was reversing again, pulling free of the patch of soft ground that had stymied it.) 'Okay, that's good. Update me if there are any developments.'

So the colonel is jittery? Good. A uniform over near the support truck from the NNSA was waving to her; local cops drafted in for crowd control and vehicle marshaling. She changed course towards him. *So he should be.* 'What's up?' she demanded.

'Uh, Agent – ' He was nervous; not used to dealing with FBI.

'Herz.' She nodded. 'You have something.'

'Yeah, there's a car at the north quadrant entrance, driver says it's for you. Name of Hall.'

'Oh.' – *What's Rich doing up* there? – 'If that's Rich Hall and Amanda Cruz, we're expecting them.' She kicked herself mentally: *Should have told them which gate to use.* 'Let them in. They've got a package we're expecting.'

'Sure thing, ma'am.' He leaned over towards the driver's window of the patrol car, talking to his partner. Herz walked on, jittery with too much poor-quality caffeine and a rising sense of tension. *We're about to fire the opening shot in a war*, she thought. *I wonder where it's going to end . . .*

*

It was dark, and the moon already riding low in the sky outside the kitchen window, when Huw yawned and conceded defeat. He saved the draft of his report, closed the lid of his laptop, picked up two glasses and a bottle of zinfandel, and went upstairs to bed.

As he closed the door and turned on the light, the bedding moved. A tousled head appeared: 'What kept you?'

'I have a report to write, in case you'd forgotten.' He put the glasses and the bottle down on the dressing table and began to unbutton his shirt. 'I hope you had a better day than I did, my lady.'

'I very much doubt it.' She sat up and plumped up the pillows. As the comforter dropped, he saw that she was naked. Catching his gaze, she smiled. 'Lock the door?'

'Sure.' He dropped his shirt on the carpet, let his jeans fall, then went to the door and shot the dead bolt. Then he picked up the wine bottle and twisted the screw cap. 'What happened?'

'Head office are going mad.' She screwed up her face. 'It's *unreal*. The council are running around like half-headed turkey fowl, the whole flock of them.'

'Well, that's a surprise.' He filled a glass, sniffed it, then held it out to her. She took it. 'Any word on the boss . . . ?'

'Olga's bringing him out within the next hour. Assuming nobody attacks the ambulance, he'll be in a hospital bed by dawn. The last word from that quarter is that he's tried to talk, since the incident.'

Huw filled his own wineglass, then sat down on the edge of the bed. 'Can we forget about politics for a few hours? I know you want me to bring you up to date on what I was doing back in New York, and I'm sure you've got a lot of stuff to tell me about what's been going on since the last time we were together, but I would like, for once, to take some time out with you. Just you and me alone, with no unquiet ghosts.'

Her frown faded slightly. 'I wish we could. But there's so much riding on this. We'll have time later, if we succeed, but' – she glanced at the door anxiously – 'there's so much that can still go wrong. If Miriam has any mad ideas about running away . . .'

'Well, that's an interesting question. While you were away, we had a chat. She seemed to need it.'

'Oh?' Brilliana drank down a mouthful of wine. 'How is she doing?'

'Not well, but I don't *think* she's going to run out on us, as long as she feels we're standing alongside her.'

'It's *that* bad? I've known her for, ah, nearly a year, and her highness does not strike me as disloyal to her friends.'

Huw did not miss the significance of the honorific. 'She hasn't acceded to that rank yet, has she?'

'No.' Brill's expression was bleak. 'I don't think she's fully realized, yet, what it means – she was having a difficult time understanding that vile business of Henryk's, much less thinking about what is going to happen . . .'

'Er, I think you're wrong.' Huw emptied his glass in one long swallow. 'Needed that. Excuse me. Did you buy her a pregnancy test kit?' He refilled her glass, then topped up his own.

'I – yes, but I haven't given it to her yet. She asked you about that?'

'She is remarkably open, but her ability to trust – anyone, I think – is badly damaged by the whole business of the succession. I . . . I offered to help her obtain an abortion if she thought she needed one.'

'Huw!' Brill clapped one hand to her mouth. Then: 'Why?'

'She raised the subject.' Huw hunched his shoulders. 'I don't think she will, but . . . if she feels pressured, what will she do?'

'React,' Brill said automatically. 'Oh. Yes, that was cleverly played, my love. But you should have warned me. That's too clever by half. What if she'd called your bluff?'

'What if it wasn't a bluff?' He shrugged. 'She's no use to our cause if she doesn't trust us. No use to anyone *at all*. That is true whether or not she has a royal bun in the oven. We're trying to break the pattern, not reinforce it.'

'Uh-huh. Winning her trust is one thing.' She leaned towards him. 'But you'd help her shoot herself in the head?'

'If I was convinced that she wanted to, and knew what she was asking for . . . yes.' He looked at Brilliana with a bleakness that sat badly with his age. 'I'd try to save her first, mind you.'

'Would you try to save *me* from my worst urges?' she asked sharply.

Huw put his glass down. 'That's one of those questions to which there's no safe answer, isn't it?'

'Yes.' She drained her own glass and reached across him, to put it down beside his. He shivered as she pushed her breasts against his side; her nipples were stiff. 'My worst urge right now says I want you to fuck me like there's no tomorrow. Because tomorrow' – she ran her hand down his chest – 'we might both be dead.'

*

Erasmus was going over the next morning's news with John Winstanley and Oliver Smith, the party commissioners for truth and justice, when word of the abdication came in.

Smith was reading down a plate, his lips moving silently as he read the raised bright mirror-text of the lead: '. . . and we call upon all right-minded men to, hang on, here's a dropped – '

'Yes, *yes*,' Erasmus said acidly. 'No need for *that*, leave it to the subs. What I need to know is, do you think it's sound?'

'Is it *sound*?' Winstanley nodded lugubriously. 'Well, that's the – '

The door rattled open. Burgeson looked up sharply. 'What is it?' he demanded.

The messenger boy – or youth – looked unabashed: 'It's Mr. Burroughs, sir! He wants you to come, quick like! 'E says it's important!'

Erasmus stared at him. 'Where is he?' he demanded.

''E's in the mayor's mansion, sir! There's news from out east – a train just came in, and there was folks on it who said the king's abdicated!'

Erasmus glanced at Smith. 'I think you'd better hold the front page,' he said mildly, 'I'm going to go see what this is all about.'

It was an overcast, gray summer's day outside, with a thin fog from the bay pumped up to a malignant brown haze by the smoke from a hundred thousand stoves and steam cars on this side of the bay. Fishing boats were maneuvering around the wharves, working their way in and out of the harbor as if the crisis of the past weeks was just a distant rumor. From the front steps, waiting as his men brought the car round to him, Erasmus could just make out the dots of the picket fleet in the distance, military yachts and korfes riding at anchor to defend the coast against the approach of French bombardiers or submarines. He eyed them warily every morning, half afraid they would finally make their move, choosing sides in the coming struggle. Word from the cadres aboard the ships was that the sailors were restive, unpaid for months now, but that the officers remained crown loyalists for the most part. Should push come to shove, it would be an ugly affair – and one that the realm's foreign enemies would be keen to exploit. Which was probably why John Frederick had not tried his luck by ordering the picket into the bay to put down the provisional government forces. It was a card he could only play once, and if it failed, he might as well dust off Cromwell's block. Although if the messenger lad was right . . .

By the time he arrived at the mayoral mansion, a light rain was falling and the onshore breeze was stiffening, blowing the smog apart. Erasmus paused for a deep breath as he stepped out of the back of the car, relishing the feel of air in lungs he'd almost despaired of a year ago. *Where are you now, Miriam?* he wondered briefly. It was her medication that had cured him, of that he was certain, even though the weird pills had turned his urine blue and disrupted his digestion. *What other magic tricks do you have up your sleeve?* It was something he'd have to explain to the chairman, sooner or later – if he could work out how to broach the subject without sounding as if he'd taken leave of his senses. 'Follow,' he said over his shoulder. The two bodyguards and the woman from the stenography pool moved hastily into position.

The committee offices on the first floor were seething – nobody was at their posts except for the militia guards, their rifles clenched in nervous hands. 'Where's the chairman?' Erasmus demanded when they came to the first checkpoint.

'He's in the committee room, sir,' said the senior man – Erasmus, being a regular enough visitor (and a member of the committee to boot), ranked above the regular interrogation such a question might have drawn from a stranger. 'Can you tell us what's going on?'

'Finding out is why I'm here.' Erasmus frowned. 'There'll be a statement later.' He glanced at his stenographer. 'Minute that for me.' He swept through the corridors towards the former dining room that Sir Adam had requisitioned as a meeting place for the committee, only pausing at the door where two heavies in the red, white, and blue armbands of internal security waited with shotguns. 'Erasmus Burgeson, commissioner for information, here to see the chairman,' announced one of his guards.

'Aye, right.' *These* guards were going by the book. Erasmus waited patiently as the senior one uncapped a speaking tube and announced him, then listened for instructions. 'You're to go in, sir. Your party' – a thumb gesture – 'can wait in the guardroom.'

Burgeson nodded at them. 'You heard him.' And then he opened the door.

The Committee for Democratic Accountability was neither accountable, nor democratic, nor even much of a committee – these words were all statements of aspiration, as much as anything else, for in the early days of building a better nation these words held power, and it was Sir Adam's hope that his institutions would grow into their names. Personally, Erasmus thought this was dangerously naïve – he'd read a number of books that Miriam had loaned him, strange books describing the historical processes of her even stranger world – but it was at least worth a try. Not *all* revolutions ended up eating their young, and heaven knew it was an opportunity to break with the dead hand of the oppressive past, but the thought that *this* revolution might go the way of some of those in Miriam's books had kept him awake into the small hours on more nights than he cared to think about.

Inside the committee room, there was an atmosphere of euphoria. Sir Adam was standing behind the lectern, and about half the delegates from the district councils seemed to have packed themselves in. Someone had opened a crate of cava and orange farmers from down south were toasting shipyard workers from the east bay with foam sparkling from their chipped tea mugs. Erasmus grabbed the first shoulder he could catch inside the doorway. 'What's going on?' he demanded.

'It's the king!' The man grinned broadly. 'He's gone! Packed up his bags in New London and ran. The garrison in Montreal picked him up!'

A sharp stab of anxiety gnawed at Erasmus. 'Are they ours?'

'They mutinied three weeks ago and elected a workers' and soldiers' council! They're with the white guards!'

Erasmus blinked. 'Excuse me.' He began to elbow his way through the crush towards the lectern where Sir Adam was earnestly holding forth to a gaggle of inner party graybeards who remained obdurately sober in the face of the collective derangement.

'Ah, Erasmus.' Sir Adam smiled. 'I gather the good news has reached you.'

'I need to know where it came from' – Erasmus pointed a thumb over his shoulder – 'if we're to get the word out where it's needed. I've got a stenographer waiting in the guardroom, and a front page to fill by three.'

'That's easy enough.' Burroughs gestured. 'You know Edward MacDonald, I take it.'

Erasmus nodded. 'We've met.' Ed, Lady Bishop's right-hand man, nodded back, cautiously.

'He brought certain other news of your activities out east, news that I personally consider would stretch the bounds of credibility – if anyone less than Lady Bishop vouched for their truth.' Burroughs contemplated Erasmus, an expression of perplexity on his face that reminded Burgeson of a school-teacher examining a pupil who had just done something that, while not actually deserving of punishment, was inexplicably wrong. 'We'll need to talk about it in due course.'

'Yes, we will.' Erasmus surprised himself with the assurance of his answer. 'But this isn't the time for addressing long-term problems. We've got to get the word of these momentous events out first. Once the loyalists realize they have been abandoned by their false monarch, that will change the entire situation!' He nodded at Edward. 'What's happened out east? What can you tell me that I can print? I need pictures, damn it! Who witnessed the events?'

*

The attack began an hour before dawn. Otto ven Neuhalle watched from a discreet distance as his men walked their precious M60s onto the front of the gatehouse from long range, firing parsimonious bursts – wary of his threats to damage any man who damaged his precious guns. The defenders declined to fire randomly into the dark, although a ghastly white glare opened its unblinking eye above the barred front gate, casting long shadows across the beaten ground before it – shadows that promised pain and death to anyone who ventured into view of the firing slits in the walls.

'Keep their heads down!' he shouted at Shutz and his men. 'But watch for our own!'

They didn't have many minutes to wait. Creaking and squealing with an ominous rumble, two large wagons rolled round the shoulder of the hill, following the road that led to the gate. The bullocks that pulled them didn't sound too happy, roaring and lowing beneath their heavy burden. Otto bared his teeth as he heard the voice of their driver and the crack of his whip.

'This should be fun,' a familiar voice commented from behind him.

Otto shivered as a chilly sweat broke out across the nape of his neck. 'Your Majesty has the better of me.' He turned around slowly – it was a faux pas to turn one's back on the monarch, and he had no desire to draw attention to it – and bowed deeply.

'Rise.' The king gestured impatiently. The lance of royal body-guards around him faced outward; the armor and colors he wore were indistinguishable from their uniform, but for the lack of an arm-band of rank. 'Two minutes, no more. They should be shooting by now.'

Otto found his tongue. 'May I ask if the carts are for men or explosives, my liege? I need to prepare my men . . .'

'Explosives.' Egon nodded towards them. 'The driver will take them up to the gate then set them off.'

'The – oh.' Otto nodded. The driver would do what he was told, or his family would be done by as the king had decreed: probably something creatively horrible, to reinforce his reputation as a strong and ruthless monarch. 'By your leave, I shall order my men to take cover just before the blast.'

'We wish them to advance and provide covering fire for the cavalry immediately afterwards,' Egon added offhand.

'Cavalry?' Otto bit his tongue, but even so the word slipped out first. Beyond the gatehouse was a wet moat, and then a steep descent into a dry moat before the gate into the castle's outer battlements. Nobody in their right mind would use cavalry against the layered defenses of a castle!

'Cavalry.' The royal grin was almost impish. 'I hope you find it educational.'

'My lord – ' One of the guards cleared his throat.

'Momentarily.' Egon stared at Otto. 'I intend to surprise *everyone*, Baron. This is just the start.'

Otto bowed his neck jerkily. 'Yes, Your Majesty.'

'Go.' Dismissed, Otto turned to warn Shutz and his gunners about the wagons – and to leave the king's disturbing presence. Behind him, Egon was mounting the saddle of a stallion from the royal stable. A pair of irreplaceable witch-clan night-vision glasses hung from his pommel.

The defenders were asleep, dead, or incompetent, Otto decided as he watched the wagons roll along the road towards the gatehouse. Or they'd been struck blind by Sky Father. The glaring hell-light cast a lurid glow across the ground before the gatehouse, but there was no shouted challenge, no crack of gunfire. *What are they* doing? He wondered. A horrid surmise began to gnaw at his imagination. *They're dead, or gone, and we're advancing into their ground while they sneak through the land of the dead, to ambush us from behind* –

Rapid fire crackled from the gatehouse, followed by a squealing roar of bovine distress: Otto breathed again. *Not dead or gone, just incompetent.* They'd shown little sign of movement earlier in the campaign, and despite their lightning-fast assault on the castle when he'd taken it, they'd failed to follow through. The witch-clan were traders, after all, lowborn tinkers, not knights and soldiers. He grinned as the wagon ground forward faster, the uninjured oxen panicked halfway to a stampede by the gunfire and the smell of blood. It had fifty yards to go, then forty – *Why aren't they firing? Are they low on ammunition?* – then twenty, then –

Otto knelt close to the ground, bracing himself, mouth open to keep his ears from hurting. The moments stretched on, as he counted up to twenty heartbeats.

'Is he dead?' called one of his gunners.

'I think – ' someone began to reply, but the rest of his comment was forestalled by a searing flash. A second later the sound reached Otto, a door the size of a mountainside slamming shut beside his head. The ground shook. A couple of seconds later still, the gravel and fragments rained down around the smoke-filled hole. 'What was *that*?' Otto shouted, barely able to hear himself. It wasn't like any powder explosion he'd ever heard, and he'd heard enough in his time. *What's the Pervert got his hands on now?* he added silently, straightening up.

The hell-light had gone out, along with the front of the gatehouse.

The wagon hadn't been small – there could have been half a ton, or even a ton, of explosives in it; whatever kind of explosives the king's alchemists had cooked up, using lore stolen from the witches.

Otto cleared his dry throat, spat experimentally. 'Break them down, get ready to move out,' he shouted at Shutz. 'The cavalry will be through here next.'

Shutz looked baffled, then pointed to his ears. Otto nodded. *'Scheisse.'* He gestured at the now-silent machine guns, miming packing them and moving forward. Shutz nodded, then opened his mouth and began shouting orders. Or at least he appeared to be telling troopers what to do: Otto found to his bemusement that he couldn't hear them.

The ground was still shaking. Peering back up the road, it wasn't hard for Otto to see why. Two more wagons were plodding grimly towards the pile of dust and smoke that had been the gatehouse – and behind them, what looked like a battalion of royal dragoons. In the predawn twilight they rode at no more than a slow walking pace. Otto shook his head; the ringing in his ears went on, but he was beginning to hear other sounds now. He raised his glasses, fumbled with the power button, and peered at the wagon. *This* one carried soldiers in helmets and half-armor, and a complicated mess of stuff, not the barrels of explosives he'd half-expected to see. 'Interesting,' he murmured, looking round for a messenger. 'You!'

'My lord!' The man shouted.

'Tell Anders to get his guns ready to move. We're to cover this force.' He pointed at the approaching dragoons. 'They're going to break in. Go!' *How* they were going to break into the castle he had no idea, but Egon clearly expected them to do so, and Otto had more than a slight suspicion that the new explosives in the oxcart weren't Egon's only surprise.

*

Strung out on caffeine and fatigue, Judith Herz suppressed a yawn as she watched the technicians with the handcart maneuver the device into position on the scaffold. There was a big cross spray-painted in the middle of the top level, and they were taking pains to move it so that it was centered perfectly. The size of a beer keg, with a briefcase-sized detonation controller strapped to it with duct tape, the FADM didn't look particularly menacing. She glanced over at Rich Hall, who was sitting patiently in a director's chair, the Pelican case containing ARMBAND between his feet. Cruz was about, somewhere, of course: They were taking pains to keep it within arm's reach at all times. *Good*, Judith thought tiredly. *Everything's ready, except for the PAL codes*. And head office, of course, but they'd be on-site shortly. The sooner they could get everything hooked up, the sooner they could all go and get some well-earned sleep.

A flicker of motion near the entrance to the tent caught her eye and she looked round. The new arrivals seemed tired: the colonel, talking animatedly to the man-in-black from the West Wing, a couple of aides following in their wake. *Oh great*, she thought: *rubberneckers*. 'Wait here,' she hold the technicians, then walked down the ramp to meet the newcomers.

'Colonel.' She smiled. 'And, uh, Dr. James.'

Smith glanced sidelong at him. 'He's our vertical liaison. With Mr. Cheney.'

'Dead straight.' Dr. James looked tired, too: The bags under his eyes suggested the lights had been burning late in the Naval Observatory grounds. 'Let's take a look at the package.'

'We haven't attached ARMBAND yet,' Judith began to say as Dr. James marched straight towards the scaffold.

'Then do it, right now. We need to get this thing done.'

What's the sudden hurry? she wondered. 'Yes. Sir.' She waved at Rich, who sat up sharply and mimed a query until she beckoned. 'What's up?'

'Change of situation.' James was clearly tense. 'I have the PAL codes.' He tapped his breast pocket. 'Colonel?'

'Dr. James is here as an official observer for the White House,' Smith reassured her. 'Also, we have Donald Reckitt from NNSA, Mary Kay Kare from, from the people who made ARMBAND, Richard Tracy from the Office of Special Plans – '

The introductions went on until the scaffolding began to creak under their weight. Finally they worked their way down through the layers of observers and their credentials to the technical staff. 'And Dr. Rand, who will confirm that the munition is release ready, check the connections to the detonation controller, and hand over to Major Alvarez and Captain Hu for deployment.'

'Certainly. If you folks wouldn't mind giving me some elbow room . . . ?' Rand, fiftyish and somewhat bohemian in appearance, looked as irritated by the institutional rubbernecking as Herz felt. As FTO's tame expert on these gadgets – indeed, as one of the nation's leading experts: he'd studied under Teddy Taylor, although the Comprehensive Test Ban Treaty meant that his expertise was somewhat abstract – he understood the FADMs as well as anyone else. And he ran through his checklist surprisingly rapidly. 'All looking good,' he announced, finally. 'Considering where it's been.'

'That's enough about that.' Dr. James spoke sharply: 'Not everyone here is briefed.'

'Oh?' Rand smiled lopsidedly as he straightened up. 'Well, that makes it all right then.' He patted the bomb, almost affectionately. 'For what it's worth, this one's ready to pop. Excuse me, ladies, gentlemen . . .'

As Rand left the platform, the colonel glanced at Herz. 'If you want to call the items . . . ?'

'Uh, yes, sir . . .' She stared at her clipboard and blinked a few times, wishing the tension between her brows would go away. Focusing was hard. 'PAL codes. I need to contact WAR – the designated release authority,' she corrected. She looked at Dr. James.

He nodded. 'This is what you want,' he said, handing her a manila envelope from his jacket pocket.

Judith slit it open with a fingernail. There was a single sheet of paper, on White House stationery, with a brief note, a pair of eight-digit numbers, and a famous signature. 'Well.' She breathed deeply. 'This looks to be in order, so' – she clipped it behind her checklist – 'we move on to ARMBAND. Rich, this is your curtain call. Major? We're ready to attach ARMBAND.'

Alvarez waved Rich Hall through to the front of the platform. 'Okay, here it is,' he said. He cleared his throat. 'I've only done this a couple of times before.'

He opened the shockproof case and pulled out four black rubber feet. 'Shoes.' Rocking the bomb carefully side to side, he wedged the feet underneath it. 'The payload needs to be electrostatically isolated from ground, or this won't work.' Next, he picked up a drab plastic box, its upper face broken only by a winking red LED, a button, and a key slot. 'Okay, now for the duct tape.' With that, he pulled out a reel of duct tape and a box cutter, and taped the box to the top of the bomb. Finally, he held up a key: 'Arming key.' He inserted it in the slot and gave it a half turn, and addressed Alvarez: 'ARMBAND is not yet armed. To activate it, it's necessary to give the key another half-turn, then push the button. It beeps, then five seconds later, it does its stuff. You do *not* want to be touching it when that happens.' He picked up his case and stepped back. 'You have control now.'

'I have control,' Alvarez echoed. He nodded at Wall: 'You'd better leave the platform now, sir.'

Is that all? Judith blinked again, feeling obscurely cheated. It was like black magic – a device that could transport a payload into another universe? – and yet it seemed so mundane.

'Agent Herz?' Colonel Smith prodded her.

'Oh? I'm sorry.' She nodded. 'Major Alvarez?' she called.

'Ma'am.' Alvarez and Hu were out of uniform – nobody wanted inconvenient questions about what army officers were doing in a field outside Concord – but nobody would mistake them for civilians, not with that crew cut and attitude. 'I have the checklist.'

He knelt down beside the package and unclipped a panel on the detonation controller strapped to the side of the bomb. Pulling open a laminated ring-bound checklist, he began to flip through pages, periodically double-checking a switch position. 'Check, please,' he told Hu.

'Check.'

'I need the PAL code now.'

'Here are your numbers.' Herz read out the eight-digit sequence from the letter. The audience fell silent, like witnesses at an execution. As, in a manner of speaking, they were: Alvarez and Hu the hangmen, adjusting the noose; Herz the prison governor, handing over the death warrant; and parties unknown standing on the trapdoor . . .

Well, at least they won't feel a thing, she told herself. *More than you can say for their victims, over the years.* 'Remember, we want a sixty-second delay. If the package doesn't disappear in front of your eyes within ten seconds, then turn the ARMBAND key to the "safe" position and enter the abort code. Are you ready?'

'We're ready,' Alvarez called.

'Ready!' Hu echoed.

Alvarez carefully closed the cover on the detonation controller, but – Herz noted – neglected to latch it shut. *That* wasn't in the checklist, at a guess.

The silence was oppressive. Finally, Dr. James cleared his throat. 'Major Alvarez, with the authority vested in me by the executive order I have received, I order you to proceed.'

*

Three days ago, the bulk of the Clan's mobile security force had concentrated in a field near Concord, arriving in buses disguised as costumed medievalists. Now, in the predawn light, they'd made it three miles down the road – riding in the backs of steam-powered livestock trucks, disguised as filthy, fight-worn anachronists. Their leader, the duke, and his paramedic and bodyguards, led by the lady Olga, had split off ten minutes ago, heading for an uncertain rendezvous and a waiting ambulance. That left Carl, captain of Security, with a reduced command and a monstrous headache; but at least it was better than being bottled up in that stone death trap.

'You're sure this is the spot.' He fixed Morgan with a well-practiced stare.

'Yuh-ess.' Morgan yawned hugely. 'My apologies, sir Captain. We are two miles southwest of the gates of the Hjalmar Palace, fifty yards north of the milestone, and the cross yonder' – he gestured – 'marks the center of the road.' The road was little more than a dirt track, but had the singular advantage of being a known quantity. 'Last night the pretender's forces were encamped a mile down the road from the gatehouse, dispersed in tents through the woods to either side. Watchers on the hill slope, of course. I cannot be sure – we have no recent intelligence – but I don't believe the camp extended more than two miles down the road to Wergatsfurt. So we *should* be a few hundred yards beyond their rear perimeter, as of last night.'

'Right.' Carl turned to Helmut. 'Are the men ready?'

'As ready as we can be.' Helmut's normally taciturn demeanor was positively stony. Which wasn't good.

'How much ammunition did we end up leaving behind?'

'For the Dragons? Most of it. Stefan's got just eight rounds. The SAWs are better – we divided up the belts. I'd say, three thousand rounds and two barrels per gun. And of course the light arms, we're fully equipped from the castle's armory. But food and water – it's not good.'

'Well, we'll just have to do the job before that becomes an issue.' Carl paused in thought. 'Have the men dose up with prophylactics before we cross over. We need a marker for the crossover point on the other side' – he pointed at the rough wooden cross that marked Morgan's survey point – 'and make sure everyone knows that if we move to retreat, that's the rendezvous point. Have Olaf's section position their M47 fifty yards forward of that marker, with one of the SAWs for covering fire' – Carl paced towards the perimeter of the fenced-in field to which the Lees' trucks had brought them – 'the M47's priority will be to take out the enemy M60s lest they bring us under beaten fire. Get Erik's people to cross over here. Hmm. If there's any sign of the Pervert's bodyguard, Little Dimmir's lance can concentrate on nailing them with support from Erik's people, and Arthur's SAW section if they're dug in *there*.' He continued laying out the deployment as Helmut and two sergeants followed him around the perimeter, making notes. It was all ad hoc, dangerously under-planned and hasty, but if there was one thing they didn't have, it was time for a careful setup. Finally, he finished: 'That's it. Brief your men and get them into position. We go in, hmm, zero-six-hundred, that's just under half an hour. Get moving!'

*

Otto's itchy sense of unease grew stronger with every step he took towards the moat. Ahead of him, the roar of the royal cannon provided a drumbeat punctuation to the sounds of advance: men shouting, chanting the king's name; boots tramping out the rhythm of the march in time to the beat of their drummers; horses clattering on the cobbled roadbed, neighing, jingling of kit; and periodically a spastic belch of machine-gun fire arcing overhead, crackling and whining off the stony roofline of the walls.

They're not shooting back, he realized, a hundred yards past the gatehouse, as he paused in a dip in the ground. Sometime in the past couple of hours the witches had cleared out. *Which means –*

'Forward for the Gruinmarkt!' The voice behind the cry was half-hoarse, but instantly recognizable as the royal life guards took up the call. 'The witches have fled before us!' The life guards flooded forward like a pack of hounds following an injured deer.

'Well, fuck it,' Otto grunted. 'Jorg!'

'Sir.'

'Tell Heidlor to set his guns up here and range in on the keep's door. Indirect fire.'

'Sir!' Jorg paused. 'But aren't we – '

'Damn your eyes, do it!'

Otto raised his glasses and studied the near horizon, shockingly close. In the predawn gloom the castle was a brooding presence up ahead, its upper ramparts topping the huge dry moat beyond the rise. *They've had two days to prepare for this, and they like blowing things up. What would I do in their shoes?* 'Jorg!'

Jorg, panting, hurried back towards him. 'Sir?'

'Tell Heidlor to range in on the keep's door *and* to keep a watch out behind us, ranged in on the road past the gatehouse.'

'The gatehouse, sir? But we came that way – '

'Exactly.' Otto bared his teeth at the man; Jorg ducked his head hastily and ran back towards the gunners and their overloaded mules.

Otto settled down, kneeling, to watch the lines of advance. The lack of fire from the castle worried him, but he had scarcely raised his glasses again when a loud and hearty hail demanded his attention. 'Ahem, my lord Neuhalle!' The interruption leaned over the pommel of his horse to look down at Otto. It was Geraunt, Earl Marlburg, one of the king's younger and more enthusiastic vassals.

'Yes, Sir Geraunt?' Otto stared up at him, annoyed.

'His majesty sends word!' Geraunt was obviously excited. He drew a message tube out of his sleeve and extended it towards Otto. 'A change to your disposition. You are to turn around and withdraw to the gatehouse, there to cover the approaches to the castle, he says.'

'Right.' Otto took the tube. A wave of palpable relief washed through him. Not that he was a coward – certainly the past month of campaigning had given the lie to that – but the idea of advancing into a booby-trapped castle did not fill him with joy. If the king wanted him to stake out the approaches to the castle, against the stab in the back with a witch's knife that Otto himself anticipated, then that was a reassuringly known quantity. More importantly it suggested that his majesty was, if not exactly sane, then no crazier than any other fox. 'Can you tell me what his majesty intends?'

Sir Geraunt hunkered down, putting his horse between Otto and the keep. Otto looked up at him: 'His majesty is most exercised; he says the witches have fled before him, and probably laid mines to bring down the keep, so he intends to secure the inner walls, then bring in sappers to find the – '

The world flashed white, twice, in a tenth of the beat of a heart. Everything glared as bright as the face of the noonday sun, except for the knife-edge shadow of Sir Geraunt, freakishly cast across Otto's upper body and head.

Otto blinked as a wave of heat washed across his skin. A giant the size of a mountain had opened the door of a kiln full of molten iron big enough to forge the hammer of the gods, and the glare surged overhead, stifling and oppressive. The sensation of heat faded over the duration of two heartbeats and he opened his eyes, but everything was blotchy and purple-white with afterimages. *Was that an explosion?* he thought numbly, as reflex or shock made him collapse back into the ground cover. What was left of Sir Geraunt's mount, with what was left of Sir Geraunt still astride it, began to fall sideways into his depression. Neither of them lived, which was perhaps a mercy, because while Sir Geraunt and his horse were intact and unblemished on the side that fell towards Otto, their opposite side – that had faced the castle – was scorched to charcoal around a delicate intaglio of bone.

The castle was no longer there. Where the keep had crouched within its courtyard, shielded by the outer walls and their rammed-earth revetments, a skull-shape of dust and fire was rising, its cap looming over the ramparts like a curious salamander crawling from its volcanic home to survey its surroundings.

As Otto fell, a tornado-blast of fiery wind pulsed across the burning grass that covered the approaches to the castle, casting aloft the calcined bodies of the men and animals who had been caught in the open at the moment of the heat flash. Burning sticks and a shotgun blast of fractured gravel caromed off the ground. A scant second later the shock front reversed, sucking back towards the roiling bubble of flames as it rose from the center of the fortification on a stem of dirt and debris.

Otto inhaled a mouth-watering stench of cooking meat and hot air and tried to collect his scattered wits. Something was holding his legs down. He couldn't see anything – just violet afterimages stubbornly refusing to fade when he screwed his eyes shut. Panicking, he tried to kick, but without vision he couldn't see the dead horse lying atop him. His back was a dull mass of pain where he'd fallen, and the smell – *Have they taken me down to Hel, the choosers of the slain?* he wondered dizzily as he turned his damaged eyes towards the furious underside of the mushroom cloud.

*

Carl stared at the turbulent caul of smoke rising above the ridgeline and swallowed, forcing back the sharp taste of stomach acid at the back of his tongue. His head pounded, but his eyes were clear. Around him, soldiers stared slack-jawed at the ominous thunderhead. The predawn sky was just turning dark blue, but the fires ignited by the bomb brought their own light to the scene, so for the moment their faces were stained ruddy with a mixture of awe and fear.

'Is that what I think it is?' asked Helmut.

Baron Hjorth cleared his throat. 'It can't be,' he said confidently. 'They're all supposed to be under lock . . . and key . . .' He trailed off into an uncertain silence.

Carl took him by the elbow. More soldiers were spilling in out of the air, staggering or bending over in some cases – two world-walks in three hours was a brutal pace, even for the young and fit – and Carl had to step around them as he steered Oliver a hundred meters up the road in the direction of the castle. 'That.' He gestured. 'Is a mushroom cloud. Yes?'

Oliver blinked rapidly. 'I think so.' He swallowed. 'I've never seen one before.'

'Well. Where the *fuck* did it come from?'

'Don't ask me!' Oliver snarled. '*I* didn't do it! God-on-a-stick, what do you take me for? All our bombs are accounted for as of last Tuesday except for the one Matthias' – he stopped dead for a moment – 'Oh dear.'

'If that *bastard* Matthias – '

Oliver cut him off with a slashing gesture. 'Trust me, Matthias is dead.' He closed his eyes, composing himself. 'This is someone else. Sending us a message.' He opened his eyes. 'How old is that . . . thing?'

Carl glanced up, uneasily sniffing the air: The tang of wood smoke spoke of pine trees on the reverse slope ignited by the heat flash. 'I don't know. Not old – see the stem? It hasn't drifted.' His guts loosened as he realized. *If I'd timed this just a little later we'd still have been there.* He licked his thumb and held it up. There was a faint breeze from the south, blowing towards the castle. 'Um. What, if anything, do you know about fallout?'

'The poison rain these things shed? I think we should forget the Pervert and get your men out of here. Forced march. If you want to set up guns south of Wergatsfurt and catch any stragglers you're welcome to them, but if they were camped a mile yonder' – he gestured towards the cloud – 'I don't know. They *might* have survived, if they dug in for the night. Although I don't give much for their chances if that fire starts to spread.'

Carl grinned humorlessly. 'Have you ever known the Pervert to refuse a chance to stab us in the back, my lord? Dawn attacks a specialty, remember?'

Oliver shook his head.

'Come.' Carl turned his back on the cloud. 'I'll leave two men to scout the area in an hour's time. The rest – let's hit the road. I'll have time to worry about whoever's sending us *messages* when I've hunted down and killed the last of the pretender's men.'

Behind them a dark rain began to fall on the battlefield, fat drops turbid with radioactive dust scorched from the stones of the castle and the bones of the men who had followed their usurper-king into the radius of the fireball. The survivors, burned and broken – those that could move – cupped their hands to catch the rain and drank greedily.

*

Otto Neuhalle, and the ten survivors of his company, were among them. They did not know – nor could they – that the man-portable nuclear weapon responsible for the fireball had a maximum yield of only one kiloton, and that such bombs are inherently dirty, and that this blast had been, by nuclear standards, absolutely filthy; that it had failed to consume even a tenth of its plutonium core, and had scooped up huge masses of debris and irradiated it before scattering it tightly around ground zero.

Dead men, drinking bitter rain.

REALIGNMENTS

'If he's dead, we're so screwed.'

Brill's fingers whitened on the steering wheel, but Miriam took Huw's gloomy appraisal as a conversational opportunity. They were coming less frequently today, as the reality of driving across a continent took hold. 'Isn't that a little pessimistic?'

Huw closed the lid of his laptop and carefully unplugged the cable from the satphone. He slid them both into their pockets in the flight case before he replied. 'It's not sounding good. They got him into the high dependency unit more than seventy-two hours after the initial intracerebral hemorrhage. He's still alive, but he's confused and only semiconscious and, uh, I've done some reading. More than forty percent of patients with that kind of hemorrhage die within a month.'

Yul, sprawled across the van's third bench seat, chose that moment to emit a thunderous snore. Elena, who'd been lying asleep with her head in his lap, shuddered and opened her eyes, then yawned. 'What?'

'He's not dead yet,' Miriam observed. 'He's not going to die of anything nonmedical, not with Olga looking out for him. And he's got the best treatment money can buy.'

'Which is not saying a lot.'

Brill hunched her shoulders behind the wheel, pulling out to inch past a big rig. 'Listen, Huw, why don't you just shut up?' she snapped.

'Wha . . . ?' Huw gaped.

'Hush, Brill, he doesn't know my uncle – his grace – like you do.' Miriam glanced in her sunshade mirror and spotted Elena sitting up, clearly fascinated. 'Sorry, but he's right. I hope he *does* pull through, but the odds aren't much better than fifty-fifty. And we ought to have some idea about what to do if we get there and . . .' She trailed off, diving back into her thoughts.

'I don't want to think about it,' said Brill. 'I'm sorry, Huw. I should not exercise myself over your words. Many will be thinking them. But I feel so helpless.' She thumped the steering column. 'I wish I could drive faster!'

'If you get pulled for speeding, and he *does* recover – ' Elena began.

Miriam snorted. 'Enough of that, kid. What's more important to you, Brill: getting there, or going fast? You don't want to pull a traffic stop. Think of the poor cop's widow and orphans, if it helps.'

'You are perfectly correct, as usual, milady.' Brill sighed. 'And I am using cruise control. What other news, Sir Huw?'

'Um.' Huw stretched, extending his legs under Miriam's seat and his arms backwards to touch the ceiling above his brother's head. 'There's a condition red lockdown. Avoid commercial flights, avoid all contact with the authorities, avoid unnecessary travel, lock the doors and bar the windows. Something about a major battle near Wergatsfurt, and something really bad happening to the Pervert's army. Sounds like my Lord Riordan opened a can of whoop-ass or something. But you'd expect them to sound a little less tense if they'd nailed the bad guys properly, wouldn't you?'

'Not necessarily.' Miriam mused. 'If there's been an army running wild through the countryside in a civil war, it could take a long time for things to get back to normal. Look at Iraq: They went in *weeks* ago and it's still a mess.' She paused. 'Egon could be down, but what about the rest of his vassals? The Duke of Niejwein, this, that and the other baron or earl or whatever. It's not over until the council hammers out a settlement that ends the fighting.' She rubbed her belly thoughtfully, then paused. 'And I need to see a doctor.' The test kit had been unequivocal, but the uncertainty over the sex of the fetus remained. 'Then get a seat at the table before they decide I'm just one of the chess pieces.'

'A chess piece with a posse!' Elena giggled.

'*Not* funny,' Huw chided her.

Her moue mirrored Brill's, for an entirely different reason. 'I suppose not,' she said. 'I was just joking.'

'Bored now,' Yul mocked, having woken up in the preceding

minute or two. 'Are we there yet?' he squeaked in a falsetto imitation.

'Bastard!' Elena thumped him over the head with a travel pillow.

'Children . . . !' Huw shook his head. 'I'm sorry,' he mouthed at Miriam by way of the mirror.

Miriam glanced sidelong at Brill. 'How long have you known these reprobates?'

'Long enough to know they're just acting out because they're over here for the first time.' She braced her arms across the steering wheel, slumping forward in evident boredom. 'They get dizzy.'

'Don't tell me you weren't like this on your first time out?' Miriam thought back to the first time she'd brought Brill over to Boston (her version of Boston – not the curious retarded twin in New Britain). She'd thought Brill was a naïve ingénue and a scion of the outer families, not able to world-walk for herself, not realizing Angbard would never have turned her loose in Niejwein without planting one or more of his valkyries on her as spy and bodyguard.

'My first time out was' – Brill looked pensive – 'I was twelve, I think. But I had a false identity in my own name by the time I was fourteen. Thanks to the duke. He believed in starting them early.'

'Lucky cow.' Elena giggled again.

I am trapped on a school bus in the middle of flyover country with a bunch of overarmed and undersocialized postadolescents, Miriam realized, *and there's no way out.* 'Starting what early?'

'Starting the doppelgänger identities. It's only sensible, you know. He wanted to put as many of us as possible through the right kinds of finishing school – Harvard, Yale, the Marine Corps – in case we ever have to evacuate.'

'Evacuate.' The gears whirred in Miriam's head. 'Evacuate the Gruinmarkt?' – if that was even on the menu – 'Why hasn't it already happened?'

'Would you voluntarily abandon your home? Your world?' Brill looked at her oddly.

'Um. It's home, right?' The idea resonated with her own experience. 'But there are no decent roads, no indoor plumbing, hedgelords have pigs in their halls, the social setup is right out of the dark ages – why would you stay?'

'Home is where everyone you know is,' said Brill. 'That doesn't mean you've got to love it – you know my thoughts, my lady! But you can't *ignore* it.'

Miriam fell silent for a couple of minutes, thinking. She'd had a taste of living another life in another world – but it had strings attached, and not ones to her liking, in Baron Henryk's captivity. Then she'd escaped during the debacle at the betrothal, and considered making a run for it when she was in New Britain; thought hard about going native, dropping out, leaving everything behind for a false identity. New Britain had big drawbacks, especially compared to home, but at least it was free of reactionary aristocrats who wanted to turn her into a dynastic slave. And if she'd done it, it would have been through her own choice. *But I decided to come back*, she realized. *I've got a family and while I was busy being independent they got their claws into me.*

'What do you need a doppelgänger identity for, then?' She paused. 'I mean, if all it's for is to maintain a toehold identity in this world . . .'

'Identity is a lever,' Huw said gnomically. 'The fulcrum is world-walking.'

'But what do you want a lever *for*?' Miriam persisted.

'So we can move the world!' Brill straightened her back, looking straight ahead.

Then Elena chirped up again: 'Are we nearly there, yet?'

*

In the end, it took them eighty-five hours to make a journey that would have taken a day if they'd been able to fly direct. Eighty-five hours and two changes of vehicle and three changes of plates, driving licenses, and other ID documents – care of certain arrangements the Clan maintained with local contractors.

With five drivers available they could have shaved a couple of hours off if they hadn't changed vehicles and taken certain other precautions, and a whole eight hours if Miriam hadn't insisted on stopping for the night at a motel outside Syracuse. 'I am going to visit the duke tomorrow,' she pointed out. 'I need to sleep properly, I need a shower, and I need to not look like I've been sleeping in a van for a week, because I don't know *who else* will be visiting the duke. This is politics. Do you have a problem with that?'

'No,' Brill agreed meekly – and the morning after the motel stop they lost another two hours in a strip mall, hunting suitable shoes, a suit, and some spray to keep Miriam's bleached hair from going in all directions.

'How do I look?' asked Miriam.

'Scary,' Brill admitted after a pause. 'But it'll do.'

'You think so?'

'Stop worrying. If any knave denigrates your topiary, I'll shoot him.'

Miriam gave her an old-fashioned look as she climbed in the cab of the new van, but Brilliana was obviously in high spirits – probably in anticipation of their arrival. *It's all right for her, she's not the one who has to confront them*, Miriam reminded herself. *She's not the one with the unwanted pregnancy.* Her stomach burned with acid indigestion, the product of stress and too much Diet Pepsi. 'Let's go,' she told Huw (for it was his turn behind the wheel). 'I want to get this over with.'

Cerebrovascular incidents were a familiar and unpleasant problem for the Clan: World-walking induced abrupt blood-pressure spikes, and far too many of their number died of strokes. But Miriam still had to grapple with her disbelief as Huw pulled up outside a discreet, shrub-fronted clinic in the outskirts of Springfield. 'Forty beds? *All* of them?'

'Yes, milady.' Huw reached for the parking brake. 'It's the price of doing business.'

She glanced at him sharply, but his expression was deadly serious. 'Nobody knows why, I suppose?'

'Indeed.' The engine stopped. 'It's on my research list. A long way down.' He swallowed. 'I suppose you're going to say, because I'm young.'

'No, it's more like I was thinking, it might tell us something about the family talent,' Miriam replied. She dabbed at a stray wisp of hair in the mirror, split ends mocking her. 'I knew it was a problem. I didn't realize it was this big a problem, though. There's too much to do, isn't there?'

'I'm working on it,' Huw said soberly. 'It's just that my to-do list is eight years long, and growing longer by about one year every seven months.'

'I beg your pardon, Miriam.' Brill sounded as tense as she felt. 'Visiting hours . . .'

'All right.' Miriam opened her door and carefully climbed down from the van. She pulled a face as she caught her reflection in the mirror: Appearances counted for a lot when dealing with the elders and the formal Clan hierarchy. 'I look a mess. Let's get on with this.'

Behind her, Yul and Elena were dismounting. 'With your permission, I'll take point, my lady.' Elena winked at her as she swung a sports bag over her shoulder. '*I* think you look just fine.'

Miriam looked at Brill in mute appeal. 'Let her do it, it's what she does best,' Brill replied. 'Yul, rear guard. Huw? Lock up and let's go.' All of them, Miriam realized, were armed – but Elena was the one with the serious firepower in her bag. *What am I doing here?* she asked herself as they crossed the car park towards the doors to reception: *How did I get into this mess?* Unfortunately, that question was easy enough to answer: *Mom dumped me in at the deep end, sink or swim.* Iris had raised her in the United States in ignorance of the world-walking families, for her own reasons – reasons that could be viewed as cold-bloodedly calculating rather than compassionate, depending on whether Iris thought of herself as a player or a fugitive. Not that she could hate Iris – or Patricia, to her extended family – either way; her mother had been under enormous pressure at the time. *But I wish she'd prepared me better.*

Getting into the small and very exclusive hospital that the Clan maintained for their brainstruck was not a simple matter of walking up to the reception desk and saying, 'Hello, I've come to visit Angbard Lofstrom.' Even leaving aside the small matter of his place on the DEA's most wanted list, Angbard had enemies, many of whom might well consider hospital visiting hours to be the perfect time to even up old scores. So Miriam was unsurprised when her introductory statement of intent, 'Hello, I've come to visit Angbard Lofstrom,' resulted in the ornamental receptionist staring vacuously up at her as if she'd demanded money with threats. A serious-faced young man whose dark suit was cut to conceal his sidearm bounced out from behind a glass screen off to one side, sized them up, then relaxed momentarily. 'Wer' isht?' he demanded.

Brill replied in machine-gun Hochsprache, too fast for Miriam to catch. The young man looked surprised, but mildly relieved as he replied. Then he turned to Miriam. 'My lady, if you please' – he pointed at a seating area off to one side – 'to wait there in?' His English was heavily accented.

'Ja – ' Brill replied at length. 'Bertil says he needs to check our identities before he can let us in,' she explained to Miriam. 'He knows who we are.'

'Good.' Miriam allowed herself to be led to the waiting area. 'Any idea how long . . . ?'

'Not long.' Brill didn't bother sitting down. 'They'll just need time to make sure we didn't bring any unwanted company.' Her posture was relaxed, but Miriam couldn't help noticing the way her eyeballs flickered from doors to windows.

A minute passed before another of the dark-suited security guards came in through a door behind the receptionist's desk. *They always look like Mormon missionaries*, Miriam noted, *or Secret Service agents. That's a* weakness, *isn't it?* Angbard's guidelines for looking inconspicuous had evolved decades earlier; after her weeks on the run and the tutorial in escape and evasion she'd received from the Leveler underground, their corporate uniform now struck her as a weakness, like wearing a flashing neon sign advertising *Clan operation here.*

'My lady?' The new guy walked straight over to Miriam and half bowed to her. 'If you would come this way, please?'

'I'm bringing my companions,' she said.

'Ah.' His eyes focused on Elena's shoulder bag. 'I would like to see that, please.'

Elena looked as if she was about to object. Miriam shook her head. 'Show him.'

Elena opened her bag reluctantly and the guard looked inside. He blinked. 'Hmm. You may come, but please unload and safe your arm.' He shrugged at Miriam apologetically. 'I am sorry but it is a matter of policy – no armor-piercing loads are allowed. The rest of you, pistols only? No concealed shotguns? Good. If you would follow me . . .'

Elena trailed behind them, her hands buried in her bag, from which muffled clicking noises were emerging.

Another hospital corridor leading to another hospital room, like a hotel with oxygen lines and diagnostic machines in place of the Internet hub and minibar. *I'm getting to hate these places*, she realized, as she followed the broad shoulders and buzz cut of her guide. 'Have you been here before?' she asked Brill.

'Yes.' Brilliana seemed reluctant to say more, so she dropped the topic.

They passed a set of fire doors, then a nursing station, and finally came to a door where another pair of machine-gun missionaries were standing easy. Their guide knocked twice, then opened the door. 'More visitors,' he said quietly.

The first thing Miriam saw in the small hospital room was a bed with a body in it and people gathered around, their backs turned to her. Then one of them looked round: 'Olga!'

Olga's expression of startled relief emboldened Miriam to take a step forward.

'Miriam – '

Then the woman beside Olga looked up. 'Miriam?' And her heart fluttered and skipped a beat.

'Mom?'

'Ach, *scheisse*. You didn't need to see him like this.'

Iris stared up at her. She looked tired, and apprehensive – guilty, perhaps – and worried. Miriam looked past her at the figure in the bed. 'Maybe not, Mom, but let me be the judge of that.' There was an ache in her throat as she looked at Olga. 'How is he?'

Olga shook her head. 'He is not good,' she said. 'Earlier, he could speak, he spoke of you – but not since we moved him. He is barely conscious.'

'Then why *did* you move – '

Iris cut in. 'They were under siege, kid. You know, bad guys with machine guns shooting at them? They wouldn't have relocated him if staying was an option. You can ask Dr. MacDonald later if you want to know more.' She nodded at Brilliana. 'Who are your companions?'

Brill gestured. 'They're mine. *Ours.*' She put an odd emphasis on the words. 'Who's seen his grace in this condition?'

'Everyone and their dog.' Iris addressed Miriam: 'I'm expecting that little shitweasel Julius Arnesen to turn up any minute now. Oliver Hjorth is making himself surprisingly useful, all things considered – I think he finally worked out how unreliable mother dearest is' – the dowager Hildegarde, who seemed to take Miriam's mere existence as a personal affront – 'and Mors Hjalmar is running interference for me. The silver lining on this particular shit sandwich is that most of the conservative tribal elders attended your betrothal, Miriam. They were in the Summer Palace when Egon staged his little divertisse-ment – we came out much better. Also, they're on the defensive now because of the troubles at home. But once they get a grip on how ill my half brother is, they're going to jump us. You can be sure of it.'

'Good!' said Miriam, surprising herself – and, from their reactions, everybody else. 'Let them.' She sidestepped around Brill and got her first good look at the duke.

Last time she'd seen him, months ago, Angbard had seemed implacable and unstoppable: a mafia don at the height of his power, self-assured and calculating, a healthy sixty-something executive whose polished exterior masked the ruthless drive and cynical out-look within. Lying half-asleep in a hospital bed, an intravenous drip in his left arm and the cables of an EEG taped to his patchily shaved head, he looked pathetic and broken. His skin was translucent, stretched thin across ancient muscles, the outline of bones showing through at elbows and shoulders; his closed eyes were half-sunk in their sockets. His breathing was shallow and slow.

Iris cleared her throat. 'Are you sure you don't want to reconsider that?'

Miriam looked her mother in the eye. 'Can you think of a better time?'

'Ladies – ' Heads turned. The Clan security officer who'd brought them here paused. 'Perhaps you would like to move to the conference room? He is not well, and the doctor said not to disturb him overly. They will try to feed him in half an hour, and need space . . .'

'That sounds like a good idea,' said Brilliana. 'Will you call us if any other visitors arrive, Carlos?'

'I'll do that. This way, please.'

*

Over peppermint tea and refreshments in the conference room, Miriam eyed Iris warily. 'You're looking healthy.'

Iris nodded. 'Over here, treatment is easier to come by.' She was making do with a single cane, moving without any obvious signs of the multiple sclerosis that periodically confined her to a wheelchair. 'And certain bottlenecks are . . . no longer present.' Months ago, she'd as good as told Miriam that she was on her own: that Hildegarde – or other members of the conservative faction – had a death grip on the supply of medicines she needed, and if Iris went against their will she'd stay in a wheelchair in the near-medieval conditions of the Gruinmarkt until she rotted.

'How nice.' Miriam managed an acid smile. 'So what happens now?'

Iris looked at her sharply. 'That depends on you, kid. Depends on whether you're willing to play ball.'

'That depends on what rules the ball game is played by.'

Her mother nodded. 'Yes, well; the rules are changing.' She glanced at the young people gathered at the other end of the room, chatting over drinks and snacks. 'There's a garden here. Are you up to pushing a wheelchair?'

'I think I can trust them, Mom.' Miriam let a note of exasperation into her voice.

'More fool you, then,' Iris said tartly. 'Your uncle trusted me, and look where it got him . . .' She trailed off thoughtfully, then shrugged. 'You may be right about them. I'm not saying you're not. Just . . . don't be so certain of people. We have met the class enemy, and they is us. You can never tell in advance who's going to betray you. And we need to talk in private, just you and me. So let's get a wheelchair and go look at the flowers.'

132

'What's to talk about that needs so much secrecy?' Miriam asked.

Iris smiled crookedly. 'Oh, you'd be surprised, kid. I've got a plan. And I figure *you've* got a plan, too. So, let's walk, and I'll tell you mine if you tell me yours.'

'After the last plan you hatched that got me sucked in . . .' Miriam followed Iris slowly into the corridor, shaking her head. 'But it got worse. You know what those bastards have done to me?'

'Yes.' A moment's pause, then: 'Mother dearest told me, right before the betrothal. She was very proud of it.' Miriam quailed at the tone in Iris's – her own mother's – voice. A stranger might not have recognized it, but Miriam had grown up knowing what it signified: the unnatural calm before a storm of coldly righteous anger. 'I'm appalled, but not surprised. That's how they play the game, after all. They were raised to only value us for our uterus. Uteri.' They reached the nursing station; an empty wheelchair waited beside it. 'If you could push . . . ?' Iris asked.

The garden was bright and empty, neatly manicured lawns bordered by magnolia hedges. 'You said the rules had changed,' Miriam said quietly. 'But I don't see much sign of them changing.'

'As I said, I've been developing a plan. It's a long-term project – you don't get an entrenched aristocracy to change how they do things overnight – and it relies on an indirect approach; the first step is to build a coalition and the second is to steer it. So I've been cutting deals, finding out what it'll take to get various parties to sign on. For it to succeed, we've got to work together, but everyone I've spoken to so far seems to be willing to do that – for their own reasons, if not for mine. Now . . . the one thing the conservatives will rely on is the sure knowledge that mothers and daughters always work at cross-purposes. They *always* stab each other in the back, because the way the Clan is structured to encourage arranged first-cousin marriages puts them in conflict. But . . . our rules are different. That's a big part of why I raised you in the United States, by the way. I wanted a daughter I could trust, a daughter who'd trust *me*. A daughter I could work with rather than against.'

Miriam stared at the backs of her hands on the handles of the wheelchair. A daughter's hands. Trusting, maybe too trusting. They'd been over this ground before, and the outcome had been unwelcome. But that was then . . . 'What do you want?' she asked.

Iris chuckled quietly. 'Well, let me see. Knowing you, you're planning something to do with business models and new worlds. Am I right? You're plotting a business revolution.' Without waiting for Miriam's assent she continued: '*My* plan is a bit different. I just want to make sure that no daughter of the families ever goes through what you've been put through ever again, for dynastic reasons. Or what I went through. That's all; nothing huge.'

Miriam cleared her throat. 'But. You'd need to break the Clan's entire structure to do that,' she said conversationally. She could hear the blood throbbing in her ears.

'Yes,' said Iris. 'You see? You're not the only one of us who wants a revolution.' Her voice dropped a notch. 'The trouble is, like I said: I can't make it work without your help. You're in a powerful position, and better still, you've got a perfect excuse for moving across social boundaries rather than obeying convention. It's not going to be obvious to onlookers whether you're doing stuff deliberately or because you don't know any better. Which gives you a certain freedom of action . . . Meanwhile, my plan depends on us agreeing to cooperate, and that's something the braid system tends to discourage. See? A year ago you wouldn't have been this suspicious of my motives. That's part of the problem. I know it's a lot to ask of you – but I want you to trust me to help you.'

Miriam stared at the back of her mother's head, her mind a whirl of emotions. Once, a year ago, she'd have trusted Iris implicitly, but now that she knew the forge her mother had been tempered in, a tiny voice urged caution. 'Tell me exactly what you're planning,' she said slowly, 'then I'll tell you what *I'm* planning.'

'And then?'

'Then perhaps we can do a deal.'

*

Working in the belly of the beast, supervising the electrically driven presses of the *Petrograd Times* and minding the telautograph senders that broadcast the message of the Committee for Democratic

Accountability up and down the western seaboard, Erasmus had little time to spare for mundane tasks (he slept under his desk, having not had time even to requisition a room in a miner's flophouse), but he had a superb perspective on the revolution. 'We're going to succeed,' he told John Winstanley one morning, over tea. 'I think this time it's actually going to *work*.'

Winstanley had stared at him. 'You thought it might not? Careful, citizen!'

'Feh.' Burgeson snorted. 'I've spent half my life in exile, *citizen*, working underground for a second chance. Ask Sir Adam, or Lady Bishop, if you doubt my commitment. And I'll willingly do it all over again and go for third time lucky, and even a fourth, if this one doesn't succeed. I'm just pleased to note that it probably *won't be necessary*, and so I am taking advantage of your discretion to vent a little steam in company where it won't fog the minds of the new fish.'

'Ahem. Well, then, I certainly can't find fault with *that*. I'm sorry, Erasmus. Sometimes it's hard to be sure who's reliable and who isn't.'

Burgeson turned his attention back to the pile of communiqués on the table, studiously ignoring the Truth Commissioner. He was rapidly developing a jaundiced view of many of his fellow revolutionaries, now that the time to come out of the shadows and march for freedom and democracy had arrived; too many of them stood revealed as time-servers and insidious busybodies, who glowingly talked up their activities in the underground struggle with scant evidence of actually having done anything. *I didn't spend twenty years underground just so the likes of you could criticize me for pessimism, citizen.* The New Men seemed to be more preoccupied with rooting out dissenters and those lacking in ideological zeal than in actually building a better nation, but Erasmus wasn't yet sure enough of his footing to speak out against them. The rot had spread far and wide in a matter of weeks. *Not so surprising, if what the membership subcommittee reports is right*, he reminded himself; the council's declared members – whose number could all count on a short drop to the end of a rope if the revolution failed – had quadrupled in the past two weeks, and just keeping Polis informers out of the rank and file was proving a challenge.

'Let's see,' he said. 'Jim, if you'd be so good . . . ?'

'Ayup.' Jim, who Erasmus had drafted as a sub-editor as soon as he'd ascertained his literacy, picked up the top of the pile. 'Lessee now. Yesterday, Telegraph Street, Cyprus Hill: A people's collective has seized control of the Jevons Ironworks and Steam Corporation factory and is restarting the manufacturing of parts for the war effort, with the arming of the Cyprus Hill militia as a first priority. The first four armored steamers have been delivered and are patrolling the Hispaniola Reaches already.'

'Bottom drawer,' Erasmus said instantly. 'Next.'

'Yesterday, Dunedin: The ships of the Ontario patrol have put into harbor and their officers and men have raised the people's flag. That's the last of the undeclared territorial and riverine patrols – '

'Get that on the wire. Hold page three, this sounds promising.'

'A moment.' Winstanley leaned forward. 'Are those ships under control of people's commissioners? Because if not, how do we know they're not planning – '

Burgeson glared at him. 'That's not your department,' he said, 'nor mine. If you want to waste your time, make inquiries; my job is to get the news out, and this is news.' He turned back to Jim. 'Get someone to look for some stock pictures of the Ontario patrol. I know: you, Bill. Go now, find pictures.'

Bill, the put-upon trainee sub, darted off through the news room towards the stairs down to the library. 'Next story,' Erasmus said wearily.

'Yesterday. People's courts in Santiago have arrested and tried sixteen Polis commissars and eleven informers for crimes against the people: Three have been executed for ordering the arrest and torture of patriots during the Andean campaign last fall. More details . . .'

'Run it. Paper only, inside pages.' Erasmus jotted down a quick note on his pad. 'Next.'

'Today. Communiqué from the New London people's committee: A people's provisional council will be voted in, by open polling next Tuesday, to form a constitutional convention that will determine the structure of the people's congress and establish a timetable for its election. Lots of details here. Um, delegates from the provinces are to attend, as are members of the inner council – '

'Stop.' Erasmus stood. 'That's the front page for you, right there, and get it on the wire. I'll need a copy for reference while I write the editorial. Go get it now.' He glanced at Winstanley, who was examining his fingernails. 'Coming?'

'What? Where?'

Erasmus closed his eyes for a few seconds, feeling every second of his years. *Give me strength.* When he opened them again, he spoke evenly. 'I don't know about you, but *I* am going to see Sir Adam, who will surely be preparing to depart *very shortly*, to attend the convention. I need to learn what he expects of me in his absence.' He paused. Winstanley was looking at him dumbly. 'I expect he'll have some errands for you to run,' he added, not unkindly.

'What – oh? But. Surely . . . ?' Winstanley looked confused.

'You weren't listening, were you? Or rather, you were listening to the *voice*, not to the *words*.'

Winstanley flinched. 'I say, there's no need for – '

'Negativism?' Erasmus smiled humorlessly. 'Get your jacket, man. We have to see the chief right away.'

'The correct salutation is "citizen".' Winstanley levered himself out of his chair with a glare.

'Certainly, *citizen.*' Erasmus headed for the door.

Over in the Committee Palace (its new name hastily hacked into a layer of fresh cement that covered the carved lintel of the former mayoral mansion), Erasmus found the usual ant-heap a-buzzing with petitioners, delegates from regional committees from places as far afield as Chihuahua and North Cascadia, guards drawn from the local militia, and the anxious families of arrested king's men. 'Commissioner Burgeson, to see Sir Adam,' he told the harried page waiting in the Hall of People's Justice (formerly the western state dining room).

'This way, sir. You're just in time.'

Am I, now? He stifled a wince as the door opened. 'Ah! Erasmus.' Sir Adam grinned and stood up, cutting off the manager or committee member who had been talking to him. 'I'd just sent a courier for you. Did he arrive?'

'A courier? No, we must have passed in the street.' Burgeson glanced round. The manager or committee member was an unfamiliar face; Burgeson's secretary Joseph MacDonald, though . . . 'I take it you're going east?'

'*We're* going, Erasmus.' Sir Adam inspected him curiously. 'Unless you have more pressing concerns to keep you in this provincial capital than the business of keeping the people appraised of the progress of the new constitutional convention?'

'I'm sure Jim and Judas between them can keep the press and the wire running, just as long as you leave orders to keep that sheep Winstanley away from the hay. But I assumed we'd be here a bit longer . . . Do you really need me merely as a stenographer or ordinary correspondent?'

'God, no!' Sir Adam looked him in the eye. 'I need you in the capital, doing what you've started here, only on a larger scale. *You* pick the correspondents – and the editors – then leave them to it unless they go off course. But we're about to up our game, man, and I want someone riding herd on the gossipmongers who knows what he's doing.'

Erasmus's cheek twitched. 'The correct salutation is "citizen", or so Citizen Winstanley keeps reminding me, but aside from that I take your point.' He grinned. 'So what's the plan?'

'The militia – rather, an army air wing who have signed to us – are arranging for a mail packet to fly from Prussian Ridge encampment tonight. You and I will be on it, along with a dozen trusted cadre – Haynes, Smith, Joe, Miss Rutherford, a few others, I've written a memo – your copy is on its way to the wrong place – and we shall arrive in New London the day after tomorrow. Andrew White is collating the lists of longtime party members for us to review when we arrive. You will take your pick of staff for a new Communications Committee, which will take over from the Truth and Justice commissioners when the congressional committee sits. Edicts are being drafted to nationalize all the telautographs and printing presses and place them under your ministry. Are you for it?'

'*All* of them?' Erasmus raised an eyebrow; Sir Adam nodded.

'Well, that's reassuring – nothing like half measures to short the stew pot.' He rubbed his hands together. 'Yes, I'm up for it. But, one question – '

'Yes? Spit it out, man!'

Erasmus scowled. 'Is there somewhere in this place where I can catch a bath and some fresh clothes? I've been living in my office for the past week – I'd rather not stand up in front of a room full of newspaper owners and tell them I'm holding their front pages to ransom while smelling like a tramp . . .'

*

The next day, Miriam visited the clinic again – this time, for her own appointment.

Brill had found her an anonymous motel suite near the interstate, along with a survival kit. 'Here's your driving license, credit card, and phone. Want to do dinner?'

'Sounds like a plan. Uh, what about you guys?'

'Oh, we'll be around.' Brill looked amused. 'I thought you'd appreciate some privacy. Tomorrow . . .'

'Yeah, that.'

Tomorrow dawned hot and early through the picture window in the suite's lounge; Miriam rolled over and buried her face in the pillow until the bedside alarm radio cut in, reminding her that she really needed to get up. She sat up slowly, fuzzy-headed and confused: *Where am I?* A concatenation of hotel bedrooms seemed to blur behind her. *What am I – oh.* And so it began – the first day of Iris's, of her own, little conspiracy.

She swallowed, feeling a mild sense of nauseous dread. *You can't avoid this step*, a little voice reminded her. *But it's too much like admitting it's real.* The result of the cheap pregnancy test kit on the road had left her feeling numb but clearheaded. Going to see an OB/GYN and finding out whether it was a boy was the inexorable next step down the road, but she wasn't ready to face up to her destination yet, or to decide whether she was going to go there or stamp on the brake pedal. As she brushed her teeth, combed out her hair – which was darkening at the roots again, after its brutal treatment in

New London – and pulled on her clothes, she found herself treasuring every remaining second of her indecision.

Brill was waiting for her downstairs in the lobby, concealed behind a newspaper. She rustled it as she rose, to signal her presence. 'Ready?' she asked.

'Let's get this over with.' Miriam managed a brittle smile.

'As my lady wishes.'

While Miriam had been held prisoner for a couple of months by Baron Henryk – held in the conditions of a most privileged prisoner, the troublesome heiress of a noble family who must needs be mewed up and married off before she embarrassed the elders enough to warrant strangling – the baron had arranged a most unpleasant medical examination for her by a doctor who specialized in making sure that the family tree always bore fruit on the right branches. And seven weeks later, give or take a couple of days, her period was *still* late, and she was regularly skipping breakfast. Not to mention the other, terrifying symptom: the loss of her ability to world-walk. There was no room for doubt in her mind, even before the test stick had shown her the treacherous blue label. *It's not like I haven't been pregnant before*, she'd told herself. But dealing with it was another matter entirely, and if it was male, potentially heir to an explosive situation . . . this wasn't about *her* doubts and fears. It was about everybody else's. *And Mom. Mustn't forget Mom.*

'Your pardon, Miriam – aren't you a bit tense?'

'Put yourself in my shoes. How would *you* feel?'

'I'd be petrified! If it's a boy it's the heir – ' Brill stopped, her hands gripping the steering wheel.

'That's what we're going to find out,' Miriam agreed. With the free run of a fertility clinic, ven Hjalmar would have been able to put his sperm samples through a sex sorting protocol, and while that wasn't a surefire guarantee, she wasn't inclined to bet against it. 'But what about me?'

Brill paused for a few seconds. 'I'm sorry.'

Miriam took a deep breath, then let it out slowly. 'Don't be. What's done is not your fault.' *What happens next, though . . .* 'Just get me there and back. Then we'll talk.'

This time there was no security cordon of bible-scholar bandits to penetrate, just a brilliant and vacuous smile from the receptionist followed by directions to a waiting room. 'Dr. Price is waiting for you,' she added as Miriam put one foot in front of the other and forced herself along the corridor. Brilliana, behind her, felt like the shadow of all her fears, come to escort her to the examination room. *I've done this before*, she reminded herself. *Yes, but you were twenty-one and indecisive and Mom guilt-tripped you* out of *having an abortion –* And *there* was a nasty thought, because how certain was she that Mom wasn't playing a riff on that same head game all over again?

Seven weeks along. All I have to do is ask. Huw said he'd sort everything out. She held the thought like the key to a prison cell as she paused on the threshold of the examination room, and the guy with curly brown hair sitting at the desk turned to look at her and then rose to greet her. 'Hello? Are you Miriam? I'm Dr. Price, Alan Price.' His eyes tracked past her. 'And this is . . . ?'

'A friend.' She practiced her smile again; she had a feeling that if she was going to go through with this she'd be needing it a lot over the next weeks and months. 'Hi. I understand you're an OB/GYN.' She shuffled sideways as he gestured towards a chair. 'Have you ever worked with Dr. ven Hjalmar?'

Price frowned. 'Van Hjelmar . . . no, doesn't ring a bell.' He shook his head. 'Were you seeing him?'

'A different practice.' Miriam sat down heavily, as if her strings had been cut; a vast weight of dread that she hadn't even been aware of disappeared. 'I really didn't like him. Hence this, uh . . .'

'I understand.' Price leaned over and dragged a third chair into position, then waved Brilliana towards it. His face assumed an expression of professional interest. 'And your mother, I gather, suggested . . . ?'

'Yes.' Miriam took another deep breath. 'My fiancé is, uh – '

' – He died last month,' Brill picked up without a pause.

'Oh, I'm sorry!' Price sat up. 'Well, that probably explains it.'

'It was a shooting accident,' Miriam said tonelessly, earning her a sharp look from Brill.

'Eh.' Price glanced back at his computer screen. 'All right. So you were on his HMO plan, but now you've moved to – oh, I see. Well. I think my receptionist's got the new release forms through – if you can sign one and get your old practitioner's details to us we can take it from there.'

'Okay.' Miriam nodded.

'Meanwhile . . . ?' Price raised an eyebrow.

'Well.' Miriam managed to get a grip on her breathing: *mustn't start hyperventilating.* 'I'm pregnant.' It was funny how you could change your script and the person who you were talking to would fall into a new pattern of their own, she thought as she watched Price visibly tense as he tried to keep up with the conversation: from polite sympathy through to curiosity to a quickly suppressed wince. Brill glanced sidelong at her again: *You're laying it on too thick, back off!* 'It wasn't planned,' she added, not backpedaling exactly but trying to fill in enough details to put Price back on ground he was comfortable with, that wouldn't raise any questions. 'We were going to wait until after the wedding. But . . .' She shrugged helplessly.

'I see.' Price was visibly trying to get a grip on the situation. 'Well, then.' He cleared his throat. 'Have you used a pregnancy test kit?'

'Yes. I assume you'll want a urine sample so you can verify . . . ?'

'Yes.' Price opened his desk drawer and removed a collection jar. 'If you wouldn't mind? The rest room is through there.'

When Miriam returned she placed the collection jar on the desk as carefully as if it were full of nitroglycerin. 'Here it is.'

'Right.' Price looked as if he was about to say something else, then changed his mind at the last moment. 'I'll run it right now and then we can take it from there. Is that okay?'

Miriam didn't trust herself to reply. She nodded jerkily.

'Okay. I'll be right back.' Price pulled on a blue disposable glove, then stood up and carried the sample jar out through a side door.

Miriam looked at Brill. 'How discreet is he going to be?'

'Very. He's on salary. Our dime.'

'Ah.'

They sat in silence for five minutes; then, as Miriam was considering her conversational options, Dr. Price opened the door again. He was, she noticed, no longer wearing the glove. There was a brief,

142

awkward silence as he sat down again, then: 'It's positive,' he confirmed. Then he picked up his pen and a notepad. 'How long ago did you last have sex?'

The question threw Miriam for a moment, bringing back unwelcome memories of Roland. She was about to say 'at least eight months ago,' when suddenly she realized: *That's not what he's asking.* 'Seven weeks,' she said. A little white lie; sex had nothing to do with her current situation, except in the most abstract imaginable sense.

'Well. You've made it through the riskiest period – most spontaneous miscarriages occur in the first eight weeks. So the next question is – I'm assuming you're here because you want to continue with it?' He paused, prompting.

Miriam could feel the blood pounding in her ears. No matter how she unpacked the question it didn't quite make sense to her: It felt like the introduction to a much larger question, monstrously large, an iceberg of possibilities. *I could say no,* she thought. *Get this over with right now. Quit the game.* Mom might disapprove, the duke might object when he recovered, but they couldn't stop her if . . . Miriam opened her mouth. 'Yes,' she heard herself whisper hoarsely. She swallowed. 'Yes,' she said again, louder; thinking, *I can change my mind later. There's still time.* 'I'm assuming you're going to want to schedule an amniocentesis appointment, for,' she swallowed, 'things like Down's syndrome and hydrocephalus? Will you be able to check on the – my baby's – sex?'

'Eh, we can do that. It's a bit early for amniocentesis right now, though, if it's only been seven weeks. I'd like to start by asking some questions about your family and medical history. Then I'm going to take a blood sample to get started with, while we're waiting for your old records to arrive. Shall we begin?'

OATH OF FEALTY

After they left the clinic, Brill drove Miriam back to the motel. Miriam could hear the questions tumbling over and over in her head: The silence was so loud that it roared. And now, the talk, Miriam thought, keyed up and tense. It had to come to this sooner or later . . .

'You said you wanted to talk,' Brill said into the abrupt emptiness that flooded the car's interior as she turned off the ignition. She studied Miriam in her mirror, carefully avoiding eye contact.

'Yes, yes I did.' Miriam opened her door. 'Do you have time to come in?'

'Of course.' Brilliana looked as if she were walking on eggshells. 'I imagine this must be hard to adjust to.'

'That's the least of it.' Miriam held her tongue as they entered the lobby and walked to her door. 'Come in.'

Brill had rented a suite for her; Miriam took the sofa, and the younger woman perched on the armchair opposite. For a few seconds they stared at each other in silence. Finally, Brill cracked and spoke first. 'It's hard, isn't it?'

'Yes.' Miriam kept her eyes on her. 'I have three questions, Brill.'

'Three? Is that all?'

'I think so.' *Because if you can't convince me I can trust you, then* . . . well, *that* was an interesting question, and not one Miriam wanted to consider just yet. 'You work directly for Angbard, don't you? Tell me, are you sworn to him personally? A vassal under his patronage?'

Brilliana looked at her warily. 'You never asked before.' She rubbed her cheek thoughtfully. 'What makes you ask?'

Miriam licked her lips. 'I'd like a straight answer. Please.'

Suddenly Brill's expression cleared. 'Oh!' The penny had clearly dropped. 'I am ranked as a sergeant in the Clan's Security, that is clear enough. But you have the rest of it, too: His grace swore me to his

144

personal service.' She looked Miriam in the eye. 'To be discharged by death, or his word.'

'Ah.' Miriam nodded, very slightly. *So Mom was telling the truth.* A tension in her chest began to unclench.

'Why do you ask?' Brill repeated.

Miriam took a deep breath. 'You – you, and Huw, and my mother, and the tooth fairy, for all I know – say you want me to trust you. Well, right now I find I'm very short on trust. I've been locked up, beaten, I've been *impregnated*' – she paused to breathe again – 'then suddenly a couple of weeks later it's all "trust us, we want you to lead us"! And – factional differences or not – I'm having a hard time buying it. So. Second question. Why did Angbard sic you onto me?'

Brill closed her eyes, startling Miriam. 'Crone give me patience' – she opened her eyes again – 'Helge, he's your *step-uncle*. He married but his wife died years ago and they produced no offspring – don't you get it?'

'But surely – '

'Surely *nothing!* Have you no idea how violent the civil war was? His line were targets! Your mother was targeted, her husband killed! The whole reason for Clan Security is to prevent anything like that happening ever again! Meanwhile, you, you – ' Brill's shoulders were shaking. 'Please!'

'Please, what?' Miriam stared, bewildered. 'It's this social thing again, isn't it? What am I doing wrong *this* time?'

With a visible effort, Brilliana collected herself. 'You're your mother's heir,' she said quietly. 'How hard is it to see that you're also your *uncle's* heir? Or at least his closest surviving descendant by distaff – you're a woman, so you won't inherit everything, but you're attached to the title to a whole damned *duchy*. God-on-a-stick, Helge, don't you get it? Henryk wanted you under his thumb because it gave him a weapon against his grace! And it shut you up, but they've always had a casual way with their women,' she added with offhand venom. Then she looked back at Miriam. 'I am a sworn vassal of your uncle, Helge. Sworn to protect his interests. You are his next of kin. Need I to draw you a diagram?'

'Uh.' *Oh boy.* Miriam turned it all over in her mind. *Damn, I'm really going to have to work on figuring out how these extended family links work!* 'But your direct loyalty is to him, not to me. Right?'

'That's the picture,' Brilliana said sharply. 'I love you like a sister, but you can be so slow at times!'

'Well, then.' Miriam glanced at the window. 'Maybe it's because I've been playing the wrong card game all along,' she said slowly. Then she looked back at Brill. 'I've been here a year and I haven't so much as sworn a swineherd to my service. Right?'

Brill's eyes widened. 'You can't. I'm sworn to his grace, unto the death – his or mine.'

Miriam nodded, satisfied. *Thanks, Mom.* 'I understand. But his grace is clearly ill – possibly on his deathbed?'

Brill nodded jerkily.

'Well, then. I believe there is a thing called an oath contingent, yes?'

'Who told you about *that?*'

'Look.' Miriam leaned forward. 'What are you going to do if – when – my uncle dies?'

'But that's different!' It came out almost as a wail.

'Not according to my mother.' Miriam pinned her in place with a stare. 'In the old days, oaths contingent were quite common – to ensure a secure succession in event of an assassination. The contingent liege's orders are overridden by those of the first lord living. Yes?'

'I suppose so. But – '

'Brill.' Miriam paused. 'This is my third question. Did his grace give you any orders that would bring you into a conflict of loyalty if you were sworn to me by an oath contingent?'

The younger woman looked at her, wide-eyed as a doe in the headlights of a truck. 'Yes,' she whispered.

'Uh-oh.' Miriam flopped back on the sofa. She rubbed her forehead. 'Well, there goes *that* good – '

'Wait.' Brill raised a hand. 'You would not have raised the oath contingent unless you planned to live among us, would you?'

Miriam steeled herself. 'I need sworn vassals to defend me if I'm going to live in the Gruinmarkt. I was hoping – '

'Well.' Brill took a deep breath. 'Then the conflict of interests

146

does not arise.' She grimaced. 'His grace directed me – while you were in New Britain – to bring you back, alive or dead. Preferably alive, but – '

'Whoa.' Miriam stared at her. 'Do I want to hear this?'

Brill shuffled, uncomfortable. 'You are not planning to offer your services to the American government. Are you?'

'I – ' Miriam flashed back to what Mike had told her in the walls of a smoldering palace. 'No. No way.'

'Well.' Brill held out her hands across the coffee table. 'In that case, I can swear to you. If' – she made eye contact – 'you still want me?'

Miriam swallowed. ('It's a bit like a marriage,' Iris had told her. 'A big, rowdy, polygamous one, arguments and all. Minus the sex.') 'This means you're going to be part of my household and responsibilities for life, doesn't it?'

'Once his grace dies or otherwise discharges me.' Brill ducked her head.

'Then' – Miriam reached out and caught her hands – 'I accept. Your oath of loyalty, contingent on the word of your first liege.' She stood, slowly, pulling Brill with her. 'We can swear to each other in front of witnesses later, can't we?'

'Whenever you ask, milady.' Brilliana bowed low and kissed the backs of both her hands. 'There, that is the minimal form. It is done.' Then she smiled happily.

'Tell me,' said Miriam. 'I was a real idiot not to do this when I first arrived, wasn't I? There are other people I should be swearing, aren't there?'

'Yes, milady.' Brill straightened up, her eyes glistening. Then she leaned forward and, surprising Miriam, kissed her on the mouth. Before Miriam could recoil or respond she took a step away. 'It's going to be so much *fun* working for you! I can tell.'

*

Barely a week had passed, but the atmosphere in this meeting was darker by far than its predecessor. The venue was the same – an air-conditioned conference room in a Sheraton hotel adjoining a conference center in the middle of downtown Boston, with heavily padded leather chairs arranged around a boardroom table. And now, as then, the attendees were dressed as conservatively as a party of merchant bankers. But there were fewer of them today, barely a round dozen; some of the faces had changed, and two of the newcomers were women. But it was none of his business, decided the hotel facilities manager who was seeing to their needs; they were good customers – quiet, serious, utterly unlikely to start shooting each other or snorting crank in the rest room.

Which just demonstrated how misleading appearances could be.

There were thirteen seats at the table today, but one of them – at its head – was vacant. The broad-shouldered man sitting to its left nodded to a younger fellow at the far end. 'Rudi, please shut the door. If you would pay attention, please?'

The quiet conversation ebbed as Rudi sat down again, the door securely locked behind him. 'I think we'll begin with a situation report,' Riordan said quietly. 'Lady Thorold, if you wouldn't mind?'

'Of course.' Olga opened the leather conference folder she'd brought to the meeting; in a severe black suit, with her long blond hair tied back, she resembled a trial lawyer rather than an intelligence officer. 'The duke's medical condition is stable. That's the good news.'

Olga read from her notes: 'The average thirty-day survival figures for subarachnoid hemorrhage are around six-tenths. His grace has already come through the main danger period, but the doctors agree his chances of full recovery are slight. He's paralyzed on the left side, and his speech is impaired. They can't evaluate his mental functioning yet. He may recover some of his faculties, but he's likely to be mobility-challenged – probably wheelchair-bound, possibly bedridden – for life. They've scheduled a second MRI for him tomorrow to track the reduction of the thrombosis, and they should have more to report on Friday.' She managed the medical terms with an ease that might have surprised Miriam, had she been present; but then, she'd checked her carefully cultivated airhead persona at the door. 'The balance of medical opinion is that his grace will definitely not be able to resume even light duties for at least thirty days. Even if he makes a significant recovery, he is unlikely to be back in the chair' – her eyes tracked to the empty seat at the head of the table – 'for half a year.'

The attentive silence she'd been speaking into dissolved in a buzz of expressions of shock and sharply indrawn breath. Earl Riordan brought his hand down on the edge of the table. 'Silence!' he barked. 'We knew it was going to be bad. Thank you, milady.' He scowled. 'We have a chain of command here. I recognize that I am not equipped to replace his grace in his capacity as director of security policy, or in his management of the intelligence apparatus, but for the former we have the Council of Lords, and for the latter' – he glanced sideways: Olga inclined her head – 'there is a parallel line of authority. For the time being I will assume operational command, until his grace resumes his duties or I am removed by order of the Council. Is that clear?'

There was a vigorous outbreak of nodding. 'Have you met with the Council yet?' asked Carl, with uncharacteristic hesitancy.

'That's where I'm going as soon as we conclude this meeting.' Riordan leaned back. 'Does anyone else wish to comment? On the record?'

'You're going to find it hard to convince the stick-in-the-muds to accept Lady Thorold as acting director of intelligence,' remarked Carl, his arms crossed.

'They'll like my second-choice candidate even less.' Riordan bared his teeth. 'Are you questioning her fitness for the role, or merely her sex?'

Carl shook his head, his expression shuttered. 'Just saying,' he muttered.

Riordan glanced round the table as Olga closed her file and leaned back, trying to keep all expression off her face.

'I've worked with her for the past six years and I would not propose her for this position if I doubted her capability,' Riordan said sharply. 'The empty pots in the conservative club can rattle as much as they please; it's as good an issue as any to remind them that this is not business as usual.'

There was a general rumble of agreement. 'You're in the saddle now,' Olga murmured in Riordan's ear. 'Just try not to fall off.'

Riordan flushed slightly. 'Right. Next item.' He glanced up. 'Rudi. Your flying machine. You are hereby ordered to prepare a report on the feasibility of equipping, supplying, training, and operating a squadron of no fewer than six and no more than twelve aircraft, within the Gruinmarkt. Tasks will be scouting and surveillance, and – if you can work out how to do it – medical evacuation. Your target corvée budget is twelve tons. I want it on my desk, with costing, in three days' time. I understand that training pilots and observers takes time, so I want a list of candidates – outer families for preference, we can't routinely divert world-walkers to a hazardous auxiliary duty. Any problems?'

Rudi looked awestruck. 'I can do it! Sir.'

'That's what I like to hear.' Riordan didn't smile. 'Kiril, Rudi's got priority over *everything* except first-class post; even ammunition resupply. We need an airborne capability; I've discussed it with Count Julius already, and it's going to happen. So. Next item, the Hjalmar Palace. Carl. What can you tell us?'

The heavyset man shrugged lazily, almost indolently. Riordan took no offense; he'd worked with him long enough to know better than to think it an insult. 'The palace is gone. Sorry, but that's all there is to say about it. Snurri and Ray took samples and we had them analyzed, and they found fallout. Cesium-131, strontium-90, lots of carbon-14. Snurri and Ray indented for new boots and fatigues, and I've sent them to the clinic, just in case.'

'*Scheisse.*' Nobody but Olga really noticed Riordan's one-word curse, because nobody but Olga was listening to anything but the sound of their own voices. Clan Security, though a highly disciplined organization in the field, tended to operate more like a bickering extended family behind closed doors. 'Silence!' Riordan whacked the tabletop. 'Let him finish, damn you!'

'Thank you, cuz.' Carl's face twisted in something horribly close to a smile. 'They couldn't measure the crater because there isn't one. The keep was blown out, completely shattered, but the inner walls of the sunken moat caught the blast, and the foundations are solid stone, all the way down. We got a best estimate of how big it was from the remains the pretender's men left on the field. Half a kiloton, and it probably went off in the vicinity of the treason room we used for the assault. Sir, do you know what's going on? Because if so, an announcement might quell some of the crazier rumors that are floating around . . .'

Riordan sighed. 'Unfortunately, the rumors hold more than a grain of truth.' This time around he didn't try to maintain order. Instead, he leaned back and waited, arms crossed, for the inevitable flood of questions to die down to a trickle. 'Are we ready now?' His cheek twitched. 'Milady, I believe you have a summary.'

Olga glanced around the table. Twelve pairs of eyes looked back at her with expressions ranging from disbelief to disgust. 'Eighteen years ago the Council, sitting in camera with the duke present, discussed the question of our long-term relationship with the United States. Of particular concern was the matter of leverage, if and when the American rulers discovered us.'

She picked up a glass and filled it from the jug on the table. Nobody spoke; curiosity was, it seemed, a more valuable currency than outrage. 'A variety of strategies were discussed. Our predecessors' reliance on the ability to access the private files of J. Edgar Hoover was clearly coming to an end – Hoover's death, and the subsequent reorganization of the American secret police, along with their adoption of computerized files, rendered that particular channel obsolete. Computers in general have proven to be a major obstacle: We can't just world-walk into the locked room full of filing cabinets stuffed with blackmail material at night. So a couple of new plans were set up.'

She saw a couple of heads nodding along at the far end of the table and tried to suppress a smile. 'I believe Piotr has just put two and two together and worked out why the duke took it upon himself to issue certain career advice. Piotr spent six years in the USAF, not as an aerial knight but as a black-handed munitions officer. Unfortunately he did not enter precisely the specialty the duke had in mind . . . but others did.' More of her audience were clearly putting two and two together. Finally, Rudi raised a hand. 'Yes?'

'I looked into this. Nukes – they're not light! You couldn't world-

151

walk one across. At the least, you'd have to disassemble it first, wouldn't you?'

'Normally, yes.' She nodded. 'But. Back in the early sixties, the Americans developed small demolition devices, the SADM, for engineers to use in demolishing bridges in enemy territory. Small is a figure of speech – a strong man could carry one on his back for short distances – but it was ideal for our purposes. Then, in the seventies, they created a storable type, the FADM, to leave in the custody of their allies, to use in resistance operations in event of a Soviet invasion of Western Europe. The friends they picked were not trustworthy' – an understatement: The Italian neo-fascists who'd blown up the Bologna railway station in the 1970s had nearly sparked a civil war – 'and the FADMs were recalled to their stores, but they weren't all scrapped. A decade ago we finally placed a man in the nuclear inspectorate, with access. He surveyed the storage site, organized the doppelgänger revetment, and we were in. Locating and stealing the pass keys to the permissive action locks took another two years. Then we had our own nuclear stockpile.'

She raised her glass, drank deeply. 'The matter rested with his grace until the last year. It appears that the traitor Matthias had access to the procedures, and to his grace's seal. He ordered one of the devices removed from storage and transported to Boston.' She waited as the shocked muttering subsided. 'More recently, we learned that the Americans had learned of this weapon. Our traitor had apparently threatened them with it. They indicated their displeasure and demanded our cooperation in retrieving it. I think' – her gaze flickered towards Carl – 'that most likely they found it by themselves and decided to send us a message. Either that, or our traitor has struck at us – but he is no world-walker. Meanwhile, we know the American secret police hold some of ours prisoner.'

'But how – '

'What are we going to – '

'*Silence!*' The word having had its desired effect, Riordan continued, quietly. 'They can hurt us, as they've demonstrated. They could have picked the Summer Palace in Niejwein. They could have picked the Thorold castle. We know they've captured couriers and forced them to carry spies over, but this is a new threat. We don't know *what* they can do. All we know for certain is that our strongholds are not only undoppelgängered, they may very well be death traps.'

He fell silent. Carl cleared his throat. Deceptively mildly, he asked, 'Can we get our hands on some more?'

Olga, who had been rolling the empty water glass between her hands, put it down. 'That's already taken care of,' she said.

'In any event, it's not a solution,' Riordan said dismissively. 'At best it's a minimal deterrent. We can hurt them – we can kill tens of thousands – but you know how the Americans respond to an attack. They are relentless, and they will slaughter millions without remorse in the name of vengeance. Worse, their councils and congresses are so contrived that *they cannot surrender*. Fighting them is like fighting a nest of hornets: Any leader who advocates surrender is ridiculed and risks removal from office. And *this* leader – ' He shook his head. 'They haven't felt the tread of conquering boots on their land in more than a lifetime, and for most of a lifetime they have been an empire, mighty and powerful; there is a level at which they do not believe it is possible for them to be beaten. If you are stung by a hornet you do not avenge yourself by hitting the hornet's home with a stick. If we're going to confront them, the *last* thing we should do is fight them openly, on ground of their own choosing.'

'Such as the Gruinmarkt,' said one of the new faces at the table, who had been sitting quietly at the back of the room until now. Heads turned towards him. 'My apologies, milady. But . . .' He shrugged, impatiently. 'Someone needs to get to the *point*.'

'Quite right,' muttered Carl.

'Earl Wu.' Riordan looked at him. 'You spoke out of turn.'

'Then I apologize.' Wu looked unrepentant.

The staring match threatened to escalate into outright acrimony. Olga took a deep breath. 'I believe his lordship is referring to certain informed speculation circulating in the intelligence committee over the past couple of days,' she said. 'Rumors.'

'What rumors?' Riordan looked at her.

'We take our ability for granted.' Olga raised a hand to her throat, to the thin gold chain from which hung a locket containing the Clan sigil. 'And for a long time we've assumed that we were limited to the two worlds, to *home* and to *here*. But now we know there are at least two more worlds. How many more could there be? We didn't know as much as we thought we did. Or rather, much of what we thought we knew of our own limits was a consequence of timidity and custom.' The muttering began again. 'The Americans have told their scientists to find out how our talent works. They've actually told us this. *Threatened* us with it. They don't believe in magic: If they can see something in front of their eyes, then they can work out how it happens. They've demanded our surrender.' She licked her lips. 'We need contingency plans. Because they might be bluffing – but if they're not, if they *have* found a way to send weapons and people between worlds by science, then we're in horrible danger. The Council needs to answer the question, what is to be done? And if they won't, *someone's* going to have to do it for them. That *someone* being us.'

*

Getting to see the colonel was a nontrivial problem; he was a busy man, and Mike was on medical leave with a leg that wasn't going to bear his weight any time soon and a wiretap on his phone line. But he needed to talk to the colonel. Colonel Smith was, if not a friend, then at least the kind of boss who gave a shit what happened to his subordinates. The kind who figured a chain of command ran in two directions, not one. Unlike Dr. James and his shadowy sponsors.

After James's false-flag ambulance had dropped him off at the hospital to be poked and prodded, Mike had caught a taxi home, lost in thought. A bomb in a cell phone, to be handed out like candy and detonated at will, was a scary kind of message to send. It said, *we have nothing to talk about.* It said, *We want you dead, and we don't care how. We don't even care much who you are.* Mike shuddered as he recalled how Olga's cynicism had startled him: 'How do we know there isn't a bomb in the earpiece?' she'd asked. Well, he'd denied it indignantly enough – and now she'd think he was a liar. More importantly, Miriam's Machiavellian mother – and whoever she was working with – would also be convinced that the diplomatic dicker-ing the colonel had supposedly been trying to get off the ground was a sting. *Dr. James has deliberately killed any chance we've got of negotiating a peaceful settlement,* he realized. *He's burned any chance of me ever being seen as a trustworthy – honorable – negotiator. And he's playing some kind of double game and going behind Smith's back. What the hell is going on?*

Mike's total exposure on the other side of the wall of worlds was measured in days, but he'd seen enough (hell, he'd smelled, heard, and tasted enough) to suspect that Dr. James was working on very incomplete information – or his plans had very little to do with the reality on the ground of the Gruinmarkt. Worse, he seemed to be just about ignoring the Clan, the enigmatic world-walkers who'd been a huge thorn in the DEA's collective ass for the past thirty years or more; it was almost as if he figured that a sufficient display of shock and awe would make them fold without a fight. But in Mike's experience, beating on somebody without giving them any way out was a great way to make them do their damnedest to kill you. Mike's instinct for self-preservation told him that pursuing the matter was a bad idea, and normally he'd have listened to it, but he had an uneasy feeling that this situation broke all the rules. If Dr. James was really off the rails someone needed to call him on it – and the logical person wasn't Mike but his boss.

It took Mike a day to nerve himself to make his move. He spent it at home, planning, running through all the outcomes he could imagine. 'What can possibly go wrong?' he asked Oscar, while making a list of bullet points on a legal pad. The elderly tomcat paused from washing his paw to give him a look of such bleak suspicion that Mike had to smile. 'It's like that, huh?'

The next morning, he shoehorned himself into his car and drove carefully to a nearby strip mall, which had seen better days, and where, if he remembered correctly, there might still be some beaten-up pay phones tucked away in a corner. His memory turned out to be correct. Staking out a booth and using his cell as an address book, he dialed a certain unlisted number. *Seven minutes*, he told himself. *Ten, max.*

'Hello?' It wasn't Colonel Smith, but the voice was familiar.

'Janice? It's Mike Fleming here. Can I please have a word with the colonel?'

There was a pause. 'Mike? You're on an unsecured line, you know that?'

'I have a problem with my home phone. Can you put me through?'

A longer pause. 'I – see. Please hold.' The hold music cut off after half a minute. 'Okay, I'm transferring you now.'

'Mike?' It was Colonel Smith. He tensed. Until now, he hadn't been entirely sure it was going to work, but now he was committed, upcoming security vetting or no. *I could be throwing my career away*, he thought, feeling mildly nauseous.

'Hi, boss.'

'Mike, you're still signed off sick. What's up?' Smith sounded concerned.

'Oh, nothing much. I was wondering, though, if you'd be free to do lunch sometime?'

'If I'd be – ' There was a muffled sound, as of a hand covering a mic. 'Lunch? Oh, right. Look, I'm tied up right now, but how about we brown bag it some time soon?'

Mike nodded to himself. Message received: The last time the colonel had dropped round with a brown bag there'd been a bomb and a gun in it. 'Sure. It's not urgent, I don't want to drag you out of the office – how about next Wednesday?' It was one of the older field-expedient codes: ignore negatives, treat them as emphasis. Mike just hoped the colonel had been to the same school.

'Maybe sooner,' Smith reassured him. 'I'll see you around.'

When he hung up, Mike almost collapsed on the spot. He'd been on the phone for two minutes. His arms were aching and he could feel the sweat in the small of his back. He pulled out the antibacterial gel wipes and applied them vigorously to the mouthpiece of the phone – he'd held the receiver and dialed the numbers with a gloved hand, but there were bound to be residues, DNA sequences, whatever – then mentally crossed it off his list of untapped numbers, for good. That left the polygraph. *But*, he figured, *raising chain-of-command concerns with one's immediate superior isn't normally a sacking offense.* And Dr. James hadn't told him *not* to, either.

He'd hoped the colonel would deduce the urgency in his invitation and he was right. Barely half an hour after he arrived home the doorbell rang. *Too soon, way too soon!* his nerves gibbered at him as he hobbled towards the entryphone, but the small monitor showed him a single figure on the front step. 'Come on up,' he said, eyeballing the top of his boss's head with trepidation. A moment later, he opened the door.

'This had better be good,' said Smith, standing on the front step with a bag that contained – if Mike was any kind of judge of smells and corporate logos – something from Burger King.

Mike hung back. 'To your knowledge, is this apartment bugged?'

'Is – ' Smith raised an eyebrow, an expression of deep concern on his face: concern for Mike's sanity, in all probability. 'If I thought it was bugged, I wouldn't be here. What's up?'

'Maybe nothing. To your knowledge, was there anything hinky about the cell phone you dropped off with me last time you visited.'

'Was there' – Mike had never really seen a man's pupils dilate like that, up close – 'what?' He could see irritation and curiosity fighting out in Smith's face.

'Let me get my coat. You're driving.'

'You bet.' Smith shook his head. 'This had better be good.'

The colonel drove a Taurus – anonymous, not obviously government issue. He didn't say a word until they were a mile down the road. 'This car is not bugged. I swept it myself. Talk.'

Mike swallowed. 'You're my boss. In my chain of command. I'm talking to you because I'm not from the other side of the fence. Is it normal for someone higher up the chain of command to do a false-flag pickup and brief a subordinate against their line officer?'

Smith didn't say anything, but Mike noticed his knuckles whiten against the leather steering wheel.

'Because if so,' Mike continued, 'I'd really like to know, so I can claim my pension and get the hell out.'

Smith whistled tunelessly between his teeth. 'You're telling me someone's been messing with you – Dr. James. Right?'

'That's the one.'

'*Shit!*' Smith thumped the center of the steering wheel so hard Mike twitched. 'Sorry. I thought I'd cured him of that.' He flicked a turn signal on, then peeled over onto an exit ramp. 'What did he want you to do?'

'It's what I've already done, as much as anything else – the cell phone you gave me, to pass on to the other side? Did you know it had a bomb in the earpiece? At least, that's what Dr. James told me. He also told me he was reassigning me to some kind of expeditionary force. Do you know anything about that?'

'You sure about the phone?' Smith sounded troubled.

'That's what he said. It gets worse. When I handed the thing over, my contact actually came out and asked me to my face whether there was a bomb in it. I said no, of course not, but it sounds like they're about as paranoid as the doctor. If they check it and find there *is* a bomb in it . . .'

'That's a matter for the policy folks to deliberate on,' Smith said as he changed lanes. 'Mike, I know what you're asking and why, and I've got to say, that's not your question – or mine – to ask. Incidentally, you don't need to worry about any fallout; we've got a signed executive order waiting to cover our asses. But let me spin you a scenario? Put yourself in the doctor's shoes. He knew the bad guys had a stolen nuke and he wanted it back, and he had to send them a message that he meant business. You were talking to their, their liberals. But we don't *want* to talk to their liberals. Liberals are predisposed to dicker; the doctor wants to get the attention of their hard-liners, get *them* to fold. We'd already told them that we wanted the weapon back. Negotiation beyond that point was useless: They could hand it over and we'd think about talking, but if not, no deal. So . . . if you look at it from his angle, a phone bomb would underline the message that we were pissed and we wanted our toy back. To the doctor's way of thinking, if they found it, no big deal: It underlines the message. If it worked, waxing one weak sister would send a message to their *other* faction that we mean business. At least, that's how he works.' He tapped his fingers on the steering wheel air bag cover.

'With respect, sir, that's crazy. The Clan doesn't work that way; what might work with a criminal enterprise or a dictatorship is the wrong way to go about nudging a hereditary aristocracy. He's talking about assassinating someone's mother or brother. They'll see it as cause for a blood feud!'

'Hmm. That's another way of looking at things. Only it's already out of date. Mike, you swore an oath. Can I rely on you to keep this to yourself?'

Fleming nodded, uncertain. 'I guess so.' Part of him wanted to interrupt: *But you're wrong!* He'd spent two stinking days running a fever in a horse-drawn carriage with Miriam's mother and the Russian ice princess with the sniper's rifle, and every instinct screamed that the colonel's scenario setup was glaringly wrong – that to those folks, the political was personal, very personal indeed, and a phone bomb in the wrong ear wouldn't be treated as a message, but as grounds for a bloody feud played out by the assassination of public figures – but at the same time, the colonel obviously had something else on his mind. And he had a sick, sinking feeling that trying to bring conflicting facts to the colonel's attention, much less Dr. James's, would lead to dismissal of his concerns at best. At worst – *don't go there*, he told himself.

'You didn't hear this from me, and you will *not* repeat it, but a few days ago we did an audit. The bad guys didn't stop at just one nuke. We're fairly certain our quiver is missing six arrows – that's how many are missing, including the one we recovered, and the MO was the same for each theft.'

'Six – shit! What happened?'

'Too much.' Smith paused for a few seconds, cutting in behind a tractor-trailer. 'The doctor sent the one we found back to them: Another of his little messages. He has, it seems, got some special friends in Special Forces, and contacts all the way up to the National Command Authority. He's gotten the right help to build his own stovepiped parallel command and control chain for these gadgets, and he's gotten the vice president's ear, and Mr. Cheney got the president to sign off on it . . . Hopefully it killed a bunch of their troops. There's been a determination that we are at war; this isn't a counter-terrorism op anymore, nor a smuggling interdiction. They've even gone to the Supremes to get a secret ruling that *Posse Comitatus* doesn't apply to parallel universes.

'To the executive's way of thinking, these guys are as much a threat to us as Chemical Ali was – hell, even more of a threat. The closest thing to a weapon of mass destruction *he* had was Saddam's head on a stick, but he had to go, visibly and publicly, and these guys have to go, too. Even when it was just one nuke, if they'd given it back to us when we asked nicely, and sued for terms . . . it was going to be difficult. Anyway, there's no use crying over spilt milk. The five remaining bombs aren't enough to hurt us significantly – but they're more than enough reason to bring the hammer down on the bad guys. There's a lab out west that's been making progress on a gizmo for moving stuff between, uh, parallel universes. And you know what the price of gas is. If we can make it work, it'll be a lot easier to get at the oil under their version of Texas than to deal with the Saudis. That'll be what Mr. Cheney is thinking, and it's going to be what he's telling James to expedite. When Wolfowitz gets through fixing up Iraq . . . do I need to draw you a diagram?'

At war. Mike shook his head. 'So you're telling me this is just another oil war? Has anyone told Congress that they're supposed to have authorized this?'

'You know as well as I do that that's not how things happen in this administration. They're looking to our national security in the broadest terms, and when they've got their ducks lined up in a row, well: They've got a majority in Congress, they're even in the Senate, and the other side have given them the most pliable minority leader in decades. Lieberman's terrified of not looking tough on security issues, and lets the VP play him like a piano. That's why the president's style of leadership works: He decides, and then Mr. Cheney gives him the leverage.'

'Not, he decides whatever Mr. Cheney wants him to?'

Smith gave him an old-fashioned look. 'That's not for you or me to comment on, Mr. Fleming. Either way, though, the narcoterrorism angle and the stolen nukes will make great headline copy if – when –

it leaks out in public. We can call them Taliban 2.0, now with nukes: It'll play well in Peoria, and the paranoia aspect – bad guys who can click their heels and vanish into thin air – is going to keep everyone on their toes. Bottom line is, those guys picked the wrong administration to play footsie with.' Smith glanced sidelong at Mike. 'But I'm a lot less happy about Dr. James's habit of going outside the chain of command.'

Mike nerved himself. 'Aren't you a bit worried that the doctor may be completely misreading how these people will react? They're not narcoterrorists and they're not hicks, they've got their own way of doing things – '

'It doesn't matter *how* they respond,' said the colonel. 'They're roadkill, son. A decision has been made, at the highest level. We don't negotiate in good faith with nuclear terrorists: We lie to them and then we kill them, no quarter given. The oil is a side issue. If you've got a problem with that, tell me now; I'll find you a desk to fly where I can keep an eye on you and you don't have to do anything *objectionable*.' The final word came out with an ironic drawl and a raised eyebrow.

For a bleak, clear moment Mike could see it all bearing down on him: a continent of lies and weasel-worded justifications, lies on both sides – Olga couldn't have been as ignorant as she'd professed, not if six of the things were missing – and onrushing bloody-handed strife. From the administration on down, policy set by the realpolitik dictates of securing the nation's borders and energy supplies . . . up against an adversary who had stolen nuclear weapons and dealt with enemies by tit-for-tat revenge slaying.

'I'm on board,' he said, holding his misgivings close to his chest. 'I just hope those missing nukes show up.'

'So do I. And so do the people we've got looking for them.'

BEGIN RECORDING

'My lord Gruen, his lordship Oliver, Baron Hjorth.'
(*Sound of door closing.*)

161

'Ah, Oliver.'

'My lord Baron! If you would care to take a seat . . . ? We are awaiting her grace, and Baron Schwartzwasser. I think then we may proceed . . .'

(*Eighteen minutes pass. More people arrive.*)

'. . . Let us begin.' (*Clears throat.*) 'I declare this session open. My lord Gruen, you requested this meeting, I believe to discuss the recent incident in the northwest?'

'Yes, yes I did! Thank you, my lord. I have reports – '

' – It's insupportable!'

'My lady? Do you have something you feel you must contribute, or can we hear Lord Gruen's report first?'

'It's insupportable!' (*Vile muttered imprecations.*) 'Ignore me. I am just an old grandmother . . .'

'Hardly only that, my lady. Lord Gruen?'

'I am inclined to agree with her grace, as it happens: Her description of it is succinct. Here are the facts of the matter. The Pervert's army split into three columns, which dispersed and harried our estates grievously. His Grace Duke Lofstrom responded by dispersing small defensive forces among the noble households, but concentrating the main body of our Security corvée in the Anglische world as a flying column. He was most insistent that at some point the Pervert would bring his arms together to invest one of our great estates, in the hope of drawing us into a battle in which, outnumbered, we would fall.

'Despite our entreaties to defend our estates adequately and wipe out the attacking columns, he deliberately starved us of troops, claiming that he must needs give the Pervert a false, weak, picture of our strength of arms, and that in any case there were insufficient soldiers to defend all our households.'

(*Sound of paper shuffling.*)

'Despite one's worst fears as to his motivation, I must concede that Isjlmeer and Nordtsman received no more succor than did Giraunt Dire and Hjalmar; the duke applied his neglect evenhandedly, failing to relieve his own party inasmuch as he also neglected our own. I do not, therefore, believe that there

162

would be support for a move to relieve him in Committee, especially in view of the accuracy of his prediction. The Pervert *did* concentrate his forces to attack the Hjalmar Palace, evidently with treachery in mind, and in doing so he placed his army within reach of the duke's flying column. Unimpeachable sources tell me that the Pervert's forces had stolen machine guns, but were inadequately supplied and poorly deployed to resist the attack that Earl Riordan was preparing.'

(*Throat clearing.*)

'Yes, my lord?'

'Are you then confirming that, that Angbard's strategy was *sound*?'

(*Pause.*)

'I would prefer to say that it wasn't obviously *un*sound, my lord. Clearly, his parsimony in the defense of our estates bled us grievously. But equally clearly, if he *had* committed troops to our defense, he would have been unable to concentrate the forces he needed for a counterattack, and he would have ceded the initiative to the Pervert. It is possible that a more aggressive strategy of engagement would have borne fruit earlier, but one cannot be certain.'

'Oh.' (*Disappointed.*)

'Indeed.' (*Drily.*) 'I am much more concerned by the unexpected outcome of the events at the fork in the Wergat. There is considerable confusion – the Anglischprache attack on the duke's forces, the duke's ictus, the exfiltration through the *other* Anglische realm with the connivance of the traitor family – and lastly, the, the *atomic bomb*. I was hoping my lord Hjorth might shed some light on that latter.'

(*Muttering.*) 'My lords, my lady. If I may speak?'

Her grace: 'You may speak until the cows come home, and convince no one.'

'Nevertheless, if I may speak . . . ?'

(*Conversation dies down.*)

'Thank you. Of the duke's condition, I shall speak later: As your representative on the security committee I believe I may brief you on the subject. But to get back to the matter in hand, my sources tell me that when the traitor Matthias fled to the Anglischprache king-president's party nine months ago, he clearly gave them much more than anyone anticipated. Previous fugitives have been taken for madmen and incarcerated, or we have been able to hunt them down and deal with them – but Matthias appeared to vanish from the face of the earth. We now know that he flung himself on the mercy of the *Drug Enforcement Agency*, and by their offices, on a dark and sinister conspiracy of spies.'

(*Shocked muttering.*)

'There is worse. As you know, with the aid of those of our younger generation who have enlisted and served in the American armies, we have gained some knowledge of, and eventually access to, their atomic bombs. The weight and complexity of these devices, and the secrecy that surrounds their activation, transport, and use, defied us for many years, but in the second year of Alexis's reign we finally infiltrated' – (*muttering*) – 'a master sergeant in the Marine Corps, yes – enlisted and received special training – man-portable devices, designed for smuggling, with which to sabotage the enemies of the Anglischprache empire overseas in time of war – the, ah, Soviet Union. And these devices were stored securely, they thought, but without doppelgängering, as is to be expected of the ignorant. It was a delicate but straightforward task to build a bunker from which a world-walker could enter the storage cells – the hardest part was obtaining a treaty right to the land from the Teppeheuan, and the maintenance schedule for the bombs. From then on, of the twelve weapons, we ensured that six were stored on our side at all times, and rotated back into the Pantex store when they were due to be repaired.

'Then Matthias stole one of them.'

(*More shocked muttering.*)

'Order! Order, I say!'

'Thank you, my lord. If I may continue?'

(*Pause.*)

'Matthias ven Holtzbrinck was *trusted*. Nobody suspected him! He was Duke Lofstrom's keeper of secrets. I must confess that in all fairness *I* thought him a man of the utmost probity. Be that as it may, Matthias ordered the removal of one of the weapons, and then hid it somewhere. We don't know where because he covered his tracks exceedingly well: Perhaps one of the dead could tell us, but . . . anyway. Need I explain what the king-president's men thought of their ultimate witch-weapon being stolen? I think we can guess. My sources tell me that they began negotiations with the duke with a threat, and that their spies have already been apprehended in the Gruinmarkt. Don't look so shocked. Did you think our missing soldiers had betrayed us and sought refuge? Captivity and slavery – they have ways of compelling a world-walker.' (*Muttering.*) 'We face a determined enemy, and they showed just *how* determined they were at the Hjalmar Palace.'

'Then it was an atomic bomb?'

'Yes.'

(*Uproar. Three minutes . . .*)

'Order! Order, I say!'

'My lady? You have the floor.'

'This is insupportable! Gentlemen, we have known for many years that one day the Anglischprache would learn of our existence. But we cannot allow them to, to think they can tamper at will in our affairs! Sending, without warning, an atomic bomb, into a castle invested only hours earlier by the pride of our army, is a base and ignoble act. It is dishonorable! To live with this threat hanging over us is intolerable, and I submit that it is unthinkable to negotiate as one ruler to another with a king-president who would deliver such a stab in the back. If negotiations were in hand then they acted with base treachery. We act, now, as the largest faction of the Clan, and as rulers of the kingdom of Gruinmarkt, though the peace is not yet settled. We must secure our kingdom from this threat; if there is one thing I have learned in more than sixty years of politics and thirty years of war, it is that you cannot sleep peacefully unless your neighbor can be relied on to obey the same law as you do. The Americans are now, like it or not, our neighbors. We must therefore compel them to obey the law of kings.'

'My lady. What are you suggesting?'

(*Coldly.*) 'One act of treachery deserves another. Do we not have
arms? Do we not have a kingdom to defend? The American
king-president has declared war upon us and through us upon
our domain and all those who live in it. We must make it clear
that we will not be trifled with. The time for petty affairs of
finance and customs is over. We must hurt the Americans, and
hurt them so badly that their next king will not meddle lightly in
our affairs.

'My lords. We have, in the course of this civil war, already found it
necessary to kill one self-proclaimed king: even, one who would
have reigned by blessing of the Sky Father. We must not, now,
balk at the death of another lord who is an even greater danger
to us than the Pervert. We must settle this matter with the
Americans before they think to send their atomic bombs into the
heart of Niejwein, aye, and every stronghold and palace in the
land. And the best way to compel their rulers to negotiate in
good faith is to demonstrate our strength with utmost clarity. My
lords, you must decapitate the enemy. There is no alternative . . .'

(*Uproar.*)

END RECORDING

166

HIGH ESTATE

There was a country estate, untouched by war, separated from the clinic in Springfield by about three blocks and two-and-a-half thousand years of divergent history. Brill had picked up a courier from somewhere nearby and driven Miriam round to a safe house on a quiet residential street; whereupon the courier had carried her across, back into the depths of someone else's history.

It was, in many respects, like her time as an involuntary guest of Baron Henryk. There was no electricity in the great stone-walled house, and no central heating or water on tap, and she was surrounded by servants who spoke to her only in Hochsprache. Brill had left her in the hands of the maidservants, and she'd felt an unpleasant tension as the chattering women dressed her in clothes from the landholder's wife's chests. *Trapped again*: She felt a quite unexpected sense of panicky claustrophobia rising as they fussed over her. It had been hard to stand still, giving no sign of her urge to bolt and run: She forced herself to recall Brill's oath. *She won't leave me here*, she told herself.

To distract herself she fought her unease by trying to puzzle out their story. The landholder, she eventually concluded, was away in the wars, a relative of the Clan families: He'd sent his dependents to safety for the duration, leaving the staff behind with instructions to look after whomever the council billeted on them. Which meant they were expecting to host one Lady Helge, house and braid and surname unspecified, not Miriam – a woman from another world. *You let yourself get trapped again*, a little corner of her worried. *They laid out a trap and let you walk right into it.*

But there were significant differences from Henryk's idea of hospitality, despite the primitive amenities and unwanted expectations. Her bedroom door had a lock, but she held the key. The afternoon after her arrival, trying to dispel the anxiety and claustrophobia of being Helge again, she'd ventured from her room to look around the grand hall and the main rooms of the estate. When she'd returned she found the battered suitcase she'd borrowed from Erasmus sitting beside the canopy bed. A quick inspection with shaking hands revealed her laptop and the revolver Burgeson had given her. And not only had they let her keep the locket James Lee had given her – Brill had winked, and given her a second, smaller locket on a gold bracelet. None of these things were of any immediate use, but collectively they conveyed a powerful message: *The trap has a key, and you are not a prisoner.*

She'd sat on the bed, holding the laptop and shaking, carefully stifling her sobs of relief lest the servants waiting outside take fright. When she'd calmed down sufficiently to function again, she checked over the small pistol, reloading it with ammunition from its case. She let the hammer down on an empty cylinder, and slid it into a pouch she'd found cunningly stitched inside the cuff of her left sleeve; *I can make this work*, she told herself. *I've* got to *make this work*. The one common drawback of both her own plan, and her mother's, was that they depended on her living as the Countess Helge voh Thorold d'Hjorth. Not playacting in fancy dress, but actually being a lady of the Gruinmarkt – at least unless and until Iris's hastily improvised junta secured its grip on power, or the US military figured out a way to claw a hole in the wall between the worlds. Which could happen tomorrow – or in ten years' time.

The alternatives on offer were all worse: a gamble on the questionable mercies of the DEA's witness protection program, an even riskier gamble on Erasmus and his ruthless political allies. Between her mother's Machiavellian proposal and the naïve optimism of the young progressive faction, there was at least some room for her to get a grip on events. 'As long as Henryk doesn't rise from the dead I'll be all right,' she muttered under her breath. (*Keep telling yourself that*, mocked her inner skeptic. *They'll find some other way to screw you* . . .)

If Roland were still alive, and had actually been the knight in shining armor he'd looked like at first sight, she wouldn't have to sort everything out for herself. But first he'd disappointed her, then he'd died trying to live up to her expectations, and now there was nothing to do but press on regardless. *No more heroes*, she resolved. *I'm going to have to do this all on my own again, damn it.* Which, semirandomly, reminded her of the old song. 'What do I have to do to get a CD player in here?' she asked herself, and managed a croak of laughter.

A tentative voice piped up somewhere behind her, near the door: 'Milady, are you all right?'

Miriam – Helge – turned her head. 'I am – well,' she managed in her halting Hochsprache. 'What is it?'

The servant, a maid of the bedchamber – evidently of a higher status than a common or garden serving woman – studiously ignored her reddened eyes. 'Milady? I beg you to receive a visitor downstairs?' The maid continued for another sentence, but Helge's Hochsprache was too patchy to catch more than a feminine prefix and an implication of status.

'In a, a minute.' Helge reached for one of the canopy posts and levered herself upright. 'Speak, tell, her I will see them.' She took a step towards the heavy oak dresser with the water jug and bowl that stood in for a sink. The door closed behind her. 'Ouch.' She'd kept the ankle boots she'd acquired in New London because they fit her feet better than any shoes in milady's wardrobe, but she'd been wearing them all day and her feet were complaining. She examined her face ruefully in the precious aluminum-framed mirror. 'I'm a mess,' she told it, and it winced, agreeing. 'Better clean up.'

Five minutes later, Helge closed her door and marched onto the landing at the head of the grand staircase, a wide wooden platform that circled the inside wall of the central hall. She gripped the handrail tightly as she descended. *It wouldn't do to fall downstairs, I might lose the baby.* She tried not to throw off the fit of dark humor: She had a feeling that if she aired that particular joke she might scare people. Not, she was determined, that she was going to bond even remotely with the kid. *That* would be too much like collusion. *I wonder who wants to see me?*

The butler, or equerry or whatever, was waiting at the foot of the stairs with a gaggle of maidservants lined up behind him. 'Milady.' He bowed, almost sweeping the floor. 'Her ladyship awaits you in the green lounge.'

Miriam nodded acknowledgement. *Who?* Two unfamiliar servants waited outside the door he indicated, standing at ease with almost military precision. 'Introduce me,' she said.

'Aye, milady.' The equerry walked towards the door, which opened before him. 'This is Lady Thorold –'

'We've met,' said Helge. She swept past the startled equerry.

Olga met her halfway in a hug. 'Helge! You look well. Have they been looking after you?'

'Well enough so far.' She hugged Olga back, then took a deep breath and stepped aside to look at her. With her hair up, wearing an embroidered riding habit, Olga almost looked like the blond ingénue Miriam had mistaken her for when they'd first met, almost a year ago. 'You're looking good yourself.' She took another deep breath, feeling the knot of anxiety begin to loosen. 'But how have you been? Brill tried to bring me up to date on some of the details, but . . .'

'It has been difficult.' Olga looked slightly pained for a moment, then her brows wrinkled into a thunderous frown. 'But leave that for later! I come to see you, and I find you in a yokel's barn with peasants for attendants and no guards for your back – how long have you been left alone here?'

'Oh, I've only been here since this morning –'

'Only this morning? Well then, I probably need not execute anyone just yet –'

'Wait!' She held up a hand. 'Brill was sorting things out for me. What are you going on about?'

'It was Lady d'Ost?' Olga's anger faded. 'She told me about your . . . arrangement. She left you here?'

'Yeah. But she was supposed to be back later in the day. Think she ran into trouble?'

'Possibly.' Olga walked over to the heavy oak sideboard that stood against one wall and opened a small valise to pull out a handset. 'I'll just check. One-two, one-two. Stefan, wer' ist?' A burst of crackling Hochsprache answered her. Miriam didn't even try to follow the conversation, but after a minute's back and forth Olga was content to shove the radio back in her bag. 'My men will ask, when they finish walking the perimeter. It could be just one of those things . . .' Olga shrugged, delicately. 'But we cannot leave you here without a staff, especially once the servants work out who you are. At a minimum you need your own ladies-in-waiting – at least two of them, to supervise the servants and look to your needs. I am able to detach Lady Brilliana from other duties, so she can serve, again . . . Then you need a lance of guards under a suitable officer, and a communications officer with a courier or two at his disposal. I'd be happier if we could add a doctor or at least a properly trained paramedic, a coachman and two grooms, and either a full kitchen staff or at least a poisontaster. The full household we can leave until later, but this is an essential minimum – '

'Olga.' Miriam – shoving Helge out of her mind – took a deep breath. 'Why?'

'Why?' Olga looked surprised. 'Because you're *carrying the heir*, dear. We have a special word for a woman who does that. We call her *the queen*.'

*

'This glorious nation of ours was not built by the landed gentry or the bastard sons of George; it was built by the sweat and love of men like you. And its future is in your hands.'

Erasmus squinted at the faces behind the fulminating glare of the limelights as the scripted applause rolled on, trying to hold an impassive expression of determination on his face. 'Thank you, citizens! And long live the commonwealth!'

The applause grew louder, sounding genuinely enthusiastic. Hungry men clinging to their best hope of a solid meal, a cynical corner of his mind observed as he bowed his head, then stepped back from the lectern and walked to the back of the stage to make way for the next speaker.

'I thought that was well enough received,' he told the fellow on the bench seat behind the backstage curtain. 'What do you think?'

Ronald Smith, the Assistant Commissioner for Justice, nodded thoughtfully. 'A good tub-thumping rant doesn't go amiss,' he conceded. 'Who's on next?'

'Brian MacDougal.' Burgeson frowned as he sat beside Smith. 'Which means he'll harangue them for three hours about the price of flour while their stomachs are rumbling.'

'I ought to go back to the front bench.' Smith showed no sign of moving.

'I ought to go back to the office.' Burgeson's frown deepened. 'There'll be new slanders and rumors from the Patriot Club to rebut before the congress is over, if I don't mistake myself . . .'

'No, you don't.' Smith fumbled in his coat pocket for a while before pulling out a villainously stained clay pipe. 'They're getting ready for something big. I can feel it in my bones. We'll have to break some heads before long, or they'll be electing a king to ride us like nags. Francis or Sir Hubert, most likely.' Both of whom were popular with the elitist thugs of the Patriot Club and their opportunist redshirted street runners – the shirts were dyed to conceal the bloodstains of their victims, Burgeson had announced in one of his more lurid editorials, and for once he was making none of it up.

'They'll break the assembly if they do that.'

'The assembly's doomed anyway, Erasmus. As long as Sir Adam sticks to his and our principles and the New Club continue to demand amnesty for John Frederick, there's going to be no compromise, and the taller the debate grows, the more bitter its fruit will be.'

'You sound as if you want to compromise. Or am I misunderstanding you?'

Smith grunted as he fumbled with his lighter. 'No, I believe there *will* be a compromise, eventually, whether we want it or no; the only question is, whose terms will it favor? The alternative is open strife, and as that would only benefit our enemies . . .'

He pulled the trigger. Sparks snapped and fell into the barrel of his pipe.

'I think you underestimate our resources and our prowess,' Erasmus murmured as Smith drew on his weed. 'We have a majority of the navy behind us.' The rigid stratification and harsh discipline of the service, combined with a recent decline in the quality of rations and an influx of conscripts, had turned the navy into a tinderbox of pro-Leveler sentiment. 'In fact, I think we'd have a majority of the people behind us, if the assembly would get round to holding the elections we were promised for our support.' Erasmus nodded to himself. 'We know we hold the people's mandate, that's why they're carrying on this rear-guard action in the popular committees. And the sooner we stop gassing at each other and patting ourselves on the back' – his nod towards the front of the stage, where Citizen MacDougal had com-menced his peroration on the price of bread, took in the invisible audience of party delegates – 'the better. This is what did for us the last time round, and if we don't seize the day it'll do for us again – '

He paused. A messenger boy was tiptoeing towards them, eyes wide. 'Citizen Burgeson?' he piped quietly.

'Yes, lad?'

'Electrogram from the Westminster Halls!' He held the message slip out, stiff-armed.

'Hmm.' Burgeson took the message and read it as fast as he could in the backstage twilight. Then he pocketed it. 'It has been good to talk to you, Citizen Smith, but I'm needed elsewhere.' He rose. 'Do keep me informed as to the substance of Citizen MacDougal's bakery, will you?' Then he turned to the messenger boy: 'Go tell the post-master to signal that I'm on my way.'

Burgeson emerged blinking from the basement of the comman-deered theater where the party caucus was in full swing. Two militiamen in the gray-and-green uniform of the Freedom Riders challenged him. 'Citizen Burgeson. Please tell Citizen Supervisor Philips that I am ready to leave on urgent business and require trans-port.'

'Sir!' One of the guards hurried off; the other stood by. Erasmus pointedly ignored the solecism: Ex-soldiers generally made the best militiamen, even when their political awareness wasn't up to scratch, and with the opposition boasting of two redshirts for every Freedom Rider the Party could muster, only a fool would make an issue of a slip of the tongue.

Presently the guard returned with Supervisor Philips following behind him. Philips, tall, stoop-shouldered, and quavery of voice, wouldn't normally have been Erasmus's idea of a military commander: He reminded him of a praying mantis. (But these weren't normal times, and Philips was, if nothing else, politically sound.) 'Ah, Citizen Burgeson. What can I do for you?'

Erasmus suppressed a twitch. Drawing himself up to his full height, he said: 'I am summoned to the Westminster Halls by Sir Adam.'

'Interesting.' He could almost see the gears meshing in Philips's mind. 'We'll have to avoid the Central Canal and Three Mile Lane, the redshirts are smashing up shop windows again, working themselves up.' The gears spun to a conclusive stop: 'Citizen, please follow me. Meng, go tell Stevens to send the armored car round to the front steps. He's to follow with the motorcycle detachment. Gray, stand guard until I send someone to relieve you.' Erasmus fell in behind Philips. 'I should like you to ride in the car for your own safety, citizen. Unless you feel the need to arrange a provocation?'

'No provocations today.' Erasmus smiled humorlessly, mentally reviewing the message that had dragged him away from the interminable speeches of the party faithful: COME AT ONCE TO DISCUSS PATRIOTS WITHDRAWAL FROM ASS BREAK NEED TO RESPOND BREAK. 'But there'll be plenty of provocations tomorrow.'

*

Miriam was still vibrating from Olga's arrival two hours later, when the Lady Brilliana d'Ost arrived with all the ceremony due to a lord's daughter, and a small army of servants, stewards, armed guards, and other retainers besides. *They can't mean it*, Miriam kept telling herself: *I'm no queen!* She'd met His Majesty King Alexis a number of times, and his mother, the dowager queen, but there'd been an empty space in that family tree for some years before Egon pulled his hostile takeover bid. She'd acquired from King Alexis a vague sense of what it was to be a monarch: much like being the CEO of a sprawling, huge, corporation with an activist and frequently hostile board. And the special angle that if you screwed up, being fired took on a whole new meaning.

Olga had dragged her on a tour of the house and its grounds – sucking two bodyguards along in her wake, and using her walkie-talkie to warn other outer guards of their progress – and had tried explaining a huge inchoate bundle of protocol to her, in between showing her round an orchard patrolled by peacocks and a huge selection of outbuildings that evidently made this site suitable for a temporary royal presence – but most of it went right over her head. Too much, too fast: Miriam was still trying to come to terms with her mother's sudden reemergence at the center of a web of diplomacy (and the huge imposition of being pregnant, much less the whole question of her status here) to grapple with anything else.

In the end, she'd just raised a hand. 'Olga. Stop. This is too much for me, right now.'

'Too much.' Olga paused. 'Helge. You need to know this. What is – '

'Back to the house. Please?'

Olga peered at her. 'You're not feeling too good?'

'I am *way* overloaded,' she admitted. 'I'm not ready for this, for any of it. Mom's plan. You're part of it, right?'

'Back to the house,' Olga said firmly, taking her in hand. 'Yes,' she confirmed as they walked, 'I have the honor of conspiring with her, as do you. But we are relying on you for so much. If you are overloaded, let me help?'

Miriam sighed. 'I'm not sure I can. Being pregnant? That wasn't in my plans. Mom's conspiracy? Ditto. Now you want me to be a queen, which is way outside my comfort zone: It's the kind of job that drives people into an early grave. And then there's the other stuff.'

'Other stuff?'

'Don't bullshit me, Olga. Angbard didn't pick you just because of your bright smile and fashion sense. You must have gotten my report through Brill. I *did* meet Mike Fleming in the palace! And he told me – '

'Yes, we know.' Olga paused while one of their silent escorts opened the orchard gate for her. 'It is a very bad situation, Helge, and I would be lying if I said it was entirely under control. You have been told what happened to Egon's men?'

'Yes.' Miriam followed Olga through the gate. 'Which means it's only a matter of time. It could all explode in our faces tomorrow, or next month.'

'Absolutely. Your uncle – while he lay sick, he told me we needed to put your business plan into action, that it was the only way. But my word carries little weight with the likes of Julius or your grand-dam. If your mother's conspiracy works, we'll see. But we are riding on a tumbrel with a broken wheel – time is scarce, so we must pursue all our options at once lest we find ourselves treading on air. You as the mother to the heir – that helps. If not with the old aristocracy, then with our own conservatives – *they* recognize the heir, it was their own scheme! And there are other materials that his grace told me to entrust to you, when I can recover them – they are another. We might be able to hold the Gruinmarkt yet, should the American scientists fail to unravel our talent. It could take them years, not months. And we will still need to defeat them in covert battle and recover our hostages from them.'

'But it's going to end sooner or later, and probably sooner than we think – '

'Yes, but every month it buys us is a month longer to find a way out of the trap. And we have plans. If the worst should fail to arrive, there is your mother's scheme. And if the worst *does* arrive, we have evacuation plans. We can flee by way of Canada, and then to other nations. We have sent spies to Europe. Your friend in New Britain might supply another option – better, if the Americans announce our existence at large. We've got *many* alternatives. Too many, in fact.' The shady garden path approached the courtyard at the rear of the house, the door leading back inside. 'Your confusion is our confusion. Brilliana told me you were working on a new plan of business. Work hard; I think we may need it very soon.'

Which was all very well, and brought Miriam back to herself, lending her the strength for another try at being Helge. Just in time to open the door onto chaos.

'Move that upstairs! No, not that, the other case! You, yes, you, go find the kitchen! Honestly, where do I get these people? Oh, hi, Miriam!'

The main hallway was full of luggage, heavy trunks and crates, and their attendant grooms, guards, and porters. Brill – Lady Brilliana d'Ost in this time and place, elegant and poised – stood in the middle of it, directing the traffic with the confidence of a born chatelaine. 'You'd better wait in the blue receiving room while I get this under control. Which reminds me.' She switched to Hochsprache: 'Sir Alasdair, your presence is required.' In English, sotto voce: 'Alasdair is in charge of your bodyguards, Helge. Yes he's Clan, a full world-walker, but the offspring of two outer families hence the lack of braid. He's reliable, and unsworn.'

'He is?' Miriam murmured, smiling with clenched teeth as a medium-sized mountain of a man shambled across the busy floor, narrowly missing two pieces of itinerant furniture and their cursing porters.

'He is. He's also my cousin.' Brill nudged. 'Alasdair, I'd like you to meet Helge – '

'Your highness, I am overwhelmed!' The mountain bowed like a landslide, sweeping the floor before Miriam's feet with his hat. 'It is an honor to meet you! My lady has told me so much – '

'Oh good.' At least the man-mountain spoke English. *Stand up*, she thought at the top of his head in mild desperation.

'Sir Alasdair, you must be able to stand in your liege's presence,' Olga interrupted, casting Miriam a sidelong look.

'Of course,' Miriam echoed. *Okay, that's two hints. I get the message. Swear your chief of security!*

'Your highness is gracious.' Brill winked at her and Olga studiously looked away as Alasdair straightened, revealing himself to be a not-unpresentable but extremely large fellow in his mid-thirties, if not for the starstruck expression on his face.

'If you do not mind, I have to be elsewhere,' Olga told Miriam. She nodded at Brill. 'You know what must be done?'

'I do.'

'Well then.' Olga ducked a brief curtsey in Miriam's direction, then sidestepped around the doorway and back into the garden.

'What was that about?' asked Miriam.

'Lady Hjorth is most peculiarly busy right now,' Brilliana commented. 'As I should be, too, if you do not mind.'

Alasdair cleared his throat. 'If your highness would care to inspect your guard of honor?'

'I'm not anyone's highness yet,' Miriam pointed out. 'But if you insist . . .'

'Alasdair and his men will see to your security,' Brill repeated, as if she thought Miriam hadn't already got the message. 'Meanwhile, I must humbly beg you to excuse me. I've got to get all the servants bedded in and the caravan unloaded – '

'Olga said something about ladies-in-waiting,' Miriam interrupted. 'Who did you pick?'

'Look no further.' Brill raised an eyebrow. 'Do you think I would put you in the hands of amateurs? I will find suitable assistants as soon as time permits.'

'Oh, thank god.' Miriam mopped at her brow in barely feigned relief. 'So, I can leave everything to you?'

'You are my *highest* priority,' Brill said drily. 'You were, even before I swore to you. Now go and meet your guards.' She turned and swept back into the chaos in the entrance hall, leaving Miriam standing alone with Sir Alasdair.

'Your highness.' Alasdair rumbled quietly when he spoke. 'Lady d'Ost has told me something of her time with you. I understand you were raised in America and have little experience of living in civilized manner here. In particular, she said you are unused to servants and bodyguards – is that correct?'

'Pretty much.' Miriam watched him sidelong as she took in the details of the room: dark, heavy furniture, tapestries on the walls, an unlit hearth, unpadded chairs built so ruggedly they might be intended to bear the weight of history. Sir Alasdair looked to be a part of these environs, save for the Glock holstered on the opposite side of his belt from his saber. 'What, realistically, can your guards do for me? Other than get in my way?'

'What indeed? Well, there are eight of them, so two are on duty at all times. And when your highness is traveling, all of them will be on duty to cover your path, before and after. We will cover your movements without getting in your way if you but tell us where you wish to go. And when the assassins come, we'll be ready for them.'

Assassins? Miriam blinked as Sir Alasdair paused for breath. 'Charming,' she muttered.

'My Lady d'Ost told me that you have killed a man who tried to kill you. Our job is to see that you never have to do that again.'

'Well, that's nice to know. And if I do?'

'Then it will be over our dead bodies,' Alasdair said placidly. 'If your highness would care to follow me?'

'If you think – ' She froze as Alasdair opened the door back onto the semi-organized chaos in the hall. 'Wait, that man. I know him.'

She was fumbling with the pouch in her sleeve as Alasdair followed her gaze. He tensed and stepped sideways to place his body in front of her and pull the door closed. He turned to face her. 'What about him? That's Sir Gunnar; he's an experienced bodyguard, used to work for – '

Miriam's heart was thundering as if she were trying to run a marathon. She moved her hands behind her back, then tried again to slide her right hand into her left wristband. This time her fingers closed around the butt of her pistol: The man whose true name she had just learned hadn't seen her yet. Talking to another guard, he'd been distracted when Alasdair opened the door.

She swallowed, her mouth unaccountably dry. 'Speaking hypothetically – if I ordered you to take that man outside and hang him from the nearest tree, would you do it?' The choking sense of panic was back with a vengeance. *The Ferret*, she'd called him. No-name. *Gunnar*.

'If he were a commoner, yes. But he's one of us,' Alasdair rumbled. 'A proven world-walker and thus a gentleman, even though he's a by-blow of an outer family lass. You'd need to accuse him of something. Hold a trial.' There was an oddly apprehensive note in his voice. *He's afraid of me*, she realized. It was like a bucket of cold water in her face: *Sir Alasdair is* afraid *of* me?

'Well, then I won't ask you to do anything you can't. But if I ordered you to send him a very long way away from me and make sure I never set eyes on him *ever again*, could you do *that*?'

'Of course.' The tension went out of his voice, replaced by something like mild amusement. 'Do you want me to do that? May I ask why?'

'*Yes*. We have a history, him and me.' For a moment she'd been back in Henryk's tower with the Ferret loitering outside her bedroom door, an unsleeping jailer – possibly an executioner-in-waiting, she had no doubt about his willingness to kill her if his master ordered it – cold-eyed and contemptuous. And her racing pulse and clammy skin told her that part of her, a part nobody else could see, would always be waiting in that cell for his key to turn and those pale eyes to flicker across her face without registering any emotion. She flexed her fingers and carefully drew her pistol, then lowered her arm to hide it in a fold of her skirts, careful to keep her eyes on Alasdair's face as she did so. 'Did you pick him? Is he a friend of yours?'

'He was on the list.' Alasdair's nostrils flared. 'One of the top three available bodyguards by ranking. I wouldn't say I know him closely.' Miriam stared into his eyes. Wheels were turning there, slowly but surely. 'You have relatives who dislike you, my lady, but do you really think they'd – '

'I think we should *find out*.' She took a deep breath. 'In a moment you're going to open the door and walk towards G-Gunnar. I'll be behind you. Close and disarm him if he so much as blinks. If he draws, you may assume he's an assassin – but if we can take him alive, I have questions I want answering.'

'Your highness.' Alasdair's nod was cursory, but he sounded worried. 'Is this wise?'

'Very little I do is *wise*, but I'm afraid it's *necessary*. If you're going to be my bodyguard, you'd better get used to it: As you yourself noted, I'm a target. After you, my lord.'

Sir Alasdair turned back to face the door and pushed it ajar. Then he surprised her.

The front hall of the country house was roughly rectangular, perhaps forty feet long and twenty feet wide. The grand staircase started at one side, climbing the walls from landing to landing in turn, linking the two upper stories of the house. At the very moment the door opened, the floor held at least nine porters, servants, guards, cooks, maids, and other workers unpacking the small mountain of supplies that Lady d'Ost had rustled up seemingly out of nowhere to furnish the Countess Helge's entourage. Gunnar was two-thirds of the way across the floor from the door to the blue room, deep in conversation with another fellow, both of them in the livery of guards of the royal household.

Miriam had expected Alasdair to approach his prey directly. Instead, he stood in the doorway for a couple of seconds, scanning the room: Then he broke into a run. But he didn't run towards Gunnar – instead he ran at right-angles to the direct line. As he ran, he drew his sword, with a great shout of *'Ho! Thief!'* that echoed around the room.

Why did he – Miriam raised her pistol, bringing it to bear on the Ferret with both hands – *oh, I see.*

At the last moment, Alasdair spun on his heel before the porter he'd been threatening to skewer – the fellow was frozen in terror, his eyes the size of dinner plates – and rebounded towards the Ferret, who was only now beginning to react to the perceived threat, reaching for a sidearm –

'Freeze!' Alasdair shouted. 'She has the better of you! Don't throw your life away!'

Miriam swallowed, carefully tightening her aim. *He knew I'd drawn. And he deliberately cleared my line of fire! When am I going to stop underestimating these people?*

The Ferret's face, framed in her sights, was corpse-gray.

'Raise your hands!' she called.

The Ferret – *Sir Gunnar, he's got a name,* she reminded herself – slowly raised his hands. Sir Alasdair stood perhaps six feet away from him, his raised saber lethally close. A healthy man could lunge across ten feet in a second, with arm's reach and sword's point to add another six – the Glock holstered at Gunnar's belt might as well have been as far away as the moon. *If you've got a gun and your assailant has a knife, don't* ever *let them get within twelve feet of you,* she distantly remembered a long-ago instructor telling her.

Miriam took a shuffling step forward, then another, feeling for solid footing with her toes. It got easier to ignore the sensation of her heart trying to climb out through her mouth with practice, she noted absently.

'Disarm him,' she heard Sir Alasdair tell the other guard, who glanced nervously over his shoulder at her – *at her* – then hastily pulled the gun and the sword from Gunnar's belt.

Miriam risked lengthening her stride. Her breath was coming hard. Amusement and hysteria vied for control. She stopped when she was about fifteen feet from her target. 'Who sent you here?' she demanded.

'I'm not going to plead for mercy.' The Ferret's eyes, staring at her over the iron sights of her pistol, seemed to drill right through her. 'You're going to kill me anyway.' He sounded curiously resigned.

He'd beaten her, once, to make a point: *Obey me or I will hurt you.* That he'd been following orders rather than giving rein to his own sadistic urge made no difference to Miriam. But – *Hold a trial. And accuse him of* what, *exactly?* Of being her jailer after Henryk had violated Clan law and process by *not* executing her for what she'd done? If she gave him a trial, stuff better swept under the rug would come out. Kill him out of hand, and her enemies – the ones who'd tried to have her raped, or killed, or maimed several times over the past year – would find a way to make use of it, but at least he wouldn't be able to rat her out. Likely they'd use it as evidence of her instability or anger – *anger* was always a good one to pin on a threatening woman. But it was nothing like as damaging as what he could reveal.

She licked her lips. 'Not necessarily.' *Don't tempt me* struggled briefly with a moment of revulsion: *Life is too damned cheap here as it is.* 'Restrain him.' The other guard was already loosening the Ferret's belt. 'Lower your arms. Slowly.'

The room was very quiet. Miriam blinked back from her focus through the sights of the gun and realized all the servants had scurried for cover. *Smart of them.* 'I hold him covered,' Sir Alasdair said conversationally.

'Oh. Thanks.' She blinked again, then lowered the gun and carefully unhooked her finger from the trigger guard, which seemed to have somehow shrunk to the gauge of a wedding ring. The guard worked the Ferret's arms behind his back and tied them together with his own belt. She glanced at Sir Alasdair. 'Tell him what I told you to do with him. I don't think he'll believe it, coming from me.'

Alasdair kept his sword raised. 'Her highness ordered me to send you a very long way away from her and make sure she never set eyes on you again. Her exact words.' His cheek twitched. 'I don't *have* to kill you.'

'Highness?' Gunnar's face slumped, defiance draining out of it to leave wan misery behind. 'So it's true?'

'Is what true?' she asked.

'You're carrying. The heir.'

She stared at Sir Gunnar. 'You didn't *know*?'

'My lord did not see fit to tell me.' He was pale, almost greenish. Miriam stared at the blue eyes set in a nondescript face, the balding head and wiry frame, trying to remember how scant seconds ago she'd looked at them and seen a monster. *Who's the* real *monster here?* she asked herself.

'It's true,' she told him. 'And what Sir Alasdair told you is true. You don't have to die; all you have to do is stay the hell away from me. And tell us how your name got on that list.'

'What list?' He looked away, at Sir Alasdair. 'What the hell is she talking about?'

'Why are you here? Look at me!' Miriam shifted her grip on her pistol.

The Ferret turned his head, reluctantly. 'What list?' he asked again.

'The master roster of available bodyguards for council members,' Sir Alasdair rumbled. 'You were right at the top of it.'

'As if I shouldn't be?' Gunnar snorted. 'What do you take me for?'

'Wait,' said Miriam. 'What did you do for Henryk? Officially?'

There was a pause. 'I was his chief of security. *Officially.*'

Ah. 'And unofficially?'

Gunnar made a small shrug. Now that he wasn't staring down the barrel of a pistol held by an incandescently angry woman he seemed to be recovering his poise. 'The same. I *was* his chief of security. Until the Pretender did for him.'

'Right.' She glanced at Sir Alasdair. 'Maybe you'd like to tell him what I asked you *first.*'

'Highness, I think he can guess.' Alasdair's smile was humorless, and it wiped the nascent defiance right off Gunnar's face. 'I am ordered, and empowered, to act with any necessary force in defense of your person. Do you consider this man a threat to your person?'

It was hard to look at the Ferret's frightened face and still want to see him swinging from a tree. It had been tempting in the abstract, but ven Hjalmar was the real villain of the piece, and beyond her reach if he was indeed dead; in the clarity of the moment she found the Ferret pathetic rather than threatening, an accomplice rather than a ringleader. 'Right now . . . no. But he knows things. And I don't trust where he's been, why he's here. It stinks.' She glanced at Sir Alasdair. 'Escort him from the premises and make sure he doesn't come back, but don't kill him. I need to talk to you later, but first I have other work to do.' Her cheek twitched as she looked back at the Ferret. 'Payback can be a bitch, can't it? Have a nice day.'

Gunnar's control finally cracked. 'High-born cunt! The doctor was right about you!' he shouted after her. But she had already turned her back on him, and he could not possibly see her shock. The sound of her guards beating him followed her up the staircase.

BEGIN RECORDING

'WELLSPRING?'

'MYRIAD?'

'No, I'm the fucking tooth fairy – who do you think? You've missed
    three calls in a row. This had better be good.'

'Oh yes? Well, that stunt you pulled with the physics package could
    have killed me! What the hell were you *thinking?*'

'Hey, *I* didn't pull the trigger on that one. We're not a monolith;
    stovepipes melt and shit falls between the cracks. Did you just
    place this call so you could bitch at me or do you have
    something concrete?'

(*Indignant snort.*) 'Certainly. Your message in a pipe bomb, up near
   Concord? It was received loud and clear.'

'Really? Good – '

'No, *bad*. You know there was a pocket-sized civil war going on over
   there? Well, your timing was *brilliant*. You wiped out an entire
   army. Only trouble is, *it was the wrong one*. You handed the
   tinkers victory on a plate – they're busy mopping up right now,
   chasing down the last stragglers. They've even got some kind of
   half-cocked claim to the throne lined up, and you killed the only
   legitimate heir who wasn't in their pocket! Did you know that?
   You've just killed off all their enemies, and let them know into
   the bargain that it's war to the knife.'

(*Silence.*)

'Hello? Are you still there?'

'Jesus.'

'The phrase they use hereabouts is "God-on-a-stick"; but, yes, I echo
   the sentiment.'

'Can you just confirm all that, please?'

'Certainly. When you blew up the Hjalmar Palace, the royalist army
   that was *fighting* the tinkers had just occupied it. *They* had
   evacuated it a couple of hours earlier. Among the casualties was
   the crown prince – '

'Hang on. You said the Clan had evacuated the structure. Are you
   certain of that?'

(*Snort.*) 'If they hadn't, then how come their soldiers are dispersed
   all around the capital? Oh, they're not stupid – they got the
   message, you won't catch them all concentrating in a
   strongpoint again. Why?'

'But how? How did they withdraw?'

'The usual way – they world-walked. Or so I infer. They certainly
   didn't fight their way through the pretender's siege works:
   Individually they outgunned his army, but quantity's got a
   quality all of its own, as they say.'

(*Silence.*)

'Are you still there?'

'Yes. Just thinking.'

'Well, think faster. I don't have long here.'

(*Slowly.*) 'If the nar – If the Clan forces exfiltrated by world-walking, how did they do it? We had the whole area blanketed.'

'You did? Well, they must have just gone through another world, then.'

'Another' – (*pause*) – 'you're shitting me.'

'Huh?'

'Other world, unquote.'

'Yes. So?'

'You mean there are more?'

'What?'

'How many worlds, MYRIAD? *How many fucking worlds?*'

'Eh, don't get sharp with me, asshole! I can always put the phone down!'

(*Heavy breathing.*) 'I need to know.' (*Pause.*) 'I'm sorry. This is – this upsets everything.'

'I thought you knew this shit. Do I have to baby you?'

'Knew – ah, shit. Look, this stuff is new to us. How many worlds are there?'

'How should I know? Last week, there was ours, there was yours, there was the other one the homicidal cousins come from – '

'Homicidal *cousins*?'

'Long story. Anyway, word just in says they've discovered a fourth, and there's a team actively looking for more. For all I know there are factions or conspiracies who've already gotten there, who've got their own private bolt-holes well stocked for a long siege; but it used to be that everybody only knew about two. I'm guessing that cat's out of the bag, and . . . nobody knows. Could be, four's the total. But are you willing to bet on that?'

'Oh Jesus. The VP is going to shit a supertanker.'

'Hey, I'm just the messenger. Didn't your other informants tell you?'

'No.' (*Pause.*) 'How do they get to these other worlds?'

'Fuck knows. I *think* there's something about using a different symbol, or maybe it's just where they start out from. I really don't – ' (*Pause.*)

'Hello?'

'Someone's coming, got to clear down now. I'll call later.'
(*Click.*)
'Wait – '
(*Dial tone.*)

END RECORDING

An attorney's office in Providence was an unlikely setting to look for a government-in-exile, but it suited Iris just fine. *The boy's smart*, she decided. *Smart* and *discreet* were interchangeable in this context: Nobody would bat an eyelid at an attorney receiving numerous visitors, some of them shady, some at odd times of day. It was the next best thing to a crack house as an interchange for anonymous visitors, with the added advantage of being less likely to attract attention in its own right.

This would be harder than dealing with Dr. Darling.

'I'll walk,' she told Mhara as her young companion opened the minivan door for her. *Bad idea to look weak.*

'Yes, milady . . .'

Something about her tone of voice caught Iris's attention. 'Yes?' she said sharply.

'By your pardon, milady, but will you be expecting me to . . . you know?'

Iris sighed. 'Absolutely not,' she said, in a more gentle tone of voice. 'I'm here to talk, not to clean up loose ends; you don't need to worry about conflict of interests. You can leave your kit in the trunk if you want.'

'Thank you, milady.' Mhara sounded relieved; but, Iris noticed, she made no move to jettison her shoulder bag. 'That won't be necessary.'

Iris made her way slowly past the unmanned reception desk towards the elevator beyond. Looking up, she noticed the CCTV camera and paused, giving it time for a good look at her. Then she shuffled forward and pressed and held the call button.

'Iris Beckstein,' she said. 'His lordship is expecting me.'

The lift doors opened. Iris gave Mhara an ironic little smile. 'After you,' she said.

'Thank you, milady.' Mhara held the lift open for her – redundantly – looking slightly puzzled. 'Why is there no security?' she asked as the doors closed.

'You didn't notice, did you?' Iris asked. Mhara shook her head. 'This used to be a level two safe house, before they let it out for commercial rent ten years ago. They recommissioned it a few months ago, at a guess, after that bastard Matthias went over the wall. If we weren't expected, the doors wouldn't have opened. And if we'd tried to force the issue' – she raised her walking stick – 'the sprinkler system isn't for putting out fires.'

'Ugh.' Mhara looked at the ceiling, her eyes widening as she noticed the black Perspex hemispheres in two corners.

Naïve, but give her time . . . Iris waited, trying to prepare herself for the coming confrontation.

The elevator car stopped and the doors slid open. 'After you.'

Iris gestured towards the door opposite, then shuffled after Mhara. A moment later, the door opened. 'Your ladyship?' The polite young man in a suit that didn't quite conceal his shoulder holster held the door open. 'They're waiting for you in the boardroom.'

'Really?' Iris smiled brightly. 'Mhara, I'm afraid you'll have to wait outside.'

'Certainly, milady – '

'I can see to her comfort.'

'You will.' Cutting their chatter dead, Iris picked up her pace and hobbled past him, leaning heavily on her stick. It would be the second door on the left, if they'd followed the standard layout . . .

The boardroom was small, dominated by a huge meeting table surrounded by chairs designed to keep their occupants from falling asleep prematurely. The door's reinforced frame, and the shuttered box on one wall – a discreet cabinet that might equally hide a projection screen or an expensive plasma TV as anything more exotic – were the only obvious signs to distinguish it from a meeting room in any other law firm's office. Iris opened the door with some difficulty and slipped through it with a sigh of relief as a very different polite young man held it open, scowling. 'You're late, aunt,' he said.

'Heavy traffic on the interstate.' She gestured at an empty chair. 'If you don't mind, Oliver?' Then she nodded at the room's other occupants. 'Ah, Captain. Or should that be Major? I gather congratulations are in order. Julius, was it your idea?'

'No idea what you're talking about!' said the turkey-necked oldster at the head of the table. 'But it's good news all the same.'

'Yes, well.' Oliver, Baron Hjorth, pulled a chair out for her. She lowered herself into it gratefully. 'I gather our number one problem has been removed from the map by our number two problem. Or is that a slight oversimplification?'

'Very probably.' The possibly newly promoted Earl Riordan put down the document he'd been studying and stared at her, his blue eyes cold as a mountain lake in winter. 'If you don't mind waiting, milady, we are expecting one more participant, in a nonexecutive capacity.'

'Oh?' Iris asked, as the door opened again.

'Hi, everybody! Am I late? Oh! Iris! How *are* you . . . ?'

Olga seemed flustered, but happy to see her – as indeed she should be. Iris suppressed a smile. 'No time for social niceties, child! We have a meeting to start.'

'Yes.' Riordan raised an eye at her. 'And what delayed you, my dear?'

'A traffic accident.' Olga's smile vanished. 'Fatal.'

'Ah.' Iris glanced sideways as Oliver scribbled something on his notepad.

'Well, we're all here now,' Iris commented. 'Aside from the absentees. So if you'd care to start? I assume you have an agenda in mind?'

'Yes.' Riordan's cheek twitched. 'Let's see: attending . . . everyone on the list, yes. Apologies, none. Absent due to death: Henryk Wu-Thorold, Peffer Hjorth, Mors Hjalmar, Erik Herzog, Lars Thorold. *Scheisse* . . . New attendees include Patricia Thorold-Hjorth, Oliver Hjorth replacing Mors Hjalmar, Olga Thorold replacing myself, myself deputizing for Angbard Lofstrom. We are quorate – just barely. The agenda – look under your notepad, it probably got covered up.

If you don't mind, as we're starting late, I'd like to begin by calling Lady voh Thorold to report on the current medical prognosis of the principal security officer. Then we'll proceed onto matters arising and work out where we go from there. Olga?'

'Oh. Right.' Olga looked almost comically blank for a moment, then reached into her handbag to remove a day planner bulging with notes. 'To recap, the duke has been in the high dependency unit for six days now, and he isn't dead. He's even showing some signs of awareness and trying to communicate. That's the good news. The bad news is, he isn't getting any better. Let me just go over what Dr. Benford told me . . .'

She rattled on for almost ten minutes. 'He is much the same,' she concluded. 'His recovery is slow, and he betrays holes in his memory. He has trouble with names, and his left arm is still very weak.'

She put her day planner down and leaned back in her chair, looking almost bored. *Well, she's had longer to adjust to this than the rest of us,* Iris conceded. Beneath the blond mop – and Olga could play the blond airhead role for all it was worth when she wanted to – there was a very sharp young mind. *She doesn't think he's coming back.* Iris suppressed a pang of horror. *Oh my brother, why did you have to do this to us* now, *of all times?*

'In short, his grace is unlikely to join Sky Father in his halls this month, but he will probably not be issuing orders in the short term. We may hope that he will recover sufficiently to conduct his private affairs, and possibly even to resume the leadership of Security – but this is likely to take months, or years.' She leaned back and crossed her arms, tired and defensive. 'All yours, cuz.'

'If I may interrupt?' Julius sat up slightly. *Oh, come on* – Iris bit back on her response. Julius had always had a sharp mind behind that slightly vague facade; as one of the last of the elder generation of power brokers, he called for a certain wary respect – but he also had a tendency towards unhurried meandering, which had grown worse in recent years.

'You have the floor.' Riordan nodded and made a note on his pad. The cassette recorder at his left hand was turning, red LED steady: Preparing the minutes would be a sensitive job.

'Thank you. As chair of the Council of Families, I would like to note on the record that in view of the current emergency, we cannot allow the seat of principal security officer to remain empty. I therefore propose that until the duke reclaims his throne, or until the council of families votes to replace him, Earl-Major Riordan should continue to execute security policy in his stead. As for the direction of that policy, I believe the best way of ensuring impartiality is to place it in the hands of a committee. Such as this one, assembled as it is to evaluate the situation – I believe all interests are adequately represented? Baron Hjorth?' He turned to Iris. 'Your grace?'

Oliver was staring at her, too. Iris nodded slowly, gathering her thoughts. 'It could fly. But you've missed someone out,' she said after a moment. 'And I want to see some limits . . . Six months, or the death of a member, and it goes to an emergency session of the full council, not just this security subcommittee.'

Oliver was nodding, but Riordan looked irritated. 'An emergency session could be difficult to arrange – '

'Nonsense. This is a policy committee, not the executive. You have an emergency? *You* handle it. But for policy – we have differences.' Oliver stopped nodding. 'I won't lend my name to an office that can outlive my approval.'

'You're talking coalition,' said Julius.

'Yes, exactly.' She winked at Oliver. 'I don't think any of us want to see a return to the old ways. Let's not leave ourselves open to temptation.' In the old days, assassination was a not-unheard-of tool for manipulating the collective will.

Riordan cleared his throat. 'You said you thought we were missing a member,' he said.

'Yes.' She picked up her water glass and took a sip. 'There are two aspects to this job: How we pacify our homeland and how we deal with the American authorities. When it comes to the former, it would appear that my daughter is' – she swallowed again – 'holding an extremely useful asset. And I gather the central committee' – she nodded at Julius – 'have already considered her potential as a tool of state. But, speaking as one who knows her mind, I must warn you that if you think you can use her purely as a puppet you're mistaken.

She's a sharp blade; if you don't want to cut yourself, you'll need to get her to wield herself. And the best way to do that is to co-opt her. Offer her a seat on this committee and listen to her input.'

'Ah.' Oliver picked up his pen, twirled it between his fingertips in thought. 'Who do you propose should step down to vacate a seat for her?'

Iris saw Olga begin to open her mouth and pushed on. 'I don't. *You*' – she pointed at the earl – 'are here to represent your circle. *He*' – Riordan – 'is Clan Security. Julius is our council overseer; *she*' – she pointed at Olga, whose eyes widened – 'happens to have new party sympathies' – *as close to a lie as I've told all day* – 'and as for me, I'm here to make sure nobody poisons my half-brother.' Her cheek twitched. 'Call me an insurance policy.' She crossed her arms and waited.

'I thought you were in favor of marrying her off? Integrating her as fast as possible,' Oliver accused.

'That was then, this is now.' Iris shrugged. *And what you think has very little to do with the truth of the matter* . . . 'You don't still think I'm trying to undercut your inheritance?'

'Ach.' Oliver shook his head. 'That's of secondary importance, compared to the mess we've got to clean up! I am prepared to set the matter aside for a period of, say, a year and a day, then submit it to mutually agreed arbitration. In the interests of ensuring that there *is* a future in which I can peacefully enjoy my inheritance, you understand. If you think her claim can be made to stick – '

'We've got some extra help there.'

Riordan spoke up. 'The betrothal was witnessed. *Not* just by our relatives, and it seems there were survivors. No less a notable than the Duke of Niejwein himself, although how he got away – and he kept what he knew to himself when Egon came calling – '

'Ah.' Julius looked relieved. 'So we have a friendly witness.'

'Not exactly.' Riordan looked pained. 'Lady Olga . . . ?'

'We've got him in a lockup in this world. I had him brought over here as a security precaution – he's less likely to escape.'

'Have him witness publicly before his execution,' Iris suggested. 'Offer him amnesty for his family and estates if he cooperates.'

'I know Oskar ven Niejwein,' Oliver muttered darkly. *His eldest living son*, Iris realized. 'Better hang 'em all afterwards. It's the only way you'd be safe from him.'

'No!' Iris's head whipped round as Riordan spoke. 'What does royalty trade in?' he asked, meeting her surprised gaze.

'Royalty trades in power.'

'Huh.' His frown deepened. 'I don't think so. Oliver?'

'It trades in law,' Baron Hjorth said easily, 'its ability to rule well.'

'No, that's wrong, too.' Riordan glanced at Olga. 'What do you think?'

'Consistency?' she offered, with a raised eyebrow.

'Close.' Riordan straightened in his chair. 'Royalty trades on *belief*. A king is just one man, but if everybody in the kingdom believes in him, with the blessing of the gods, he reigns. *We* know this – we have been touched by this *Anglischprache* world – even if our benighted countrymen remain ignorant. Kings only reign if people believe they are kings. The belief follows the actions, often as not – the exercise of power, the issuing of laws – and is encouraged by consistency in leadership.

'We need Niejwein alive and *believing* we hold the throne by right of inheritance, not conquest, and reminding anyone who asks. If he's dead, people will forget his words if it conveniences them to do so. So I second Patricia Thorold-Hjorth's recommendation that Countess Helge be offered a seat on the security committee. And while we can and must make an example of some of the rebels, Niejwein must live.'

'So do we have a general agreement?' Iris asked. 'An ad hoc policy committee to sit for six months until relieved by a full council session, ruling in the name of Helge's unborn child, with Helge co-opted as a member of the committee and responsibility for Clan security resting with the major?'

Riordan glanced at the agenda in front of him. 'There's a lot more to it than that,' he pointed out.

'Yes. But the rest is small print – these are the big issues. I call for an informal show of hands: Is a solution along the lines I just outlined acceptable in principle to you all?'

She glanced around the table. Riordan nodded. 'Votes, please.

Non-binding, subject to further negotiation on the details,' he added, heavily. 'So we know whether it is worth our while to continue with this meeting.'

Hands began to go up. Iris raised hers; a moment later, Oliver Hjorth grimaced and raised his.

'I see nobody objects.' Riordan nodded. 'In that case, let us start on the, ah, small print. I believe you submitted a draft list of actions, my lord Julius . . . ?'

CORONATION

It had been a busy three weeks for Mike Fleming. An enforced week of idleness at home – idleness that was curiously unrestful, punctuated by cold-sweat fear-awakenings at dead of night when something creaked or rattled in the elderly apartment – was followed by a week of presenteeism in the office, hobbling around with a lightweight cast on his foot and a walking stick in his hand, doing make-work to ease him back into the establishment. Then one morning they'd come for him: two unsmiling internal affairs officers with handcuff eyes, who told him that his security clearance was being revalidated and escorted him to an interview suite on the thirteenth floor of an FTO-rented office building.

The polygraph test itself was almost anticlimactic. It wasn't the first time that Mike had been through one; *and I've done nothing to be ashamed of,* he reminded himself as they hooked him up. He focused on the self-righteous truth: Unless the system was so corrupted that sharing honest concerns with his superior officer was now an offense, he was in the clear.

So the questions about his alcohol consumption, political leanings, and TV viewing habits came as something of an anticlimax.

They sent him home afterwards, but early the next day a courier dropped by with a priority letter and a new identity badge, clearing him to return to duty. So Mike hobbled out to his car again and drove to work, arriving late, to find he'd missed a scheduled meeting with Dr. James and that there was a secret memo – one he wouldn't have been allowed to set eyes on two days earlier – waiting for him to arrive at his desk.

'I'm supposed to give you access to the GREEN SKY files,' Marilyn Shipman said, her lips pursed in prim disapproval. Mike couldn't tell whether it was him she disapproved of, or merely the general idea of giving someone, anyone, access to the files. 'For transcription purposes only. Room 4117 is set up with a stand-alone PC for you to use, and I can bring the files to you there one at a time.'

'Ah, right.' Mike gestured at his desk. 'I've got a lexicon and some other research materials. Can I bring them along?'

'Only if you don't mind leaving them there.' Shipman paused. 'Paper goes into the room but *nothing* comes out until it's been approved by the classification committee. Depending on their classification, I could make an authorized copy and have it added to the room's permanent inventory. But if they're another codeword project . . .'

'I don't think so, but I'll have to check.' Mike suppressed a momentary smile at her expression of shock. Some of the spooks who'd ended up in FTO were halfway human, but others seemed to take the form of their procedures more seriously than the actual substance. Like Ms. Shipman, who – he had a mental bet going with his evil twin self – would probably be less offended if he exposed himself to her than by his momentary forgetfulness about the classification level of his own notebook.

An entire working day (and three meetings) later, Mike finally got the keys to Room 4117 and its contents, including his carefully photocopied lexicon and handwritten notes on Hochsprache. There was other material, too: an intimidating row of nonclassified but obscure works on proto-Germanic and Norse linguistics. The room itself was sparsely furnished and windowless, half filled by the single desk. The PC, and an audio-typist's tape deck, were fastened to it by steel cables, and as if to drive home the point, a framed print on the wall behind the PC reproached him: SECURITY, IT'S MORE THAN YOUR JOB THAT'S AT STAKE.

Then Marilyn brought him the box of material he was supposed to be working with.

'You're kidding me. I've got to sign for a bunch of *cassette tapes*?'

'You got it. Here and here.' She pointed to the relevant lines on the form.

'Some of these look like they've been chewed by a dog.'

'You're working with primary source material now. You'd be

amazed at some of the stuff we get coming in from Pakistan and the Middle East.' She paused while he signed the clipboard. 'These are originals, Mr. Fleming. They've been backed up – they're in the library if anything goes wrong – but most of our analysts work with primary recordings wherever possible. Just in case anything's missing from the backup copy. There shouldn't be any problems of that kind, but you can never be quite sure. As to why it's on cassette tape, I couldn't possibly say. Perhaps that's all the field officer had to hand. They're still common in some parts of the world.' She smiled tightly and tapped the yellowing plastic lid on the secretarial recorder with a fingertip. 'Do you remember how to use one of these?'

'I think I can cope.' Mike looked at the headset doubtfully. 'What's that?' He pointed at a hole that had been drilled through a red button on the machine's control panel.

'That was the record button. They disconnect the erase head, too, just in case; this one's for playback only.'

'What, in case I slip and accidentally delete something?'

'No, it's in case you try to record a message for the accomplice you've got working down in library services to smuggle out of the establishment, Mr. Fleming. That should have been in your security briefing materials. We are very methodical here.'

'I can see that.' Mike picked up the first of the cassettes; a thin patina of dust grayed the hand-scribbled label. 'Has this been in your archives for long?'

'I don't know and I couldn't say.'

After Marilyn left, Mike sorted through the box. There were ten cassettes in all, and some of them were clearly years old. Most were identified only by a serial number scribbled on one side; a couple of them showed signs of the tape having been crumpled, as if they had unspooled and been painstakingly reassembled from a tangle of twisted Mylar. It had been years since Mike had last bothered with a cassette in everyday life; his last two automobiles had come with CD players. They were an obsolete technology, analog recordings on thin ribbons of tape. It seemed very strange to be working with them again, inside a windowless cell in a huge concrete office block in Maryland. But then again, a little voice reminded him: *They're robust.*

The equipment's cheap, and doesn't have to look like a spy tool. And you can replace them easily. Why fix something if it isn't broken?

And so he slotted the first tape into the player, donned the headset, and pressed the PLAY button.

And it made very little sense whatsoever, even on the third replay.

By the third day, Mike had just about worked out what his problem was. It wasn't just his grasp of the language, poor as it was. It wasn't the clarity of the recordings, either – the microphone had been reasonably well placed, and it was of adequate sensitivity. The men (and occasional women) he heard discussing things in what sounded like an office suite – these were regular business meetings, as far as he could tell – were audible enough, and he could make out most of their words with a little effort. Many of their terms were unfamiliar, but as if to balance things out, the speakers used familiar English words quite often, albeit with an accent that gave Mike some trouble at first.

'It's the context,' he told the security awareness poster. 'Knowing what they're talking about is as important as knowing what they're saying.' He waved his hands widely, taking in the expanse of his empire – the desk, the chair, the walls – and declaimed, 'Half of what gets said in any committee meeting doesn't get expressed verbally, it's all body language and gestures and who's making eye contact with whom. Jesus.' He looked at the box of tapes disgustedly. 'Maybe these would be some use to a secretary who sat in on the meeting, fodder for the minutes . . .'

His eyes widened as he remembered lying on the floor in an empty office, Matthias – source GREENSLEEVES – standing over him with a gun: 'If you'd gone after the Clan as a police operation, that would have given the thin white duke something more urgent to worry about than a missing secretary, no?'

Jesus. He stared at the tapes in surprise. *Matthias was their boss man's – the thin white duke's – secretary, wasn't he? These are probably his transcripts.* Not that he'd recognized the defector's voice – it had been months since he'd died, and Matt's voice wasn't distinctive enough to draw his attention, not on an elderly tape recording of a meeting – but the implications . . . *GREENSLEEVES didn't bring any*

tapes with him when he defected, so how did these get here? We have a
spy in the Clan's security apparatus, high enough up to get us these
tapes. I wonder who they are? And what else they've brought over ... ?

*

In a shack attached to the stables at the back of Helge's temporary palace, a man in combat fatigues sat on a swivel chair and contemplated failure.

'It's not working,' he complained, and rubbed his aching forehead. 'What am I doing wrong, bro?'

'Patience.' Huw carried on typing notes on a laptop perched precariously on one knee.

This experiment was Helge's idea. 'The first time I world-walked I was *sitting down*,' she'd told him. 'That's not supposed to be possible, is it? And then, later, I' – a shadow crossed her face – 'I was brought across. In a wheelchair.' Her frown deepened. 'There's stuff we've been lied to about, Huw. I don't know whether it's from ignorance or deliberate, but we ought to find out, don't you think?'

Angbard had said *get to the bottom of it*, and while the duke was hors de combat, Huw was more than happy to keep on following the same line of inquiry for Helge. 'Okay, that's test number four. Let's try out the next set of casters. You want to stand up while I fit them?'

'Yah.' Yul stood, then picked up the chair, inverted it, and planted it on the workbench.

Huw put down the laptop then went to work on the upturned chair's wheels with a multi-tool, worrying them until they came loose. He pulled another set of feet from a box and began installing them. 'This set should work better, if I'm right,' he explained as he worked. 'High density polyethylene is a very good insulator, and they're hard – reducing the contact area with the ground.'

'What about the mat?' asked Yul.

'That, too. We'll try that first: you, me, then Elena. Then without the mat.'

'You think the mat has something to do with it?'

'I'm not sure.' Huw straightened up. 'She world-walked in an office chair. We don't do that because it never occurred to anyone.

They tried wheelbarrows, and on horseback, back in the day. Even a carriage plus four. All we know is that nobody world-walks in a vehicle, because when they tried to do it, it didn't work. But we do it on foot, wearing shoes or boots. So what's going on? What's different about boots and wheels?'

'Horses weigh a lot,' Yul pointed out. 'So do wooden barrows, or carriages.'

'Yes, but.' Huw reached for a mallet and a wooden dowel, lined them up carefully, and gave a recalcitrant caster a whack. 'We don't *know*. There are other explanations, like: Most shoes are made to be waterproof, yes? Which makes them nonconductive. Whereas anyone who tried horses would have used one that was properly shod, with cold iron . . . I just want to try again, from first principles.'

'Why not get Rudi to try it in midair?' asked Yul.

Huw snorted. 'Would you like to give yourself a world-walker's head in midair, while trying to fly a plane? And what if it works but doesn't take the plane with the pilot?'

'Oh.' Yul looked thoughtful. 'Could he try it in a balloon? With a parachute, set up to unfold immediately if he fell? Or maybe a passenger to do the world-walking?'

Huw stopped dead. 'That's a *good* idea. Hold this.' He passed the chair to his brother while he opened up the laptop again and hastily tapped out a note. 'You volunteering?'

'What, me? No! I can't skydive! I get dizzy wearing platform soles!'

'Just asking.' Huw shut the laptop again. 'Whoever does it, that intrepid adventurer, they'll get lots of attention from the ladies.'

'You think?' Yul brightened slightly.

'Absolutely,' Huw said blandly. *Especially from her majesty*, but best not to swell Yul's head. 'Hand me that test meter then get the carpet protector . . .'

It was, he figured, a matter of getting the conditions right.

'There are a couple of possibilities,' he'd told Helge earlier in the morning, when she'd appeared in the stables, unannounced and unexpected, just like any other country squire's wife making her daily rounds of the estate. 'It could be the exclusion effect.' It was well known that you couldn't world-walk if there was a solid object in the way in the destination world. 'What if the ground pressure of feet or shoes doesn't set up a potential interpenetration, but wheels do? There's a smaller contact area, after all.'

'Can women world-walk in stiletto heels?' Helge had thrown back at him, looking half-amused.

'What? Have you – '

'I've never tried. I'm not good in heels, and world-walking in them isn't something I'd do deliberately.' She paused. 'But it's one for your list, isn't it?'

'I'll do that,' he agreed. 'Would you like to sit in on the experiment today? You might spot something I wouldn't . . .'

'I wish I could.' A pained expression crept across her face. 'They're keeping me busy, Huw, lots of protocol lessons and meetings with tedious fools I can't afford not to be nice to. In fact, I'd better be going now – otherwise I'll be late for this morning's first appointment. I think I've got an hour free before dinner, maybe you could fill me in on the day's progress then?'

He'd asked Lady d'Ost about the stiletto thing over lunch: The answer turned out to be, 'Yes – you'll likely twist an ankle, so you always take your shoes off first.'

As for the chair and the matters in hand . . . 'I'm seeing no conductivity at all,' Huw muttered. 'Good insulators.' Bare feet were insulators, too, of course, albeit not that good, and damp leather shoes were piss-poor, but dry rubber-soled boots or bare feet didn't seem to make any difference to world-walking. 'Okay, you want to try these?'

'All right.' Yul sighed and tugged the chair onto the middle of the plastic carpet-protector mat. 'I'm getting tired, though, bro.' He sat down and glanced at the back of his left wrist.

Huw looked at the floor. 'Hey, you're off the target – '

He stopped. Yul, and the chair, had disappeared.

'Shit.' Elena will fucking kill me, he thought incoherently. He slid a foot forward, then stopped. Opening the laptop again, he tapped out a quick note. Then he stood on the correct spot – not a foot to one side, where Yul had been – and looked at the knotwork he carried on a laminated badge, ready to world-walk.

The headache was sudden and harsh, a classic interpenetration blast. 'Ow.' *He's moving about.* Huw swore a bit more, then went and stood precisely where Yul had put the chair, and tried again.

The walls of the shack vanished, replaced by trees and sunlight and a warm summer breeze. Huw staggered, jostling Yul, who spun round with pistol drawn. 'Joker's bane, bro! Don't *do* that!'

'Sorry.' Huw bent double, the headache and visual distortions coinciding with a huge wave of nausea. He barely noticed the chair, lying to its side. The grass around its wheels was almost knee-length. *Should have surveyed more thoroughly*, he thought, then lost his attention to the desperate problem of hanging onto his lunch.

After a minute, he got things under control. 'You going to be all right?' Yul asked anxiously. 'Because one of us needs to go back.'

'Yes.' Huw stayed bent over. 'Not just yet.'

'I fell over when I came across. I think I bruised my ass.'

'I'm not surprised.' He retched again, then wiped his mouth. 'Ow.' Shuffling round, he knelt, facing the tussock Yul had stood in. 'We missed an angle.'

'We did?'

'Yeah.' Huw pointed. 'You had a foot on the ground.'

'So?'

'So you brought the chair over. And you were grounded. When you sat in it, you were fiddling with one armrest.' Huw shuffled towards it. 'Right. You had your fingers curled under it. Were you touching it?'

'I think so.' Yul frowned.

'Show me.' Huw was nearly dancing with impatience.

Hulius raised the chair and sat in it slowly. He lowered one foot to touch the ground, then shuffled for comfort, leaned forward with the fingers of his left hand curled under the armrest.

'Okay, hold that position.' Huw contorted himself to look under the armrest. 'I see. Were you fidgeting with the post?'

'Post?'

'The metal thing – yeah, that. The fabric on the armrest cover is stapled to the underside of the arm. And that in turn is connected to the frame of the chair by a metal post. Huh. Of course if you try to world-walk home, holding the chair up by the underside of those arms, it'll go with you, as long as the wheels aren't fouling anything.'

'You think that's all there is to it?' Yul looked startled.

'No, but it's a start. We go across, we take ourselves – obviously – and also the stuff we're carrying, the stuff we're physically connected to, but not the earth itself. The planet is a bit too big to carry. The question is, how far does the effect propagate? I've been thinking electrical or capacitive, but that's wrong. I should probably be thinking in terms of quantum state coherence. *And* the exclusion effect, as a separate spoiler, to make it more complicated. What *is* a coherent quantum state in a many-worlds Everett-Wheeler cosmology, anyway?'

Yul yawned elaborately. 'Does it matter? Way I see it, the lords of the post won't be enthusiastic about folks realizing they're not needed for the corvée. It could be a power thing, bro, to bind us together by misleading us as to the true number of participants required to set up a splinter network. If it only takes two guys and a wheelbarrow to do the work of six . . . that might present a defection problem, yes? On top of which you're the only relative I know who's mad enough to try to disprove something that everyone *knows* is the way things work, just in case everyone else is wrong. Must be that fancy education of yours.' He paused. 'Not that I believe a word of it, but I wouldn't mention it to anyone except her majesty if I were you, bro. They might not understand . . .'

*

The next day, Miriam received the visitor she'd been half dreading and half waiting for. Rising that morning, she'd donned Helge like a dress even as her maids were helping her into more material garments. Then she'd started the day by formally swearing Brilliana and Sir Alasdair to her service, before witnesses, followed by such of her guards as Sir Alasdair recommended to her. Then she'd gone out into the garden, just to get out of the way of the teeming servants – Brill's self-kicking anthill was still settling down and sorting out its various niches in the house – and partly to convince herself that she was free to do so. And that was where her mother found her, sitting on a bench in an ornamental gazebo. And proceeded to lecture her about her newfound status.

'You're going to have to be a queen widow for a while,' the Duchess Patricia voh Hjorth d'Wu ab Thorold explained to her. Wearing a voluminous black silk dress that she had somehow squeezed into the seat of an electric wheelchair, which in turn must have taken two strapping couriers to carry across in pieces, she posed an incongruous sight. 'Probably not forever, but you should plan on doing it for at least the next nine months. It'll give you a lot of leverage, but don't misunderstand – you won't be ruling the country. There's no tradition of rule by women in this culture. We – the junta – have agreed we're going to present ourselves in public as a council of regents. They'll be the ones who do the ruling – making policy decisions – but I've held out for you to have a seat on the council. You'll have title and nobility in your own right, and the power of high justice, the ability to arraign and try nobles. You'll sign laws agreed by the assembly of lords, as a member of the council of regents. Which in turn means the Clan council can't ignore you.'

'Yes, Mom,' Helge said obediently.

'Don't patronize me and I won't patronize you, kid. The quid pro quo is that there's a lot of ceremonial that goes with the job, a *lot* of face time. You're going to have to be Helge in public for ninety percent of that. Also, the Clan council will expect you to issue decrees and perform administrative chores to order. They say rabbit, you hop – at least at first. How much input you manage to acquire into *their* decisions is up to you, but my advice would be to do it very slowly and carefully. Don't risk overrunning your base, as you did last time. I'm going to be around to help. Our enemies won't be expecting that. And you'll have Brilliana. Olga and Riordan seem to *like* you, Sky Father only knows why, but that's another immense advantage because those two are holding Security together right now. I'd advise against trying to swear them to you – nothing's likely to scare the backwoods conservatives into doing something stupid like the fear that you're trying to take over Clan Security – but Riordan leans our way and Olga is one of us.'

'Define *us*,' Helge challenged.

'*Us* is you and me and everyone else who wants to drag the Clan kicking and screaming into the modern world.' Her mother's cheek dimpled. 'Hot and cold running water, votes for women, that sort of thing. *Next* stupid question?'

'So you tell me you've fixed up this situation where I'll have a lot of leverage but I'm going to be a figurehead, and I have the power to basically try the nobility, even pass laws, but I can't go head-to-head with the council, and if I push the limits too hard the reactionaries might try to assassinate me, and by the way, I'm going to be on public display as a storybook princess almost all the time. Is that the picture?' Helge stood up. 'What else am I missing?'

'Your own power base,' Patricia said crisply. She peered at Miriam. 'Have you sworn Brilliana yet? Your head of security?'

'Yes – '

'That young whippersnapper Huw? Or his brother and *his* doxy?'

'Ma!' She sat down again.

'You're not thinking ahead. You need them on your side, they're young and enthusiastic and willing – what's stopping you?'

'Um. An opportunity?'

'Exactly! So manufacture one. Invite them to a party. Better still, invite all the progressives. Be visible.'

'But I don't know who – '

'Brilliana does. Rely on her!'

'You think I can do that?' Helge asked disbelievingly.

'No.' Her mother grinned. 'I *know* you can. You just need to make up your mind to do it.' The grin faded. 'But. On to other matters. It's been a long time since we talked about the birds and the bees, hasn't it?'

'Oh, Ma.' Helge kicked her skirts out. 'I'm not a teenager any-more.'

'Of course not.' Patricia nodded. 'But you didn't grow up here. Can I offer some blunt advice?'

'You're going to, whether I want it or not, right?'

'Oh M– Helge. You slay me. Very well, it's this: You're a grown woman and you've got needs. And if you wait until the bun's finished baking and are reasonably discreet, nobody will look askance. Once you've been publicly acknowledged as the queen-widow, you're . . . in effect you're married, to a dead, absentee husband. Marriage is about property, and status, and rank, and if you're fool enough you can throw it all away. So don't do that, okay? Take a lover, but be discreet, use contraception. And whatever you do, don't mess with the help, *especially* don't mess with your sworn vassals. Pick a man who's respectably married and owes you no obligation, and what you get up to harms no one. But unmarried men, or vassals? They're trouble.'

Helge gaped, speechless. After a moment she managed to shut her mouth. 'Mother!'

Patricia sighed. 'Kid, the rules are *different* here. What have I been trying to beat into that thick skull of yours?'

'But, but – '

'You're confusing love and marriage. That old song, love and marriage, horse and carriage? It's rubbish.' She snorted dismissively. 'At least, that's not how any self-respecting aristocracy comports itself. You marry for power and heirs and you take your fun where you find it.' For a moment she looked wistful: 'That's one of the things I'm *really* going to miss about not living in the United States anymore. But just because a society runs on arranged marriages, it doesn't mean people don't fall in love. Just as long as they're discreet in public.'

'Oh god.' Helge made to run a hand through her hair, stopped at the last moment as she touched the jeweled pins that held it in place. 'That is just so screwed up . . .'

'I realize it must seem that way to you. The rules here are *very* different.'

'Ick.'

'It's not that bad, kid.' Patricia stage-managed a smile from somewhere. 'You're a *widow*. You've graduated from the marriage market, *summa cum laude*.'

'I don't need to hear this right now,' said Helge. 'I am *so* not interested in men right now – '

'But you *will* be, if not now then next year, and you need to know this stuff before it happens. Unless you want to let being a victim define you for the rest of your life, you're going to look back on this one day and shrug and say, "but I moved on."'

Helge stared at her mother sharply. 'What do you mean?'

Patricia looked her in the eye. 'Your – my husband – was a real piece of work. But I didn't let that get between *us*, between you and me, kid.'

Helge looked away. 'I'm not – '

'You're *my* daughter. *Mine*, not his. That's all the revenge that's good for me.'

After a moment, Helge looked back at her mother. Her eyes were dark, glistening with unshed tears. 'I had no idea.'

'I didn't want you to. I *really* didn't want to lay that on you.' Patricia held out a hand. After a moment, her daughter took it. 'But you wanted to know why I want to change the Clan. I'm doing it so no granddaughter or great-granddaughter of mine ever has to go through what I went through.'

'Oh, Mom.' Helge rose, then knelt in front of the wheelchair. She laid her head on her mother's lap, hugging her. 'I'm sorry.'

'Hush. It's not your fault.'

'But I thought you – '

'Yeah, I know what you thought. It's the usual Clan mother/ daughter rivalry. But like I said, we're not going to play by their rules. Are you with me?'

'Yes,' said Helge.

'Excellent.' Her mother stroked the nape of her neck lightly. 'You and me, kid. Together we'll make this thing work.'

*

In the end, the coup came down to simple economics. The emergency government had neglected to pay their employees for three weeks; whereas Sir Adam's party had, if not put a chicken in every pot, at least put a loaf of bread and tripe in dripping on every table that was spread with yesterday's copy of *The Leveler* in lieu of a cloth. They didn't have money but they had plenty of guns, and so they'd sent the party militia to seize control of the dockside warehouses. Wherein they found plenty of bulk grain that had been stockpiled for export, and which they lost no time in distributing to the people. It was a short-term gambit, but it paid off: Nothing buys friends in a famine like a full belly.

The morning of the coup came three days after the Patriot Club withdrew from the emergency assembly. Patriot gangs had taken to the streets of New London, protesting the Levelers' presence in the debating chamber with paving stones and pry bars. They'd scoured the army barracks, recruiting the wrong kind of soldiers – angry, unpaid young men, their bellies full of looted beer, looking for some-one to blame. 'We can't allow this to continue,' Sir Adam had said, his voice tinny over the crackling electrograph conference call. 'They'll cause chaos, and the people will blame us for losing control of the situation. So they must be stopped. Tomorrow morning, I want to see every man we've got turned out and ready for action. The Freedom Riders will patrol the streets around Parliament and the government buildings on Grosvenor Street; those of you in charge of departments will go to your offices with your guards and secure them against intrusion.'

'What about the New Party and the other opposition groups?' asked one of the delegates on the line.

'I don't think we're going to waste our time worrying about them,' said Sir Adam. 'They're either broadly for us and our program, in which case we will listen to their input before we act – once the emer-gency is over – or they're against us, in which case they are part of the problem. The Freedom Riders will bar access to the Commons while we debate and pass the Enabling Act; let them protest once we've saved their necks from the noose. I'm more concerned about the Patriot mob. As soon as they work out what's going on they'll attempt to storm the citadel, and I want us to be ready for them.'

Which was why, at four o'clock in the morning, instead of being sound asleep in bed, Erasmus was sitting in the passenger cab of a steamer, facing backwards, knee to knee with two strapping militia-men and nose to nose with Supervisor Philips, as it screamed up the broad boulevard fronting the East River at the head of a column of loudly buzzing motorcycle combinations. They were heading for the Propaganda Ministry offices in Bronckborough, to catch them at the tail end of a quiet graveyard shift. For lack of any other distraction, he scrutinized Philips closely; in his long black coat and forage cap he resembled a hungry crow.

'Soon be over, eh, sir?'

Philips's eyes swiveled sideways, towards the serg– *No, under-officer*, Erasmus reminded himself – *must keep the new ranks straight – underofficer* who had spoken. 'One expects so, Wolfe, unless anyone tipped a wink to the traitors.'

'Not me, sir!'

Erasmus suppressed his momentary amusement at the man's discomfort. Someone *might* have done so, despite the Party's control over the Post Office and the central electrograph exchanges, and if that was the case they might be heading straight into a field of beaten fire between heavy machine guns. *In which case we'll pay with our lives.* But Philips's reference to the Patriots as traitors – *that* was interesting. *So easily do our names twist and bite us*, Erasmus mused cynically.

The ministry offices stood at the crest of a north–south ridgeline at the intersection of two broad boulevards lined with plane trees; with clear fields of fire in all directions and no windows below the third floor, it was a characteristic example of the governmental architectural style that had arrived in the wake of the Black Fist Freedom Guard's assassination of King George Frederick's father. The steps fronting the building were guarded, but the railway sidings and loading docks at the back, through which huge rolls of newsprint arrived every evening to print the next day's edition of the *Parliamentary Gazette*, were another matter. By the time Burgeson's car drew up beside a gap-doored loading bay, there wasn't a red shirt in sight: All the guards on duty wore the black pea coats and helmets of the Freedom Riders.

'Ah, good.' Erasmus unwound to his full height as Philips hurried into the warehouse and conferred with his junior officers. 'Underofficer Wolfe.'

'Sir?'

'As soon as it's safe, I intend to go to the minister's office. I need guards.'

'Yes, sir. Allow me to petition Supervisor Philips?'

Erasmus nodded. 'Make it fast.'

The second staff car arrived, disgorging a claque of radical journalists and sub-editors handpicked by Erasmus earlier in the week just as Philips strutted over. 'Sir, the building appears to be in our hands for now. There was only a skeleton crew on duty, as the Patriots appear to have been shorting the staff to pay their thugs. I can't *guarantee* there isn't an assassin lurking in the minister's dining room until my men have searched the place top to bottom, but if you'll let me assign you a guard you can have the run of it.' He grinned beakishly, as if claiming ownership of a particularly juicy piece of roadkill.

'Good.' Erasmus addressed his editorial staff: 'Jonas, Eric, I want you to go to the speaking-room and see that the pulpit is ready for a morning broadcast. I'll be addressing the nation on Voice of New England as soon as we have a program. Milo, get the emergency broadcast filler ready to run. Stephen, coordinate with Milo on developing a schedule of news announcements to run round the clock. I will be on hand to read proclamations and announce emergency decrees as we receive them from Freedom House through the day. Jack, the print floor is yours. Let's go to work!'

They stormed through the Ministry building like children in a sweet shop, capering around the huge printing presses and the broadcasting pulpits of the king's own mouthpiece; marveling at the stentorian voice of the state that fate, audacity, and Sir Adam's brash plan had put at their disposal. ''T's going ter be glorious, sorr,' Stephen confided in Erasmus as they walked the editor's gallery overlooking the presses that had until recently spun the *Gazette*, official mouthpiece of John Frederick's despotic agenda. His eyes gleamed. 'All them years hiding type-trays in us basement, an' it come to this!'

'Enjoy it while you can, Steve. Seize the front page!' They came to the door leading to the third-floor landing, and the stairs up to the soundproofed broadcasting pulpits. 'You'll have to excuse me: I've got a speech to record for the nine o'clock news, and then I'll be in the Minister's office, working up our schedule for the next week.'

'A speech? What's in it?'

'Just some announcements Sir Adam charged me with making,' Erasmus said blandly. Then he relaxed slightly: No point in *not* confiding in his new subordinate, after all! 'We're taking the People's Palace' – the Houses of Parliament, renamed by raucous consensus earlier in the week – 'this morning, to pass an Enabling Act. It'll give the Executive Council the power to rule by decree during the current emergency, and we'll use it to round up the Patriots as soon as they raise their heads and start yelling for our blood. The sooner we can shut the opposition down for a while, the faster we'll be able to set up a rationing system and get food to the people again. And the faster we do that, the sooner we'll have their undivided support.

'By winter, we'll be building the new Jerusalem! And you, my friend, are going to tell the world that's what we're going to do.'

*

Pomp, circumstance, and matters of state seemed inseparable; and the more tenuous the state, the more pomp and circumstance seemed to surround it, Miriam reflected. 'I hope this is going to work,' she murmured.

'Milady, it looks perfect!' Gerta, her recently acquired lady of the wardrobe, chirped, tugging at the laces of her left sleeve. 'You are the, the model of a queen!' Her English was heavily accented and somewhat hesitant, but at least she had some; Brill had filtered the candidates ruthlessly to ensure that Miriam wasn't left floundering with her rudimentary Hochsprache.

I don't feel like one, Miriam thought, but held her counsel. *I feel more like a wedding cake decoration gone wrong. And this outfit weighs more than a suit of armor.* She was still ambivalent about the whole mad scheme; only the certain knowledge of what could happen if this masquerade failed was holding her on course – on course for weeks of state audiences and banquets and balls, and seven months of sore feet, morning nausea, aching back, and medical worries. 'Continue,' she said tonelessly, as Gerta continued to wind a seemingly endless silver chain around her collar, while three other maids – more junior by far – fussed around her.

She'd lain awake for most of the previous night, listening to the

wind drumming across the roof above her, and the calls of the sentries as they exchanged watch, and she'd worried at the plan like a
dog with a mangy leg. If this was the right thing to do, if this was the
right thing for *her*, if, if . . . If she was going to act a part in a perilous
play, if she was going to have another baby – at her age – not with a
man she loved, but by donor insemination, as a bargaining chip in
a deadly political game, to lay claim to a toxic throne. *Poor little
bastard*, she thought – and he would, indeed, be a bastard except
for the elaborate lies of a dozen pre-briefed and pre-blackmailed
witnesses who would swear blind to a secret wedding ceremony –
doomed to be a figurehead for the throne. *Damn, and I thought I had
problems . . .*

Miriam had no illusions about the fate awaiting anyone who
aspired to sit on the throne of the Gruinmarkt. It would be an unstable and perilous perch, even without the imminent threat of
invasion or attack by the US government. *If I wanted the best for him
I'd run away, very fast, very far*, she'd decided. But the best for him
would be the worst for everyone else: The Gruinmarkt would fall
apart very fast if a strong settlement wasn't reestablished. *It would
trigger a civil war of succession*, she realized. And her life, and her
mother's, and – *nearly everyone I care for* – would be in danger. *I can't
do that*, she thought hopelessly, punching the overstuffed bolster as
she rolled over in the night. *Where did I get this sense of loyalty from?
What do I owe them, after what they did to me?*

'My lady?' She blinked back to the present to see Gerta staring at
her. 'And now, your face?'

The women of the Clan, and their relatives in the outer families –
recessive carriers of the gene that activated the world-walking ability
– had discovered cosmetics, but not modernism or minimalism.
Miriam, who'd never gone in for much more than lip gloss and eye-
liner, forced herself to stand still while Gerta and a small army of
assistants did their best to turn her into a porcelain doll, using so
many layers of powder that she was afraid to smile lest her face crack
and fall off. *At least they're using imported cosmetics rather than white
lead and belladonna*, she consoled herself.

A seeming eternity of primping preparations passed before the door crashed open, startling her considerably. Miriam, unable to simply turn her head, maneuvered to look: 'Yes? Oh – '

'My lady. Are you ready?' It was Brilliana, dressed to the nines and escorted by two young lords with swords and MP5Ks at their waists, and three more overdressed girls (one to hold the train of her gown, the others evidently for decoration).

Miriam sighed. 'Gerta. Am I ready?'

Gerta squawked and dropped a curtsey before Brill. 'My lady! Another half hour, please? Her grace is *nearly* – '

Brill looked Miriam up and down with professional speed. 'No. Stick a crown on her head and she's done,' she announced, with something like satisfaction. 'How do you feel, Helge?'

'I feel' – Miriam dropped into halting Hochsprache – 'I am, am ready. I am like a hot, blanket? No, sheet, um, no, dress – '

Brill smiled and nodded – somehow she'd evaded the worst excesses of the cosmetological battalions – and produced a small crystal vial with a silver stopper from a fold in her sleeve, which she offered. 'You'll need this,' she suggested.

Miriam took it and held it before her face, where the flickering lamps in the chandelier could illuminate it. 'Um. What is it?'

'Crystal meth. In case you doze off.'

'But I'm pregnant!'

'Hist. One or two won't hurt you, you know? I asked a *good* doctor.' (Not, by her emphasis, Dr. ven Hjalmar, who Miriam had publicly speculated about disemboweling – especially if, as Gunnar had implied, he was still alive.) 'The damage if this act of theater should go awry is far greater than the risk of a miscarriage.'

'I thought you had an iron rule, don't dabble in the cargo . . .'

'This isn't dabbling, it is your doctor's prescription, Helge. You are going to have to sit on that throne looking alert for more than four hours, without caffeine or a toilet break, and I am warning you, it is as hard as a board. How else are you going to manage it?'

Miriam shook one of the tablets into the palm of her hand and swallowed. 'Uck. That was vile.'

'Come now, your grace! Klaus' – Brill half-turned, and snapped

213

her fingers – 'Menger, attend! You will lead. Jeanne and you, you will follow me. Sabine, you take my train. We will practice our order on the way to the carriage. Her grace will walk ten paces behind you, and you – yes, Gerta – arrange her attendants. When we arrive at the palace, once we enter the hall, you will pass me and proceed to the throne, Helge, and be seated when the Green Staff is struck for the third time and Baron Reinstahl declares the session open. I'll lead you in, you just concentrate on looking as if I'm not there and not tripping on your hem. Then we will play it by ear . . .'

They walked along the passageway from the royal receiving room at a slow march. Brill paced ahead of her, wearing an ornate gown dripping with expensive jewelry. The walls were still pocked with the scars of musket balls. The knights Brilliana had brought to her dressing room paced to either side, and behind them came another squad of soldiers – outer family relatives, heavily armed and tense. It was all, Miriam thought, a masque, the principal actors wearing costumes that emphasized their power and wealth. Even the palace was a stage set – after the explosion at the Hjalmar Palace, none of the high Clan nobles would dare spend even a minute longer than absolutely necessary there. But you had to hold a coronation where people could *see* it. The whole thing, right down to the ending, was as scripted as a Broadway musical. Miriam concentrated on keeping her face fixed in what she hoped was a benevolent half-smile: In truth, her jaw ached and everything shone with a knife-edged crystal clarity that verged on hallucination.

Before them, a guard detail came to attention. A trumpet blatted, three rising notes; then with a grating squeal, the door to the great hall swung open. *The hinges*, Miriam thought distantly, *they need to oil the hinges.* (The thought gnawed at her despite its irrelevance – glued to the surface of her mind.)

'Her grace the Princess Royal Helge Thorold-Hjorth, widow of Creon ven Alexis du –' the majordomo's recitation of her name and rank rolled on and on, taxing Miriam's basic Hochsprache with its allusions and genealogical connections, asserting an outrageous connection between her and the all-but-expired royal family. She swayed slightly, trying to maintain a dignified and expressionless poise, but was unable to stop her eyes flickering from side to side to take in the assembled audience.

It looked like half the surviving fathers of the Clan had come, bringing their sons and wives with them – and their bodyguards, for the rows of benches that rose beneath the windows (formerly full of stained glass; now open to the outside air, the glaziers not yet rounded up to repair them) were backed by a row of guards. Here and there she could pick out a familiar face amidst the sea of strangers, and they were all staring at her, as if they expected her to sprout a second head or start speaking in tongues at any moment. Her stomach clenched: Bile flooded into the back of her mouth. For an instant Miriam trembled on the edge of panic, close to bolting.

Brill began to move forward again. She followed, instinctively putting one foot in front of the other.

'The throne, milady,' the girl behind her hissed, voice pitched for her ear only. 'Step to your left, if you please.'

There was another cantonment of benches, dead ahead, walled in with wooden screens – a ladies' screen, Miriam recognized – and within it, a different gaggle of nobles, their wrists weighted with iron fetters. And there was a raised platform, and a chair with a canopy over it, and other, confusing impressions –

Somehow she found herself on the raised chair, with one of her maids behind each shoulder and the lords Menger and Klaus standing before her. A priest she half recognized (he'd been wearing a pinstriped suit at the last Clan council meeting) was advancing on her, swathed in robes. A subordinate followed him, holding a dazzling lump of metal that might have been a crown in the fevered imaginings of a Gaudí; behind him came another six chanting subordinates and a white calf on a rope which looked at her with confused, long-lashed eyes.

The chanting stopped and the audience rose to their feet. The calf moaned as two of the acolytes shoved it in front of the dais and a third thrust a golden bowl under its throat. There was a moment of reverential silence as the bishop turned and pulled his gilt sickle through the beast's throat; then the bubbling blood overflowed the basin and splashed across the flagstones to a breaking roar of approval punctuated by stamping feet.

The bishop raised his sickle, then as the assembled nobles quieted their chant, he began to shout a prayer, his voice hoarse and cracked with hope. *What's he saying* – Miriam burped again, swallowing acid indigestion – *something about sanctification* – she was unprepared when he turned to her and, after dipping a hand into the bowl, he stepped towards her and daubed a sticky finger on her forehead. Then the second priest knelt beside him, and the bishop raised the crown above her head.

'It's the Summer Crown,' he told her in English. 'Try not to break it, we want it back after the ceremony.'

When he lowered his arms his sleeves dangled in front of her. The hot smell of fresh blood filled her nostrils as the crowd in the bleachers roared their – approval? Amusement? Miriam closed her eyes. *I'm not here. I'm not here. You can't make me* be *here*. She wished the earth would open and swallow her; the expectations bearing down on her filled her with a hollow terror. *Mom, I am* so *going to kill you*.

Then the bishop – *It's Julius, isn't it?* she recalled, dizzily – receded. She opened her eyes.

'Milady!' hissed the lady-in-waiting at her left shoulder. 'It's time to say your words.'

Words? Miriam blinked fuzzily, the oppressive weight of the metal headgear threatening to unbalance her neck. *I'm meant to say something, right?* Brill had gone over it with her: She'd practiced with Gerta, she'd practiced with a mirror, she'd practiced until she was sure she'd be able to remember them . . .

'I, the Queen-Widow Helge, by virtue of the power vested in me by Sky Father, do declare this royal court open . . .' her memory began.

Oh, that, Miriam remembered. She opened her mouth and heard someone begin to recite formal phrases in an alien language. Her voice was steady and authoritative: She sounded like a powerful and dignified ruler. *I wonder if they'll introduce me to her after the performance?*

BEGIN TRANSCRIPT

(*Cockpit voice recorder.*)

(*Rotor noise in background.*)

'Climbing two five to flight level three zero, ground speed 150. GPS
    check.'

'GPS check, uh, okay.'

'TCAS clear. Ready to engage INS.'

'INS ready, fifty-mile orbit at three zero.'

'Okay. How's the datalink to that – that – '

'FLIR/DIMT is mapping fine.'

'Right. INS engaged. Racetrack. You boys ready back there?'

'ARMBAND is ready.'

'Ready.'

'Coming up on way point yankee one in fifty seconds, boys. On my
    mark, activate translation black box.'

'Arming translation circuit . . . okay, she's ready on your command.'

'Mark.'

'We have translation.'

'Radar altimeter check, please. What's the state of ARMBAND?'

'Sir, we've got two translations left, three hours to bingo time – '

'Tower, mike-mike-papa-four, do you read.'

'Two translations, three hours, check. You gentlemen will doubtless
    be pleased to know that as we've only got fuel for 140 minutes
    we'll be going home well before then.'

'Inlet temperature four. External temperature ten and dropping, was
    fifteen. Cloud cover was six, now four. Holy shit, *the ground* – it's
    completely different – '

'FLIR/DIMT is mapping fine. Uh, INS shows six meter z-axis
    anomaly. INS red light. INS red light. Looks like he took us
    with him okay.'

'Tower, mike-mike-papa-four, do you read.'

'INS reset. INS breaker reset. Damn, we're back to dead reckoning.
    Speed check.'

'Ground speed 146. Altitude three zero nine zero by radar altimeter. Lots of trees down there, whole lotta trees.'

'Okay, let's do an INS restart.'

'Captain, confirmed, tower does not respond.'

'FLIR/DIMT lock on north ridge corresponds to INS map waypoint 195604. Restarting. Restarted. Returning to orbit.'

'Tower on crest of ridge via FLIR. Got battlements!'

'Fuel, nine thousand. Throttle back on two, eighty percent. Okay, you've got an hour from my mark.'

'Got any candidates on IDAS?'

'Not a whisper. It's dead down there. Not even cell phone traffic. Why am I getting this itchy feeling between my shoulder blades?'

'Time check: three hours twenty-nine minutes to dawn. Altitude four one hundred, ground speed 145, visibility zero, six on FLIR. Stop worrying about MANPADs, lieutenant.'

'Roger. Waypoint yankee two coming up, turning on zero two zero.'

'I'm still getting nothing, sir. Trying FM.'

'Use your judgment.'

'Fuel eighty-six hundred. Throttle on eighty, inlet temperature three.'

'Quiet as the grave. Hey, some traffic on *shortwave*. Twenty megahertz band, low power. Voice traffic . . . not English.'

'Waypoint yankee three coming up, turning on zero nine zero. Climb to flight level five zero.'

'Okay, that's enough. We're in class E airspace on the other side, so let's get out of here. ARMBAND?'

'Ready to roll whenever you call, captain.'

'Okay, we're going home. Prepare to translate on my mark – '

END TRANSCRIPT

DECEPTIVE PRACTICES

A week had passed since the bizarre coronation ritual, and it had been a busy period. Miriam found herself at the center of a tornado of activity, with every hour accounted for. There were banquets with lord this and baron that, introductions until her cheeks ached from smiling and her right hand was red from scrubbing: Their kisses left her feeling unclean, compromised. The dressmakers had moved in, altering garments borrowed from some remnants of the royal wardrobe and fitting her for gowns and dresses suitable for a dowager queen-widow and a mother-to-be. Brill had found time, for a couple of hours every day, to bring a bottle of wine and sit with her while she explained the finer points of political and personal alliances; and Gerta engaged her in conversational Hochsprache, nervous and halting at first, to polish her speech. (Which, with total immersion in a sea of servants, few of whom spoke English, was beginning to improve.)

Being Helge was becoming easier, she found. Practice had diminished the role to a set of manners and a half-understood language that she could summon up at need, rather than a claustrophobia-inducing caul. Perhaps she was getting used to it, or perhaps her mother's private crusade and promise of mutual support had given her the impulse she needed to make it work. Whatever the cause, the outcome was that whenever she paused to think about her position Miriam was startled by how smoothly her new life had locked in around her, and with how little friction. Perhaps what she'd needed all along was a key to the gilded cage, and the reassurance that people she could trust were minding the door.

It had not been Miriam's idea to put on the gilded robes of state today, to sit on an unpadded chair in a drafty hall and read aloud a variety of prearranged – bloodcurdling and inevitably fatal –

sentences on assorted members of the nobility who had been unlucky enough to back the wrong horse. But it had shown up on her timetable for the week – and Brill, Riordan, and her mother had visited *en masse* to assure her that it was necessary. They'd even hauled in Julius, to provide a facade of Clannish unity. 'You need to sit in on the court and pronounce judgment, without us whispering in your ear all the time,' Brill explained, 'otherwise people will say you're a figurehead.'

'But I *am* a figurehead!' Miriam protested. 'Aren't I? I get the message, this is the council's doing. It's just, I don't approve of the death penalty. And this, executing people just because they did what Egon told them to, out of fear – '

'If they think you're a figurehead, they won't fear you,' Iris explained, with visibly fraying patience. 'And that'll breed trouble. People hereabouts aren't used to enlightened government. You need to stick some heads on spikes, Helge, to make the others keep a low profile. If you won't do it yourself, the council will have to do it for you. And everybody will whisper that it's because you're a weak woman who is just a figurehead.'

'There are a number of earls and barons who we definitely cannot trust,' Riordan added. 'Not to mention a duke or two. They're mortal enemies – they didn't act solely out of fear of Egon's displeasure – and we can't have a duke sitting in judgment over another duke. If you refuse to read their execution order we'll just have to poison them. It gets messy.'

'But if I start out by organizing a massacre, isn't that going to raise the stakes later? I thought we were agreed that reinforcing the rule of law was essential . . .'

'It's not a massacre if they get a fair trial first. So give them a fair trial and fill a gibbet or two with the worst cases, to make an example,' Iris suggested. 'Then offer clemency to the rest, on onerous terms. It worked for dad.'

'Really?' Miriam gave her mother a very old-fashioned look. 'Tell me more . . .'

Which had been the start of a slippery-slope argument. Miriam had fought a rearguard action, but Helge had ultimately conceded the necessity of applying these medieval standards of justice under the circumstances. Which was why she was sitting stiff as a board on a solid wooden throne, listening to advocates argue over a variety of unfortunate nobles, and trying not to fall asleep.

For a man with every reason to believe his fate was to be subjected to *peine forte et dure*, the Duke of Niejwein was in remarkably high spirits. Or perhaps the reddening of his cheeks and the twinkle in his eye were signs of agitation and contempt. The resemblance he bore to the Iraqi dictator Ali Hassan, who'd been on all the news channels a few weeks ago when the Marines finally got their hands on him, was striking. Whatever the case, when he raised his fettered hands and spat something fast at Miriam she had no problem interpreting his intent.

'He says he thanks you for your hospitality but it is most unnecessary,' murmured Gerta.

'Tell him he's welcome, all the same.' Miriam waited while her assistant translated. 'And I view his position with sympathy.'

'Milady!' Gerta sounded confused. 'Are you sure?'

'Yes.' Miriam glared at her. *I am your queen, damn it. Even if I'm fronting for a committee.* 'Do it.'

'Yes, milady.' Gerta addressed the duke; he seemed confused.

'Have another sweet,' Miriam offered the Duke of Niejwein by way of her translator.

It was, Olga had explained, the polite way to do business with noble prisoners: Offer them candied peel and a silk rope to sweeten the walk to the scaffold where, if his crimes were deemed minor, he could expect the relative mercy of a swift hanging. But Niejwein, for some reason, seemed not to have much of an appetite today. And after having sentenced two earls to death earlier in this session – in both cases they had massacred some of her distant relatives with more enthusiasm than was strictly called for, and Riordan had been most insistent on the urgent need to hang them – she could see why. The earls and their retainers were hired thugs; but Niejwein, as head bean counter, had expedited Egon's reign of terror in a far deadlier way.

'We wanted to speak with you in private,' Miriam added, trying to ignore the small crowd of eavesdroppers. 'To discuss your future.'

Niejwein's short bark of laughter turned heads; more than one guard's hand hovered close by a weapon. 'I have no future,' Gerta translated.

'Not necessarily. You have no future without the grace and pardon of the crown, but you should not jump to conclusions about your ultimate fate.'

For the first time the Duke of Niejwein looked frightened. And for the first time Miriam, watching him, began to get an edgy feeling that she understood him.

Niejwein was outwardly average: middle-aged, of middling stature, heavy-faced, and tired-looking. He sat on a stone bench before her, arms and legs clanking with wrought iron whenever he moved, wearing a nobleman's household robes, somewhat the worse for wear, ingrained with the grime of whatever cellar they'd warehoused him in for the run-up to her coronation. He'd been there a week ago, Miriam remembered, staring at her with hollowed eyes, among the other prisoners in the guarded block on the floor of the great hall.

He'd never been much of a warrior or a scholar, according to Brill. She'd asked for – and, for a miracle, been given – Angbard's files on the man, and for another miracle they'd been written in English. (Angbard, it seemed, insisted on Clan secrets being written in English when they were to be kept in the Gruinmarkt, and in Hochsprache if they were to be used in the United States.)

Oskar Niejwein was a second son, elevated into his deceased brother's shoes after a boar hunt gone wrong and a lingering death from sepsis. He'd distinguished himself by maintaining and extending the royal estates and by tax farming with a level of enthusiasm and ruthlessness not spoken of in recent memory. It was no wonder that Egon hadn't sent him into the field as a commander, and no surprise that Riordan's men had seized him with such ease – Niejwein had all the military acumen of a turkey. But that didn't make him useless to an ambitious monarch planning a purge: quite the opposite. As the old saying had it, knights studied tactics, barons studied strategy, and dukes studied logistics. Oskar was an Olympic-grade tax farmer. Which meant . . .

'Your majesty plays with me,' said Niejwein. 'Have you no decency?'

Miriam kept her face frozen as a ripple of shock spread through her audience. That was *not* how a vassal should address a monarch, after all. *How do I deal with this without looking weak . . . ?*

(Iris – showing a coldly cynical streak Miriam had seldom seen any sign of back home – had laid it out for her in the privy council meeting the morning after the coronation performance: 'There are certain rules you've got to obey in public. You can't afford to look like a patsy, dear. If they give you backchat it either means they're scared to death or they think you're weak. The former is acceptable, but if it's the latter, you must be ruthless. The rot spreads rapidly and the longer you leave it the harder it becomes to fix the damage. Put it another way: Better to flog them on the spot for insubordination than let things slide until you have to have them broken on the wheel for rebellion.')

'We are not playing games,' Miriam said evenly. 'We are simply trying to decide whether you can be of use to us. But if you insist on seeing malice in place of mercy, you *will* seal your own fate.' She waited while Gerta translated. The color drained slowly from Niejwein's cheeks as she continued: 'We understand that circumstances placed your neck under our brother-in-law's boot. We are prepared to make allowances – to a degree. A prudent woodsman does not chop down all the trees in his forest when autumn comes; he harvests the old and rotten, and keeps the healthy for another year. Only the rotten need fear the axe in this demesne.'

She'd stiffened up again, sitting on this damnable hard-as-a-board throne. Shifting her thighs, she leaned forward as Gerta worked through to the end of the speech. 'Are you a rotten bough?' she asked, raising an eyebrow. 'Or would you like a chance to demonstrate how sound you are?'

Abruptly, Niejwein was on his knees; she didn't need the blow-by-blow translation to grasp the gist of his entreaties. Her Hochsprache was still stilted and poor, but she got the sense that he'd only gone along with Egon's mad usurpation out of terror while unaware of her majesty's survival, and he was of course loyal to the crown and he'd be her most stalwart vassal forever and a day if, if only, if –

Damn, he could give lessons in crow-eating to the CEO of a Fortune 100 corporation facing a record loss-making quarter. Miriam managed a faint, slightly perplexed smile as Gerta tried to keep up with the storm of entreaties. Right now, with a royal pardon dangling before his eyes, Niejwein would promise her just about anything to keep his head atop his shoulders and his neck unstretched. Which meant that she'd have to take anything he said with a pinch of salt big enough to pickle a sperm whale. Her eyes narrowed as she considered her options. *I can't kill him* now, *even if he deserves it – not without looking capricious.* But in his undignified hurry to ingratiate himself, the duke was impressing her with his unreliability. *Why would he misjudge me like that?* she wondered. Chalk it up to another of the gaps between Gruinmarkt and American mores: The political over here was *very* personal indeed, as everybody kept reminding her.

'Enough.' She raised her right hand and he stopped so suddenly he nearly swallowed his tongue. Miriam took a deep breath. 'Rise, your grace. We will not hang a man for a single honest mistake.' *Two mistakes in a row and I might change my mind . . .* 'We would, however, be delighted if you would stay here as our honored guest, while we restore the kingdom to order. Perhaps your wife and eldest son would care to join us as well. We shall take full responsibility for their safety.' In Hochsprache, there were no separate words to distinguish *safety* from *security.* 'And we would be pleased if you would attend us in session with the council of regents to decide in what manner you can assist us in securing the realm.'

There. She waited for Gerta to translate, watching the succession of expressions flit across Oskar ven Niejwein's face, starting with stark relief, then fading into apprehension as he realized just how onerous his rehabilitation was to be. *You, your wife, and your eldest son are to be hostages under the Clan's control. You will devote precisely as much time and money to cleaning up this mess as the council demands. And if you don't play along, we've got you where we want you.*

Well, it beat the usual punishments for high treason, which included the aforementioned *peine forte et dure*, or just a straightforward impalement-and-burning-at-the-stake, the traditional cutting of the blood eagle being considered too barbaric for this effete and gentle age.

Miriam suppressed a slight shudder as Niejwein bowed deeply, then bowed again, stuttering a mixture of gracious thanks and praise for her mercy, insight, wisdom, deportment, wit, and general brilliance. She merely nodded. 'Take him away,' she said, for the benefit of his jailers, 'to suitable accommodation for a high noble whose loyalty to the crown is understood by all.' Which was to say, a cell with a view.

*

It took three more weeks of ceremonial duties, horse-trading with noble descendants of real (but successful) horse thieves, sitting in court sessions and trying to show no sign of discomfort when her judges pronounced bloodcurdling sentences upon the recalcitrant few – not to mention diplomacy, shouting, and some pigheaded sulking – but at last they agreed to book her into a suite in a boutique hotel near Quincy, with an ob/gyn appointment for the following day. The ob/gyn exam was the excuse; the real purpose was to give her a weekend off, lest she explode.

'I think you can take two, or at most three days off before too many questions asked,' Riordan had said. 'Then it will be getting close to Hedge-Wife's Night and you'll be expected to officiate – '

'Four,' said Brill, just as Iris said: 'Two.' They stopped and glared at each other warily, like cats sizing each other up for a fight.

'People.' Miriam rubbed her forehead tiredly. 'I've had too much of this.' She waved a tired hand, taking in the high ceiling, the ornate tapestries and rugs that did little to soften the wood and plaster of the electricity and aircon-free room, the discreet chamber pots. They were in private, having exiled the servants for the duration of the brief discussion; they'd be back soon enough, like the rats in the walls that kept her awake in the dead of night with their scuttling and fighting. 'I need to decompress, just for a couple of days – '

'We can bring doctors to you, there is no need for you to go to them. If we are secure by winter, then you can retreat to the Winter

225

Palace and spend most of your time in Manhattan,' Iris pointed out.

'That's months away. And anyway, you can hold down some of my appointments right now if I'm not here,' Miriam told her. 'Her grace, the Dowager Duchess Patricia Thorold ven Hjorth, mother of the queen-widow, who is indisposed due to her confinement. Isn't that the formula?'

Iris grunted, displeased. 'Something like that,' she conceded.

'Admit it, *you* want some time off, too, don't you?'

Her mother shook her head. 'Coming back to this life hasn't been easy. If I give up now . . .'

After much haggling they had arranged that an anonymous carriage would leave town in the morning with Miriam inside, disguised as an anonymous lady-in-waiting of noble rank. An hour later, by way of the Clan's highly organized courier service, Miriam – wearing jeans and a cotton blouse, feeling almost naked after weeks in court gowns – checked into a four-star hotel near Quincy, with no servants and no visible guards – and no pomp, ceremony, or stench of open sewers outside the windows.

(That the Clan owned the hotel via a cutout investment company, and that it was carefully monitored for signs of external surveillance, and discreetly guarded by much better than normal security, was another matter entirely. There was a tacit agreement: As long as Miriam agreed not to test the bars on her cage, everyone could pretend they didn't exist.)

It had come as a welcome, but monumental, relief to have *electricity* and *air conditioning* and *toilets* and *jacuzzis* and *daytime television* and other miracles that had not yet reached the Gruinmarkt. Or even New Britain. It was enough to leave her head spinning and half-dizzy with sudden culture shock: Aside from her brief stay in the safe house out west, she'd been living in strange, backward cultures for months on end. *I ought to start with a shower,* she thought, almost salivating with the pornographic luxury of it. *And turn the air con up to max. And I'll wash my hair. And then* . . . the phone rang.

'What the – ' She looked round, then made a dive for the room phone. 'Yes?' she demanded.

'Ms. Beckworth?' (That was the name.) 'This is the front desk, you have a visitor . . .'

Oh hell. Miriam glanced at her watch. *Twenty minutes.* 'Can I talk to them, please?'

'Certainly, ma'am . . .'

'Miriam?'

'Olga?' Miriam sat down hard on the edge of the bed.

'Hi! It's me! I heard you were in town and figured I'd drop in. Mind if I come up?' There was a bright, slightly edgy tone to her voice that set the skin on Miriam's nape crawling.

'Sure, pass me back to reception and I'll tell them. Okay – '

A couple of seconds later the handset was back on its cradle. Miriam stared at it, hard. 'Damn,' she muttered. Her vision blurred: *It's one thing after another.* Her carefully fostered illusion of stolen time wavered: *What's happened now?*

There was a knock on the door. Miriam, far less trustful than she'd been even a couple of months ago, checked the spy hole: A familiar face winked at her.

'Come in.'

'Thank you.' Olga smiled reflexively. Then, as the door closed, her smile slipped. 'Helge, I am so terribly sorry to impose on you, but we need to talk. Urgently.'

'Oh hell.' Miriam sat down again, her own face freezing in a smile that mirrored Olga's in its insincerity. 'I guessed.' *Something's come up in the past three hours, and they want my input, even though I'm just a front for the policy committee.* Plaintively: 'Couldn't it wait?'

'I don't think so.' Olga took a deep breath. 'It's about your mother.'

'She's not ill, is – '

'No, it's not that.' Olga paused.

'Yes?' Miriam's heartbeat settled back to normal. Iris's multiple sclerosis hadn't been far from her mind for years now; she'd thought she'd gotten used to the knowledge that sooner or later she'd have a really bad relapse, but all it took was Olga's ambiguous statement to drag her to the edge of an anxiety attack. 'It's not her health?'

'No.' Olga glanced around the room, her expression wooden. 'I think – there is no easy way to say this.'

'Yes?' Miriam felt her face muscles tense unpleasantly.

'Your uncle. When he was ill. He told me to collect certain documents and, and bring them to you.'

'Documents?' Miriam sat up.

'About the' – Olga licked her lips – 'the fertility clinic.' She stared at Miriam, her expression clear but unreadable.

'You know about it.'

'Know – ' Olga shook her head. 'Only a bit. His grace told me something, after the, the war broke out. It has been closed down, Helge, the program ended and the records destroyed.'

'My uncle,' Miriam said very slowly, 'would *never* destroy that program.'

'Well.' Olga wet her lips again. 'Someone did.'

'Eh.' Miriam shook her head. 'I don't get it.'

'His grace shut down the program, that's true enough. He had the records copied, though – taken out of the clinic, physically removed to a medic's practice office pending transfer to Niejwein. He wanted to keep track of the names, addresses, and details of the children enrolled in the program, but while there was fighting in Niejwein it was too risky to move the records there. And it was too risky to leave everything in the clinic. So . . .'

'You'd better tell me what happened.'

'I went to see Dr. Darling.' Olga shivered for a moment, then walked across the room and sat down in the solitary armchair. 'He's dead. It was a professional hit, almost a month ago. And his office was cleaned out, Helge. The records are missing.'

'But he – ' Miriam stared. 'Where does Mom come into this?'

'I had orders to get those records to *you*.' Olga looked unhappy. 'And your mother took them.'

'She was in the same town at the same time, right?'

'Yes.' The set of Olga's shoulders relaxed. 'On its own that would not be conclusive, but – '

'You're telling me my mother, who spends half her time in a wheelchair these days, assassinated a doctor, stole several thousand sets of medical records, and made a clean getaway? And why? To stop me from getting my hands on the *breeding program's records*?' Her emphasis on the last three words made Olga wince.

'I am uncertain as to her motive. But – your mother knew of the program, no? And you must needs be aware of her views on the balance of powers within our circle of families, yes?'

Miriam sighed. '*Of course* I know what she thinks of – of all that stuff. But that breeding program was just plain odious. I know why they did it, I mean – we're dangerously short on world-walkers, and if we can use a fertility clinic as a cover to spread the recessive trait around, then pay some of the first-generation women to act as donors – but I tend to agree with Mom that it's destabilizing as hell. And ethically more than questionable, too. But why would she destroy the records or kill Darling? Was there something else we don't know about?'

'I don't know.' Olga looked troubled.

'Then why don't you ask her?' Miriam crossed her arms.

'Because.' Olga bit her lip. 'She killed Dr. Darling,' she said, conversationally. 'She had her woman Mhara do it, in direct contravention of Security protocols. The other thing, Helge, that you did not let me get to, is that there was another witness present.'

'Really?' Miriam's shoulders tensed.

'Dr. ven Hjalmar,' said Olga.

'I want him dead.' Miriam's voice was flat.

'We need to find out why she killed Dr. Darling first, don't we?'

'But – ' Miriam changed tack. 'Brill thought ven Hjalmar was dead,' she said. 'In fact, she told me so.'

'Hmm. There was some confusion after the palace – perhaps she was not in the loop?' Olga leaned back and met Miriam's eyes. 'I am telling you this because Mhara's first loyalty is to Security; she was most upset when she learned her actions were unauthorized. What is your mother doing, Helge? How many games is she playing?'

'I . . . don't . . .' Miriam fell silent. 'Dr. ven Hjalmar,' she said faintly. 'Is she cooperating with him?'

Olga stared at her for a long time.

*

Summer in the suburbs. The smell of honeysuckle and the creaking of cicadas hung heavy in the backyard of the small house on a residential street in Ann Arbor; there was little traffic outside, the neighbors either already in bed or away from their homes, dining out or working late. But inside the house, behind lowered blinds, the lights were on and the occupants were working. Not that a casual interloper would have recognized their activities as such.

Huw sat in front of a laptop in the day room at the back of the house, staring at the Mathematica workbook running in a window as it stepped through variations on a set. Wearing goggles and an oxygen mask, with a blood pressure cuff on his upper arm and a Glock on his belt, he squinted intently as the program flashed up a series of topological deformations of a familiar knot.

On his left wrist, he wore an electronic engineer's grounding strap, which he had attached to a grounding spike in the backyard by a length of wire – and tested carefully. Two camcorders on tripods monitored his expression and the screen of the laptop. The medical telemetry gear was on order, but hadn't arrived yet; it would have to wait for the next run. There were other watchers, too, equipped as best as he'd been able to manage in the time available.

'Ouch.' Huw tapped the space bar on the keyboard, pausing the run. 'Sequence number 144. I definitely felt something there.' He glanced round. 'Elena? You awake back there?'

'This thing stinks.' Her voice buzzed slightly. 'And I give you seven more minutes until changeover time, my lord. Would you mind hurrying up and getting it over with?'

Huw stretched, rotating his shoulder blades. 'Okay,' he agreed. 'Resuming with sequence number 145 in three, two, one' – he tapped the space bar again – 'ouch! Ow, shit!' – and again. Then he reached down and hit the start button on the blood pressure monitor. 'That was a definite . . . something. Ow, my head.'

The machine buzzed as the cuff inflated. Thirty seconds passed, then it began to tick and hiss, venting compressed air. Finally it deflated with a sigh. 'Shit. One fifty-two over ninety-five. Right, that's it for this run. I got a *definite* contact.'

Huw closed the workbook, then removed his goggles and

unclipped the oxygen mask. 'Ow.' He rubbed at his cheeks and the bridge of his nose, where the rubber had chafed. 'How are you coping?'

'Help me out of this thing?' Elena asked plaintively.

Huw stood up, detached the grounding strap, and stretched again. 'Okay, let's see . . .' Elena was fumbling with the gas regulator under her visor. 'No, let me sort that out.' A moment later he had the visor unclipped and her helmet swinging open.

'That's better!' She took a deep breath and began to unfasten her gloves as he attacked the straps holding her backpack in place. 'Are you sure the real thing will be lighter?'

'No,' Huw admitted. 'And that's if we can get our hands on one in the first place. I think we're going to end up having one custom made.' Pressurized suits with self-contained air circulation weren't exactly an off-the-shelf item, and some of the suppliers he'd approached had responded with alarming questions; the line between certain civilian and military uses was rather thin, it seemed. 'Here, you should be able to get your helmet off now.'

'Oh, that's nice.' Elena began to work at the high-altitude suit's catches. It had been a random find in a somewhat peculiar store, and had taken almost a week to restore to working order; so far it was the only one they had, which had put a serious cramp on experimentation until Huw had bitten the bullet and decided to work with an oxygen bottle and goggles as minimal safety precautions. 'How do you feel?'

'Head's splitting,' Huw admitted. 'Hmm. Let me just check again.' He ran the blood pressure monitor again. It was roughly the same – alarmingly high for a fit twenty-something – but he was standing up and moving, rather than slouched over a computer: *Good.* 'I think I'm coming down.'

'It was definitely a tingle? Stronger than the last?'

'I think,' Huw paused for thought, 'I'm going to skip forward a couple of notches, see how far this sequence runs. I got two weak ones, then this' – he winced – 'like tuning in an old radio.'

'A radio? A radio tuned to new worlds?'

'Maybe.' He detached the blood pressure cuff and walked over to the archway leading to the kitchen. 'I'm more interested in knowing what class of knot we're dealing with.'

'What kind of . . . ? But it's a knot! How many kinds *are* there?'

'I don't know.' Huw glanced at the coffee machine, then the wine bottle sitting next to it. 'Huh. Where's – ' The door chime pinged for attention.

'I'll get it.' Elena was out of the boots and gloves; she'd managed to unzip the pressure suit as far as the crotch, revealing the rumpled tee shirt and jeans she was wearing inside it. Huw shook his head. 'That'd better not be the Jehovah's Witnesses; they're going to think we've got a *really* weird family life.'

'You say that like it's a *bad* thing – oh hello there!' Her voice rose to a happy chirp as Huw looked round. 'Come in, be you welcome! He's in the kitchen, over there, *Huw* – '

Making a snap decision, Huw palmed the corkscrew and picked up the bottle. Turning, he paused in the doorway. 'Sigfrid? What are *you* doing here?'

Sigfrid – lanky, tall, with a mustache that resembled a corpulent caterpillar asleep on his upper lip – unslung his shoulder bag and grinned. 'Eh, his lordship the major sent me. Said you needed spare hands for some kind of project?'

'Well.' Huw raised the bottle. 'It's about time. Do you know if he was sending anyone else?'

'No.' Sigfrid looked uncertain. 'At least, he didn't tell *me*.'

'Right.' He turned to Elena: 'Can you phone Yul? Tell him to pick up food for four this time.' Back to Sigfrid. 'So what have you been doing in the meantime?'

'Oh, you know.' Sigfrid shrugged his jacket back from his shoulders and let it slide to the floor. 'I was with his lordship of Markford's household when the pretender went on his rampage? So I had a busy couple of weeks. First a siege, then an evacuation through the backwoods, then lots of running around, hurry up and wait, until they stuck me in Castle Hjorth with the guards detachment.'

'But you're here now.' Huw nodded to himself. 'Want to fetch some glasses?' Elena was on her mobile phone. 'Top cupboard, to the left of the kitchen sink.' Sig was never the scholarly sort, but he was bright enough to learn. 'Let me fill you in on what we're trying to achieve here.'

'Surely. The major said something about trying to *find other worlds*. Does that mean . . . ?'

Huw nodded. 'Yes. And tomorrow we're going to try to open up another one.' He pulled the cork free with a pop. 'We live in interesting times!'

*

On their first day in the enemy capital, the reconnaissance team checked into their hotel and commenced operations. Disguised as a family of Dutch tourists, Sir Gunnar ven Hjorth-Hjalmar, accompanied by his married younger cousin Beatrice and her infant son (the elder was back at the family estate, in the care of his nurse), purchased day passes on the double-decker tourist busses that rumbled incessantly through the boulevards and avenues of the city. Sitting on the top deck with a camcorder glued to his right eye, his 'wife' gaping in bucolic awe at the colonnaded classical buildings and low office blocks to either side, Gunnar found it amusing to contemplate the police and security checkpoints that swarmed defensively around the federal buildings. *They call* this *security?* he asked himself ironically. *Hmm. Target-rich environment, maybe.*

'What's *that*?' asked Beatrice, pointing at the Washington Monument. She spoke Hochsprache, the better to aid the disguise; a strawberry blonde with a two-year-old on her hip wasn't anybody's idea of an Al-Qaeda terrorist. She hadn't spent much time over in the Anglischprache world, beyond the minimum required for the corvée, and her emulation of an awestruck tourist was entirely genuine – because Niejwein, the largest city with which she was familiar, was less than a tenth the size of downtown Washington, D.C.

'It is a memorial to their founding king-emperor, the duke who led their armies during their rebellion against the king across the water.' Gunnar sniffed. 'He refused to take the throne, but their aristocrats honor him to this day.'

'How very stupid of him,' Beatrice agreed. 'Was he mad?'

'I don't know.' Gunnar zoomed in on the monument, then panned

233

slowly sideways to take in the neoclassical palaces of bureaucracy to either side of the wide plaza and the shallow pool. Eight and nine stories high, none of them exceeded the height of the spire. *Interesting*, he noted. 'Mark a waypoint, please.'

Beatrice fumbled obediently in her handbag, then produced a tissue and wiped little Anders's nose. Anders bubbled sleepily as his mother wadded up the tissue with mild distaste and stuffed it back in her bag, along with the GPS machine. 'He will need cleaning soon,' she told Gunnar.

'It cannot be helped. A single man, making notes and filming, would attract attention.'

'Of course, cousin. But we will need to stop the carriage to do so.'

Gunnar panned back across the Mall, slowly scanning a frontage of museum buildings. 'There are public toilets in all the museums and public buildings here, well-kept and as luxurious as any palace back home.'

'Good.' She glanced behind her. 'These buildings. The *people* own them?'

'Only indirectly. Just as they rebelled against their king and replaced him with none, so they tried to abolish their aristocracy. It grew back, of course, but not in the same image – there is a ruling class here, but its members are not named count this or lord that.'

'How very confusing! How is one to recognize a superior . . . ?'

'You don't.' Gunnar ignored her evident discomfort. 'It's *very* confusing at first. But eventually you learn to spot the signs. Their wealth, for one thing. And the way the laws that leash the ordinary people slip past them. They don't carry arms; other people carry arms for them, it's a sign of how rich and powerful this empire has become.' *Too many words*, he thought. The words wouldn't stop coming; relief at being here, at not worrying about being murdered by the bitch-queen back home, had loosened his tongue.

Beatrice shifted Anders across her lap. 'It's huge,' she said, her voice wavering slightly.

'Of course. This city, Washington, D.C., has nearly two-thirds the population of the entire Gruinmarkt. And it rules over everything from the outer kingdom in our west through the badlands and the mountains to the Sudtmarkt and the Nordmarkt – well, part of the Nordtmarkt belongs to these Americans' northern neighbor, but that kingdom is also vast, by our lights. But it is still a kingdom and it is still run by a king-emperor of sorts, albeit one of their elite who is formally proclaimed by his peers to rule for four or eight years. And we know how to talk to power.'

'Huh. My tutor told me their king-emperor is elected, that the people choose him. Is this not so?'

'It looks like that, yes, but it's not so simple. The little people are presented with two contenders, but the ruling elite would never tolerate the candidacy of an outsider. Sometimes a contender tries to *look* like an outsider, but it's purely a rabble-rousing pretense. This current king-emperor doesn't even go that far; his father was king-emperor before last.'

'Huh. Again, how stupid! Sir Gunnar, I think we should move now, before Anders disgraces himself. If it pleases you?'

Gunnar lowered the camcorder and switched it to standby. The tour guide was still droning on in a nasal voice, mangled by the loud-speakers behind the windshield at the front of the open upper deck of the bus. 'Yes, let us do so.' The bus swayed as it moved forward then turned in towards the curb. 'Follow me.'

The sky was clear and blue, the sun beating down on the sidewalk as Beatrice stepped off the bus with Anders, waiting while Gunnar – determinedly staying in character – collected the pushchair. As he unfolded it, Anders sent up a sleepy moan: Beatrice bounced him, shushing. 'Please let us get him indoors.'

'In a moment.' Gunnar glanced round. The bus had stopped close by a huge concrete and stone facade – back home, it would have been the stronghold of a noble family, but here it was most likely a museum of some sort. 'Ah yes. We'll try there.' *Holocaust Memorial Museum?* Gunnar had a vague recollection that it might be connected with some historic massacre in these Anglischprache folks' history, but that didn't matter to him; it was a museum, so obviously it would have toilets and baby-changing facilities. 'Record a waypoint. And another one in the baby-changing room, if the machine functions adequately indoors.'

The museum had security guards and one of those annoying contraptions that let them peer into visitors' possessions next to a metal detecting arch. Gunnar was sufficiently familiar with such precautions to have left his weapons back at the hotel, but they still irritated him, reminding him that he was not free to comport himself as a gentleman in this place. If the business of governance was to maintain a monopoly on lethal force, as his baron had once asserted, then the Anglischprache clearly understood this message. Still, discreet signs pointed to the toilets beyond the obstruction, and the little one's needs must be attended to.

Gunnar cooled his heels in the atrium for a few minutes while his sister-in-law dealt with the child. It was a peculiar museum, he decided, very strange – more like a mausoleum. This holocaust was clearly a most unsavory affair, but why dwell on it? It was confusing: It didn't even seem to have happened to the Anglischprache themselves, but to some other people. So why bother commemorating it with a museum? *But it's in the right place*, he reminded himself. *And it'll be easier to get onto the roof than any of the government offices. If it's high enough . . .*

Beatrice finally emerged from the rest room, carrying a quieter Anders. Gunnar smiled, trying to look relieved. 'I think I would like to go upstairs here,' he told her quietly. 'Let's go find the elevator and ride it to the top. Did you get a waypoint?'

'I'm sorry, cousin; the machine balked. I think the walls are too thick.'

'Then you will try again on the highest floor. And I shall look for access doors to the roof. If there's a window, I will film landmarks through it, to estimate the elevation.'

'You have plans for this place?'

'Oh yes, indeed.' Gunnar nodded. 'We're well into Sudtmarkt territory here, but for what I think we shall be doing, that should be no obstacle.'

'You want to doppelgänger a *museum*?'

'It's a possibility – I want to look at some shops, too. As long as the land is accessible, it will fit my needs. And I don't recall any cities in the middle of swamps down there. The Sudtmarkt can be bullied, bought, or bribed, and along with elevation that's all that matters.'

*

A month had passed since the disastrous mission into Niejwein; Mike had been back in the office for two weeks, alternating between inter-departmental meetings and frustrating sessions in room 4117 when he got an e-mail from the colonel: 'Tomorrow we're taking a day trip to the Otis Air National Guard Base on Cape Cod. I've got a meeting there, and there are some folks I want to introduce you to.'

The aircraft hangar was dim and cavernous after the bright day-light outside. Mike blinked, slightly dazzled, at the thing squatting on the stained concrete in front of him. It seemed misshapen and mal-formed, like a fairy-tale dragon sleeping in its cave. Sure enough it was green and scaly and spiky – a huge refueling probe jutting lance-like from the chin beneath its cockpit windows, and infrared sensors bulging like enormous warts from the deformed forehead beneath the hunched shoulders of its engine cowls.

Dragons, however, did not traditionally have high-visibility warning tags dangling from their rotor blade tips, or an array of maintenance trolleys and tractors parked around them. And dragons most especially didn't have a bunch of Air Force officers chattering next to the huge external fuel tank slung from their port winglet.

Mike had hobbled halfway to the chopper before anyone noticed him. An arm waved: 'Mike. Over here, I want you to meet these folks.' He picked up his pace as much as he dared. 'Gentlemen, this is Mike Fleming. Mike is a special agent on assignment to our organiza-tion from DEA. His specialty is getting under enemy skin. He's our HUMINT guy, in other words, and he picked up that broken leg in the same line of work as you guys – only on foot. Mike, this is Lieutenant John Goddard, and Captain Simon MacDonald. They're in charge of flight operations for this little test project – staff and execution both, they sit up front in the cockpit.' More faces and more introductions followed, warrant officer this and tech specialist that, the guys in charge of making the big helicopter work. Mike tried to commit them all to memory, then gave up. The half dozen guys and one or two women in fatigues standing around here were the crew chiefs and flight crew – it took a lot of people to keep a Pave Low helicopter flying.

'Pleased to meet you.' Mike shook hands all round. He caught Eric's eye. 'I'm impressed.' Which statement, when fully unpacked, meant *How the* hell *have you been keeping this under wraps?* The implications weren't exactly subtle: *So this is Dr. James's breakthrough. What happens next?*

'Good,' said Smith, nodding. Quietly: 'I told them you're not up to serious exertion, they'll make allowances. Just try to take it all in.' He paused for a moment. 'Simon, why don't you give Mike here the dog and pony show. I'll go over the load-out requirements with John and Susan in the meantime. When Mike's up to speed, we can meet up in the office, uh, that's room R-127, and share notes.'

'Yes, I'll do that, sir.' MacDonald turned to Mike and waved a hand at a door some way back along the flank of the green monster. 'Ever seen one of these before?' he asked breezily.

'Don't think so. On the news, maybe?' Mike followed the captain across the stained concrete floor towards the door, going as fast as he could with his cast. The chopper was the size of a small airliner. Blades big enough to bridge a freeway curved overhead in the dimness. The fuel tanks under the stubby wings proved, on closer acquaintance, to be nearly as tall as he was, and as long as a pickup truck. 'I don't know much about helicopters,' he admitted.

'Okay, we'll fix that.' MacDonald flashed a smile. 'This is a modified MH-53, descended from the Jolly Green Giant. Back about twenty years ago it was our biggest cargo helicopter. This one's been rebuilt as an MH-53J, part of the Pave Low III program. It's still a transport chopper, but it's been tailored for one particular job – low-level, long-range undetected penetration of enemy airspace, at night or in bad weather, in support of special forces. So we've got a load of extra toys on this ship that you don't normally see all in one place.'

The side door was open. MacDonald pulled himself up and stood, then reached down to help Mike into the cavernous belly of the beast. 'This is a General Electric GAU-2/A, what the army call an M134 minigun. We've got three of them, one in each side door and one on the ramp at the back.' He walked forward, towards the open cockpit door. 'Night, bad weather, and enemy territory. That's a crappy combination and it means flying low in crappy visibility conditions. So we've got terrain-following radar, infrared night vision gear, GPS, inertial navigation, an IDAS/MATT terminal for tactical datalink – ' He stopped. 'Which isn't going to be much use where we're going, I guess. Neither is the GPS or the missile warning transponders or a whole load of stuff. So I'll not go over that, right? What you need to know is, it's a big chopper that can fly low and fast, at night, while carrying three infantry squads or two squads and a dozen prisoners or six stretcher cases. We can put them down fast, night or day, and provide covering suppressive fire against light forces. Or we can carry an outside load the size of a Humvee. So. Have you got any questions?' He seemed amused.

'Yeah.' Mike glanced around. 'You've crossed over before, as I understand it. How'd it go?'

MacDonald's face clouded. 'It went okay.' He gestured at a boxy framework aft of one of the flight engineer's positions. 'I'd studied all the backgrounders – but still, it wasn't like anything I'd expected.' He shook his head. 'One thing to bear in mind is that it would be a really bad idea to do that kind of transition too close to the ground. The air pressure, wind direction, weather – it can all vary. You could be in a world of hurt if you go from wet weather and low pressure to a sudden heat wave without enough airspace under your belly.' He registered Mike's expression. 'You get less lift in high temperatures,' he explained. 'Affects rotary-winged ships as well as fixed-wing, and we tend to fly low and heavy. With all the graceful flight characteristics of a grand piano, if we lose engine power or exceed our load limit.' He sat down in the pilot's chair. 'Go on, take a seat, she won't bite as long as you keep your hands to yourself.'

'I don't think I'd fit. Not 'til I get this thing off my leg.' Mike leaned across the back of the copilot's seat, staring at the controls. 'Last time I saw this many screens was when I had to arrest a share trader – it's like a flying dealer desk!'

'Yeah, that's about right. Of course, if any of it goes wrong it adds a whole new meaning to the phrase, "my computer crashed."'

MacDonald grinned. 'Look, out there. And down. Get a feel for the visibility. What do you think our main problem is going to be?'

'What do I – oh.' Mike frowned. 'Okay, there's no GPS where we're going. The Clan don't have heavy weapons, at least nothing heavier than machine guns – as far as we know. Unless they've somehow bought some missiles, and they're pretty much limited to whatever they can carry by hand from one side to the other. So – ' He glanced up at the rotor blade arching overhead and followed it out into the middle distance. 'Hmm. Where we're going there are a lot of trees. And the places we want to get inside of are walled. Is that going to be a problem?'

'You ever seen *Black Hawk Down*?' It was a rhetorical question. 'We've got ways of dealing with trees. What we really don't like – our second worst nightmare – is buildings with armed hostiles overlooking the LZ. Just don't go there. The ground pounders can secure the target, *then* we can land and pick them up. The alternative is to risk us taking one on the rotor head, in which case we all get to walk home.'

'What's your worst nightmare?'

'MANPADs,' he said bluntly. 'Man-portable air defense missiles, that is. Not your basic SAM-7, which is fundamentally obsolete, but late-model Stingers or an SA-16 Igla – that's Russian-made and as deadly as a Stinger – can really ruin your day. From what I've been reading, your bad guys could carry them across, they only weigh about fifty pounds. We've got countermeasures and flare dispensers, of course, but if they've bothered to get hold of a bunch of MANPADs and learn how to use them properly, we could be in a world of hurt.'

Mike nodded. 'That wouldn't be good.'

'Well.' MacDonald slapped the top of the instrument console affectionately. 'It's not as bad as it sounds. Because they won't be expecting anyone to come calling by chopper. It's never happened to them before, right? So they've got no reason to expect it now. Plus, we have God *and* firepower on our side. As long as the ARMBAND supply holds up we can ship over spec-ops teams and their logistics until the cows come home. You do not want to get between a Delta Forces specialist and his ticket home, if you follow my drift, it doesn't improve your life expectancy. So it's all down to the guys with the black boxes.'

'I don't know anything about that side of things.' Mike shrugged. 'For that, you need to talk to the colonel. But I would guess that we've got a bunch of GPS coordinates you can feed into your magic steering box of tricks; sites the Clan used as safe houses in this world, so they're almost certainly collocated with their installations in the other place. We don't know what they look like over there, but that's beside the point if we know where to find them.'

'Well, it also helps to know what we're meant to do when we get there. Although that oughta be obvious – otherwise they'd have sent someone else. So what *do* you know that you can tell me?'

'I don't. Know, that is. What you're cleared for, for example.' Mike paused. 'I'm just the monkey – Colonel Smith, he's the organ-grinder. You've been over to the other world, you've got the basics, right? This is new to me. Until this morning, I hadn't had more than a hint that you guys even existed.'

'There are too many Chinese walls in this business. Not our fault.'

'Yeah, well, you know this didn't come out of nowhere, did it?' Mike decided to take a calculated risk. 'The folks who live over there found us first. And they're not friendly.'

'No shit? I'd never have guessed.'

'Well, that's the punch line. Because the target where they live – it's another version of North America, only wild and not particularly civilized. I've been over there on foot and, hell, we're not getting very far if we get stuck down there. So I would *guess* that's where you guys come in. But I don't know for sure because nobody's told me' – he shrugged – 'but I think we're about to find out. Maybe we should go find that office now. Find out what the official line is.'

PARTY TO CONSPIRACY

Throwing a party and inviting all your friends and family was not, Miriam reminded herself ruefully, a skill that she'd made much use of over the past few years – especially on the scale that was called for now.

For one thing, she had status; as a member of the council of regents that had assembled itself from the wreckage of the Clan Council's progressive faction, and as a countess in her own right, she wasn't allowed to do things by half. A low-key get-together in the living room with finger food and quiet music and a bring-your-own-bottle policy was right out, apparently. If a countess – much less a queen-widow – threw a party, arrangements must be made for feeding and irrigating not only the guests, but: their coachmen, arms-men, and servants; their horses; their hangers-on, courtiers, cousins, and children in the process of being introduced to polite society; her *own* arms-men and servants; and the additional kitchen and carrying staff who it would be necessary to beg, borrow, or kidnap in order to feed all of the above. Just the quantity of wine that must be brought in beggared the imagination.

'Old King Harald, he had a reputation for bankrupting any lord who made trouble for him. He used to invite himself and his court to stay for a couple of weeks, paying a house call – with six hundred mouths to feed.' Brill grinned at Miriam over the clipboard she was going through. 'Two thousand three hundred bottles of spiced wine and eighty casks of small beer is *nothing* for a weekend retreat, my lady.'

'Oh god. Am I going to bankrupt myself if I make a habit of this?'

'Potentially, yes.' Brill lowered her clipboard. 'You must know, a third of the royal budget was spent on food and drink for the court. I know this sounds insane to you, but this is the reality of our economy

– peasants produce little surplus, knowing that it can be taken from them in taxes. However.' She made a note on her checklist: 'Four oxen, two hundred turkey-fowl, twelve pigs, a quarter-ton of fresh-caught cod, six barrels of salted butter, two tons of wheat . . . yes, you can afford this from your household funds. Monthly, even. It increases your outgoings tenfold, but only for three days. And once you have demonstrated your hospitality, there is no reason to hold such entertainments merely for your courtiers: Say the word and those you wish to see will visit to pay their respects. Next week's festivity demonstrates your wealth and power and establishes you on the social circuit.'

'You make that sound as if it's something I'm going to have to repeat.'

'My lady.' Brilliana's tone was patient rather than patronizing: 'Nothing you do now can divert you from your destiny to become a shining star in the social firmament – well, nothing short of barking at the moon – but how seriously the other stars of the stratum take you depends on how you comport yourself in this affair. Many of your peers are shallow, vapid, prone to superficial gossip, and extremely malicious. Yet you – or I – cannot exist without their sanction. Your status as queen-widow depends on their consent and their consent is contingent on you being the queen-widow they expect – in public.'

'Huh. By throwing a huge party I give them lots of stuff to gossip about, though.' Miriam frowned. 'But if I *don't* throw a huge party they'll gossip anyway, with even less substance and possibly more malice because I haven't stuffed their stomachs with good food. I can't win, can I?'

Brill nodded. 'My humble advice is to treat it as a matter of gravest business, and to attend to every plaint and whine that your supplicants – and you will have many – bring to your attention. Then ignore them, as is your wish, but at least let them talk at you.'

'I'm not going to ignore them.' Miriam picked moodily at a loose thread on the left sleeve of her day-dress. 'Damn it. You remember my Dictaphone? I need it, or one like it. Make it one that runs on micro-cassettes, and make sure there's a spare set of batteries and spare tapes for, oh, let's go mad and say twenty-four hours. Add a pair of

243

desktop recorders with on/off pedals to the shopping list, and another laptop, and some kind of printer. We've got the generator, right? Let's use it. Can you find me a couple of people who know how to use a keyboard and speak both English and Hochsprache who we can trust? I need an office staff for this job . . .'

Brill closed her mouth with a snap. 'Uh. An office?'

'Yeah. You've framed it for me: This is a political do, isn't it? And I've got to be a politician. So I'm going to listen to everybody, and because I can't memorize it all, I'm going to record what they say and respond later, off-line. But somebody's got to type up all those petitions and turn them into stuff I can deal with.'

'You need secretaries.' Brill picked up her clipboard, flipped over a page, and began making notes. 'Trustworthy – I know. Second sons or daughters of allies? To assist the queen-widow's household? I believe . . . yes, I can do that. Anything else?'

'Yes. I want a photographer.'

'A photographer.' Brill frowned. 'That is very unusual. May I ask why?'

'Yes, well. If anyone makes trouble, tell the truth: I need to learn to recognize people, and because I'm new around here and don't want to give offense by *not* recognizing people the second time I see them, I want photographs with names attached. But otherwise – hmm. It's a party. People are on display, right? So have a photo printer to hand, and offer to take portraits. Do you think that would work?'

'We don't have a photo printer . . .' Brill trailed off. She blinked, surprised. 'You offer portraits, as a cover while you compile mug shots?'

'Old political campaign trick, kid, Mom told me about it. She did some campaigning back in the eighties when she was married to – ' Miriam stopped, her throat closing involuntarily. *Dad*, she thought, a black sense of despair suffocating her for a moment. 'Shit.'

Brill stared at her. 'Helge?'

Miriam shook her head.

'Hara!' Brill snapped her fingers. 'A cup of sack for my lady, at once.' The maidservant, who had been hiding in some dark recess, darted away with a duck of her head that might have been a bow. 'Helge?' Brill repeated gently.

'A memory.' Miriam stared at the backs of her hands. Smooth skin, unpainted nails – nail polish was an alien innovation here – and she remembered holding her father's hands, years ago; it seemed like an eternity ago. A happier, more innocent lifetime that belonged to someone else. 'You know how it is. You're thinking about something completely different and then – bang.'

'Your father.' Brill cleared her throat. 'You do not speak of Lord Alfredo, do you.'

Miriam sighed. 'The man is dead, and besides, it was in another country a long time ago.' She glanced at Brill. 'He died nearly ten years ago. He was a good man.' She tried to swallow. 'It seems so long ago. I'm being silly . . . !'

'No you're not.' Brill laid her clipboard down as the door opened. It was the maid, bearing a tray with a bottle and two cups on it. 'You've been driving yourself hard today, my lady; a cup and a pause to refresh your nerves will not delay you any more than overtiring yourself would do.'

'A cup.' Miriam focused on the tray as Hara placed it on the table and retreated, bowing. Over the weeks she'd been working on her ability to ignore the omnipresent servants; or rather, to avoid embarrassing anyone – herself or them – by recognizing them as social individuals. Her long habit of politeness vied with newly learned behavior as she held herself back from thanking the woman (which would only push both of them into a possibly disastrous social minuet of interaction, that might result in the maid losing her job or being flogged for insolence if she misspoke). 'Pour one for yourself, Brill. I'm – you're right. Anyway, what am I meant to be doing next?'

Brilliana produced a pocket watch from her sleeve. 'Hmm. You were due for a fitting half an hour ago, but that doesn't matter. The seamstresses already have all the toiles they need, they can embroider while they wait. Hmm again. There is the menu to consider, and your household's clothing, and the fireworks, and small gifts and largesse, but' – her gaze flickered to Miriam's face – 'we can do that tomorrow. Milady? Right now, you're going to take a break. Please?'

*

Ding-dong.

The doorbell chime died away. The short dark-haired woman swore quietly and put down the vegetable knife she'd been using on a handful of onions. 'What now?' she asked herself rhetorically, wiping her hands on a towel as she walked towards the front door. Last week it had been the Jehovah's Witnesses, the week before . . . *Well, at least it won't be* them. They *never ring*. They just appeared in her living room, disturbingly self-possessed and always armed.

'Yes?' she said, opening the door.

'Hi, Paulie,' said Brilliana, smiling hesitantly.

Paulette gaped for a moment. 'You'd better come in.' She took in Brill's companion: 'You, too?'

'Thank you,' said Olga, as they retreated into the front hall. She closed the door carefully. 'Miriam sent us.'

'Looks nice,' Brill added offhand as she looked around. 'That wallpaper, is it new?'

'I put it up six months ago!' Paulette stared at her in exasperation and muted fear. At her last visit, Brill had hinted darkly about the extremes the Clan would go to in order to preserve their secrecy. 'How is she? Did you find her?'

'Yes.' Brilliana nodded. 'Luckily I found her before things went too badly awry. And there is gold at the end of this tunnel.'

'Politics! Who needs it?' Olga chirped brightly, momentarily slipping into her airhead role. 'One needs must be patient while these things work themselves out. But in any case, we thought we ought to visit. It's well past time we had a talk.'

'Um.' Paulette backed towards the kitchen. 'Sure. How would you like to do it over an iced tea?'

'I'd like that just fine.'

Ten minutes later, with mugs in hand, they were seated around the coffee table in the lounge. 'Have you had any official visits?' asked

Brill. 'Men in black, that sort of thing?' She said it lightly, as if half-joking, but Paulette knew how serious it was.

'No, nothing I've noticed. No visits, no strange mini-vans, none of that sort of thing.'

'Fine.' Brill sounded reassured. Olga, however, looked thoughtful.

'Don't you want to check the phone lines?' she asked, unable to help herself.

'Already done.' Brill's smile was unsettling. 'I left a device behind on my last visit. It would have told me if there was any sign of tampering.'

'We hope,' Olga added.

'Oh.' Paulette took a mouthful of her drink to stop herself saying anything she might regret later. 'Well that's all right then.' Brill showed no sign of noticing any irony. 'So you came to have a little chat. After months of nothing at all.' She squinted at Brill. 'And you brought Olga. How nice.' Sarcasm was risky, but Paulette was a realist: If the news was really bad, these two wouldn't have invited themselves in for a social. There had to be a *value proposition* in play here, an offer too good to refuse. But at least they were here to make an offer, not to simply shoot her out of hand. The Clan were comparatively civilized, for a bunch of barely postmedieval gangsters.

'She sent us,' said Olga. 'She told us to tell you, you were right. But that is not why we are here. It appears the US government has noticed us.'

'Oh.' Paulette put her glass down. 'Shit.'

There was a moment's heartfelt silence.

'Just *how much* have the feds noticed you guys?' Paulette asked carefully, meaning: *Am I likely to get any of that attention?*

'Thoroughly.' Olga looked tired for a moment. 'Brill?'

'There's an entire new federal agency devoted just to us.' Brill took a mouthful of tea, frowned. 'Super-black, off the books, siphoning money off the war appropriations and the NSA and the CIA, as far as we can tell. They've captured couriers and used them as mules to get into our world. Most recently they' – she swallowed – 'used a backpack nuke to send us a message.'

'Oh Jesus.' There didn't seem to be anything else to say to that. 'That's not policing, that's *war*.'

'Exactly,' Brilliana agreed.

'Which leaves us with problems.' Olga picked up the thread. 'We can no longer do business over here as usual' – *business* being the somewhat less legal side of the import–export trade – 'and further-more, this mess coincided with a political upset back home. Everything's up in the air.'

'And you're off the reservation,' Paulette said drily.

'Yes, there is that.' Olga glanced sidelong at Brill. 'There's no telling how long it'll last.' Brill shook her head slightly. 'But anyway . . . we came to apologize for dragging you into this mess.'

'Isn't it a bit late for that?'

'Not necessarily. We can cut you loose. You were never directly involved in our principal business operations. There's no record of you outside of a few handwritten ledgers in Niejwein, and the office Hel–Miriam bought, and there's no sign that the feds are aware of what she was up to on her own behalf. I think if we cover your tracks we can be confident that they won't stumble across you.' She halted awkwardly for a moment. 'The flip side is, if they identify you as a person of interest, we won't be able to do anything to protect you. We won't even know.'

'Ah.' Paulette contemplated screaming, but it didn't seem like it would do any good. 'What *could* you do to help?'

'Well, that depends.' Olga put her hands between her knees, clearly uneasy. 'Whatever happens next, the Clan won't be acting as, as an extradimensional drugs cartel anymore. The feds consider us to be a hostile government: Should we not act upon our status? Fur-thermore, the changes among the all-highest mean that they are not entirely wrong. Anyway, I didn't come here merely to say we are cutting you loose.'

Here it comes. 'What have you got in mind?' Paulette asked wearily. 'And is it going to just evaporate under me again, three months down the line . . . ?'

'That wasn't Miriam's doing.' Olga shook her head. 'You should not underestimate the power of the enemies she made. She spent months under house arrest. Later, you can ask her yourself if you are so inclined. But this is different.'

'In what way is it different?' *Why am I doing this?* Paulette asked herself. *Am I trying to get myself sucked in again?* It was true, the money had been good – and Miriam was a friend, and it beat the ordinary daily grind she'd had before, and the tedious admin job she'd had to take up since; but the downside, attracting the attention of the government, and not in a good way, was almost enough to make her short-circuit the process and say 'no' immediately. Only residual curiosity was keeping her going.

'Miriam has both a secure position and a plan,' said Olga. 'She is in a position where, if she plays her hand correctly, she can set policy for the whole Clan. I am not entirely clear on her design, but she said I should tell you that unlike the old trade, this one is both legal and ethically sound. She said it would also need a lot of organizing at this end, materials and books and journals and specialist expertise to buy in . . . and to be firewalled completely from the Clan's historic operations. Is that of interest to you?'

Paulette nodded. She'd visited New Britain once at Miriam's behest, found it a strange and disorienting experience, like a trip to another century. 'Well, it's a plan. But what makes this time different?'

Olga glanced at Brill, as if for support. 'She's the queen,' she said.

Paulette blinked. 'Queen,' she repeated. It was the last thing she'd have expected to hear.

'Yes. You know, woman who sits on a throne? Sometimes wears a crown?'

'Eh.' Paulette blinked again, then looked at Brilliana. Who was watching her, a flicker of tightly controlled amusement twitching her lips. 'She's not joking, is she?'

'Power is no joking matter.' The younger woman's eyes were cold. 'We've just fought a civil war over it. And now Helge is carrying the heir to the throne – long story, you do not need to look shocked – so we would be fools not to seize the moment. And we need a new world to exploit, now that this one has shown itself hostile. That much has now become glaringly clear even to the most reactionary of the conservative wing.'

'Okay.' Paulette licked her lips. 'So what's in it for me?' *If you say old times' sake I may just punch you* . . . This was the proverbial offer too good to refuse. *No way will they just let me go now.*

'A tenth of a point of gross,' said Olga. 'But you don't have to make up your mind just yet. Miriam is holding a meeting in a few days, for her accomplices and confidants. If you are interested, you may attend.' She slid a business card across the table. 'Phone this number no later than four o'clock tomorrow afternoon and say yes or no, then follow the post officer's instructions; they will see you across. The nature of the business, and your role in it, is such that if you choose to decline the offer, you have nothing to fear – you could spill everything you know as of this moment, and the US government would learn nothing they don't already know. Oh, and she sends you this. You can treat it as a nonreturnable advance against wages.' She slid a checkbook across the table to rest atop the card. 'Half a million bucks in the account, Paulie. Try not to spend it all at once.'

*

It was just another summer party, held on the afternoon of a muggy, humid summer day twelve miles outside of Niejwein, in the grounds of a fortified mansion out near what would – in another world – be Lincoln, Massachusetts. Summer parties were a seasonal fixture among the aristocracy of Niejwein, required to live in proximity to their ruler and lacking in any kind of civil society that might host more public entertainments; but this was also the first Miriam had ever held. *Just a summer party,* Miriam reminded herself, glassy-eyed, as yet more carriages and their obligatory escorts of footmen and mounted guards drew up, disgorging men and women in the peacock finery of the nobility: It was like the Academy Awards, minus the onlookers and the network television presence, but with added cock-fighting behind the woodshed.

Sir Alasdair had a third of his men dispersed around the perimeter of her commandeered residence, another third staking out the doppelgänger house in Lincoln, and the remaining cadre of guards on alert downstairs. Brilliana had the receiving line under control, looking for all the world like the lady of the house herself – and leaving Miriam (again wearing the persona of Helge, Prince Creon's puta-tive widow) free to focus on those she wished to talk to. Two teenage scions of the inner family lines, Barbara and Magraet, had been intro-duced into the household for transcription and translation and ensconced in a back room with a bottle of wine and a supply of spare batteries and Dictaphone tapes. And Earl Riordan – no, *Baron* Rior-dan, a reward by order in council for his support, paid out of the estates of several drastically pruned noble family trees – had sent her a dozen hard-eyed Security agents in the livery of waiters and other domestics. There'd be no trouble here, clearly. 'It's all under control,' Brill had assured her that morning. 'Just relax and enjoy the affair.'

'Relax? In the middle of *this*?' Miriam had taken in the organized chaos.

'Yes, Helge, it's your job to be serene. Leave the panicking to me.' And Brill had left her to the mercy of her wardrobe staff, who had spent weeks preparing their idea of a party dress for her, and who had never heard of the word *excess*.

Which left her standing still in an attempt not to perspire in the stuffy warmth of the blue receiving room, trying to smile and make small talk and juggle a glass of wine and a peacock-feather fan that barely stirred the air in front of her. She was surrounded: With Sir Alasdair standing discreetly to one side, and a permanent floating mob of relatives and hangers-on trying to approach her from the front, she was unable to move, reliant on the two ladies-in-waiting hovering nearby.

' – The effect on the harvest will, unfortunately, be bad, your high-ness, with so many destitute; the pretender's army ate what they could and burned the rest, and banditry and famine follow such as night follows day.'

Miriam – *no, Helge* – smiled politely as Lord Ragnr and Styl droned on, talking *at* her rather than *to* her, but most accurately delivering his report to the small condenser mike hidden in her corsage. 'And how much has been lost, exactly?' she nudged, shaking her head minutely as Sir Alasdair raised an eyebrow and mimed a shoving motion.

'Oh, lots! I myself counted – ' That was Lord Ragnr and Styl's vice,

Miriam remembered. In another world he'd have been an adornment to a major accountancy firm's boardroom. In this one, he was a liability to his profession (lord oath-sworn to Duke Lofstrom and ruler of some boring fishing villages, a small chunk of forest, and a bunch of peasant hamlets; performance appraisal based on ability to hunt, drink, and kill the duke's enemies). But she'd listened to him before, and he seemed to think this gave him license to bend her ear in future, and what he had to say was deeply tedious but clearly a matter of profound importance for the business of future good governance. And so, she stood and smiled, and listened to the man.

' – By your leave, my lord?' Miriam blinked back to the present as Sir Alasdair gently interrupted. 'My liege, your grandam is about to be announced.'

'She is?' Miriam felt the color draining from her cheeks. *I thought she was dead!* 'You're certain about that?'

'Absolutely.' Sir Alasdair's expression was imperturbable: She noted the colorless wire coiling from his left ear to the collar of his tunic.

'Oh. Well.' She took a breath of musty, overheated air. 'My lord, you must, please, forgive me? But I have not seen my grandmother since before the insurrection, and' – *If I clap eyes on her before I die of old age it's too soon* – 'I really must pay my respects.' *I'd rather piss on her grave, but I suppose I'd better find out why she's here.*

Ragnr and Styl seemed disappointed for some reason, but took it in good spirit, and after much backing and flowery commiseration she was free. More backing and sidling and some whispered instructions and her ladies-in-waiting formed a flying wedge, or at any rate a creeping one. As they moved towards the door with Miriam in their wake she recognized a gaggle of familiar faces. 'Sir Huw?' she called.

'Milady!'

She smiled, unforced: 'Did you bring your results?'

Huw nodded. 'I'm ready to speak. Whenever you want me to.'

'Good. Upstairs, half an hour?'

Huw ducked his head and vanished into a knot of younger Clan members. Miriam blinked as she noticed Elena, almost unrecognizable in a red gown with a long train. *Are they an item?* Miriam wondered, before dismissing the question. *Where's Mom? I need her advice before I confront Hildegarde.*

'Milady?' It was Gerta, pressed into service as an attendant. 'If it please you . . .'

'I need to circulate,' she mouthed over her shoulder. 'Sir Alasdair . . . ?'

The press around her began to give way as she made progress towards the main hall. Despite the open doors and windows the air was no less close, thanks to the milling clusters of visitors and their attendants, and the copious quantities of rose water and other perfumes with which they attended to their toilet. Out here in the countryside, the humidity and stink of summer was a mere echo of conditions in the capital; though the gods had little to say against bathing, the smell of old sweat and unwashed clothing was unpleasantly noticeable.

'Make way for her grace!' called one of her servants. 'Make – '

'So the rumors were accurate. You *did* survive.'

Miriam turned to face the speaker. 'I could say the same of you, Grandmother.'

The Grand Dowager Duchess Hildegarde was in her eighties, one of those octogenarians who seemed to persist through a process of mummification. She stared at Miriam, her eyelids drooping as if in disinterest. 'I find that interesting,' she said flatly. 'The odds were not in your favor.'

For a moment Miriam flickered back to that bewildering and fearful night, remembering James Lee's evident flattery – and offer of a locket bearing the Lee clan's deviant knotwork: In retrospect an incitement to defect. She managed a polite smile. 'I try to make a habit of beating bad odds.'

'Hah. You'll continue to face them, girl, as long as you keep playing your fancy games. You ignore the old ways at your peril; others cleave to them, and your fingers can be burned just as easily by the fire you didn't light. Although you seem to have a fine talent for getting others to rescue you from situations of your own devising. But on another matter, have you seen your dam? I must have words with her. We need to clear the air.'

Her grandmother's offhanded condescension didn't surprise Miriam; but the suggestion that the air needed clearing was something else. 'What's there to talk about? I thought you'd disowned her!'

'Well.' Hildegarde's cheek twitched. 'That was then; this is politics, after all.'

'On the contrary, this is my party, and I'm shocked, absolutely shocked, that anybody might want to discuss matters of politics here.' Miriam glared at her grandmother. 'Or haven't you worked it out yet?'

Hildegarde looked her up and down. 'Oh, Patricia raised you well,' she breathed. 'And I could ask exactly the same of you, but you wouldn't listen. Best save my breath. You'll understand eventually.' Then, before Miriam could think of a suitable response, she turned and shuffled aside.

'What was *that* about?' asked Brill, materializing at her elbow: 'I could have sworn – '

'I wish I knew.' Miriam stared after the dowager, disturbed. 'I have the strangest feeling that she was trying to send me some sort of message I'm meant to understand. Only somebody forgot to tell me how to read her mind.'

'She is' – Brill stared at the broad shoulders of the dowager's arms-men – 'a most powerful and dangerous lady.'

'And what makes it worse is the fact that she thinks I ought to be on her side.' Miriam curled her lower lip.

'Really?' Brill glanced sidelong at her. 'I was going to say, I believe she thinks she is looking out for *your* best interests. Being your grandam, after all.'

Miriam shrugged uncomfortably. 'Save me from people acting in my best interests. Without asking first,' she added.

'I wouldn't – ' Brill paused and cupped a hand to her left ear. Like Sir Alasdair, she was wearing a wire. 'Ah, Baron Isserlis is soon to arrive, my lady. I must leave you for a while. Where should I tell him you want to meet, again?'

'With the others: in the red room, upstairs, at six o'clock. That's where I told Laurens to put the projection screen and laptop, anyway.'

'Does that goes for all of them?'

'It does. Except for the obvious exceptions.'

'The B-list.'

'Exactly. Wine 'em, dine 'em, and keep 'em out of my hair while I'm making the pitch. That includes my grandmother.' Miriam fanned herself. 'Can you do that?'

Brill smiled. 'Watch me,' she said. 'It's your job to relax and enjoy yourself. Then give a good presentation!'

*

In a mosquito-infested marsh on the banks of a sluggish river, a draft of peasants from the estates of the Earl of Dankfurt had assembled a scaffold. The framework of stout timber and planking bore a winch and some additional contrivances, and despite its crude appearance it had been positioned very carefully indeed. Blood and sweat had gone into its location, and the use of imported surveying tools to measure very precisely indeed its distance and altitude relative to the four reference points where Clan couriers had established accurate GPS locations before crossing over from Washington D.C.

(Accurately locating anything in the Sudtmarkt was problematic, but where there was a need – and urgency – there was a way: and with four reference points, theodolites, and standardized lengths of chain, positioning to within a couple of inches at a distance of up to a mile was perfectly achievable. Besides, Gunnar had insisted on three-inch precision with the icy certainty of punishment from above to back him up. And so it was done.)

'This is the entry point?' asked the visitor.

'Yes, my lord.' Gunnar turned and gestured towards a nearby copse of trees, climbing the gentle slope. 'And right over – there, past the tree line – you should just be able to see the tower for the department store on Pennsylvania Avenue. Site three is, I'm afraid, not visible from here, being on the other side of the river, but construction is complete. We carried out our intrusion tests yesterday shortly after closing time and everything worked perfectly.'

'Intrusion tests?'

'A courier, outfitted with cover as a tourist, to make sure our proposed sites were workable. He crossed over ten minutes after the museum closed, to ensure there were no human witnesses, then made his way out when the alarm system went off. His story was that he'd been in the rest room and hadn't noticed the time. Along the way, he checked for motion detectors in the rest rooms, that sort of thing, to ensure a witness-free transit point.'

'Excellent. And the others?'

'Shops are a little bit harder to probe, so I checked the store in reverse, myself – I crossed over from the other side. Found we were three inches too low on this side, so I raised the platform accordingly. We will have to risk their store security noticing that they lost a shopper, but they are most likely to assume that I was simply an artful thief.'

One of the visiting lord's companions was making notes in a planner; another of them held a large parasol above his lordship's head. His lordship looked thoughtful for a few seconds. 'And how do you probe the third site?'

'Ah, well.' Gunnar froze for a few seconds. '*That* one we can't send a world-walker into. We can fool store security guards who are looking for shoplifters, but soldiers with machine guns are another matter. We will just have to do it blind and get it right first time. On the other hand, I managed to get a verified GPS reading and a distance estimate to the facade from the car park by pretending to be lost tourists, and the outer dimensions of the building itself are well-known. I am certain – I place my honor on it – that site three is within four or five feet of the geometric center of the complex, at ground level.'

'What about the subway station?'

'It's been closed since 9/11, unfortunately, otherwise that would be ideal. Damned amateurs with their box-cutters . . .'

'Leave me. Not you, Gunnar.'

Gunnar stared at his visitor. 'My lord?'

The parasol- and planner-bearers and the bodyguards were also staring at his lordship. 'All of you, go and wait with the carriage a while. I must talk with Sir Gunnar in confidence.'

Heads ducked; without further ado, the servants and guards backed away then turned and filed towards the edge of the clearing.

His lordship watched with ill-concealed impatience until the last of them was out of easy earshot, before turning to Gunnar.

'You must tell me the truth, sir. I'm informed that our superiors have a definite goal in mind, for which they require certain assurances. *Both* our necks – and those of others – are at risk should this scheme fail. If, in your estimate, it is doomed, please say so now. There will be censure, certainly, but it will be nothing compared to the punishment that will fall on both of us should we make the attempt and fail.'

Gunnar nodded thoughtfully. 'Your staff, how many of them . . . ?'

'At least two spies, for opposing factions.'

'Ah, well that makes it clear, then.' Gunnar took a deep breath. 'This is a huge risk we're taking. And you just revealed your internal security coverage. You know that, don't you?'

'The spies in question will have a boating accident involving alligators around sunset this evening.' His lordship smiled humorlessly. 'We – my superiors – have chewed the plan to pieces. Our other choices are no better. The pretender saw to that with his betrothal-day massacre and the radicals have been happy to complete his work. But. My question. Can you make it work?'

'Well.' Gunnar raised his hat to run fingers through his hair. 'I believe so, given the men and the machines. Sites one and two are not professionally secured. The Anglischprache, they rely too much on machines to do the work of men. I will need a team of four world-walkers for each of those two sites, including two Security men who can kill without hesitation if necessary. And the, ah, janitor's carts we discussed. They will need to synchronize their time in advance, and if anyone is out of position it will fail. And you will need to supply the devices and they must work, and at least one man on each team must be trained in setting their timers. But I am, um . . . I believe we have a one-in-fifty chance of failure for sites one and two. It's a solid plan.'

'And site three?'

Gunnar wiped the sweat from his forehead. 'Site three is the tricky one. Unlike one and two, it's going to happen in full view of a whole bunch of soldiers who have been on the alert for terrorist attackers for the past two years, ever since a couple of hundred of their comrades were slain. We need two world-walkers – one to get them in, and one to get himself and his partner out – and the device must be pre-set with a very short timer, no more than one minute. And even then, I would only give the insertion team a fifty-fifty chance of getting out in one piece. The only thing in its favor is surprise.'

'Hmm.'

'What about team four?' Gunnar asked slyly.

'Team four?' His lordship raised one sculpted eyebrow. 'There is no team four.'

'Really?' Gunnar fanned himself with his hat. 'I find that hard to believe, my lord. Or perhaps our superiors are holding something in reserve . . . ?'

His lordship snorted. 'They're targeting the White House, the Capitol, and the Pentagon – what more do you want?'

'That bitch in Niejwein.'

His lordship winked. 'Already taken care of, Sir Gunnar. But I advise you to forget I told you so. Too much knowledge can be a dangerous thing.'

*

Room 4117 was scaring Mike. Not the room itself, but what its contents implied.

Matthias's – source GREENSLEEVES's – voice featured prominently in his dreams as he doggedly plowed through the box of cassette tapes, transcribing and backing up, listening and rewinding, making notes and cross-checking the dictionaries and lexicons that other, more skilled linguists were working on with the detainees FTO had squirreled away in an underground dungeon somewhere. FTO had access to some of the NSA's most skilled linguists, and they were making progress, more progress in weeks than Mike had made in months. Which realization did not fill him with joy; rather, it made him ask: *Why has Dr. James stuck me in here to do this job when there are any number of better translators available?*

There were any number of answers to that question, but only the most paranoid one stood up to scrutiny: that this material was toxic or contagious, and only a translator who was already hopelessly compromised by exposure to secrets and lies should be given access to it. Mike had worked with source GREENSLEEVES in person, had been infiltrated into a Clan palace in the Gruinmarkt, and knew some of the ugly little truths about Dr. James and his plans. *James wants me here so he can keep an eye on me,* Mike realized, staring at the calendar behind his monitor one afternoon. *He gets some use out of me and meanwhile I'm locked down as thoroughly as if he'd stuck me in one of those holding cells.* He shivered slightly, despite the humid warmth that the air conditioning was fighting a losing battle to keep at bay.

The further into the tapes he got, the dirtier he felt. Someone – probably Matt, but he had an uneasy feeling that there was someone else in the loop – had wired a number of offices, both in the Gruinmarkt and, it appeared, in locations around the US. And they'd recorded a whole bunch of meetings in which various deeply scary old men had talked business. Much of it was innocent enough, by the standards of your everyday extradimensional narcoterrorist ring – move shipment X to port Y, bribe such a local nobleman to raise a peasant levy to carry it, how many knights shall we send, sir? – but every so often Mike ran across a segment that made him sit bolt upright in alarm, doubting the evidence of his own ears. And some of this stuff went back *years.* These recordings were anything but new. And bits of them, mixing broken English with Hochsprache, were unambiguous and chilling in their significance:

'Another five hundred thousand to the Partnership for a Drug-Free America,' said the old guy with the chilly voice and the accent like a fake Nazi general in a 50's war movie. 'Feed it through the top four pressure trusts.'

'What about the other items . . . ?'

'Commission those, too. I believe we can stretch to sixty thousand to fund the additional studies, and they will provide valuable marketing material. Nobody looks at the source of this funding too closely, the police and prisons lobby discourage it.' A dry chuckle. 'The proposal on drug-screening prisons will be helpful, too. I think we should encourage it.'

Mike paused the tape again and sat, staring at the computer screen for a while. The skin in the small of his back felt as if it was crawling off his spine. *Did I just hear that?* He wondered. *Did I just hear one of the biggest cocaine smugglers in North America ordering his accountant to donate half a million dollars to a zero-tolerance pressure group? Jesus, what is the world coming to?*

It made economic sense, if you looked at it from a sufficiently cynical perspective; it was not in the Clan's interest for the price of the commodity they shifted to drop – and drop it surely would, if it was legalized or if the pressure to keep up the war on drugs ever slackened. But for Mike Fleming, who'd willingly given the best years of his life to the DEA, it was a deeply unsettling idea; nauseating, even. *Bought and sold: We're doing the dealers' work for them, keeping prices high.*

His fingers hunted over the keyboard blindly, stabbing for letters as he stared through the glass screen, eyes unfocused. Eventually he stopped and pressed PLAY again.

' – Tell them first, though: They'll need to make suitable accounting arrangements so that it doesn't show up in the PAC's cash flow if they're audited.'

A grunt of assent and the conversation switched track to inconsequentialities, something about one of the attendees' – a count's – daughter's impending wedding, gossip about someone else's urgent desire to obtain the current season of *Friends* on tape or DVD. And then the meeting broke up.

Mike hit the PAUSE button again and massaged his forehead. Then, glancing mistrustfully at the screen, he scribbled a note to himself on the legal pad next to the mouse mat: LOOK INTO CREATIVE ACCT. RE. PAC PAY-OFFS? And: COUNT INSMANN'S DAUGHTER'S MARRIAGE -> POLITICAL IMPLICATIONS. It was a tenuous enough lead to go on, but the Clan's political entanglements were sufficiently personal that the wedding gossip might actually be the most important news on this tape.

Then he pressed PLAY again.

Whatever device Dr. James's mole had been using to bug these meetings seemed to be sound-triggered, with about a thirty-second delay. Mike waited for the beep as the machine rolled on to the next recording, ready to laboriously translate and transcribe what he could. It was the old man, the duke, again, talking to a woman – younger, if Mike was any judge of such things, but . . .

'I'm not happy about the situation in D.C., my lady.'

'Is there ever anything to be happy about in that town, your grace?'

'Sometimes. The trouble is, the people with whom we do business change too fast, and this new gang – this *old* gang, rather, in new office – they get above themselves.'

'Can you blame them? They are fresh in the power and glory of the new administration. "The adults are back in charge."' (A snort.) 'Once they calm down and finish feeling their oats they will come back to us.'

'I wish I could share your optimism.'

'You have reason to believe they'll be any different, this time?'

(Pause.) 'Yes. We have worked with them before, it's true, and most of the team they have picked works well to protect our interests. For example, this attorney general, John Ashcroft, we know him well. He's sound on the right issues, a zealot – but unlikely to become dangerously creative. He knows better than to rock the boat. An arm's-length relationship is sufficient for this term, no need to get too close . . . our friends will keep him in line. But what concerns me is that some of the other positions are occupied by those of a less predictable disposition. These Nixon-era underlings, seeking to prove that they could have – yes, like the vice president, yes, exactly.'

'You don't like the current vice president? You think he is unfit?'

'It's not *that*. You know about the West Coast operation, though – '

'Yes? I thought we terminated it years ago?'

'We did. My point is, he was our partner in that venture.'

(Long pause.) 'You're joking.'

'I'm afraid not. He's one of our inner circle.'

'But how – it's against policy! To involve politicians, I mean.'

(Sigh.) 'At the time, he was out of office. Swore blind he was going to stay out, too – that's when he began developing his business seriously. The complaints of financial opacity in Halliburton that came out during the Dresser Industries takeover – whose interests do you think those accounting arrangements served? And you must

261

understand that from our point of view he looked like the perfect cutout. A respectable businessman, former defense secretary with heavy political and business contacts – who'd suspect him?'

'Crone Mother's tears! This should *not* have been allowed.'

'May I remind you again that nobody saw it coming? That if we had, it wouldn't have happened?'

'What are you going to do about it?'

'What we always do, when they're too big to take down: I'm afraid we're going to have to pay him tribute.'

'It's going to be expensive, Angbard. He's their king-in-waiting – indeed, he may actually be their king-emperor in all but name. The dynastic child they've placed on the throne does not impress with his acumen. Someone must be issuing the orders in his stead.'

'Oh, I wouldn't be so sure, my lady; he's strong-willed and I'm told he's brighter than he looks when the glare of the public gaze is shuttered. And I am not certain you're right about the cost of tribute, either. But Mr. Cheney is as rich as one of our first circle, and from his office in the Old Executive Office Building he has more power than many of our relatives can even conceive of. So we cannot buy him with money or cow him with threats. However, there is a currency a man of his type craves, and he knows we can pay in it.'

'What – oh, I see.'

'He is, it seems, setting up his own private intelligence group – by proxy, through Defense – this Office of Special Plans. He is one of those seekers for power who have a compulsive need for secrecy and hidden knowledge. We know exactly how to handle such men, do we not?'

'As long as you're cautious, Angbard. He knows too much already.'

'About us? We won't be feeding him tidbits about *us*. But the fellow has enemies, and he knows it, and as long as we make ourselves discreetly indispensable we'll be safe from investigation by any agency he can touch. That's how it worked with Hoover. We've never had a vice president before, my lady; I hope to make it a mutually profitable arrangement.'

(Pause.) 'As long as he doesn't turn on us, your grace. Mark my words. As long as he doesn't turn on us . . .'

The tape clicked to an end. Mike stared at the poisonous thing, unwilling to rewind it and listen again. It wasn't as if he hadn't had his suspicions, but . . . *This is* Art Bell Show *material,* he told himself. *The vice president is in cahoots with the Clan?*

Slowly a new and even more unwelcome supposition inserted itself into his mind. *No. The vice president* was *in cahoots with the Clan. Now he's* – Mike flashed over on a vision of Dr. James, in a meeting with the VPOTUS himself, giving orders from his shadowy web – *now he's set on* destroying *them. When Matthias defected, he didn't realize the reports would end on Mr. Cheney's desk and the VP would have to kill him and turn on the Clan to destroy the evidence of his collusion* –

The thoughts were coming too fast. Mike stood up tiredly, stretched the kinks out of his shoulders, glanced at the clock. It was four in the afternoon: a little early to go home, normally, but . . .

The Clan take politics personally – *when they figure out what's happened they'll treat it as a* personal *betrayal. But if I even hint that I know this shit, Dr. James will have me rubbed out. What the hell am I going to do?*

Buy time. Sign myself out as sick. And hope something turns up . . .

COUP

Miriam cleared her throat. *Begin with a cliche:* This was the part she was edgy about. 'I expect you're all wondering why I asked you here,' she said, and smiled. Deathly silence. She studied her audience: forty or so of the most important movers and shakers of the inner families, mostly allies of the progressive faction. They were rapt, waiting for her explanation and uninclined to social chatter. *Oh well, moving swiftly on . . .* 'It's been a year since I turned up with a plan and a business and asked my uncle to call a meeting of the Clan Council.'

Heads nodded. Many of them had been at that particular meeting.

'You probably think I asked you here today because a lot has happened in the past year. In particular, *that* plan is dead in the water. I'm not going to assign blame or complain about it. Rather, I'd like to describe the situation we face right now, and propose a new plan. It's drastic, because we're in a bad position, but I think we can make it work. It'll mean major changes to the way we live, but if we go through with it' – she shrugged – 'we'll be in a better position, going forward.' *Too much padding*, she thought nervously.

She leaned over the laptop – sitting on a lectern borrowed from the shrine to the household deities – and tapped the space bar. PowerPoint was running, but the projector – 'Someone check that – '

Huw poked at the projector. 'It's on,' he confirmed. A moment later the screen beside her (a bleached, lime-washed canvas stretched flat within a monstrously baroque gilt picture frame) flickered to life.

'Okay.' Miriam focused on her notes. She'd spent almost twelve hours working on this presentation, far less than the subject deserved but as much as she'd been able to steal between her other duties over the past week. 'Here's what we know for sure: Almost ten months ago,

Sir Matthias, who had been participating in at least one little conspiracy against his grace the duke, vanished. We've subsequently learned that he handed himself in to the DEA in return for immunity' – shocked muttering from the back of the room told her that not everybody present had known even that much – 'and the DEA handed him on to some kind of black intelligence team called the Family Trade Organization. They're the folks behind the series of raids that shut down the east coast network. A number of us have been compromised, including myself and her grace my mother. FTO subsequently captured at least two of our number and coerced them to act as mules, and at least one of their agents was in the grounds of the Summer Palace earlier this year when the pretender made his bid for the succession.'

She paused. The muttering hadn't died down. 'Can you save it for later?' she called.

'Silence!' This a deep bellow from Sir Alasdair, at the back corner of the room. 'Pray continue, milady.'

'Thank you . . . As I was about to say, anything we decide to do now has to take account of the facts that the US government is aware of us; considers us to be a threat; has developed at the very least a minimal capability to send operatives over here: and we can presume that the explosion at the Hjalmar Palace was also their work. And the news doesn't get any better from there. Um.'

Next slide. 'Now, I'm going to assume that we are all familiar with the long-lost cousins and the rediscovery of their, ah, home world. Before his illness, his grace the duke observed that one extra world might be an accident, but two were unlikely to be a coincidence; accordingly, he tasked Sir Huw here with conducting some preliminary research into the matter. What Sir Huw established, very rapidly, was that our early attempts to use the cousins' variant knotwork design on the east coast of the United States had failed because of a doppelgängering effect of some kind. The cousins' knotwork does in fact work, if you go far enough south and west. The world Sir Huw and his fellows discovered was – well, we don't know that it's uninhabited, but the presence of ruined buildings suggests that it used to be inhabited. Now it's cold; Maryland is sub-arctic, with pine forests, and there's residual radioactivity around the ruins – ' She paused again, as the chatter peaked briefly. 'Yes, this is, *was*, a high-tech world. *Very* high-tech.'

She ran the next slide. A photograph of a shattered white dome on a forested hillside. Fast forward again: structures inside the dome, indistinct in the gloom but clearly showing how enormous it was. Next slide: a sealed metal door set in a concrete wall. 'On the other side of this door, Sir Huw discovered hard vacuum.' Next slide: a view down into the valley, thick mist swirling around the crack in the dome's side. 'A door into an apparently endless vacuum. The cloud you're looking at is condensation where the air pressure around the dome drops. It's too dangerous to approach closer, or we'd have gone back to try and seal it – our people were lucky to get away alive. Our best guess is that it's a gate that maintains a permanent connection between two worlds, rather than the transient connection we make when we world-walk. But we have no idea how it works or why there's no, uh, world there. Maybe there used to be and the gate needs to be anchored in some way? We don't know.'

The chatter had subsided into a stunned silence. Miriam glanced round the shocked faces in front of her. 'Sir Huw has also conducted some topological analysis on the family knotworks,' she continued. 'He generated a series of variants and checked them – not to world-walk, but to see if he could feel them. He generated them using Mathematica. It turns out that the family knots can be derived by following a fairly simple formula, and there are three constants that, if you vary them, give rise to different knots that give him the family headache.' Next slide: a polynomial equation. 'Apparently, this is the key to our ability – it's the Alexander polynomial describing the class of knots to which ours belong. No, I don't understand it either, but it turns out that by tweaking some of these coefficients we get different knots that include the two we already know of.

'Any given knot, starting in any given world, seems to act as a binary switch: Focus on it and you can walk from your starting world into a single destination determined by the knot you use.'

Someone had thoughtfully placed a wine goblet by her laptop. used to take a sip.

'There's more. The conventional wisdom about how much we can carry, about the impossibility of moving goods using a carriage or a wheelbarrow? It's somewhat . . . wrong. It's true that you can't *easily* carry a larger payload, but with careful prior arrangement and some attention to insulators and reducing contact area you can move about a quarter of a ton. Possibly more, we haven't really pushed the limits yet. I suspect that this was known to the postal service but carefully kept quiet prior to the civil war; the number of world-walkers who'd have to cooperate to establish a rival corvée, independent of our Clan authorities, is much smaller than the conventional wisdom would have it. If this was widely known it would have made it harder to control the young and adventurous, and consequently harder to retain a breeding population. So the knowledge was actively suppressed, and experimentation discouraged, and during the chaos of the civil war everyone who knew the truth was murdered. Maybe it was a deliberate strategy – knowledge is power – or just coincidence, or accident. It doesn't matter; what I want to impress on you is that there are big gaps in our knowledge, and some of them appear to have been placed there deliberately. Only we've begun to piece things together, thanks to the recent destabilization. And the picture I'm building isn't pretty.'

She hit the key for the next slide. 'You heard – a year ago you heard – my views on the Clan's business and its long-term viability. Smuggling drugs only works as long as they stay expensive, and as long as the people you're smuggling them past don't know what's going on. We've seen evidence of a technology to build gates between worlds, and if there's one thing the US government is good at, it's throwing money at scientific research and making it stick. They know we're here, and I promise you that right now there is a national laboratory – hell, there are probably ten – trying to work out how world-walking works. Worst case, they've already cracked the problem; best case . . . we may have years rather than months. But once they crack it, here in the Gruinmarkt, we're *finished*. Those people can send two million tons of heavy metal halfway around the world to kick in doors in Baghdad, and we're right on their doorstep.'

She paused to scan the room again. Forty pairs of eyes were staring at her as if she'd sprouted a second head. Her stomach knotted queasily. 'I think we need to get used to the idea that it's *over*. We can't stay here indefinitely; we don't have the leverage. Even if we can negotiate some kind of peaceful settlement with them – and looking at the current administration I'm not optimistic – it'd be like sleeping with an elephant. If it rolls over in its sleep . . . well. We need some ideas about what we *can* do. New Britain is a first approximation of an answer: It's got vastly more resources than the Sudtmarkt to Nordmarkt coastline, and we've got contacts there.

'So. I propose that we should collectively go into the technology-transfer business. We've got access to American libraries and know-how, and if we put our muscle into it we can jump-start a technological revolution in New Britain. Operating under cover in the United States has brought very mixed results – it's encouraged us to act like criminals, like gangsters. I propose that our new venture should be conducted openly, at least in New Britain. We should contact their authorities and ask for asylum. We *could* do it quietly, trying to set up cover identities and sneak in – but it would be much harder while they're in the middle of a war and a major political upheaval. If we were exposed by accident, the first response would likely be harsh, just as it has been in the United States.

'But anyway. That's why I invited you here today. Last year I told you that I thought the Clan's business was unsustainable in the long term. Today, I'm telling you that it has become a lethal liability in the present – and to explore an alternative model. I can't do this on my own. It's up to you to help make this work. But if it doesn't, if we don't pull ourselves together and rapidly start up a new operation, we're going to be crushed like bugs. Probably within a matter of months.'

She took another sip from her wineglass. 'Any questions?' A hand waved at the back, then another. The first, Huw, was one of her plants, but the other . . . 'Earl Wu? You have something to say?'

'Yes,' rumbled the Security heavy. 'You are an optimist. You think we can change our ways, yes? We will either have to run from the Americans, or negotiate with them.'

Miriam frowned. 'Isn't that obvious? There's nothing else – '

' – They will want to strike back,' Carl interrupted. 'Our back-woods hotheads. They are used to power and they do not spend enough time in America to understand how large the dragon is that they think they have cornered.' He tapped his forehead. 'I got my education in the US Marine Corps. And I know our idiots, the ones who stayed home.'

'But how *can* they strike back?' Miriam stared at him. Brooding and grim as a warrior out of a Viking saga, Carl exuded absolute certainty and bleakly pessimistic skepticism.

'They can aim a sniper's rifle as well as anyone. And there are always the Clan's special weapons.' A ripple of muttering spiraled the room, rapidly ascending in volume. 'Whose principle military value lies in *not* using them, but the conservatives have never been good at subtle thinking.'

'The Clan's – ' Miriam bit her tongue. 'You've got to be joking. They wouldn't dare use them. Would they?'

'You need to talk to Baron Riordan,' said Carl. 'I can say no more than that. But I'd speak to him soon, your majesty. Immediately, if possible. For all I know, the orders might already have been signed.'

*

It was early evening; the store had closed to the public two hours ago, and most of the employees had long since checked out and gone to do battle with the rush-hour traffic or the crowds on the subway. The contract cleaners and stock fillers had moved in for the duration, wheeling their handcarts through the aisles and racks of clothing, polishing the display cases, vacuuming the back offices and storerooms. They had a long, patient night's work ahead of them, as did the two-man security team who walked the shop floor as infrequently as they could. 'It creeps me out, man,' Ricardo had explained once when Frank asked him. 'You know about the broad who killed herself in the third-floor john ten years ago? This is one *creepy* store.'

'You been drinking too much, man,' Frank told him, with a snort. 'You been listenin' to too many ghost stories, they ain't none of your business. Burglars, *that's* your business.'

'Not slipping and breaking my fool neck on all that marble, that's my business,' Ricardo grumbled. But he tried to follow Frank's advice all the same. Which was why he wasn't looking at the walls as he slouched, face downturned, past the rest rooms on the third floor, just as the door to the men's room gaped silently open.

D.C. played host to a whole raft of police forces, from embassy guards to the Metro Police to the secret service, and all of them liked to play dress-up. If Ricardo had noticed the ghost who glided from the rest-room doorway on the balls of his feet, his first reaction might have been alarm – followed by a flood of adrenaline-driven weak-kneed shock as he registered the look: the black balaclava helmet concealing the face, the black fatigues, and the silenced pistol in a military holster.

But Ricardo did not notice the mall ninja stepping out into the gallery behind him. Nor did he notice the second man in SWAT-team black slide out of the toilet door, scanning the other way down the aisle between knitware and ladies' formals with his pistol. Ricardo remained oblivious – for the rest of his life.

The first intruder had frozen momentarily in Ricardo's shadow. But now he took two steps forward, drawing a compact cylinder from his belt. One more step, and Ricardo might have noticed something for he tensed and began to turn; but the intruder was already behind him, thrusting hard.

The security guard dropped like a sack of potatoes, twitching as the illegally overcharged stunner pumped electricity through him. At the thud, the second intruder twitched round hastily; but Ricardo's assailant was quick with a hand signal, and then a compact Syrette. He bent over the fallen guard and picked up his left hand, then slid the needle into a vein on the inside of the man's wrist and squeezed the tube. Finally he looked round.

'Clear,' said his companion.

'Help me get this into the stalls and position him.'

Together they towed Ricardo – eyes closed, breathing slowly, seemingly completely relaxed – back into the men's room. A quick crisis conference ensued.

'You sure about this?'

'Yes. Can't risk him coming round.'

'Shit. Okay, let's get him on the seat and make this look good. On my word – '

'God-on-a-stick, he's heavy.'

'Roll his sleeve up, above the elbow, while I find the kit.'

'You're really going to do this.'

'You want to explain to the earl why we didn't?'

'Good point . . .'

There was a janitor's trolley in front of the row of washbasins, with a large trash bin and storage for cleaning sundries. Drawing on a pair of disposable gloves, the second intruder retrieved some items from one of the compartments: a tarnished Zippo lighter, a heat-blackened steel spoon, a syringe (already loaded with clear liquid), and a rubber hose.

'Right, let's do this.'

Ricardo twitched slightly and sniffed in his sleep as the men in black set up the scene. Then the syringe bit cold into his inner arm. 'Wuh,' he said, dozily.

'Hold him!'

The first intruder clamped his hands around Ricardo's shoulders; but the guard wasn't awake enough to put up any kind of struggle. And after drawing blood, his executioner was finished. The intruders stepped back to examine their handiwork: the ligature around the upper arm, the empty syringe, the addict's works on the floor by his feet.

'Shit. Never had to do that before.'

'Neither have I. Easier than a hanging, isn't it?'

'Uglier, maybe. Let's get this over with.'

Leaving the cubicle and its mute witness behind, the two men removed their masks and gloves and unhooked their holsters, stowing them in the janitor's cart. 'Okay, we've got six minutes before his number two notices that he hasn't finished his round – if we're unlucky. Let's go find the freight elevator and get out of here.'

Intruder number one wheeled the heavy janitor's cart out of the toilet block while his partner stood watch. This was the riskiest part of the procedure: The security guard was a known quantity, and one they'd been prepared for, but if they ran into a real cleaner they'd have to play things by ear. If there were too many disappearances overnight someone might think to ask urgent questions in the morning. But they didn't run into anyone else as they wheeled the cart over to the unmarked door leading to the service passages behind the shop floor, and the battered and scraped freight elevator arrived without undue fuss.

The sales floors – the sections of the store open to the public – occupied the first through fifth floors, but it was an eight-story building. The upper levels housed a restaurant, then administrative offices and storage rooms for stock and old documents. When the elevator stopped on the eighth floor, intruder number one was the first to exit. He glanced both ways along the empty corridor. 'Clear.'

'All right, let's shift this.'

Together they wheeled the cart along the corridor towards the building's northeast edge. Most of the rooms on this level were offices, prized by the store managers for their view of Penn Avenue; none of these would do. But where there are offices there are also facilities – mail rooms, sluices for the janitors, storerooms. And presently the intruders found what they were looking for: a locked door which, once they opened it using the guard's master key, proved to conceal a small, cluttered closet stacked with anonymous brown cardboard boxes. The odor of neglect hung over them like a mildewed blanket. 'This one's perfect – hasn't been cleaned in weeks.'

'Good, let's get this thing in here.'

Together they manhandled the cart into the room, then busied themselves moving and restacking the boxes, which proved to be full of yellowing paper files. By the time they finished, the cart was nearly invisible from the doorway, concealed behind a stack of archives. 'Okay, setup time. Let's see. Epoxy glue first . . .'

Intruder number one busied himself applying fat sticks of epoxy putty to the wheels of the cart. By the time he finished, anyone attempting to remove it would find the wheels more than reluctant to budge: another mild deterrent to anyone wondering what an abandoned janitor's cart was doing in the back of a storeroom. Then intruder number two went to work on the contents of the trash can, with a pen-sized flashlight and a checklist with an olive-drab cover bearing the words TOP SECRET.

'Power lead one, positive . . . safety to "armed". Countdown, see table three. Yes. Yes, that's right. Power lead three to input four. Armed. Timer self-test – green. PAL code is set to the default, eight zeroes. Let's see if that works. Okay, that works. Timer master key to "set". Here goes . . .' The intruder carefully twisted a butterfly nut, unscrewing a small cover that concealed a thumbwheel. The detonation controller on the device predated LEDs: no bright lights and digital countdown here, just six plastic dials and a push button to latch the timer into place. Finally, after checking his wristwatch and double-checking his calculation he replaced the cover. 'Okay, switching safety to "live".' He winced slightly as he twisted the switch, but the only thing that happened was that a dull red pilot lamp next to the main power switch went out. 'That looks okay. You got the putty?'

'Here.'

He took the tube of epoxy putty, squeezed a strip out, and pressed it into place over the thumbwheel securing the timer wheels, then under and around the safety switch. Once the putty hardened, it would take a hammer and chisel to free up the controls – and the device itself was tamper-resistant: pulling out wires or cracking the case would trigger it.

Intruder number one looked at him with wide, spooked eyes. 'You realize what we've just done, cuz?'

'Yeah. Let's get the hell out of here!'

Methodical as always, his last action before they caught the elevator back down to the toilet – and thence to the wooden scaffold in a swamp in the Sudtmarkt – was to lock the door, and then empty half a tube of Krazy Glue into the keyhole.

The dead guard would be discovered, but the body of a junkie was unlikely to trigger a tear-down search of an entire department store. The locked door might be noticed, but if so, would either be ignored or generate a low-priority call to Facilities, who might or might not respond the same day. The rearranged boxes might be noticed, but probably wouldn't be – nobody cleaned inside that room on a regular basis. And the out-of-place janitor's cart might irritate someone into trying to move it, but in that case they'd discover its wheels were stuck and its contents were inconveniently heavy. *True stealth,* intruder number one's superior had explained, *is made of lots of little barriers that are not apparent to the enemy.*

If anyone penetrated the final barrier and actually looked inside the waste bin in a janitor's cart in a locked room on the top floor of a department store, they would discover a sleeping horror.

But they'd have to do it fast: The timer would count down to zero in less than eighteen hours.

*

'What have you not been telling me?'

Miriam leaned on the back of the visitor's chair in the wood-paneled office, unwilling to sit down or comply with the usual polite rituals of an office visit. For his part, the office's owner looked equally unhappy. Miriam's arrival (accompanied by a squad of personal retainers, including both Brilliana and Sir Alasdair) had clearly disrupted his plans for the day.

'Lots,' Riordan snapped. Then he paused to visibly gather his wits. 'Please excuse me, this is *not* a good time . . .'

'It never is.' Miriam's stomach churned. Dyspepsia was a constant companion right now, along with weird aches and odd food cravings. And she'd had to ride piggyback on one of her guards to get here, which indignity didn't improve her mood. 'I'm talking about the special weapons. I gather there are *complications.*'

Behind her, Brilliana shifted from foot to foot; Riordan leaned back in his chair, steepled his fingers, and stared at her. It was a mannerism blatantly modeled on Angbard's style, but he didn't have the gravitas to carry it off. *The poor bastard's as out of his depth as I am,* she realized. *We're both aping the absent experts.*

'Someone blabbed,' he said flatly. 'Tell me. I need to know.'

'It was – ' Brill stopped abruptly at Miriam's look.

'You don't need to answer him,' Miriam told her. 'Baron.' She fixed him with a stare of her own – this one not modeled on anyone, even her mother. 'Here are the facts as I know them. Some idiot a generation ago sneaked a couple of our people through an Army or Air

274

Force technical school and got them qualified in the care and handling of special weapons. More recently, someone else, also an idiot, decided that having a brace of special weapons to hand was a good idea; just knowing where to steal them in a hurry wasn't good enough. Angbard trusted Matthias, Matthias had the keys to the kingdom, and when he defected he took at least one of the weapons as a fallback insurance policy. The Family Trade Organization sent it back to us, up near Concord. But it wasn't the only weapon we'd stolen, and they want the others back. So where *are* they? *You* know who's supposed to be in charge of them. What's going on?'

Riordan wilted suddenly. 'My lady. Please. Have a seat.'

'You've lost them, haven't you?'

'*Scheisse*,' murmured Sir Alasdair. 'Sorry.'

Riordan glanced at her bodyguard, then back at Miriam. 'Not . . . exactly. I'm not in charge of them. The Clan Council entrusted them to someone else.'

'Oh.' Miriam rolled her eyes. 'You're going to tell me that after Angbard's illness and in the absence of a track record showing where you stood they didn't see fit to entrust you with them. So they gave them to that fuckup Oliver Hjorth to sit on.'

'Oliver's not a fuckup.' Riordan's tone was distinctly defensive. 'I appreciate that you and he got off to a very bad start, that he's seen fit to align himself with a faction that you have a predisposition against, and all the rest of it. But he is neither stupid or lazy, much less unreliable. Usually.'

'Usually.'

It hung in the air for a moment, before Riordan replied. 'Nobody has seen him for two days.'

'Nobody has – ' Miriam blinked. 'You're kidding. You're *Clan Security*. You're telling me you've lost track of the official the Council put in charge of half a dozen atom bombs?'

'Milady – ' It was Brill.

'What is it?'

'He can't – ' Her eyes were pleading.

'Nobody can keep track of every member of the inner families,' rumbled Alasdair. 'We don't have the manpower.' Miriam looked round, to see him watching Riordan. 'Nevertheless . . . something happened, did it not?'

'I was awaiting a report,' Riordan admitted reluctantly, 'before calling a meeting of the Committee of Regents. And the full Council, if necessary. It is not just his lordship who is proving hard to contact.'

'Who's missing?'

'Oliver, Baron Hjorth. Baron Schwartzwasser. His lordship of Gruen, Baron ven Hjalmar. About half a dozen past and present soldiers of this very office who are absent without leave, two-thirds of the Postal Committee, various others – don't look so shocked; it's a goodly cross section of the conservative faction, but not all of them. I happen to know that Baron Julius is sitting on the bench in the royal assizes today, and when I raised the matter he professed ignorance convincingly. My lady, they might be attending a private party, for all I know. Their political views are not a sufficient reason to condemn them, in the absence of any other evidence.'

'But you don't know where the bombs are.' Riordan looked pained. Miriam leaned towards him. 'And there are *rumors*,' she hissed. 'A lot of whispering about revenge and honor. I'm not deaf, I've got ears to hear this stuff with. What do you think is going on?'

Riordan tensed, and she thought for a moment that he was about to reply, but at that moment the door opened. 'I said we weren't to be – oh. My lady.' He rose to his feet as Miriam turned.

'Helge? What are you doing here?' Olga glanced round tensely as she closed the door. 'I see.' She focused on the office's owner. 'My lord, we need to talk about Plan Blue, *right now*. Helge, I beg of you, please excuse us – '

'It's too late for that.' Riordan frowned. 'Helge was just asking me about – about Plan Blue.'

'Plan Blue?' Miriam echoed.

Alasdair cleared his throat. 'Is that the contingency plan for – ' He cleared his throat again, and raised an eyebrow.

'Oh *scheisse*,' said Brill, despair in her voice.

'The bastards have activated it,' said Olga, her voice tightly controlled. 'And I do not recall being invited to a plenary session to approve such action. Do you? It's unforgivable!'

'Plan Blue?' Miriam repeated.

'Excuse me.' Riordan nodded at her. 'My apologies, my lady, but I must make a call.' He lifted the telephone handset and began to dial, then paused. 'That's funny. There's no tone.'

'Give that to me.' Miriam reached for it. The handset was dead, mocking her. 'Um, you've got a dead line. Could you have been cut off by accident, or is that too improbable?'

'Enemy action,' said Sir Alasdair. 'My lady, over here.' He moved swiftly, gesturing Miriam away from the window and moving to stand where she'd been a moment before.

'Otto Schenck admitted it to, to one of my sources,' Olga added as Riordan poked at his desktop computer, a frown spreading on his face. 'Boasted, belike, he said they're going to send the enemy their king's head on a plate – '

'It's not going to work,' Brill whispered.

'What's not going to work?' Miriam rounded on her. 'What are you talking about?'

'Why now? Why are they doing this *now*?' Brill looked at Miriam. 'It's something to do with your grandmother, my lady. Her visit the other day. That was no coincidence!'

'What do you – '

'We need to get out of here!' Brill raised her voice, piercing and urgent. 'Listen, everybody! This is a setup! We need to leave the building *right now*!'

'Why – ' Riordan was standing up.

'She's right, *go, now*!' Olga grabbed his arm.

'My lady. This way.' Alasdair yanked the door open and pulled Miriam along behind him.

'But where are we – ' Miriam stopped arguing and concentrated on not stumbling as he powered along the corridor towards a fire door. 'Alasdair! *No!*' Visions of claymore mines flashed through her mind as he stopped dead.

'Oh, I don't think so,' he assured her with a sharkish grin. 'I checked this one before you arrived. Besides, I don't think they want to *kill* us. Immobilize us and send us a message, perhaps, but they're not going to risk killing the heir.' He shoved down on the emergency

277

bar and pushed the door open. In the distance behind them, a tinny siren began to wail. 'After me, if you please.'

Sir Alasdair ducked round the door, then pronounced the area clear. They piled down the fire escape to the car park at the back of the small office building, Brill and Olga trailing behind. 'What exactly is Plan Blue?' Miriam demanded breathlessly. 'Where's Riordan?'

'He's got other things to do,' said Olga. 'My lady Brilliana, please take your mistress somewhere safe.'

'Where – '

' – Plan Blue?'

'Plan Blue is the usage case for the Clan deterrent,' Brill explained as they climbed into Sir Alasdair's Explorer. 'A decapitation strike at the enemy.'

'Oh Jesus. Tell me that doesn't mean what I think it means.'

'I fear I cannot.'

'Olga, what is Riordan doing?'

'He's going to find a phone.' She frowned. 'Oh, there he is now . . .'

Miriam turned her head to see Riordan round the side of the building, holding a briefcase. He was walking towards them. Olga popped the door.

'Drive,' he said, climbing in. 'I've got to make a call. Once it connects, they'll be trying to trace us, so on my word pull into a car park so I can ditch this thing.'

Brill stared at the case as if it contained a poisonous reptile. 'Is this safe?' she asked.

'No. You were right about it, Olga.'

The truck was already moving as Riordan opened the briefcase. 'What's that?' asked Miriam.

'A special phone.' Brill looked upset. 'Not safe.'

'Indeed.' There was a tray in the case, with a cell phone – in several pieces – nested in separate pockets. One of them contained a small, crude-looking circuit board with a diode soldered to it; another contained a compact handset.

'Why did we leave the office?' asked Miriam.

'Can't use this phone while stationary,' Riordan grunted. 'And the opposition cut our lines. A nuisance measure, I think, but the timing is worrying; I think they were watching you to see if you would take their bait. And you did.'

'Bait?' She shook her head, bewildered.

'You came to see me, about Plan Blue. I do not believe that is an accident.'

'Bastards,' she mumbled under her breath. Louder: 'It was your man Carl.'

'Thank you,' Riordan said gravely. 'All right, I am going to talk to the enemy now.' He picked up the handset, flicked a switch on the small circuit board, and poked at the exposed keypad of the vivisected phone. 'Dialing . . .' The sound of a ringing phone filled the truck's cab, coming from a speaker in the briefcase.

'Hello?' The voice answering the phone was cold.

'I was told that you can send a message to the White House,' said Riordan. 'Is that correct?'

Miriam's skin crawled as she waited for the reply.

'Correct,' the voice said drily. 'To whom am I speaking?'

'You can call me the Chief of Security.'

'And you may call me Dr. James. Are you calling to surrender?'

'No, I'm calling to warn you that your meddling has produced an overreaction from our conservative faction. They've activated a plan which – *fuck*.'

The line had gone dead; simultaneously, the LED on the circuit board had lit up, burning red.

'They did it,' Brill said, fascinated. 'The *bastards*.' Her actual word, in Hochsprache, was considerably stronger.

'Next drive-through, please,' Riordan called to Sir Alasdair. 'I am afraid you are right, milady.'

'What was that?' Miriam asked, staring at the LED.

'Something one of our artificers put in to replace the ten grams of C-4 wired across the earpiece,' said Olga. 'Is it not an ingenious little assassination weapon?'

'But we' – Miriam stared in horror – 'we were going to warn them!'

'Maybe they don't want warning?' Sir Alasdair asked.

'But we – ' Miriam stopped. 'We've got to do something! Do you know where the bombs are?'

'No,' said Olga.

'That's the whole point of Plan Blue,' Riordan added. 'It's a procedure for deployment. Nobody knows everything about it; for example, I don't know the precise target locations. It was designed so that it can't be disrupted if the commanders are captured, or if one of the bomb emplacement teams is captured.'

'But that's insane! Isn't there any way of stopping it?'

'Normally, yes, if the chain of command was operating. But someone appears to have decided to cut us out of the loop. I fear we are facing a coup assisted by people inside Security, my lady. I have some calls to make . . .'

'We can warn them,' said Olga, causing at least three people to ask, 'how?' simultaneously.

'Your friend, Mr. Fleming,' she added, glancing sidelong at Miriam. 'He is inside their security apparat.'

'So was that, that man. On the phone.' Miriam stared at Riordan, who was busily unplugging components in the briefcase and fiddling with something that looked alarmingly like a pyrotechnic flare.

'Yes, but Fleming will know how to bypass him,' Brill said thoughtfully. 'He will know how to escalate a bomb threat and sound a general alert. His superior may be playing foolish games, but I believe he is still trustworthy.'

The Explorer turned a corner. 'Stopping in a minute,' called Sir Alasdair. 'Are you ready?'

'Yes,' said Riordan, depressing a button on the flare and closing the briefcase. He latched it shut, then spun the combination wheels. 'We have two minutes until we require a fire extinguisher.'

'You won't need them.' Alasdair was already slowing, his turn signal flashing. 'Okay, go.' The car park outside a 7-Eleven was deserted.

Riordan popped the door, lowered the briefcase, and then kicked it away from the truck. 'Go yourself,' he said. He was already opening another mobile phone, this one reassuringly unmodified. 'Duty chief? This is the major. I have some orders for you. The day codes are – '

Miriam rubbed her temples. 'Anyone got a cell phone?' she asked.

'I have,' said Olga. 'Why?'

'Unless you can't live without it, I want to call Mike.'

'But we can – '

'I said *I want to call Mike!*' Miriam snarled. 'When I've spoken to him you can put me back in my padded box to gestate while you get down to finding those fucking bombs and arresting or shooting whoever stole them, but *I* should be the one who talks to Mike.'

'Why – '

'Because I'm the only one of us he's got any reason to trust,' she said bleakly. 'And I'm afraid I'm going to burn him.'

*

The clinic room could have been a bedroom in a chain hotel, if not for the row of sockets on the wall behind the bed – piping in oxygen, vacuum, and other, less common utilities – and for the cardiac monitor on a stand beside it, spreading leads like creepers to each of the occupant's withered branchlike limbs. Outside the sealed window unit, the late afternoon sunshine parched the manicured strip of grass that bordered this side of the clinic; beyond it, a thin rind of trees dappled the discreet brick wall with green shadows.

The man in the bed dozed lightly. He'd been awake earlier in the day, shaking in frustration as the speech therapist tried to coax words out of his larynx, and the effort – followed by an hour with the physiotherapist, working on the muscles in his damaged left arm, and then a light lunch served by a care assistant who carefully spooned each mouthful into his mouth – had tired him out. He'd been in his late sixties even before the stroke, his stamina reduced and his aches more noticeable with every morning. Since the stroke, things had only gotten worse. Afternoon naps, which he'd once disdained as suitable only for kindergartners, had become a regular daily fixture for him.

Something – a small movement, or an out-of-place noise – brought him to consciousness. Perhaps the shadow of a bird fluttering before the window glass disturbed him, or footsteps in the corridor outside: In any case, his eyelids flickered open, staring at the ceiling overhead. 'Urrr.' He closed his mouth, which had fallen open as he slept, and reached for the bed's motor controller with his left hand. His eyes twitched from side to side, scanning the angles and planes of the space surrounding him, looking for intrusions. His thumb twitched, pushing the headboard motor control, and the bed began to whine, raising him towards a sitting position.

'Good afternoon, old man.' The visitor closed the clinic room door carefully, then approached the bed, standing where its occupant could see him.

'Urr . . . doc.' Surprise and doubt sparked in the old man's eyes. 'Doc-tor!'

'I wanted to take a last look at you. You know, before the end.'

'You. End?' The visitor had to lean close to make out the words, for Angbard's speech was garbled, the muscles of his lips and tongue cut loose by the death of nerves in his brain. 'Wher' guards?'

'They were called away.' The visitor seemed amused. 'Something to do with an emergency, I gather. Do you remember Plan Blue?'

'Wha –'

The visitor watched as Angbard fumbled with the bed's controller. 'No, I don't think so,' he said, after a moment. Reaching out, he pulled the handset away from the duke's weakened fingers. 'Your aunt sends her regards, and to tell you that our long-standing arrangement is canceled,' he said, and stood up. 'That may be sufficient for her, but some of us have been waiting in line, and now it's *my* turn.'

'*Scheisse!*'

The duke made a grab for the emergency cord, but it was futile; he was still deathly weak and uncontrolled on his left side, and his right hand clawed inches short of the pull. Then the visitor grabbed the pillow from behind his head and rammed it down onto his face. It was a very uneven struggle, but even so the old man didn't go easily. 'Fucking lie down and *die*,' snarled the visitor, leaning on him as he tried to grab the duke's flailing left hand. 'Why can't you do something right for once in your life?'

He was answered by a buzzer sounding from the heart monitor.

Breathing heavily he levered himself off the bed; then, lifting the pillow, he shoved it under the duke's lolling head before turning to stare at the monitor. 'Hmm, you do appear to have lost your sinus rhythm altogether! Time to leave, I think.' He stared at the corpse in distaste. 'That's a better end than you deserved, old man. Better by far, compared to the normal punishment for betrayal . . .'

He breathed deeply a few times, watching the buzzing heart monitor. Then Dr. ven Hjalmar opened the door, took a deep breath to fill his lungs, and shouted, 'Crash cart, stat! Patient in cardiac arrest!' before turning back to the bed to commence the motions of resuscitation.

*

Mike had been accumulating leave for too long; taking some of it now wouldn't strike anyone in human resources as strange, although it was a fair bet that someone higher up the tree would start asking questions if he didn't show up for work within a week.

In the meantime he went home, still numb with shock from the disclosures buried on the cassette tapes. It was, he thought, time to make some hard choices: Collusion between officials and the bad guys was nothing particularly new, but for it to go so high up the ladder was unprecedented. And it would be extraordinarily dangerous for someone at his level to do anything about it. Or not – and that was even worse. *Dr. James is in Mr. Cheney's pocket*, Mike reminded himself. *And he gave me those tapes, not some other, more qualified analyst. If I'm lucky, he did it because he considers me trustworthy. More likely* . . . A vision kept flickering in his mind's eye, of Colonel Smith, in all candor, telling Dr. James, 'Mike's a bit squirrelly about you. Nothing to worry about, but you should keep an eye on him.' And Dr. James, with that chilly reserved look in his eye, nodding and making a note by his name on the org chart: *disposable resource*.

Mike was under no illusions about the taskmaster Dr. James worked for: a determined, driven, man – *ruthless* would not be an exaggeration. He had a fire in his belly and a desire to bend history to his will. With his doctrine of a unitary executive and his gradual arrogation of extraordinary powers granted by a weak presidency, he'd turned the office of vice president into the most powerful post in the government. And he had good reason to silence anyone who knew of his covert connection to the Clan: good reason, even, to silence the

Clan themselves for good. *He's an oilman, and he knows they're sitting on all the oil that was ever under Texas, untapped,* Mike realized. *And now he's got a machine for getting there. It's crude today, but who knows what it'll be like tomorrow? He's got to be thinking, who needs Iraq, anyway? Or Saudi Arabia?*

Mike wasn't naïve: He knew that the most addictive drug, the deadliest one, the one that fucked people up beyond redemption every time, was money. *And I'm between an addict and the most powerful fix in history . . .*

That afternoon and evening, he meticulously searched his apartment, starting by unplugging all the electrical appliances and checking sockets and power supplies for signs of tampering. Then he began to search the walls and floors, inch by inch, looking for bugs. And while he searched, he thought.

The big picture looked grimmer the longer he pondered it. Thinking back, there'd been the horror-flick prop they'd found in a lockup in Cambridge, thick layers of dust covering the Strangelovian intrusion of a 1950s-era hydrogen bomb, propped up on two-by-fours and bricks with a broken timer plugged into its tail. Nobody ever said what it had been about, but the NIRT inspectors had tagged its date: early 1970s, Nixon administration. *What kind of false-flag operation involves nuking one of your own cities? How about one designed to psyche your country up for a war with China?* Except it hadn't happened. *But the Clan have a track record of stealing nukes from our inventory.* Mike shuddered. And the VP had backed the plan to invade Iraq, even after Chemical Ali had offed his cousin Saddam and sued for peace on any terms. And according to some folks who Mike wasn't yet prepared to write off as swivel-eyed loons, the oil had something to do with it.

He slept uneasily that night, his dreams unusually vivid: an injured princess in a burning medieval palace, her face half-melted by the nuclear heat-flash, telling him, 'I'll call when I can', as he tried to pull his leg from a mantrap and reached down to lever apart its jaws, only to find it was a skull, a skull biting his legs, Pete Garfinkle's skull, horribly charred by the bomb that had set this off, and if he couldn't get away the next nuke would fry him –

The next morning he rose, late and groggy, and went back to work. Around ten o'clock he finally found what he'd been looking for: a pinhole in the living room wall that had been all but concealed by the frame of a cheap print that had come with the apartment. Mike passed it by, continuing his search. It would be perfectly obvious what he was doing, and there was no point in showing any sign of having discovered the camera. Either it was being monitored, in which case they'd simply replace it with another the next time he went out, or the survey had been terminated, in which case there was nothing to worry about. He leaned towards the latter case (keeping a watch on an apartment was an expensive business, requiring at least six full-time agents on rotation, even without the overheads of being ready to tail the occupant if they left), but he had to assume the former, especially if Dr. James considered him unsound. *He could have farmed it out to Internal Affairs, told them I'm suspected of espionage,* he thought bleakly. In which case, he was providing them with lots of circumstantial evidence that he was overdue for a vacation in Club Fed; but that couldn't be avoided. Federal prison might actually be an improvement over the alternatives, if Dr. James decided Mike needed to be silenced.

He'd finished the bug hunt – without finding any additional devices – and had moved into the washroom to process the pile of shirts and underwear that had been building up, when the phone rang.

Swearing, he made a grab for the handset and caught it before the answering machine cut in. He was half-expecting a recorded telesales announcement for his pains, but years of fielding out-of-hours emergencies had made him wary of dropping messages. 'Mike?' asked a woman's voice. 'Are you there?'

'Yes – ' It took a moment for the voice to register. 'Don't say your name!' he said hurriedly. 'The line is probably being monitored.'

'And this cell phone is going down a storm drain as soon as I end the call.' She sounded nervous.

'Is it about the talk we had? Because if so, there've been some changes – '

'No, it's not about that. Listen, Olga told me what you told her.'

'*Olga* told' – he paused, his tenuous train of thought perilously close to derailment – 'what's your situation?'

'I'm okay, my mom's okay, and we know about the surprise in the cell phone your boss left for us.' Cold sweat drenched Mike's back as she continued relentlessly: 'It's about the nukes. Your boss didn't stay on the line long enough to let us pass on the news that all this *send them a message* shit has just blown up in a big way. The conservative faction are attempting to stage a coup and as part of their preparations they've stolen' – a pause – 'no, they've *deployed* at least three, possibly four, of the bombs in their possession. Hang on' – the line went silent for a few seconds – 'word is that *they* have decided to send *you* a message, the same type your people sent *them*, and you've probably got less than twenty-four hours to find it.'

'If this is some kind of joke – '

'No, hang on, I'm relaying stuff. The target is probably Washington D.C., and the bombs only dial up to about one kiloton each. The bad guys are inside our chain of command; they activated a contingency plan and changed the targets. We're currently trying to reestablish control and find out where the new target locations are, and as soon as we figure that out I will phone this landline number and pass the information on. I want you to know that we're treating this as treason and it is not our intention to blow up any cities. Have you got that?'

'Wait, *listen!* Did you try telling – did you talk to Dr. James? Did you talk to him – '

'Yes, that's the name. Can you pass this – '

Mike tried to swallow, his mouth was dry and sticky, and his heart was hammering. 'Dr. James works directly for the vice president. Mr. Cheney has been in collusion with someone in your inner families for a very long time – more than ten years – and he wants you all dead. There are tapes . . . I'm not trusted, I'm a disposable asset. Just saying. If what you're telling me is true, Dr. James doesn't care about losing a city block or two – it would make it easier to justify what's coming down the line. Think of Pearl Harbor, think of 9/11. If I pass this up the line, they'll bury it and I'll show up in the morgue one morning.'

'Shit.' Her voice cracked. 'Mike, I'm going to have to put the phone down in a minute, I've been on the line too long. What can we do?'

'Find the bombs. Drag them back to the Gruinmarkt and dump them in a swamp or something.' He stared bleakly at the kitchen sink. 'I'm going to put the answering machine on now and go out. Got to go outside the chain of command and talk to some folks who might be able to do something useful.'

'If there's anything we can do – '

'Just find the fucking bombs!' he snarled, and slammed the handset down on its charge point so hard that the battery cover pinged off.

'Shit.' He breathed deeply, staring at the phone. Coming from anyone else, he'd have questioned the sanity of the bearer of such news – but he knew Miriam. And he'd let his mouth run away with him, blabbing the truth about the tapes Dr. James had him listening in on. Never mind the pinhole camera: The phone line *was* bugged and even if nobody was monitoring it in real time, the word would be out soon.

Mike went through into the living room, and then his bedroom, as fast as his cast would let him. (It was still itching, but nearly ready to come off; give it two weeks, said the doctor he'd seen the week before.) He collected his jacket and a small go-bag from under the bed, which held (among other things) a gun, a couple of fully charged and never-used cell phones, and a handwritten paper address book. 'Who first?' he asked the air as he headed for the front door. *I could try the colonel again*, he thought dismally. Or . . . *Agent Herz. She might go for it.* But whether she'd listen to him was another matter: *They'll put the word out on me within an hour.* That left the usual channels – he could go talk to the FBI or his former boss at the DEA field office in town, but again: *They'll think I'm crazier than a fruitbat once Dr. James gets through with them.* He opened the front door.

I'm going to have to go to the press, he thought, and raised the remote on his car key chain, and had already begun to press the button just as a second thought crystallized in his mind: *James is an old hand. What if he's playing by pre-Church Commission rules –*

In the aftermath of the explosion, every car alarm within three blocks began to sound, accompanied by a chorus of panicking dogs and, soon enough, the rising and falling of sirens; but they were too late.

NORTHWOODS

Morning, July sixteenth.

In a locked store room on the eighth – top – floor of a department store off Pennsylvania Avenue, a timer counted down towards zero.

Another timer matched its progress – in a janitor's store on the top floor of a museum building near the Mall, behind a door jammed by cyanoacrylate glue in the lock and hinges.

And unfathomably far away, on a scaffold by the swampy banks of a slow-moving river, two men labored over a third timer, readying it for delivery to a target in the looking-glass world of the United States of America.

Nobody understood yet, but the worlds were about to change.

*

'Duty Chief? This is the major. I have some orders for you. The day code is: Echo, Golf, Zulu, X-ray, five, nine, Bravo. Did you get that?'

'Yes, my lord. One moment . . . yes, that is correct. What do you have for me?'

'Flash priority message to all Internal Security posts. Message begins: Traitors to the Clan have activated Plan Blue without authorization. Any security officers in possession of special weapons are to secure and disarm them immediately. Anyone not in possession but with knowledge of the disposition of special weapons must report to me immediately. Use of lethal force to secure and disarm special weapons in the possession of unauthorized parties is approved.' Riordan swallowed and shifted his grip on the cell phone. 'Anyone who is unaware of Plan Blue or the nature of the special weapons – you should execute Plan Black *immediately*. I repeat, Plan Black, immediate effect. Order ends. Please copy.'

The stunned silence at the other end of the connection lasted almost a second. 'My lord. Plan Blue? Plan Black?'

'Copy, damn your eyes!'

'Sir.' The duty officer pulled himself together: 'I copy . . .' He repeated Riordan's orders. 'I'll put that out immediately, by your leave?'

'Do it. Riordan out.'

He closed the phone with a snap and glanced sidelong at Lady Olga. She was staring across her seat back at Miriam, who was talking intently into her own phone, her face a study in strain. He opened his mouth, but she raised a finger. Half a minute passed as their driver, Alasdair, carried them ever closer to the turnpike; then Miriam held the phone away from her face and shook her head. 'Trash,' she said, holding it out to Brill, who popped the battery before sliding it into a waste bag. 'We are so fucked,' she said tonelessly.

'Plan Black?' Olga asked.

'What did Mr. Fleming say?' asked Riordan, ignoring her to focus on Miriam.

'It's – ' Miriam shook her head, punch-drunk. 'Crazy talk. He says Dr. James works for the vice president! And *he's* been in collusion with someone in the Clan for years! It's insane! He said something about tapes, and about them *wanting* an excuse, a Pearl Harbor.'

'Can Fleming do anything for us?' Riordan stared at Miriam as she shook her head again. 'Why not?'

'He says he's disposable. He's going to try and find someone to talk to, but there's no point going through the chain of command. We're trying to negotiate with people who want us dead – tell me it's not true?'

'Figures,' Olga said tartly. Everyone stared at her – even Sir Alasdair, by way of the rearview mirror.

'What do you mean, my lady?' Riordan's return to exaggerated courtesy was a sign of stress, screamingly clear to Miriam even in her punch-drunk state.

'We've been looking for a second mole, ever since Matthias went over the wall, nearly a year ago. But we haven't been looking very *hard*, if you follow. And I heard rumors about there being a former politician, now retired, chief executive of a major logistics corporation, who was cooperating with us to provide doppelgängered locations and distribution hubs, back in the good years, in the late eighties and early nineties. The West Coast operation – back when he was out of politics. Before his comeback as VP. The crown fits, does it not?'

'But why – ' This from Brilliana, unable to contain her curiosity.

'We don't work with politicians,' Riordan said tiredly. 'It's too hard to tell good from bad – the ones who stay bought from the ones who don't. There's too much potential for blowback, as the CIA can attest. But Mr. Cheney was out of politics, wasn't he?'

Miriam nodded, brooding. 'He was in the wilderness until . . .' Her eyes widened. 'Oof. So, he got a second start in politics, and the duke would have pulled the plug. Am I right? But then Matthias went over the wall, and his report would have ended up where the VP – or one of his people in his intelligence operation – could read it, and he'd have to take out Matthias and then try to – oh *no* – '

'He'd have to try to kill us all,' Olga finished the sentence, nodding, 'or not even the president could keep him from impeachment, yes? Our mole, for whom we have not been looking with sufficient vigor, isn't a low-level functionary; he's the vice president of the United States. And now he fears exposure.'

Riordan reached over to tap Sir Alasdair on the shoulder. 'Do you know where your Plan Black site is?' he asked.

'Yes, my lord.' Alasdair nodded, checking his side mirror as he floored the accelerator to merge with the traffic on the interstate. 'I'm taking us there.'

'What's Plan Black?' Miriam tried to make eye contact with Olga.

Riordan cleared his throat. 'My lady, we need to get you to a place of safety. But it's not just you; in light of the current situation we *all* need to get clear. Plan Black is a defensive measure, put in place by his grace after the mess last year. It's a complete withdrawal – everyone in this world is to proceed to a safe site, collect essential equipment, and cross over.'

'But that's – ' Miriam paused. 'What about the conservative faction? Baron Hjorth, the duchess, whoever took the bombs and activated Plan Blue, will they – '

'No.' Riordan bared his teeth. 'And I'm counting on it. Because if they disobey a directive from the acting head of Clan Security in the middle of an emergency, that's all I need to shoot them.'

'It's the civil war, my lady, all over again.' Olga whistled tunelessly. 'They've been begging for it – and now they're going to get it.'

*

Four hundred miles from D.C., in a quiet residential street in Boston, the first bomb of the day detonated.

It wasn't a very large bomb – just a repurposed concussion grenade – but it was right under the driver's seat of the parked Saturn it was attached to. There was a bright flash; every window shattered as the car heaved on its suspension. Mike Fleming, standing in his doorway with key-fob remote raised, had no time to blink; the pressure wave shoved him backward and he stumbled, falling against the doorframe. In the ringing moment of silence after the blast, car alarms went off up and down the street and panicking dogs added their voices to the chorus. The hot yellow light of burning plastic and seat cushions filtered through the empty windows of the car, warmth beating on Mike's face as he struggled to work out why he was sitting down with his legs askew, why the back of his head hurt –

They want me dead, he realized, coldly. And then: *Dr. James screwed up.*

It was an easy mistake to make. The technician who'd planted the bomb had meant to wire it to the ignition circuit, but they'd got the central locking instead. The fine art of car bombing had gotten positively esoteric in the past few years, with the proliferation of in-car electronics, remote-control engine starters, and other bells and whistles; and US government agents were more used to defusing the things than planting them. Then: *But that means they're complicit for sure.* The thought was shocking. *It's like Operation Northwoods! Only this time they're going through with it for real.*

Mike reached up gingerly and felt the back of his head. There was going to be a nasty lump in a few hours, but his fingers came away dry. No bleeding. Taking stock, limb by limb, he took deep breaths, pushing down the wave of impending panic. *I'm alive,* he told himself. *Shaken but intact.* He'd been lucky; if he hadn't changed the batteries in his key-fob remote three months ago he might have been closer to the car, or even reduced to using the door key, with fatal results. As he stood up, something crunched underfoot. Fragments from the rear window, pea-sized pellets of safety glass. Bending down stiffly, he picked up his go-bag. His leg twinged hard inside its cast. What now? *Clear the killing zone,* the instructors had insisted, years before. But they'd been talking about a different kind of ambush – a car bomb was a passive trap. *Probably they were relying on it. Probably . . .* Mike pulled his pistol from the bag and duck-walked towards the street, edging around the burning car as he scanned for threats. In the distance, a siren began to scream.

Less than twenty seconds had elapsed.

*

In another world, in a mansion overlooking a lawn that swept downhill to the banks of a small river, an elderly man sat at a writing desk in a room off to one side of the great hall. It was a small room, walled in bare stone and floored with planks, which the tapestries and rugs failed to conceal; the large window casements, built for light but featuring heavy oak shutters with peepholes and iron bolts, suggested the architect had been more concerned with security than comfort. Despite the summer heat he held his robes of office tight about his shoulders, shivering as he stared at the ledger before him with tired eyes. It was a balance sheet of sorts, but the items tallied in its columns were not quantities of coin but the living and the dead. And from time to time, with the slow, considered strokes of his pen, Baron Julius Arnesen moved names from one column to the other.

Arnesen was a survivor of seventy-some years, most of which he had experienced in a state of barely suppressed existential terror. Even now, in a house his security chief assured him was securely doppelgängered from both the known alternate worlds (in the United States by a convenient interstate off-ramp, and in New Britain by a recently acquired derelict warehouse), and at the tail end of his years, he could not bring himself to sit with his back to door or window. Besides, an instinct for trouble that had served him well over the decades whispered warnings in his ears: Not all was right in the Gruinmarkt, or within the uneasy coalition of Clan radicals and conservatives who had agreed to back the Baroness Helge Thorold-Hjorth and her claim to bear the heir to the throne. *It's all going to come apart again, sooner or later,* he told himself gloomily, as he examined the next name in the ledger. *There are too many of them . . .*

Egon was dead, blown to bits along with most of his army, and Helge – pregnant as a result of the gynecological skullduggery of one of the Clan's own doctors – was acknowledged as the dead Prince Creon's widow. But a goodly chunk of the backwoods nobility wouldn't believe a word of it, even if she presented them with a baby who was the very spitting image of Creon in six months' time. To them, Helge was simply an impostor, a willing puppet for the Clan's avarice and ambition. They were keeping their mouths shut right now, out of fear, but that wouldn't last forever; and weeding out the goats from the sheep was proving to be a well nigh impossible task. As magister of the royal assizes, Julius had considerable freedom to arraign and try hedge-lords whom he might suspect of treasonous intent; but he also had to walk a fine line between rooting out threats and conducting a witch hunt that might itself provoke another uprising.

Here in the countryside eight miles outside the capital Niejwein, in a house seized from the estate of the lord of Ostrood – conveniently missing with his sons since the destruction of the royal army at the Hjalmar Palace – Julius had established a crown court to supervise the necessary unpleasantness. To arraign and execute nobles in the capital would be inflammatory; better by far to conduct the grim job beyond the city walls, not so far out of sight as to invite accusations of secrecy, but remote enough to deter casual rubbernecking. With selected witnesses to testify to the fairness of the proceedings, and a cordon secured by imported American security devices as well as armed guards, he could proceed at his leisure without fear of the leading cause of death among judges in the Gruinmarkt – assassination by an angry relative.

Take the current case in hand, for example. Sir Euaunt ven Pridmann was a hedge-knight, titular liege lord to a village of some ninety souls, a house with a roof that leaked, three daughters with dowries to pay, one son, and a debt run up by his wastrel grandfather that exceeded the village's annual surplus by a factor of fifteen. Only a writ of relief from usury signed by the previous king's brother had spared him the indignity of being turfed out of his own home.

For such a man to show up in the army of the late pretender to the throne might be nothing more than simple desperation, for Egon had promised his followers a half-share in the Clan lands that they took for him – not that ven Pridmann had done much looting and pillaging. With gout and poor eyesight he'd spent three-quarters of the war in his sickbed, and another fourth groaning with dysentery. That was why he hadn't been present at the destruction of the Hjalmar Palace by the god-cursed 'special weapon' Clan Security had apparently detonated there, and his subsequent surrender and protestations of loyalty to the true heir were just another footnote to the whole sordid affair. But. *But.* Julius squinted at the ledger: How could you be *sure*? Could ven Pridmann be what the otherworld Americans called a *werewolf*, one who stayed behind to fight on in secret, after the war? Or might he have lied about his culpability, claiming innocence of very real crimes?

Julius sighed and laid his pen down beside the ledger. You couldn't be sure; and speculation about intangibles like loyalty in the absence of prior evidence was a good way to develop a raging case of paranoia. You could end up hanging thousands, as a preventative measure or in the hope of instilling a healthy fear in the survivors – but in the end, would it work? Would fear make them keep their heads down, or provoke a further uprising? *He's got gout,* Julius reasoned. *And he's too poor to buy a gun or pay a lance of infantry. Low risk.* And reasoning thus, he crossed ven Pridmann off the death list.

There was a knock.

'Yes? Yes?' Julius said querulously, looking up.

An apologetic face peeped round the door. 'Sorry to bother you, my lord, but you have a visitor? Philip ven Holtz-Hjalmar from the Office of the Post, with dispatches from the Crown.'

'Tell him to leave them – ' Julius paused. *That's funny, I wonder what it is?* The post office in question was the Clan's courier service, manned by members of the six families and their close relatives who held in common the talent of walking between worlds. Normally he could expect at most one courier delivery a day, and today's had arrived some hours ago. 'Show him in.'

'At once, my lord.'

The manservant withdrew. After a moment's muted conversation, the door opened again.

'My lord Arnesen.' Julius didn't recognize the courier. The brief-case he held was expensive and flashy: brushed aluminum with a combination lock and other less obvious security measures. 'May we speak in private?'

'Of course.' Julius waved at his servant: 'Be off, and keep everyone away from the door.'

'Thank you, my lord.' The courier didn't smile.

'Well? What is it?' Julius strained to sit up, pushing back against the weight of his years.

'Special message, for your eyes only, from Her Grace the Dowager Thorold-Hjorth.' He put the briefcase down on the side table.

This should be good, Julius thought. The Duchess Hildegarde hadn't had the time of day for him since the disaster at the Summer Palace three months ago. *If she's decided to kiss and make up now it must mean –*

He was still trying to articulate the thought when the messenger shot him in the face, twice. The gun was fitted with a suppressor, and Baron Arnesen was seated; there was barely any noise, and the second bullet was in any case unnecessary.

'She sent her best wishes,' said the courier, sliding his pistol back into the padded sleeve and picking up his briefcase in his left hand. 'Her *very* best wishes.'

Then he rolled his left sleeve up, focused his eyes on the temporary tattoo on the back of his wrist, and vanished into the locked and derelict warehouse that Julius Arnesen had been so reassured to hear of from his chief of security.

*

Meanwhile in another world, a doctor of medicine prepared himself for his next house call – one that would destroy families, rewrite wills, and quite possibly generate blood feuds. *They deserve it,* he thought, with a bitter sense of anticipation. *Traitors and bastards, the lot of 'em.*

For Dr. Griben ven Hjalmar, the past six months had brought about a disastrous and unplanned fall from grace and privilege. A younger child of the same generation as the Duchess Patricia, or Angbard ven Lofstrom, born without any great title or fortune to his outer-family-derived name, Griben had been quick-witted and ambitious enough to seize for himself the opportunity to study needful skills in the land of the Anglischprache, a decade before it became the common pattern of the youth of the six families. In those days, the intelligent and scholarly were viewed with circumspection, if not outright suspicion: Few paths were open, other than the military – a career with direct and useful benefits to the Clan's scions.

Griben aimed higher, choosing medicine. In the drafty palaces of the Gruinmarkt, the allure of Western medicine held a mesmeric attraction to the elders and the high ladies. With open sewers in the streets, and middens behind many houses, infection and disease were everyday killers: Childbed morbidity and infant mortality robbed the Clan of much of its vigor. Griben had worked hard to convince Angbard's dour predecessor of his loyalty, and in return had been given some slight experience of life in America – even a chance to practice medicine and train after graduation, so long as he packed his bag and scurried home at the beck and call of his betters.

Antibiotics and vaccines raised many a soul from death's bed, but the real returns were quite obviously to be found in obstetric medicine. He realized this even in pre-med; the Clan's strength lay in its numbers, and enhancing that would find favor with its lords. As for the gratitude of its noblewomen at being spared a difficult or even fatal labor . . . the favors so endowed were subtler and took longer to redound, but no less significant for all that. One day, Griben reasoned, it was likely that the head destined to wear the crown would be there solely because of his intervention – and the parents of that prince would know it. So for two decades he'd worked at his practice, patiently healing the sick, attending to confinements, delivering the babies (and on occasion discreetly seeing to the family-planning needs of their mothers), while keeping abreast of the latest developments in his field.

As his reputation burgeoned, so did his personal wealth and influence. He bought an estate in Oest Hjalmar and a private practice in Plymouth, growing plump and comfortable. Duke Lofstrom sought his advice on certain technical matters of state, which he dealt with discreetly and efficiently. There was talk of an earldom in his future, even a petty barony; he began considering the social advantages of taking to wife one of the ladies-in-waiting who graced the court of her majesty the queen-widow.

Then everything inexplicably and rapidly turned to shit.

Dr. ven Hjalmar shrugged, working his left shoulder in circles to adjust the hang of the oddly styled jacket he wore, then glanced at the fly-specked mirror on the dresser. His lip curled. *To fall this far ...* He glanced sidelong at the battered carpetbag that sat on the hotel room bed. *Well, what goes down can come right up again,* he reminded himself.

It was all the Beckstein women's fault, mother and daughter both. He'd first heard it from the mouth of the haughty dowager duchess herself: 'The woman's an impostor of course,' Hildegarde voh Thorold-Hjorth had snapped at him. 'Do you really think it likely that an heiress has been living secretly in exile, in the, the barbarian world, for all these years? Just to surface *now*, when everything is finally settling down again? This is a plot, you mark my words!'

Well, the Beckstein woman *wasn't* an impostor – the dowager might not know a DNA paternity test from a rain of frogs, but he was under no such illusions – but the emergence after so long of her black-sheep mother certainly suggested that the dowager was right about it being some sort of conspiracy. And the bewildering ease with which Miriam had destroyed all the obstacles set in her path and then taken on the Clan Council like some kind of radical reformist firebrand was certainly suggestive. *Someone* was clearly manipulating the woman. And her exposure of the lost cousins, and this strange world which they had made their own, was a thunderbolt out of the blue. 'She's a loose cannon,' Baron Henryk ven Nordstrom had muttered angrily over a glass of port. 'We shall have to take her out of play, Robard, or she's going to throw the board on the floor and jump on the pieces.'

'Do you want me to neutralize her permanently?' ven Hjalmar had asked, cocking his head slightly to one side. 'It seems unsubtle . . .'

Henryk snorted in reply. 'She's a woman, we can tie her down. If necessary, you can damage her a little.' He didn't mention the other business, with the boy in the palace all those years ago; it would be gauche. 'Marry her off and give her some children to keep her busy. Or, if she won't back off, a childbed accident. Hmm, come to think of it, I know a possible husband.'

Well, *that* hadn't worked out for the best, either. Griben snorted again, angry and disquieted. He'd seen what the Pervert's army had left of the pretty little country house he'd bought, kicked the blood and ashes of Oest Hjalmar from his heels for a final time after he'd made the surviving peasants build a cairn from the ruins. He'd done his bit for Henryk, ensuring the rebellious cow got knocked up on schedule for the handfasting after she stuck her nose in one too many corners where it didn't belong; how was he to know the Pervert would respond by committing regicide, fratricide, patricide, homicide, and generally going crazy enough to justify his reputation?

But after that, things went even more askew. Somehow Angbard's minions had conspired to put her *on the fucking throne*, the throne! – of all places – with a Praetorian guard of hardline progressivist thugs. And she *knew*. She'd dug and dug until she'd turned up the breeding program, figured out what it was for – almost as if she'd been pointed at it by someone. Figured out that Angbard had asked him to set up the liaison with the clinic, no doubt. Figured out that what was going on was a power struggle between the old bitches who arranged the marriage braids and the macho phalangist order of the Clan Security organization. Figured out that *he* was the fixer, the enabler, the Clan's own medic and expert in reproductive technology who had given Angbard the idea, back when he was a young and foolish intern who didn't know any better . . .

His idea. The power of it still filled his age-tempered heart with bitter awe: The power to raise an army of world-walkers, to breed them and train them to obedience. It could have made him the most powerful man in the six – now unhappily seven – families. If he'd waited longer, realized that he stood on the threshold of his own success, he'd never have sought Angbard's patronage, much less learned to his dismay how thoroughly that put him under the thin white duke's thumb.

Stolen. Well he had, by god – by the Anglischprache's dead god on a stick, or by Lightning Child, or whichever thrice-damned god really mattered (and who could tell) – he had stolen it back again. The bitch-queen Helge might have it in for him, and her thugs wouldn't hesitate with the hot knives if they ever discovered his role in Hildegarde's little gambit – but that was irrelevant now. He had the list. And he had a copy of the lost family's knotwork emblem, a passport for travel to New Britain. And lastly, he had a piece of paper with a name and address on it.

James Lee had done his job well, during his exile among the Clan.

Finally satisfied with his appearance, Dr. ven Hjalmar walked to the door and opened it an inch. 'I'm ready to go,' he said quietly.

Of the two stout, silent types standing guard, one remained impassive. The other ducked his head, obsequious – or perhaps merely polite in this society; Griben was no judge of strange mores – and shuffled hastily towards the end of the corridor.

The doctor retreated back to his room to wait. These were dangerous times, to be sure, and he had nearly fallen foul of muggers on his way here as it was; the distinction between prison guard and bodyguard might be drawn arbitrarily fine. In any case, the Lees had done him the courtesy of placing him in a ground-floor room with a window overlooking a walled garden; unless Clan Security was asleep at the switch and the Lees had been allowed to set up doppelgänger installations, he was free to leave should he so choose. Of course, that might simply be yet another of their tests . . .

There was a knock; then the door opened. 'Good afternoon, Doctor.'

Ven Hjalmar nodded affably. 'And the same to you, sir.' The elders were clearly taking him seriously, to have sent James Lee to conduct him to this meeting. James was one of the principal heirs. One-quarter ethnic Han by descent, he wouldn't have raised any eyebrows in the other Anglische world: but the politics of race and ethnicity were very different here, and the Lee family's long sojourn on the west coast of the Clan's world among the peasants of the Middle Empire had rendered them conspicuous in the whitebread northeast of New Britain. 'Chinee gangsters' was perhaps the nicest term the natives had for them, and despite their considerable wealth they perforce kept a low profile – much like Griben himself. 'I trust it *is* a good afternoon?'

'I've had worse.' Lee held the door open. 'The elders are waiting to hear your proposal in person, and there's always the potential for – misunderstandings, in such circumstances. But we are all men of goodwill, yes?'

'Yes.' Ven Hjalmar nodded. 'And we all hold valid insurance policies. After you, no, I must insist . . .'

*

The Lee family had fallen out of contact with the rest of the Clan most of two centuries ago – through betrayal, they had thought, although the case for cock-up over conspiracy was persuasive – and in that time they had come to do things very differently. However, some aspects of the operation were boringly familiar: an obsession with the rituals of hierarchy, pecking order, and tiresome minutiae of rank. As with the Clan, they relied on arranged marriages to keep the recessive genetic component of the world-walking trait strong. Like the Clan, they had fractured into a loose formation of families, first and second cousins intermarrying, with a halo of carriers clinging to their coattails. (Again, like the Clan, they practiced a carefully controlled level of exogamy, lest inbreeding for the world-walking trait reinforce other, less desirable ones.) *Unlike* the Clan, Mendelian genetics had made a late arrival – and actual modern reproductive genetics as practiced in the clinics of America was an unknown black art. Or so ven Hjalmar believed; in fact, he was betting his life on it.

*

'Speak to me of this breeding program,' said the old man on the mattress.

Ven Hjalmar stared at his beard. It straggled from the point of his chin, wispy but not too wispy, leaving his cheeks bare. *Is that spirit gum?* he wondered. The cheeks: There was something unnatural about their smoothness, as if powdered, perhaps to conceal the pattern of stubble. It would make sense perhaps, in an emergency, to be able to shed the formal robes, queue, and beard, to dissolve in the crowd . . . 'It was established by the Clan's security division a generation ago,' he said slowly. 'Normally the, the braid of marriages is managed by the elder womenfolk, matchmakers. But with a civil war only just dying down, the Clan's numbers were diminished drastically.' It was surprisingly easy to slip into the habit of speaking of them as a third party, as *them* not *us*. Another creeping sign of exile.

'In America, to which they have access, medical science is very much more advanced than in the Gruinmarkt – or in New Britain. Childless couples can make discreet use of medical services to arrange for a child to be born, with one or other parent's *genes*' – he used the alien word deliberately, throwing it into conversation without explanation – 'to the wife, or to a host mother for adoption. The duke came to an arrangement with such a clinic, to discreetly ensure that a number of such babies were born with the ability to pass on the world-walking *gene* to their own offspring. Records were kept. The plan was to approach the female offspring, as adults, and offer to pay them to be host mothers – paid handsomely, to bear a child for adoption. A child who would, thanks to the clinic, be a true world-walker, and be fostered by the Clan.'

The old lady to the right of the bearded elder tugged her robe fastidiously. Despite the cultivated air of impassivity, the stench of her disapproval nearly made the doctor cough. 'They are unmarried, these host mothers?' she asked querulously.

Ven Hjalmar nodded. 'They do things very differently in the United States,' he added.

'Ah.' She nodded; oddly, her disapproval seemed to have subsided. *Must be some local custom* . . . He took note of it.

'As you can imagine, the Clan's, ah, matchmakers' – he'd nearly said *old women* but caught himself at the last moment – 'did not know of this scheme. It undermined their authority, threatening their rank and privilege. Furthermore, if it went to completion it would hugely undermine the noble families, for these new world-walkers would be brought into the Clan by the duke's security apparatus, with no hereditary ties to bind them to the braids. The scheme found favor with the radical reformers who wished to integrate the Clan more tightly into America, but to those of us who had some loyalty to the old ways' – *or who preferred to be bigger fish in a smaller pond* – 'it was most suspicious.'

The old man – Elder Huan, James Lee had whispered in his ear as they approached the chamber – nodded. 'Indeed.' He fixed ven Hjalmar with a direct and unwavering gaze that was entirely at odds with the image he had maintained throughout the audience up to this point, and asked, 'What do you want of us, Doctor?'

Ven Hjalmar did a double take. 'Uh, well, as a doctor, the duke commanded my attendance. I obeyed, with reservations; however, I consider myself to be released from his service by the occasion of his death. The family loyalists and the radicals are currently tearing each other apart. I come to you in the hope that you might better exercise the wisdom needed to guide and integrate a generation of new world-walkers.' He paused. 'I do not have the list of host mothers on my person, and indeed it would be no use to you without a physician licensed to practice in the United States – which I happen to be. There will be expenses, and it will take some time to set up, but I believe my identity over there is still secure. And I have in any case taken steps – '

Elder Huan glanced sideways at the sour-faced old woman. 'Aunt Mei?'

Aunt Mei sniffed. 'Get to the *point*, boy. We don't have all day!' Elder Huan produced a pocket watch from one sleeve of his robe and glanced at it. 'You are trying to sell us something. Name your price.'

Sweat broke out on Griben's hands. *Not so Chinese*, he realized. Either that, or the directness was a snub, unconscionable rudeness to someone of professional rank. 'I can give you world-walking babies,' he finally admitted. 'I will have to spend some time and considerable money in the United States, and it will take at least eighteen months to start – this can't be hurried, not just the pregnancies but the appearance of legitimate medical practice – but once the operation is up and running, I can deliver up to fifty new world-walkers in the first two years, more later.' *Lots* more with harvested eggs and sperm and an IVF clinic; times had moved on since the first proposal to use AID and host mothers. 'The money . . . I believe on the order of two million US dollars should cover start-up costs, and another hundred thousand per baby. That would be eight thousand pounds and eight hundred pounds. You'll need to build a small shipping operation along similar lines to the Clan's to raise the money – but you have the advantage of being utterly unknown to and unsuspected by the federal agencies. If you stay out of their exact line of business you should thrive.'

Aunt Mei's eyes narrowed. 'And *your* price?' she asked.

It was now or never. 'I want somewhere to live,' he said. 'My patron is dead, the Clan is in turmoil, and I doubt their ability to survive what is coming. I know the Americans – I've worked among them for years – the Gruinmarkt will not be safe. If the loyalist faction wins, they will try to continue as before, a big mistake. If the progressives win . . . they'll want to live here.' He smiled, as ingratiatingly as he could. 'We are distant cousins. Can we put past misunderstandings behind us and work together? Consider me a test case.'

'You ask of us accession to our family,' declared Aunt Mei. 'Money and status besides, but principally refuge from your enemies.' She turned and nudged Elder Huan. 'Is that *all*?' She sounded mildly scandalized.

Elder Huan stared at ven Hjalmar. 'Is that all, indeed?' he echoed ironically. 'You would betray your own family . . . ?'

'*They* betrayed *me*!' Ven Hjalmar was beyond containment. 'I was placed in an intolerable position! Obey the duke and earn the undying hatred of a woman who was to be married to the heir to the throne, or disobey the duke and – well!' He swallowed. 'I gather there is a curse: *May you come to the attention of important people.* At first it looked like a simple problem to solve. The girl was an idiot, naive, and worse, was poking her nose into places it did not belong. But then the civil war started, the duke was incapacitated, and she . . . well. My household was destroyed in the war: My parents are dead, I

304

have no brothers or sisters. What is a man at the end of his affairs to do?'

There it was, on the table. Spun as neatly as he could manage, admittedly, no hint that his own actions had been motivated by anything but the purest obedience to his elders and betters; but soon there would be no one alive to gainsay his account. (The duke was reliably dead, and as for the dowager Hildegarde, she had followed the most insane imaginable 'strategy of tension' with the Americans, obviously lacking even the remotest idea of the magnitude of their inevitable response – she would follow him soon, and certainly long before she'd move to New Britain, of that he was certain.) Robard sweated some more, waiting for the elder Huan to give some indication of his thoughts. Then, after a moment, the elder inclined his head, and looked at Aunt Mei. 'As you will.'

Aunt Mei looked at ven Hjalmar. 'We shall consider your proposal,' she said. 'Such matters are best decided on after full discussion: You may enjoy our hospitality while we search for consensus. But I shall tell you this minute that if we agree with it, there will be another price you must pay.'

'Another . . . ?' Ven Hjalmar was at a loss.

'Yes.' A crinkling around her eyes that hinted at amusement. 'If you are to stay with us, you will have to find a wife.' She clapped her hands. 'Nephew.' James Lee bowed. 'Take the doctor back to his room.'

*

Erasmus Burgeson strode through the portico of the People's Palace as if he owned it, his brown leather duster swinging around him. His usual entourage followed him – a pair of guards in the black peacoats and helmets of Freedom Riders, a stenographer and a pair of messenger boys to race his orders to the nearest telautograph, three secretaries and assistants. It was impossible to fart without his entourage recording the event and issuing a press release to reassure the masses that the commissioner of state propaganda had eaten a healthy breakfast and his bowels were in perfect working order. *Such is the price of being on the winning side,* he reminded himself whenever it became uncomfortable; the alternative – a short walk off the end of a long rope – was far less attractive.

Just one month had wrought great changes. The pompous neo-classical building was crawling with Freedom Riders and guards from the newly formed Security Committee, checking passeportes and getting underfoot: but with some justification, for there had been three assassination attempts on members of the Radical government by Patriot renegades in the past week alone – one of them successful to the extent of having cost Commissioner of Industry Sutter half the fingers on one hand and the use of his left eye, not to mention a secretary and a bodyguard. Erasmus had made much of this shocking martyrdom, but it was hardly the most onerous fate the Patriot mob had in mind for any commissioner who fell into their hands, as the full gibbets in royalist-held Rio de Janeiro could attest.

But the guards didn't impede Burgeson's progress through the entrance and up the stairs to the Avenue of Ministries; they stood aside and saluted with alacrity, their faces expressionless. It was only at the door to the receiving room that he encountered a delay: Commissioner of Security Reynolds's men, of course. 'Citizen Burgeson! You are expected, but your colleagues must identify themselves. Your papers, please!'

Erasmus waited impatiently while the guards confirmed that his aides were indeed on the privileged list, then nodded amiably to the underofficer on door duty. 'If you please?' he asked. The man practically jumped to open the door, avoiding eye contact: Erasmus was of the same rank as the head of his entire organization. Erasmus nodded and, not waiting for his escort, walked through into the outer office. It was crammed with junior people's commissioners and bureaucrats awaiting instruction, cooling their heels in the antechamber to the doctor's surgery. Not pausing for idle chatter, Burgeson walked towards the inner door.

A stout fellow who overtopped him by a good six inches stepped sideways into his path, blocking the doorway. 'You can't – ' he began.

Erasmus stopped and looked up at him. 'Don't you recognize me?' It was genuinely curious, to be stopped by anyone – even a bruiser in the uniform of the Security Committee.

The bodyguard stared down at Erasmus. Then, after a second, he began to wilt. 'No sir,' he admitted. 'Is you expected by 'is citizenship this mornin'?'

'Yes.' Burgeson smiled, showing no teeth. 'Why don't you announce me?'

The ability to intimidate secret policemen didn't come easily or lightly to Erasmus; he still found it a thing of wonder as he watched the big bodyguard turn and push the door ajar to announce his arrival. He'd spent years in the camps, then more years on the run as a Leveler underground organizer in Boston, periodically arrested and beaten by men of this selfsame type, the attack dogs of power. It was no surprise after all these years to see these people rising in the armed wing of the revolutionary democratic cadres, and leaders like Reynolds gaining a certain reputation – especially in view of the unfolding crisis that had first provoked an abdication and then enabled the party to hold its coup – but it was a disappointment. *Meet the new boss, same as the old boss*: Erasmus remembered the Beckstein woman's cynical bon mot. Then he dismissed it from his mind as the thug threw the door wide open before him and stood aside.

'Hail, citizen.' Sir Adam Burroughs smiled wearily at him as the door closed at his back. 'Have you been keeping well?'

'Well enough.' Erasmus lowered his creaking limbs into one of the ornate chairs that faced Sir Adam's huge, gilt-tooled leather-topped barge of a desk. And indeed, it was true: With the tuberculosis that had threatened to kill him cured by Miriam's magic medicine, he felt like a new man, albeit a somewhat breathless one upon whose heels middle age was treading. 'Drowning in paperwork, of course, but aren't we all? My staff are just about keeping on top of the routine stuff, but if anything out of the ordinary comes up they need their reins held.' Barely a square inch of Sir Adam's desk was occupied, but that was one of the privileges of office: There was another, discreet servants' door in the opposite wall, and behind it a pool of stenographers, typer operators, and clerks to meet his needs. 'What can I do for you, citizen?'

'It's the French business.' Sir Adam sounded morose. 'I've asked

Citizens Wolfe and Daly to join us in a few minutes.' Wolfe was the commissioner for foreign affairs, and Daly was the commissioner for the navy: both cabinet posts, like Burgeson's own, and all three of them – not to mention Sir Adam – were clinging on to the bare backs of their respective commissariats for dear life. Nobody in the provisional government knew much about what they were supposed to be doing, with the questionable exception of the Security Committee, who with gusto and zeal were going about doing unto others as they had been done by. Luckily the revolutionary cadres were mostly used to living on their wits, and Sir Adam was setting a good example by ruthlessly culling officials who showed more proficiency in filling their wallets than their brains. 'We can't put them off for any longer.'

'What are your thoughts on the scope of the problem?' Erasmus asked carefully.

'What problem?' Sir Adam raised one gray eyebrow. 'It's an imperialist war of attrition and there's nothing to be gained from continuing it. Especially as His Former Majesty emptied the coffers and mismanaged the economy to the point that we can't *afford* to continue it. The question is not whether we sue for peace, it's how – ah, John, Mark! So glad you could join us!'

So am I, Erasmus thought as the two other commissioners exchanged greetings and took their seats. Being seen to proceed by consensus on matters of state was vital – at this point, to take after the king's authoritarian style would be the quickest way imaginable to demoralize the rank and file. 'Are we quorate?' he asked.

'I believe so.' Wolfe, a short, balding fellow with a neat spade-shaped beard, twitched slightly, a nervous tic he'd come out of the mining camps with – Erasmus had had dealings with him before, in Boston and parts south. 'Is this about the embassy?' he asked Sir Adam.

'Yes.' Sir Adam reached into a desk drawer and withdrew a slim envelope. 'He insisted on delivering his preliminary list of demands to me, personally, "as acting head of state," as he put it.' He made a moue of distaste. Wolfe grunted irritably as Sir Adam slid the envelope across the desk towards him. 'I don't want to preempt your

considered opinion, but I don't consider his demands to be acceptable.'

Erasmus frowned: Daly, the naval commissioner, looked startled,
but Wolfe took the trespass on his turf in good form, and merely
began reading. After a moment he shook his head. 'No, no . . . you're
absolutely right. Impossible.' He put the paper down. 'Why are you
even considering it?'

Sir Adam smiled with all the warmth of a glacier: 'Because we
need peace abroad. You know and I know that we cannot accept these
terms, but neither can we afford to continue this war.'

'May I?' Erasmus reached for the letter as Sir Adam nodded.

'But the price they're demanding – ' Erasmus scanned quickly.
After the usual salutations and diplomatic greetings, the letter was
brusque and to the point. 'It's outrageous,' Wolfe continued. 'The
money is one thing, but the loss of territory is wholly unacceptable,
and the limitation on naval strength is – '

'Choke them,' Erasmus commented.

'Excuse me?' Wolfe stared at him.

'There is stuff here we can't deal with, it's true. War reparations . . .
but we know we can't pay, and they must know we can't pay. So buy
them off with promissory notes which we do not intend to honor.
That's the first thing. Then there's the matter of the territorial
demands. So they want Cuba. *Give* them Cuba.' He grinned humorlessly at Wolfe's expression. 'Hasn't the small matter of how to put
down the Patriot resistance there exercised us unduly? It all depends
how we give them Cuba. Suppose we accede to the French demands.
The news stories at home will run, the French have *taken* Cuba. And
to the Cubans, our broadcasts will say, sorry, but the Patriots stabbed
us in the back. And there is nothing to stop us funneling guns and
money to the Patriots who take up arms against the French, is there?
Let it bleed them, I say. They want Nippon? Let them explain that to
the shogun. It's not as if he recognizes our sovereignty in any case.'

'What naval concessions are they demanding?' asked Daly. 'We
need the navy, the army isn't politically correct – '

'They want six of our ships of the line, and limits on new construction of such,' Erasmus noted. 'So take six of the oldest prison

hulks and hand them over. Turn the hulls in the shipyards over to a new task – not that we can afford to proceed with construction this year, in any case – those purpose-built flat-topped tenders the air-minded officers have been talking about.' Miriam had lent Erasmus a number of history books from her strange world; he'd found the account of her nation's war with the Chrysanthemum Throne in the Pacific most interesting.

'These are good suggestions,' Sir Adam noted, 'but we cannot accede to this – this laundry list! If we pay the danegeld, the Dane will . . . well. You know full well why they want Cuba. And there are these reports of disturbing new weapons. John, did you discover anything?'

Daly looked lugubrious. 'There's an entire *city* in Colorado that I'd never heard of two weeks ago,' he said, an expression of uneasy disbelief on his face. 'It's full of natural philosophers and artificers, and they're taking quantities of electricity you wouldn't believe. Something about a super-petard, made from chronosium, I gather. Splitting the atom, alchemical transformation of chronosium into something they call osirisium in atomic crucibles. And they confirm the French intelligence.' He glanced at Erasmus: 'I mean no ill, but is everyone here approved for this news?'

Sir Adam nodded. 'I wouldn't ask you to report on it if I thought otherwise. The war is liable to move into a new and uncertain stage if we continue it. The French have these petards, they may be able to drop them from aerodynes or fire them from the guns of battleships: a single shell that can destroy a fleet or level a city. It beggars the imagination but we cannot ignore it, even if they have but one or two. We need them likewise, and we need time to test and assemble an arsenal. Speaking of which . . . ?'

'I pressed them for a date, but they said the earliest they could test their first charge would be three months from now. If it works, and if ordered to, they can scale up production, making perhaps one a month by the end of the year. Apparently this stuff is not like other explosives, it takes months or years to synthesize – but in eighteen months, production will double, and eighteen months after that they can increase output fourfold.'

'So we can have four of these, what do you call them, corpuscular petards? – corpses, an ominous name for an ominous weapon – by the end of this year. Sixteen by the end of next year, thirty-four by the end of the year after, and hundreds the year after that. Is that a fair summary?' Daly nodded. 'Then our medium-term goal is clear: We need to get the bloody French off our backs for at least three and a half years, strengthen our homeland air defenses against their aerodynes, and work out some way of deterring the imperialists. In which case' – Sir Adam gestured irritably at the diplomatic communiqué – 'we need to give them enough to shut them up for a while, but not so easily that they smell a rat or are tempted to press for more.' He looked pointedly at Erasmus. 'Finesse and propaganda are the order of the day.'

'Yes. This will require care and delicacy.' Erasmus continued reading. 'And the most intricate maintenance of their misconceptions. When do you intend to commence direct talks with the enemy ambassador?'

'Tomorrow.' Sir Adam's tone was decisive. 'The sooner we bury the hatchet the faster we can set about rebuilding that which is broken and reasserting the control that we have lost. And only when we are secure on three continents can we look to the task of liberating the other four.'

*

An editor's life is frequently predictable, but seldom boring.

At eleven that morning, Steve Schroeder was settling down in his cubicle with his third mug of coffee, to work over a feature he'd commissioned for the next day's issue.

In his early forties, Steve wasn't a big wheel on the *Herald*; but he'd been a tech journalist since the early eighties, and he had a weekly section to fill, features to buy from freelance stringers, and in-depth editorial pieces to write. He rated an office, or a cubicle, or at least space to think without interruption when he wasn't attending editorial committee meetings and discussing clients to target with Joan in advertising sales, or any of the hundred and one things other than editing that went with wearing the hat. Reading the articles he'd asked for and *editing* them sometimes seemed like a luxury; so he frowned instinctively at the stranger standing in the entrance to his cubicle. 'Yes?'

The stranger wore a visitor's badge, and there was something odd about him. Not the casual Friday clothes; it took Steve a moment to spot the cast on his leg. 'You're Steve Schroeder?'

'Who wants to know?'

The stranger shrugged. 'You don't know me.' He produced a police ID card. Steve sat up, squinting at the badge. *Drug Enforcement Agency?*

'Not my department; crime's upstairs on – '

'No, I think I need to talk to you. You commissioned a bunch of articles by Miriam Beckstein a couple of years ago, didn't you?'

Huh? 'What's this about?' Steve asked cautiously.

'Haven't heard from her for a while, have you?'

Alarm bells were going off in his head. 'Has she been arrested? I don't know anything; we had a strictly business relationship – '

'She hasn't been arrested.' Fleming's gaze flickered sidelong; if Steve hadn't been staring at him he might not have noticed. 'She mentioned you, actually, a couple of years ago. Listen, I don't know anyone here, and I've got very limited time, so I thought I'd try you and see if you could direct me to the right people.' He swallowed. 'She pointed me at a story, kind of, before she disappeared. I need to see it breaks, and breaks publicly, or *I'm* going to disappear too. I'm sorry if that sounds overdramatic – '

'No, that's all right.' *Jesus, why me? Why now?* Steve glanced at his workstation for long enough to save the file he was reading. *Do I need this shit?* Building security mostly kept the nuts out with admirable efficiency; and paranoids invariably headed for Crime and Current Affairs. If this guy *was* a nut . . . 'Mind if I look at that?' Fleming handed him the badge. Steve blinked, peering at it. *Certainly looks real enough . . .* He handed it back. 'Why me?'

'Because – ' Fleming was looking around. 'Mind if I sit down?'

Steve took a deep breath and gestured at the visitor's chair by his desk. 'Go ahead. In your own time.'

'Last year Miriam Beckstein lost her job. You know about that?'

312

Steve nodded, guardedly. 'You want to tell me about it?'

'It wasn't the regular post-9/11 slowdown; she was fired because she stumbled across a highly sophisticated money-laundering operation. Drug money, and lots of it.'

Steve nodded again. Trying to remember: What had Miriam said? She'd been working for *The Industry Weatherman* back then, hadn't she? Something wild about them canning her for uncovering – *Jesus*, he thought. 'Mind if I record this?' he asked.

'Sure. Be my guest.' Fleming chuckled as Steve activated his recorder. It was a hoarse bark, too much stress bottled up behind it. 'Listen, this isn't just about drugs, and I know it's going to sound nuts, so let me start with some supporting evidence. An hour ago, my car was blown up. The news desk will probably have a report on it, incident in Braintree – ' He proceeded to give an address. 'I'm being targeted because I'm considered unreliable by the organization I've been working for on secondment. You can check on that bombing. If you wait until this afternoon, I'm afraid – shit. There's going to be a terrorist strike this afternoon in D.C., and it's going to be bigger than 9/11. That's why I'm here. There's a faction in the government who have decided to run an updated version of Operation Northwoods, and they've maneuvered a narcoterrorist group into taking the fall for it. I'm – I was – attached to a special cross-agency task force working on the narcoterrorist ring in question. They're the folks Miriam stumbled across – and it turns out that they're big, bigger than the Medellín Cartel, and they've got contacts all the way to the top.'

'Operation – what was that operation you mentioned?' Steve stared at his visitor. *Jesus. Why do I always get the cranks?*

'Operation Northwoods. Back in 1962, during the Cold War, the Chiefs of Staff came up with a false-flag project to justify an invasion of Cuba. The idea was that the CIA would fake up terrorist attacks on American cities, and plant evidence pointing at Castro. They were going to include hijackings, bombings, the lot – the most extreme scenarios included small nukes, or attacks on the capitol; it was all "Remember the *Maine*" stuff. Northwoods wasn't activated, but during the early seventies the Nixon administration put in place the equipment for the same, on a bigger scale – there was a serious

313

proposal to nuke Boston in order to justify a preemptive attack on China. This stuff keeps coming up again, and I'd like to remind you that our current vice president and the secretary for defense got their first policy chops under Nixon and Ford.'

'But they can't – ' Steve stopped. 'They've just invaded Iraq! Why would they want to do this now? If they were going to – '

'Iraq was the president's hobbyhorse. And no, I'm not saying that 9/11 was stage-managed to drag us into that war; that would be paranoid. But there's a whole new enemy on hand, and a black cross-agency program to deal with them called the Family Trade Organization, and some of us aren't too happy about the way things are being run. Let me fill you in on what's been going on . . .'

EVACUATION

The marcher kingdoms of the East Coast, from the Nordtmarkt south, were scantily populated by American standards: The Gruinmarkt's three to four million – there was no exact census – could handily live in New York City with room to spare. The Clan and their outer families (related by blood, but not for the most part gifted with the world-walking talent) were at their most numerous in the Gruinmarkt, but even there their total extended families barely reached ten thousand souls. The five inner families had, between them, a couple of thousand adult world-walkers and perhaps twice that many children (and some seniors and pregnant women for whom world-walking would be a hazardous, if not lethal, experience).

At one point in the 1930s, American style, the inner families alone had counted ten thousand adult world-walkers; but the Clan's long, festering civil war had been a demographic disaster. To an organization that relied for its viability on a carefully preserved recessive gene, walking the line between inbreeding and extinction, a series of blood feuds between families had sown the seeds of collapse.

Nearly twenty years ago, Angbard, Duke Lofstrom, the chief of the Clan's collective security agency, had started a program to prevent such a collapse from ever again threatening the Clan. He'd poured huge amounts of money into funding a network of fertility clinics in the United States, and the children of that initiative were now growing to adulthood, ignorant of the genes (and other, more exotic intracellular machinery) for which they were carriers. Angbard's plan had been simple and direct: to approach young female carriers selected from the clinics' records, and pay them to act as host mothers for fictional infertile couples. The result was to be a steady stream of world-walkers, raised in the United States and not loyal to the quarreling families, who could be recruited in due course. Miriam, Helge, had been raised in Boston by Angbard's sister as an experiment in cultural assimilation, not to mention a political insurance policy: Other children of the Clan had been schooled and trained in the ways and knowledge of the exotic West.

But Angbard had planned on being around to coordinate the recruitment of the new world-walkers. He hadn't expected Matthias's defection, or the exposure of the clinics to hostile inspection, and he hadn't anticipated the reaction of the Auld Bitches, the gaggle of grandmothers whose carefully arranged marriages kept the traditional Clan structure afloat. Their tame gynecologist, Dr. ven Hjalmar, was a stalwart of the conservative club. He'd been the one who, at Baron Henryk's bidding, had arranged for Helge's involuntary pregnancy. He'd also acquired the breeding program records for his faction and, most recently, taken pains to ensure that Angbard would never again threaten their prestige as gatekeepers of the family trade. And now the surviving members of the Clan's conservative clique – the ones who hadn't been massacred by Prince Egon at the ill-fated betrothal feast – were cleaning up.

On that July morning, approximately one in every hundred world-walkers died.

In his private chambers in the Ostrood House, Baron Julius Arnesen was shot dead by Sir Gavaign Thorold.

Lord Mors Hjalmar, his eldest son Euen, and wife Gretyl were blown up by a satchel charge of PETN delivered by a courier who, not being a member of the clique responsible, also died in the blast – neither the first nor the last collateral casualty.

There were other, less successful assassination attempts. The young soldier detailed to slay Sir Helmut Anders had second thoughts and, rather than carrying out his orders, broke down and confessed them to his commander. The assault team targeting Earl-Major Riordan arrived at the wrong safe house owing to faulty intelligence, and by the time they located the correct headquarters building it had already been evacuated. And the poison-pen letter addressed to Lady Patricia Thorold-Hjorth – lightly spritzed in dimethyl mercury, a potent neurotoxin – never left the postal office, owing to an unusual shortage of world-walkers arriving to discharge their corvée duties that day.

In fact, nearly two-thirds of those targeted for assassination survived, and nearly a third of the would-be assassins were captured, killed, or failed to carry out their missions. As *coup d'état* attempts went, this one might best be described as a halfhearted clusterfuck. The conservative faction had been under siege since the betrothal-night massacre, many of their most effective members slain; what remained was the rump of the postal committee (cleaving to the last to the trade that had brought them wealth and power), the scheming grandmothers and their young cat's-paws, and a bedraggled handful who had fallen upon hard times or whose status was in some other way threatened by the new order.

Only one element of the conspiracy ran reliably to completion. Unfortunately, it was Plan Blue.

*

In a humid marsh on the banks of a broad river, there stood a scaffold by the grace of the earl of Dankfurt. The scaffold lacked many of the appurtenances of such – no dangling carrion or cast-iron basket of bones to add to the not inconsiderable stench of the swamp – but it provided a stout and very carefully surveyed platform. Here in the Sudtmarkt most maps were hand-scribed in ink on vellum, and accurate to the nearest league. But this platform bore stripe-painted measuring sticks at each corner, and had been carefully pinned down by theodolites borne by world-walkers. Its position and altitude were known to within a foot, making it the most accurately placed location in the entire kingdom.

Five men stood on the scaffold beside a cheap wheelbarrow that held an olive-drab cylinder the size of a beer keg. Two of them wore US army fatigues, in the new desert pattern that had come in with the Iraq war: outer-family world-walkers both, young and more tenuously attached to the Clan than most. The other three were clad in fashions that had never been a feature of that time line. 'Are you clear on the schedule?' demanded one fellow, a thin-haired, thin-faced man whom Miriam had once likened to a ferret.

'Sir.' The shorter of the two uniformed men bowed his neck formally.

'Tell us, please,' said one of the other fellows, resting his hand on the pommel of his small-sword.

'At T minus eight minutes, Erik takes his place on the barrow. I then cross over. Emergence is scheduled for level two, visitors' car park block delta three. There will be cameras but no internal guard patrols inside the car park – active security is on the perimeter and at the doors.'

The ferret-faced man nodded. 'Kurt?'

The tall, sandy-haired soldier nodded. 'I dismount. We have sixty seconds to clear down any witnesses. Then we wheel the barrow to the stairwell. By T minus six the payload is to be emplaced in the place of the red fire extinguisher, which we will place in the barrow. We are then to proceed back to our arrival point, whereupon Jurgen will take his place in the barrow and I will bring us home no later than T minus five.'

'What provisions for failure have you made?' asked the fellow with the small-sword.

'Not much,' the Ferret admitted. 'Jurgen?'

Jurgen shrugged. 'We shoot any witnesses, of course.' He tapped one trouser pocket, which was cut away to reveal the butt of a silenced pistol peeping out of a leg holster. The uniforms weren't very authentic – but then, they only had to mislead witnesses for a few seconds. 'If we can't cross back because of a surveyor's error, we turn the barrow upside down and Kurt stands on it. I ride him. Yes?'

The Ferret nodded to his companion. 'My lord earl, there we are. Simple, sweet, with minimal room for things to go wrong.'

The earl nodded thoughtfully. His eyes flickered between the two soldiers. Did they suspect that the thumbwheel on the payload's timer-controller had been modified to detonate six minutes earlier than the indicated time? Probably not, else they wouldn't be standing here. 'If we'd been able to survey inside this, this five-sided structure . . .'

'Indeed. Unfortunately, my lord Hjorth, it is the most important administrative headquarters of their military, and it was attacked by their enemies only two years ago. The visitors' car park is as close as we could get. The payload' – the Ferret patted the stubby metal cylinder – 'is sufficient to the job.'

'Well, then.' Baron Oliver Hjorth managed a strained smile. 'I salute your bravery. Good men!'

Jurgen nodded. 'I'm certain that there will be no trouble, my lord.'

'Everyone in the witch-kingdom expects to see fire extinguishers in stairwells,' added the Ferret, not bothering to explain that the keg-sized payload looked utterly unlike a fire extinguisher. 'And it won't be there long enough for anyone to tamper with it.' Strapped to the detonation controller, it weighed nearly ninety kilos; there was a reason for the carefully surveyed crossing point, the wheelbarrow, and the two strong-backed and incurious couriers.

'Good,' the earl said briskly. He pulled out a pocket watch and inspected the dial. 'Fifty-six minutes, I see. Is that the time? Well, I must be going now.' He nodded at the Ferret. 'I expect to see you in Dankfurt by evening.'

'And the men, sir,' prompted the Ferret.

'Oh yes. And you.' Hjorth glanced at the uniformed couriers. 'Yes, we shall find a suitable reward for you. I must be going.'

With that, he turned and clambered down the ladder, followed by his bodyguard. Together, they squelched towards the rowboat that waited at the water's edge. It would carry them to the other side, and thence to the carriage waiting to race him away down the post road, so that he would be a couple of leagues distant before the clocks counted down to zero.

Just in case something went wrong at the last moment. You could never be too sure, with these devices.

*

The Explorer rumbled slowly down a narrow road near Andover, thick old-growth trees blocking the view to either side. Harold Parker State Forest wasn't exactly the back end of nowhere, but with thousands of acres of hardwood and pine forest, campground and logging roads, and day trippers moving in and out all summer, it was a good place to disappear. Miriam sat back with her eyes closed, trying to fend off the sickening sense of impending dread. It was happening again: the sense of her life careering out of control, in the hands of – *Stop that,* she told herself. Half the occupants of the big SUV were sworn to her, bound by oaths of fealty; the rest were – *If I can't trust them, I can't trust* anybody. So here they were, bumping along a logging road towards a secret, undisclosed location where Clan Security maintained a cache of equipment and a doppelgängered transfer house –

The SUV was slowing. Miriam opened her eyes. 'Nearly there,' Sir Alasdair grunted.

Riordan was still glued to his cell phone, nodding occasionally between bursts of clipped Hochsprache. Miriam tapped him on the shoulder. He held up a hand. 'Be right back,' he told his absent conversationalist. 'What is it?'

'If there's a mole inside ClanSec, how do you know your Plan Black site hasn't been rigged?' she asked. 'If I was trying to mousetrap you, I can't think of a better way to do it than scaring you into running for a compromised rendezvous.'

Riordan looked thoughtful. Miriam noticed Sir Alasdair's shoulders tense. Brilliana chirped up from the back row of seats: 'She's right, you know.'

'Yes,' Riordan said grudgingly. 'But we need to evacuate – '

'It can be booby-trapped here, or in the Gruinmarkt,' Olga pointed out. 'If here, we can deal with it. Over there – we shall just have to reconnoiter, no?'

'Sounds like a plan,' said Sir Alasdair. 'Who are we expecting here, my lord?'

'This site is meant to be held by Sir Helmut's second lance,' Riordan said as he stared at the screen of the tablet PC in his lap. 'Two over here, six over there with two active and four in recovery or ready for transfer. The site on the other side is a farmhouse: burned out during the campaign, I'm afraid, but defensible.'

'Can you identify them?' asked Brilliana.

'By sight, yes, most probably. Outer-family aspirants, a couple of young bloods – I can show you their personnel files, with photographs. Why?'

'Because if I see the wrong faces on duty I want to be sure before

I shoot them.'

The Explorer was slowing. Now Sir Alasdair took a sharp left onto a dirt trail barely any wider than the SUV. 'We're about two hundred yards out,' he warned. 'Where do you want me to stop?'

'Right here.' Riordan glanced at Brilliana. 'Are you ready, my lady?'

Brill nodded, reaching into her shoulder bag to pull out a black, stubby gun with a melted-looking grip just below the muzzle and a box magazine stretching along the upper surface of the barrel. 'Sir Alasdair – '

'I'm coming too,' rumbled Miriam's bodyguard. He pulled the parking brake. 'My lord, would you care to take the wheel? If a quick withdrawal is required – '

'I can drive,' Miriam heard herself saying. 'You don't need me for anything else, and I'm sure you need your hands?'

Riordan glanced at her, worried, then nodded. 'Here's the contact sheet.' He passed the tablet PC back to Brill, who peered at it for a few seconds.

'Okay, I am ready,' she announced, and opened her door.

For Miriam, the next few minutes passed nightmarishly slowly. As Alasdair and Brill disappeared up the track and into the trees along-side it, she took Sir Alasdair's place behind the wheel, adjusting the seat and lap belt to fit. She kept the engine running at a low idle, although what she'd do if it turned out to be an ambush wasn't obvi-ous – backing up down a dirt trail while under fire from hostiles didn't seem likely to have a happy outcome. She sighed, keeping her eyes on the road ahead, waiting.

'They know what they're doing,' Olga said, unexpectedly.

'Huh?' Miriam swallowed.

'She's right,' added Riordan. 'I would not have let them go if I thought them likely to walk into an ambush.'

'But if they – '

Someone was jogging down the track, waving. Miriam focused, swallowing bile. It was Brill. She didn't look happy.

'Wait here.' Olga's door opened; before Miriam could say any-thing, she was heading towards Brill. After a brief exchange, Brill turned and headed back up the path. Olga returned to the Explorer.

'She says it's safe to proceed to the shack, but there's a problem.' Her lips were drawn tight with worry.

'You'd better go,' Riordan added. 'We're on a timetable here.'

'We're – ' *Oh.* Miriam put the SUV in gear and began to crawl forward. *It's an evacuation plan; they've got to figure on hostiles blowing it sooner or later, so . . .* She'd seen enough of the Clan's security machinations in action to guess how it went. Wherever they were evacuating through, the safe house – shack? – would be anything but safe to someone arriving after the cutoff time.

The track curved around a stand of trees, then down an embankment and around another clump to terminate in a clearing. At one side of the clearing stood a windowless shack, its wooden slats bleached silvery gray by the weather. Brilliana stood in front of the padlocked door, white-faced, her P90 at the ready in clenched hands. 'Park here,' said Olga, opening her door again.

Miriam parked, then climbed down from the cab. 'Where's Alasdair?' she asked, approaching Brill.

Brill shook slightly. 'Milady, he's gone across already. Please *don't go there* – ' But Miriam had already seen what was round the side of the shack.

'What happened?' she demanded. 'Who are they?' Riordan had also seen; he knelt by the nearer of the two bodies, examining it. Lying facedown, dressed in hunting camouflage jacket and trousers, they might have been asleep. Miriam stared at Riordan, then back at Brill. 'What happened?' she repeated.

'They were waiting for us.' Brill's voice was robotic, unnaturally controlled. 'They were not the guards we expected to see. That one' – Riordan was straightening up – 'I recognized him. He worked for Henryk.'

Riordan was holding something at arm's length. As he came closer, Miriam recognized it. 'Silenced,' Riordan told her, his voice over-controlled as he ejected the magazine and worked the slide to remove the chambered round. 'An assassin's weapon.'

Brill nodded, her face frozen; but something in the set of her shoulders unwound, slumping infinitesimally.

322

'Oh my god.' Miriam felt her knees going weak. 'What's Sir Alasdair walking into?'

'I don't know.' Brill took a deep breath. 'I wouldn't want to be in their shoes. Don't worry, my lady, he'll try to save one of them for questioning.'

Miriam shivered. Her sense of dread intensified: not for herself, but for Alasdair. The man-mountain had already saved her life at least once; deceptively big and slow, he could move like an avalanche when needs must. 'What are they doing here?'

'If I had to guess, I'd say the conservatives think they're inside our OODA loop.' Olga looked extremely unhappy. 'This has to have been planned well in advance. My lady, I beg your indulgence, but would you mind waiting in the truck? It has been modified – there is some lightweight armor – it would set my mind at ease.'

'Really?' Miriam fought back the urge to scream with frustration.

'Lady Olga, allow me.' Brill touched Miriam's arm. 'Walk with me.'

Brill led Miriam back up the track, just beyond the bend.

'What's going to – '

Brill cut across her. 'Listen, my lady. In a couple of minutes, two of us – I would guess the earl and myself – will have to cross over, piggyback. *If* the map is truthful, *if* Sir Alasdair has been successful at his task, I will return. Then Lady Olga will have to carry you across, while the returnee recovers their wits. If I don't come back, you should assume that we are both dead and that before we died we betrayed your presence here to your enemies. In which case you and Lady Olga must *drive like hell* then go to ground and lose yourselves as thoroughly as you can imagine. Because if Earl-Major Riordan is dead or captured, our enemies will have accomplished their end, and all they need you for is to bring the heir to term and then . . . they won't need you anymore. Do you understand? Do you *understand*?'

Brill's grip on her wrist was painful. Miriam nodded, jerkily. 'How long?' she managed.

'About . . . hmm. No more than five minutes.' Brilliana pursed her lips. 'If Sir Alasdair ran into trouble and we can't fix it, we'll come back. No false heroics. So you see? If I don't come back soon, it's because I can't.'

'You could be walking into an ambush.'

'We could but we won't.' Brill nodded her head at the uphill slope. 'What do you think that is?'

'That's a – ' Miriam stopped. 'Oh. *Clever.*'

'Yes.' The ground level in the Gruinmarkt didn't always match the level in this world. World-walking tended not to go too well if the world-walker arrived several meters above ground level; and it didn't work at all if they tried to cross over inside a solid object. 'The shack is the primary location, but there's a secret secondary. At the crest of the ramp, step off the track to the left, about six feet, then cross over. There's an outhouse, and you come out at roof level with a clear field of fire.' Brill hefted her gun. 'Listen, go back to the truck and wait with Lady Olga.' She smiled diffidently: 'It will work out, you see.'

*

Near a small town in Pennsylvania, six miles north of Camp David, Highway 16 runs through rolling hills and open woodland, past the foot of a low mountain called Raven Rock.

A casual visitor turning off the highway onto Harbaugh Valley Road wouldn't see much: a chain-link fence and a narrow track off to one side, and a sign warning of a restricted area. But if they drove up the road a couple of miles it would be another story – assuming the armed guards didn't stop them first. Tucked away behind the trees on top of the mountain there was a huge array of satellite dishes and radio masts. And beneath the ground, buried under many meters of bedrock, lay the Raven Rock Mountain Complex, home of the Alternative National Military Command Center, the 114th Signal Battalion, and the emergency operations centers for the army, navy, air force, joint staff, and secretary of defense.

Of course, a casual visitor wouldn't have seen the visitors arriving in the back of unmarked black Lincoln Town Cars with smoked windows that sat oddly low on their suspension. They wouldn't have seen the thick steel doors that opened inside the low, windowless buildings, or the downward-sloping tunnel that cut into the ground, or the elevators and cranes and the blast doors set into the side of the tunnel. Indeed, there was no such thing as a casual visitor at the concrete-and-steel-lined installation embedded in the ground beneath the motel and golf club buildings.

Welcome to the Undisclosed Location.

In a compact, brightly lit conference room ninety feet below the ground, the vice president sat with his advisors, watching television. They had a lot of television to watch; a rack of six sets covered half a wall, flicking through channels on a twenty-second cycle. Bloomberg, CNN, Fox News, and C-SPAN played tag with the Cartoon Network and Discovery Channel on four monitors; two others were permanently tuned to NBC and the view from a traffic camera overlooking a street intersection in Dupont Circle.

The vice president leaned back in his chair, stretching his arms, and glanced at the skinny Yalie with his lapel-pin crucifix and rimless spectacles. 'This is the boring part,' he confided. 'We used to come down here and game these scenarios every month or so during the nineties, you know. All weekend long. Used to be the Russkies on the other side, or the Iranians. They'd set up their opening move, we'd set up our response, and then we'd see how it all played out, whether or not we locate and kill the threat before it activates, which branch of the crisis algorithm we go down. The trouser legs of terror.' He chuckled, a throaty laugh that terminated in a bubbling cough. 'So. Do you think they're bluffing?'

Dr. Andrew James glanced past his boss, at the empty chair where State's assistant secretary ought to be sitting if this session wasn't classified FAMILY TRADE ONLY. 'I couldn't say for sure, sir, but that phone call sounded promising.' He gestured at the desk telephone in front of him, beige and stuffed with buttons with obscure labels that only made sense to the NSA eggheads who designed these gadgets. 'The call terminated promptly.'

'Good,' the VP said vehemently. 'Gutless bastards.'

'We don't know for sure that it terminated as intended, sir,' James warned. 'The adversary's INFOSEC is pretty good for an amateur operation, and the bugging transcript from contact FLEMING indicates at least one of them was concerned about the bait phone.'

'They got the message, either way. Bart, is there any noise on the Continuity side?'

325

'Nothing new, sir.' Bart, a graying DISA apparatchik, was hunched over a laptop with a trailing cable patched into a wall jack – a SIPRNet connection. 'They're all just standing by. SECDEF is aboard KNEECAP on the ramp at Andrews AFB, standing by for JEEP with short-notice takeoff clearance. The president is in the EOB as usual. Uh, message from SECDEF. He wants to know if you've got an update.'

'Tell him no' – the vice-president stared at the wall of televisions, then reached behind his left ear to adjust the multichannel earpiece – 'but if they don't send us a message within the next twenty-four hours I think they're probably going to fold. I just want him where – want backup. This *could* go wrong.'

Dr. James's BlackBerry buzzed for attention. Glancing down at its screen, he froze. 'Sir.'

'Speak.'

'SIGTRADE just issued a RED FLASH – some kind of coded signal. It's running through their network – ' The machine buzzed again. 'Uh, right. Something is going on. Post six reports surveillance subjects all just freaked. They're moving, and it's sudden.'

The vice-president closed his eyes. 'Round 'em up, then. That's plan – which plan – '

Another aide riffled hastily through a ring binder. 'Would that be HEAD CRASH, sir? Track and disable immediate, then hood and ship?'

'That's the one.' He nodded. 'Send it,' he told Bart. 'And tell them I want hourly head counts and updates on everything – misses as well as arrests.'

*

In private, behind locked doors, the discussion took a different shape.

'Sit down, Jim. Have a whisky?'

'Yes, please.' James Lee settled into the overstuffed armchair and waited while his father – Elder Huan's nephew Shen – filled two crystal tumblers from a hip flask and ensconced himself in the room's other armchair. His den was furnished in conventional Western style, free of exotic affectations or imported reminders of the Middle Empire here; just two overstuffed armchairs, a battered mahogany bureau from the inventory of a retired ship's captain, and a wall of pigeonholes and index files. The Lee family's decidedly schizophrenic relationship with New Britain was tilted to the Occident here; but then, Dad had always been an Anglophile. 'How's Mother keeping? And Angelina? I haven't seen them lately – '

'Neither have I, Jim. We write, regularly – Xian says all is well and they're enjoying the peace in the summer house near Nan Shang.' Nan Shang in what would be California, two worlds over – or the Middle Empire in the world where the eastern seaboard belonged to the marcher kingdoms. With the fiscal crisis in full flow, and latterly the riots and disorder, many of the family's elders had deemed it prudent to send their dependents away to safety. While the Lee extended family were nothing like as prominent in the West as the six Eastern families had become in the East, their country estates were nevertheless palatial. 'The postal service is still working. Do you want me to – '

'No, I'm sorry, Father. Just curious. You wanted a chat?'

'Yes.' His father was silent for a few seconds. Then: 'What is your opinion of the doctor? Did you have an opportunity to form an opinion of him during your stay with the cousins?' During the six months during which James had been a pampered hostage.

'I didn't know him well, Father. But – you want my honest opinion? He's a worm. A dangerous, slimy, treacherous worm.'

'Strong words.' The lightness of his father's tone was belied by his sour face. 'Do you have reason for it?'

'I believe so. I don't think he told Eldest any outright untruths, but nothing he said was quite right, either. He was telling the truth when he said he was the personal physician to many of the Eastern cousins' womenfolk, but he was also . . . not as put-upon as he would have you believe. He said he earned the undying hatred of the woman Helge – and he was telling the truth there, too. But Helge didn't impress me as being anybody's fool. She's neither naive nor stupid – we had time to talk – there's something unpleasant underneath this excess of servility on his part, Father. I can't tell you precisely what he's hiding, but he's hiding *something*.'

'That much was obvious from his performance.' Shen took a sip of whisky. 'I don't think Mei is serious about finding him a wife – unless she means to set the Widow Ting on him.' James flinched; avoiding cousin Ting and her dangerous games had been one of his wiser moves. 'I gather she's itching to marry again. That would make . . . three? Four? No matter. It is perfectly clear that the doctor is as twisty as a hangman's noose. What your uncle would like to know is – can he deliver what he offered?'

'I don't know.' James paused. 'You may know more than I, Father. Is it true that Helge is with child?'

For a long moment his father stared into his tumbler. 'It might be so.'

'Because.' James licked his lips. 'Before the Per– before the youngest son's rebellion, she was held prisoner and securely chaperoned. And I met the heir to whom she was betrothed. *He* wasn't going to do any begetting on her. There was unsavory whispering about some of ven Hjalmar's works, among the servants I cultivated. Some said that the man was an abortionist. Others accused him of drugging and raping noblewomen – a story I find incredible, under the circumstances described. What is true is that the Clan's ladies, whom he served, made use of a hospital or clinic in the United States, which he helped run. I know *that* much. And Helge was leashed for poking her nose into some business that sounds very like this baby clinic he offered to elder Yuan. So: I believe he is mostly telling the truth – again, only mostly.'

'What do you think he plans?'

'What he – ' James stopped. 'You can't be thinking of working with him! He's a viper. He's stung two masters already, why would he stop short of making it three? It's in his nature!'

'Calm down, boy, I'm not making that decision!'

'I'm sorry, Father.'

'That is good. Don't worry unduly – we trust him no more than you do. But we need to have some idea of his goals before we can decide whether to make use of him or not. If he can deliver what he offers – perhaps as many as five hundred world-walkers within ten years – that is a matter of enormous significance! We would not have to worry about the Eastern cousins after that. It would open up new business possibilities, ways of making ourselves useful to those in authority – whomever they may be, when the current incivility dies down – new blood in our thinning arteries. *Can he do it?* That is what my uncle asks. If he can, then we can use him: tie him down, shadow his work, and eventually take it over. But if he's a mere charlatan' – Shen made a dismissive gesture, casting the shadow of ven Hjalmar over his left shoulder – 'we know how to deal with that, too.'

James tried again: 'I think it's unwise – '

'You have made that clear already!' his father snapped. 'Your opinion is *noted*. But the decision-making is for your elders; they must balance the safety and needs of the family against the risks involved in taking this asp to our breast. All my uncle needs from you now is an assessment – is what he says *possible?*'

James took a deep breath, embarrassment and anger warring. 'I . . . I can't deny it. From what the Eastern cousins were saying, when they had no reason to guard their tongues – yes, very possibly.'

'Thank you.' Shen lifted his tumbler. 'I think it best if we do not include you in the discussion; you are, perhaps, too close to its subjects. I agree with your assessment of the doctor's character – but even serial traitors may be useful to us on occasion. Especially if we know their weaknesses. Which is why I ask again: What do you believe his goals are?'

'What goals? Beside keeping his head on his shoulders?'

Shen leaned forward. 'Has it gone that far?'

'He did something to Helge that angered her greatly. And she is pregnant, with an heir to the throne of Gruinmarkt that is universally acknowledged as such by the Eastern cousins, who say something about a, uh, *DNA paternity check,* whatever that might be. Are they fools, Father? Is *she* a fool? I think those rumors about drugs and rape are . . . not true, exactly, but close. Ven Hjalmar got Lady Helge pregnant with seed from the royal line – then his patron died, and he must run for his life. He wants money, sanctuary, and time to continue his work – which is this breeding program. He wants to use us, Father, that's what I think.'

'Ah.' His father relaxed, smiling at last. He raised his glass. 'And you think that's all?'

'I wouldn't swear to it, but – '

'It'll do.' Shen took a sip. 'Thank you, son. I think I can discuss this with Eldest now.'

James's shoulders sank. 'You think Uncle will take Dr. ven Hjalmar on.'

'Yes.' Shen's smile widened. 'But don't worry. He will be under control . . .'

*

The second thing to catch Miriam's attention was the mingled smells of scorched wood and warm blood. The first was managing to control her fall; being carried piggyback was hard enough when the steed was a strapping young soldier, never mind a physically fit but lightly built younger woman. As Miriam and Olga disentangled themselves, Miriam looked around curiously. They'd come through in the target area once a deeply relieved Brill had confirmed that the zone was secure, and it was Miriam's first chance to see the havoc that the Pervert's army had inflicted on the Clan's outlying minor steadings.

One farmhouse looked much like another to her eye – in the Gruinmarkt they tended to be thick-walled, made from heavy logs or clay bricks depending on the locally available materials – but this one bore clear signs of battle. The roof of one wing was scorched and blackened, and the window shutters on the central building had been wrecked. More to the point –

'Who – ' she began, as Olga raised a hand and waved at the armed man standing guard by the door.

'My lady!' He went to one knee. 'Lord Riordan awaits you in the west wing.'

'Rise, Thom. Where are Knuth and Thorson?' Olga was all business, despite what had to be a splitting headache.

'We haven't seen ear nor tail of them since they crossed over yesterday.' The guard's eyes widened as he looked at Miriam: 'Is this – '

'Yes, and you don't need to make a scene over me,' she said hastily. Turning to Olga: 'The other two – they're your missing guards?'

'Let us discuss that indoors.' Olga nodded at the farmstead's front door, which stood ajar. Thom followed behind like an overeager dog, happy his mistress was home. 'I think Knuth and Thorson are probably dead,' she said quietly. 'The two who were waiting for us definitely weren't them.'

Miriam nodded, jerkily. 'So they were assassins? Just there to kill whoever turned up?'

'Whoever turned up at the duty staff officer's primary evacuation point, yes.' The picture was clear enough. The evac point had been guarded by a lance of soldiers, two on the American side and six in the Gruinmarkt. The assassins had murdered the two guards in the state park, then planned on catching Earl Riordan and his colleagues as they arrived, one by one. They hadn't anticipated a group who, forewarned, arrived expecting skullduggery. 'I expect Lady d'Ost will try and find where they hid the bodies before she comes hither to report. Come on inside, my lady.'

The farmstead was a wreck. The guards had made a gesture towards clearing up, pushing the worst of the trashed furniture and shattered kitchenware up against one wall and sweeping the floor – the pretender's cavalry had briefly used it as a stable – but the scorch marks of a fire that had failed to take hold still streaked the walls, and there was a persistent, faint aroma of rotting meat. The guards had brought out camp chairs and a folding table, and Riordan had set up his headquarters there, organizing the guards to man a shortwave radio and track unfolding events on a large map. He looked up as Miriam arrived. 'Welcome, Your Majesty.'

'How bad is it?' Miriam asked.

'We're getting reports. The evac plan is running smoothly and I've ordered all stations to check out the other side for unwelcome visitors. Didn't want to say why – things will be chaotic enough without setting off a panic about a civil war. The trouble is, we're fifteen miles out of Niejwein – the eye of the storm – half a day's ride; and I'm not happy about disclosing your location. In the worst case our enemies may have direction-finding equipment, and if they've got their hands on Rudy's ultralight . . . we've got to sit tight as long as possible. I've ordered Helmut to bring a couple of lances here as soon as he's nailed down the Summer Palace and I've put orders out for the arrest of the entire postal committee and, I regret to say, your grandmother. We

331

can weed that garden at our leisure once we've got it fenced in. Unless you have any other suggestions?'

'Yes.' Miriam swallowed. 'Is there any word of my mother? Or, or Dr. Griben ven Hjalmar? I think they're in cahoots . . .'

Riordan glanced at one of his men and barked a question in Hochsprache too fast for Miriam to follow. The reply was hesitant. 'No reports,' he said, turning to Miriam. 'I'll let you know if anything turns up. I assume you're talking about the duke's special, ah, medical program?' Miriam nodded. 'I'm on it. Now, if you wouldn't mind – ' He looked pointedly at the security guard with the radio headset, who was waving urgently for attention.

'Go to it.' Miriam shuffled awkwardly aside, towards the doorway into the burned-out wing of the farmhouse. 'What do we do now?' she asked Olga.

'We wait, my lady. And we learn. Or *you* wait, I have orders to send. Please.' She gestured at the bedrolls on the hard-packed floor. 'Make yourself comfortable. We may be here some time.'

*

Twenty years ago, in the rookeries of a town called New Catford, Elder Huan had known a young and dangerous radical – a Leveler and ranter called Stephen Reynolds.

In those days, Huan had been the public face of the family's business involvements – a discreet railroad for money and dispatches that the underground made use of from time to time. Reynolds had been Huan Lee's contact, and for a while things had gone swimmingly. Few organizations had as great a need for secrecy as the Leveler command, and indeed Huan had toyed with the idea of disclosing the family's secret to him – for the family's singular talent and the needs of the terrorists and bomb-throwers and other idealists were perfectly aligned, and the pogroms and lynchings of the English, tacitly encouraged by the government (who knew a good target for the mob's ire when they saw it – and skin of the wrong color had always been one such), did nothing to endear the authorities to him. At least the revolutionaries preached equality and fraternity, and an end to the oppression of all races.

A series of unfortunate events had closed off that avenue before Huan started down it; raids, arrests, and executions of Leveler cells clear across the country. He, himself, had been forced to world-walk in a hurry, one jump ahead of the jackboots of the Polis troopers. And that had been the end of *that*. The first duty of the family was survival, then profit – martyrdom in the name of revolutionary fraternity wasn't part of the package. In the wake of the raids he'd thought Stephen Reynolds dead – until he heard the name again, in a broadcast by the revolutionary propaganda ministry. Reynolds had survived and, it seemed, prospered in the council of the Radical Party.

This didn't entirely surprise Elder Huan. As he had described it to his brothers, some time later, 'The man is a rat – sharp as a wire, personally courageous, and curious. The Polis will have a hard time taking him.' And now the fox was in charge of a hen coop of no small size, having emerged in charge of the Annapolis Freedom Riders, then promoted to organize the Bureau of Internal Security that the party had formed to replace the reactionary and untrustworthy Crown Polis.

Now Elder Huan – through conduits and contacts both esoteric and obscure – had arranged for a meeting with the man himself. The agenda of the meeting was to be the renewal of an old alliance. And Elder Huan intended to make Reynolds an offer that would secure the safety of the family throughout the current crisis.

*

For his part, Reynolds – a thickset fellow with brown hair, thinning at the crown, and half-moon pince-nez that gave him an avuncular appearance even when supervising interrogations – was looking forward to the meeting for entirely the wrong reasons.

'I want you and two squads to be ready outside the front door. Place another squad round the back. Plain clothes, two steamers ready for backup.' He smiled, not warmly. Brentford, his secretary, nodded and scribbled in his notebook. 'You should arrest everyone in the building or leaving it after my departure, *unless* I indicate otherwise by displaying a red kerchief in my breast pocket. Special Regime Blue, with added attention. The charges will be resisting arrest, treason, membership of a proscribed organization, and anything else that occurs to you. Have the Star Tribunal ready to sit on them and I'll sign off on the execution warrants immediately. Do you have that?'

Brentford nodded, impassive. These were not unusual orders; Citizen Reynolds took a very robust approach to dealing with subversives. 'The, ah, exception, sir? Do you have any other instructions to deal with that case?'

'No.' Reynolds made a fist, squeezing. 'If anything comes up I'll handle it myself.'

'The danger, sir – '

'They're petty smugglers and racketeers, citizen. I dealt with them before, during the Long Emergency; it's almost a certainty that they want to deal themselves a hand at the table, in which case they're in for a short, sharp surprise. I merely reserve the final judgment *in case* there's something more serious at hand.' He stood, behind his desk, and straightened his uniform tunic, flicking invisible dust motes from one black lapel. 'Plain clothes, I say again. I'll see you at eight.'

Reynolds strode to the door as Brentford saluted. He didn't look back. Brentford was a reliable party man, a typical functionary of the new organization: He'd do as he was told, and look up to Reynolds as a bluff fellow who led from the front, as long as he occasionally indulged in eccentricities such as periodically going into the field to gather up nests of vipers and traitors with his own hands.

Reynolds didn't smile at the thought. There were risks attached to this behavior, and he didn't hold with taking risks unless there was something he held to be personally important at stake. Maintaining his carefully constructed public image was all very well, but placing himself in front of a desperate fugitive's knife was . . . it was *undignified*. On the other hand, sometimes it was necessary to deal with former Polis informers himself, to ensure that they courageously swallowed their suicide pills or jumped out of a high window. He considered it to be a small mercy – far less unpleasant than what fate held in store for them in the ungentle hands of his enthusiastic staff in Interrogations and Inquiries.

Citizen-Commissioner Stephen Reynolds was more than willing

to go into the field in person and meet past friends – especially if it meant that he could silence them before they could spill their guts to the interrogators in the BIS basements.

*

The venue Elder Huan had chosen for the meeting was a tiny front-room bar in a public house in Menzies Gate, a run-down suburb on the edge of what, in another world, would be called Brooklyn. His foot soldiers had paid the owner handsomely to take his wife and six children and two servants and move out for the night: a three-month amnesty from protection money, *and* a wallet bulging with ration coupons. 'I want privacy,' Huan had told One-Eye Cho, 'and I want a safe exit. See to it.' The pub, unbeknownst to its owner, was collocated with a trackless forest clearing in the northern Sudtmarkt – one carved out with sweat and axe and saw by Cho's sons. Elder had dealt with Reynolds before, and with the Polis, and was under no illusions about the hazards of dining with devils in Secret Security Police uniforms. 'Place two reliable bearers in the exit, and two armed guards. Find someone who can pass as white, and put him behind the bar with a shotgun to cover my retreat. He can be the bartender. Put another in the kitchen, who can at least provide cold cuts and soup if our guest is hungry.'

The pub was a theater: Reynolds and Huan had both prepared scripts for the other's benefit. The only question remaining to be answered was whose review would be more favorable.

*

Eight o'clock; the sky was still bright, but the shops were mostly shuttered, the costermongers and peddlers and rag-and-bone men and beggars had mostly slunk away, and the front windows of the pub were dark. Reynolds surveyed it professionally as he approached along the pavement. He'd swapped his uniform for a suit of clothes as ill-fitting – even moth-nibbled – as any he had worn during the long desperate years on the run. On the far side of the road, a couple of dusty idlers clustered near a corner; he glanced away. Down the street, a steamer sat by the curb, curtains drawn in its passenger compartment. All was as it should be. He nodded, then turned back towards the door and rapped the head of his cane on it twice.

A spy-slot slid aside. 'We're shut.'

'Tell your master an old friend calls.' Reynolds kept his voice low. 'Remember New Catford to him.'

The spy-slot closed. A moment later, the door opened. Reynolds slid inside.

The pub was indeed short on customers, but as the barman shot the bolts and returned to his place, Reynolds was intrigued by the appearance of the couple sitting at the one sound table, each with a glass of beer to hand. The old Chinaman he recognized, after a pause: It was indeed the gangmaster and smuggler from New Catford who had called himself Cheung. But who was the middle-aged white man? *Questions, questions.* Reynolds smiled broadly as he approached the table and Cheung stood.

'Ah, Citizen Reynolds!' cried Cheung – Reynolds suppressed a wince – and the other fellow stood, somewhat slowly. 'How wonderful to see you prospering so in these harsh times. Please, this is my associate Dr. ven Hjalmar, a physician. Please have a seat. Beer? Spirits? Have you eaten?'

Reynolds negotiated the social minefield and sat, without glancing at the bartender – whose impassivity told him more than he needed to know about his loyalties. *Most professional,* he decided: Cheung clearly knew what he was about. Which suggested a simple wrap-up might be difficult – but then, the presence of the doctor implied that this might be rather more complex than the usual pathetic blackmail attempt. 'A beer would be welcome. I gather you had a business proposal you wanted to bring to my attention?'

'Oh yes, indeed.' Cheung smiled happily. 'To your very good health!' He raised his glass. Reynolds perforce followed suit and submitted to another five minutes of trivial niceties. 'We considered putting some elements of this proposal to you all those years ago, in Catford, but the unfortunate excess of zeal displayed by the Polis at that time impressed upon us the need for discretion. Now, however, anything we choose to confide in you is unlikely to be beaten out of you by the royalist inquisitors. So: another toast, to our future business success!'

Reynolds blinked as he answered the toast: This was very much *not* what he'd been expecting. 'I'm afraid you have the better of me,' he admitted. 'What business do you have in mind?'

Cheung glanced around before he replied. 'You must have realized that I had a most effective way of moving dispatches and contraband between locations, without fear of interception.' Reynolds nodded guardedly. 'Well, that . . . mechanism . . . is still available. And I believe that, given the nature of your current engagement, you might very well find a use for it.' Reynolds nodded again, slightly perturbed. *What's he on about?* he wondered. Cheung beckoned at the bartender. 'Scott. Please come and stand in front of Citizen Reynolds, then make yourself scarce. Have Ang report to me in five minutes.'

The bartender – Scott – bowed slightly, then stepped in front of the table. 'Observe,' he told Reynolds. He looked away, in the direction of the archway leading to the kitchen. Then he vanished.

'This is our family secret,' Reynolds heard Cheung saying behind him as he waved his arms through the thin air where Scott had stood: 'We can walk between worlds. We have had to hold this to ourselves, in utter confidence, for generations; I'm sure you can imagine the consequences if word were to leak out in public. However, I know you to be a man of utmost probity and integrity, and in your new and elevated rank, I am certain you will recognize the desirability to keep this a secret as close to your chest as any matter of state. I brought the doctor along because he can explain to you the origins, transmission, and limits of our family talent better than I; it is hereditary, and we have never met any people to whom we are not blood kin who can do it . . .'

Reynolds swallowed: His heart was hammering. 'Business,' he said hollowly. '*What* business?' He turned round slowly. Where had Scott gone? Was he behind him? Waiting with an axe –

'I want to put my family at your service,' said Cheung. His expression was bland. 'I am certain you will find our unique talent very valuable indeed. These are dangerous times; the party has many

337

enemies. I hope that you – we – will better be able to defend it if we can come to a working agreement?'

Reynolds licked suddenly dry lips. 'How many of you are there?' he asked.

'Seventy adults, able to perform at will, and their children. Two hundred other relatives, some of whose offspring may be able to do so. And Dr. ven Hjalmar has a proposal that will, I am sorry to say, strike you as something out of a philosophical romance, but which may revolutionize our capacity in the longer term, ten years or more.'

Reynolds glanced round again, just as a young man – half a head shorter than the absent Scott – appeared out of thin air, bowed deeply to him, and moved to take up his station behind the bar. He swallowed again, mind churning like a millrace. 'How much do you want?' he asked.

Cheung smiled again. 'Perhaps Dr. ven Hjalmar should start by telling you exactly what is on sale. We can discuss the price later . . .'

On the eighth floor of a department store just off Eighteenth Street NW in Washington, D.C., there was a locked janitor's closet. Earlier that morning the police had been busy downstairs. A security guard had been found dead in a customer restroom, evidently the victim of an accidental heroin overdose. Nobody, in the ensuing fuss, had felt any need to fetch cleaning supplies from this particular closet, and so nobody had discovered that the door was not only locked but the lock was jammed, so that the key wouldn't turn.

Because nobody had visited the room, nobody had called a locksmith. And because the door remained locked, nobody had noticed the presence of an abandoned janitor's trolley, its cylindrical plastic trash can weighted down by something heavy. Nor had anyone, in an attempt to move the trolley, discovered that its wheels were jammed as thoroughly as the lock on the door. And nobody had raised the lid on the trash can and, staring inside, recognized the olive-drab cylinder for what it was: a SADM – storable atomic demolition munition – in its field carrier, connected to a live detonation sequencer (its cover similarly glued shut), a very long way indeed from its designated storage cell in a bunker at the Pantex plant in West Texas.

The janitor's store was approximately 450 meters – two blocks – away from Lafayette Square and, opposite it, the White House; and it was about ten meters above the roofline of that building.

The detonation sequencer was little more than a countdown timer – a milspec timer, with a set of thumbwheels to enter the permissive action codes, and more thumbwheels to enter the countdown time and desired yield. Beneath the glued-down cover were additional test and fault lights and switches. From the timer emerged a fat cable that screwed onto a multi-pin socket on the outside of the bomb carrier. Inside the carrier nestled one of the smallest atomic bombs ever assembled, so compact that a strong man with a suitable backpack frame could actually carry it. But not for long, and not for much longer.

Eleven-sixteen and twelve seconds, on the morning of July 16, 2003.

Stop all the clocks. *All of them.*

*

It was a regular summer day in Washington, D.C. Open-topped tourist buses carried their camera-snapping cargo around the sights on Capitol Hill – itself something of a misnomer, for the gentle slope of the Mall was anything but mountainous – past the reflecting pool, the Washington Monument, the museums and administrative buildings and white stone-clad porticoes of power. In hundreds of offices, stores, restaurants, and businesses around the center ordinary people were at work.

Like Nazma Hussein, aged twenty-six, daughter of Yemeni immigrants, married to Ali the cook, cleaning and setting out tables in the front of her family's small lunch diner on K Street NW, worrying about her younger sister Ayesha who is having trouble at school: Papa wants her to come and work in the restaurant until he and Baba can find her a suitable husband, but Nazma thinks she can do better –

Like Ryan Baylor, aged twenty-three, a law student at GWU, hurrying along H Street to get to the Burns Law Library and swearing quietly under his breath – overslept, forgot to set his alarm, got a reading list as long as his arm and a hangover beating a brazen kettledrum counterpoint to the traffic noise as he wonders if those cans of Coors were really a good idea the evening before a test –

Like Ashanda Roe, aged twenty-eight, working a dead-end shelf-stacking job in a 7-Eleven on D Street NW, sweating as she tears open boxes of Depends and shoves them into position on an end galley, tossing the packaging into a wheeled cage and whistling under her breath. She's worrying because her son Darrick, who is only seven, is spending too much time with a bunch of no-good kids who hang out with –

Six thousand, two hundred and eighty-six other people, ordinary

340

people, men and women and children, tourists and natives, illegal immigrants and blue bloods, homeless vagrants and ambassadors –

Stop all the clocks.

*

In the grand scheme of things, in the recondite world of nuclear war planning, a one-kiloton atomic bomb doesn't sound like much. It's less than a tenth of the yield of the weapon that leveled the heart of Hiroshima, a two-hundredth the power of a single warhead from a Minuteman or Trident missile. But the destructive force of a nuclear weapon doesn't correspond directly to its nominal yield; a bomb with ten times the explosive power causes rather less than ten times as much destruction as a smaller one.

Oliver Hjorth's first bomb detonated at twelve seconds past eleven-sixteen, on the eighth floor of a steel-framed concrete department store about a third of a mile from the White House.

Within a hundredth of a second, the department store building and everything else on its block vanished (along with fifty-seven staff and one hundred and fourteen shoppers), swallowed by a white-hot sphere of superheated gas and molten dust. The department store's neighbors, out to a radius of a block, survived a fraction of a second longer, their stone and concrete facades scorching and beginning to smoke until the expanding shock wave, air compressed and flash-heated to thousands of degrees, rammed into them like a runaway train.

Beyond the immediate neighborhood, the shock wave dissipated rapidly, reflecting off concrete and asphalt and thundering skywards in a bellowing roar that would, a little over a minute later, be audible in Baltimore. And beyond a couple of blocks' radius, only the most unlucky bystanders – those standing in the open with a direct line of sight down Seventeenth Street or H Street – would be exposed to the heat pulse, their skin charring and their eyes burned out by the flash.

But within a third of a mile, the destruction was horrendous.

Nazma Hussein saw a flash out of the corner of her eye, like a reflection from the noonday sun, only more brilliant. Looking up, she glanced at the window: But it was nothing, and she looked back at the

341

table she was laying out cutlery on, and deposited another fork on the place mat just as the shock wave arrived to throw a thousand glittering plate-glass knives through her face and abdomen.

Ryan saw a flash on the ground in front of him, and winced, closing his eyes as a wave of prickly heat washed over the back of his head and neck. He inhaled, his nostrils flaring. Flashes sparkled inside his eyelids as he smelled burning hair. His scalp ablaze, he drew breath to scream at the excruciating pain. But then the wind caught him with one hand, and the law library building with another, and clapped them together. And that was all he knew. A small mercy: He would not live to suffer the slow death of a thousand REMs that he had been exposed to, or the fourth-degree burns from the heat flash.

Ashanda was lucky. Working in the back of the store, she saw no flash of light, but heard a roar like a truck piling into the front of the building. The ground shook as the lights failed, and she fell to the floor, screaming in alarm. The rumbling went on for much too long, and she closed her eyes and prayed that it wasn't an earthquake; but who in D.C. had ever imagined an earthquake striking here? As the vibration faded, she pulled herself to her knees, then up to her feet. People were moaning in the front of the shop, but without lights she might as well be blind. She began to fumble her way back to the stockroom door, still shaky, praying that Darrick was all right.

*

The White House, although originally built in the late eighteenth century, had been reconstructed in the mid-twentieth around a steel load-bearing frame. With stone walls and a steel skeleton, it was by no means as fragile as its age might suggest; but the Truman-era structure wasn't designed to withstand a nuclear blast at close range, and in time of war the president was supposed to be elsewhere.

The White House survived the heat flash, but the shock wave took barely a second to surge down the street. By the time it hit the West Wing it was traveling at just over three hundred miles per hour, with an overpressure slightly over six pounds per square inch – funneled by the broad boulevard – and an impact to rival an F5 tornado.

The forty-third president of the United States was chatting informally with his deputy chief of staff and special assistant (whose windowless office in the middle of the first floor of the West Wing was perhaps the most eavesdropper-proof location in the entire federal government) when the shock wave hit.

It would never be determined precisely why the president was visiting his campaign manager, chief political strategist, and senior advisor, rather than vice versa; it was perhaps a reflection of the importance of this secretive political operative to the administration. But the location of this lair, in the middle of a warren of offices on the first floor, meant that none of its occupants could have had any warning of the catastrophe. Perhaps the lights flickered and dimmed as the White House's backup power supply kicked in, and perhaps they stared in annoyance at the dead phones in their hands; but before anyone had time to walk as far as the office door, the masonry, concrete, and stone of the West Wing was struck by a pile driver of compressed air. Just over six pounds per square inch sounds far less impressive than nine hundred pounds per square foot, but they are the same thing. Worse: The compressed air in the wave had to come from somewhere. As the shock wave passed, it left behind an evacuated zone, where the air pressure had dropped precipitously, swinging the strain on the building's structure from positive pounds to negative. It was a lethal whiplash of pressure, far worse than even a direct strike by a tornado.

Had the West Wing been built of modern reinforced structural concrete it might have survived, albeit with severe damage. But it wasn't, and the falling ceiling respected neither rank nor titles of nobility.

*

Eleven seconds later, the second bomb detonated.

This one had been planted on the top floor of the Holocaust Museum on Fourteenth Street SW, just off Independence Avenue and two blocks away from the Mall.

Perhaps Baron Hjorth had meant to target Congress; if so, he'd been overoptimistic – situated more than a mile away, the Capitol suffered external blast damage and many of its windows were blown in, but aside from shrapnel injuries, a number of flash fires ignited by the detonation, and severe damage to the outside of the dome, the Capitol was not seriously affected.

Not so the cluster of federal agencies around the Mall. FEMA and the FBI were both less than three thousand feet from ground zero; and pity the employees of the Department of Agriculture, across the road from the museum. More than eleven thousand people, mostly government employees and tourists, were directly affected by the second bomb, half of them killed by heat flash or shock wave as the rippling blast tore the heart out of the federal government.

And then there was the third device.

*

Eleven-sixteen and thirty-eight seconds. Two figures in desert fatigues bearing sergeant's stripes – Kurt and Jurgen, who were in fact, by grace of his lordship Baron Griben ven Hjalmar, sergeants-at-arms of the post – appeared out of nowhere on the second floor of a car park adjacent to the Pentagon, one of them standing and the other sprawling atop a wheelbarrow that also contained an olive-drab cylinder.

'*Scheisse*,' said Jurgen, as Kurt swung his feet over the side of the barrow and stood up. Beneath the low concrete roof half the theft alarms of half the vehicles in the park were shrilling in an earsplitting cacophony that filled his head and threatened to overflow when he opened his mouth, a profoundly unnatural counterpoint to the low rumbling from outside.

'This way.' Kurt, eyes flickering side-to-side, pointed along a line of parked trucks and SUVs towards a bare concrete wall with a fire door. Jurgen swallowed bile, picked up the handles of the wheelbarrow, tried to ignore the nausea in his stomach. His feet lurched side-to-side as he shoved the heavy load towards the stairwell. '*Two minutes.*'

'Two? Okay.' Jurgen nodded. Everything was crystal clear, suffused with a luminosity of migraine. The Boss couldn't be blamed for taking these little precautions, he could see that. 'How about here – '

'No, we want a stairwell – '

344

'You! Freeze!' Jurgen stumbled. The guard who had just stepped out of the stairwell – *Why is there a guard here?* – had his M16 raised. 'Identify yourselves! Sir!' The military courtesy didn't in any way detract from the pointed message of the assault rifle. This wasn't in the plan. Jurgen's head pounded.

'What's happening?' called Kurt.

'Full lockdown. Badges, *now!*' Another siren joined the clamoring car alarms – this one full-voiced and deep, the stentorian honking of a building alarm.

Kurt raised his left hand, then reached inside a trouser pocket. Time slowed to a crawl as he rolled sideways towards a parked F-250. Jurgen dropped the barrow's handles and broke right, diving for the opposite side of the row to take cover behind a Toyota compact. As he reached for his Glock, an earsplitting crackle of full-auto fire echoed from one end of the car park to the other. Grounded behind the Toyota, he rose to kneel, raised his pistol, and returned fire through the car's windows – not aimed, but suppressive. He winced with each pull of the trigger as the reports rammed ice picks into his already aching head. He couldn't be sure, but Kurt seemed to be shooting, too. Another hammer-drill burst of automatic fire, then the guard's weapon fell silent.

'*Kurt, wer ist –* '

The harsh bang of another pistol shot was followed almost immediately by the irregular snap of rifle fire, and Jurgen ducked, heart hammering and mouth dry. *There's more than one of them,* he realized, icy horror settling into his belly. The plan was simple enough – he'd brought Kurt over, Kurt was to carry him back – but with him pinned down behind this automobile, there was no way that was going to work. He swallowed and rubbed his left sleeve against the car, trying to expose the temporary tattoo on his wrist. If world-walking twice in five minutes didn't kill him, there was a good chance a three-floor fall would do the job, but the ticking nightmare in the barrow was an even more certain exit ticket.

'*Ish' vertrich nu!*' He shouted, then stared at the knot on his wrist until it expanded into a white-hot pain between his eyes.

Falling. Into silence.

Behind him, ten meters up the aisle from where Kurt's bleeding body lay and twenty meters from the sentries crouched behind a Humvee, the thing in the wheelbarrow emitted a click, then a muffled bang, and finally a wisp of smoke that coiled towards the ceiling. The detonation sequencer had done its job, but this particular FADM had missed its last maintenance check due to a bookkeeping irregularity. The constant warm rain of neutrons from the high-purity plutonium pit had, over the years, degraded the detonators distributed around its shell of high explosives. Overdue for tear-down and reconstruction half a decade ago, the bomb failed to explode; instead, the long-term storable core began to burn, fizzing and smoldering inside its casing.

Not all the detonators had degraded. When the high explosive sphere finally blew seventy seconds later, it killed four marine guards as they advanced from truck to truck, closing in on the hostiles' last known location. But the blast was unsequenced and asymmetric. Rather than imploding the weapon's pit and triggering a fission chain reaction, it merely fragmented it and blasted chunks of hot plutonium shrapnel into the surrounding cars and concrete structure of the car park.

*

July 16, 2003, eleven o'clock and thirty minutes, local time; fighters roared, circling overhead. Beneath the leaden, smoldering skies the clocks had stopped; all electronics had been killed by the electromagnetic pulses. And though the survivors were stirring, shocky and dazed but helping one another shuffle away from the burning holes of the city in every direction – north, south, east, and west – nothing now would ever come to any good.

Stop all the clocks.

DAMAGE CONTROL

It had taken Steve nearly an hour to get Fleming out of his office, during which time he'd gotten increasingly irritated with the skinny, intense agent's insistence that some insane conspiracy of interdimensional nuclear narcoterrorists was about to blow up the Capitol. *Why do the fruitcakes always pick on* me? he kept wondering.

Of course the explosion in Braintree checked out – gas mains, according to the wire feed. But that was no surprise: It was the sort of detail a paranoid would glom onto and integrate into their confabulation, especially if it happened close to their front door. One of the first warning signs of any delusional system was the conviction that the victim was at the center of events. Tom Brokaw wasn't reading the news, he was sending you a personal message, encrypted in the twitches of his left eyebrow.

Sure Fleming didn't seem particularly unhinged – other than insofar as his story was completely bugfuck insane and required the listener to suspend their belief in the laws of physics and replace it with the belief that the government was waging a secret war against drug dealers from another dimension – but that meant nothing. Steve had been a beat journalist for years before he found his niche on the tech desk. Journalists attract lunatics like dog turds attract flies, and he'd listened to enough vision statements by dot-com CEOs to recognize the signs of a sharp mind that had begun to veer down a reality tunnel lined with flashing lights and industrial espionage. So he'd finally cut Fleming off, halfway down a long, convoluted monologue that seemed to be an attempt to explain how Beckstein had got his attention – not without qualms, because Fleming sounded halfway to stalkerdom when he got onto the subject of rescuing her from some kind of arranged marriage – and raised his hand. 'Look,' he said wearily, 'this is a bit much. You said they made you translate tapes.

And there are these lockets they use for, what did you call it, world-walking. Do you have any kind of, you know, physical evidence? Because you can appreciate this is kind of a complex story and we can't run it without fact-checking, and – '

Fleming stood up. 'Okay.' He looked exasperated. 'I got it.'

Steve peered up at him owlishly. 'I don't want to blow you off. But you've got to see – they'll laugh me out of the meeting if I can't back this up with something physical. And this isn't my department. I'm not the desk editor you're looking for – '

Fleming nodded again, surprising him. 'Okay. Look,' he glanced at his watch, 'I'll phone you again after they make their move. I don't think we'll have long to wait. Remember what I said?'

Steve nodded back at him, deadpan. 'Atom bombs.'

'You think I'm nuts. Well, I'm not. At least I don't *think* I am. But I can't afford to stick around right now. Let's just say, if a terrorist nuke goes off in one of our cities in the next week, I'll be in touch and we can talk again. Okay?'

'You got it.' Steve clicked his recorder off. 'Where are you going?'

'That would be telling.' Fleming ducked out of his cubicle without looking back. By the time Steve levered himself out of his chair and poked his head around the partition, he was gone.

'Who was that?' asked Lena from real estate, who was just passing with a coffee.

'J. Random Crank. Probably not worth worrying about – he seemed harmless.'

'You've got to watch them,' she said worriedly. 'Sometimes they come back. Why didn't you call security?'

'I wish I knew.' Steve rubbed his forehead. The shrill buzz of his phone dragged him back inside the cubicle. He picked up the receiver, checking the caller ID: It was Tony in editorial. 'Steve speaking, can I – '

'Turn on your TV,' Tony interrupted. Something in his tone made Steve's scalp crawl.

'What channel?' he demanded.

'Any of them.' Tony hung up. All around the office, the phones were going mad. *No, it can't be*, Steve thought, dry-swallowing. He

348

moused over to the TV tuner icon on his desktop and double-clicked to open it. And saw:

*

Two lopsided mushroom clouds roiling against the clear blue sky before a camera view flecked with static, both leaning towards the north in the grip of a light breeze –

'Vehicles are being turned back at police checkpoints. Meanwhile, National Guard units – '

A roiling storm of dust and gravel like the aftermath of the collapse of the Twin Towers –

'Vice president, at an undisclosed location, will address the nation – '

A brown-haired woman on CNN, her normal smile replaced by a rictus of shock, asking someone on the ground questions they couldn't answer –

People, walking, from their offices. Dirty and shocked, some of them carrying their shoes, briefcases, helping their neighbors –

'Reports that the White House was the target of the attack cannot be confirmed yet, but surviving eyewitnesses say – '

A flashback view from a surveillance camera somewhere looking out across the Potomac, *flash* and it's gone, blink and you've missed it –

'Residents warned to stay indoors, keep doors and windows closed, and to drink only bottled – '

*

Minutes later Steve stared into the toilet bowl, waiting for his stomach to finish twisting as he ejected the morning's coffee grounds and bile. *I had him in my office,* he thought. *Oh Jesus.* It wasn't the thought that he'd turned down the scoop of a lifetime that hurt like a knife in the guts: *What if I'd listened to him?* Probably it had been too late already. Probably nothing could have been done. But the possibility that he'd had the key to averting this situation sitting in his cubicle, trying to explain everything with that slightly flaky twitch – the man who knew too much – that was too much to bear. Assuming, of course, that Fleming was telling the truth when he said he wasn't the guy behind the bombs. *That* needed checking out, for sure.

When he finally had the dry heaves under control he straightened up and, still somewhat shaky, walked over to the washbasins to clean himself up. The face that stared at him, bleary-eyed above the taps, looked years older than the face he'd shaved in the bathroom mirror at home that morning. *What have we done?* he wondered. The details were in the dictaphone; he'd zoned out during parts of Fleming's spiel, particularly when it had been getting positively otherworldly. He remembered bits – something about medieval antipersonnel mines, crazy stuff about prisoners with bombs strapped to their necks – but the big picture evaded him, like a slippery mass of jelly that refused to be nailed down, like an untangled ball of string. Steve took a deep breath. *I've got to get Fleming to call in,* he realized. A faint journalistic reflex raised its head: *It's the story of a lifetime.* Or the citizen's arrest of a lifetime. *Is a nuclear unabomber even possible?*

J. Barrett Armstrong's office on the tenth floor was larger than Steve Schroeder's beige cubicle on the eighth. It had a corner of the building to itself, with a view of Faneuil Hall off to one side and a mahogany conference table the size of a Marine Corps helicopter carrier tucked away near the inner wall of the suite. It was the very image of a modern news magnate's poop deck, shipshape and shining with the gleaming elbow grease of a dozen minimum-wage cleaners; the captain's quarters of a vessel in the great fleet commanded by an Australian news magnate of some note. In the grand scheme of the mainstream media J. Barrett Armstrong wasn't so high up the totem pole, but in the grand scheme of the folks who signed Steve's paychecks he was right at the top, Thunderbird-in-chief.

Right now, J. Barrett Armstrong's office was crowded with managers and senior editors, all of whom were getting a piece of the proprietor's ear as he vented his frustration. 'The fucking war's *over,*' he shouted, wadding up a printout from the machine in the corner and throwing it at the wall. 'Who did Ali get the bomb from? There's the fricking story!' A bank of monitors on a stand showed the story unfolding in repeated silent flashbacks. 'How did they smuggle them in? Go on, get digging!'

Nobody noticed Steve sneaking in until he tapped his boss, Riccardo Pirello, on the shoulder. Rick turned, distractedly: 'What is it?'

'It's not Iraq,' said Steve. He swallowed. 'It's narcoterrorists, and the nukes were stolen from our own inventory.'

The boss was belting out orders to his mates and boatswains: 'Bhaskar, I want an in-depth on the Iranian nuclear program, inside spread, you've got six pages – '

Steve held up his dictaphone where Riccardo could see it. 'Scoop, boss. Walked into my office an hour ago.'

'A – what the fuck – ' Riccardo grabbed his arm.

Nobody else had noticed; all eyes were focused on the Man, who was throwing a pocket tantrum in the direction of enemies both Middle Eastern and imaginary. 'Let's find a room,' Steve suggested. 'I've got my desk line patched through to my mobile. He's going to call back.'

'Who – '

'My source.' Steve's cheek twitched. 'He told me this would happen. I thought he was crazy and kicked him out. He said he'd phone after it happened.'

'Jesus.' Riccardo stared at him for a moment. 'Why *you*?'

'Friend of a friend. She went missing six months ago investigating this, apparently.'

'Jesus. Okay, let's get a cube and see what you've got. Then if it checks out I'll try and figure out how we can break it to Skippy without getting ourselves shitcanned for making him look bad.'

*

The atmosphere in the situation room under Raven Rock was a toxic miasma of fury, loss, and anticipation: a sweaty, testosterone-breathing swamp of the will to triumph made immanent. From the moment the PINNACLE NUCFLASH alert came in, the VP hunched over one end of the cramped conference table, growling out a torrent of unanswerable questions, demanding action on HEAD CRASH and CLEANSWEEP and other more arcane Family Trade projects, issuing instructions to his staff, orders for the Emergency Preparedness and Response Directorate and other subagencies within the sprawling

DHS empire. 'We're still trying to raise the EOB, sir,' said one particularly hapless staffer.

'I don't want to hear that word *trying*,' he snarled. 'I want *results*. Success or failure. Clear?'

The TV screens were clear enough. Andrew James couldn't help staring at the hypnotic rewind footage from time to time, the sunny morning view of downtown D.C., the flash and static-riddled flicker, the rolling, boiling cloud of chaotic darkness shot through with fire rising beyond the Capitol. The close-ups replaying every ten minutes of the Washington Monument blowdown, chunks of rock knocked clear out of the base of the spire as the Mach wave bounced off the waters of the reflecting pool, cherry trees catching fire in a thousand inglorious blazing points of light. Inarticulate anchormen and women, struggling with the enormity. Talking heads, eyes frozen in fear like deer in the headlights, struggling to pin the blame on Iraqi revenants, Iranian terrorists, everyone and anyone.

'Dr. James.'

He tore his eyes away from the screen. 'Sir?'

The VP glared at him. 'I want to know the status of SCOTUS as of this morning. I very much fear we'll be needing their services later today and I want to know who's available.'

James nodded. 'I can find out. Do you want me to expedite the draft order on Family Trade just yet?'

'No, let's wait for confirmation. George will want to pull the trigger himself once we brief him, assuming he survived, and if not, I need to be sworn in first. Otherwise those bastards in Congress will –'

'Sir?' Jack Shapiro, off the NSA desk just outside the conference room, stuck his head round the door. 'We've got eyeballs overhead right now, do you want it on screen?'

Cheney nodded. 'Wait one, Andrew,' he told Dr. James. 'Put it on any damn screen but Fox News, okay?'

Two minutes later the center screen turned blue. Static replaced the CNN news crawl for a moment; then a grainy, gray, roiling turbulence filled the monitor from edge to edge. A flickering head-up display scrawled barely readable numbers across the cloudscape.

Shapiro grimaced, his face contorted by the telephone handset clamped between neck and shoulder. 'That's looking down on the Ellipse,' he confirmed. 'The chopper's standing off at six thousand feet, two thousand feet south of ground zero – it's one of the VH-3s from HMX-1, it was on station at Andrews AFB when . . .' He trailed off. The VP was staring at the picture, face frozen.

'Where's the White House?' he demanded hoarsely.

'About' – Shapiro approached the screen, pointed with a shaking finger – 'there.' The splash of gray across more gray was almost unrecognizable. 'Less than six hundred yards from ground zero, sir. There *might* be survivors – '

Dr. James quietly pushed his chair back from the table, turned away from the screens, and stood up. A DISA staffer took over the chair even before he cleared the doorway. The corridor outside was cramped and overfull with aides and officers busily waiting to see the Man. All of them showed signs of agitation: anger and fear and outrage vying for priority. *Patience*, James told himself. *The end times haven't begun – yet.* The VP would be a much better president than his predecessor; and in any case, a presidential martyrdom pardoned all political sins.

Dr. James headed for the communications office. His mind, unlike almost everyone else's, was calm: He knew exactly what he had to do. Find out where the surviving Supreme Court justices were, locate the senior surviving judge, and get him here as fast as possible to swear in the new president. *Then we can clean house.* Both at home and in the other world God had provided for America, as this one was filling up with heathens and atheists and wickedness. *There will be a reckoning*, he thought with quiet satisfaction. *And righteousness will prevail.*

*

Steve Schroeder had barely been back at his desk for ten minutes when he received another visit. This time it was Riccardo, with two other men Steve didn't recognize but who exuded the unmistakable smell of cop. 'Mr. Schroeder,' said the tall, thin one. 'Mr. Pirello here tells me you had a visitor this morning.'

Steve glanced at Riccardo. His boss's forehead was gleaming under the fluorescent tubes. 'Tell him, Steve.'

'Yes,' Steve admitted. 'Do you have ID?'

The short fireplug in the double-breasted suit leaned towards him: 'You don't get to ask questions,' he started, but the thin man raised a hand.

'Not yet. Mr. Schroeder, we're from the FBI. Agent Judt.' He held an ID badge where Steve couldn't help seeing it. 'This is my colleague, Agent Fowler. It would make things much easier if we could keep this cordial, and we understand your first instinct is to treat this as a news investigation, but right now we're looking at an unprecedented crime and you're the first lead we've found. If you know anything, *anything* at all, then I'd be very grateful if you'd share it with us.'

'If there's another bomb out there and you don't help us, you could be charged with conspiracy,' Agent Fowler added in a low warning rumble. Then he shut up.

Steve took a deep breath. The explosions kept replaying behind his eyelids in slow motion. He breathed out slowly. 'I'm a bit . . . freaked,' he admitted. 'This morning I had a visit from a man who identified himself as a DEA agent, name of Fleming. He spun me a crazy yarn and I figured he was basically your usual run-of-the-mill paranoid schizophrenic. I didn't check his ID at the time – tell the truth, I wanted him out of here. He said there'd be nukes, and he'd call back later. I've got a recording' – he gestured to his dictaphone – 'but that's about it. All I can tell you is what he told me. And hope to hell he gets back in touch.'

Agent Fowler stared at him with an expression like a mastiff contemplating a marrowbone. 'You sent him away.'

Fear and anger began to mix in the back of Steve's mind. 'No, what I sent away was a *fruitcake*,' he insisted. 'I write the information technology section. Put yourself in my shoes – some guy you don't know comes to visit and explains how a secret government agency to deal with time travelers from another universe has lost a bunch of atom bombs accidentally-on-purpose because they want the time travelers to plant them in our cities – what would *you* do? Ask him when he last took his prescription? *Show him the door*, by any chance?'

354

Fowler still stared at him, but after a second Agent Judt nodded. 'Your point is taken,' he said. 'Nevertheless . . .'

'You want to wait until he makes contact again, be my guest.' Steve shivered. 'He might be a fruitcake, or he might be the real thing; that's not my call. I assume you guys can tell the difference?'

'We get fruitcakes too,' Judt assured him. Riccardo was being no help: He just stood there in front of the beige partition, eyes vacant, nodding along like a pod person. 'But we don't usually get them so close to an actual, uh, *incident.*'

'Act of war,' Fowler snarled quietly. 'Or treason.'

Fleming didn't ask for anonymity, Steve reminded himself. Which left: handing a journalistic source over to the FBI. Normally that would be a huge no-no, utterly immoral and unjustifiable, except . . . this wasn't business as usual, was it? 'I'll help you,' Steve said quietly. 'I want to see you catch whoever did it. But I don't think it's Fleming you want. He said he was trying to get the word out. If he planted the bombs, why spin that cock-and-bull story in the first place? And if he didn't plant them, but he knew where the bombs were, why *wouldn't* he tell me?'

'Leave the analysis to us,' suggested Agent Judt. 'It's our specialty.' He pointed at the dictaphone. 'I need to take that, I'm afraid. Jack, if you'd like to stay with Mr. Schroeder just in case the phone rings? I'm going to bring headquarters up to speed, get some backup in.' He looked pointedly at Riccardo. 'You didn't hear any of this, Mr. Pirello, but it would be very helpful to me if you could have someone in your building security department provide Agent Fowler and me with visitor badges, and warn the front desk we're expecting colleagues.'

Riccardo scuttled away as soon as Judt broke eye contact. Then he turned back to Steve. 'Just wait here with Jack,' he said reassuringly.

'What if Fleming phones? What do I do?' Steve demanded.

'Answer it,' said Fowler, in a much more human tone of voice. 'Record it, and let me listen in. And if he wants to set up a meeting – go for it.'

*

In a cheap motel room on the outskirts of Providence, Mike Fleming sat on the edge of an overstuffed mattress and poured a stiff shot of bourbon into the glass from the bathroom. His go bag sat on the luggage rack, leaking the dregs of his runaway life: a change of underwear, a set of false ID documents, the paperwork for the rental car in the parking lot – hired under a false name, paid for with a credit card under that name. The TV on the chest of drawers blatted on in hypermanic shock, showing endless rolling reruns of a flash reflecting off the Potomac, the collapsing monument – for some reason, the White House seemed to be taboo, too raw a nerve to touch in the bleeding subconscious of a national trauma. He needed the bourbon, as a personal anesthetic: It was appallingly bad tradecraft, he knew, but right now he didn't feel able to face reality without a haze of alcohol.

Mike wasn't an amateur. He'd always known – always – that a job could blow up in his face. You didn't expect that to happen, in the DEA, but you were an idiot if you didn't take precautions and make arrangements to look after your own skin. It was surprisingly easy to build up a false identity, and after one particular assignment in Central America had gone bad on him with extreme prejudice (a local chief of police had turned out to be the brother-in-law of the local heroin wholesaler), he'd carefully considered his options. When Pete Garfinkle had died, he'd activated them. It made as much sense as keeping his gun clean and loaded – especially after Dr. James had earmarked him for a one-way ticket into fairyland. They weren't forgeries, they were genuine, legal ID: He didn't use the license to get off speeding tickets, and he paid the credit card bill in full every time he used it. They were simply an insurance policy for dangerous times, and ever since he'd gotten back home after the disastrous expedition into Niejwein a couple of months ago, he'd been glad of the driving license and credit card taped inside a video cassette's sleeve in the living room.

From Steve Schroeder's office he'd taken the elevator down to street level, caught a bus, switched to the Green Line, changed train and commuter line three times in thirty minutes, then hopped a Chinatown bus to New York, exiting early and ultimately ending up in a motel in Providence with a new rental car and a deep sense of foreboding. Then, walking into the motel front desk, he'd seen the endless looping scenes of disaster on CNN. It had taken three times as long as usual to check in. One of the two clerks on duty was weeping, her shoulders shaking; the other was less demonstrative, but not one hundred percent functional. 'Why do they *hate* us?' the weeping one moaned during a break in her crying jag. 'Why won't they leave us alone?'

'Think Chemical Ali did it?' Three months ago it would have been Saddam, before his cousin's palace coup on the eve of the invasion.

'Who cares?'

Mike had disentangled himself, carefully trying not to think too hard about the scenes on the TV. But once he got to his room, it hit him.

I tried to prevent it. But I failed.

A vast, seething sense of numbness threatened to swallow him. *This can't be happening, there must be some way out of here, some way to get to where this didn't happen.* But it *had* happened; for better or worse – almost certainly for worse – Miriam's enemies had lashed out at the Family Trade Organization in the most brutal way imaginable. Not one, but two bombs had gone off in D.C.: Atomic bombs, the all-time nightmare the DHS had been warning about, the things Mike had been having nightmares about for the year since Matthias walked into a DEA office in downtown Boston with a stolen ingot of plutonium in his pocket.

No way of knowing if Schroeder had taken him seriously. He'd felt the argument slipping away, Schroeder's impatience visibly growing as he tried to explain about the Clan, and about the FTO project to wrap them up and then to infiltrate and attack their home bases. He hadn't even gotten as far as his contact with Miriam's mother, Olga the ice princess, the business about negotiation. He could see Schroeder's attention drifting. And if he couldn't convince one man who'd known Miriam and wondered where she'd gotten to, what hope was there?

Maybe if I hadn't asked the colonel, weeks ago, he speculated. Colonel Smith was Air Force, on secondment to FTO by way of a posting with the NSA. He understood chains of command and accountability and what to do about illegal orders. Not like that shadowy spook-fucker, Dr. James. *But they blew up my car.* They'd *expected* him to run somewhere. Smith might already be dead. *If I'd smuggled some of the tapes out* – tapes of conversations in Hochsprache, recorded by someone with access to the Clan's innermost counsels – but that was nuts, too. The whole setup in that office was designed to prevent classified materials from going AWOL.

Where do I go, now?

Tired and sweaty and stressed and just a little bit numb from the bourbon, Mike sank back against the headboard and stared at the TV screen. Two diagonal columns of smoke, one of them almost forming the classic mushroom, the other bent and twisted out of recognizable shape. Again and again, the Washington Monument's base blasted sideways out from under it, the peak falling. Helicopter footage of the rubble, now, eight- and nine-story office blocks stomped flat as if by a giant's foot. Preliminary estimates of the death toll already saying it was worse than 9/11, much worse. Anchormen and women looking shocked and almost human under their makeup, idiotically repeating questions and answers, hunting for meaning in the meaningless. Interviews with a survivor on a gurney, bandaged around one side of their head, medevac'd to a hospital in Baltimore.

What's left that I can do?

The vice president, somber in a black suit – someone had found a mourning armband for him somewhere – mounting a stage and standing behind a lectern. Balding, jowly, face like thunder as he answered questions in a near-constant waterfall of flashbulb flickering. Promising to find the culprits and punish them. Make them pay. This man whom the Clan's consigliere had named as their West Coast connection. A whey-faced Justice Scalia stepping forward to administer the oath of office. President Cheney. Dire warnings about the Middle East. Appeals for national unity in the face of this terrorist threat. Promises of further legislation to secure the border. State of emergency. State of complicity.

Where can I run?

Mike lifted his glass and took another mouthful. Knowing too much about the Family Trade Organization was bad enough; knowing too much about the new president's darker secrets was a one-way ticket to an unmarked roadside grave, for sure. And the hell of it was, there was probably no price he could pay that would buy his way back in, even if he *wanted* in on what looked like the most monstrously cynical false-flag job since Hitler faked a Polish army attack on his own troops in order to justify the kickoff for the Second World War. *I need to be out of this game,* he realized blearily. Preferably in some way that would defuse the whole thing, reduce the risk of escalation. *Stop them killing each other, somehow.* It seemed absurdly, impossibly utopian, as far beyond his grasp as a mission to Mars. So he took another sip of bourbon. He had a lot of driving to do tomorrow, and he needed a good night's sleep beforehand, and after what he'd seen today . . . it was almost enough to make him wish he smoked marijuana.

*

Even revolutions need administration: And so the cabinet meeting rooms in the Brunswick Palace in New London played host to a very different committee from the nest of landowning aristocrats and deadwood who'd cluttered John Frederick's court just three months earlier. They'd replaced the long, polished mahogany table in the Green Receiving Room with a circular one, the better to disguise any irregularities of status, and they'd done away with the ornate seat with the royal coat of arms; but it was still a committee, and Sir Adam Burroughs presided in his role as First Citizen and Pastor of the Revolution.

Erasmus arrived late, nearly stepping on the heels of Jean-Paul Dax, the maritime and fisheries commissioner. 'My apologies,' he wheezed. 'Is there a holdup?'

'Not really.' Dax stepped aside, giving him a sharp glance. 'I see your place has moved.'

'Hmm.' Burgeson had headed towards his place at the right of Sir Adam's hand, but now that he noticed, the engraved nameplates on the table had been shuffled, moving him three seats farther to the right. 'A mere protocol lapse, nothing important.' He shook his head, stepping over towards his new neighbors: Maurits Blanc, commissioner of forestry, and David McLellan, first industrial whip. 'Hello, David, and good day to you.'

'Not such a good day . . .' McLellan seemed slightly subdued as Erasmus sat down. He directed his gaze at the opposite side of the round table, and Erasmus followed: *Not much chivalry on display there*, he noticed. A tight clump of uniforms sat to the left of Sir Adam: Reynolds, along with Jennings from the Justice Directorate, Fowler from Prisons and Reeducation, and a thin-faced fellow he didn't recognize – who, from his attitude, looked to be a crony of Reynolds. A murder of crows, seated shoulder-to-shoulder: What kind of message was *that*?

'Is Stephen feeling his oats?' Erasmus murmured, for McLellan's ears only.

'I have no idea.' Burgeson glanced at him sharply: McLellan's expression was fixed, almost ghostly. Erasmus would have said more, but at that precise moment Sir Adam cleared his throat.

'Good morning, and welcome. I declare this session open. I would like to note apologies for absence from the following commissioners: John Wilson, Electricity, Daniel Graves, Munitions – ' The list went on. Erasmus glanced around the table. There were, indeed, fewer seats than usual – a surprise, but not necessarily an unwelcome one: the cumbersome size of the revolutionary cabinet had sometimes driven him to despair.

'Now, to the agenda. First, a report on the rationing program. Citizen Brooks – '

Erasmus was barely listening – making notes, verging on doodles, on his pad – as the discussion wandered, seemingly at random, from department to department. He knew it was intentional, that Sir Adam's goal was to ensure that everyone had some degree of insight into everyone else's business – *transparency*, he called it – but sometimes the minutiae of government were deathly boring; he had newspapers and widecasters to run, a nagging itch to get out in front and cultivate his own garden. Nevertheless he sat at ease, cultivating stillness, and trying to keep at least the bare minimum of attention on the reports. Tone was as important as content, he felt: You could often tell fairly rapidly if someone was trying to pull the wool over your eyes simply by the way they spun out their words.

It was halfway through Fowler's report that Erasmus began to feel the first stirrings of disquiet. 'Construction of new reeducation centers is proceeding apace' – Fowler droned portentously, like a well-fed vicar delivering a slow afternoon sermon – 'on course to meet the goal of one center per township with a population in excess of ten thousand. And I confidently expect my department to be able to meet our labor obligation to the Forestry Commission and the Departments of Mines and Transport – '

Did I just hear that? Burgeson blinked, staring at Fowler and his neighbors. *Did I just hear the minister for prisons boast that he was supplying labor quotas to mines and road-building units?* The skin on the back of his neck crawled. Yes, there were a lot of soldiers in the royalist camp, and many prisoners of war – and yes, there was a depression-spawned crime wave – but handing a profit motive to the screws stuck in his throat. He glanced around the table. At least a third of the commissioners he recognized had done hard time in the royal labor camps. Yet they just sat there while Fowler regurgitated his self-congratulatory litany of manacles refastened and windows barred. *That can't be what's going on,* he decided. *I must have misheard.*

Next on the agenda was Citizen Commissioner Reynolds's report – and for this, Erasmus regained his focus and listened attentively. Reynolds wasn't exactly a rabble-rousing firebrand, but unlike Fowler he had some idea about pacing and delivery and the need to keep his audience's attention. 'Thank you, citizens. The struggle for hearts and minds continues' – he nodded at Erasmus, guilelessly collegiate – 'and I would like to congratulate our colleagues in propaganda and education for their sterling work in bringing enlightenment to the public. However, there remains a hard core of wreckers and traitors – I'd place it at between two and eight percent – who cleave to the discredited doctrine of the divine right of kingship, and who work tirelessly and in secret to undermine our good works. The vast majority of these enemies work outside our ranks, in open opposition – but as the party has grown a hundredfold in the past three months, inevitably some of them have slipped in among us, stealthy maggots crawling within to undermine and discredit us.

'A week ago, Citizens Fowler, Petersen, and I convened an extraordinary meeting of the Peace and Justice Subcommittee. We agreed that it was essential to identify the disloyal minority and restrain them before they do any more damage. To that end, we have begun a veterinarian process within our own departments. Security is particularly vulnerable to infiltration by saboteurs and former revenants of the Crown Polis, as you know, and I am pleased to say that we have identified and arrested no fewer than one hundred and fifty-six royalist traitors in the past three days. These individuals are now being processed by tribunals of people's legates appointed by the Department of Law. I hope to report at the next cabinet meeting that the trials have been concluded and my department purged of traitors; when I can make such an announcement, it will be time to start looking for opportunities to carry the fight to the enemy in other departments.' Reynolds smiled warmly, nodding and making eye contact around the table; there was a brief rumble of agreement from all sides.

Erasmus bobbed his head: but unlike his neighbors, he was aghast. Among the books Miriam Beckstein had lent him the year before, he had been quite taken aback by one in particular: a history of revolution in the East, not in the French Empire-in-being in the Russias, but in a strange, rustic nation ruled by descendants of Peter the Great. The picture it painted, of purges and show trials followed by a lowering veil of terror, was one of utmost horror; he'd taken some comfort from the realization that it couldn't happen here, that the bizarre ideology of the Leninists was nothing like the egalitarian and democratic creed of the Levelers. *Was I wrong?* he wondered, watching Citizen Commissioner Reynolds smiling and acknowledging the congratulations of his fellow commissioners with a sense of sickness growing in his belly: *Is corruption and purgation a natural product of revolutions? Or is there something else going on here?*

His eyes narrowing, Erasmus Burgeson resolved to order some discreet research.

*

362

It wasn't a regular briefing room: They'd had to commandeer the biggest lecture theater in the complex and it was still packed, shoulder-to-shoulder with blue and brown uniforms. Security was tight, from the Bradleys and twitchy-fingered National Guard units out on the freeway to the military police patrols on the way in. Everyone knew about the lucky escape the Pentagon had had, if only via the grapevine. The word on the floor was that the bad guys were aiming for a trifecta, but missed one – well, they *mostly* missed: Half a dozen guards and unlucky commuters were awaiting burial in a concrete vault with discreet radiation trefoils once Arlington got back to normal. But nobody in the lecture theater was inclined to cut the bad guys any slack. The mood, Colonel Smith reflected, was hungry. He tried to put it out of his mind as he walked to the podium and tapped the mike.

'Good morning, everyone. I'm Lieutenant Colonel Eric Smith, lately of the air force, seconded to NSA/CSS Office of Unconventional Programs, and from there to an organization you haven't heard of until now. I've been instructed to bring you up to speed on our existence, mission, and progress to date. I'll be happy to take your questions at the end, but I'd be grateful if you could hold on to them for the time being. Just so you know where we're going, this is about the attack yesterday, and what we – all of us – are going to be dealing with over the next months and years.'

He hit the remote button to bring up the first slide. The silence was broken by a cough from the audience; otherwise, it was total.

'For the past year I've been seconded to a black ops group called the Family Trade Organization, FTO. FTO is unlisted and draws on assets from Air Force, NSA, FBI, CIA, DEA, NRO, and the national laboratories. We're tasked with responding to a threat which was only identified thirteen months ago. That's when this man walked into a DEA office in Boston and asked for witness protection.'

Click. A new slide, showing a polyethylene-wrapped brick of white powder, and a small metal ingot, side by side on a worktop. 'He was carrying a kilogram of China White and a hundred-gram lump of plutonium 239, which we subsequently confirmed had been produced in one of our own breeders. This got our attention, but his story was so crazy that DEA nearly wrote him off as a kook – they didn't take the plutonium brick seriously at first. However, it checked out.'

Click. Surveillance video, grainy black-and-white, showing a view of a jail cell. A prisoner is sitting on the edge of a plastic bench, alone. He glances around. Then, after a few seconds, he rolls back his left sleeve to reveal some kind of tattoo on his wrist. He raises it in front of his face. Abruptly, the cell is empty.

'Our witness claimed to be a member of a group or tribe of illegal aliens with the ability to travel between worlds. The place of origin of these aliens was initially unknown, but backward. They can will themselves between their own world – or location – and ours, by staring at a special knotwork design. They speak a language not familiar to anyone in the linguistics department at NSA, but related to Low German. And they use their ability to smuggle narcotics.'

Click. A slide showing an odd, crude knotwork design.

'DEA would have written source GREENSLEEVES off as a nut, but they raided one of his suggested locations and hit paydirt – a major transfer location for a cocaine distribution ring they'd been hunting for two years. At this point they began following up his leads and arrested a number of couriers. One of whom you just saw pulling a vanishing trick in front of a spy camera in a locked cell.'

Click. A windowless laboratory, white glove boxes and racks of electronics bulking beside workbenches.

'The initiative came from DEA but was escalated rapidly with the backing of OSP and NSA, to establish a cross-disciplinary investigative unit. About five months ago our collaborations at Livermore confirmed that there is indeed a physical mechanism at work here. What we're looking at is not teleportation, but some sort of quantum tunneling effect between our world and a world very much like our own – a parallel universe. Other worlds are also believed to exist – many of them.'

Click. Video from a camera bolted to the rear bulkhead of a helicopter's flight deck, grainy and washed out from beneath by the low-light-level radiance spilled from the instrument consoles: a view of darkened ridgelines.

'Project ARMBAND is now delivering prototype transfer units that can displace aircraft – or limited-scale ground forces – to what we have confirmed is this other world. There's virtually no radio traffic or sign of advanced civilization other than stuff that these – the hostiles call themselves the Clan – have stolen from us. Our intelligence take is that this is a primitive version of our own world, one where the dark ages were very dark. The Clan, as they're called, people with a biologically mediated ability to tunnel through into our world and back again – we don't know where they came from, and neither do the prisoners we've been able to question. But they exist within a high medieval civilization along the east coast of North America, former Viking colonies. They're not Christian: Christianity and Islam are unknown in their world. They've been using their access to us to build up their own power back home.'

Click. Aerial photographs of a small city. Forests loom in an untamed blanket beyond the edge of town. Only a couple of narrow roads wind between the trees. Smoke rises from chimneys. There are walls, meandering along the hilltops around the center. Some way outside them, there is a small harbor.

'This is the capital city of the local power where the Clan holds most authority, a small state called Niejwein, located roughly where downtown Boston is. Four months ago we were able to use our captured prisoners to transport a SPECOPS forward recon team into position. We've confirmed this story six ways: I'd like to emphasize this, we have an intelligence briefing on the enemy culture and you'll find it in your in-tray when you check your e-mail. What we're dealing with is a hostile power considerably more primitive and less well organized than Afghanistan, but sitting physically right on our doorstep – collocated with us geographically, but accessible only by means of ARMBAND devices or at will to the Clan's members.'

Click. An olive-drab cylinder approximately the size of a beer keg, with a green box strapped to it and connected by fat wires.

'This is an FADM, field atomic demolition munition. Third-generation descendant of the W53 tactical device used in the Davey Crockett. Twelve of them were supposed to be in storage in Pantex. Source GREENSLEEVES claimed to have stolen and emplaced one in downtown Boston as insurance when he walked in and asked for witness protection – ' Smith paused. 'May I continue?' He leaned close to the mike but kept his tone mild: Most of the audience outranked him considerably.

'Thank you. There was an accident subsequently when GREEN-SLEEVES panicked and tried to escape custody, and GREENSLEEVES was killed; and there was some question over whether he was in fact lying. A routine inventory check reported that all the FADMs were present and accounted for. However, a month ago FTO personnel located and subsequently disarmed a device in downtown Boston, confirming that the FADM audit report was faulty. This triggered a PINNACLE EMPTY QUIVER and a full-up inspection, in the course of which it became apparent that no less than six FADMs had been stolen from Pantex at some time in the preceding three years. FADMs are on the inactive inventory and the plant was following standard asset risk management procedures for the weapon storage areas, with layered security, patrols and sensors, and secure vaults. Unfortunately our existing ARM failed to take into account the possibility that extradimensional narcoterrorists might appear *inside* the storage vaults, remove the weapon assemblies from their carriers, and replace them with dummies.'

Smith paused. There was no point continuing right now – not with the muttering wave of disbelief and outrage – and besides, his throat was becoming sore. He raised his water bottle, then tapped the mike again.

'If I may continue? Thank you. Those of you tasked with nuclear weapons security know more about the consequences of that particular event than I do; to those who aren't, we're in the process of upgrading our risk management model and temporarily escalated security is already in place for those parts of the inventory which suffer from compromised ARM. We're not going to lose any more nukes, period.

'Meanwhile, the background to this particular empty quiver event is that DEA's initial approach to the Clan was that they were a major narcotics ring and should be dealt with accordingly. We're talking about narcoterrorists on the same scale as the Medellín Cartel, with turnover in the four-to-six-billion-dollar-per-year range, and a membership in excess of a thousand individuals. What became apparent only later was that the scope of the threat, intrusions from another world, a parallel universe, is unprecedented and carries with it many unknown unknowns, if I may steal a phrase from the top. What we failed to appreciate at first was that the Clan were effectively a parallel government within their own nation, but not *the* government – an analogy with al-Qaeda and the Taliban in Afghanistan is apposite – and that the local authorities wanted rid of them. The situation was highly unstable. I am informed that negotiations with the Clan for return of the stolen weapons were conducted, but internal factional disputes resulted in the, the consequences we've all witnessed this week.'

Which was flat-out half-truths and lies, but the real story wasn't something it was safe to talk about even behind locked doors in Crypto City: Smith's boss, Dr. James, had anticipated a response, but not on this scale. Calculations had been botched, as badly as the decision in early 2001 to ignore the festering hatred in the hills around Kabul. 'We need to get the hard-liners to talk to us, not the liberals,' Dr. James had explained. Nobody had anticipated that the hard-liners' idea of a gambit would be a full-dress onslaught – or if they had, they were burying the evidence so deep that even thinking that thing was a career-limiting move.

'I can't discuss the political response to the current situation,' Smith continued, speaking into a hair-raising silence, 'but I've been told I can mention the legal dimension. Other FTO officials are briefing their respective departments today. As of now, FTO and the existence of the extradimensional threat are no longer super-black, although the content of this briefing remains classified. The briefing process is intended to bring everyone up to speed before the orders start coming down. I've been told to alert you that a military response is inevitable – the president is meeting with the survivors of the House of Representatives and there is a briefing going on behind closed doors right now – and the War Powers Act has been invoked. Our NATO partners have already come through and invoked Clause Six of the North Atlantic treaty, meaning that we can count on any necessary assistance. White House counsel and the attorney general's office agree that the usual treaty obligations requiring a UN mandate for a declaration of war do not apply to territory physically located within our own national borders, and *posse comitatus* does not apply to parallel universes – this remains to be confirmed by the Supreme Court, but we anticipate a favorable outcome.'

As three of the four justices who died in the attack were from the liberal side of the bench – by sheer bad luck, they'd been attending an event at GWU that morning – this was an extreme understatement: The new Supreme Court, when it could be sworn in, would be hand-picked to make Chief Justice Scalia happy.

Smith took a deep breath. 'So, to summarize: We have been attacked by a new kind of enemy, using our own stolen weapons. But we've been studying them covertly, and we've got the tools to reach out and touch them. And we're going to show them *exactly* what happens when you fuck with the United States.' He stared straight at one of the generals in the front row, who had been visibly containing himself for several minutes. 'Thank you for your patience. Now are there any questions?'

The floodgates opened.

*

The day after his failed attempt to leak all over Steve Schroeder's news desk, Mike Fleming deliberately set out to tickle the dragon's tail. He did so in the full, cold foreknowledge that he was taking a huge personal risk, but he was running short on alternatives.

Driving from motel to strip mall and around and about by way of just about any second-rate road he could find that wasn't an interstate or turnpike, Mike watched the news unfold. The sky was blue and empty, contrail-free except for the occasional track of a patrolling F-15; as on 9/11, they'd shut down all civilian aviation. The fire this time had not come from above, but few people knew that yet, and as gestures went, grounding the airliners was a trivially easy way to signal that something was being done to protect the nation. It was the old security syllogism: *Something must be done, this is something,* ~~~ *this must be done.* Mike drove slowly, listening to the radio. There were police checkpoints on roads in and out of D.C.; the tattered remnants of Congress and the Supreme Court were gathering at an Undisclosed Location to mourn their dead and witness the somber inauguration of the new president. A presidential address to the nation was scheduled for the evening against a drum-beat of unreassuring negatives leaking from the Pentagon, *This isn't al-Qaeda, this isn't the Iranians, this is something new.* The pro-forma groundswell rumble of rage and fury at yet another unheralded and unannounced cowardly attack on America was gathering momentum. The nation was on the edge of its nerves, terrified and angry. Continuity of Government legislation was being overhauled, FEMA managers stumbling bleary-eyed to the realization that the job they'd been hired for was now necessary –

At a pay phone in the back of a 7-Eleven, Mike pulled out a calling card and began to dial, keeping a nervous eye on his wristwatch. He listened briefly, then dialed a PIN. '*Hello. You have no new messages.*'

He hung up. 'Shit,' he muttered, trudging back towards the front of the shop, trying hard not to think of the implications, not hurrying, not dawdling, but conserving the energy he'd need to carry him through the next day. He was already two miles away when the first police cruiser pulled up outside with its lights flashing, ten minutes too late: driving slowly, mind spinning as he tried to come up with a fallback plan that didn't end with his death.

If only Miriam's mother had left a message, or Olga the ice princess, he'd have more options open – but they hadn't, and without a contact number he was out in the cold. The only lines he could follow led back into an organization answering to a new president who had been in cahoots with the Clan's worst elements and wanted the evidence buried, or to a news editor who hadn't believed him the first time round – and who knew what Steve would think, now that the White House was a smoking ruin?

I blew it, he thought bleakly. *Dr. James has likely declared me a rogue asset already.* Which was technically correct – as long as one was unaware that James himself was in it up to his eyeballs. The temptation to simply drive away, to take his papers and find a new life in a small town and forget he'd ever been Mike Fleming, was intense. *But it wouldn't work in the long term,* he realized. The emergency administration would bring in the kind of internal ID checks that people used to point to when they wanted to denounce the Soviets. They'd have to: It wasn't as if they could keep world-walkers out by ramping up the immigration service. *What can I do?*

His options seemed to be narrowing down. *Work within the organization* had gone out the window with that car bomb. *Talk to Iris Beckstein* – about what? *Talk to the press* – no, that had seemed like a good idea yesterday: funny how rapidly things changed. He could guess what would happen if he fixed up another meeting with Steve Schroeder any time soon. Steve would try to verify his source, be coopted, spun some line about Mike being a conspirator, and reel him in willingly; and Mike had no tangible evidence to back up his claims. *Try to turn a coworker* – look how well that had worked for Pete Garfinkle. Pete had confessed misgivings to Mike; shortly thereafter he'd been put in a situation that killed him. Mike had confessed misgivings to Colonel Smith; shortly thereafter – *join up the dots.* The whole organization was corrupt, from the top down. For all he knew, the bombs – his knuckles whitened upon the steering wheel – did the new president have big enough balls to deliberately maneuver the Clan into giving him everything he wanted, on a plate? To have helped them get their hands on the bombs, and then to have provoked them into attacking the United States? Not a crippling attack, but a beheading one, laying the groundwork for a *coup d'état*?

The scale of his paranoia was giving Mike a very strange sensation, the cold detachment of a head trip into a darkened wilderness of mirrors: the occupational disease of spies. *If you can't trust your friends, the only people left to trust are your enemies,* he reminded himself. Miriam had tried to warn him; that suggested, at a minimum, something to hope for. *But FTO'll be watching her house. And her mother's. In case anyone shows.* He forced himself to relax his grip on the wheel and pay attention to his surroundings as a pickup weaved past him, horn blaring. *How* many *watchers?* Maintaining full surveillance on a building was extremely expensive – especially if nobody had bothered to look in on it for months.

An ephemeral flash of hope lit up the world around him. If FTO had been watching Miriam's house before, they might well have pulled out already – and yesterday's events would have shaken things up even more. *But what if they're wrong?* He remembered Matthias's advice, from months ago: *They think like a government. And Miriam's* important *to them. She's an insider – otherwise she wouldn't have been able to warn me. Would we put a watch on a cabinet official's house if we knew enemies had it under surveillance? Even if we were under attack?* Trying to work through that line of thought threatened to give him a headache, but it seemed to be worth checking out. Best case, there'd be a Clan security post discreetly watching her place, and nobody else. Worst case, an FTO surveillance team – but knowing how FTO worked in the field, he'd have a good chance of spotting them. *Find Miriam. Try to cut a deal: Warn her faction about the spy, about the president's plans – in return, try to get them to hand over the murderers. Maybe find some way to cut a deal.*

I just hope I'm not too late.

LEAKING EVERYWHERE

In a stately house four miles outside Niejwein, two noble ladies sat beside an unlit hearth, awkwardly eyeing each other. Between their angled chairs an occasional table stood like a frontier fence, punctuated by the border tower of a fortified wine decanter. The afternoon sun slanting through the lattice window stained the wood-paneled walls with a deep golden warmth; a pair of fat flies buzzed in erratic circles below the ceiling, swooping and tracing out the lines of their confinement.

'Have you been keeping well?' asked the older of the pair, her age-spotted eyelids drooping as she watched her sixty-two-year-old visitor. 'Do you have any complaints?' She spoke abruptly, her tone brusque.

The younger one snorted. 'Only the obvious, Mother.' The last word came out with an odd emphasis, falling just short of making an insult of it. 'Your hospitality is impeccable but, I hope you'll excuse me for putting it so crudely, oppressive. I would ask, though, is my maid Mhara unharmed?'

The dowager frowned, her crow's-feet wrinkles deepening. 'I do not know.' She extended a shaky hand and tugged on a braided bell cord. A discreet servants' door opened behind her. 'My daughter inquires of her maid.'

'Yes, my lady.' The attendant bowed his head.

'Was she taken? If so, is she well?'

'She, ah, escaped, my lady. After she shot one of the dragoons in the, ah, thigh.'

'Well then.' The dowager gave her daughter a wintry smile. 'Satisfied?'

Her daughter stared back at her for a long moment, then nodded fractionally. 'Satisfied.'

'Go away,' the dowager announced to the air. The servants' door opened and closed again, restoring the illusion of privacy. 'Such a show of compassion,' she added, her tone of voice dripping with irony.

'There's no show about it, *Mother*.' Patricia Thorold-Hjorth, herself dowager duchess and mother to the queen-widow, stared back at her own dam, the Duchess Hildegarde. 'We bled ourselves white in your lifetime. Every one of us of the true blood who dies, especially the women, is a score fewer grandchildren to support our successors. If you don't feel that –'

She stopped, as Hildegarde's palm rattled the crystal on the table. '*Of course* I feel that!' the duchess exploded. 'I've known that since long before I whelped you, you ungrateful child. I've known that ever since my sister –' She stopped, and reached for a glass of wine. 'Damn you, *you're* old enough to know better, too.'

Hildegarde stopped. They sat in silence for a minute, eyeing each other sidelong. Finally Patricia spoke. 'I assume you didn't bring me here for a friendly mother-daughter chat.'

'I brought you here to save your life, girl,' Hildegarde said harshly.

Patricia blinked. 'You did?'

'If you were elsewhere, I could not ensure that certain of the more enthusiastic members of the conservative club would leave you be,' the dowager pointed out. 'And I feel some residual family loyalty to this day, whatever you may think of me.'

'Eh. Well, if you say so. Do you expect that will make Helge think better of you?'

'No.' The dowager stared at her daughter. 'But it will be one less thing for me to take to my grave.' For a moment her eyes unfocussed, staring vaguely into some interior landscape. 'You corrupted her most thoroughly. My congratulations would be in order, were the ultimate effect not so damaging.'

Patricia reached slowly for the other wineglass. 'Why should I thank you for saving my life?' she asked. 'Are your faction planning a return to the bad old days? Cousin killers?'

'No. Not really.' Hildegarde took a sip from her glass. 'But it was necessary to break the back of your half-brother's organization, to

373

buy time while we deal with the harvest he was about to bring in from the field. Test-tube babies, what an idea. I gather I should thank you for helping deal with it – Dr. ven Hjalmar was quite effusive in his praise for your assistance. But in any case: The program is secure, as is our future. We shall make sure that the infants are raised by trustworthy families, to know their place within the Clan – better than your wildcat, anyway – and in the next generation our numbers will increase fivefold.'

'Where is the doctor?'

'Oh, who cares?' Hildegarde waved a shaky hand: 'He doesn't matter now that the program records are destroyed.'

'Really?' Hildegarde's grasp of computers was theoretical at best, shaky at worst. 'He's not tried to blackmail you?'

'No.' Hildegarde's grin was not reassuring. 'I think he might be afraid to show his face. Something to do with your hoyden.'

'So you took action against Security?' Patricia nudged.

'Yes. I had to, to preserve the balance. I know you harbor Anglischprache ideas about "equality" and "freedom", but you must understand, we are *not* a meritocracy – we live or die by our bloodlines. Certainly Angbard had the right idea thirty years ago, to clamp a lid on the interminable feuding, but his solution has become a monster. There are young people who pledge their loyalty to the Security directorate, would you believe it? If he was allowed to bring the, the changelings into his organization, within a generation we'd be done for. This way is better: With the Security organization cut back to its original status, and other threats dealt with, we can resume our traditional – ' Patricia was whey-faced. 'What is it?'

'*Other* threats. *What* other threats?'

'Oh, nothing important.' Hildegarde waved the back of her hand dismissively, prompting a fly to dodge. 'We sent a message to the Anglischprache leadership, one that they won't ignore. Once we've got them out of our hair – '

'A message the Anglischprache won't ignore? What kind of message?'

'Oh, we used those bombs Oliver had lying about.' Hildegarde sniffed. 'How else do you deal with a hostile king? They'll make the

374

point quite well: Once the new Anglischprache president-emperor ascends the throne, he won't be under any illusions about the consequences of threatening us. We'll talk to him, I'm sure. We've done it before: This will just set negotiations off on the right foot.'

'*Sky Father . . .*' Patricia stared at her mother, aghast, then raised her wineglass and knocked it back in a single swallow. 'Those were atomic weapons,' she said slowly. 'Where were they set?'

'Oh, some white palace, I gather,' Hildegarde said dismissively. 'In a town named after a famous soldier.'

'Oh dear Trickster Cousin,' Patricia muttered under her breath. 'You said "used". I suppose it's too much to hope that you misspoke, and there's still time – '

Hildegarde stared at her daughter, perplexed. 'Of course not. This was yesterday. Are you all right?'

'I – a moment.' Patricia shrugged uncomfortably. 'This is not a criticism I speak now, but – I lived among them for nearly a third of a century, Mother. *You did not.* You don't know them the way I do.' Patricia nodded at the decanter: Her mother reached for the bell-pull once more. 'I'm telling you, you've misjudged them badly.'

'We had to get rid of their current king-emperor somehow; he's an idiot.' Hildegarde paused while her footman refilled both goblets and retreated. 'His next-in-line is far more intelligent. He understands power and its uses.'

'Granted. But their president is not a king, as we understand the term, he is merely a first citizen, elected by his people. They run everything by a system of laws.'

'I know that – '

'The trouble is, simply attacking them on their home field is . . . it's a declaration of war. And *they don't know how to surrender*, Mother. They *can't*. There is no law in their constitution that says "if attacked by an irresistible force it is permissible to offer a limited surrender: To do so invoke this clause." Once they're at war, any leader who tries to stop it will be impeached – removed. It's like stabbing a hornets' nest: Every one you kill just makes the others angrier. I'm not making this up. The last time they lost a war, nearly thirty years ago, they left it to an unelected temporary regent to take the barrage of rotten fruit, and there are *still* people who think they could have won in Vietnam if only they'd fought harder. There are still many in the South who think they could have won the slaveowners' treasonous rebellion against the North, a century and a half ago. They're all quite mad, you know. Just now they're fighting two wars on the other side of the world, all because a ranting priest sent his idiot followers to blow up a couple of towers. *Two* wars – because they're not sure who did it.' Patricia picked up her glass again. 'Do you know how powerful these bombs are?' she asked. 'I'm told they can be made more or less damaging – '

'Oh, I'm sure they used the most powerful available,' Hildegarde said dismissively. 'No point tapping your enemy on the head with a twig when there's a club to hand, is there? As you say, it only makes them angry. But the enemy's intentions, you must understand – they don't matter. What can they do to us? Certainly they may kidnap one or two of our own, ride them like mules, and they may even bring more of their bombs, but we are on our home ground here. We must be firm and deliver our ultimatum, and they must learn to leave us alone!'

'Mother.' Patricia looked at Hildegarde: 'You're not the only person who's been sending messages. I – at the rump Council's orders – I've been trying to negotiate with them for some time. They don't want to haggle; they want our total surrender. They sent a final démarche and cut me dead.'

'Really.' Hildegarde didn't bother to feign interest.

'They're working on a *machine*, Mother dearest. A machine that does what we do, a machine for walking between worlds. Yes, they told us this. Also that it might take months or years, but when they succeeded, they would come here, and how they would treat with us would depend entirely on how we treated with *them*.'

'And you believed that?'

'Yes. As a matter of fact, I did – and do. You've never lived among them. You don't know what they're capable of.'

Hildegarde sniffed. 'Well, it will probably never happen. And if it does, we'll think of something. But for now, our internal factional dispute is settled. The Security apparat is back in its box, we have found a satisfactory solution to Angbard's silly little breeding program, and we – you and I – are back on course to meet our braid's long-term goal. Your diversion has had no real long-term effect. That's always been your besetting problem – always wanting to hare off and do things your own way, even when it forces you to do something silly, like hide yourself away in a foreign scholar's hovel for thirty years instead of enjoying the rightful fruits of your rank. I know, you're not going to apologize. I don't expect you to. Will you believe me if I tell you that I bear you no ill will? Or your daughter? Or *her* child, be it boy or girl? But you have been a sore trial to your elderly mother, these years, more even than the prodigal stepson. Even now. Not even asking why I wanted to see you.'

There was an uncomfortable pause. 'Why?' Patricia finally asked.

'Because I'm dying,' Hildegarde said, so offhandedly that it took Patricia a moment to do a double take. 'Nothing that the Anglisch-prache doctors can repair, I assure you – I have been poked and prodded by Drs. ven Skorzeman and ven Hjalmar, and they have attempted to convince me to visit the other side for blood treatments that will make my hair fall out and my gums bleed, to no avail. I am a goodly age, Patricia. I may even live to see a world-walking great-grandchild of mine take the throne, which is more than my half-sister managed. And I never managed to settle my affairs with Angelin. So there is a canker in my guts and I should not want to impose overlong on your patience, but I am an old and impatient woman and I ask you to indulge my sentiment.'

Patricia stared at the dowager. 'But Angelin refused to speak to you – '

'She might have eventually, had she not died at the hands of her own grandchild's men.' Hildegarde turned unfocussed eyes on the window. 'Which just goes to show the unwisdom of schooling our young in alien ways: Never forget that – we are foreigners wherever we live, whether we be ruler or servant. Angelin failed to look to Egon's schooling. She left him to go native. You . . . made the opposite error with Helge, I think, schooling her to think she was Anglisch. I never took the time to set things right with my sister. So, I thought I should at least make a gesture . . . Don't make me reconsider the wisdom of this meeting.'

'Oh, Mother.' Patricia put her wineglass down. 'This is most harsh, this news.' A hesitancy crept into her voice.

'Bear with me.' Hildegarde raised a slightly shaky hand and closed her eyes, as Patricia picked up the decanter with both hands and refilled their glasses. 'I have always acted for what I perceived to be the best interests of our braid. I had hoped you would understand that, and at least not stand in my way, but by poisoning my natural heir against me . . . Well, it's too late to undo that.' She opened her eyes and blinked rheumily at her daughter. 'May you have better luck with your grandchild. Angelin's great-grandchild.'

'If it arrives. Consanguinuity – '

'It will be all right, child. Helge and Creon were second cousins, and Creon's ailment was a consequence of poisoning, not inbreeding. We risk worse with every twist of the braid. The hazard is minimal.'

'Miriam won't see it that way, you know.'

'*Miriam* – what an odd name. Where did you get it from?'

'The same place I got Iris. And Beckstein. She answers to it, you know. You might have gotten better results from her if you'd called her by the name she prefers.'

'Perhaps. But it's not her name, it's a disguise. Where would we be if people could pick and choose their own names? Nobody need recognize their seniors – there would be anarchy! Or another strong man like Angbard would grab everybody by the throat and rule by *force majeure*. A rogue, that boy. But listen, I have a few months, perhaps a year or two. And seeing that Angbard was ill, I decided to move now, to detach his slippery followers' fingers from the reins of power and hand them back to their rightful owner – a woman of the line, or a lord working as her agent, as is right and proper. *You*, Patricia. You have a grandchild in the great game, or you will soon – you will act in their name. Once the hangers-on and opportunists are purged, once Angbard's security apparatus is emptied of dangerous innovators and cut back to its original size and scope, you will inherit the full power of my position, and they'll love you. Complete freedom of action. I never had that, girl, but *you will*.'

Patricia stared at Hildegarde for almost a minute. Presently, she closed her mouth. 'You're not joking.'

'You know me, girl. Do I ever joke?'

Patricia opened her mouth for a moment, then closed it again. 'Let me get this straight. You had your granddaughter forcibly inseminated with your sister's grandson's sperm so that you could reassert our cadet branch's claim to the throne. You had me kidnapped and brought here so that we could kiss and make up. You're dying of cancer, so you decided to set up Miriam's kid for the throne by destroying Angbard's security organization, just as the old nobility are getting over the civil war and wondering what we're going to unleash on them next. And you nuked the White House to send a message to Dick Cheney. Am I missing anything?'

'Yes.' Hildegarde's self-satisfaction came to the fore: 'Who do you think taunted Egon about his younger brother's marriage? Someone had to do it – otherwise we'd never have pried his useless ass off the throne! It would have set us back at least two generations.'

Patricia picked up her wineglass and drained it for the third time. 'Mother, I have a confession to make. Miriam once told me she thought you were a scheming bitch, and I'm afraid I defended your honor. I take it all back. You're *completely* insane!'

'Let us pray that it runs in the family, then. As for your confession – consider yourself forgiven. I shall be relying on your cunning once I surrender to you, you realize.' Hildegarde reached out and pulled the bell rope – '*More wine, damn your eyes!* I insist on getting drunk with my daughter at least once before I die. Yes, I'm insane. If insanity is defined by wanting to put my great-grandchild on the throne, I'm mad. If it's crazy to want to strangle the ghouls that crowd around the royal crib and break the private army that threatens our autonomy, I'm all of that. I bent the Clan and the Kingdom to serve you and your line, Patricia, and I find at the end of my days that I regret nothing. So. Once you are in charge of the Clan, what do you think you will do with it?'

'I haven't made my confession yet, Mother.' Patricia looked at the dowager oddly. 'It would have been good to have had this heart-to-heart a little earlier – perhaps a year ago. I'm afraid we're both too late . . .'

*

An hour after Miriam and her guards and allies arrived at the farmstead, the place was abuzz with Clan Security. There were several safe transfer locations in the state forest, and one of Earl-Major Riordan's first orders had been to summon every available soldier – not already committed to point defense or the pursuit of the renegade elements of the postal service and the conservative club – to establish a security cordon.

Miriam, sick at heart, sat in one corner of the command post, listening – the fast, military Hochsprache was hard to follow, and she was catching perhaps one word in three, but she could follow the general sense of the discussion – and watching as Riordan took reports and consulted with Olga and issued orders, as often as not by radio to outlying sites. The headquarters troops had set up a whole bunch of card indexes and a large corkboard, startlingly prosaic in a field headquarters in a fire-damaged farmhouse, and were keeping a written log of every decision Riordan handed down. A hanging list of index cards had gone up on one wall, each card bearing a name: Baron Henryk, Baron Oliver, Dowager Duchess Thorold-Hjorth. Miriam carefully avoided trying to read the handwritten annotations whenever a clerk updated one of them. Ringleaders they might be, and in some cases bitter enemies, but they were all people she knew, or had known, at court. A similar list hung on the opposite wall, and it was both longer and less frequently updated – known allies and their disposition.

'Why not computerize?' she'd asked Brill, in a quiet moment when the latter had sat down on the bench beside her with a mug of coffee.

'Where are we going to get the electricity to run the computer from?' Brill replied. 'Batteries need charging, generators need fuel. Best not to make hostages to fate. Besides,' she glanced at the communications specialist bent over the radio, 'computers come with their own problems. They make treachery easier. And it's a small enough squabble that we don't need them.'

'But the Clan – ' Miriam stopped.

'We know all the main players. By name and by face. We know most of our associates, too.' The world-walkers, children of latent, outer-family lines, not yet fully integrated into the Clan of which they were branches. 'We are few enough that this will be over – ' Brill stopped. The communications specialist had stood up, hunching over his set. Suddenly he swore, and waved urgently at Olga. Olga hurried over; a moment later Riordan joined her.

'What's going on?' Miriam stood up.

'I don't know.' Brill's face was expressionless. 'Nothing good by the look of it.'

Olga turned towards them, mouthed something. She looked appalled.

'Tell me,' Miriam demanded, raising her voice against the general hubbub of urgent questions and answers.

Olga took two steps towards her. 'I am very sorry, my lady,' she said woodenly.

'It's Plan Blue?'

Olga nodded. 'It is all over the television channels,' she added softly. 'Two nuclear explosions. In D.C.'

For a moment everything in Miriam's vision was as gray as ash. She must have staggered, for Brilliana caught her elbow. 'What.' She swallowed. 'How bad?'

'We do not know yet, my lady. That news is still in the pipeline. We have' – she gestured at the radio bench – 'other urgent priorities right now. But there are reports of many casualties.'

Miriam swallowed again. Her stomach clenched. 'Was this definitely the work of, of the conservative faction?'

'It is reasonable to suppose so, but we can't be certain yet.' Olga was peering at her, worried. 'My lady, what do you – '

'Because if it was their doing, if it was anything to do with the Clan, then we are *fucked*.' She could see it in her mind's eye, mushroom clouds rising over the Capitol, and a bleak vision of a future far more traumatic than anything she'd ever imagined. 'We're about to lose all access to the United States. They won't rest until they've found a way to come over here and chase us down and kill us. There won't be anywhere we can run to in their world or this one that's far enough away for safety.'

'Even if it was not Baron Hjorth's doing, even if we had nothing to do with it, we would not be secure,' Brilliana pointed out. 'We know that the vice president has reason to want us dead. This could be some other's work, and he would still send his minions to hunt us.'

'Damn.' Miriam swallowed again, feeling the acid tang of bile at the back of her mouth. 'Think I'm going to throw up.'

'This way, milady' – everyone was solicitous towards the mother-to-be, Miriam noted absentmindedly, up to and including making decisions on her behalf, as if she were a passive object with no will of her own –

It was raining outside, and the stench from the latrines round the side of the house completed the job that the news and the anxiety and the morning sickness had started. Her stomach cramped as she doubled over, spitting bile, and waited for the shooting pain in her gut to subside. Brill waited outside, leaving her a token space. *I'm alone,* she realized despondently. *Alone, surrounded by allies and sworn vassals, some of whom consider themselves my friends. I don't think any of them truly understand . . .* Her thoughts drifted back towards the sketchily described horrors unfolding down south, and her stomach clenched again. By the time she finished, she found she had regained a modicum of calm. *They don't know what's going to happen,* she realized. *But I do.* Miriam had been living in Boston through the crazy days that followed 9/11. And she'd seen the lock-step march to the drumbeat of war that followed, seen the way everybody rallied to the flag. In the past few weeks and months, a tenuous skepticism had been taking hold, but nothing could be better calculated to extinguish it than a terrorist outrage to dwarf the fall of the Twin Towers. The only question was how long it would take the US military to gear up for an invasion, and she had an uneasy feeling that they were already living on borrowed time.

'Milady?' It was Brill.

'I'm better. For now.' Miriam waved off her offered hand and took a deep breath of rain-cleansed air. 'I'm going to lie down. But. I need to know how bad it is, what the bastards have done. And as soon as Riordan and Olga have a free minute I need to talk to them.'

'But they're going to be – ' Brill stopped. 'What do you need to dis-tract them with?'

'The evacuation plan,' Miriam said bluntly.

'What plan – '

'The one we need to draw up *right now* to get everyone across to New Britain. If we don't' – she raised her head, stared across the seared fields towards the tree line at the edge of the cleared area – 'we're dead, or worse. I know what my people – sorry, the Americans – are capable of. We don't stand a chance if we stay here. One way or another, the Clan is finished in the Gruinmarkt; this whole stupid cockamamie scheme to put a baby on the throne is pointless now. The only questions remaining are which direction we run, and how far.'

*

A steady stream of couriers, security staff, and refugees trickled into the farmstead over the hours following Miriam's evacuation. By midafternoon, Earl Riordan had sent out levies to round up labor from the nearest villages, and by sunset a large temporary camp was taking shape, patrolled by guards with assault rifles. The farm itself was receiving a makeover in the shape of a temporary royal residence: However humble it might be by comparison with the palaces of Niejwein, it was far better than the tents and improvised bivouacs of the soldiers.

Despite her ongoing nausea, Miriam followed Riordan and Olga and their staff when they moved into a pavilion beside the farmhouse. 'You should be lying down, taking things easy,' Brilliana said, halfheartedly trying to divert her.

'The hell with that. These are my people, aren't they? I need to be here.' *And I need to know . . .* The sense of dread gnawing at her guts was beyond awful.

In the late afternoon, despite the apparent defection of most of the Clan postal office's lords to the traitors' side – at least, it was hard to put any other interpretation on their total failure to comply with the executive head of Clan Security's increasingly heated orders to report – they managed to establish a solid radio network with the other security sites in the Gruinmarkt; and the New York office was still sufficiently functional to arrange a three-hourly courier run with digital video tapes from the Anglischprache world's news feeds. Shortwave and FM didn't have the bandwidth to play back video, but the headlines off the wire services were more than enough to make Miriam sick to her stomach and leave Brilliana and Sir Alasdair anxious for her health.

REUTERS: THIRD ATOMIC WEAPON FAILS TO DETONATE AT PENTAGON

AP: FLIGHTS, STOCK MARKET TRADING SUSPENDED INDEFINITELY

REUTERS: VICE PRESIDENT SWORN IN AS WHITE HOUSE CONFIRMED DESTROYED: PRESIDENT WAS 'AT HOME'

UPI: IRAN CONDEMNS 'FOOLISH AND ILL-ADVISED' ATTACK

REUTERS: SADR LEADS NIGHTTIME DEMONSTRATION IN BAGHDAD: MILLION PROTESTORS IN FIRDOS SQUARE

AP: PRESIDENT TO ADDRESS NATION

But there was even more important news.

At first there was nothing more than a knot of turmoil around the table where Olga and three clerical assistants were coordinating intelligence reports and updating the list of known survivors and victims of the coup attempt. 'I don't believe it,' said Sir Alasdair, making his way back towards Miriam. 'It can't be a coincidence!' His expression was glazed, distant.

'What's happened?' Brill, who had been leaning over a clipboard crossing off the names of couriers who had made too many crossings for the day, looked up at the tone in Miriam's voice.

'The duke,' said Sir Alasdair. He cleared his throat. 'I am very sorry, my lady. Your uncle. The latest report from the clinic says. Um. He went into cardiac arrest this morning.'

'This *morning*?' Miriam caught Brilliana staring at her. She clutched the arm of her folding director's chair. 'Can't be. Can't possibly be. Are they *sure*?' She swallowed. Angbard, the thin white duke: For over thirty years he'd been the guiding will behind the Clan Security operation, the hand that held the reins binding the disparate squabbling families together. Since his stroke two months ago his duties had been carved up and assigned to Olga and Riordan, but not without question or challenge: The Clan Council was not eager to see any individual ever again wield that much power. 'He's dead?' She heard her voice rising and raised a hand to cover her mouth.

'If it's a coincidence I'll eat this table. I'm sorry, my lady,' Sir Alasdair added, 'but it can't possibly be an accident. Not with a revolt in progress and, and the other news. From the Americans.'

'Brill, I'm sorry – ' Miriam's voice broke. Angbard hadn't *felt* like an uncle to her – more like a scary Mafia godfather who, for no obvious reason, had taken a liking to her – but he'd been a huge influence on Brilliana. *And Olga*, Miriam reminded herself. 'Is there any word on who killed him? Because when we find them – '

'It wasn't a killing, according to the clinic,' Sir Alasdair said. 'Although it beggars belief to suppose it a coincidence, for now it must needs be but one more insult to avenge at our convenience. One of our doctors was in attendance, Dr. ven Hjalmar – '

'Shit. *Shit!*' Miriam clenched her fist. Brill was watching her, a dangerous light in her eyes.

Sir Alasdair paused. 'Is there a problem?' he asked.

'Dr. ven Hjalmar is a wanted man,' Brilliana said, her tone colorless.

'Very,' Miriam added, her voice cracking. 'Sir Alasdair. Should you or your men find Dr. ven Hjalmar . . . I will sleep better for knowing that he's dead.'

Sir Alasdair nodded. 'I'm sure that can be arranged.' He paused. 'Is there a reason?'

Brilliana cleared her throat. 'A necessary and sufficient one that need not concern you further. Oh, and his murder of Duke Angbard should be sufficient, should it not?'

'Ah – really?' Sir Alasdair's eyebrow rose. 'Well, if you say so – ' He noticed Miriam's expression. 'You're sure?'

'Very sure,' she said flatly.

'In that case, I'll put the order out. By your leave.' Sir Alasdair beat a hasty retreat.

Miriam glanced at Brill, trying to gather her wits. 'Come on, I want to find out what's happening.'

The card indexes, divided by faction members and known status, were growing in size and complexity – and a third list had joined the first two: known fatalities. Earl Riordan was deep in conversation with one of his lieutenants as Miriam approached him – 'Then tomorrow morning, we shall relocate to Koudrivier House. Assign two lances to establish a security cordon and a third for courier and doppelgänger duties. The rest of your men I want – my lady?' He straightened up. 'What can I do for you?'

'My uncle is dead,' Miriam managed, the words feeling strange in her mouth. *The uncle I never had time to get to know has been murdered* . . . 'Is my mother accounted for? Or my grandmother?'

Earl Riordan looked irritated for a moment, then thoughtful. 'Your grandam is unaccounted for. Along with several of her friends, who appear to be involved in the insurrection.' He turned to one of the clerks and asked a question in rapid Hochsprache. 'We shall find out about her grace your mother shortly, I trust. Is there anything else?'

'Yes.' Miriam gripped her hands tightly behind her back. 'The duke is dead. How fast can we get a quorum of the Clan Council together? Just enough to confirm' – she caught Olga's head turning towards her, the warning look too late – 'you as official head of Clan Security,' she continued. 'And an extraordinary meeting to discuss policy.'

'We'll do that as soon as – ' Riordan glanced at the map table across the aisle from his clerks. 'We have a cabal of insurrectionists to arrest first – '

'No.' The firmness in her voice surprised Miriam. Even though her guts were burning, acid bile and churning stress in her belly: *Can't stop now.* 'I don't think you grasp how far this has gone. Dick Cheney has just been sworn in as president. You know he worked for the duke: This is a comprehensive clusterfuck. This president will need to destroy us, destroy the evidence, and the fuckwit faction have just handed him the perfect excuse. The American military are going to find a way to come over here and they will kill *everybody.* You're thinking months or weeks. We probably don't have that long.' Miriam stared at Riordan. He was not entirely an enigma, but she couldn't say that she knew him well; another of the younger generation, like Roland, educated to college level or higher in the United States, but bound to serve in the traditional family trade. 'We just nuked the White House,' she reminded him. 'What would *you* do in their shoes?'

'I'd – ' His expression would have been funny if the situation hadn't been so serious. 'Oh. *Scheisse.*' A momentary expression of despair flickered across his face. 'What do you suggest?'

'We need to establish safe locations in New Britain right now, today. Get our people across there, start setting up an evacuation pipeline. You're right about suppressing the, the rebels – but we're not going back to business as usual over here. Never again. They won't give us time; if we want to survive we need to evacuate. There are folk I know who might be able to help us, if we can – '

Riordan raised a hand. 'There will be no cutting and running,' he said firmly. 'Your point is well taken, but if we "cut and run" while the houses are divided, our organization will . . . it won't remain viable. The rebels will harry us and our less loyal relatives will desert us, until there's nothing left. The Clan stands or dies as a group. But.' He looked at Brilliana. 'My lady, this world is not safe for her royal highness, not now, and probably not for some time. And she is quite right about the need for us to prepare an evacuation pipeline, against the hazard she so vividly identifies. Can you take her to New Britain and see to her safety?'

'Now wait a – ' Miriam began, but Brill cut in before she could get going.

'Yes, I can do that. I'll need muscle. Sir Alasdair, her royal highness's household, a number of other people. And we'll need money. Lots of it, if we're setting up an evacuation pipeline.'

'You've got it.' Riordan took a deep breath. 'My lady?' He looked back at Miriam. 'The rebels want you under their thumb. If they have you, they hold the monarchy here, and they truly don't realize what they've unleashed in America. Your goal of preparing a, a fallback for us, in New Britain, is a worthy one, and my second-highest priority after rounding up the traitors. I see no reason for it not to be *your* highest priority. If nothing else, it puts you beyond the insurrectionists' easy reach – and the Americans', if your fears come to pass.' He glanced at Brilliana. 'Look after her and see that her orders in this enterprise are carried out. Make sure to keep me informed of your location: We may need to move the Continuity Council there as well, or at least hold audiences. If anyone obstructs you, you have my authority on this matter, on the orders of the Clan Security executive.' To Miriam: 'Is that what you desire, my lady?'

Miriam nodded, swallowed. The nausea was quite severe; she shoved it out of her mind. 'I've got some plans already nailed down,' she said. 'Come on, Brill. Let's find somewhere to work. There's a list of people and things we need.' She swallowed again, feeling a cramp in her belly. 'Oh. Oh shit. I don't feel good . . .'

BEGIN RECORDING

'Shalom, Mordechai.'

'And you, my friend. This must be a fraught time for you; I can't say how much these outrages pain me, I can barely imagine how much worse it must be for you.' (*Pause.*) 'I assume this is not a casual visit?'

'No, I – I've been very busy, as you can imagine. I've got about an hour out of the office, though, and I think you need to know. First, tell me – the attacks. Who do you think carried them out?'

(*Pause.*) 'If I tell you who I think did it, you'll assume it's inside information. And I can't give you inside information even if I have it to give, my friend. But I don't think it was the usual clowns, if that's what you're fishing for? Because they're simply incapable of pulling something like this off. Let me tell you, everyone in the Institute is doing their nut right now – '

'Oh *hell*. They haven't officially told your people, then? Who did it?'

'You *know* who did it? Who?'

(*Slowly.*) 'You're going to think I'm crazy if you don't get this through official channels, I swear – they briefed everybody yesterday and this morning, half of us thought they were mad but they have evidence, Mordechai, hard evidence. It's a new threat, completely unlike anything we imagined.'

'Really? My money was on a false-flag operation by the Office of Special Programs.'

'No, no, it wasn't us: we're not criminals! Well, the bombs were ours. But they were stolen from the inactive inventory.'

'*Stolen?* Tell me it's not true, Jack! Nobody "just steals" special weapons like they're shoplifting a candy store – '

'Take a deep breath, man. There are other universes, parallel worlds, like ours but where things happened differently. Different people, different history. There's a secret project under Livermore building machines for transiting between parallel worlds: They've got the photographs to prove it. The way they briefed us – a bunch of, of drug lords from another dimension, can you believe it? Illegal aliens, emphasis on the alien, whatever. They stole half a dozen backpack nukes, they just *appeared inside* the secure storage cells and walked off with them! The White House has been studying the situation for a year now. Negotiations broke down, and this was their idea of a Dear John.'

'Oy. From anyone else I would not believe it, Jack, but from you, I take it as gospel. Tell me, have you been working too hard lately?'

'Fuck off, I'm not jerking your chain. Listen, I expect you'll hear about it officially through diplomatic channels within a day or two. It's a huge mess – a whole fucking sewage farm has hit the windmill. D.C. was blowback, just like al-Qaeda, let's not kid ourselves – and the president means to put an end to it, and do it hard and fast.'

'What do you mean by hard and fast, in this context?'

'They've indented for a hundred and sixty B83s from Pantex, with an option on another two hundred in two weeks, that's what I mean. And the Fifth Bomb Wing have gone onto lockdown. I mean, everyone's on alert everywhere, but the Fifth have canceled all leave and there's a complete communications blackout. Half of them moved to Fairford in England for Iraq, and the grapevine says the rest are staging out there with B83s aboard, just to keep them out of enemy hands. I just saw orders

reactivating the Seventy-second Bomb Squadron and pulling in
ground staff.'

'Out of *enemy* – what the fuck is going on?'

'Like I said, it's a whole new ballgame. These fuckers can just
appear out of thin air, anywhere! Inside your security perimeter!
My guess is that the Fifth Bomb Wing is being readied for a
counterstrike mission into a, a parallel universe, just as soon as
they can load up with B83s, fit the transit machines, and as soon
as the U2s deliver accurate target maps. Keeping them overseas
in England is a security measure: They can move sideways
between worlds, show up inside the perimeter of our bases – but
if the bombers aren't home they can't touch them. Watch for the
KC-10s moving too. I tell you, they're getting ready for an attack
on North America – just not *our* North America.'

'Okay, Jack, I've got to hand it to you. You are either taking far more
LSD than is good for you, or you have completely spoiled my
afternoon, because you just aren't imaginative enough to make
up a story like that without chemical assistance. I say that as a
compliment, by the way – an excessively active imagination is a
liability in our line of work. I'm going to have to escalate this,
and that's going to make my head hurt because, my boss, it's
going to make *his* head hurt. So I hope you won't take this the
wrong way when I ask, what have you got for me? What concrete
evidence have you got to back these claims up?'

(*Rustling.*) 'It's classified, but not top-secret. I mean, this stuff is
general dissemination for about a hundred thousand soldiers, as
of this morning – it *was* top-secret, but they're realists, there's no
way to keep a lid on something like this indefinitely. So I, uh,
there's a classified briefing pack that I need to lock back in my
office drawer tonight. I assume you've got a camera or
something?'

'Of course. Jack, you're a mensch. Listen, I am just about to go to the
toilet, I'll be back in a few minutes and your briefing pack can go
right back to the office after lunch while I go find some
headache pills before I call Tel Aviv. Are you sure this isn't just a
prank to make Benny Netanyahu shit himself . . . ? No? Too bad.

Because I'd love to be there to see his face when this lands on his desk.'

END RECORDING

Oliver, Baron Hjorth had spent a sleepless night in a co-opted tax farmer's mansion in a country estate, near the site of Baltimore in the United States. The rooms two stories up, under the eaves, were uncomfortably hot in the summer miasma; but they lent a good view of the approaches to the house, and more importantly, good radio reception for a location so far south of the Gruinmarkt.

In his opinion, it was only sensible to take precautions: He had played his part in the operation in good faith, but there was a significant risk that some ne'er-do-well or rakehell anarchist of the progressive creed might seek him out with murder in mind. So the baron sat in a sweltering servants' room, his head bowed beneath the roof beams, while next door his man Schuller poked at the scanner, waiting.

On the other side of the wall of worlds from this mansion there was a modest, suburban family home. In its car port waited a black Lincoln, fully fueled for the dash up the interstate to Boston. But once he took to the wide American highways he'd be trapped, in a manner of speaking; committed to Niejwein, by hook or by crook. He could be at the palace in a matter of hours, there to take charge of a troop of cavalry as befitted a gentleman: but while he was on the road he'd be unable to listen in on the upstart Riordan's increasingly desperate messages.

Impatient and irritable with tiredness, Oliver stood – for perhaps the fifth time that morning – and walked to the window casement. Below him, a cleared slope ran downhill to the wood line: Nobody stirred on the dirt track leading to the house. *Good.* He glanced at the doorway. Schuller was a reliable man, one of the untitled worldwalkers of outer family breeding that Riordan had sacked from Angbard's organization in the wake of the fiasco at the Hjalmar Palace.

Let's see what news . . . Oliver walked to the doorway and shoved the curtain aside. 'How goes it?' he demanded.

Schuller glanced up, then nodded – overfamiliarly, in Oliver's opinion, but fatigue made churls of all men – and shoved one headphone away from an ear. 'Nothing for the past fifteen minutes, my lord. Before that, something garbled from Lady Thorold's adjutant. A call for reinforcements from their Millgartfurt station, where they reported word of an attack – cut short. Orders from Major Riordan's command post, demanding that all units hold their station and report by numbers. There were three responses.'

'*Good.*' The baron laced his fingers together tightly. 'What word from the Anglischprache?'

'Riordan told the post to keep reporting hourly on the attack; it is by all accounts total chaos over there. All air flights are grounded, but the roads are open – outside of the capital, of course. They're clucking like headless chickens.' Schuller's expression was stony. 'As well they might. Fools.'

'Did I pledge you for your opinions?' The baron raised an eyelid: Schuller recoiled slightly.

'No, sir!'

'Then kindly keep them to yourself, there's a good chap. I'm trying to think.' Oliver dabbed at his forehead, trying to mop away the perspiration. *The limousine is air-conditioned,* he reminded himself. 'You have a log, yes? Let me see it.' Schuller held up a clipboard. The pages were neatly hand-scribed, a list of times and stations and cryptic notes of their message content. 'Careless of them. They're not encrypting.'

'They are probably shorthanded, sir.' Schuller looked up at the baron as he paged through the sheet. 'Their traffic has been tailing off all morning.'

'Well then.' The baron smiled as he saw the time stamps grow thinner, the broadcasts more desperate. 'I think it's time to move headquarters. Tell Stanislaw and Poul we're moving, then hail Andrei and tell him to ready the troops to move this afternoon. Shut up shop and meet me downstairs in ten minutes: I must change first.' It wouldn't do to be stopped and searched by the Anglische police while dressed as a Sudtmarkt cousin's guest, but he had a business suit laid out next door.

The plan was simple, as such things went: Baron Hjorth would transfer to the United States, drive north – covering a distance of hundreds of miles in a mere afternoon – and reemerge in the Gruinmarkt, on his own estate, with a bodyguard of cavalrymen in time to ride to the flag of the postal lords and her grace the dowager duchess. Who, if things were going to plan – as appeared to be the case – would have coaxed the Idiot's hoyden widow into a suitably well-guarded retreat and arranged for her confinement, in every sense of the word. Having managed the successful delivery of the atomic bombs to their targets (an expensive process, as Jurgen could attest), he was, if nothing else, in line for the reward for a job well done. *Probably more of the same,* he thought, as he dressed in American fashion, mildly irritated by the lack of body servants. *The sacrifices we make . . .*

Oliver made his way through the empty servants' quarters, passing the room recently vacated by Schuller, before descending by way of a back staircase and a dressing room to reach the main staircase. His men had dismissed most of the regular staff, banishing them to the village over the hill in the name of security. The great house was almost deserted, sweltering in the noon heat. Air-conditioning and the milder Northern climate beckoned, putting a spring in the baron's step. As he reached the bottom step, one shoe touching the mosaic floor of the central hall, he paused. It was, if anything, *too* quiet. 'Poul?' he called quietly. 'Stanislaw – '

'They won't be answering.' Schuller stepped out of the shadows.

Oliver's left hand tightened on the handrail. 'What is this?' His right hand was already shoving aside his jacket, reaching for the small of his back –

Schuller shot him. In the confines of the high-ceilinged room the blast of the shotgun was deafening: it launched a screeching flight of frightened birds from the grounds outside. Oliver Hjorth collapsed, eyes staring, his chest flayed open as any victim of the blood eagle. Schuller racked the pump on his weapon, ejecting the smoking cartridge, his eyes red-rimmed and tired, his face still expressionless.

'Fucking aristocratic traitor,' he muttered, inspecting the baron's body for any sign of residual life; but there was not so much as a toe-twitch, and the pool of blood was spreading evenly now, no longer spurting but beginning to soak into the rug at the center of the hall. Turning on his heel, Schuller walked slowly towards the front door of the hall; raising his left hand to stare at something cupped within his palm, he vanished. An instant later he reappeared in a linoleum-floored utility room, windowless. Walking over to the telephone, he dialed a number from memory: 'Message to the major,' he said, swallowing back bile. 'Cuckoo Four has hatched three eggs. Cuckoo Four is going home.'

There was a moment's delay, and then a woman's voice spoke: 'Got that, and good luck. The major says you did well.'

'Bye.' He hung up, carefully unloaded his shotgun, and deposited it on the workbench. Then, taking a pair of car keys from his pocket, he headed for the carport. It would be a long drive for one man sticking religiously to the speed limit; but if he hurried, he could be back with his unit by sundown. Unlike the baron, Earl-Major Riordan didn't think of his agents as expendable embarrassments.

*

It took more than a war, a liquidity crisis, and a revolution to stop the dogs. The morning after his father explained the new arrangement to him – the identity of their new political patron, the reason for backing ven Hjalmar, and the ruling council of elders' plans for the future – James Lee, his hat pulled down as low as his spirits, walked to the track to put some money on the greyhounds.

It was not, of course, entirely safe for a man with Asian features to walk these streets alone; but Lin, his favorite younger brother, was eager to get out of the house for a few hours. With smoked glasses and the beard he'd been cultivating of late, James didn't feel too out of place; and in addition to his cane, he had a pistol and a locket on a ribbon around his left wrist.

'Look – I'll put two shillings on Red Leinster in the next race,' said Lin, pointing at one of the muzzled and hooded hounds, being led back to the kennels in the wake of a near-miss. 'How about you?'

'Huh. Three and six on Bottle Rocket, I think.' James glanced around, looking for a tout's man. 'And a pint of mild.'

'Make that two pints.' Lin flashed him a brief grin. 'What's gotten into you, brother? I haven't seen you this low since . . .' He trailed off.

James shook his head. Another glance: 'Not in English,' he said quietly. 'Later, maybe.'

'Oh.' Slightly crestfallen, Lin subsided. But not for long: 'Look! There's your bookmaker.' He pointed excitedly, at a sharply dressed figure surrounded by a court of supplicants, and not a few stone-faced gentlemen with stout walking sticks – some of them doubtless concealing blades. 'Are you going to – '

James shook his head. 'Life's a gamble,' he said quietly. A moment later his mood lifted. 'Yes, I think I shall take a flutter.' He worked his way over towards the bookmaker, Lin following along in his wake. A few minutes later, by way of a tap-man who dispensed mild straight into battered pewter pots from the back of a cask-laden dray, he made his way towards the back of the trackside crowd. The audience was abuzz with anticipation as the fresh dogs were led out to the stalls. 'Which do you think is more important: filial obedience, or honor?' he asked.

Lin's eyes crossed briefly. 'Uh. Beer?' he hazarded.

James shook his head minutely. 'Imagine I'm being serious.'

'Well, then.' Lin took a gulp of the black beer. 'This is a trick question, isn't it? Filial obedience, obviously, because that's where your honor comes from, right?'

'Wrong.' James took a sip from his own mug. 'And yes it *is* a trick question, but not the kind you're expecting. Let me see. Try this one: Why does honor come from filial obedience?'

'Because it does?' Lin rolled his eyes this time, making it clear that he was honoring his elder brother precisely inasmuch as the free beer required. 'This is boring – '

'No it isn't,' James said, quietly urgent. 'Listen. Firstly, we obey because it's the right and traditional thing to do. Secondly, we obey because it is what we shall want for ourselves, when *we* are elders. And thirdly, we obey because the old farts are usually right, and they are making decisions with our family's best interests in mind. They know what they're doing. Except when they *don't*. So let me rephrase: If you found out that the elders were doing something really stupid, *dangerously* stupid, and you couldn't talk them out of it – what would you do?'

A rattling clangor of gates and the shrill of a whistle: The dogs were off, bolting up the track in pursuit of the mechanical hare. 'Oh brother.' Lin was uncharacteristically quiet. 'This isn't theoretical, is it?'

'No.' Shouting and hoarse cheering rose on all sides as the crowd urged their hounds on. 'They've bet the family's future on a wild black dog. *Our* future, Lin.'

'They wouldn't do that,' Lin said automatically. He raised his tankard, drank deeply as the gongs clashed and the crowd roared their approval. 'Would they?' He wiped his mouth with the back of a hairless wrist.

'They would, and they did, with the best of intentions.' James shook his head. 'Huh, there goes my three and six. But looks like you lucked out.'

'What have they done?' Lin asked as they queued to collect his winnings – not so much, for he'd bet on a favorite – from the men with clubs.

'Later.' James waited patiently while his younger brother swapped his ticket for five shillings; the tout's men looked disapprovingly on, but made no move to pick a fight. They headed back to the dray for a refill, then over to the fence near the bleachers to watch. The racing dogs were kenneled, while dogs of another kind were brought out, along with a bear for them to bait in a wire-fenced enclosure in the middle of the track. 'You met the enemy heir, Helge, Miriam. What did you think of her?'

Lin shook his head. 'She's a crazy woman,' he said admiringly. A shadow crossed his face. 'I owe her, brother. It shames me to say.'

'The elders sent you to kill her, and she ended up saving your life. That's a heavy obligation, isn't it? What if I said the elders have settled on a harebrained scheme to make us safe and rich – but one that will kill her? Where's your honor there, eh?'

'They wouldn't do that!' Lin glanced from side to side. 'That would restart the war, wouldn't it?'

'They may not realize what they're doing,' James said quietly. 'They're entering into an arrangement with one of her enemies, though, a man who she told me had wronged her grievously. Another of the cousins, their feuds are hard to keep track of . . . but what makes this different is that they're *also* talking to a government man.' His younger brother's eyes were bulging with disbelief. 'I know, I know. *I* think they've taken leave of their senses, you know the rules – but Dad and Uncle Huan are agreed. They figure the revolution's going to turn into a bloody civil war, and I think they're probably right about that – and they think we need political patronage to survive it. Well, that goes against the old rules, but they're the elders: They *make* the rules, and sometimes you have to throw out the old rules and bring in new rules. The trouble is, they're hoping to use a mad scheme of Dr. ven Hjalmar's to breed extra world-walkers – don't ask me how it works, it's magic medicine from the other world the cousins go to – and they're hoping to use their political patron's offices to make it work. Ven Hjalmar is poison: Miriam hates him. And the patron they've picked – ' James shook his head. 'I don't trust him. Uncle doesn't trust him either, but I think Uncle underestimates how untrustworthy he is. *And* ven Hjalmar. They'll cut a deal behind our backs and we'll be at their mercy.'

'A deal. What sort of deal? What do they want us to do?' Lin stared at his elder brother.

'Assassination. Spying. Smuggling. What do *you* think the Levelers' secret Polis might want of us? And then they'll own us, match, lock, and trigger. But more importantly – the cousins will be looking for sanctuary here, and this will put them at our throat, and we at theirs: The Polis won't tolerate a different group of world-walkers beyond their control, once they learn of the cousins' existence. We'll be right back where we started, but this time under the thumb of the Polis – who despise us because we're children of the Inner Kingdom.'

'We could go back there – ' Lin stopped.

'Could we?' It was James's turn to raise an eyebrow. 'Where would we be, if we couldn't move freely through New Britain? How would we prosper? And that's assuming we *can* go back there. What the cousins have stirred up – ' He shook his head. 'No, it wouldn't work. That's why I'm asking you: Which comes first, your honor or your filial loyalty?'

Lin stared for a few seconds; then his shoulders slumped. He took a deep mouthful of beer. 'I defer to your elder wisdom,' he finally said. Another pause. 'What are you going to do?'

'I'm going to watch.' James whistled tunelessly between his front teeth. 'Hopefully I won't have to do anything. Hopefully Uncle is right and I am wrong. But if it turns out that Uncle Huan *isn't* right . . . will you obey him to the end, or will you do what's right for the family?'

Lin looked away. Then he looked back and nodded: a minute inclination of the head, but a significant one – the precise degree of submission that he might otherwise give his father. 'What are you considering?'

'Nothing specific, as yet.' James raised his tankard. 'But if the elders' plans go astray – we'll see.'

*

As he turned in to Miriam Beckstein's street, Mike Fleming felt an uncontrollable shudder ripple up the small of his back: an intense sensation of guilt, as if he'd done something unforgivable. Which was ridiculous. *Why do I feel like a stalker?* he wondered ironically. *I'm not the guy who's been lurking in the bushes with a phone and a camera for the past six months, hoping she'll come home.* He drove carefully up the road, not slowing and not staring at the houses, trying to tag the parked cars as memories battered for his attention.

Mike had a history: not uncommon. Single cop, married to the job. He had another history, too: dates, girlfriends, brief excursions into the alien world of domesticity that never quite seemed to gain traction. Three or four years ago he'd met a woman journalist – *how?* he could remember the where, but not the why – and asked her out, or maybe she'd asked him to ask her out, or something. And they'd gotten to know each other and she'd asked him home and then it all seemed to cool off, over the space of a couple of months.

Nothing new there; and he could easily have written it off. *She's a civilian, it wasn't going to work.* But for some reason, he hadn't gotten over her as easily as all that. He'd thought about looking her up. Seeing if he could make her change her mind. Then he realized he was getting close to some creepy headspace, and asked himself if that was really who he wanted to be, took a vacation and went on a cruise, drank too much, and had a couple of one-night stands. Which seemed to fix things, but he'd teetered on the fine edge of obsession for a few weeks, and now here he was driving down her street, and it felt weird. Creepy. Blame FTO for sucking him in and Miriam for concealing her secret other life from him – assuming that was what she'd been doing? – but this felt *wrong*. And what he was going to do next was even more wrong.

Burgling Ex-Girlfriend's House 101: First make sure there's nobody watching it, then make sure there's nobody home. Mike took a long loop around the neighborhood, killing five minutes before he turned back and drove down the street in the opposite direction. One parked car had departed; of the remaining ones, two were occupied, but hadn't been on his first pass. Ten minutes later, he made a third pass. A truck had parked up, with two workmen sitting inside, eating their lunch or something. Someone was messing with the trunk of another parked car. The two that had been occupied earlier were vacant. *If there's a watch, they're using a house or a camera.* But not sitting in a car, waiting to pounce.

Mike pulled in, several doors down from Miriam's. He'd stopped at a Kinko's on his way. Now he hung a laminated badge around his neck, and stuck a fat day planner under his left arm. The badge bore a photograph but gave a false name and identified him as working for a fictional market research company, and the bulging day planner's zipped compartment held tools rather than papers, but to a casual bystander . . . well.

Now came the tricky part. He climbed out of his car and locked it; stretched; then walked up the street, trying not to hobble. He paused at the first door he came to, deliberately trying to look bored. There was a doorbell: J & P SUTHERLAND. He pushed it, waited, hoping nobody was in. If they were, he had a couple of spiels ready; but any exposure was a calculated risk. After a minute he pushed the buzzer again. The Sutherlands were obviously out; check one house off the list – he ritually made a note on the pad clipped to the back of his planner – and move on.

As Mike moved up the road, ringing doorbells and waiting, he kept a weather eye open for twitching curtains, unexpected antennae. A bored Boston grandmother at one apartment threatened to take too much interest in him, but he managed to dissuade her with the number-two pitch: Was she satisfied with her current lawn-care company? (For telecommuting techies, the number-one pitch was a nonstick-bakeware multilevel marketing scheme. Anything to avoid having to actually interview anybody.) Finally he reached Miriam's doorstep. The windows were grimy, and the mailbox was threatening to overflow: good. *So nobody's renting.* He rang the doorbell, stood there for the requisite minute, and moved on.

This was the moment of maximum danger, and his skin was crawling as he slowly walked to the next door. If FTO *was* watching the Beckstein house, they'd be all over him if they suspected he was trying to make contact. But they *wouldn't* be all over a random street canvasser, and Mike had taken steps to not look like Mike Fleming, rogue agent and wanted man, from his cheap suit to the shaven scalp and false mustache. It wouldn't fool a proper inspection, but if he had to do that he'd already lost; all he had to do was look like part of the street furniture.

Three doors. Nobody coming out of the houses opposite, no sedan cruising slowly down the road towards him. His mind kept circling back to the ingrained grime on the windows, the crammed mailbox. *Let them have dropped the watch,* he prayed. A 24/7 watch on a person of interest was a costly affair: It took at least five agents working forty hours a week to minimally cover a target, and if the target was expecting it and taking evasive measures – jumping next door's backyard fence, for example – you could double or triple that watch before you had a hope of keeping the cordon intact. Add management and headquarters staff and vacation and sick leave and a pair of tail cars in case the target went shopping and you could easily use up twenty personnel – call it a cool million and a half per year in payroll alone. And Miriam hadn't been back, that much he was fairly sure of. Another sixty seconds passed. Mike made an executive decision: *There's no watch. Party time!*

The houses adjacent to the Beckstein residence were all vacant at this time of day. Mike turned and walked back to the next one over, then rang the doorbell again. When there was no response, he shrugged; then instead of going back to the sidewalk he walked around the building, slowly, looking up at the eaves. (Cover story number three: Would you like to buy some weatherproof gutter lining?)

The fence between their yard and the next was head-high, but they weren't tidy gardeners and there was no dog; once he was out of sight of the street it took Mike thirty seconds to shove an empty rainwater barrel against the wooden wall and climb over it, taking care to lower himself down on his good leg. The grass in Miriam's yard was thigh-high, utterly unkempt and flopping over under its own weight. Mike picked himself up and looked around. There was a wooden shed, and a glass sliding door into the living room – locked. *Think like a cop. Where would she leave it?* Mike turned to the shed immediately. It had seen better days: The concrete plinth was cracked, and the window hung loose. He carefully reached through the window opening, slowly feeling around the frame until his questing fingers touched a nail and something else. He stifled a grin as he inspected the keyring. This was almost *too* easy. *What am I missing?* he wondered. A momentary premonition tickled the edge of his consciousness. *Miriam has enemies in the Clan, folks like Matthias.* And Matthias had an extra-special calling card. Mike looked at the sliding door. So it wasn't going to be easy, was it?

The key turned in the lock. Mike opened his case and removed a can of WD-40, and sprayed it into the track at the bottom of the door. Then he took out another can, and a long screwdriver. First, he edged the door open a quarter of an inch. Then he slowly ran the screwdriver's tip into the gap, and painstakingly lifted it from floor to ceiling. It met no resistance. *Good.* It was a warm day, and the cold sweat was clammy across his neck and shoulders and in the small of his back as he widened the entrance. Still nothing. *Am I jumping at shadows?* When the opening was eighteen inches wide, Mike gave the

ray can a brisk shake, then pointed it into the room,
ceiling, and held the nozzle down.

...ing – quick-setting plastic foam – squirted out and drifted
...ards the floor in loops and tangles. About six inches inside the
doorway, at calf level to a careless boot, it hung in midair, draped over
a fine wire. Mike crouched down and studied it, then looked inside.
The tripwire – now he knew what to look for – ran to a hook in the
opposite side of the doorframe, and then to a green box screwed to
the wall.

Mike stepped over the wire. Then he breathed out, and looked
around.

The lounge-cum-office was a mess. Some person or persons
unknown had searched it, thoroughly, not taking pains to tidy up
afterwards; then someone else had installed the booby box and tripwire. It was dusty inside, and dark. *Power's probably out,* he realized.
A turf'n'trap sting gone to seed, long neglected by its intended victim:
Better check for more wires. Before touching anything, he pulled on a
pair of surgical gloves. A poke at a desk lamp confirmed that the
power was out – no surprises there. Hunting around in the sea of
papers that hands unseen had dumped on the office floor was going
to take some time, but seemed unavoidable: Empty sockets in a main
extension block under the desk, and an abandoned palmtop docking
station, suggested the absence of a computer and other electronic
devices. Mike checked the rest of the house briefly, squirting Silly
String before going through each doorway: There was another wire
just inside the front door, beyond a toppled-over bookcase, but there
were no other traps as far as he could see.

Getting down to work on the office, he wondered who'd turfed the
scene. The missing computer was suggestive; going by the empty
shelves and the boxes on the floor, it didn't take long to notice that all
the computer media – Zip disks, CD-ROMs, even dusty old floppy
disks – were missing. 'Huh,' he said quietly. 'So they were looking for
files?' Miriam was a journalist. It was carelessly done, as if they'd been
looking for something specific – and the searchers weren't cops or
spooks. Cops searching a journalist's office wouldn't leave a scrap of
paper behind, and spooks wouldn't want the subject to know they

were under surveillance. 'Amateurs.' Mike took heart: It made his job that bit easier, to know that the perps had been looking for something specific, not trying to deny information to someone coming after.

Fumbling through the pile of papers, sorting them into separate blocks, Mike ran across a telephone cable. It was still plugged in, and tracing it back to the desk he discovered the handset, which had fallen down beside the wall. It was a fancy one, with a built-in answerphone and a cassette tape. Mike pocketed the tape, then went back to work on the papers. Lots of cuttings from newspapers and magazines, lots of scribbled notes about articles she'd been working on, a grocery bill, invoices from the gas and electric – nothing obviously significant. The books: there was a pile of software manuals, business books, some dog-eared crime thrillers and Harlequin romances, a Filofax –

Mike flipped it open. 'Bingo!' It was full of handwritten names, numbers, and addresses, scribbled out and overwritten and annotated. Evidently Miriam didn't trust computers for everything; either that, or he'd latched on to a years-out-of-date organizer. But a quick look in the front revealed a year planner that went as far forward as the previous year. *Why the hell didn't they take it?* he wondered, looking around. 'Huh.' Assuming the searchers were from the Clan . . . would they even know what a Filofax was? It looked like a book, from a distance; perhaps someone had told the brute squad to grab computers, disks, and any loose files on her desk. *They don't think like cops* or *spooks.* He looked round, at the green box on the wall above the door, and shuddered. *Time to blow.*

Outside, with the glass door shut and the key back on its nail in the shed, he glanced at the fence. His leg twinged, reminding him that he wasn't ready for climbing or running. There was a gap between the fence and the side of the house, shadowy; he slipped into it, his fat planner (now pregnant with Miriam's Filofax) clutched before him.

There was a wooden gate at the end of the alley, latched shut but not padlocked. He paused behind it to peer between the vertical slats. A police car cruised slowly along the street, two officers inside. *Two?* Mike swore under his breath and crouched down. The car seemed to take forever to drive out of sight. Heart pounding, Mike checked his watch. It was half past noon, near enough exactly. He straightened up slowly, then unlatched the gate and limped past the front of the house as fast as he could, then back onto the sidewalk outside. He fumbled the key to his rental car at first, sweat and tension and butterflies in his stomach making him uncharacteristically clumsy, but on the second try, the door swung open and he slumped down behind the steering wheel and pulled it to just as another police car – or perhaps the same one, returning – swung into the street.

Mike ducked. *They're not running a stakeout but they've got police surveillance,* he told himself. Adding the Beckstein residence to a regular patrol's list of places of interest would cost FTO virtually nothing – and they'd missed spotting him by seconds. He stayed down, crouched over the passenger seat as the cruiser slowly drove past. They'd be counting heads, looking for the unexpected. His cover was good but it wouldn't pass a police background check if they went to town on him – and they would, if they found Miriam's purloined Filofax. Ten seconds passed, then twenty. Mike straightened up cautiously and glanced in the rearview mirror. The cops were nearing the end of the road. Thirty seconds; they paused briefly, then hung a left, and Mike breathed out. *Okay, back to the motel,* he told himself. *Then we'll see what we've got here . . .*

BEGIN RECORDING

'My fellow Americans, good evening.

'It pains me more than I can say to be speaking to you tonight as your president. There are no good situations in which a vice president can take the oath of office; we step into the boots of a fallen commander-in-chief, hoping we can fill them, hoping we can live up to what our dead predecessor would have expected of us. It is a heavy burden of responsibility and, God willing, I shall do my utmost to live up to it. I owe nothing less to you, to all our citizens and especially to the gallant men and women who serve the cause of freedom and democracy in our nation's armed forces; and I say this – I shall not sleep until our enemies, the enemies who murderously attacked us a week ago, are hunted down wherever they hide and are destroyed.

'In time of war – and this is nothing less – it is the job of the commander-in-chief to defend the republic, and it is the job of the vice president to stand ready to serve, which is why I have appointed to the vacant office of the vice president, as my replacement, a man well-qualified to fight for freedom: former Secretary of Defense Rumsfeld. I trust that his appointment to this post, vacated by my succession, will be approved by the House. The future of the republic is safe in his hands.

'But I can already hear you asking: Safe from whom?

'In the turmoil and heroism and agony of the attacks, it was difficult at first for us to ascertain the identity of our enemies. We have many enemies in the Middle East, from al-Qaeda and the terrorists in Iraq and Afghanistan, to the mullahs of Tehran, and naturally our suspicions first fell on those quarters. But they are not our only enemies; and the nature of the attack made it hard to be sure who was responsible. The two atomic bombs that exploded in our capital, and the third that misfired in the Pentagon visitors' lot, were stolen from our own stockpile. This was not only a cowardly and heinous act of nuclear terrorism, but a carefully planned one. However, we have identified the attackers, and we are now preparing to deal with them as they have dealt with us.

'There is no easy way for me to explain this because the reality lies far beyond our everyday experience, but the scientists of our national laboratories assure me that this is true: We live in what they call a multiverse, a many-branched tree of reality. Scientists at Los Alamos have for a year now been probing techniques for traveling to other universes – to other versions of this, our own Earth. They had hoped to use this technique for peaceful ends, to solve the environmental and climatic problems that may arise in future decades. But we have discovered, the hard way, that we are not alone.

'Some of the alternate earths we have discovered are inhabited. And in at least one of these, the inhabitants are hostile. Worse: They, too, have the technological tools to travel to other universes. The enemy who attacked us is the government of a sovereign nation in another America, a Godless feudal despotism ruled by terror and the lash. They know no freedom and they hate our own, for we are a living refutation of everything they hold to be true. Agents of this enemy have moved unseen among us for a generation, and they have been instrumental in the narcotics trade, using it to fund their infiltration of our institutions, their theft of our technologies. They are followers of an alien ideology and they seek to bring us down, and it is to that end that they stole at least six atomic weapons from their storage cells on military bases – gaining access from another unseen universe even as our guards vigilantly defended the perimeter fences.

'We have a name for this enemy: They call themselves the Clan, and they rule a despotic kingdom called Gruinmarkt. And we know what to do to them, for they attacked us without warning on the sixteenth of July, a date that will live in infamy with 9/11, and 12/7, for as long as there is a United States of America.

'To you of the Clan, the cabal of thieves and drug smugglers who have attacked America, I have a simple message: If you surrender now, without preconditions, I will guarantee you a fair trial before the military tribunals now convened at Guantánamo Bay. Only those of you who are guilty of crimes against the United States need fear our justice. But you should think fast. This offer expires one week from today. And then, in the words of my predecessor, Harry S. Truman, you face prompt and utter annihilation.

'Good night, and God bless America.'

END RECORDING

BED REST

It was beyond belief how far things could change in just a week.

Sir Huw, beanpole-skinny and a bit gawky, reined his horse in and dismounted painfully while he was still a hundred yards short of the farmstead. He stretched, trying to iron the kinks out of his thigh and calf muscles.

'Is this it, bro?' rumbled the man-mountain driving the cart and pair behind him. 'In the middle of nowhere?'

Huw glanced around. 'On the other side, we're near Edison,' he said. 'I'll go first. We're expected, but . . .' No point saying it: *The guards are jumpy.* Because, this week and forevermore, *all* the guards were jumpy. *Probably expecting Delta Force to drop in,* Huw mused. Not, in his estimate, likely to happen just yet – although in the long run it couldn't be ruled out. Anxiety battled caution, and set his feet in motion. 'I wonder how Her Majesty is.'

'Nearly three months gone by now,' chirped another voice from the back of the cart, emanating from beneath a blanket that covered its passenger and a mound of wheeled luggage – all Tumi-branded, expensive but ultralightweight ballistic nylon. 'Sick as a mule on a fishing boat.' Huw didn't look round: Trust Elena to interpret it as a political question. Because Miriam's pregnancy *was* political – and that was all it was. 'Did you pack the books?'

'Yes.' Huw had, in fact, packed the books. Two hundred kilograms of them, paper that was worth far more than its weight in gold, or cocaine, where they were going. The Rubber Bible, *The Merck Manual*, the US Pharmacopeia; and more recondite references, science and engineering and medicine all, with a side order of mathematics and maps. They weighed a bundle, but when he'd messaged ahead to ask if they should go digital, the reply had been a terse *no*. Which made a certain sense. CD-ROMs and computers weren't durable enough for what Miriam was planning – if, in fact, he was reading her intentions aright.

Huw walked towards the farmyard, leading his horse. It was a hedge-laird's place; the hearth smoke of a small village rose beyond it, and he could see stooped backs in the fields, some of them pausing and turning to stare at the visitors. But then two guards stepped out in front of him from the barn, and he stopped. The middle-aged sergeant raised a hand: 'Who hails?' The other stood by tensely, his rifle pointed at the ground before Huw's feet.

'Sir Huw Thoms, lieutenant by order of his grace, accompanied by Hulius Thoms and the Lady Elena of Holdt, in the service of the Council.' He halted; his horse exhaled noisily, neck drooping.

'Approach and be identified.' Huw took a step forward. The sergeant peered at him, then glanced at a clipboard cautiously. 'You are welcome, sir.'

Huw stood where he was. 'The password of the day is "banquet",' he stated. '*Now* can we come in? The horses are tired.'

The armsman with the rifle relaxed visibly as his sergeant nodded. 'Very good, sir, the countersign is "mullet".' He gestured towards the stables. 'We'll be pleased to sort you out. Sorry about the precautions – you can't be too careful these days.'

Huw waved a hand at the machine gun dug in just inside the tree line, ready to enfilade the approach to the farm. 'Any rebels try you so far?'

'Not yet, sir. Ah, your companions. If you don't mind – '

Elena and Yul climbed down from the cart and consented to be inspected and compared to their photographs. 'Is it that bad?' Elena asked brightly, shaking out her skirts.

'Some of Lord Ganskwert's retainers attacked the house at Doveswood last night, using a carriage and disguises to cover their approach. Three dead, plus the traitors of course. We can't be too careful.'

'Indeed.' Elena grinned and flashed the sergeant a glimpse of what she had inside her capacious shoulder bag. He blanched. 'Sleep tight!' She added, 'We're on your side!'

'Lightning Child, can't you keep it to yourself for even a minute?'

Huw complained. To the sergeant: 'We won't be staying overnight – we're wanted by Her Majesty, as soon as possible.'

'Ah, we'll do our best, sir. I'll have to confirm that first.' His tone didn't brook argument.

'We can wait awhile,' Huw conceded. 'Got to sort out the horses first, grab something to eat if possible, that sort of thing.'

'There is bread and sausages in the kitchen. If you'd like to wait inside I can have my men deal with your mounts? I take it they're security livery?'

'Yes,' Huw agreed. 'All yours.' He handed his reins to the man. 'We'll be inside if you need us.'

'Excellent,' added Yul, following his elder brother towards the farm building.

Huw and his small team had been well away from the excitement when the putsch by the conservatives and the lords of the Postal Service broke; following up a task assigned to him by Angbard, Duke Lofstrom, back before his stroke – the urgency of which had only become greater since. Huw had been in a rented house outside Macon, recovering from an exploration run, when Elena had erupted into the living room shouting about something on the television and waking up Yul (who had a post-walk hangover of doom). He'd begun to chastise her, only to fall silent as the mushroom cloud, red-lit from within, roiled skyward behind a rain of damaged-camera static.

They'd spent the first hour in shock, but then had come Riordan's Plan Black; and that had presented Huw with a problem, because they were nearly a thousand miles from the nearest evacuation point. Flights were grounded; police and national guard units were hogging the highways. It had taken them three days to make the drive, avoiding interstates and major cities. Finally they'd reached the outskirts of Providence and crossed over, taking another four days to finish the journey from Huw's family estates to this transit point, barely seventy miles away. A thousand miles – two hours by air. Or three days by back roads in the United States. Seventy miles – four days, in the Gruinmarkt. It was an object lesson in the source of the Clan's power – and a warning.

They didn't have long to wait; true to his word, the sergeant ducked in through the kitchen door barely half an hour later. 'By your leave, sir, we have confirmed your permission to travel. If you are ready to go now . . . ?'

'I suppose so,' said Yul, reluctantly setting aside a mug of game soup and a half-eaten cornbread roll. Elena was already on her feet, impatient; Huw set down his wine – a half-drained glass, itself exotic and valuable in this place – and stood.

'Have you got a level stage?' he asked. 'We need to take the cart's contents.'

'We have something better, sir.' The guard turned and headed towards the barn. Huw followed him. Opposite the stalls – he saw a lad busily rubbing down the horses – someone had installed a raised platform, planks stretched across aluminum scaffolding. A ramp led up to it, and at the bottom –

'That's a *good* idea,' Elena said admiringly.

Three big supermarket trolleys waited for them, loaded up with bags. 'The regular couriers will bring them back once you unload them,' said the sergeant. He picked up his clipboard. 'In view of the current troubles we have no postmaster, but I'm keeping score. For later.'

'All right.' Huw set his hands to one of the trolleys and pushed it up the ramp. 'What's the other side like?'

'It's in a cellar.' The sergeant looked disapproving. 'Good thing too. You don't want to be seen coming and going over there – it's a zoo. But you'll be safe enough here.' He caught Huw's expression and nodded. 'I'll go first, see if I don't.' He climbed onto the platform and waited while Hulius and Elena pushed their laden trolleys up the ramp. 'Here, you let me take that one, young miss. Why don't you ride for once?' Laying one hand on the trolley's metal frame, he reached up and tugged a cord leading to a blind on the opposite wall. The blind rose –

The basement was brick-walled, and the ceiling low, but the Clan's surveyors had done their job well and the raised floor was a perfectly level match for the platform in the barn. As Huw hauled the first of his suitcases out of the trolley, trying to ignore the nausea and migrainelike headache, he heard voices from the top of the staircase: Elena, and someone else, someone familiar and welcome.

'My lady Brilliana,' he said. He deposited his case beside the top step – the cellar stairs surfaced in what seemed to be a servants' pantry – and bowed. 'I'm glad to see you.'

'Sir Huw! How wonderful to see you, too.' She smiled slightly more warmly than was proper: Huw held himself in check, ignoring the impulse to hug her. He'd been worried about her for the past week; to find her here, her hair in blond curls, dressed after last year's New London mode, lifted a huge weight from his heart. She held out her hand, and, somewhat daringly, he bent to kiss it. 'Have you had a troublesome time?' she asked, gripping his fingers.

'Not as bad as some.' Huw straightened up, then gestured at the bags: 'I bought the books Miriam wanted. And a few more besides. Yul is' – footsteps creaked on the stairs and he stepped aside as his brother hauled two more suitcases over the threshold – 'here, too.'

'And all these damned bits of paper,' his brother complained, shoving the cases forward. 'Lightning Child damn them for a waste of weight – ' He stepped forward, out of the path of the sergeant from the other side of the transit post, who heaved another two bags towards Huw.

'Trig tables,' Huw added. 'Have you any idea how hard it is to find five-digit trigonometry tables in good condition? Nobody's printed them for years. I also threw in a couple of calculators – I found a store with old stock HP-48GXs and a thermal printer, so I bought the lot. They take rechargeable batteries so the only scarce resource is the thermal paper,' he added defensively. 'I'm still running the one I bought for my freshman year – they run forever. They predate the ban on lead in solder, so there's no problem with tin whiskers forming in the ICs and shorting them out.'

'Oh, Huw.' Brill shook her head, still smiling. 'Listen, I'm sure it's a good idea! It's just' – she glanced over her shoulder – 'we may not be able to resupply at will, and you know how easily computers break.'

'These aren't computers; they're programmable calculators. But they might as well be mainframes, by these people's standards. And we brought rechargeable batteries and solar chargers.' He was burbling, he realized: a combination of post-world-walking sickness and the peculiar relief of finding Brill alive and well in the wake of the previous week's events. 'Sorry. Been a stressful time. Is Miriam – '

'She's in bed upstairs. Resting.' An unreadable expression flickered across Brill's face. 'I'll give you the tour, if you like. Who else . . . ?'

'Me, ma'am.' The sergeant reappeared, carrying two more suitcases, wheezing somewhat. 'One more to go, sirs, ladies.'

'No need to overdo it, Marek, the last cases will wait half an hour if you want to put your feet up.' Brill's concern was obvious: 'You've already been over today, haven't you?'

'Yes, ma'am, but it needs moving and we're shorthanded – '

'You'll be even more shorthanded if you work yourself into a stroke! Go and sit yourself down in the parlor with a mug of beer and a pill until your head clears. Go on, I'll get Maria to look after you – ' Brill dragged the sergeant out of the servants' stairwell, seemingly by main force of will, then returned to lead Huw into the downstairs lounge. 'He's right that they're badly undermanned over there, but he insists on trying to do everything,' she said apologetically. 'There's too much of that around here.'

'Too much of it *everywhere*!' Elena said emphatically. 'Why, if I hadn't forced Huw to let me drive – but how is her royal highness?' She looked at Huw: 'Won't she want to – '

'Yes, how is she?' Huw began, then stopped. Brill's expression was bleak. 'Oh. Oh dear.'

'The lady Helge is perfectly all right.' Brilliana's voice was emotionless. 'But she's very tired and needs time to recover.'

'Recover from what?' Yul chipped in before Elena could kick his ankle.

'Her express instructions are that you are to tell no one,' Brill continued, looking Huw straight in the eye. 'Nobody is going to leave this house who cannot keep his or her mouth shut, at least until it no longer matters.'

'Until *what* matters?' Yul asked, head swiveling between Brilliana and Huw with ever-increasing perplexity.

'Was it spontaneous?' Huw demanded.

Brill nodded. 'The day of the putsch.'

'Let me see her?' demanded Elena. 'My mother was midwife to the district nobility when I was young and she taught me – '

Yul stood by, crestfallen and lost for words. 'Give me your locket,' Brill said to Elena. 'And you too,' she added to Yul. She spared Huw but a brief narrow-eyed glance that seemed to say, *If I can't trust you, then who?* 'You're not to tire her out, mind,' she added for Elena's benefit. 'If she's sleeping, leave her be.' Then she turned towards the door to the owner's rooms. 'Leave the cases for now, Huw. Let me fill you in on what's been going wrong here . . .'

*

In the end, there was no siege: The house surrendered without a shot being fired, doors and windows flung wide, a white flag running up the pole that rose from the apex of the steeply pitched roof.

That wouldn't have been enough to save the occupants, of course. Riordan was not inclined towards mercy: In the wake of a hard-fought civil war against the old nobility, it was quite obvious to one and all that the Clan divided must fall, and this rebellion could be seen as nothing but the blackest treachery. But by the same token, the families were weak, their numbers perilously low – and acts of gratuitous revenge would only weaken them further, and risk sowing the seeds of blood feud to boot. 'Arrest everyone,' he'd instructed his captain on the ground, Sir Helmut: 'You may hang Oliver Hjorth, Griben ven Hjalmar, or' – a lengthy list of confirmed conspirators – 'out of hand, and you may deal as you wish with anyone who resists, but we must avoid the appearance of revenge at all costs. We can afford to spare those who did not raise arms against us, and who are guilty only of following their sworn liege – and their dependents.'

Helmut's mustache quivered. 'Is this wise, sir?' he asked.

'Probably not,' Riordan retorted, 'But the alternative is even less so – unless you think we should undertake our enemies' work for them by cutting each other's throats to the last?'

And so: This was the third great holding of a rebel family that Sir Helmut had ridden into in two days. And they were getting the message. At the last one, the house of Freyn-Hankl, a minor outer family connected with the Hjorth lineage, the servants had risen up and locked their upstart landowners in the wine cellars, and sued for mercy. Sir Helmut, mindful of his commanding officer's advice, had rewarded them accordingly, then sent them packing to spread the word (before he discreetly executed his prisoners – who had, to be fair, poisoned the entire staff of the local Security post by treachery). Facing the open windows and doors of the summer house at Judtford, with his soldiers going in and coming out at will, he was pleased with the outcome of this tactic. Whether or not it was wise or necessary, it was certainly proving to be effective.

'Sir! If you please, to the drawing room.' A startled-looking messenger boy, barely in his teens, darted from the front door.

Sir Helmut stared at him. 'In whose name?' he demanded.

'Sir! Two duchesses! One of them's the queen's mum, an' the other is hers! What should we do with them, Jan wants to know?'

Sir Helmut stared some more, until the lad's bravado collapsed with a shudder. Then he nodded and glanced over his shoulder. 'Sammel, Karl, accompany me,' he snapped. The two soldiers nodded and moved in, rifles at the ready. 'Lead me to the ladies,' he told the messenger. 'Let's see what we've got.'

The withdrawing room was dark, and cramped with too much overstuffed furniture, and it smelled of face powder and death. Flies buzzed near the ceiling above the occupants, a pair whom Sir Helmut could not help but recognize. One of them was sleeping. 'What happened here?' he demanded.

The younger of the pair – the one who was mother to the queen-widow – looked at him from beneath drooping eyelids. 'Was 'fraid you wouldn't get here,' she slurred.

'What – '

'Poison. In tha' wine. Sh-she started it.' A shaking hand rose slowly, pointed at the mounded fabric, the shriveled, doll-like body within. 'Tha' coup. 'S'hers. Did it for Helge, she said.'

'But – ' Helmut's eyes took in the empty decanter, the lack of motion. 'Are you drunk, or – '

'Dying, prob'ly.' She wheezed for a second or two; it might have been laughter. 'Poisoned the wine with pure heroin. The trade of queens.'

'I see.' Helmut turned to the wide-eyed messenger lad: 'You. Run along and fetch a medic, *fast.*' To the duchess: 'There's an antidote. We'll get you – '

'No.' Patricia closed her eyes for a long moment. 'Ma, Hilde – Hildegarde. Started this all. Leave her. No trial. As for me . . .' She subsided, slurring. A rattling snort emanated from the other chair and Helmut glanced at the door, before leaning to listen to the old woman's chest.

Helmut rose and, turning on his heel, strode towards the door. *Crone save me,* he subvocalized. The messenger was coming, a corpsman following behind. 'I have two heroin overdoses for you,' Helmut told him. 'Forget triage; save the younger one first if at all possible.'

'Heroin overdose?' The paramedic looked startled. 'But I don't have – are you sure – '

'Deliberate poisoning. Get to it.' Helmut stepped aside as the medic nodded and went inside. Helmut breathed deeply, then turned to the messenger. 'Here.' He pulled out his notepad and scribbled a brief memo. 'Tell comms to radio this to Earl-Major Riordan in day code purple, stat.' The lad took the note and fled. Helmut stared after him for a moment then shook his head. *What a mess.* Poisoning and attempted matricide versus kidnapping: petty treason versus high treason. How to weigh the balance? 'Jester's balls, if only I'd been delayed an hour on the road . . .'

*

Miriam lay in bed, propped up on a small mountain of pillows, staring blankly at the floral-patterned wallpaper behind the water jug on the dresser and thinking about death.

I never wanted it. So why am I feeling so bad? she wondered. *What the hell is* wrong *with me?*

It wasn't as if she'd wanted to have a baby: Griben ven Hjalmar's artificial insemination was, if not actual rape, then certainly morally equivalent. Only Huw's offer to help her obtain a termination – if that was what she willed – had kept her from running, and not stopping until she arrived at the nearest available abortion clinic. As the immediate rage and humiliation and dread faded, she began to reevaluate the situation: not from an American woman's perspective, but with the eyes of a Clan noblewoman catapulted headlong into the middle of a fraught political dilemma. *I don't have to love it. I don't have to raise it. I just have to put up with eight months of back pain and morning sickness and get it out of my body. And in return . . .*

She'd signed a fraught compromise with her conscience. Perhaps she was just rationalizing her situation, even succumbing to Stockholm syndrome – the tendency of the abducted to empathize with their kidnappers – and while she hated what had been done to her, she was no longer eager to dispose of the unwanted pregnancy. She'd done it before, many years ago; it had been difficult, the situation looming no less inconveniently in a life turned upside down, but she'd persevered. She'd even, a year ago, harbored wistful thoughts about finding a Mr. Right and –

Her body had betrayed her.

I'm thirty-five, damn it. Not an ideal age to be pregnant, especially in a medieval backwater without rapid access to decent medical care. Especially in the middle of a civil war with enemies scheming for her demise, or worse. She'd been stressed, anxious, frightened, and still in the first trimester: and when the cramps began she'd ignored them, refusing to admit what was happening. *And now it's not going to happen.* The royal dynasty that had ruled the Gruinmarkt for the past century and a half had bled out in a bedpan in New Britain, while the soldiers watched their maps and the nobles schemed. It wasn't much worse than a heavy period (aside from the pain, and the shock, and the sudden sense of horror as a sky full of cloud-castle futures evaporated). But it was a death sentence, and not just for the dynastic plans of the conservative faction.

She'd managed to hold her face together until she was away from Riordan's headquarters, with Brill's support. Ridden piggyback across to a farmhouse in the countryside outside small-town Framingham – not swallowed by Boston's suburbs, in New Britain's contorted history – that Sir Alasdair had located: abandoned, for reasons unclear, but not decayed.

'We've got to keep you away from court, my lady,' Brill explained, hollow-eyed with exhaustion, as she steered her up the staircase to an underfurnished bedroom. It had been a day since the miscarriage: a day of heavy bleeding, with the added discomfort of a ride in an oxcart through the backwoods around Niejwein. She'd begun shivering with the onset of a mild fever, not taking it all in, anomalously passive. 'When word gets out all hell will follow soon enough, but we can buy time first. Miriam? How do you feel?'

Miriam had licked her lips. 'Freezing,' she complained. 'Need water.' She'd pulled the bedding over her shoulders, curling up beneath without removing her clothes.

'I'll get a doctor,' Brill had said. And that was about the last thing Miriam remembered clearly for the next forty-eight hours.

Her fever was easily banished by bootleg drugs – amoxicillin was eerily effective in a world that hadn't been overexposed to antibiotics – and she lay abed, weak but recovering. Brilliana had held the center of her world, drafting in her household staff as they surfaced after the coup, organizing a courier link to the Niejwein countryside, turning her muttered suggestions into firm orders issued in the name of the security directorate's highest office. *I don't deserve these people*, Miriam thought vaguely. Depression stalked her waking hours incessantly, and her mood fluctuated from hour to hour: She couldn't tell from moment to moment whether she was relieved or bereft. *Why do they put up with me? Can't do* anything *right. Can't build a business, can't have a baby, can't even stay awake –*

There was a knock at the door.

She cleared her throat. 'Enter.' Her voice creaked like a rusting hinge, underused.

The door opened. 'Miriam?'

She turned her head. 'Ah! Sir Huw.' She cleared her throat again. 'Sorry. Not been well.' Huw was still wearing Gruinmarkt-casual: leather leggings, linen blouson. She saw another face behind him: 'And, and Elena? Hello, come on in. Sorry I can't be more hos– hospitable.' She tried to sit up.

'Your Majesty!' trilled Elena. Miriam tried not to wince. 'Oh, you look so ill – '

'It's not that bad,' she interrupted, before the girl – *Girl? By Clan standards she's overdue to be married* – started gushing. 'I had a fever,' she added, to Huw. 'Caught something nasty while I was having the miscarriage. Or maybe I miscarried because . . .' She trailed off. 'How have you been?' she asked. *When at a loss for small talk, ask a leading question.* That was what her mother, Iris – or Patricia, to her long-lost family – had brought her up to do. Once, it had made for a career –

Huw took a deep breath. 'We found more,' he said, holding up three fingers. 'And two viable knots. Then all hell broke loose and we only just got here.'

'*Three* worlds?'

'Yes!' Elena bounced up and down on the linen press she'd taken for a seat. She, too, was wearing native Gruinmarkt dress; she and Huw would have faded right into the background at any Renaissance Faire, if not for the machine pistol poking from her shoulder bag. 'Three! It was very exciting! One of them was so warm Yul nearly fainted before he could get his oxygen mask off! The others – '

Huw cleared *his* throat, pointedly. 'If I may? *That* one was subtropical, humid. Lots of cycads and ferns, very damp. We didn't see any people, or any animal life for that matter – but insects. Big dragonflies, *that* big.' He held his hands a foot apart. 'I was pretty light-headed by the time we left. I want to measure the atmospheric gas mix – I think it's way on the high side of normal, oxygen-wise. Like the carboniferous era never ended, or came back, or something. And then there was another cold pine-forest world. Again, no life, no radio transmissions, no sign of people.' He shook his head.

'The third?' Miriam pushed herself up against the pillows, fascinated.

'We nearly died,' Elena said very quietly.

'You nearly – ' Miriam stopped. 'Huw, I thought you were taking precautions? Pressure suits, oxygen, guns?'

'We were. *That* one's inhabited – but not by anything familiar to us.' He clammed up. 'Miriam. Uh. Helge. My lady. What's going on? Why are we here?'

Miriam blinked. 'Inhabited? By what?'

'Robots, maybe. Or very fast minerals. Something surprised Yul so he shot it, and it ate his shotgun. After that, we didn't stick around.

418

Why are we here? The major said you were in charge of, of something important – '

'I need to get out of bed.' Miriam winced. 'This wasn't part of the plan. Huw, we're here to make contact with the government. Official contact, and that means I need to be in there doing it.'

'*Official* contact?' His eyes widened.

'Yes. We're finished in the United States. The Clan, I mean. Those mindless idiots in the postal arm, Baron Hjorth, my grandmother – they've completely wrecked any hope of us *ever* going back, much less normalizing relations. The US will follow us to the ends of the universe if necessary. Ends of *every* universe. Certainly they had agents in the Gruinmarkt . . . Riordan's not stupid, he saw this coming. That's what we're doing here. We're to open negotiations with the Empire of New Britain and sue for asylum. They've got problems too, stuff we can help with – the French, that is, the Bourbon monarchy in St. Petersburg. We've got access to science and technology that's half a century ahead of anything they've got in the laboratory here, much less widely deployed. That gives us a bargaining tool, much better than a suitcase full of heroin.' She chuckled softly. It made her ribs hurt. 'You know all the Roswell, Area 51, alien jokes? Crashed flying saucers, secret government labs full of alien technology? We're going to be their aliens. Except there's a slight problem.'

'A problem?' Huw's expression was a sight. 'I can see several potential problems with that idea. What kind of problem do you find worrying enough to single out?'

'We're not the only people who've had a *coup d'état*.' Miriam sat up, bracing her arms against the headboard of the bed. 'The king's under arrest, the country is in a state of crisis, and the contacts I'd made are high up in the new government. Which may sound like a great opportunity to you, but I'm not sure I like what they're doing with it. And before we can talk to them we need to square things with the cousins.'

'The cousins – '

'Yes. Or they'll assume we're breaking the truce. Tell me, Huw – have you ever met James Lee?'

*

419

The huge, wooden radio in the parlor of the safe house near Framingham was tuned permanently to Voice of England, hissing and warbling the stentorian voice of Freedom Party-approved news as and when the atmospheric conditions permitted. The morning of the day after his arrival, Huw opened it up and marveled at the bulky tubes and rat's nest of wires within. It was a basic amplitude-modulated set, the main tuning capacitor fixed firmly in position by a loop of wire sealed with a royal crest in solder: comically easy to subvert, *if* the amateur engineer had been partial to five years in a labor camp next time it was inspected by the Polis. Huw shook his head, then added a crate of pocket-sized Sony world-band receivers to his next supply run shopping list, along with a gross of NiCad batteries and some more solar-powered chargers.

'How do you use it?' asked Brilliana, looking at it dubiously.

'You plug it back in' – Huw demonstrated, clipping the battery wire to the bulky lead-acid cell that filled much of the radio's plinth – 'and turn it on like so.' Hissing static filled the room.

She frowned. 'It sounds horrible. How do you tune it?'

'You don't. I mean, we can adjust it slightly, within a permitted frequency range.' Huw straightened up. 'But the state owns the airwaves.' Someone was talking in portentious tones through the wrong end of a trombone. 'Welcome to the pre-transistor era, when radio engineers needed muscles.'

'What use is a radio you can't – '

Miriam stopped in the doorway. 'Wait!' She held up a hand. She was looking better this morning, Huw decided: There was color in her cheeks and she'd bothered to get dressed in native drag, something like an Indian shalwar suit, only with frightening amounts of embroidery and lace. 'Can you turn that up?'

'I guess.' Huw tweaked the fine-tuning pot, then cranked up the volume.

'I know that voice!' Miriam stared at the radio, her eyes wide. 'It's Erasmus!'

'Really?' Brill cocked her head. 'I suppose it might be.'

' – Our enemies. Only through unceasing vigilance can we ensure our safety in the face of the brutal attacks of the aristocratic gang and

420

their lickspittle toadies. But be of good heart: They are a minority, and they swim against the current of history. The slave owners and gang-masters and mercantilists cannot bully us if we stand firm against them. The party is the backbone of the people, and we shall bear the full weight of the struggle against totalitarian monarchism on your behalf – '

'Yes, I think you're right,' Brilliana said thoughtfully. 'He's wordy enough . . .'

'Jesus.' Miriam swayed slightly. 'It's too early for this. Is there any coffee?'

'In the kitchen, I think.' Brill looked at Huw. 'Enough with the radio,' she said. Huw could take a hint: He switched it off, and waited for the glowing tubes to fade before he followed them towards the waiting pot.

Miriam was sitting on one of the two chairs, her hands clutching an earthenware mug of black coffee. The kettle still steamed atop the coal-fired cast-iron cooking range. 'He's on the *radio*,' she said, as if she didn't quite believe it. 'Voice of England. That's the official news channel, isn't it? He must have made it to California and come back. This will make everything so much simpler.' Her hands were shaking slightly. 'But it also means we need to talk to the cousins now, not later.'

'It's too dangerous.' Brill looked mulish. 'Travel, I mean! There are roving gangs, and we don't have a car, or – '

'They don't use cars here,' Miriam pointed out. 'At least not the way they do in our – my – America. There are trains. We're about three miles outside city limits and there's a railway station. You can catch a train to, to – where are the Lees? Do we have an address for them in Boston? If the service is running right now, and if they aren't demanding travel papers. But there's a small-scale civil war going on. They don't – neither side – have the resources to lock down travel, except across contested borders. We're on the east coast city belt here, the paper says it's all Freedom Party territory – '

'You've got newspapers?' Huw demanded, incredulity getting the better of him.

'Yes, why wouldn't we?' Miriam was nonplussed. 'They don't have domestic television, Huw, no internet either. How do you expect they get their news?'

'But, but – there's a civil war going on!'

'Yes, but that's not stopping the local papers. We get visitors, Huw. We've had knife-grinders and pan-sellers and we get a book merchant who carries the weekly paper. As far as our neighbors know, we're a bunch of squatters who moved in here when the farmer and his family ran away – they're royalists, he was a snitch, apparently. They don't mind having us around: Alasdair and Erik saw off a gang of hobos – probably deserters – the day before yesterday. So we, we try to keep informed. And we're trying to fit in.' She frowned. 'Got to get you some local clothes.'

'I'll sort him out.' Brill rose and poked at the firebox in the range cautiously. Between the summer warmth and an active fire the kitchen was unpleasantly warm, although Miriam still looked as if she was cold. 'There's a lot of work involved in establishing a safe house,' she said, looking at Huw speculatively. 'I've got a list. If you want to stick around, make yourself useful – '

'No,' said Miriam. Brill looked at her. 'I need to see Erasmus. In person.' She tapped a finger on the table. 'We need to send a message to James Lee, fix up a conference.' Another tap. 'And we need to get as many of our people as possible over here right now. And set up identities for them.' A third finger-tap. 'Which feeds back to Erasmus. If he'll help us out, *all* our immediate troubles here go away.'

'And if he doesn't?' asked Brill.

'Then we're so screwed it isn't funny.' Miriam took a sip of coffee. 'So we're not going to worry about that right now. I'm not well enough to travel today, but I'm getting better. Huw? I want you and Yul – you're the expeditionary research team, aren't you? – to go into Framingham today. Yeah, I know, so find him some clothes, Brill. Huw, I'll give you a couple of letters to post, and a shopping list. Starting with a steamer. We've got gold, yes? More of the shiny stuff than we know what to do with. So we're going to spend some of it. Get a steamer – a truck, not a passenger car – and buy food and clothing, anything that's not nailed down, anything you can find from thrift stores. Some furniture, too, chairs and beds if you can get them – we're short on stuff here – but that's a secondary consideration.' She was staring past him, Huw realized, staring into some interior space, transcribing a vision. 'Along the way you're going to post those letters, one to James Lee, one to Erasmus.'

She cleared her throat. 'Now here's the hard bit. If you're stopped by Freedom Riders, drop my name – Miriam Beckstein – and say I'm working for Erasmus Burgeson and Lady Margaret Bishop. Remember that name: Margaret Bishop. It'll get their attention. If it doesn't get their attention, *don't* resist if they take you into custody, but make sure you emphasize that you're working for me and I'm working for their bosses – Lady Bishop and Erasmus know about me, and about the Clan, at least in outline. Then get the hell away. You know how to do it, you've got your temp tats, yes?'

Huw cleared his throat. 'Do you want that to happen?' *Or is this just micromanagement due to nerves?*

'No.' Miriam shook her head. 'We want to make contact at the highest level, which means ideally we go straight to Erasmus. But if things go wrong, we *don't* want to start out with a firefight. Do you see where I'm going here?'

'Six different directions at once, it seems.' Huw rolled his eyes. 'Yeah, I *think* I get it. These people are going to be our patrons, so don't start the relationship by shooting the servants, right?'

'That's it. If you run into real trouble, don't hang around – just world-walk. We can afford to try again at making contact; we can't afford to lose you.'

*

'Conflicting mission objectives: check.' *Click.* Yul shoved another cartridge into the magazine he was filling. 'Flashing wads of money around in the middle of a revolution while guilty of looking foreign.' *Click.* 'Micromanaging boss trying to run things on impulse.' *Clack.* He squeezed down on the last cartridge with a quiet grunt, then laid the magazine aside. 'Have I missed anything, bro?'

'Yes.' It was either the coffee or pre-op nerves: Huw was annoyed to find his hands were shaking slightly as he checked the battery level on the small Pentax digital camera. 'We've got a six-month deadline to make BOLTHOLE work.' (BOLTHOLE was the name Brill had pinned on the current project; a handy identifier, and one that anticipated Miriam's tendency to hatch additional projects.) 'Then all the hounds of Hel come belling after our heels. And that's before the Americans –'

'I don't see what you and Her Maj are so worked up about, bro. They can't touch us.' Hulius stood, shrugging his coat into shape.

'We disagree.' Huw slid the camera into an inner pocket of his own jacket. 'You haven't spent enough time over there to know how they think, how they work.' He stood up as Yul stowed his spare magazines in a deep pocket. 'Come on, let's go.' He slung a small leather satchel across his chest, allowed it to settle into place, then gave the strap a jerk: Nothing rattled.

It was a warm day outside, but the cloud cover threatened rain for the afternoon. Huw and Yul headed out into the run-down farmyard – now coming into a modicum of order as Helge's armsmen cleared up after the absent owners – then down the dirt track to the highway. The road into town was metaled but only wide enough for one vehicle, bordered by deep ditches with passing places every quarter mile. 'They make good roads,' Yul remarked as they walked along the side. 'Not as good as the Americans, but better than us. Why is that?'

'Long story.' Huw shook his head. 'We're stuck in a development trap, back home.'

'A what trap?'

A rabbit bolted for safety ahead of them as the road curved; birds peeped and clattered in the trees to either side like misconfigured machinery. 'Development. In the Americans' world there are lots of other countries. Some of them are dirt-poor, full of peasants. Sort of like home, believe it or not. The rich folks can import automobiles and mobile phones but the poor are just like they've always been. The Americans were that way, two hundred years ago – but somewhere along the way they stumbled on a better way of doing things. You've seen how they live today. Turns out – they've tried it a lot, in their world – if you just throw money at a poor country and pay for things like roads and schools, it doesn't automatically *get better*. Their economists have a bunch of theories about why, and how, and what

424

you need to do to make an entire nation lift itself up by its own b
straps . . . but most of them are wrong. Not surprising, really; m
economists say what the rich people who pay them want to hear.
If they knew for sure, if there was one true answer, there'd be *no*
underdeveloped nations. *We'd* have developed, in the Gruinmarkt,
too, if there was a well-defined recipe. It's probably some combination of money, and institutions like the rule of law and suppression of
corruption, and education, and a work ethic, and fair markets, and
ways of making people feel like they can better themselves – social
inclusion. But nobody knows for sure.'

A high stone wall appeared alongside the road, boundary marker
to a country estate. 'People have to be able to produce a bit more
than they consume, for one thing. And for another, they have to know
that if they *do* produce it – well, what does a lord do if his peasants
are growing more food than they need?'

Yul shrugged. 'What do you expect me to say, bro? They're his
tenants!'

'Well, yeah, but.' They passed a spiked iron gate, head-high and
closed, behind which a big house squatted with sullenly shuttered
windows. The wall resumed. 'Here's the thing. Our families became
rich, and bought titles of nobility, and married into the aristocracy.
And after a generation or two they *were* noble houses. But we're still
stuck in a sea of peasants who don't make anything worth shit, who
don't generate surpluses because they know some guy in a suit of
armor can take it away from them whenever he likes. We've got towns
and artisans and apothecaries and some traders and merchants
and they're . . . you've seen the Americans. They're not smarter than
us. They don't work harder than the peasants on your father's land.
They're not – most of them – rich because they inherited it. But two
hundred years ago things over there took a strange turn, and now
they're overwhelmingly wealthy. These people are . . . they're better
off than us: not as good as the Americans, but doing well and getting
better, if you look beyond the current crisis. So *what are they doing
right?*'

Huw stopped. The wall had come to an end, and ahead of them
the road ran straight between a burned-out strip of row houses and a

425

cleared field; but a group of four men had stepped into the highway in front of them, blocking the way ahead. They had the thin faces and hungry eyes of those who had been too long between hot meals.

'Yer bag. Give it 'ere,' said the thinnest, sharpest man. He held out a hand, palm-up. Huw saw that it was missing two fingers. The men to either side of the speaker, hard-faced, held crudely carved shillelaghs close by their sides.

'I don't think so,' replied Huw. 'Would you like to reconsider?' From behind his left shoulder he heard a rip of Velcro as Yul freed up his holster.

'They's the strangers wot moved on ole Hansen's farm,' the skinny man – barely more than a teenager – at the left of the row hissed sharply.

The speaker's eyes flickered sideways, but he showed no sign of attention. 'Git 'em, lads,' he drawled, and the highwaymen raised their clubs.

Yul drew and fired in a smooth motion. His Glock cracked four times while Huw was persuading his own weapon to point the right way. The two club-men dropped like sacks of potatoes. The skinny lad's jaw dropped; he turned and bolted into the field.

'Aw, *shit*,' said the sharp-faced speaker. He sounded disgusted, resigned even, but he didn't run. 'Yez party men, huh?' Huw strained to make the words out through a combination of ringing ears, the thunder of his own heartbeat, and the man's foreign-sounding accent.

'That's right!' He kept his aim on the highwayman's chest. Yul stayed out of his line of fire, performing an odd, jerky duck-walk as he scanned the sides of the road for further threats. 'And you are . . . ?'

'Down on me luck.' Abruptly, the highwayman sat down in the middle of the road and screwed his eyes shut. 'G'wan, shoot me. Better'n' starvin' to death like this past week. I'm ready.'

'No. You're not worth the bullet.' Huw stared at the highwayman over the sights of his pistol. An idea came to him. 'You are under arrest for attempted robbery. Now, we can do this two different ways. First way is, we take you for trial before a people's court. They won't show you any mercy: Why should they? You're a highwayman. But the other way – if you want to make yourself useful to us, if you're very *useful*, my colleague and I can accidentally look the other way for a few seconds.'

'Forget it, citizen. He's a villain: Once a villain always a villain. Let's find a rope – ' Yul was just playing bad cop. Probably.

'What do ye want?' The highwayman was looking from Yul to Huw and back again in fear. 'Yer playin' with me! Yer mad!'

'Dead right.' Huw narrowed his eyes. 'On your feet. We're going into town and you're going to walk in front of us with your hands tied behind your back. The people's foe. And you know what? I'm going to ask you for directions and you're going to guide us truthfully. Do it well and maybe we won't hand you over to the tribunal. Do it badly – ' He jerked his neck sideways. 'Understand?'

The highwayman nodded fearfully. It was, Huw reflected, a hell of a way to hire a tour guide.

*

Framingham was a mess. From burned-out farmsteads and cottages on the outskirts of town to beggarmen showing their war wounds and soup kitchens on the curbsides, it gave every indication of being locked in a spiral of decline. But there were no further highwaymen or muggers; probably none such were willing to risk tangling with two openly armed men escorting a prisoner before them. Huw kept his back straight, attempting to exude unconscious authority. *We're party men, Freedom Riders. If nobody here's seen such before* . . . Well, it would work right up until they ran into the real thing; and when that happened, they could world-walk.

'We're going to the main post office,' Huw told the prisoner. 'Then to' – he racked his memory for the name they'd plucked from a local newssheet's advertising columns – 'Rackham's bookmaker. Make it smart.'

The main post office was a stone-fronted building in a dusty high street, guarded by half a dozen desperadoes behind a barricade of beer casks from a nearby pub. Rackham's was a quarter mile past it, down a side street, its facade boarded over and its door barred.

They turned into an alleyway behind the bookmaker's. 'You have ten seconds to make yourself invisible,' Huw told his shivering prisoner, who stared at him with stunned disbelief for a moment before taking to his heels.

'Was that clever?' asked Yul.

'No, But were you really planning on walking into a people's tribunal behind him?'

'Um. Point, bro. What do we do now?'

'We sell this next door.' Huw tightened his grip on the satchel, feeling the gold ingots inside. 'And then we go to the post office and post a letter.'

'But it's not running! You saw the barricades? It's the Freedom Party headquarters.'

'That's what I'm counting on,' Huw said, more calmly than he felt. 'They've got a grip on the mass media – the phones, the e-mail equivalents, the news distribution system. They're not stupid, they know about controlling the flow of information. Which means they're the only people who can get a message through to that friend of Miriam's – the skinny guy with the hat. Remember the railway station?' Brilliana had coopted Huw and his team, dragged them on what seemed at first like a wild goose chase to a one-platform stop in the middle of nowhere. They'd arrived in the nick of time, as Miriam's other pursuers – a political officer and a carload of police thugs – had surrounded the ticket office where she and Erasmus Burgeson were barricaded inside. 'The problem is getting their attention without getting ourselves shot. Once we've got it, though . . .' He headed towards the bookmaker's, where a pair of adequately fed bouncers were eyeing the passersby. '. . . we're on the way.'

*

The committee watched the presidential address, and the press conference that followed it, in dead silence.

The thirty-two-inch plasma screen and DVD player were alien intrusions in the wood-and-tapestry-lined audience room at the west of the royal palace. The portable gasoline generator in the antechamber outside throbbed loudly, threatening to drown out the recorded questions, played through speakers too small for a chamber designed for royal audiences in an age before amplification. The flickering color images danced off the walls, reflecting from the tired faces of the noble audience. Many of them still wore armor, camouflage surcoats over bulletproof vests and machine-woven titanium chain mail. They were the surviving officers of the Clan's security organization, and such of the Clan's other leaders as were deemed trustworthy, ignorant of or uninvolved in the abortive putsch mounted by the lords of the postal corvée. Wanted men, one and all.

Finally, Olga paused the DVD – recorded off-air by one of the few communications techs Riordan had ordered to stay behind in Cambridge. She looked around the semicircle of faces opposite, taking in their expressions, ranging from blank incomprehension to shock and dismay. 'Does anyone have any questions, or can I move on to present our analysis?' she asked. 'Strictly questions, no comment at this time.'

A hand went up at the back. Olga made eye contact and nodded. It was Sir Ulrich, one of the progressive faction's stalwarts, a medic by training. 'Can they do it?' he asked.

'You heard him.' Olga's cheek twitched. Dread was a sick sensation in the pit of her stomach. 'Let me remind you of Mr. Cheney's history; he's a hawk. He was one of the main sponsors of the Project for a New American Century, he's the planner behind the Iraq invasion, and he's an imperialist in the old model. What most of you don't know is that back in the 1980s he was one of our main commercial enabling partners in the Western operation. And he's gone public about our existence. Getting back to your question: He's defined the success of his presidency in terms of his ability to take us down. The Americans will follow their king-emperor unquestioningly – as long as he delivers results. President Bush used Iraq as a rallying cry after 9/11; Mr. Cheney has pinned the target on us.'

'So you think – ' Ulrich paused. 'Sorry.'

'It's quite all right.' Olga gestured at the front rank. 'My lord Riordan, I yield the floor.'

Riordan walked to the front of the room. 'Thank you, Lady voh Thorold,' he started. Then he paused, and looked around at his audience. 'I'm not going to tell you any comforting lies. We have lost' – he raised a folio and squinted at it – 'thirty-nine world-walkers of our own, and sixty-six of the conservative faction. Eleven more are in custody, awaiting a hearing. Most of them we can do naught with but hang as a warning. Remaining to us in the five great families' – he swallowed – 'we have a total of four hundred and sixteen who can world-walk regularly, and another hundred and nineteen elderly and infants. Twenty-eight womenfolk who are with child and so must needs be carried. In our offshoots and cadet branches there are perhaps two thousand three hundred relatives, of whom one thousand and seven hundred or thereabouts are married or coming into or of childbearing age. One hundred and forty-one of their children are world-walkers.'

He stopped, and exchanged the folio for a hip flask for a moment.

'The American army is largely occupied overseas, for which we should be grateful. They have more than six hundred thousand men under arms, and five hundred warships, and with their navy and air forces their military force numbers two warriors for every peasant in the Gruinmarkt. Our account of Baron Hjorth's treachery is that he purloined no less than four but certainly no more than six of their atomic bombs. That leaves them with' – he consulted the folio – 'ah, *six thousand* or thereabouts, almost all of which are more powerful than those Oliver Hjorth absconded with, to our two.' He closed the folio and stared at his audience.

'The technical term for our strategic situation is: *fucked.*

'The only ray of hope is the possibility that their new king-emperor is bluffing about their ability to visit destruction upon our heads. But we believe there is no way that he could afford to threaten us politically unless he has the capability to follow through, so the Anglischprache probably *do* have a world-walking ability. It might be a matter of captured cousins, but I doubt it. There's the destruction of the Hjalmar Palace to consider, and they had Special Forces soldiers scouting around Niejwein as long ago as the betrothal feast between Prince Creon and Her Majesty. They had the ability to maintain a small scouting force over here four months ago. That implies they could not, back then, send a major expeditionary force across at that time. What they can do now – '

A hand went up in the front row. Riordan stopped. 'Your grace,' he said, with labored and pointed patience.

'Believe them,' Patricia Thorold-Hjorth called tiredly from her wheelchair. She clasped her hands on top of her walking stick and frowned, her face still haggard. The medic's intervention had kept her breathing, but the poisoning had taken its toll. 'During the late civil war, I was – with the express consent of my late brother – negotiating with the current president. His agent broke off communications with a sudden ultimatum: our immediate surrender in return for our lives. He spoke of a mechanical contrivance for world-walking, for moving vehicles. One of my daughter's protégés was tasked by my brother with investigating the nature and limitations of world-walking, and has made a number of discoveries; in particular, some wheeled contrivances can – under some circumstances – be carried along.' A muttering spread through her audience. 'And to this date, four more worlds have been discovered, and two new knots.' The muttering grew louder.

'Silence!' shouted Riordan. 'Damn you, I will hear one speaker at a time!' He looked at the dowager. 'You have more?'

'Not much.' She looked pensive. 'Wheelbarrows – it was suppressed by the lords of the post, I presume, during the civil war. Too much risk of a few youngsters going over the wall, if they realized how few bodies it would take to start a rival operation; we would have faced dissolution within months. But there is no obvious size limit; the limit was imposed by the exclusion problem, the risk of wheels intersecting with matter in the other world. Given a suitably prepared staging area, machined to high precision, who knows what they could send. Tanks? Helicopters? We are on their doorstep. These people can send a hundred thousand soldiers halfway around the world. What can they send an hour's drive down the road?'

'I don't think we need worry about that just yet,' Riordan declared, trying to regain control of the briefing. 'But.' He paused a moment, looking around the anxious faces before him. 'At a minimum, we face teams of special forces with backpack atomic bombs, like the ones that have already been used. At worst, if they have truly worked out how to travel between worlds, we may see a full-scale invasion. I

431

think the latter is a very real threat, and we have the example of their recent adventure in the distant land of Iraq to learn from. If we sit and wait for them to come to us, we will be defeated – they outnumber all the Eastern kingdoms, not just the Gruinmarkt, by thirty bodies to one, and look what they did to Iraq. This is not a matter for chivalrous denial; it is a fight we cannot possibly win.'

He gestured in the direction of Baron Horst of Lorsburg, one of the few conservatives to have been conclusively proven to have been on the outside of the coup attempt – a tiresomely business-minded fellow, fussy and narrowly legalistic. 'Sir, I believe you wish to express an opinion?'

Lorsburg removed his bifocals and nervously rubbed them on his shirt sleeve. 'You appear to be saying that Clan Security can't protect us. Is that right?'

'Clan Security can't take on the United States government, no, not if they develop world-walking machines.' Riordan nodded patiently. 'Do you have something more to say?'

Lorsburg hunkered down in his seat. 'If you can't save us, what good *are* you?' he asked querulously.

'There's a difference between saying we can't win a direct fight, and not being able to save you. We *can* save the Clan – but not if we sit and wait for the Anglischprache to come calling. What we can't save are the fixed assets: our estates and vassals. Anything we can't carry. We are descended from migrant tinkers and traders, and I am afraid that we will have to become such again, at least for a while. Those of you who think the American army will not come here are welcome to go back to your palaces and great houses and pretend we can continue to do business as usual. You might be right – in which case, the rest of us will sheepishly rejoin you in due course. But for the time being, I submit that our best hope lies elsewhere.

'We could cross over to America, and live in hiding among a people who hate and fear us. The Clan has some small accumulated capital; the banking committee has invested heavily in real estate, investment banks, and big corporations over the past fifty years. We would be modestly wealthy, but no longer the rulers and lords of all we survey, as we are here; and we would live in fear of a single loose-tongued cousin unraveling our network, by accident or malice. We could only survive if all of us took a vow of silence and held to it. And I leave to your imagination the difficulty of maintaining our continuity, the braids –

'But there is a better alternative. My lady voh Thorold?'

Olga stood up. 'I speak not as the director of intelligence operations, but as a confidante of the queen-widow,' she said, turning to face the room. 'As we have known for some time, there are other worlds than just this one and that of the Anglischprache. Before his illness, Duke Lofstrom detailed a protégé of Helge's to conduct a survey. Helge has continued to press for these activities – we now know of four other worlds beyond the initial three, but they are not considered suitable for exploitation. If you desire the details, I will be happy to describe them later. For the time being, our best hope lies in New Britain, where Her Majesty is attempting to establish negotiations with the new revolutionary government – ' Uproar.

'I say! *Silence!*' Riordan's bellow cut through the shouting. 'I'll drag the next man who interrupts out and horse-whip him around the walls! Show some respect, damn you!'

The hubbub subsided. Olga waited for the earl to nod at her, then continued. '*Unlike* the Anglischprache of America, we have *good* relations with the revolutionaries who have formed the provisional government of New Britain. We have, if nothing else, a negotiable arrangement with our relatives there; I'm sure a diplomatic accommodation can be reached.' She stared at Lorsburg, who was looking mulishly unconvinced. 'Her Majesty is a *personal friend* of the minister of propaganda. We supplied their cells in Boston with material and aid prior to the abdication and uprising. Unlike the situation in the United States, we have no history of large-scale law-breaking to prejudice them against us; nothing but our aristocratic rank in the Gruinmarkt, which we must perforce shed in any case if we abandon our way of life here and move to a new world.' She paused, voluntarily this time: Lorsburg had raised a hand. 'Yes? What is it?'

'This is well and good, and perhaps we would be safe from the Americans there – for a while. But you're asking us to abandon everything, to take to the roads and live like vagabonds, or throw ourselves on the mercy of a dubious cabal of regicidal peasants! How do you expect us to subsist in this new world? What shall we do?'

'We will have to work.' Olga smiled tightly. 'You are quite right; it's not going to be easy. We will have to give up much that we have become accustomed to. On the other hand, we will be alive, we will be able to sleep at night without worrying that the next knock on the door may be agents of the state come to arrest us, and, as I said, there is a *business plan*. Nobody will hold a gun to your heads and force you to join those of us who intend to establish first a refuge and then a new trade and source of wealth in New Britain – if you wish to wait here and guard your estates, then I believe the Council will be happy to leave you to it. But there is one condition: *If* the Americans come, we don't want you spilling our plans to their interrogators. So I am going to ask everyone to leave the room now. Those of you who wish to join our plan, may come back in; those who want no truck with it should go home. If you change your minds later, you can petition my lord the earl for a place. But if you stay for the next stage of this briefing you are committing yourselves to join us in New Britain – or to the silence of the grave.'

WAR TRAIN ROLLING

Holed up back in a motel room with a bottle of Pepsi and a box of graham crackers, Mike opened up his planner and spread his spoils on the comforter – room service had tidied the room while he'd been burglarizing Miriam's booby-trapped home. He was still shaking with the aftermath of the adrenaline surge from the near-miss with the police watch team. *Thirty seconds and they'd have made me.* Thirty seconds and – *Stop that: you've got a job to do.*

Two items sat on the bed: a cassette and a bulging organizer, its edges rounded and worn by daily use. He added the remaining contents of his shopping bag, spoils of a brief excursion into a Walgreens: a cheap Far Eastern walkman, and a box of batteries. 'Let's get you set up,' he muttered to the machine, then did a double take. *Talking to myself. Huh.* It wasn't a terribly good sign. It had been a couple of days – since his abortive meeting with Steve Schroeder – since Mike had exchanged more words with anyone than it took to rent a car. It wasn't as if he was a gregarious type, but hanging out here with his ass on the line had him feeling horribly exposed. And there were loose life-ends left untied, from Oscar the tomcat (who had probably moved in with the neighbors who kept overfeeding him by now) to his dad and his third wife (whom he didn't dare call; even if they weren't in custody, their line was almost certainly on a fully-staffed watch by now). 'The time to throw in the towel is when you start talking back to yourself, right? Oh no it isn't, Mike . . .' The batteries were in, so he hit the playback button.

A beep, then a man's voice: 'Miriam? Andy here. Listen, a little bird told me about what happened yesterday and I think it sucks. They didn't have any details, but I want you to know if you need some free-lance commissions you should give me a call. Talk later? Bye.'

Mike paused, then rewound. *Andy* went on his notepad, along with *freelance commissions*. Probably nothing useful, but . . .

Click. 'Hi? Paulette here, it's seven-thirty, listen, I've been doing some thinking about what we dug up before they fired us. Miriam, honey, let's talk. I don't want to rake over dead shit, but there's some stuff I need to get straight in my head. Can I come around?'

He sat up. *Fired*, he wrote on his pad, and underlined the word twice. This Paulette woman had said *we*. So Miriam had been fired. 'When?' That was the trouble with answerphones; the new solid-state ones had timestamps, but the old cassette ones were less than useful in that department. On the other hand, she hadn't wiped these messages. So they'd arrived pretty close to whatever had brought her into contact with the Clan.

Next message: a man's voice, threatening. 'Bitch. We know where you live. Heard about you from our mutual friend Joe. Keep your nose out of our business or you'll be fucking sorry.'

Mike stopped dead, his shoulders tense. *Joe*, he wrote, then circled the name heavily and added a couple of question marks. *Not Clan?* he added. The Clan weren't in the cold-call trade; concrete overcoats and car bombs were more their style. Still, coming on top of Paulette's message this was . . . suggestive. Miriam had been fired from her job, along with this Paulette woman, for digging up something. 'She's a journalist, it's what she does.' Next thing, there was a threatening phone call. Some time not long after, Miriam disappeared. Some time after that, her house was systematically searched for computers and electronic media, by someone who wasn't interested in old paperwork. And then it was booby-trapped and staked out by the FTO . . . 'Stop right there!' Mike flipped the organizer open and turned to the address divider. 'Paulet, Paulette, Powell-et? How do you spell it, it's a first name . . .'

He read for a long time, swearing occasionally at Miriam's spidery handwriting and her copious list of contacts – *She's a journalist, it's what she does* – until he hit paydirt a third of the way through: *Milan, Paulette. Business intelligence division, The Weatherman.* That was where Miriam had worked, last time he looked. 'Bingo,' Mike muttered. There was a cell number *and* a street address. He made a note of it; then, systematic to the end, he went back to the cassette tape.

The next message was a call from Steve Schroeder – his voice familiar – asking Miriam to get in touch. It was followed by an odd double beep: some kind of tape position marker, probably. Then the rest of the tape: a farrago of political polls, telesales contacts, and robocalls that took Mike almost an hour to skim. He took notes, hoping some sort of pattern would appear, but nothing jumped out at him. Probably the calls were exactly what they sounded like: junk. Which left him with a couple of names, one of which seemed promising, and a conundrum. Someone had threatened Miriam, right after she'd been fired for stumbling over something. Was it Clan-related? And was this Paulette woman involved? 'There's only one way to find out,' Mike told himself unhappily. His stomach rumbled. 'Time to hit the road again.'

*

The coded electrogram from Springfield followed a circuitous course to Erasmus Burgeson's desk.

Huw's bluff had worked; the cadre at the post office were inexperienced and undisciplined, excited volunteers barely out of the first flush of revolutionary fervor, more enthusiastic than efficient. There was no command structure as such, no uniforms and no identity papers, and as yet very little paranoia: The threats they expected to defend the post office against were the crude and obvious violence of counterrevolutionary elements, fists and guns rather than the sly subtlety of wreckers and saboteurs from within. Their revolution had not yet begun to eat its offspring.

When Huw claimed to be part of a small reconnaissance cell in the countryside and asked to send a message to the stratospheric heights of the party organization, he was met at first with gape-jawed incomprehension and then an eagerness to oblige that was almost comically servile. It was only when he and Yul prepared to slip away that anyone questioned the wisdom of allowing strangers to transmit electrograms to New London without clearance, and by the time old Johnny Miller, former deputy postmaster of the imperial mail (now wearing his union hat openly), expressed the doubtful opinion that perhaps somebody ought to have detained the strangers pending the establishment of their bona fides, Huw and Yul were half a mile down the road.

Despite deputy postmaster Miller's misgivings, the eighty-word electrogram Miriam had so carefully crafted arrived in the central monitoring and sorting hall at Breed's Hill, whereupon an eagle-eyed (and probably bored) clerk recognized the office of the recipient and, for no very good reason, stamped it with a PARTY PRIORITY flag and sent it on its way.

From Breed's Hill – where in Miriam's world one of the key battles of the American War of Independence had been fought – the message was encrypted in a standard party cypher and flashed down cables to the Imperial Postal Headquarters building on Manhattan Island, and thence to the Ministry of Propaganda, where the commissioner on duty in the message room saw its high priority and swore, vilely. Erasmus was not in town that day; indeed, was not due back for some time. But it was a PARTY PRIORITY cable. What to do?

In the basement of the Ministry of Propaganda were numerous broadcasting rooms; and no fewer than six of these were given over to the letter talkers, who endlessly recited strings of words sapped of all meaning, words chosen for their clarity over the airwaves. So barely two hours after Huw and Yul had shown the cadre in Springfield two clean pairs of heels, a letter talker keyed his microphone and began to intone: 'Libra, Opal, Furlong, Opal, Whisky, Trident' – over the air on a shortwave frequency given over to the encrypted electrospeak broadcasts of the party's network, a frequency that would be echoed by transmitters all over both Western continents, flooding the airwaves until Burgeson's radio operator could not help but hear it.

Which event happened in the operator's room on board an armored war train fifty miles west of St. Anne, which stood not far from the site of Cincinatti in Miriam's world. The operator, his ears encased in bulky headphones, handed the coded message with his header to the encryption sergeant, who typed it into his clacking, buzzing machine, and then folded the tape and handed it off to a messenger boy, who dashed from the compartment into the train's main corridor and then along a treacherous, swaying armored tunnel to the command carriage where the commissioner of state propaganda sat slumped over a pile of newspapers, reading the day's dispatches as he planned the next step in his media blitz.

'What is it now?' Erasmus asked, glancing up.

The messenger boy straightened. 'Sor, a cript for thee?' He presented the roll of tape with both hands. 'Came in over the airwaves, like.'

'I see.' The train clanked across a badly maintained crossing, swaying from side to side. Erasmus, unrolling the tape, drew the electric lamp down from overhead to illuminate the mechanical scratchings as he tried to focus on it. It had been under at least three pairs of eyeballs since arriving here; over the electrograph, that meant . . . He blinked. *Miriam? She's here? And she wants to talk?* He wound back to the header at the start of the message that identified the sending station. *Springfield.* Burgeson chuckled humorlessly for a moment. HAVE INTERESTING PROPOSAL FOR YOU RE TECHNOLOGY TRANSFER AND FAMILY BUSINESS. To put that much in an uncoded message was a giveaway: It reeked of near-panic. She'd said something about her relatives being caught up in a civil war, hadn't she? *Interesting.*

Burgeson reached out with his left hand and yanked the bell rope, without taking his eyes off the message tape. A few seconds later Citizen Supervisor Philips stuck his head round the partition. 'You called, citizen?'

'Yes.' Burgeson shoved the newspaper stack to one side, so that they overflowed the desk and drifted down across the empty rifle rack beside it. 'Something urgent has come up back East. I need to be in Boston as soon as possible.'

'Boston? What about the campaign, citizen?'

'The campaign can continue without me for a couple of days.' Burgeson stared at Philips. Dried-out and etiolated, the officer resembled a praying mantis in a black uniform: but he was an efficient organizer, indeed had pulled together the staff and crew for this campaign train at short notice. 'We've hit New Brentford and Jensenville in the past two days, you've seen how I want things done: Occupy the local paper's offices, vet the correspondents, deal with any who

439

are unreliable and promote our cadres in their place. Continue to monitor as you move on.' The two-thousand-ton armored war train, bristling with machine guns and black-clad Freedom Riders, was probably unique in history in having its own offset press and typesetting carriage; but as Erasmus had argued the point with Sir Adam, this was a war of public perception – and despite the technowizardry of the videography engineers, public perceptions were still shaped by hot metal type. 'Keep moving, look for royal blue newspapers and ensure that you leave only red freedom-lovers in your wake.'

'I think I can do that, sir.' Philips nodded. 'Difficult cases . . . ?'

'Use your discretion.' *Here, have some rope; try not to hang yourself with it.* 'I'll be back as soon as I can. Meanwhile, when's the next supply run back to Lynchburg departing?'

'If it's Boston you want, there's an aerodrome near Raleigh that's loyal,' Philips offered. 'I'll wire them to put a scout at your disposal?'

'Do that.' Burgeson suppressed a shudder. Flying tended to make him airsick, even in the modern fully-enclosed mail planes. 'I need to be there as soon as possible.'

'Absolutely, citizen. I'll put the wheels in motion at once.' And, true to his word, almost as soon as Philips disappeared there came an almighty squeal of brakes from beneath the train.

*

The past week had been one long nightmare for Paulette Milan.

She'd been a fascinated observer of Miriam's adventures, in the wake of the horrible morning a year ago when they'd both lost their jobs; and later, when Miriam had sucked her into running an office for her – funneling resources to an extradimensional business start-up – she'd been able to square it with her conscience because she agreed with Miriam's goals. If the Clan, Miriam's criminal extended family, could be diverted into some other line of business, that was cool. And if some of their money stuck to Paulie's fingertips in the form of wages, well, as long as the wages weren't coming in for anything illegal on her part, that was fine, too.

But things hadn't worked out. First Miriam had vanished for nearly six months – a virtual prisoner, held under house arrest for much of that time. The money pipeline had slammed shut, leaving Paulie looking for a job in the middle of a recession. Then things got worse. About six weeks ago Miriam's friends – or co-conspirators, or cousins, or whatever – Olga and Brill had turned up on her doorstep and made her the kind of offer you weren't allowed to refuse if you knew what was good for you. There was a fat line of credit to sweeten the pill, but it left Paulie looking over her shoulder nervously. You didn't hand out that kind of money just to open an office, in her experience. And there had been dark hints about internal politics within the Clan, a civil war, and the feds nosing around.

All of this was *bad*. Capital-B bad. Paulie had grown up in a neighborhood where the hard men flashed too much cash around, sometimes checked into club fed for a few years at a time, and snitches tended to have accidents . . . She'd thought she had a good idea what was coming until she'd turned on the TV a few days ago and seen the rising mushroom clouds. Heard the new president's broadcast, glacial blue eyes twinkling as he came out with words that were still reverberating through the talk shows and news columns ('PENTAGON SPOKESMAN: PRESIDENT "NOT INSANE",' as the *Globe* had put it).

It made her sick to her stomach. She'd spent the first two days in bed, crying and throwing up on trips to the bathroom, certain that the FBI were going to break down her door at any moment. The stakes she'd signed up for were far higher than she'd ever imagined, and she found she hated herself for it: hated her earlier moment of pecuniary weakness, her passive compliance in following Miriam down her path of good intentions, her willingness to make friends and let people influence her. She'd caught herself looking in the bathroom cabinet at one point, and hastily shut it: The temptation to take a sleeping pill, or two, or enough to shut it out forever, was a whispering demon on her shoulder for a few hours. 'What the fuck can I *do*?' she'd asked the bourbon bottle on the kitchen table. 'What the *fuck* can I do?'

Today . . . hadn't been better, exactly; but she'd awakened in a mildly depressive haze, rather than a blind panic, knowing that she had two options. She could go to the feds, spill her guts, and hope a jail cell for the rest of her life was better than whatever the Clan did to their snitches. Or she could keep calm and carry on doing what Miriam had asked of her: sit in an office, buy books and put them in boxes, buy *stuff* (surveying tools, precision atomic clocks, laboratory balances: What did she know?) and stash it in a self-storage locker ready for a courier collection that might never arrive.

Get up. Drink a mug of coffee, no food. Go to the office. Order supplies. Repackage them with an inventory sheet, to meet the following size and weight requirements. Drive them to the lockup. Consider eating lunch and feel revulsion at the idea so do some more work, then go home. Keep calm and carry on (it beats going to Gitmo). Try not to think . . .

Paulette drove home from the rented office suite in a haze of distraction, inattentive and absentminded. The level of boxes in the lockup had begun to go down again, she'd noticed: For the first time in a week there'd been a new manila envelope with a handwritten shopping list inside. (She'd stuffed it in her handbag, purposely not reading it.) So someone was collecting the consignments. Her fingers were white on the steering wheel as she pulled up in the nearest parking space, half a block from her front door. She was running short on supplies, but the idea of going grocery shopping made her feel sick: Anything out of the routine scared her right now.

She unlocked the front door and went inside, switched the front hall light on, and dumped her handbag beside the answering machine. It was a warm enough summer's day that she hadn't bothered with a jacket. She walked through into the kitchen to start a pot of coffee, purposely not thinking about how she was going to fill the evening – a phone call to Mother, perhaps, and a movie on DVD – and that was when the strange man stepped out behind her and held up a badge.

'Paulette Milan, I'm from the DEA and I'd – '

She was lying down, and dizzy. He was staring at her. Everything was gray. His mouth was moving, and so was the world. It was confusing for a moment, but then her head began to clear: *I fainted?* She was looking up at the living room ceiling, she realized. There was something soft under the back of her head.

'Can you hear me?' He looked concerned.

'I'm – ' She took a couple of breaths. 'I'm – Oh God.'

'I'm sorry, I didn't mean to scare you like that – are you all right? Listen, do you have a heart condition – ' *No. No.* She must have shaken her head. 'Do you know Miriam Beckstein?'

Paulie swallowed. 'Shit.'

Everything, for an instant, was crystal clear. *I'm from the DEA. Do you know Miriam Beckstein?* The next logical words had to be, *You're under arrest.*

'I need to talk to her; her life's in danger.'

Paulie blinked. *Does not compute.* 'You're from the DEA,' she said hesitantly. Pushed against the carpet. 'I fainted?'

'Uh, yes, in the kitchen. I never – I carried you in here. I'm sorry, I didn't mean to scare you. I wanted to talk, but I was afraid they might be watching.'

Watching? 'Who?' she asked.

'The FTO,' he said. *Who?* she wondered. 'Or the Clan.'

The brittle crystal shell around her world shattered. 'Oh, them,' she said carelessly, her tongue loosened by shock. 'No, they ring the front doorbell. Like everyone else.' Bit by bit, awareness was starting to return. Chagrin – *I can't believe I fainted* – was followed by anxiety – *Who is this guy? How do I know he's DEA? Is he a burglar?* – and then fear: *Alone with a strange man.*

The strange man seemed to be going out of his way to be non-threatening, though. 'Do you want a hand up?' he asked. 'Figure you might be more comfortable on the sofa – ' She waved him away, then pushed herself upright, then nodded. Things went gray again for a moment. 'Listen, I'm not, uh, here on official business, exactly. But I need to talk to Miriam – ' She rose, took two steps backwards, and collapsed onto the sofa. 'Are you sure you're okay?'

'No,' she heard herself say, very distinctly. 'I'm *not* okay. Who are you, mister, and what are you doing in my house?'

He hunkered down on the balls of his feet so that he was at eye level to her. 'Name's Fleming, Mike Fleming. I used to know Miriam. She's in a whole bunch of trouble; if you know what she's been doing this past year, you'd know that – if you know about the Clan, you're in

443

trouble, too. That goes for me, also.' He paused. 'Want me to go on?'

'You're.' She stopped. 'Why did you tell me you're DEA?'

'I was, originally – I still carry a badge they issued. I'd prefer you not to phone them just yet to verify that. See, I'm willing to put my neck on the line. But I want to get to the truth. You know about the Clan?'

Paulie shook her head. 'If I say anything, you know what those people will do?' She was saying too much, she vaguely recognized, but something about this setup smelled wrong.

'Which people? The Clan, or the Family Trade Organization?' Fleming paused. 'I'm not in a position to arrest you for anything – I'm not here on official business. I need to talk to Miriam – '

'Wait.' Paulette tried to pull herself together. 'The *what* organization? You want to talk to her? About what?'

Fleming looked at her quizzically. 'The FTO is a cross-agency operation to shut down the Clan. I was part of it until, uh, about a week ago. It was an attempt to get all the agencies whose lines the Clan crossed to sing from the same hymn book. I came in from the DEA side when source GREEN – a Clan defector called Matthias – walked in the door. I've seen Miriam, about three months ago, in a palace in a place called Niejwein – want me to go on?'

Oh Jesus, save me – he's the real thing. She shook her head numbly. 'What do you want?'

'Like I said, I need to talk to Miriam. She's in terrible danger – FTO has been penetrated. The president used to work with the Clan, back in the eighties and early nineties. He's the one behind this mess, he goaded them into using those nukes, and there's worse to come. He's running FTO. All the oil in Texas – *every* version of Texas – that's what he's after, that and a state of emergency at home to give him carte blanche to do whatever the hell he likes. I've tried to put out a warning via the press, but my contact didn't believe me until the attacks, and now – '

'You went to the press?' Paulette stared at him as if he'd grown a second head. 'What did you have?'

'Nothing!' His frustration was visible.

'But you found me,' she pointed out.

'Yeah, after I turfed her house. Which is under police watch *and* booby-trapped; I found an old planner of hers, played back the answering-machine tape – '

'Shit.' She tried to stand, failed for a moment, then got her suddenly shaky knees to behave. 'There was a tape?' *If* you *found me*, they *could find me.*

'Relax. Those agencies you're thinking about don't talk to each other at that level. You're probably safe, for now.'

Probably safe and her cousin *Don't worry* had helped many a girl get pregnant, in Paulie's opinion, and when the canoodling in question might lead to the queue for the execution chamber at Gitmo rather than a hospital delivery room, chancing it was not on her roadmap. 'No, forget that: If they catch you they'll backtrack to me. Thanks a million, Mr. Fleming, you just doubled my chances of not getting out of this alive. I didn't ask for this shit! It just landed on my lap!' Her heart was hammering, she could feel her face flushing: Fleming was leaning away from her sudden vehemence. 'Fucking wiseguys, I grew up in their backyard, you know what I'm saying? The old generation. You kept your nose out of their business and didn't do nothing and they'd mostly leave you alone, especially if you knew their cousin's wife or walked their sister's dogs or something. But if you crossed them it wouldn't be any fucking horse's head at the end of your bed, no fucking wreath at your funeral; you wouldn't *have* a funeral, there wouldn't be a body to bury. There were rumors about the meat-packing plant, about the cat and dog food. And the cops weren't much better. Shakedown money every Tuesday, free coffee and bagels at the corner, and you better hope they liked your face. And that was the *local* cops, and the old-time *local* hoods, who didn't shit in their backyard 'case someone took exception, you know where I'm coming from?'

Fleming just squatted on his heels and took it, like a giant inflatable target for all her frustration. 'Yes, I know where you're from,' he said quietly when she ran down. 'Keep a low profile and don't rock the boat and you think maybe you can get by without anyone hurting you. But where *I'm* coming from – that's not an option anymore. It's not Miriam's fault that she's descended from them and has their ability, not her fault about those bombs – she tried to warn me. There are back channels between governments: That was before my boss's boss decided to burn me. No; what *I'm* telling *you* is that we're caught in the middle of a fight that's been fixed, and if I don't get to talk to Miriam, a lot of people are going to die. The new president wants the Clan dead, because it's a necessary condition to cover up his own past connection with them: He ran their West Coast heroin-distribution arm for about seven years. He's had his fingers deep into their business since then, for all I know he's the one who nudged them into acquiring nukes and then prodded them into using them, and he's just been sworn in – we probably don't have much time to get the warning out. So are you going to help me? Or are you going to sit in your foxhole and stick your fingers in your ears and sing "La la la, I can't *hear* you"?'

'You're telling me it's the *president's* fault?' She stared. Fleming didn't *look* mad –

'Yes. I know where too many bodies are buried, that's why they tried to car bomb me four days ago. FTO itself is still secret: I know enough to blow the operation sky high. Black underground prisons on US soil, captured Clan members being forced to act as mules with bombs strapped to their necks, vivisection on human subjects to find out what makes them tick, helicopters with black boxes containing bits of brain tissue – don't ask me how they got them – that can travel to the Gruinmarkt. There's an invasion coming, Ms. Milan, and they've been gearing up to attack the Clan in their own world for at least six months.'

Paulette opened her mouth, then shut it again.

Fleming sighed. 'I can see we're going to be here some time,' he said. 'Any chance of a coffee?'

*

Two days after Huw and Yul hiked into Springfield to post a letter at great personal peril (two days in which six more ClanSec world-walkers and a full half-ton of requisitioned supplies reached the safe house, two days during which the neighbors kept a remarkably low profile), Miriam was sitting in the makeshift living room, single-mindedly typing up her to-do list, when something strange happened.

With no warning, the bulky wooden cabinet in the corner of the room crackled into life. 'This is the emergency widecast network. Repeat, this is the emergency widecast network. The following message is for Miss Beckstein, last known in Springfield. Will Miss Beckstein please go to the shop in Boston where her sick friend is waiting for her. Repeat – '

The repetition of the message was lost in a clatter. 'Shit!' Miriam applied some other choice words as she bent to pick up the dropped laptop and check it for damage.

'What's happened?' Brill called from the direction of the kitchen.

'Dropped my – we've got contact!'

'What?' A second later Brill pushed the door wide open.

'The radio.' Miriam pointed at it. 'Huw didn't say there's an emergency broadcast channel! Erasmus wants to see me. In Boston.'

Brill looked at her oddly. Miriam realized she was cradling the laptop as if it were cut glass. 'Are you sure – '

'This is the emergency widecast network. Repeat – '

'I told you!'

'Okay.' Brill nodded, then paused to listen. Her face tightened as she unconsciously clenched her jaw. 'Oh yes. Well, it certainly worked. My lady, you got what you wanted. What do we do now?'

'I'd think it was obvious – '

The other door opened; it was Sir Alasdair. 'Hello? I heard shouting?'

Miriam stood up, shut the laptop's lid, and placed it carefully on the side table. 'We're going to Boston,' she announced. 'Erasmus has made contact – '

Alasdair cleared his throat. 'Made contact how – '

'Now look here!' Miriam and Alasdair both stopped dead. 'Have I your full attention?' Brilliana demanded. 'Because as your loyal retainer I think we should consider this with care. My lady, what do you intend to do? Need I remind you these are dangerous times?'

'No.' Miriam looked at Sir Alasdair, who was watching Brilliana with the patience of a hound. 'But this is exactly what we should have expected, isn't it? Erasmus is high in their ministry of propaganda, and we didn't tell him where I was. How else would he contact me, but a broadcast? So now the ball's back on our side of the court. I need to go visit him at the shop, because that's where he'll be. Unless you've got any better ideas?' Alasdair cleared his throat again. 'Yes?' she asked.

'My lady d'Ost.' He glanced at Brill. 'What is your threat assessment?'

'Hard to say. Getting there – dangerous because all travel in this land is risky in the season of civil war. Once there . . . I do not believe Burgeson means ill of my lady; he is as close to a friend, in fact, as any in the world.'

'But?' His word hung in the air for a few short seconds.

'Assuming the message is from Burgeson,' Brilliana said reluctantly. 'There is no word of his disposition. Should he be the victim of an internal plot, this might be a trap. I'd think it unlikely, but stranger things happen. And then, should he in fact be the speaker – what then?'

'Wait a minute.' Miriam raised a hand. 'The idea is to make contact. Then put my proposal to him and see what he thinks is achievable. At that point, once we've got a channel, it's down to diplomacy.'

'And capabilities.' Alasdair lowered himself onto one of the wooden dining chairs Huw and Yul had scared up in the furniture-hunting expedition. 'Their expectation of our abilities must view us as a potential threat, just as the Americans do. They will want to know why we seek refuge here. If we tell them the unvarnished truth – '

'We *must*.' Miriam was forceful. 'Yeah, we may have to admit the Clan fucked up royally in the United States. But you know something? It's nothing but the truth. If we tell them we fucked up and we want to start afresh and turn over a new leaf, it's not only believable – it's true, and they'll get the same story from everyone they ask. If we start telling white lies or trying to bamboozle them . . . how many of our people have to remember to tell the same lie? *Someone* will get confused and let something slip over a glass of wine, and then Erasmus's people will let their suspicions run riot. And let me remind you this country is in the middle of a revolution? Maybe they're going to come out of it peacefully, but most revolutions don't – we have a chance to try and influence it if we're on the inside, but we won't have a leg to stand on unless we're like Caesar's wife, above reproach. So my goal is simple: get us *in* with the temporal authorities, so deeply embedded that we're indispensable within months.'

'Indispensable?'

'I've been doing some reading.' Miriam turned tired eyes on Alasdair. 'Revolutions eat their young, especially as they build new power structures. But they *don't* eat the institutions that prop them up. Secret police, bureaucrats, armies – that's the rule. They may hang the men at the top, and go hard on their external enemies, but the majority of the rank and file keep their places. I think we can come up with a value proposition that they can't ignore, one that would scare the crap out of them if we didn't *very obviously* need their help.'

Sir Alasdair looked at Brill. 'Do you understand her when she starts talking like this?' he grumbled.

'No. Isn't it great?' Brill flashed him a grin. 'You can see why the duke, may he rest peacefully, wanted her for a figurehead upon the throne. My lady. What do you propose to do? Let us say we get you to Boston to meet with your man. What do you need?'

'I've got a list,' said Miriam, picking up the laptop. 'Let's get started . . .'

BEGIN RECORDING

' – Latest news coming in from Delhi, the Pakistani foreign minister has called off negotiations over the cease fire on the disputed Kashmir frontier – '

(*Fast forward.*)

' – Artillery duels continuing, it looks like a long, tense night for the soldiers here on the border near Amritsar. Over to you in the studio, Dan.'

'Thank you, Bob Mancini, live from the India–Pakistan border region near the disputed Kashmir province, where the cold war between the Indian and Pakistani militaries has been running hot for the past month. A reminder that the catastrophic events of 7/16 didn't stop the shooting, may in fact have aggravated it. With rumors flying that the quantum effect used by the attackers is being frantically investigated by military labs all over the world, we go to our military affairs expert, Erik Olsen. Hello, Erik.'

'Hello, Dan.'

'Briefly, what are the implications? Mr. Mukhtar's accusation that the Indian secret service is sneaking saboteurs across the border via a parallel universe is pretty serious, but is it credible? What's going on here?'

'Well, Dan, the hard fact is, nobody knows for sure who's got this technology. We've seen it in action, it's been used against us – and nobody knows who's got it. As you can imagine, it's spoiling a lot of military leaders' sleep. If you can carry a nuclear weapon through a parallel universe and have it materialize in a city, you can mount what's called a first strike, a decapitation stroke: You can take out an enemy's missiles and bombers on the ground before they can launch. Submarines are immune, luckily – '

'Why are submarines immune, Erik?'

'You've got to find them first, Dan, you can't materialize a bomb inside a submarine that's underwater unless you can find it. Bombers that are airborne are pretty much safe as well. But if they're on the ground or in dry dock – it upsets the whole logic of nuclear deterrence. And India and Pakistan both have sizable nuclear arsenals, but no submarines, they're all carried on bombers or ground-launched missiles. Into the middle of a hot war, the conflict over Kashmir with the artillery duels and machine gun attacks we've been hearing about these past weeks, it's not new – they've fought four wars in the past thirty years – the news about this science-fictional new threat, it's upset all the realities on the ground. India and Pakistan have both got to be afraid that the other side's got a new tool that makes their nuclear arsenal obsolete, the capability to smuggle nukes through other worlds – and they're already on three-minute warning, much like we were with the Soviets in the fifties except that their capital cities are just five minutes apart as the missile flies.'

'But they wouldn't be crazy enough to start a nuclear war over Kashmir, would they?'

'Nobody ever wants to start a nuclear war, Dan, that's not in question. The trouble is, they may think the other side is starting one. Back in 1983, for example, a malfunctioning Russian radar computer told the Soviets that we'd launched on them. Luckily a Colonel Petrov kept his head and waited for more information to come in, but if he'd played by the rule book he'd have told Moscow they were under attack, and it's anyone's guess what could have happened. Petrov had fifteen minutes' warning. Islamabad and New Delhi have got just three minutes to make up their minds, that's why the Federation of American Scientists say they're the greatest risk of nuclear war anywhere in the world today.'

'But that's not going to happen – '

(*Fast forward.*)

'Oh Jesus.' (*Bleeped mild expletive.*) 'This can't be – oh. I'm waiting for Bob, Bob Mancini on the India–Pakistan border. We're going over live to Bob, as soon as we can raise him. Bob? Bob, can you hear me? . . . No? Bob? We seem to have lost Bob. Our hearts go out to him, to his family and loved ones, to everyone out there . . .

'That was the emergency line from the Pentagon. America is not, repeat *not*, under attack. It's not a repeat of 7/16, it's . . . it appears that one of the Pakistani army or the Indian air force have gone – a nuclear bomb, a hydrogen bomb on Islamabad, other explosions in India. Amritsar, New Delhi, Lahore in Pakistan. I'm Dan Rather on CBS, keeping you posted on the latest developments in what are we calling this? World War Two-point-five? India and Pakistan. Five large nuclear explosions have been reported so far. We can't get a telephone line to the subcontinent.

'Reports are coming in of airliners being diverted away from Indian and Pakistani airspace. The Pentagon has announced that

America is not, repeat *not*, under attack, this is a purely regional conflict between India and Pakistan. We're going over live to Jim Patterson in Mumbai, India. Jim, what's happening?'

'Hello Dan, it's absolute chaos here, sirens going in the background, you can probably hear them. From here on the sixth floor of the Taj Mahal Palace Hotel there's traffic gridlocked throughout the city as people try to flee. In just a minute we're going down into the basements where – ' (*Click.*)

'Jim? Jim? We seem to have lost Jim. Wait, we're getting – oh no. *No.*'

END RECORDING

THE VIEW FROM FORTY THOUSAND FEET

'I don't know if this will work,' said Paulette. 'I've never done it before.'

'Don't worry, they'll have set this up to be fail-safe. Believe me, we had enough trouble cracking their communication security – they know what they're doing. You may not get an immediate answer, but they'll know you paged them.'

'I don't know how you can sit there and be so calm about it!'

Mike shrugged. 'I've had a long time to get used to the idea,' he said. Not exactly true: He'd had a couple of weeks. But the stench of bureaucratic excess, the penumbra of the inquisition, had clouded his entire period of service at the Family Trade Organization. 'Sometimes you can smell it when the place you work – when there's a bad atmosphere? When people are doing stuff that *isn't quite right*? But nobody says anything, so you think it's just you, and you're afraid to speak out.'

Paulie nodded. 'Like Enron.'

'Like – more than Enron, I guess; like the CIA in the early seventies, when they were out of control. Throwing people out of helicopters in Vietnam, mounting coups in South America. It's like they say, fish rot from the head down.'

She lifted the phone handset she'd been gripping with bony fingers and hesitantly punched in an area code, and then a number. 'We did an in-depth on Enron. It was just unbelievable, what was going on there.' The phone rang, unanswered; she let it continue for ten seconds, then neatly ended the call. 'What's next?'

Mike consulted the handwritten list she'd given him. 'Second number, ring for four seconds, at least one minute after ending the first call.' She didn't need him to do this: She could read it herself, easily enough. But company helped. 'The hardest part of being a whistle-blower is being on your own, on the outside. Everybody telling you to shut the hell up, stop rocking the boat, keep your head down and work at whatever the wise heads have put in front of you. Hmm. Area code 414 – '

Paulie dialed the second number, let it ring for four seconds, then disconnected. 'I did an interview with Sherron Watkins, you know? When the whole Enron thing blew up. She said that, too, pretty much.' She stabbed the phone at him. 'Harder to blow the whistle on these guys, let me tell you. Much harder.'

'I know it.' He stared at the third number on the list. 'On the other hand, they're not your regular gangsters: They think like a government.'

'Some folks say, governments *are* gangsters. A bunch of guys with guns who demand money, right?'

'There's a difference of approach. Gangsters aren't part of the community. They don't put anything back into it, they don't build roads and schools, they just take the money and run. Governments think differently. At least, working ones do.'

'But the Clan take money out of *our* communities. They don't spend it on *us*, do they? From our point of view they're like gangsters.'

'Or an empire.' Mike turned the thought around, examining it from different angles. 'Like the Soviet Union, the way they drained resources from outlying territories.' There was something not quite right with the metaphor, if he could just figure it out. 'Oh, next number time. Area code is 506 – '

They worked down the list over the course of an hour, as the jug of coffee cooled and the evening shadows lengthened outside. There were five numbers to call for varying lengths of time, at set minimum intervals; the third had an annoying voice menu system to navigate, asking for a quotation for auto insurance, and the fifth – answered in an Indian call center somewhere – was the only one with human interaction required: 'Sorry, wrong number.'

The whole tedious business was necessary for several reasons. A couple of random numbers to make traffic analysis harder; a couple of flags to say *I need to talk* and *I am not under duress*; and words spoken into a recording device to prove that the contact was, in fact,

Paulette Milan, and not an agent in an FTO office. There were other rituals to perform: the curtains to be left undrawn in the spare bedroom but drawn in the main, a light to be left on inside the front door. Rituals of tradecraft, the magic rite of summoning spies, impenetrable to outsiders but practiced for good reason by those on the inside. *Someone sets up a small but highly professional intelligence agency. Question: Where do they get their training? Given that we know their soldiers use the USMC as a finishing school . . .* Mike pondered the question for a moment, then gave up. Every single one of the possible answers that sprang to mind was disturbing.

Finally they were done. 'I should hear back within twenty-four hours,' Paulie said diffidently. She paused. *What now?* he wondered.

'I've been staying in a motel.' It would be racking up another night's charges. The idea of driving back there to spend another night in silence abruptly made him nauseous. 'Don't get me wrong, but I think I should be here if they come unexpectedly – '

She looked at him thoughtfully, then nodded. 'You can use the spare bedroom if you like. There's bedding in the closet.'

'Thank you.' To fill the potentially awkward silence he added, 'I feel like I'm imposing on you.' He'd had his fill of silence: Silence concealed lies. 'Can I buy you dinner?'

'Guess so.' The set of her shoulders relaxed slightly. 'Where did you meet Miriam, the first time?'

*

The sky was overcast, and the muggy onshore breeze blew a stink of fish guts and coal smoke across the streets, gusting occasionally to moan and rattle around the chimney stacks – the barometer was falling, a rain front threatening to break the summer heat.

Driving sixty miles over the poor-quality roads in a pair of steamers with leaf-spring suspensions had taken them the best part of four hours, but they'd started early and the purposeful-looking convoy had apparently convinced the more opportunistic highwaymen to keep a low profile. The only delays they encountered were a couple of checkpoints manned by volunteer militias, and as these were mostly concerned with keeping the starving robber gangs out of their suburbs, Miriam's party were waved through – a rapid progress doubtless greased by the low-denomination banknotes interleaved between the pages of the inkjet-forged Vehicle Pilot's Warrants that Huw and Alasdair presented when challenged. It was, perhaps, for the best that the militiamen's concupiscence avoided the need for a search: much better to hand over a few hundred million New Crown notes than to risk a brisk and very one-sided exchange of gunfire.

'Did you see that?' Brill asked Miriam indignantly as they left the second checkpoint: 'Half of them were carrying pitchforks! And the one with the bent nose, his tines were rusty!'

There were few obvious signs of revolution as they drove through the outskirts of Boston. More men and women in the streets, perhaps, hanging out in small groups; but with the economy spiraling into a true deflationary depression and unemployment nearing fifty percent, that was hardly surprising. There were soup kitchens, true, and the street cars bore banners proclaiming that the People's Party would feed the needy at certain listed locations – but there were also fishmongers and grocery stalls with their wares laid out in front, and the district farmer's market they passed was the usual chaos of hand-carts and wagons piled high with food. *Someone* was keeping things moving, between town and country – a good sign, as far as Miriam could tell.

And then they were into familiar streets and the second car turned off, heading for its prearranged rendezvous point. 'I'll get out here and walk the rest of the way,' Miriam said quietly as they sat behind a streetcar that had stopped for a horse-drawn wagon to unload some crates. 'You know the block. I'll remember to press once every ten minutes while things are going well.'

'Check it now,' said Brilliana, holding up her own earpiece.

'Check.' Miriam squeezed her left hand, inside a coat pocket. Brill's unit buzzed. 'Okay, we're in business.'

Brilliana caught her arm as she opened the door. 'Take care, my lady. And if you sense trouble – '

'There won't be any trouble,' Miriam said firmly. *Not with Sir Alasdair and his team watching my back.* If there was any trouble, if she was walking into a baited trap rather than a safe meeting, things would get spectacularly messy for the troublemakers. It wasn't just a matter of them having modern automatic weapons, two-way radios, and the ability to world-walk out of danger: Alasdair had cherry-picked the best men he could find in Clan Security for her bodyguard, and they'd planned and rehearsed this meeting carefully. 'I'll be fine.'

There was an alleyway, off the high street between two shuttered shop fronts; partway along it stood a tenement with its own shuttered frontage, and the three gilt balls of a pawnbroker hanging above the doorway. Miriam walked back along the pavement and turned in to the alleyway. There were no obvious watchers, nor loitering muggers. She marched up to the door beside the wooden shuttered window and yanked the bell-pull.

A few seconds later the door opened. 'Come in, come in!' It was Erasmus, his face alight with evident pleasure. Miriam drew a deep breath of relief and stepped across the threshold. 'How have you been?' he asked. 'I've been worried – '

The door swung to behind her, and she took a step forward, ending up in his arms with her chin on his shoulder. He hugged her gingerly, as if afraid she might break. 'It's been crazy,' she confessed, hugging him back. 'I've missed you too.' Erasmus let go and straightened up awkwardly. 'There's been a lot happening, much of it bad.'

'Indeed, yes – ' He took a step back, into the shadowy interior of the shop. 'Excuse me.' He turned and pushed a button that had been screwed crudely to the wall beside the door. A buzzer sounded somewhere below, in the cellars. 'An all-clear sign. Just a precaution.' He shrugged apologetically. 'Otherwise they won't let me out of their sight.'

Miriam glanced round. 'I know that problem.' The shop was just as she'd last seen it, albeit dustier and more neglected. But there was a light on in the back room, and a creaking sound. 'Do you want to talk in front of company?'

'We'll be in the morning room upstairs, Frank,' Erasmus called through the doorway, his voice a lot stronger than when she'd first met him.

'Are you sure?' Frank, staying unseen in the back room, had a rough voice.

'You've got the exit guarded. You've got the area covered. I will personally vouch for Miss Beckstein's trustworthiness; without her I wouldn't be alive for you to nanny me. But your ears are not safe for this discussion. Do you understand?'

Frank chuckled grimly. 'Aye, citizen. But all the same, if I don't hear from you inside half an hour, I'll be coming up to check on you by and by. It's what Sir Adam would expect of me.'

Erasmus shrugged apologetically at Miriam. 'This way,' he mouthed, then turned and opened the side door onto the tenement stairwell. Halfway up the staircase he added, 'I should apologize for Frank. But he's doing no less than his duty. Even getting this much time to myself is difficult.'

'Uh, yes.' Miriam waited while Erasmus opened the door to the morning room. Dust sheets covered the piano and the villainous, ancient sofa. He stripped the latter one off, sneezing as he shook it out and cast it atop the piano stool. 'My, I haven't been back here in months.'

Miriam sat down carefully. Then, remembering, she reached into her pocket and pulled out the walkie-talkie. 'Miriam here. Stand down, repeat, stand down. Over.' She caught Erasmus staring at the device. 'I have guards, too.' It buzzed twice, Brill acknowledging; she slid it away. 'Please, sit down,' she asked, gesturing at the other side of the sofa.

'You have a habit of surprising me.' Erasmus folded himself into the far corner. 'Please don't stop.'

'Not if I can help it.' She tried to smile, belying the tension in her stomach. 'How's it going, anyway?'

'How's what going?' He waved a hand at the piano, the dusty fly-specked windows, the world beyond. 'I never thought I'd live this long. Never thought I'd see the end of the tyranny, either. Nor that Sir Adam would come back and form a government, much less that he'd ask me to – well. How about yourself? What has happened to you since we last met? Nothing too trying, I hope?' His raised eyebrow was camouflage, she realized. *He's worried. About me?* She pushed the thought aside.

'Madness – bedlam,' she translated. 'Let me see if I can explain this . . . I told you about the Clan? My relations?' He nodded. 'Things went bad, very fast. You know what I was trying to do, the business. Brake pads, disk brakes. Their conservatives – they spiked it. Meanwhile, they tried to shut me up. Apparently a full-scale civil war broke out back home. And the conservative faction also discovered that the other – you know the world I came from isn't the one the Clan live in? – that other America, they found out about the Clan. To cut a long story short, the Clan conservatives tried to decapitate the American government, and at the same time, tried to kill the progressive faction. They failed on both counts: my faction, the progressives, ended up killing *them*. But now the US military are winding up for war on the Clan, and it looks like they might be able to build machinery for moving their weapons between worlds. It's not magic, Erasmus, it's some kind of physical phenomenon, and their scientists – they're better than you can imagine.'

Burgeson shook his head. 'This isn't making much sense – '

'I'm telling it wrong.' She screwed up her eyes and took a deep breath. 'Erasmus, let me start again?'

'For you, anything.' He smiled briefly.

'Okay.' She opened her eyes and exhaled. 'The Clan exists as a family business, trading between worlds. A group of us – several hundred – believe that we have irrevocably fouled up our relationship with the world of the United States. That the United States military will soon have the power to attack the Gruinmarkt, as well as the strongest possible motivation. Nowhere in the world the Clan lives in is safe. We are fairly certain that the US military *doesn't* know about your world, or at least has no way of reaching it directly – you can't get there from here without going via the Gruinmarkt. So I've got a proposal for you. We need somewhere to live – somewhere relatively safe, somewhere we haven't shat in the bed. Somewhere like New Britain. In return, we can offer you . . . well, my people have been busy grabbing all the science and engineering references they can get their hands on.

'The United States is sixty to eighty years ahead of you in science and technology, although it might as well be two hundred – we can't promise to bridge that gap instantly, but we *can* show your engineers and scientists where to look. Right now you've got a hostile French empire off your shore. There are strategies and weapons technologies we can look up in the American history books that are decades ahead of anything the French – or your – navy can muster. And other stuff; see what their economists say, for example, or their historians.'

'Ah.' Erasmus nodded to himself. 'That's an interesting idea.' He paused. 'What do your aristocratic cousins say about this idea? You are aware that we have recently held a revolution against the idea of autocracy and the landed gentry . . . ?'

'The ones you're worried about won't be coming, Erasmus. We're on the edge of a permanent schism. The people who're listening to me – the progressives – well, the United States had their revolution more than two hundred years ago, remember that history I gave you?' He nodded. 'For decades, the Clan has been educating its children in the United States. I'm unusual only in degree – my mother went the whole way, and raised me there from infancy. There's a pronounced split between the generation that has been exposed to American culture, education, and ideas, and the backwoods nobility of the Gruinmarkt; the Clan has found it increasingly hard to hold these two factions together for decades now. Those are the people I'd be bringing – those Clan members who'd rather be live refugees in a progressive republic than dead nobles clinging to the smoking wreckage of the old order. People whose idea of a world they'd like to live in is compatible with your party's ideology. All they want is a reasonable expectation of being able to live in peace.'

'Oh, Miriam.' Erasmus shook his head. 'I would be very happy if I could offer you the assurance you want. Unfortunately' – she tensed – 'I'd be lying if I said I could.' He held out his hand towards her. She stared at it for a moment, then reached out and took it. 'There is *no* certainty here. *None.* Those books you gave me, the histories of your America, they offer no reassurance. We are at war with an internal enemy who will show us no quarter if we lose, and our people are hungry, angry, and desperate. This is a governance of emergency. We hold the east coast and the west, and the major cities, but some of the small towns – ' He shook his head. 'The south, the southern continent, the big plantations there – the fighting is bloody and merciless. You shouldn't expect aid or comfort of us, Miriam. It's going to get a lot worse before it gets better. One of your American wise men said, the tree of liberty has to be watered with the blood of patriots. He wasn't exaggerating. My job is to, to try and hide what goes into the watering can. To put a good face on murder. You shouldn't expect too much of me.'

Miriam stared at him for a long moment. 'All right.' She pulled on his hand gently. 'Let's forget the living-in-peace bit. Can you protect us if we deliver? During the crisis, I mean. We help you develop the industrial mechanisms to defeat your external enemies. Can you, in return, keep the police off us?'

'The police, Reynolds and his Internal Security apparatus – ' His expression clouded. 'As long as I'm not arrested myself, *that* I can manage. I've got leverage. Bentley and Crowe owe me, Williams needs my support – but best if it comes from the top, though, from Sir Adam and with the approval of the steering committee of the People's Council. It would be best if we kept it under wraps, though, especially if your first task is to build new factories and laboratories for the war effort. Hmm.'

There was a creak from outside the morning-room door, then a throat-clearing: 'Be you folks decent?'

Erasmus's head whipped round. 'Yes, everything is fine,' he called.

'Just so, just so.' It was Frank, the unseen bodyguard. He sounded amused.

'You can go away now,' Erasmus added sharply.

A moment later Miriam heard a heavy tread descending the stairs, no longer stealthy. She looked at Erasmus, wide-eyed. 'Does he think we're – '

Erasmus looked back at her. 'I don't *know* he thinks that, but it would make a good cover story, wouldn't you agree?'

'If we – ' She stopped, feeling her ears heat. *Sitting on the sofa, holding hands.* She let go of his fingers hastily.

'I'll need to make inquiries,' said Erasmus. He let his hand fall. 'Meanwhile, that big house you bought – I'll see it's left alone. If you follow me.'

Miriam swallowed. 'How long?' she asked, trying to regain control.

'You called me back from a, a marketing campaign. I'll have to see it's running smoothly. Then report to the Council, and talk to certain people. It could take months.'

'I'm not sure we've got months.'

'If you can come up with concrete proposals, I can probably hasten the process. Nothing too amazing, but if you can think of something concrete: smaller telautographs, better aircraft engines . . . ?'

'We can do that.' Miriam swallowed. 'I can have a written proposal ready next week.' *That sort of target should be easy enough,* she thought: Someone had mentioned a flyer in the Clan who'd smuggled an ultralight into the Gruinmarkt against orders. *Find him, tell him what's needed, and pull the trigger.* Even a Second World War-era fighter plane would make an impressively futuristic demo in the skies above New London. 'Let's meet here again. Next week?'

He nodded conspiratorially. 'Come at the same time. I'll have something for you.'

'I'll do that,' she said automatically, then thought, *What?* 'What kind of something?'

'Documents. A warrant pass. A tele number to call on.' Erasmus rose to his feet, then offered her a hand. She took it, levering herself out of the collapsed cushion.

'Do you really think Frank believes we're having an affair?'

He leaned close to her ear. 'Frank reports regularly to Oswald Sartorius, who is secretary in charge of state intelligence. He doesn't realize I know, and I would appreciate your not telling him. It would be safest for you if Oswald thinks we are having an affair; that way you need only worry about being arrested if he decides to move on me, and he will believe you to be of more value alive than dead. If he learns you represent a power center . . . Oswald wants what's best for state intelligence; he is no more dangerous than a shark, as long as you stay out of the water.'

Miriam froze, feeling his breath on her cheek. 'Is it that bad?'

'I don't know.' He sounded uncertain. 'So please be careful.'

'You're the second person who's said that to me today.' It was disturbing: It meant more to her than she'd anticipated. 'You be careful too.'

'I will be.' He gestured at the door. 'After you . . .'

BEGIN PHONE TRANSCRIPT

(*Groggy.*) 'Yes? Who is this?'

'Sir? This is BLOWTORCH. Duty officer speaking. Can you confirm your identity, please?'

(*Pause.*) 'I'm KINGPIN. Is this line secure – '

'Not yet sir, if you'd like to press button four on your secure terminal now – '

(*Click.*) 'Okay, I'm scrambling. What time – Jesus, this had better be good. What's the call, son?'

'Sir, we've, uh, there's a medical alert over the president.'

'It's definitely medical? The usual problem?'

'Sir, it may be worse this time. Don Ensenat says it would be best if you were up and alert – '

'Damn. How bad is it?'

'Sir, we have, uh, the cardiac crash team are trying to resuscitate, but as of now Mr. Cheney is medically unfit. They've got him in transit to PIVOT and there's an operating theater standing by, but it doesn't look good. Sir, we're trying to contact Chief Justice Scalia as per the new continuity of government provisions but it's four in the morning in New York where he's – '

'Son. Stop right there.' (*Rustling.*) 'I'm just waking up here. I'll be in the operations center in five minutes: Get a team ready to take me to PAVILION, ready to leave in fifteen. Keep me informed if there's any change in Richard's condition, if he recovers or . . . not.'

'Yes, sir.'

'He'll hang in there. He's a tough old bird.'

'I sure hope so, sir. Hell of a thing. Is there anything else I can do for you?'

'No, son, just get me that transport.'

'Thank you sir. Goodbye and God bless.'

(*Click.*)

(*Softly.*) 'Christ on a crutch.'

END PHONE TRANSCRIPT

'Ah, Erasmus. Come in, sit down. How are you?'

'I'm well, citizen. Thank you.' It was a small office, surprisingly cramped in view of the seniority of its occupant. Windowless, which was clearly one of the features that had commended it to Sir Adam's security detail. Burgeson lowered himself into a spindly court chair and laid his folio on the chief commissioner's desk. 'There's no end of rushing about, it seems. I really ought to be back to my train, but, well. The matter of our alien friends came up again.'

Sir Adam's expression blanked for a moment, assuming the vacuity of information overload. Then he blinked. 'Ah. The Beckstein woman?'

'And her allies.'

Sir Adam looked past Erasmus, to his bodyguard. 'Seumas, if you could go and rustle up tea for two, please? I think we may be a while.' He paused until the stout fellow had left the room. 'I've got a session of the defense policy review board at three, but I can give you half an hour right now. Will that suffice?'

'I hope so.' Erasmus held his hands together to keep from fidgeting. 'They've got more than gold, as I believe I told you; did you have time to read the book?'

'Yes, as a matter of fact . . .' The chief commissioner removed his spectacles and carefully laid them on the blotter in front of him. Gold-rimmed, they gleamed in the harsh radiance cast by the electrical chandelier overhead. 'It was very strange. Erasmus, either this is a most remarkable confidence trick, or – '

Burgeson shook his head. 'There's more than just books. I've seen some of their machines. Yes, they're very strange. Frighteningly advanced. They have guns that – I've seen a young lady with a gun the size of that pen box, Sir Adam, I've seen it mow down polis thugs like a sewing engine. A battery gun you could fit in your coat pocket.'

'Aliens. With advanced technology. How much of a threat to us are they, in your estimate?'

Erasmus spread his hands wide. 'I think they're an opportunity, if we handle them carefully.'

'What kind of opportunity? And what kind of care do you have in mind?'

'They're in trouble, Sir Adam. Which gives us leverage. My understanding of their plight is admittedly incomplete, but you can rest easy: They are not from the United States and they did not invent these near-magical engines that they use. Rather, they are traders – ours is not the only world they can reach – and they have infiltrated the United States you read about and use it as a source of wealth. Mercantilists, in other words. They have historically been an irritant to their host – smugglers and criminals – and now the host has discovered their existence. Miss Beckstein is entangled in a progressive faction among them, modernizers and democrats if not actual Levelers. They recognize the bankruptcy of their former position and would seek sanctuary. In return, what they offer is *technology transfer*. They can stealthily filch the secrets of the United States' engineers and scientists, and bring them to us for development. More: They have for years been training their children in modern management techniques.'

'Just so. Very well, how many of these refugees are they?'

'Miriam says two to three thousand, at the outside. Most of them cannot travel to the other world – there are only a few hundred who can – but they're blood relatives. Which suggests an angle, doesn't it?'

Sir Adam nodded. 'What are they running from? Enemies at home, or this United States of America?'

'The latter. It appears they were careless and drew themselves to the attention of the authorities there. I have a distinct and unpleasant impression that the US authorities are building machines that can travel between other worlds, for purposes of invasion. In which case – '

'Hmm.'

'Indeed.'

'What would you do with these people, Erasmus?'

'I think we have room for a couple of thousand refugees, and it's easy enough to be generous under the circumstances. We shall keep them isolated and under wraps, of course. The ones who can't world-walk – as they call it – are as important as those who can: Apparently their children may acquire the trait. In the meantime, they can be used to compel cooperation. Sir Adam: I propose to use the world-walking refugees to acquire a library of scientific and technological material stolen from the United States. It may also be necessary to recruit human resources, doctors, skilled professionals, a library of experts: voluntarily if possible, but otherwise – '

'You're talking about abduction.'

The door opened: Seumas and a silent palace servant entered, bearing a tea trolley. Sir Adam and Erasmus waited patiently for them to leave; then Erasmus picked up where he'd left off.

'If necessary, and only in service to our war effort, but . . . yes, if push comes to shove. May I continue? I envisage setting up a network of design bureaus and academies around this library of the future. They will act as a shield around this resource, filtering it out into our own industries. The United States is, well . . . it's hard to say, but I think their world is between fifty and a hundred years ahead of us in some respects. We won't close the gap in a decade, or even two or three, because they're moving forward as well. But we can close the gap *faster than the French*. If nothing else, knowing what played-out mines to avoid pouring treasure and sweat into will help us. This is a strategic resource, Sir Adam.'

The first citizen nodded slowly. 'You don't need to convince me further, Erasmus: It's preposterous on first hearing but the world is indeed a strange place. But let's see, when this hits the central committee . . . argue me this: Why *you*? Why Propaganda? Why not Industry? Give me ammunition.'

Erasmus picked up his teacup. It's rim clattered against the saucer it was balanced on. 'Firstly, because they know me. Miss Beckstein trusts me, and she is their figurehead or leader or at least highly influential among them. These people are not beholden to us and we can't hope to corral them if they take fright. Secondly, because I'm *not* Industry. What we learn from these aliens will have effects everywhere – Industry is only the beginning of it. The Schools of Health, for instance, and the Directorates of Agriculture and Transportation – they'll all be affected. The complex I propose to establish will not be building battleships or aerodynes or setting up experimental farms; it will merely provide scientific advice on these topics. It is indubitably a subdivision of Propaganda – Information. And then there's the final thing. This, this *Clan*, they are not the only people who travel between worlds. The United States are building time machines and may stumble upon us one day; and there may be others. Our treatment of these refugees will set a precedent for future diplomatic contacts with other worlds – and also our treatment of refugees from elsewhere on this one. Do you really think that hock-fist Scott, or perhaps Oswald the Ear, would handle the nuances of disclosure effectively?'

Sir Adam's smile was frozen. 'Of course they wouldn't. Erasmus, you have convinced me of most of your case, but you're wrong on this last single point.'

'Really?'

'Yes. If these people are as valuable as you tell me, we can't possibly disclose their existence in public. Not now, not in twenty years' time. Erasmus, I'm counting on you to reel them in and put them in a deep, padded box – and build your institute and your complex of design bureaus and all the rest of the complicated machinery. We're not going to breathe a word of this to anyone, including the rest of the commission. Not the Peace and Justice puritans – they'll just find a way to use your world-travelers as a stick to stir up trouble. Not the Radicals: I've no idea what they'd do, but it'd probably be as stupid as those land-reform proposals they keep coming up with. And Foreign Affairs: If the Bourbon gets so much as a whisper that they exist, he can make them an offer that would bankrupt our coffers to match. No. This needs to be kept secret, so secret that nobody gets a whiff of their existence.

'These aliens must belong to us – and us alone. Make it so.'

*

467

The morning after the night before: Mike Fleming jolted abruptly awake to the sensation of the world falling away beneath his back. His eyes flickered open from uneasy, distorted dreams of pursuit, a panicky sense of disorientation tearing at his attention. He glanced sideways beneath half-closed lids; the light filtering in through the thin curtains showed him a floral print hanging on pastel-painted walls, strange furniture, someone else's decor. The jigsaw pieces of memory began to fill themselves in. *Paulie Milan's spare room.* They'd ordered in a Chinese meal, sat up late talking. There ensued an uneasy tap-dance as he – unused to hospitality, living for too long without that kind of life – borrowed towels and bedding, showered, prepared for an uneasy night's sleep. (Which largely consisted of taking off his shoes and pants, but keeping his pistol close to hand and checking out the yard from an unlit window before lying down atop the comforter.) It felt strange to be consigned to the guest room, like a one-night stand gone weirdly askew down some strange dimension of alienation. *Don't sleep too deep,* he'd warned himself, only to close his eyes on darkness and open them in daylight. *Well damn, but at least nobody tried to cut my throat in the night –*

He was up and standing with his back to the wall beside the door, pistol in hand, almost before he realized he'd moved. Something was amiss. His nostrils flared as he breathed in, then held his breath, listening: not to the sound of someone moving in the bathroom, or clattering in the kitchen, or voices on the radio, talking. *Not.* He'd slept through the normal noises of another person's morning. What he'd noticed was their absence, and it was infinitely more disturbing.

Voices on the radio? Talking? He could hear voices. *Who –*

Mike did a double take and closed his eyes. Tried to visualize the kitchen layout. Was there a –

Creak of a footstep on the landing. Then a tentative voice: 'Mike? Are you awake yet?'

His muscles turned to jelly as he sagged, lowering the pistol. He'd been unaware of the tension in his neck and shoulders, the totality of focus, his heart hammering with a flashback to a cheap motel room in Tijuana that stank of stale cigarette smoke and claustrophobia. He pointed the gun at the floor beside him, letting its weight drag his wrist down. 'Yeah?'

'We have a visitor. There's coffee in the kitchen. Do you want me to pour you one?'

Coffee plus visitor equals – 'Yes.' He glanced across the room to the bedside table where he'd left his holster. Coming down from the jittery adrenaline spike, he added, 'I'll be down in a couple of minutes. I need to freshen up first.'

'Okay.' Paulie's footsteps receded down the stairs.

Mike let out a breath, quietly shuddering, still winding down. The radio, the sudden silence, whatever had triggered his ambush reflex – it was all right. Moving carefully, he placed the pistol beside the holster, then picked up his pants from where he'd hung them over the back of a chair. *A visitor* almost certainly meant one of Miriam's relatives. Paulette had admitted knowing a few of them: the ice princess, another woman called Brill. He dressed hurriedly, then slid the pistol in its holster into his trouser pocket, just in case. Not that he didn't trust Paulette – he trusted her enough to sleep under her roof – but experience had taught him not to make assumptions when dealing with the Clan.

He descended the stairs, carefully keeping his left hand on the rail, and glanced sideways through the kitchen doorway. The ice princess, Olga, was sitting at the breakfast bar drinking coffee. She nodded at him coolly. 'Mr. Fleming.'

The kitchen radio was babbling headline chatter about someone in the hospital. His jaw tensed as he stepped inside the room. 'Good morning.' He noticed Paulette leaning against the kitchen worktop, her eyes worried. 'Someone mentioned coffee.' Paulette reached out and flicked off the radio as he glanced from side to side. A big leather shoulder bag gaping open on the table, something dark and angular inside it – she wouldn't come here unarmed – slatted blinds drawn down across the window onto the backyard –

'It's right here.' Paulette gestured at a mug on the breakfast bar. Mike walked over and pulled a stool out, then sat down awkwardly opposite the ice princess.

'How does it feel to be one of the most wanted people in the world?' he remarked.

469

'Why ask me? Surely you already know.' She kept a straight face, but the chill in her voice made his pulse speed.

'I didn't murder eighteen thousand people.'

'Neither did I,' said Olga. She took a mouthful of coffee, then put her mug down. 'The people who did that are dead, Mr. Fleming. My people took them down. Do you have a *problem* with that?'

Mike opened his mouth, then closed it again.

'They didn't stop at detonating bombs in your capital city,' Olga added. 'They tried to murder everyone who stood in their way. It was a coup attempt.' Her minute nod made his stomach shrink. 'They tried to kill me, and Miriam, and everyone aligned with us. Luckily we had a tip-off. They failed; the last of the plotters was crucified yesterday morning.'

'*Crucified?*' Paulette's expression was rigid.

'Oh yes. After the executioners blinded and castrated them,' Olga added, and bowed her head. 'My father was killed in the struggle, Mr. Fleming. I'd thank you not to place your *eighteen thousand dead* on my shoulders.'

Mike almost asked which faction her father had belonged to; a vestigial sense of shame stilled his tongue for a few seconds. 'I'm sorry to hear that,' he said eventually.

'But crucifixion – ' Paulette stopped.

'It was no better than they deserved. The traditional punishment for such high treason is to spread the wings of the blood eagle, then quarter the parts,' Olga added. 'But that hasn't been practiced since my grandfather's time.'

Mike stared at his mug of coffee, and dry-swallowed. This wasn't what he'd expected to hear. 'You failed to stop them,' he accused, knowing it signified nothing.

'You failed too. So we're even. Failures all round.' The silence stretched on for half a minute. Finally Olga broke it. 'Why did you call for help?'

Mike shuffled on his stool uncomfortably. 'Did you find your mole?'

'We have more urgent problems right now.' It was an evasion.

Olga looked at Paulette. 'Thank you for continuing to source provisions for us; it has been more useful than you can know, but there are some new arrangements I need to discuss with you. Things are going to be busy for a while. Mr. Fleming, there have been reports of contrails over the Gruinmarkt. We don't have much time for idle chatter. Do you know anything about them?'

'They've been planning some kind of incursion for at least six months,' Mike told her. The secret, divulged, left him feeling naked. 'I saw a spec-ops helicopter. That was before the bombs went off. They know where all the oil is, and you're a threat to national security. But since the bombs – now – I don't think they'll be satisfied with their original plans.'

'Do you believe they'll use nuclear weapons?'

'Will they?' It was Mike's turn to frown. 'They already did: that castle up near Concord. The question isn't whether, the question is when and how many.' Stripped of the bloody shirt of *eighteen thousand dead*, these events acquired a logic of their own. 'They'll kill a lot of people who have nothing to do with your extended family.'

'Yes.' Olga emptied her coffee mug. 'And so, we are taking steps to leave, to put ourselves forever beyond contact with the US government. Those of us with any sense, that is. Some refuse to see the writing on the wall, as you would say. The Clan is breaking up, you know; a generation ago the mere suggestion of an open split would have been seen as treason.'

'Where are you going?' asked Paulette.

'You've been there, I seem to recall. On a visit.' Olga raised an eyebrow. 'Excuse me for not describing it in front of Mr. Fleming. When we go – I am allowed to offer you a payoff in money, or asylum if you are afraid of the authorities here: We look after our friends. But it'll be a one-way trip.'

'They'll come after you. They'll hunt you down wherever you run to,' Mike predicted.

'Let them try.' Olga shrugged. 'Mr. Fleming, *I* didn't choose to fight the US government; I'm not Osama bin Laden. Your former president, he – well. We have a rule. When we do business with outsiders, we have a rule: *no politicians*. Mr. Cheney quit politics, in the late

471

eighties: That's when our West Coast subsidiary approached him – well. Water under the bridge. It was a serious oversight, but one we are in the process of rectifying. My question to you is, what are you going to do now? Paulette tells me your agency has tried to kill you. What do *you* want? I can give you money – we've got more than we know what to do with, we can't take it where we're going – or I can offer you asylum – '

'I want the files,' said Mike.

'The. What?'

'Your files on the president.'

'Huh?' Paulette looked confusedly between them.

'Mr. Cheney started this. I wouldn't be here now if I didn't know a deliberate provocation when I saw one. This is all happening because he wants to cover up his past complicity with the Clan, and because the existence of the Clan is now a matter of public record. An awful lot of people are going to die to cover up his secret.' Mike's frustration sought a way out. 'People who have nothing to do with your nasty little family trade, or with me, or with the president. Listen, I don't much care for you. If it was business as usual I'd arrest you *right now* and put you away on racketeering, money laundering, and drugs charges. Oh, and the illegal firearm.' He gestured at Olga's bag and she twitched a hand towards it; he shrugged. 'But it's not business as usual – never will be, ever again. The man who you guys have fallen out with is *running my country*. He's *corrupted my government*, built a secret unaccountable agency with the capability to bypass the national nuclear command authority, disappeared people into underground prisons, instituted torture of state enemies; you name it, he's done it. He's wiped his ass on the Constitution and it's all thanks to dirty drugs money: not directly, oh no, but you're complicit. I don't care *what* happens to you people – but I swore an oath to protect the constitution of the United States, and it looks like for the past year I've been working for an organization designed from the get-go to undermine it. So I want your files on Mr. Cheney, now they're no use to you any more if you're serious about pulling out. I want the dirt. And if you won't give it to me, you're worse than I think you are – and my opinion of you is pretty low right now.'

'What are you going to do with the files if we give them to you?' Olga asked.

'Well, that depends.' He glanced at Paulette. 'I take it your work here is mostly done, or you wouldn't have told me even that much?' He didn't wait for a reply. 'I need someone who knows how the press works. And I need ammunition. Someone's got to blow the lid on him before he eats the US government from inside – and I don't see anyone else volunteering.'

'But – ' Paulette stopped and looked bleakly at Olga.

'What?' Mike glanced between them.

'Do you want to tell him?' asked Olga.

Paulette shook her head wordlessly and reached across to flick on the radio.

' – Cardiac arrest on the way to Bethesda Naval Hospital. Doctors worked for three hours to try to resuscitate the president but he was declared dead at five-fourteen this morning. The vice president is meeting with advisors but is expected to appear at a press conference to make a statement imminently; we understand that Supreme Court Chief Justice Scalia is on his way to the vice president's location to administer the oath – '

'Fuck.' Mike stared at the radio. All his carefully considered plans crumbled. *'Fuck.'*

'That's two presidents in a month,' said Olga. 'I understand it's a stressful job.'

'Jesus fuck.' Paulette looked at Mike reproachfully. 'Sorry,' he muttered.

Olga was imperturbable: 'Do you think your people will care about the misdeeds of KINGPIN's predecessor?'

Mike shook his head. 'Fuck. Sorry.' He stared at the radio. The presenter was babbling on about previous presidential emergency successions. 'He's dead. Why did the bastard have to die *now*?'

'What will this new president do?' Olga leaned toward him.

'KINGPIN? He'll – ' Mike chuckled weakly. 'Oh dear god.'

'Dick Cheney was Mr. Rumsfeld's assistant, wasn't he?' Paulette blinked, her eyes watery. 'Back in the Ford era, or something. They're more like partners, were more like partners, the past couple of years.

Partners in crime – politics, not the Clan. President Rumsfeld is going to be just like President Cheney, only without the personal history.'

Mike nodded. 'You had a handle on Mr. Cheney. Mr. Rumsfeld is the same – only you've lost your handle.'

'Oh.' Olga sat motionless for a few seconds. 'This fact needs to be reported.'

'What are you going to do?' Mike asked.

'I'm going to tell certain people.' Olga flashed him a bright, brittle smile. 'I'm going to see if I can get you those papers – if you still want them. Then those of us with even half an ounce of self-preservation are going to run very fast . . .'

NEVER COMING BACK

The row of big town houses set back behind their high walls and hedges had seen better days. Every other building showed boarded-up windows to the street, the blank-eyed, gape-doored stare of ruination and downfall. Some of them – some very few – had been squatted, but for the most part the Freedom Riders had kept the dusty workless poor out of the houses of the bourgeoisie, for this was not solely a revolution of the working class.

The big steamer huffed and bumped across last winter's potholes, then slowed as Yul wrestled with the wooden steering wheel, swearing at it as he worked the brake handle and tried to lever the beast between stone gateposts. Miriam sat up in the back, trying to see over his shoulders for a first glimpse of the house she'd bought in this city using smuggled Clan bullion, a little over a year ago. 'Is it – ' she swallowed her words as the front of the building came into view.

'It seems intact.' Brilliana, next to her, added, 'Let us examine it, my lady.'

The boarded-up windows were still sealed, the front door barred and padlocked as one of her armsmen held the car's door open for Miriam. 'By your leave, my lady?' Alasdair slid round in his jump seat. 'I should go first.'

Miriam bit back an instinctive irritated response. 'Yes,' she agreed. 'Thank you.' Sir Alasdair unfolded his legs and stood, interposing his not-inconsiderable frame between her and the facade of the building.

'Wait,' Alasdair rumbled without looking round as he moved forward. 'Schraeder, left and rear. Yul, you stay with the car. Brunner, with me . . .' They spread out around the house purposefully, their long coats still closed despite the summer humidity. It looked empty, but appearances could be deceptive and Sir Alasdair was not inclined to take risks with Helge's life: He'd sworn an oath to protect her, and his people took such things seriously.

Miriam stared at the front door as Alasdair approached it, slowing on the steps, then bending close to peer at the door handle. Beside her, Brill shifted on the bench seat, one hand going to the earpiece tucked discreetly under her hat. 'Clear behind,' she said suddenly. 'Schraeder's in.'

I bought that house, Miriam told herself. Right now it looked as unfamiliar as her father – her adoptive father – had looked in the funeral parlor. Houses took as much of their character from the people who filled them as racks of meat on bone took from their animating personality. It had once been her home; but for the miscarriage she might now be looking to raise a child in it. Now it was just a big neglected building, a cumbersomely inanimate corpse –

Alasdair interrupted her morbid stream of consciousness by straightening up. He unlocked the door, opened it slowly, and stepped inside.

'All clear,' said Brill, tapping Miriam on the shoulder. 'Let's go inside.'

The house was much as Miriam had last seen it, only dusty and boarded-up, the furniture looming beneath dust sheets. 'Who organized this?' she asked, pausing at the foot of the stairs.

'I did,' said Brill. 'When Baron Henryk assigned the business operation to Morgan I assumed they'd want you back in charge sooner or later. Morgan didn't like it here, he preferred to spend as much time at home as he could.'

'Right. This way.' Miriam headed upstairs in the dark, a flashlight guiding her feet. Opposite the top of the stairs was the door to the main bedroom. She pushed it open, saw daylight: The upper windows at least were not boarded up. 'I need a hand with this.'

'With what – '

Miriam was already kneeling near the skirting board beside the bed. Stale dust and a faint smell of mouse piss wrinkled her nose. 'In here. Here, hold this.' She passed Brill the loose piece of woodwork. Behind it, the brickwork was visible. 'Pass me your knife . . .' It took a little work, but between them they levered the two half-bricks out of their niche. Then Miriam reached inside and grabbed. 'Got it.'

The black cloth bag was about the size of a boot, but much heavier. Miriam grunted and lifted it onto the bed.

'How much is it?' asked Brilliana.

'I'm surprised it's still here.' Miriam untied the knotted drawstring then thrust her hand inside. 'Yep, it's the real thing.' The gold brick glinted in the afternoon light; she returned it to the bag hastily. 'About six kilos of twenty-three-carat. It was worth a hell of a lot a year ago – God only knows what it's worth right now.' Stuck in a deflationary cycle and a liquidity crash with a revolution on top, gold – with or without seigniorage – was enormously more valuable than it had been when it was merely what the coin of the realm was made of. The national treasury had been stripped bare to pay for the war: That was what had started the crisis.

She straightened up and dusted herself down. 'Job number one for Alasdair is to get someone who knows what they're doing to hide this *properly*. We lucked out once, but sooner or later one of Erasmus's rivals will probably try and shake us down to see where the leverage is coming from. They won't believe the truth, and if they find this here we'll be for the chop. Revolutionary governments hate hoarders; it's a law of nature.'

'I'll see to it, my lady – '

'That's another thing.' Miriam glanced at the windows. 'It's not "my lady" anymore – I mean it. Drop the honorific, and tell everyone else: It's Miriam, or ma'am, but not "my lady".'

Brill's dismay was palpable. 'But you *are* my lady! You are my liege, and I owe you an acknowledgment of that fact! This isn't the United States, this is – '

'This is a continent *in the grip of revolution*.' Miriam walked towards the wardrobe and lifted one corner of its dusty shroud. 'What do you know about revolutionary governments?'

'Not much; we hang rebels, my lady.' Brill lifted back the top of the dust sheet from the bed, wrinkling her nose.

'Well, I've been doing some reading this week. Remember the books?' Miriam had given Brill a list of titles to order from Amazon. 'There's a general pattern. First there's a crisis – usually fiscal, often

ry. The old government is discredited and a coalition of inter-
move in and toss the bums out. Then they start trying to govern
coalition, and it goes to hell quickly because just changing the
government doesn't solve the underlying crisis unless it was a crisis of
legitimacy.' Brill looked perturbed, as Miriam continued: 'This means
that the new government has to try and fix the crisis at its height
while they're at their weakest, under conditions where it's very easy to
replace them. Most post-revolutionary regimes are overthrown by
their own hard-line radicals, the ones with the most blinkered ideological outlook – precisely because they're also the ones most willing
to murder anyone who stands between them and a solution to the
crisis. It happened during the French revolution, the Russian revolution, it happened in Iran . . . that's how revolutions roll.'

She tugged the dust sheet down from the wardrobe and stepped
aside.

'The revolution here was against the autocratic monarchy,
but there's also a fiscal crisis and a war. That's the trifecta – crisis of
currency, conflict, and legitimacy in one go. The aristocracy, such as it
is, gets its legitimacy from the Crown – for centuries, John Frederick
and his family have sold titles as a way of raising revenue – so anyone
with a noble title is going to be automatically suspect to the hard-
liners in the new government. And unless Sir Adam can end the war
with France and fix the economy in, oh, about six months, the hard-
liners are going to get restive.' She turned worried eyes on Brilliana.
'That's why I want everyone to stop using titles of nobility and similar
honorifics *immediately*. If I'm wrong, they'll get over it. But if I'm
right . . .'

'I understand,' Brill said tiredly. 'There's no need to repeat yourself. Miriam. Ma'am.' She peeled back the blankets and sheets that
had stayed on the bed, exposing them to air for the first time in
months. 'What else is going to happen here?'

'I don't know. It depends on whether they successfully tackle the
economy, the war, or the constitutional problems – any or all of
them.' She opened the wardrobe, sniffed. 'I think something died in
here. Where's the flashlight?'

'Here.' Brill waited while Miriam shoved aside the dresses on the

478

rail and shone the beam around the interior of the wardrobe. 'What do you think?'

'I think they'll have to execute the king, and a lot of his supporters, or the French would use him as an excuse to make mischief. And they won't rest with a revolutionary superpower on the other side of the world – Sir Adam Burroughs's Leveler ideology is an existential threat to any absolute monarchy, much like the Soviet Union was to the United States' capitalist system. Which leaves the economy.' Miriam straightened up. 'Lots of radical ministries jockeying for preeminence, a permanent emergency in foreign affairs, a big war effort. Central planning, maybe, lots of nationalization. At the worst, they might degenerate into outright fascism. They're going to have to industrialize properly if they're going to dig their way out of this mess. War spending is always a good way to boost an economy. And land reform, let's not forget the land reform – they'll probably expropriate the big slave plantations in South America, the duchies of the Midwest.'

'My – Miriam, you can't sleep here: The bedding's mildewed.'

'Wha – oh? Damn. There should be spare sheets in the laundry – ' Miriam wound down. 'Oh. No servants.'

'I could hire bodies easily enough, if you think it necessary?'

'No.' Miriam frowned. 'Flashing around cash would be really dangerous right now. Huh. Need to know if the electricity's working . . . listen, let's go see if the office is intact and the power still works. If so, we ought to go look at the factory. Then I can electrograph Erasmus and tell him we're ready to start work whenever he comes up with those passes he was talking about.'

*

In an office near the northern end of Manhattan, with a window overlooking the royal navy dockyard, Stephen Reynolds set aside the stack of death warrants at his left hand and stood, smiling warmly, as commissioners Jennings and Fowler walked in.

'Good morning, citizens.' He gestured at the seats beside his desk as he walked around it, placing himself on the same side of the table as his visitors: 'Nice to see you. Are you both well? Edward, is your wife – '

'She's fine,' Jennings said, a trifle brusquely, then cleared his throat. 'Nothing to worry about, and the would-be assassin is already in custody.' As the citizen inquisitor supervising the Justice Directorate, Jennings (not to mention his family) had become accustomed to being the principal target of the regime's enemies (not to mention their surviving relatives). 'I gather your people have identified his conspirators already.'

'Ah, excellent.' Fowler cleared his throat. 'Time is short, I'm afraid: Got a meeting of the Construction Subcommittee to chair in an hour. You have something that calls for extreme measures?'

'Yes.' Reynolds smiled again, concealing his minor irritation at being so preempted. 'Alas, we have a minor problem. That fine fellow Mr. Burgeson is apparently trespassing on our turf. I've had a tip-off from certain sources' – *not* mentioning Elder Cheung and his magical powers, or his strange associate, the Dutch doctor – 'that Erasmus is, not to put too fine a point on it, dealing with *persons of interest.* There's some question as to what he is doing; I haven't been able to get an informer into his organization. But the secrecy with which he is conducting his affairs is suggestive. Certainly it's not any activity that falls within the portfolio of the commissioner for state truth. I believe he is in league with wreckers and subversives, and I would appreciate the cooperation of your departments in, ah, distinguishing the sheep from the goats.'

Jennings tilted his head on one side thoughtfully. 'I'm sure we can work together on this matter – *if* Citizen Burgeson is acting against the best interests of the people.' A caveat from Justice was to be expected.

Reynolds nodded. It didn't signify opposition as such, merely that Jennings knew exactly what was going on and had no intention of being strung up as a scapegoat for Reynolds's move against the rival directorate. 'Of course,' he said unctuously. 'There must be proceedings with all due process to confirm or disprove guilt, absolutely! But I think it would be best if they were handled in the Star Court with all available precision, and discretion' – in other words, secretly and hastily – 'and the prisoners segregated. If there's actual subversion within the party's highest echelons, we will need to obtain absolute proof before we arrest a party commissioner. And if not – again, it would be best if it were handled quietly. The scope for embarrassment is enormous and it would reflect badly on the party as an institution.'

'It can be done, but it'll cost you,' Fowler said bluntly. 'There's a new interrogation and processing block scheduled for development on Long Island. Or I could get you a prison hulk.'

'A prison hulk?' Reynolds's eyes lit up: 'Capital! That would be just the ticket!' After the initial shock, he'd paid close attention to Cheung's sales pitch – and spent time in subsequent meetings attempting to deduce the limitations of the world-walkers' abilities. A steam yacht with decent owner's quarters and a train with sleeping car were already on his department's budget – officially to make it easier for the commissioner for internal security to travel safely between offices, unofficially to ensure his safety against world-walking killers. 'Do you have anything offshore near the Massachusetts coastline? Preferably with an anti-mutiny plug?' (Explosive scuttling charges had proven a most effective tool in preventing prison mutinies under the *ancien régime*.)

'I think something along those lines can be provided.' Fowler pulled out a notebook. 'How many berths do you need, and when and where will the arrests take place?'

'Number: unknown, but not more than a thousand at the absolute maximum. More likely under a hundred in the first instance, then a flow of stragglers for processing. Somewhere within a couple of hours of Boston. To be moored in deep water – not less than thirty feet beneath the keel – and not less than a mile offshore. If you could set it up within the next two days I would be eternally grateful . . . ?'

'I'll see what we can do.' Fowler put his notebook away. 'I take it the detainees are, er, disposable?'

'If necessary.' Reynolds nodded.

'I didn't hear that,' Jennings said fastidiously.

'Of course not.'

'Jolly good, then.' Jennings stood. 'I'll see that a circuit tribunal under Star Rules is at your men's disposal in Boston two days hence. Now if you don't mind, I have a dreadful pile of paperwork to catch up on . . .' He sighed. 'These wreckers and subversives! I swear we're going to run out of rope before they're all hanged.'

*

The fortified great house had seen better days: Its walls were fire-scorched, half the downstairs windows were bricked up, the hastily applied mortar was still weeping salts across the stone blocks of its facade, and the stable doors had been crudely removed. But it was still inhabitable – which counted for something – and the ten-meter radio mast sprouting from the roofline made it clear who its inhabitants must be.

'You wanted to see me, sir.'

The office on the second floor had once been a squire's wife's boudoir; it still smelled faintly of rosewater and gunpowder. The bed had been broken up for firewood and scrap, used to reinforce the shutters during the brief siege, and today the room was dominated by a green folding aluminum map table.

'Yes. Come in, sit down, make yourself comfortable. I've got Pepsi if you need a drink.'

'That would be wonderful, sir.'

Rudi sat tensely on the narrow edge of the camp chair while Earl-Major Riordan poured him a mug of foaming brown soda with his own hands. The lack of a batman did not escape his notice, but if Riordan wanted to preserve the social niceties . . . *It must be bad news,* he decided, a hollowness below his ribs waiting to be filled by the exotic imported beverage.

'I want to pick your brains about aircraft,' Riordan said stiffly. 'Think of this as an informal brainstorming session. Nothing we discuss is for ears beyond this room, by the way.'

Really? Rudi leaned forward. 'Brainstorming, sir?'

Riordan sighed. 'Her Majesty' – he paused, and poked at a paper on his desk – 'has written me a letter, and you're the man to answer it.' He looked slightly pained, as if his lunch had disagreed with his digestion.

'Sir.'

'You know about the *British*.' They spoke Hochsprache. 'She is

482

talking to them. She wants an aircraft. Something that can be built for them within two years and that outstrips anything they can imagine. Something for war.'

'To be built *there*?' Rudi shook his head. 'I thought they were stuck in the steam age?'

'They have aircraft. Two wings, spaced above each other like so' – Riordan gestured – 'slow, lumbering things. Made of wood and sail-cloth.'

'Really?' Rudi perked up. 'And Her Majesty wants to build something better? What for?'

'They've got a war on.' Riordan finally sat down in the chair opposite, and Rudi relaxed slightly. 'The French are blockading them, there is a threat of bombardment from aerial tenders offshore. I told her to give the *British* something for their navy, one of those submarines – you've seen *Das Boot*, No? – but she says ships take too long. They understand not to expect too much of aircraft, so build something revolutionary.' He took a deep breath. 'Give me an eagle's view. What should I be asking?'

'Huh.' Rudi rubbed his chin. It was itching; he hadn't had a chance to shave for three days, scurrying hither and yon trying to arrange bodies to haul across the ultralight parts he'd been buying. 'What engines do they have? That's going to limit us. And metallurgy. Electronics . . . I assume they've got vacuum tubes? It'll have to be something from the late nineteen-thirties or early forties. A warbird. Two engines for range, if it's going offshore, and it needs to be able to carry bombs or guns.' He paused. 'You know a plane on its own isn't going to do much? It needs tactical doctrine, pilot training, navigation tools and radar if they can build it, ideally an integrated air defense – '

Riordan waved an impatient hand. 'Yes, that's not the point. We need what Her Majesty calls a *technology demonstrator*.'

'Can they do aluminum engine blocks?' Rudi answered his own question: 'Maybe not, but aluminum goes back to the nineteenth century – we can work on them. Hmm. Engines will be a bottleneck, but . . . P-38? No, it's a pure fighter. Hard to fly, too. If they're still doing wood – ' He stopped.

'Wood?' Riordan frowned.

'We'd need to work out how to produce the engines, and we'd need modern epoxy glues instead of the shit they had back then, but. But.' Rudi shook his head. 'I think I know what you want,' he said.

'Do you?'

'The de Havilland Mosquito. The British built tons of them during the war, kept them flying until the nineteen-sixties – it was originally a fast two-seat bomber, but they hung guns on it and used it as a fighter too. Made out of plywood, with two Merlin engines – they were a nineteen-thirties design, so the metallurgy might be up to it. Long range, fast; if they're still using biplanes it'll run rings around anything they've ever imagined. If the metallurgy is better and quality control is up to it, I'd go for the P-51D, the Mustang. Faster, single-engined, similar range, more maneuverable. But for a first cut, I'd go for something made of wood with two engines. Safer that way.'

Riordan nodded. 'Could you build one?'

'Could.' Rudi carefully placed his half-full mug on the map table. He tried not to exhale Pepsi. '*Build* one?'

'For the British.' Riordan wasn't smiling. 'With *unlimited* resources, but a knife over your head.'

'Urk.' Rudi thought for a while. 'Maybe. But I'd hedge my bets.'

'How?'

'I'd start by talking to their existing aircraft designers. And bring the biggest damn library of metallurgy, electronics, materials, and aerodynamics textbooks I can find. The designs for those nineteen-forties warbirds – you can buy them on eBay for a couple of hundred dollars – CD-ROMs with just about everything on them, technical manuals, patents, blueprints, everything. But you'll probably take longer to build an exact replica of one from the blueprints than it would take a clued-up manufacturer on a war footing to invent a new one and build it from scratch. Much better to grab all the textbooks and histories, copies of *Jane's Aircraft*, manuals, ephemera – *everything* – and drop them in front of a team who're already used to working together. Hell, give them a history of air warfare and blueprints of the aircraft and they'll have a field day.'

'Huh.' Riordan's frown deepened. 'That may not be possible.'

'Oh.' Rudi deflated. 'That would make it a lot harder. If we can only use Clan members, it's nearly impossible. There aren't even a dozen of us who know an aileron from a slotted flap. But we could do the liaison thing, act as librarians, figure out what a design team needs to know and get it for them. Hell. We could go recruiting, you know? Look for aerospace engineers in trouble with the law, offer them a bolt-hole and a salary and a blind eye if they'll work for us.'

'Not practical. That last idea, I mean. But the liaison idea, hmm. Can you get me a list of names?'

'Certainly, sir. When do you need it by?' *But what about the ultralights?* he wondered.

'You have two hours. Here's a pad and a pen; Comms and Crypto are downstairs on the left if you need to ask any questions. You have my seal.' Riordan tossed a heavily embossed metal ring on the table in front of Rudi. Rudi flinched, as if from a poisonous mushroom. 'I'll be back at five and I need to send the answer to Her Majesty by six. Your task is to identify those of our people who you will need in order to help the British develop their aerospace sector. Oh, and remember to include runway construction, fuel and repair equipment and facilities, munitions, bombsights, gunsights, training, and anything else I've forgotten. That's a higher priority than your ultralight squadron, I'm afraid, but it's a much bigger job: You have an air force to build. The Pepsi's all yours.'

*

Late afternoon on a golden summer day: On a low ridge overlooking a gently sloping vale, a party of riders – exclusively male, of gentle breeding, discreetly armed but not under arms – paused for refreshment. To the peasants bent sweating over sickle and sheaf, they would be little more than dots on the horizon, as distant as the soaring eagle high above, and of as little immediate consequence.

'I fear this isn't a promising site,' said one of the onlookers, a hatchet-faced man in early middle age. 'Insufficient cover – see the brook yonder? And the path over to the house, around that outcrop? – we'd stick out like pilliwinksed fingers.'

'Bad location for helicopters, though,' said a younger man. 'See, the slope of the field: makes it hard for them to land. And for road access, I think we can add some suitable obstacles. Caltrops, pits. If the major is right and they can bring vehicles across, they won't have an easy time of it.'

Earl Bentbranch hung back, at the rear of the party. He glanced at his neighbor, Stefan ven Arnesen. Ven Arnesen twined his fingers deep in his salt-and-pepper beard, a distant look on his face. He noticed Bentbranch watching and nodded slightly.

'Do you credit it?' Bentbranch murmured.

Ven Arnesen thought for a moment. 'No,' he said softly, 'no, I don't.' He looked at the harvesters toiling in the strip fields below. It didn't *look* like the end of the world as he knew it. 'I can't.'

'They may not come for a generation. If ever. To throw everything away out of panic . . .'

Ven Arnesen spared his neighbor a long, appraising look. 'They'll come. Look, the harvest comes. And with it the poppies. Their war dead – their families used to wear poppies to remember them, did you know that?'

'You had your tenants plant dream poppies in the divisions.'

'Yes. If the bastards come for us, it's the least I can do. Give it away' – he looked out across his lands, as far as the eye could see – 'for free.' He coughed quietly. 'I'm too old to uproot myself and move on, my friend. Let the youngsters take to the road, walk the vale of tears as indigent tinkers just like our great-great-grandfathers' grand-sires once more. These are my lands and my people and I'll not be moving. All this talk of *business models* and *refugees* can't accommo-date what runs in my veins.'

'So you'll resist?'

Ven Arnesen nodded tiredly. 'Of course. And you haven't made your mind up yet.'

'I'm . . . wavering. I went to school over there, do you remember? I speak Anglische, I *could* up sticks and go to this new world they're talking of, I'd be no more or less of a stranger there than I was for seven years in Baltimore. But I could dig my own midden, too, or run to Sky Father's priests out of mindless panic. I could do any number of stupid or distasteful things, were I so inclined, but I don't generally do such things without good reason. I'd need a *very* good reason to abandon home and hearth and accept poverty and exile for life.'

'The size of the reason one needs becomes greater the older one gets,' ven Arnesen agreed. 'But I'm not convinced by this nonsense about resisting the American army, either. I've seen their films. I've spent a little time there. Overt resistance will be difficult. Whatever Ostlake and his cronies think.'

'I don't think they believe anything else, to tell you the truth. If – when – they come, the Americans will outgun us as heavily as we outgunned the Pervert's men. And there will be thousands of them, tens of thousands. With tanks and helicopters. Sure, we'll kill a few of them. And that will make it worse, it'll make them even angrier. They're not good at dealing with locals, not good at native tongues. They'll kill and they'll burn and they'll raise every man's hand against them and their occupation, and it will still take a bloody five years of pain and tears and death before they'll even think about changing their approach. By which time – '

'Look.' Ven Arnesen raised his arm and pointed.

'Where?'

'Look *up*.' A ruler-straight white line was inching across the turquoise vault of the sky, etching it like a jeweler's diamond on glass. A tiny speck crawled through the air, just ahead of the moving tip of the line. 'Is that what, what I think it is?'

'A contrail.' Bentbranch's cheeks paled. 'It's them.'

'Are you sure? Could it be something else? Something natural – '

'No. Their jets make those cloud-trails, when they move through the sky.'

'And they look down on us from above? Do you suppose they can see us now? Lightning Child strike them blind.'

'I very much fear that they're anything but blind.' Bentbranch looked away as the aircraft's course led it westwards, towards the sunset. 'Though how much detail they can see from up there . . . well, that tears it, of course. They will be drawing up maps, my lord. And they care naught that we know their mind. I find that a singularly ominous sign. Do you differ, can I ask?'

'No.' Ven Arnesen shook his head as he stared after the aircraft.

'No.' But Bentbranch was unable to discern whether he was answering the question or railing against the sign in the heavens.

Ahead of them, the main group of riders, Lord Ostlake and his men, had noticed the contrail; arms were pointing and there were raised voices. 'We should warn them,' Bentbranch said, nudging his horse forward. Ven Arnesen paid him no attention, but stared at the sky with nerve-struck eyes.

Out over the ocean in the east, the contrail was already falling apart, like the dreams of future tranquility that it had so carelessly scrawled across.

It would not take many more thirty-thousand-foot overflights to update the air force's terrain maps.

*

The old woman had been reading a book, and it still lay open on her lap, but her attention was elsewhere. There was a discreet knock at the door. She looked up as it opened, and adjusted her spectacles, unsurprised at the identity of her visitor. 'Yes?'

'Your grace.' The door closed behind him. 'I hope I'm not interrupting anything?'

'No, no . . .' She slid a bookmark into place, then carefully closed the book and placed it on the table beside her. 'I've got plenty of time. All the time in the world.'

'Ah, yes. Well, I'd like to apologize for leaving you to your own devices for so long. I trust you have been well-attended?'

'Young man, you know as well as I do that when one is in a jail cell, however well furnished, it does little good to grumble at the jailer.'

'It might, if you harbor some hope of release. And might reasonably expect to be in a position of authority over your captor, by and by.' He waited.

She stared at him grimly. 'Release?' She raised her right hand. It shook, visibly. She let it fall atop the book. 'Release from what?' The palsy was worse than it had been for some time. 'What do you think I have to look forward to, even if you give me the freedom of the city outside these walls? Without imported medicines my quality of life

488

will be poor. I can't use that liberty you hint at.' She gestured at the wheelchair she sat in. 'This is more of a jail than any dungeon you can put me in, Riordan.'

Rather than answering, the earl crossed the stone-flagged floor of the day room and, picking up the heavy armchair from beside the small dining table, turned it to face her. Then he sat, crossing one leg over the other, and waited.

After a while she sighed. 'Credit me with being old enough to be a realist.' She paused. 'I'm not going to see the right side of sixty again, and I've got multiple sclerosis. It's gaining on me. I'd like to go back home to Cambridge, where I hear they've got stuff like hot and cold running water and decent health care, but thanks to my dear departed mother and her fuckwitted reactionary conspirators that's not a terribly practical ambition, is it? I'm too old, too ill, and too tired to cast off and start up anew in another world, Riordan. I did it once, in my youth, but it was a terrible strain even with Angbard's connivance. Besides, you need me here in this gilded cage. Rule of law, and all that.'

'The rule of law.' Riordan leaned forward. 'You've never been much for that, have you?'

Patricia's face flickered in something that might have been the ghost of a smile. 'I've never been much of one for bending the neck to authority.' She shook her head. 'If I had been born to a lower estate I'd have been lucky to have made it to adulthood. As it is, the lack of highborn bloodlines taking precedence over mine – well. Easier to be rebellious when you're the daughter of a duke, not a slave. What did you want to talk to me about?'

Her attempt to wrong-foot Riordan failed. 'To ask you what I should do with you, your grace.'

'Well, that's an *interesting* question, isn't it? I suppose it depends what you want to achieve.'

'I want to keep our people alive.' He crossed his arms. 'What do *you* want?'

'Huh.' Her smile slipped away. 'It's come to that?'

'You know it has. I'm not going to charge you with petty treason, your grace; the only evidence against you is your own word, and

489

besides, the victim had abducted you and was a conspirator at *high* treason. To hold her poisoning against you would be ungrateful, not to mention sending entirely the wrong message. But there is a question to which I would like some answers.'

'My brother?'

Riordan shook his head. 'I know you didn't kill him. But Dr. ven Hjalmar is missing. And so is a certain set of medical records.'

'A set of – ' Patricia stopped dead. 'What do you know about them?'

'I've been reading Angbard's files.' Riordan's tone was quiet but implacable. 'I know about the fertility clinics and the substituted donor sperm. Five thousand unwitting outer-family members growing up in the United States. The plan to approach some of them and pay them to bear further children. I'm not stupid, Patricia. I know what that plan would mean to the old ladies and their matchmaking and braid alliances. The files are missing, your grace. Do you happen to know where they are?'

She shook her head. 'Not exactly, no.'

'And inexactly?'

'I don't think I should answer that question. For your own good.'

Riordan made a fist of his left hand and laid it quietly down on the table beside him. '*Why?*'

'It's an insurance policy, kid. *I* don't know exactly where the records are any more, only where they're going to surface. Griben ven Hjalmar – if you see him, shoot him on sight, I beg you. He may have made off with a copy of the breeding program records too.'

'Why?' repeated the earl. 'I think you owe me at least an explanation.'

'Our numbers are low. If they dip lower, the trade – our old trade – may no longer be viable. But at the same time, Angbard's plan was destabilizing in the extreme. If Clan Security suddenly acquired an influx of tractable, trained world-walkers with no loyalty to family or braid – it would overbalance the old order, would it not? We agree that much, yes?'

Riordan nodded reluctantly. 'So?'

'So Hildegarde tried to smash the program, at least by seizing the

490

infants and having them adopted by conservative families. Griben was her cat's-paw. It was a power play and countermove, nothing more. But her solution would give us other problems. There is a reason why we are six high families and their clients, why each group numbers less than three hundred. An extended family – a clan, not *our* great collective Clan, but a normal grouping – is of that order, you know? Anthropologists have theories to explain why humans form groups of that size. Tribes, clans. Dunbar's number defines the largest number of personal relationships a human being can easily keep track of, and it's somewhere between 150 and 300. We knit our six tribes together into one bigger group, to permit the braiding of a recessive genetic trait without excessive inbreeding. But if you triple our numbers – well, there was a reason we were susceptible to civil war eighty years ago. If a tribe grows too large it splinters along factional lines.'

'But you're – ' Riordan stopped. 'Oh.'

Patricia nodded. 'Yes. If Hildegarde's idea – bring the newborn world-walkers into the Clan's client families and raise them among us – had worked, we'd have grown much too fast to maintain control. It would have set us up for another damaging civil war.'

'Have you destroyed the records, then?'

She shook her head. 'No need. We may even need them later. I leave that to the Council's future deliberations; but in the meantime, I took steps to ensure that nobody would use them to breed an army of world-walkers. It has to be done openly, with the consent of the entire Clan, or not at all. And if it happens, we won't be able to operate as a family business any more: We'll need a system of governance that scales up to manage larger numbers.'

'I can live with that – if you can guarantee it.'

'The problem is ven Hjalmar.' She turned her face to the window. A beam of sunlight splashed through it, lengthening across the floor. 'The sleazy little tapeworm's stolen a set of the records. And now he's gone missing. *You* know that Helge will hang him as soon as look at him. Put yourself in his shoes – where would you go?'

Riordan stared at her. 'You think he'd defect to . . . who? The Lees?'

'I wouldn't bet against it. He might be lying low in America, but what's he going to do? He can't fake up a good enough identity to practice as an ob/gyn – the full academic and employment track record would be a *lot* harder than a regular cover – so he can't simply jump the wall and hide there, not unless he's willing to take a big cut in his standard of living. So he needs sponsorship. The breeding program is . . . well, it'd be more useful to the Lees than it is to us: They're not far from extinction, did you know that? They've got less than a hundred world-walkers. He might have gone to the US government a couple of weeks ago, but he can't do that now: They wouldn't need him once they get their hands on the breeding program records and they're in no mood to be accommodating. That leaves the Lee family, or maybe the authorities in New Britain, but the latter won't have a clue what he's offering them without a working demonstration.'

'God-on-a-stick.' Riordan ran one hand through his thin hair. 'I'll point Olga after him. One more damn thing to worry about.'

'I have a question.' Patricia waited.

'Yes?'

'My daughter's *interest* in Roland last year.' She licked suddenly dry lips. 'And Olga was betrothed to him. And that nasty business Helge told me about, in the old orangery. Which was that to do with – Mr. Cheney or the breeding program?'

'Cheney – ' For a moment Riordan looked confused. He shook his head. 'Let me think. There was something about it in the files. The old man knew there was a leak; Olga was investigating. I think he may have set her on him – she was still under cover so she could run the fresh-faced ingénue pumping her fiancé – to see if he was the leak. *Someone* on the inside was still colluding with the vice president after we officially cut him off, and Roland was considered unreliable. But you may be right. Economics was his big thing, wasn't it? If he was talking to ven Hjalmar . . .' He trailed off.

'A tame army of world-walkers,' Patricia said tartly. 'If Roland had been planning to defect, and if he could get his hands on the breeding-program records and take them to the Family Trade Organization, he could have named his own price, couldn't he? Was that why he had to die?'

Riordan gave her a flat stare. 'You might think that, but I couldn't possibly comment.'

Patricia met his gaze. After several long seconds she nodded, very slightly. 'In any case, there are other plausible explanations. My mother, for example. There's no way she would have allowed her granddaughter to marry a mere *earl*. Not with a pliable prince on offer, and her own elder sister – the queen-mother – happy to match-make for her grandson.'

'That is true.' Riordan inclined his head. Then he took a deep breath. 'I find the weight of your half-brother's secrets inordinately onerous, my lady. I wish I could confide fully in you; it's only those matters concerning your bloodline which give me cause for hesitation. I hope you can forgive me – but can you put yourself in my place?'

Patricia nodded again. 'I beg your forgiveness. I don't believe even for a moment that you might have arranged the liquidation of your elder brother Roland, not even on the duke's orders. I don't think Angbard would have given such a – but we live in paranoid times, do we not? And we *know* Dr. ven Hjalmar is a lying sack of shit who liked to incriminate other people.'

'Indeed. Did I mention it was his signature on your brother's death certificate?'

'Was it really?' Patricia breathed.

'Yes. Really.' Riordan cleared his throat. 'Just so you understand what – who – we're dealing with here. I gather Helge has given her retainers certain orders in his regard. I'm inclined to declare him outlaw before Clan Security. If you, and the committee, concur?'

Patricia nodded emphatically. 'Oh, yes.'

They sat in contemplative silence for a minute.

'Are you sure I can't convince you to go to New Britain?' asked Riordan. 'Your daughter could use your support.'

'She's a grown woman who can make her own mistakes,' Patricia said sharply. 'And I'll thank you for not telling her what I had to do to give her that freedom.' Softly: 'I think it better for the older generation to retire, you know. Rather than fighting, kicking and screaming, against the bitter end.'

'I'm certain they could take care of you, over there,' the earl pointed out. 'If you stay behind when the Americans come . . .'

'I'll die.' She sniffed. 'I've been there, to the other world, Frederick. It's backward and dangerous. With my condition it's just a matter of time. Did I tell you, my mother was dying? She thought she had a year to live. Didn't occur to her to ask how *I* was doing, oh no. If it had, and if she'd won, she might have outlived me, you know.'

'You're not that ill, are you?'

'Not yet. But without my medication I will be. And when the Americans come, it won't matter whether I'm hale and hearty or on my deathbed. If I evacuate, those medicines I need to sustain me will run out by and by. And if I stay . . .' She fixed him with a gimlet stare. 'I hope you're going to evacuate yourself before the end. My daughter doesn't need old dead wood like me clogging up her household and draining her resources; but a young, energetic lord of security is another matter.'

Riordan stared back at her. 'This land is my land. And enough of my people are staying that I'd be derelict if I abandoned them.'

'My mother said something like that. My mother was also a damned fool.' Patricia took a deep breath. 'She shot a man-eating tiger in the tip of its tail, where the wound is calculated to cause maximum pain and outrage, but to do no lasting harm. Do you really expect the tiger not to bite?'

'Oh, it's going to bite all right.' Riordan looked as resigned as a condemned man on his way to the scaffold. 'You are correct, your grace. And I am encouraging every man and woman I meet to make their way to the evacuation points. But it's an uphill battle, and many of our less well-traveled cousins are skeptical. If I go, my powers of persuasion are vastly reduced. So, like the captain of a sinking ship, my station is on the bridge until all are saved.'

'Exactly.' Patricia folded her hands. 'But I'm not going anywhere, even if you throw wide the doors to this gilded cell. So why not let me help?'

*

On the other side of the sprawling metropolis, a steamer drove slowly along a road lined with big houses, set back behind the wire-topped fences and overgrown hedges of a mostly absent bourgeoisie. Those with royalist connections or a history with the Polis or sympathies with the Patriot Party had mostly decided that they had pressing business out of town, far from urban militias who might recognize them and Leveler Party commissioners who might think the city better off without their ilk.

Sitting in the back of the steamer, James Lee stared pensively at the padlocked gates from behind smoked glass pince-nez spectacles. There, but for the lubrication of certain palms and the careful maintenance of appearances, were his own family's estates; in time of civil war, nobody suffered quite like foreign merchants, despised for their race and resented for their imagined wealth. Only the Lee family's dedication to concealing their true nature had kept them from attracting the mob's attention so far. 'This next,' he called ahead to the chauffeur and his companion, a heavyset fellow with a nose that had been broken so many times that it was almost flat. 'She's at home.' There was a trickle of smoke from one chimney pot, no doubt a flue venting from the kitchen range.

The thick hedge fronting the Beckstein estate was unkempt and as bushy as its neighbors, but the gate wasn't chained shut – and the hut beside it showed signs of recent use. As the car hissed to a halt in the roadway, the hut's door opened and a fellow stepped out, making no attempt to conceal his breech-loading blunderbuss.

'Ahoy, the house,' called the chauffeur.

The gatekeeper stayed well clear of the car. 'Who calls?' he demanded.

James leaned forward to rap the head of his cane once on the back of the driver's partition, then opened the car door and stepped out. 'James Lee,' he said easily in Hochsprache. The gatekeeper jumped. 'I have come to visit my cousin, Helge of Thorold-Hjorth.'

'Wait, if it pleases you.' The gatekeeper raised his left hand and held something to his mouth, muttering. Then he shook his head, as if hearing an answer. His face froze. 'Please wait . . . My lord, I am told that you are welcome here. But your men will please leave their arms in the vehicle.' Two more men appeared, hurrying along the driveway from the direction of the house. 'If that is acceptable . . . ?'

James nodded. 'Take the car where he directs you and wait with it,' he told his chauffeur.

'Are you sure?' the bodyguard asked edgily.

'We're safer here than we were on the way,' James pointed out. Which was true: Three men who would be taken as foreigners driving an expensive motor through a British city in time of revolution would not have been safe if they had been stopped. 'They won't lay a finger on us, Chang. They don't know what we are capable of. And besides, I am an honored guest.' He closed the car door and walked towards the gate as it swung open.

The house Miriam had purchased for her first foray into the business world in New Britain was large enough to conceal a myriad of sins, and James Lee was not surprised when the suspiciously un-obsequious butler who met him at the front door rushed him into a parlor off to one side. 'If you'd wait here, sir, her – my lady sends her apologies, and she will see you shortly.' He began to move towards the door, then paused. 'Can I fetch you anything? Tea, coffee, whisky?'

'I am perfectly all right,' James said blandly. The not-butler frowned, then bowed briskly and hurried out of the room. He was clearly unused to playing this role; his stockings were creased and his periwig lamentably disordered. James sat in the solitary armchair, glancing round curiously. Aside from the presence of the armchair and a small box attached to the wall close to one ceiling corner, there was nothing particularly unusual about the room – for a butler's pantry. *Someone is not used to entertaining,* he decided. *Now, what does that signify?*

As it happened, he didn't have long to wait. Barely ten minutes later, the not-butler threw the door open in a rush. 'They're ready for you now,' he explained. 'In the morning room. If you'll follow me, sir.'

'Certainly.' James stood and followed the fellow along a gloomy passage, then out into a wood-paneled hall and through a doorway into a day-lit room dominated by a large mahogany table set out with nearly a dozen seats. *Dining table or conference table?* He nodded politely at the occupants, reserving a small smile for their leader. 'Good morning, Your Majesty – your grace – however I should address you? I must say, I'm glad to see you looking so well.' *Well* was questionable; she looked as if she had recently been seriously unwell, and was not yet back to full health.

She nodded. 'Thank you, my lord baron. Uh – we are trying to make a practice of avoiding titles here; the neighbors are less than understanding. You may call me Miriam and I shall call you James, or Mr. Lee, whichever you prefer. Unless you insist on formalities?'

'As you wish.' The not-butler stepped forward, drawing out a chair for him. 'Perhaps you could introduce your companions? I don't believe we've all met.'

'Sure. Have a seat – everybody? Brilliana I think you've met. This is Sir – uh, Alasdair, my – '

'Chief of security,' the not-butler rumbled mildly. He, too, sat down. 'Your men are being taken care of with all due hospitality,' he added.

'Thank you.' *Message received.* James nodded and concentrated on remembering names as Miriam – the former Duchess Helge – introduced another five members of the six traitor brothers' families – *Stop that,* he reminded himself. It was a bad habit, born of a hundred and fifty and more years of tradition built on the unfortunate belief that his ancestor had been abandoned to his fate by his wicked siblings. A belief which might or might not be true, but which was singularly unhelpful in the current day and age . . .

'I assume you're here because of my letter,' Miriam finished after the naming of names. Then she simply sat back, watching him expectantly.

'Ah – yes.' *Damn.* He hadn't expected quite such an abrupt interrogation. He smiled experimentally. 'My father was most intrigued by it – especially by what it left unsaid. What is this threat you referred to?'

Miriam took a deep breath. 'I don't want to mince words. The Clan fucked up.'

Brilliana – Miriam's chief of staff, as far as he could tell – glanced at her liege. 'Should you be telling – '

Miriam shook her head. 'Leave this to me, Brill.' She looked back at James Lee, her shoulders slumping slightly. 'You know about our internal factional splits.' He nodded cautiously. The blame game

497

might be easy enough to play at this point; gods knew, his parents and grandparents had done their best to aggravate those disputes in decades past. 'But you don't know much about the Clan's trade in the United States.'

He cocked his head attentively. 'No. Not having been there, I couldn't say.'

More euphemisms; the Lee family knotwork enabled them to travel between the worlds of the Gruinmarkt and New Britain, while the Clan's knot had provided them with access to the semi-mythical United States.

'The US government discovered the Clan,' Miriam said carefully. 'The Clan has earned its power over there through criminal enterprise – smuggling. The US government sent them a message by means of an, a, a super-weapon. The conservatives decided to send a message right back using stolen weapons of the same class – and at the same time to decapitate the Clan security apparatus and council. Their coup failed, but they *really* got the attention of the US authorities. Like climbing over the railings at a zoo and stamping on the tail of a sleeping tiger.'

James tried not to wince. 'But what can they do?'

'Quite a lot.' Miriam frowned and glanced at the skinny young fellow called Huw. 'Huw? Tell him about the project my uncle gave you.'

Huw fidgeted with his oddly styled spectacles. 'I was detailed to test other knotwork designs and to systematically explore the possibility of other worlds.' He rested a hand on a strange device molded out of resin that lay on the table before him. 'I can show you – '

'No,' Miriam interrupted. 'Just the summary.'

'*Okay*. We found and visited three other worlds before the coup attempt – and identified fifteen different candidate knots that look promising. One of the worlds was accessible using your, the Lee family, knotwork from the United States. We found ruins, but very high-tech ruins. Still slightly *radioactive*.' James squinted a little at the unfamiliar jargon. 'The others were all stranger. Upshot: The three worlds we know of are only the tip of an iceberg.'

'Let me put Huw's high technology in perspective.' Miriam's smile tightened with a moue of distaste: 'He means high tech in comparison to the United States. Which is about as far ahead of New Britain as New Britain is ahead of the Gruinmarkt. There is strange stuff out there, and no mistake.'

'Perhaps, but of what use is it?' James shrugged, trying to feign disinterest.

'Well, perhaps the fact that the United States government has threatened us, and appears to have the ability to build machines that can move between worlds, will be of interest to you?' Miriam looked at him expectantly.

'Not really. They can't find us here, after all.' James crossed his arms. 'Unless you've told them where to look . . . ?'

'*We* haven't – we wouldn't know who to talk to, or how.'

James froze in response to her flat stare.

'Why are you *here*?' Alasdair asked pointedly.

Miriam held up a warning hand. 'Stop,' she told him. Looking back at James: 'Let me see. This *might* just be a social visit. But on balance, no, I don't think so. You're here to deliver a message.'

James nodded.

'From your elders – ' Miriam stopped, registering his expression. 'Oh shit. You're *not* here on your uncle's behalf?'

'You are not the only people with a problem,' James confessed ruefully. 'I am afraid my elders have made an error of judgment, one that is in nobody's best interests – not ours, nor yours.'

'An error – '

'Shut up, Huw.' This from Brilliana. 'What have they done, and what do you think we can do about it?'

'These are dangerous, turbulent times.' James stopped, hunting for the least damaging way of framing his confession. *These are dangerous, turbulent people*, he reminded himself. *Who were until a year ago enemies of our blood.* 'They sought a patron,' he confessed.

'A patr – ' Miriam stared at him. 'Crap. You mean, they've gone public?'

'Yes.' *Wait and see.* James crossed his arms.

'How public?' asked Miriam. 'What have they done?'

'It started nearly a month ago.' James met her eyes. 'When they

499

learned of the upheaval in the Eastern states, the elders became alarmed. Add your cousins' manifest difficulties with their own strange world, the America, and there was . . . cause for concern. My uncle sought advice on the wisdom of maintaining the rule of secrecy. His idea was that we should seek out a high-ranking minister within the provisional government, provide them with discreet services – ideally to the point of incrimination, to compel their cooperation later – and use their office to secure our safety. Does this sound familiar?'

They were all nodding. 'Very,' said Miriam. 'We made the same mistake.' She glanced sidelong at Brill. 'Getting involved in local politics. Hmm.'

'Don't blame *me*,' Brill said with some asperity.

'I'm not. But if the Council hadn't wanted to place a world-walker on the throne, or to do business with local politicians in Wyoming, we wouldn't be in this fix now.'

Fascinating, thought James. There was familial loyalty on display here, and also a strangely familiar bitterness. He cleared his throat. 'Then a defector from your own ranks showed up.'

'Who?'

'A doctor – ' He stopped. They were staring at him. ' – I believe you know him. Ven Hjalmar, he's called.' *Their faces* – cold sweat sprang out in the small of his back. 'Why? Is something wrong?'

'Please continue.'

'But you – '

'It's a personal matter.' Miriam made a cutting gesture. James took in the other signs: Sir Alasdair, Lady Brilliana – sudden focus, as attentive as hounds at the trail of a fox. 'What happened?'

Suddenly lots of things slid into place. 'You have reason to hate him?' *Good.* 'He has convinced my uncle that it is necessary to conspire with a political patron, and to sell him a, a *breeding program* he says your families established in America. Preposterous nonsense, but . . .' He trailed off. Miriam's expression was deathly.

'He did, did he?'

'Yes – ' James took a deep breath. 'It's true? He's telling the truth? There *is* a breeding program? The American doctors can breed world-walkers the way a farmer breeds sheep?'

'Not *exactly* like that, but close enough.' Miriam made eye contact with Alasdair. 'We're in so much shit,' she said quietly. She looked back to James: 'Which commissar is your uncle doing business with?'

'Commissioner Reynolds, overstaff supervisor in charge of the Directorate of Internal Security.' James took no pleasure from their expressions. 'A man I love even less than the doctor. He carries a certain stink; if I was a Christian I'd say he's committed mortal sins, and knows himself for one of the damned.' He crossed his arms. 'I was in at their last meeting, yesterday; to my eternal shame my uncle believes my loyalty knows no limits, and I have not yet disabused him of this notion. Yesterday. The meeting . . . the doctor told Reynolds that your acquaintance Mr. Burgeson was trying to acquire world-walkers of his own. I'm not entirely sure whether he was telling the truth or not, and this is purest hearsay and gossip – I know nothing specific about your arrangements, my lady, and I don't want to. But if the doctor was telling the truth, you'd better warn your patron sooner rather than later . . .'

RSS HEADLINE NEWS FEED

UN SECRETARY GENERAL FLIES TO AFFECTED REGION: SE ASIA FACES 'UNPRECEDENTED CRISIS': UN Secretary General Kofi Annan today flew to Chandrapur, temporary capital of India, to start talks with the emergency government about efforts to enforce the cease-fire and relieve human suffering in the fallout zone to the north and west of the country . . .

PRESIDENT RUMSFELD SWORN IN: President Donald H. Rumsfeld was today sworn into office as the 45th President of the United States of America. The oath was administered by Supreme Court Chief Justice Antonin Scalia in a somber ceremony conducted at an undisclosed location . . .

HANNITY: ARE LIBERALS ALIENS FROM ANOTHER UNIVERSE? Sean Hannity says it's open season on liberals because they're obviously intruders from a parallel universe and therefore not genuine Americans . . .

SARS OUTBREAK: WHO QUARANTINES TORONTO, FLIGHTS DIVERTED: A World Health Organization spokesperson denied that the respiratory disease is spread by travelers from parallel timelines. Meanwhile, the outbreak in Ontario claimed its fourth . . .

SAUCERWATCH: GOVERNMENT TESTING UFOS AT GROOM LAKE: Observers who have seen curious shapes in the sky above Area 51 say the current cover story is an increasingly desperate attempt to divert attention from the truth about the alien saucer tech . . .

HOUSE MEETS TO REVIEW EMERGENCY BILL: Congress is meeting today to vote on the Protecting America from Parallel Universe Attackers (PAPUA) bill, described by former president Cheney (deceased) as 'vital measures to protect us in these perilous times'. The bill was drafted by the newly sworn-in president last week in the wake of . . .

COULTER: NOW IS THE TIME TO INTERN TRAITORS

RUSSIA: PUTIN DENOUNCES 'AUTHORITARIAN CONSPIRACY': Russian President Vladimir Putin today denied former President Cheney's account of the terrorist nuclear attack on the Capitol, describing it as implausible and accusing US authorities of concocting a 'fairy tale' to provide cover for a coup . . .

END NEWS FEED

THE FINAL COUNTDOWN

The track from Kirschford down to the Linden Valley – which also defined the border of the duchy of Niejwein and Baron Cromalloch's ridings – was unusually crowded with carriages and riders this day. A local farmer out tending his herd might have watched with some surprise; the majority of the traffic was clearly upper-class, whole families of minor nobility and their close servants taking to the road in a swarm, as if some great festival had been decreed in the nearby market town of Glantzwurt. But there was no such god's day coming, nor rumor of a royal court tour through the provinces. The aristocracy were more usually to be found on their home estates, staying away from the fetid kennels of the capital at this time of year.

But there were no curious farmers, of course. The soldiers who had ridden ahead with the morning sunrise had made it grimly clear that this procession was not to be witnessed; and in the wake of the savagery of spring and early summer's rampage, those tenants who had survived unscathed were more than cooperative. So the hedgerows were mostly empty of curious eyes as the convoy creaked and squealed and neighed along the Linden Valley – curious eyes which might, if they were owned by unusually well-traveled commoners, recognize the emblems of the witch-families.

The Clan was on the move, and nothing would be the same again.

A covered wagon or a noble's carriage is an uncomfortable way to travel at the best of times, alternately chill and drafty or chokingly, stiflingly hot (depending on the season), rocking on crude leaf springs or crashing from rut to stone on no springs at all, the seats a wooden bench (perhaps with a thin cushion to save the noble posterior from the insults of the road). The horsemen might have had a better time of it, but for the dust clouds flung up by the hooves of close to a hundred animals, and the flies. To exchange a stifling shuttered box for biting insects and mud that slowly clung to sweating man and horse alike was perhaps no choice at all. But one thing they agreed: It was essential to move together, and the path of least resistance was, to say the least, unsafe.

'Why can't we go to 'Mer'ca, Ma?'

Helena voh Wu gritted her teeth as one carriage wheel bounced across a stone in the road. Tess, her second-youngest, was four years old and bright by disposition, but the exodus was taking its toll after two days, and the question came out as a whine. 'We can't go there any more, dear. I told you, it's not safe.'

'But it's where Da goes when he travels?'

'That's different.' Helena rested a hand lightly on the crib. Markus was asleep – had, in fact, cried himself to sleep after a wailing tantrum. He didn't travel well. 'We can't go there.'

'But why can't we – '

The other occupant of the carriage raised her eyes from the book she had been absorbed in. 'For Sky Lady's love, leave your ma be, Tess. See you not, she was trying to sleep?'

Helena smiled gratefully at her. Kara, her sister-in-law, was traveling with them of necessity, for her husband Sir Leon was already busied with the residual duty of the postal corvée; his young wife, her pregnancy not yet showing, was just another parcel to be transferred between houses in this desperately busy time. Not that Sir Leon believed the most outlandish warnings of the radical faction, but there was little harm in sending Kara for a vacation with her eldest brother's family.

Now Kara shook her head and glanced at Helena. The latter nodded, and Kara lifted Tess onto her lap, grunting slightly with the effort. 'Once upon a time we could all travel freely to America, at least those of us the Postal Service would permit, and it was a wondrous place, full of magic and treasure. But that's not where we're going, Tess. There are bad men in America, and evil wizards; they are hunting our menfolk who travel there, and they want to hunt us all down and throw us in their deepest dungeons.'

The child's eyes were growing wider with every sentence. Helena was about to suggest that Kara lighten up on the story, but she continued, gently bouncing Tess upon her knee: 'But don't worry, we have a plan. We're going on a journey somewhere else, to a new world like America but different, one where the k– where the rulers don't hate and fear us. We're going to cross over there and we'll be safe. You'll have a new dress, and practice your Anglischprache, and it'll be a great adventure! And the bad men won't be able to find us.'

Tess looked doubtful. 'Will the bad men get Da?'

Helena's heart missed a beat. 'Of course not!' she said hotly. Gyorg ven Wu would be deep underground, shuffling between doppelgängered bunkers with a full wheelbarrow as often as the blood-pressure monitor said was safe: a beast of burden, toiling to carry the vital necessities of life between a basement somewhere in Massachusetts and a dungeon or wine cellar beneath a castle or mansion in the Gruinmarkt. Ammunition, tools, medicine, gold, anything that Clan Security deemed necessary. The flow of luxuries had stopped cold, the personal allowance abolished in the wake of the wave of assassinations that had accompanied the horridness in the Anglischprache capital.

'Your da is safe,' Kara reassured the child. 'He'll come to see us soon enough. I expect he'll bring you chocolate.'

Helena cast her a reproving look – chocolate was an expensive import to gift on a child – but Kara caught her eye and shook her head slightly. The effect of the word *chocolate* on Tess was remarkable. 'Want chocolate!' she exclaimed. '*All* the chocolate!'

Kara smiled over Tess's head, then grimaced as one of the front wheels thumped over the edge of a rut and the carriage crashed down a few inches. Markus twitched, clenched a tiny fist close to his mouth uneasily as Helena leaned over him. 'I wish we had a smoother road to travel,' she said quietly. 'Or that we could walk from nearer home.'

'The queen's men have arranged a safely defended house,' Kara reminded her. 'They wouldn't force us to travel this way without good reason. She wouldn't let them.'

'She?'

'Her Majesty.' An odd look stole across her face, one part nostalgia to two parts regret. 'I was one of her maids. She was very wise.'

So you never tire of reminding us, Helena thought, but held her tongue; with another enervating day's drive ahead, there was nothing to gain from picking a fight. Then Tess chirped up again: 'Tell me about the queen?'

'Surely.' Kara ruffled her hair. 'Queen Helge was the child of Duke Alfredo and his wife. One day when she was younger than your brother Markus, when her parents were traveling to their country estates, they were set upon by assassins sent by – '

Helena half-closed her eyes and leaned against the wall of the carriage, looking out through the open window at the tree line beyond the cleared roadside strip. *I wonder if this is what it was like for Helge's mother,* she wondered. *She escaped just ahead of her attackers, didn't she? I wonder if we'll be so lucky . . .*

*

Arranging a meeting was much easier the second time round. Miriam handed Sir Alasdair a hastily scribbled note for the telautograph office to dispatch: NEED TO TALK URGENTLY TOMORROW AGREED LOCATION STOP. One of Alasdair's men, and then the nearest post office, did the rest.

Not that imperiously demanding a conversation with the commissioner for propaganda was a trivial matter; receiving it in New London only two hours after it was transmitted, Erasmus swore under his breath and, before departing for his evening engagement – dinner with Victor McDougall, deputy commissioner for press approval – booked a compartment on the morning mail train to Boston, along with two adjacent compartments for his bodyguards and a communications clerk. By sheer good luck Miriam had picked the right day: He could see her and, provided he caught the following morning's train for the return journey, be back in the capital in time for the Thursday Central Committee meeting. 'This had better be worth it,' he muttered to himself as he clambered into the passenger compartment of his ministerial car for the journey to McDougall's home. However, it didn't occur to him to ignore Miriam's summons. In all the time he'd known her, she'd never struck him as being one to act impetuously; if she said something was urgent, it almost certainly was.

Attending the meeting was also easier, second time round. The morning after James Lee's visit, Miriam rose early and dressed for a public excursion. She took care to look as nondescript as possible; to be mistaken for a woman of particular wealth could be as dangerous here as to look impoverished, and the sartorial class indicators were much more sharply defined than back in the United States. 'I'm ready to go whenever you've got cover for me,' she told Sir Alasdair, as she entered the front parlor. 'Two guards, one car, and a walkie-talkie.'

'Emil and Klaus are waiting.' Sir Alasdair didn't smile. 'They'll park two streets away and remain on call.' He gestured at the side table: 'Lady d'Ost prepared a handbag for you before she went out.'

'There's no – ' Miriam paused. 'You think I'll need this?' She lifted the bag, feeling the drag of its contents – a two-way radio and the dense metallic weight of a pistol.

'I hope you won't. But better safe than unsafe.'

The steamer drove slowly through the streets and neighborhoods of a dense, urban Boston quite unlike the city Miriam had known; different architecture, different street names, different shops and businesses. There were a few more vehicles on the roads today, and fewer groups of men loitering on street corners; they passed two patrols of green-clad Freedom Rider militiamen, red armbands and shoulder-slung shotguns matching their arrogant stride. Policing and public order were beginning to return to the city, albeit in a very different shape. Posters had gone up on some of the high brick walls: the stern-jawed face of a balding, white-haired man. CITIZEN BURROUGHS SAYS: WE WORK FOR FREEDOM! Miriam hunched her shoulders against an imperceptible chill, pushing back against the bench seat. Erasmus had spoken glowingly of Citizen Burroughs. She found herself wishing fervently for him to be right, despite her better reservations.

Miriam covered the last hundred yards, from the deceptive safety of the car to the door of Burgeson's tenement building, feeling naked despite the contents of her bag and the presence of her backup team. It was odd: She couldn't *see* any bodyguards or observers, but just knowing Erasmus wouldn't be able to travel alone left her feeling watched. This time, however, she had a key. After turning it in the lock, she hastily closed the door behind her and climbed the stairway Burgeson's apartment shared with half a dozen other dwellings.

His front door was locked. Miriam examined it carefully – it had become a habit, a kind of neurotic tic she'd picked up in the year-plus since she'd discovered her distinctly paranoid heritage – then opened it. The flat was much as it had been on her last visit; dustier, if anything, sheets covering most of the furniture. Erasmus wasn't here yet. For no reason she cared to examine too closely, Miriam walked from room to room, carefully opening doors and looking within. The bedroom: dominated by a sheeted bed, walled with bookcases, a fireplace still unraked with white ash caked and crumbling behind the grate. A former closet, a crude bolt added inside the door to afford a moment's privacy to those who might use the flushing toilet. The kitchen was big and empty, a tin bath sitting in one corner next to the cold coal-fired cooking range. There wasn't much here to hang a personality on, aside from the books: Burgeson kept his most valued possessions inside his head. The flat was a large one by local standards – family-sized, suitable for a prosperous shopkeeper and his wife and offspring. He must have rattled around in it like a solitary pea in a pod. *Odd,* she thought. *But then, he* was *married. Before the last clampdown.* The lack of personal touches . . . *How badly did it damage him?* She went back to the living room, which with its battered piano and beaten-up furniture gave at least a semblance of domestic clutter.

It was distinctly unsettling to her to realize how much she didn't know. Before, when she'd been an unwilling visitor in the Gruinmarkt and an adventurer exploring this strange other-Boston in New Britain, she'd not looked too deep beneath surface appearances. But now – now she was probably going to end her days *living* in this nation on the other side of time – and the thought of how little she knew about the people around her troubled her.

Who are you dealing with and how do you know whether you can trust them? It seemed to be the defining paradox of her life for the past year or so. They said that blood was thicker than water, but in her experience her relatives were most likely to define themselves as enemies; meanwhile, some who were clearly supposed to be her enemies weren't. Mike Fleming should have shanghaied her to an interrogation cell; instead, he'd warned her off. Erasmus – she'd originally trusted him as far as she could throw him; now here she was, waiting for him anxiously in an empty apartment. And she'd wanted to trust Roland, but he'd been badly, possibly irreparably, broken. She sniffed, wrinkling her nose, eyes itching – whether from a momentary twist of sorrow or a whiff of dust rising from the sofa, she couldn't say.

The street door banged, the sound reverberating distantly up the stairwell. Miriam stood, moving her hand to the top of her handbag, just in case. She heard footsteps, the front door opening, familiar sounds – Burgeson breathed heavily, moved just so – and she stood up, just in time to meet him in the living-room doorway.

'You came,' she said, slightly awkwardly.

'You called.' He looked at her, head tilted sidelong. 'I could hardly ignore you and maintain that cover story?'

'Yes, well – ' She caught her lower lip between her teeth: *What will the neighbors say? 'The commissioner is visiting his mistress again'?* – 'I couldn't exactly come and fetch you, could I? Hey, get your breath back. Do you have time to stay?'

'I can spare a few hours.' He walked past her and dragged a dust sheet off the battered sofa. 'I really need to sell up. I'm needed in the capital almost all the time; can't stay here, can't run the shop from two hundred miles away.' He sounded almost amused. 'Can I interest you in a sherry?'

'You can.' The thought of Erasmus moving out, moving away, disturbed her unaccountably. As he rummaged around the sideboard, she sat down again. 'A sherry would be nice. But I didn't rattle your cage just for a drink.'

'I didn't imagine you would.' He found a bottle, splashed generous measures into two mismatched wineglasses, and brought one over to her. He seemed to be in high spirits, or at least energized. 'Your health?' He sat down beside her and she raised her glass to bump against his. 'Now, what motivated you to bring me to town?'

They were sitting knee-to-knee. It was distracting. 'I had a visitor yesterday,' she said carefully. 'One of the, the other family. The Lees.

He had some disturbing news that I thought you needed to know about.'

'Could you have wired it?' He smiled to take the sting out of the question.

'I don't think so. Um. Do you know a Commissioner Reynolds? In Internal Security?' Nothing in his facial expression changed, but the set of his shoulders told her all she needed to know. 'James Lee came to me because, uh, he's very concerned that his uncle, the Lee family's elder, is cutting a deal with Reynolds.'

Now Burgeson's expression changed: He was visibly struggling for calm. He placed a hand on her knee. 'Please, do carry on.'

Miriam tried to gather her thoughts, scattered by the unexpected contact. 'The Lees have had a defector, a renegade from our people. One with a price on his head, Dr. ven Hjalmar. Ven Hjalmar has stolen a list of – look, this is going to take a long time to explain, just take it from me, it's bad. If the Lees can get the breeding program database out of him, they can potentially give Reynolds a couple of thousand young world-walkers within the next twenty years. There are only about a hundred of them right now. I don't like the sound of Reynolds, he's the successor to the old Polis, isn't he?'

'Yes.' Burgeson nodded. 'It's a very good thing you didn't wire me. Damn.' He took another breath, visibly rattled. 'How much do the Lees know? About your people?'

'Too much for comfort.' Despite the summer humidity, Miriam shivered. 'More to the point, ven Hjalmar is a murderous bastard who picked the losing side in an internal fight. I told you about what happened to, to me before I escaped – '

'He's the doctor you mentioned. Yes?' She felt him tense.

'Yes.'

'Well, that tells me all I need to know just now. You say he's met Stephen Reynolds?'

'That's what James Lee says. Listen, I'm not a reliable source; I don't usually bear grudges but if I run into the doctor again . . . and then there's the question of whether James was telling the – '

'Did he have any obvious reason to lie to you?' Burgeson looked her in the eye. 'Or to betray confidences?'

Miriam took a sip from her glass. Now Erasmus knew, she felt unaccountably free. 'I met him while I was being held prisoner. He was a hostage against his parents' behavior after the truce – yes, that's how the noble families in the Gruinmarkt do business. He helped me get away. I think he's hoping I can save his people from what he sees as a big mistake.'

'Very well.' He took his hand away: She felt a momentary flash of disappointment. 'I'm sorry. He was right to be afraid. Reynolds is not someone I would want to put any great faith in. Do you know what the Lee elders have in mind?'

'Spying. People who can vanish from one place and reappear in another.' Miriam shrugged. 'They don't have access to the United States, at least not yet, not without the doctor – they don't have the technology transfer capability I can give you, and they don't have the numbers yet. But they *do* have a track record as invisible assassins.' She put the glass down on the floor. 'How afraid should I be?'

'Very.' He took her hand as she straightened up, leaning close; his expression was foreboding. 'He's having me followed, you know.'

'What, he – '

'Listen.' He leaned closer, pitching his voice low: 'I've met men like Reynolds before. As long as he thinks I'm in town to see my mistress he'll be happy – he thinks he's got a hand on my neck. But you're right, he's dangerous, he's an empire-builder. He's got a power base in Justice and Prisons and he's purging his own department and, hmm, the books you lent me – made me think of Felix Dzerzhinsky or Heinrich Himmler. Expert bureaucrats who build machineries of terror inside a revolutionary movement. But he doesn't have absolute power yet. He may not even have realized how much power he has at his fingertips. Sir Adam doesn't realize, either – but I'm in a position to tell him. Reynolds isn't invulnerable but he *is* dangerous, and you have just given me a huge problem, because he is already watching me.'

'You think he's going to use me as a lever against you?'

'It's gone too far for that, I'm afraid. If he knows about your relatives and knows about our arrangement, he will see me as a direct threat. He'll have to move fast, within the next hours or days. Your household is almost certainly under surveillance as an anomaly, possibly suspected of being a group of monarchists. Damn.' He looked at her. 'I really should inform Sir Adam immediately – if Stephen has acquired a secret cell of world-walking assassins, he needs to know. I wouldn't put a coup attempt beyond him. Normally we should stay here for two or three hours at least, as if we were having a liaison. If I leave too soon, that would cause alarm. But if he's moving against your people right now – '

'Wait.' Miriam took his arm. 'You're forgetting we have radios . . .'

*

The morning had dawned bright with a thin cloudy overcast, humid and warm with a threat of summer evening storms to follow. Brilliana, her morning check on the security points complete, placed the go-bag she'd prepared for Helge on the table in the front guard room; then she went in search of Huw.

She found him in one of the garden sheds behind a row of tomato vines, wiring up a row of instruments on a rough-topped table from which the plant pots had only just been removed. He didn't notice her at first, and she stood in the doorway for a minute, watching his hands, content. 'Good morning,' she said eventually.

He looked up then, smiling luminously. 'My lady. What can I do for you?'

She looked at the row of electronics. 'It's a nice day for a walk into town. Will your equipment suffer if you leave it for a few hours?'

Obviously conflicted, Huw glanced at his makeshift workbench, then back at her. 'I suppose – ' He shook his head. Then he smiled again. 'Yeah, I can leave it for a while.' He rummaged in one of the equipment boxes by the foot of the table, then pulled a plastic sheet out and began to unfold it. 'If you wouldn't mind taking that corner?'

They covered the electronics – Brilliana was fairly certain she recognized a regulated power supply and a radio transceiver – and weighted the sheet down with potsherds in case of rain and a leaky roof. Then Huw wiped his hands on a swatch of toweling. 'This isn't a casual stroll, is it?' he asked.

'No, but it needs to look like one.' She eyed him up, evidently disapproving of his choice of jeans and a college sweatshirt. 'You'll need

512

to get changed first. Background story: You're a coachman, I'm a lady's maid, and we're on a morning off work. He's courting her and she's agreed to see the sights with him. I'll meet you by the trades' door in twenty minutes.'

'Are you expecting trouble?'

'I'm not expecting it, but I don't want to be taken by surprise. Go!'

(An observer keeping an eye on the Beckstein household that morning would have seen little to report. A pair of servants – he in a suit, worn but in good repair, and she in a black dress, clutch bag tightly gripped under her left elbow – departed in the direction of the streetcar stop. A door-to-door seller visited the rear entrance, was rebuffed. Two hours later, a black steamer – two men in the open-topped front, the passenger compartment hooded and dark – rumbled out of the garage and turned towards the main road. With these exceptions, the household carried on much as it had the day before.)

'Where are we going?' Huw asked Brilliana as they waited at the streetcar stop.

'Downtown.' She stared along the tracks. 'Boston is safer than Springfield, but still . . . I want to take a look at the docks. And then the railway stations, north and south both. It's best to have a man at my side: less risk of unwelcome misunderstandings.'

'Oh.' He sounded disappointed. 'What else?'

She slid her fingers through his waiting hand. 'I thought if there is enough time after that, we could visit the fair on the common.'

'That's more like it.'

'It'll look good to the watchers.' She squeezed his thumb, then leaned sideways, against his shoulder. 'Assuming there are any. If there aren't – by then we should know.'

'Indeed.' He paused. 'I'm carrying, in case you were wondering.'

'Good.' With her free hand she shifted the strap of her bag higher on her shoulder. 'Your knot . . . ?'

'On my wrist-ribbon.'

'That too.' She relaxed slightly. 'Oh look, a streetcar.'

They rode together in silence on the open upper deck, she sitting primly upright, he discreetly attentive to her occasional remarks.

513

There were few other passengers on the upper level this morning, and none who might be agents or Freedom Riders; the tracks were in poor repair and the car swayed like a drunk, shrieking and grating round corners. They changed streetcars near Haymarket Square, again taking the upper deck as the tram rattled its way towards the back bay.

'What are we looking for?' asked Huw.

'Doppelgänger prisons.' Brill looked away for a moment, checking the stairs at the rear of the car. 'They use prison ships here. If you were a bad guy and were about to arrest a bunch of world-walkers, what would you – '

Rounding the corner of a block of bonded warehouses, the streetcar briefly came in sight of the open water, and then the piers and cranes of the docks. A row of smaller ships lay tied up inside the harbor, their funnels clear of smoke or steam: In the water beyond, larger vessels lay at anchor. The economic crash, and latterly the state of emergency and the new government, had wreaked havoc with trade, and behind fences great pyramids and piles of break-bulk goods had grown, waiting for the flow of shipping to resume. Today there was some activity – a gang of stevedores was busy with one of the nearer ships, loading cartloads of sacks out of one of the warehouses – but still far less than on a normal day.

'What's that?' asked Brill, pointing at a ship moored out in the open water, past the mole.

'I'm not sure' – Huw followed her direction – 'a warship?' It was large, painted in the gray-blue favored by the navy, but it lacked the turrets and rangefinders of a ship of the line; more to the point, it looked poorly maintained, streaks of red staining its flanks below the anchor chains that dipped into the water. Large, boxy superstructures had been added fore and aft. 'That's an odd one.'

'Can you read its name?'

'Give me a moment.' Huw glanced around quickly, then pulled out a compact monocular. 'HMS *Burke*. Yup, it's the navy.' He shoved the scope away quickly as the streetcar rounded a street corner and began to slow.

'Delta Charlie, please copy.' Brill had her radio out. 'I need a ship class identifying. HMS *Burke*, Bravo Uniform Romeo – ' She finished, waited briefly for a reply, then slid the device away, switching it to silent as the streetcar stopped, swaying slightly as passengers boarded and alighted.

'Was that entirely safe?'

'No, but it's a calculated risk. We're right next to the harbor and if anyone's RDFing for spies they'll probably raid the ships' radio rooms first; they don't have pocket-sized transmitters around here. I set Sven up with a copy of the shipping register. He says it's a prison ship. Currently operated by the Directorate of Reeducation. That would be prisons.'

'You don't know that it's here for us.' Huw glanced at the staircase again as the streetcar began to move.

'Would you like to bet on it?'

'No. I think we ought to head back.' Huw reached out and took her hand, squeezed it gently.

She squeezed back, then pulled it away. 'I think we ought to make sure nobody's following us first.'

'You think they might try to pick us up . . . ?'

'Probably not – this sort of action is best conducted at night – but you can never be sure. I think we should be on guard. Let's head back and tell Helge. It's her call – whether we have to withdraw or not, whether Burgeson can come up with a security cordon for us – but I don't like the sound of that ship.'

*

Brilliana and Huw had been away from Miriam's house for almost an hour. Miriam herself had left half an hour afterwards. An observer – like the door-to-door salesman who had importuned the scullery maid to buy his brushes, or the ticket inspector stepping repeatedly on and off the streetcars running up and down the main road and curiously not checking any tickets – would have confirmed the presence of residents, and a lack of activity on their part. Which would be an anomaly, worthy of investigation in its own right: A household of that size would require the regular purchase of provisions, meat and milk and other perishables, for the city's electrical supply was prone to brownouts in the summer heat, rendering household food chillers unreliable.

An observer other than the ticket inspector and the salesman might have been puzzled when, shortly before noon, they disappeared into the grounds of a large abandoned house, its windows boarded and its gates barred, three blocks up the street and a block over – but there were no other observers, for Sir Alasdair's men were patrolling the overgrown acre of Miriam's house and garden and keeping an external watch only on the approaches to the front and rear. 'If you go outside you run an increased risk of attracting attention,' Miriam had pointed out, days earlier. 'Your job is to keep intruders out long enough for us to escape into the doppelgänger compound, right?' (Which was fenced in with barbed wire and patrolled by two of Alasdair's men at all times, even though it was little more than a clearing in the backwoods near the thin white duke's country retreat.)

Sir Alasdair's men were especially not patrolling the city around them. And so they were unaware of the assembly of a battalion of Internal Security troops, of the requisition of a barracks and an adjacent bonded warehouse in Saltonstall, or the arrival on railroad flatcars of a squadron of machine-gun carriers and their blackcoat crew. Lady d'Ost's brief radio call-in from the docks was received by Sven, but although he went in search of Sir Alasdair to give him the news, its significance was not appreciated: Shipping in the marcher kingdoms of the Clan's world was primitive and risky, and the significance of prison ships was not something Sir Alasdair had given much thought to.

So when four machine-gun-equipped armored steamers pulled up outside each side of the grounds, along with eight trucks – from which poured over a hundred black-clad IS militia equipped with clubs, riot shields, and shotguns – it came as something of a surprise.

Similar surprise was being felt by the maintenance crew at the farm near Framingham, as the Internal Security troops rushed the farmyard and threw tear-gas grenades through the kitchen windows; and in a block of dilapidated-looking shops fronting an immigrant rookery in Irongate – perhaps more there than elsewhere, for Uncle Huan had until this morning had every reason to believe that Citizen Reynolds was his protector – and at various other sites. But the commissioner for internal security had his own idea of what constituted protection, and he'd briefed his troops accordingly. 'It is essential that all the prisoners be handcuffed and hooded during transport,' he'd explained in the briefing room the previous evening. 'Disorientation and surprise are essential components of this operation – they're tricky characters, and if you don't do this, some of them will escape. You will take them to the designated drop-off sites and hand them over to the Reeducation Department staff for transport to the prison ship. I mentioned escape attempts. The element of surprise is essential; in order to prevent the targets from raising the alarm, if any of them try to escape you should shoot them.'

Reynolds himself left the briefing satisfied that his enthusiastic and professional team of Polis troops would conduct themselves appropriately. Then he retired to the office of the chief of Polis, to share a lunch of cold cuts delivered from the commissary (along with a passable bottle of Chablis – which had somehow bypassed the blockade to end in the Polis commissioner's private cellar) and discuss what to do next with the doctor.

*

Huw's first inkling that something was wrong came when the streetcar he and Brilliana were returning on turned the corner at the far end of the high street and came to a jolting stop. He braced against the handrail and looked round. 'Hey,' he began.

'Get *down*,' Brill hissed. Huw ducked below the level of the railing, into the space she'd just departed. She crouched in the aisle, her bag gaping open, her right hand holding a pistol inside it. 'Not a stop.'

'Right.' Taking a deep breath, Huw reached inside his coat and pulled out his own weapon. 'What did you see?'

'Barricades and – '

He missed the rest of the sentence. It was swallowed up in the familiar hammering roar of a SAW, then the harsh, slow thumping of some kind of heavy machine gun. 'Fuck! Let's bail.' He raised his voice, but he could barely hear himself; the guns were firing a couple of blocks away, and he flattened himself against the wooden treads of the streetcar floor. Brill looked at him, white-faced, spread-eagled farther back along the aisle. Then she laid her pistol on the floor and reached into her handbag, pulling out the walkie-talkie. Fumbling slightly, she switched channels. 'Charlie Delta, Charlie Delta, flash all units, attack in progress on Zulu Foxtrot, repeat, attack in progress on Zulu Foxtrot. Over.'

The radio crackled, then a voice answered, slow and shocky: 'Emil here, please repeat? Over.'

Brill keyed the transmit button: 'Emil, get Helge out of there right now! Zulu Foxtrot is under attack. Over and out.' She looked at Huw: 'Come on, we'd better – '

Huw was looking past her shoulder, and so he saw the head of the IS militiaman climbing the steps at the rear of the carriage before Brilliana registered that anything was wrong. Huw raised his pistol and sighted. The steps curled round, and the blackcoat wasn't prepared for trouble; as he turned towards Huw his mouth opened and he began to raise one hand towards the long gun slung across his shoulder.

Huw pulled the trigger twice in quick succession. 'Go!' he shouted at Brill. 'Now!'

'But we're – ' She flipped open the locket she wore on a ribbon around her left wrist, for all the world like a makeup compact.

More machine-gun fire in the near distance. Shouting, distant through tinnitus-fuzzed ears still ringing from the pistol shots. Huw shoved his sleeve up his arm and tried to focus on the dial of the handless watch, swimming eye-warpingly close under the glass. The streetcar rocked; booted feet hammered on the stair treads. Brilliana rose to a crouch on her knees and one wrist, then disappeared. Something round and black bounced onto the floor where she'd been lying, mocking Huw. He concentrated on the spinning, fiery knot in his eyes until it felt as if his head was about to explode; then the floor beneath him disappeared and he found himself falling hard, towards the grassy ground below.

Behind him, the grenade rolled a few inches across the upper deck of the streetcar, then stabilized for a second before exploding.

*

The man behind the desk was tall, silver-haired, every inch the distinguished patriarch and former fighter pilot who'd risen to lead a nation. But it was the wrong desk; and appearances were deceptive. Right now, the second unelected president of the United States was scanning a briefing folder, bifocals drooping down his nose until he flicked at them irritably. After a moment he glanced up. 'Tell me, Andrew.' He skewed Dr. James with a stare that was legendary for intimidating generals. 'This gizmo. How reliable is it?'

'We haven't made enough to say for sure, sir. But of the sixteen ARMBAND units we've used so far, only one has failed – and that was in the first manufactured group. We've got batch production down and we can swear to ninety-five-percent effectiveness for eighteen hours after manufacture. Reliability drops steeply after that time – the long-term storable variant under development should be good for six months and self-test, but we won't be able to swear to that until we've tested it. Call it a year out.'

'Huh.' The president frowned, then closed the folder and placed it carefully in the middle of the desk. 'CARTHAGE is going to take sixty-two of them. What do you say to that?'

Is that it? Dr. James lifted his chin. 'We can do it, sir. The units are already available – the main bottleneck is training the air force personnel on the mobile biomass generators, and that's in hand. Also the release to active duty and protocol for deployment, but we're basically repurposing the existing nuclear handling protocols for that; we can relax them later if you issue an executive order.'

'I don't want one of our planes failing to transition and executing CARTHAGE over domestic airspace, son. That would be unacceptable collateral damage.'

Dr. James glanced sidelong at his neighbor: another of the ubiquitous blue-suited generals who'd been dragged on board the planning side of this operation. 'Sir? With respect I think that's a question for General Morgenstern.'

The president nodded. 'Well, General. How are you going to ensure your boys don't fuck up if the doctor's mad science project fails to perform as advertised?'

The general was the perfect model of a modern military man: lean, intent, gleaming eyes. 'Mark-one eyeball, sir: that, and radio. The pilot flying will visually ascertain that there are no landmarks in sight, and the DSO will confirm transition by checking for AM talk-radio broadcasts. We've done our reconnaissance: There are no interstates or railroads in the target zone, and their urban pattern is distinctively different.'

'That assumes daylight, doesn't it?' The president had a question for every answer.

'No sir; our cities are illuminated, theirs aren't, it's that simple. The operation crews will be tasked with activating the ARMBAND units within visual range of known waypoints and will confirm that they're not in our world anymore before they button up.'

'Heavy cloud cover?'

'Radio, sir. There's no talk radio in fairyland. No GPS signal either. Sir, they aren't going to have any problem confirming they're in the correct DZ.'

The president nodded sagely. 'Make sure they check their receivers before they transition. We don't want any systems failures.'

'Yes sir. Is there anything else you want me to add?' Normally, Dr. James thought, handing the man a leading question like that might border on insolence, but right now he was in an avuncular, expansive mood; the bright and shiny gadgets were coming out of the cold warrior's toy box, and playing up to the illusion of direct presidential control over the minutiae of a strike mission was only going to go down well. *A very political general,* he told himself. *Watch him.*

'I think there is.' The president looked thoughtful. 'Doctor. Can you have a handful more ARMBAND units ready two days after the operation? We'll want them fitting to a passenger aircraft suitable for giving some, uh, *witnesses,* a ringside seat. It's for the review stand at the execution – diplomatic witnesses to show the Chinese and the Russians what happens if you fuck with the United States. It'll need to be an airframe that's ready for the boneyard, it'll need a filtered air system, good cabin visibility, and nothing too sensitive for commie eyes. Except ARMBAND, but you'll be keeping the guests out of the cockpit. General, if you could get your staff to suggest a suitable aircraft and minute my office on their pick, I'll see you get an additional order via the joint command.' He grinned impishly. 'Wish I was going along with it myself.'

REFUGEES

The walkie-talkie in Miriam's bag squawked for attention.

'What's that?' Burgeson, startled, let go of her arm as she turned to the table.

'Bad news, I think.' She pulled the radio out. 'Mike Bravo, Mike Bravo, sitrep please, over.'

A buzz of static, squelched rapidly: 'Boss? Emil here. I just got a call from Delta Charlie. Zulu Foxtrot is under attack, repeat, the house is under attack. We're bringing the truck round, you need to get out now, over.'

Miriam stared at Erasmus. 'My house is under attack. Do you know anything about it?' She knew the answer before the words were finished: The widening of his pupils and the paleness of his face told her all she needed. 'Damn. It's got to be Reynolds, hasn't it?'

'I need to get to the railway station.' Erasmus stood up, unfolding sticklike limbs as he glanced at the window. 'If he's doing this now, he means to be back in New London by nightfall, which means this is the start of something bigger. There's a Council of People's Commissioners – cabinet – meeting tomorrow morning. He'll either present the arrests as a fait accompli, and impeach me for treason and conspiracy on the spot, or go a step further and arrest the entire Mutual wing of the Council in the name of the Peace and Justice Committee. It'll be a coup in all but name: Either way, he takes me out and weakens Sir Adam enormously.'

'What are you going to do?' Miriam positioned herself between Erasmus and the doorway. 'Do you have a plan?'

'Yes, if I can get to the station.' He paused. 'You should go into hiding, in your other world – they can't reach you there – '

'The hell I will.' She picked up her bag and slung it over her shoulder, then the walkie-talkie. 'Emil, Mike Bravo here. I'm coming out with a passenger. We need a ride. Over.' She pushed the door open. 'What's at the station?'

'I have a train to catch. Once I'm on it, Reynolds can't touch me and can't stop me from telling the truth.'

'A train – '

'*My* train.' His smile widened, sharkishly. 'Steve has *no idea* what I'm capable of doing with it.'

'You'll have to tell me on the way.' She paused, by the door. 'Reynolds knows you're here, right?'

'Yes. But Josh and Mark are waiting down in the shop and his men won't get past them silently – '

'Reynolds has the Lee family working for him; or some of them.' She held up a hand, then stood still, listening.

'What are you – '

She walked across to the window casement and looked out along the alley, keeping her body in the shadows. 'Do you hear a steamer?' she asked quietly.

'No. Why?'

'Because we *should* be hearing one by now.' She froze, listening, for a moment. 'Emil and Klaus were just round the corner. Do you have some way of calling your bodyguards?'

'The shop bell-pull in the hall – it works both ways. What are you thinking?' He pitched his voice low.

'That we're very isolated right now. I may be jumping at shadows, but if Reynolds is raiding my house, why isn't he also here?'

'Oh dear.' Erasmus returned to the sideboard. 'In that case, we'd better go.' A muffled click, and he turned around, holding a small pepperpot pistol. A barely glimpsed gesture made it vanish into a sleeve or a pocket. 'For once, I'm not going to let you go first.'

'I don't think' – they collided in front of the doorway – 'so?'

'My apologies.' Looking her in the eye, Erasmus added, 'It would be best if my bodyguards saw me first.'

'Maybe.' Miriam stepped aside reluctantly. He crossed the hall and turned the key, then pulled the front door open as she followed him.

'Stop or I shoot!' Erasmus froze in the doorway. The teenager on the landing kept his pistol in Burgeson's face, but went wide-eyed as he looked past the older man and saw Miriam. 'What are *you* doing here?'

Heart in mouth, she looked the youth in the eye: 'Point the gun at someone else, Lin, or I will be *very angry* with you.'

'I'm not supposed to do that.' His voice was shaky. 'I'm supposed to kill everyone in this apartment.'

'Who told you to do that?' Miriam asked quietly.

'The man Elder Huan told me to obey without question.' Erasmus stood stock-still as Lin stepped back a pace and lowered his pistol to waist level. 'I didn't know you'd be here,' he added, almost petulantly.

Pulse hammering, Miriam took a step forward and placed a hand on Erasmus's shoulder. 'Everything is going to be all right,' she said quietly. 'Lin, I want you to meet Mr. Burgeson. He's a, a friend of mine.' She could feel his shoulder through the cloth of his jacket, solid and real and seeming to her as delicate as a fine bone-china teacup caught in midfall; she felt faint, this was so close to Roland's end. 'I will never forgive you if you kill him.'

Lin nodded. 'I am dishonored either way. But I won't shoot him. For your sake.' His elders had once sent Lin to kill Miriam. She, capturing him, had not only spared him, she'd sent him back to them with a truce offer.

'Did the man who sent you here wear a black coat, by any chance? A party commissioner called Reynolds?'

Lin shook his head. 'Oh no,' he said earnestly. 'The doctor sent me.' His nostrils flared with evident disdain: 'Dr. ven Hjalmar.'

'Would someone,' Erasmus said quietly but forcefully, 'explain to me what exactly is happening?'

'I think I can put it together,' said Miriam. 'Lin, Dr. ven Hjalmar is working with Commissioner Reynolds, isn't he? No need to confirm or deny anything – your brother and I had a conversation.'

Lin nodded. 'I was sent to remove a, a party radical who was opposed to our ends, in the doctor's words.' He stared at Erasmus. 'What will you do now?'

'Have you met Stephen Reynolds?' Erasmus asked quietly. 'He isn't one for whom loyalty is a two-way street.'

'I've discussed this with James,' said Miriam. 'Lin, I've been negotiating a, a deal with Mr. Burgeson here. It's similar to the arrangement your elders came to with the security commissioner.'

'The difference is, I don't send death squads to murder my rivals,'
Erasmus added.

Miriam looked straight at Lin: 'That's why I've been dealing with
him. The arrangement can be extended to include your relatives.
But not if you shoot him, or hand us over to the Internal Security
directorate. Or Dr. ven Hjalmar.'

Lin looked straight back at her. 'You say this man is a friend of
yours,' he said. 'Do you mean that? Are you claiming privilege of
kinship? Or is it just a business arrangement to which no honor
attaches?'

Miriam blinked. She tightened her grip on Erasmus's shoulder as
she felt him breathe in, preparing to say something potentially disastrous – 'Erasmus is a personal friend of mine, Lin. This isn't just
business.' Which was true, she realized as she said it; not that they
had gotten up to anything, not that there was substance to the cover
story Burgeson's bodyguards and enemies believed, but she could
conceive of it, at some future time. 'So yes, I claim privilege of kinship, and if you touch one hair on his head I'll claim blood feud on
you and yours. Is that what you want?'

Lin looked away, then shook his head.

'Good. We understand each other, I hope? Do you and yours claim
Dr. ven Hjalmar?'

Lin's eyes widened. 'Not yet. Aunt Mei was talking about finding
him a wife, but – '

'Then you have no problem if I declare him outlaw and anathema
as a traitor to my family and deal with him accordingly?'

He began to smile. 'If your arrangement for the security of your
clan can stretch to some more bodies – none whatsoever. What do
you have in mind?'

'First, I need to deliver Mr. Burgeson safely to South Station,
where a train is waiting for him.' She felt Erasmus preparing to speak
again. 'And then I and my sworn retainers have an appointment with

Dr. ven Hjalmar, and possibly with Commissioner Reynolds. Would you like to come along?'

'It will be my pleasure,' Lin said gravely. He looked directly at Erasmus. 'If you'd both care to come downstairs, my cousins and I have a wagon waiting on the other side of the wall of worlds. We were to use it to dispose of the evidence, but I think it will work just as well with living passengers.' He returned his pistol to a pocket holster, then raised an eyebrow. 'Which platform do you want?'

*

The miracles of modern communication technology: With two-way radios, the survivors of Reynolds's simultaneous raids called in and made contact within an hour. Miriam, her head pounding, hugged Erasmus briefly. 'Try to take care,' she murmured in his ear.

'My dear, I have every intention of doing so.' He grinned lop-sidedly.

'What are you going to do?'

'Get to my train on time, with the help of these fine fellows.' Behind her, Lin was filling two of his fellows in on the turn events had taken. 'Then I shall first signal Sir Adam. Stephen's gone too far this time – setting up a parallel arrangement with these cousins of yours and trying to frame me for subversion. I have my own supporters within the Freedom Guard; if necessary we can take it to the street.' His face fell. 'But that has its own price. What do you intend?'

'I'm going to find my people,' she told him. 'And then we're going to take out the trash. Stay away from the old Polis headquarters building for a couple of hours, Erasmus. You might want to turn up later – around six, maybe – to take charge of the cleanup operation and to assemble a cover story.' She bit her lip. 'It's not going to be pretty. Reynolds is a problem, but the doctor is a worse one: a sociopath with the background and intellect to raise his own version of the Clan, given half a chance.'

'You think your doctor is more important than Reynolds?'

'I know it.' She looked him in the eye. 'You and your boss can deal with Reynolds; he's an attack dog, but if you put a chain on his collar

526

you can keep him under control. But ven Hjalmar doesn't wear a collar in the first place.'

'Then you should take care,' he said gravely. 'I should be going. But . . . take care. I would very much like to see you again.'

'You too.' She leaned forward and, trying not to think too hard about her intentions, kissed him. She was aiming for his cheek, but he turned, and for a moment their lips touched. 'Oh. Go on.'

'Until this evening,' he said, coloring slightly as he took a step backwards, turning towards the cart, his temporary chauffeurs, and the somnolent mule between the traces.

Miriam waited until he looked away, then walked over to Lin's side. 'Let's do it,' she said. 'My people first; then the Polis building.'

*

Three o'clock in the afternoon, and for Commissioner Reynolds the day was not going terribly well.

In the communications room downstairs the telautographs were buzzing and clattering like deranged locusts; telespeakers clutching their earpieces hammered away on their keyboards, transcribing incoming messages from the snatch squads and the delivery teams charged with ferrying the detainees to the *Burke*. Periodically one of the supervisors or overofficers would collate a list of the most important updates and hurry them upstairs, where Reynolds would receive them in stony silence.

'Ninety-six subjects isolated at Irongate and consigned for detention. Thirty-one confirmed as received by the *Burke*, the others still being in transit. Slow, too slow. Site B in Boston, heavy gunfire – damn you, man, what do you mean, *heavy* gunfire returned? That group has gun carriers! What's going on out there?'

The doctor, placidly munching on a dessert platter, paused to dab at his lips with a napkin. 'I told you to expect organized resistance from that crowd,' he reminded Reynolds.

'What is Site B putting up against our people?' Reynolds demanded.

The overstaffofficer paled: 'Sir, there is word of machine-gun fire from inside the grounds. Casualties are three dead and eight injured so far; the supervisor-lieutenant on site has cordoned off the area and our men are exchanging fire with the defenders. One of the gun carriers was damaged by some sort of artillery piece when it tried to force the front gates.'

'*Damaged*, by god?' Reynolds glared at him. 'This was how long ago? Why haven't you called on the navy?'

'Sir, I can't order a shore bombardment of one of our own cities! If you want to request one it has to go up to the Joint Command Council for authorization – '

Reynolds cut him off with a chopping gesture. 'Later. They're pinned down for now, yes? What about Site C?'

'Site C was overrun on schedule, sir. One casualty, apparently self-inflicted – negligent discharge. Six prisoners consigned for detention and received by the *Burke*. Two dead, killed resisting arrest or attempting to flee.'

'Good.' Reynolds nodded jerkily. 'Site S?'

'I don't have a report for Site S, sir.' The overstaffofficer riffled through his message sheets, increasingly concerned. 'Sir, by your leave – '

'Go. Find out what happened. Report back. Dismissed.' Reynolds turned to ven Hjalmar as his adjutant made himself scarce. 'Damn it, you'd almost think – '

'They have radio – telautograph, I think you call it? Between sites. Between people.' Ven Hjalmar was clearly irritated. 'I told you that timing was essential.'

'But how can they have notified the – my men cut all the wires! The transmission wires are vulnerable, yes?'

'Transmission wires?' Ven Hjalmar squinted. 'What, you mean for transmitting the wireless signal? They don't use wires for that – just a stub antenna, so big.' He spread the fingers of one hand. 'I think we may have found a regrettable source of confusion: Their radios – the telautograph sets – are pocket-sized. They'll all be carrying them, at least one per group when they're off base – '

'Nonsense.' Reynolds stared at him. 'Pocket *telautographs*? That's ridiculous.'

'Really?' Ven Hjalmar pushed his chair back from the table. 'I was under the impression that the Lee family had taught you that when visitors from other universes come calling it's a good idea to keep an open mind.' He stood up. 'Sitting around up here and trying to convey the appearance of being in charge of the situation is all very well, but perhaps it would be a good idea to take a more hands-on approach before the enemy get inside your decision loop – '

A deep thudding sound vibrated through the walls and floor, rattling the crockery and shaking a puff of plaster dust from the ceiling.

'Damn.' Reynolds flipped open the lid of his holster and headed towards the door. 'We appear to have visitors,' he said dryly. He glanced back at ven Hjalmar. 'Come along, now.'

The doctor nodded and bent to pick up his medical bag, which he tucked beneath one arm, keeping a grip on the handle with his other hand. 'As you wish.'

The lights flickered as Reynolds marched out into the corridor. The two guards snapped to attention. 'Follow me,' he told them. 'This fellow is with us.' He strode towards the staircase leading down to the operations and communications offices below, just as a burst of rapid gunfire reverberated up the stairwell. 'Huh.' Reynolds drew his gun.

'We need to get to ground level as fast as possible,' ven Hjalmar said urgently. 'If we're at ground level I can get you out of here, but if we're – '

'The *enemy* are at ground level,' Reynolds cut him off. 'They appear to be – ' He listened. More gunfire, irregular and percussive, rattled the walls like an out-of-control drummer. 'We can stop them ascending, however.' He gestured his guards forward, to take up positions to either side of the stairs. 'We wait here until the communications staff have organized a barricade – '

'But we've got to get down!' Ven Hjalmar was agitated now. 'If we aren't at ground level I can't world-walk, which means – '

But Commissioner Reynolds was never to hear the end of ven Hjalmar's sentence.

*

Sir Alasdair and his men – just two had stayed behind at Site B to keep the security militia engaged – had exfiltrated to the backwoods landscape of the Gruinmarkt. The vicinity of Boston was well-mapped, crisscrossed by tracks and occasional roads and villages: maps, theodolites, and sensitive inertial platforms had built up a good picture of the key landmarks over the months since Miriam had pioneered a business start-up a couple of miles from Erasmus Burgeson's pawnbroker shop (and Leveler quartermaster's cellar). The Polis headquarters building, not far from Faneuil Hall, was a site of interest to Clan Security; with confirmation from Lin Lee that Reynolds and ven Hjalmar were present, it took Sir Alasdair less than an hour to arrange a counterattack.

Griben ven Hjalmar was not a soldier; he had no more (and no less) knowledge of the defensive techniques evolved by the Clan's men of arms over half a century of bloody internicine feuding than any other civilian. Stephen Reynolds was not a civilian, but had only an outsider's insight into the world-walkers. Both of them knew, in principle, of the importance of doppelgängering their safe houses – of protecting them against infiltration by enemy attackers capable of bypassing doors and walls by entering from the world next door.

However, both of them had independently made different – and fatal – risk assessments. Reynolds had assumed that because Elder Huan's 'Eastern cousins' came from a supposedly primitive world, and had demonstrated no particular talent for mayhem within his ambit, the most serious risk they presented was the piecemeal violence of the gun and the knife. And ven Hjalmar had assumed that the presence of armed guards downstairs (some of them briefed and alert to the risk of attackers appearing out of nowhere in their midst) would be sufficient.

What neither of them had anticipated was a systematic assault on the lobby of the headquarters building, conducted by a lance of Clan Security troops under the command of Sir Alasdair ven Hjorth-Wasser – who had been known as Sergeant Al 'Tiny' Schroder, towards the end of his five years in the USMC – troops in body armor, with grenades and automatic weapons, who had spent long years honing their expertise in storming defended buildings, in other worlds. Nor had they anticipated Sir Alasdair's objective: to suppress the defenders for long enough to deliver a wheelbarrow load of

ANNM charges, emplace them around the load-bearing walls, and world-walk back to safety. Two hundred kilograms of ammonium nitrate/nitromethane explosives, inside the six-story brick and stone structure, would be more than enough to blow out the load-bearing walls and drop the upper floors; building codes and construction technologies in New Britain lagged behind the United States by almost a century.

It was an anonymous and brutal counterattack, and left Sir Alasdair (and Commissioner Burgeson) with acid indigestion and disrupted sleep for some days, until the last of the bodies pulled from the rubble could finally be identified. If either ven Hjalmar or Reynolds had realized in time that their location had been betrayed, the operation might have failed, as would the cover story: a despicable royalist cell's attack on the Peace and Justice Subcommittee's leading light, the heroic death of Commissioner Reynolds as he led the blackcoats in a spirited defense of the People's Revolution, and the destruction of the dastardly terrorists by their own bombs. But it *was* a success. And as the cover-up operation proceeded – starting with the delivery of the captives held on board the *Burke* to a rather different holding area ashore, under the control of guards outside the chain of command of the Directorate of Internal Security – the parties to the fragile conspiracy were able to breathe their respective sighs of relief.

The worst was over; but now the long haul was just beginning.

*

It was a humid morning near Boston; with a blustery breeze blowing, and cloud cover lowering across the sky, fat drops of rain spattered across the sidewalk and speckled the gray wooden wall of the compound.

The wall around the compound had sprung up almost overnight, enclosing a chunk of land on the green outskirts of Wellesley – land which included a former Royal Ordnance artillery works, and a wedge of rickety brick row houses trapped between the works and the railroad line. One day, a detachment of Freedom Guards had showed up and gone door to door, telling the inhabitants that they

531

were being moved west with their factory, moving inland towards the heart of the empire, away from threat of coastal invasion. There had been no work, and no money to pay the workers, for five months; the managers had bartered steel fabrications and stockpiled gun barrels for food to keep their men from starvation. Word that the revolutionary government did indeed want them to resume production, and had prepared a new home for them and would in due course feed and pay them, overcame much resistance. Within two days the district's life had drained away on flatbeds and boxcars, rolling west towards a questionable future. The last laborers to leave had pegged out the line of the perimeter; the first to arrive unloaded timber from the sidings by the arsenal and began to build the wall and watchtowers. They did so under the guns of their camp guards, for these men were prisoners, captured royalist soldiers taken by the provisional government.

After they'd built the walls of the prison they'd occupy, and the watchtowers and guardhouses for their captors, the prisoners were set to work building their own cabins on the empty ground between two converging railroad tracks. These, too, they built walls around. They built lots of walls; and while they labored, they speculated quietly among themselves about who would get the vacant row houses.

They did not have long to wait to find out.

Family groups of oddly dressed folk, who spoke haltingly or with a strong Germanic accent, began to arrive one morning. The guards were not obsequious towards them, exactly, but it was clear that their position was one of relative privilege. They had the haunted expressions of refugees, uprooted from home and hearth forever. Some of them seemed resentful and slightly angry about their quarters, which was inexplicable: The houses were not the mansions of rich merchants or professionals, but they were habitable, and had sound roofs and foundations. Where had they come from? Nobody seemed to know, and speculation was severely discouraged. After a couple of prisoners disappeared – one of them evidently an informer, the other just plain unlucky – the others learned to keep their mouths shut.

The prisoners were kept busy. After a few more carriageloads of displaced persons arrived, some of the inmates were assigned to new building work, this time large, well-lit drafting offices illuminated by overhead skylights. Another gang found themselves unloading wagonloads of machine tools, lightweight precision-engineering equipment to stand beside the forges and heavy presses left behind by the artillery works. Something important was coming, that much was clear. But what?

*

'What is this – *hovel*?' demanded the tall woman with the babe in arms, pausing on the threshold. She spoke Hochsprache, with an aristocratic Northern accent; the politicals in their striped shirts, burdened beneath her trunk, didn't understand her.

Heyne shrugged, then turned to the convicts. 'Leave it here and report back to barracks,' he told them, speaking English. He watched as they deposited the trunk, none too softly, and shuffled away with downturned faces. Then he gestured back into the open doorway. 'It's where you're going to live for a while,' he told her bluntly. 'Be thankful; this nation's in the grip of revolt, but you've got a roof over your head and food on the table, and guards to keep you safe.'

'But I – ' Helena voh Wu stepped inside and looked around. Raw brick faced with patches of crumbling plaster stared back at her; bare boards creaked underfoot.

The other woman was more practical. 'Help me move this inside?' she said, looking up at him as she bent over one end of the trunk. The boy, free of her hand, dashed inside and thundered up the stairs, shouting excitedly.

'Certainly, my lady.' Heyne picked up the other end of the trunk and helped her maneuver it past the other woman. It gave them both a polite excuse to ignore her hand-wringing dismay.

'Is there any bedding? Or furniture?' she asked.

'Probably not.' They finished shoving the trunk against the inner wall of the front room, and Heyne straightened up. 'The previous tenants shipped out a week since, and stripped their houses of anything worth taking. The matter's in hand, though. We've got plenty of labor from the politicals in the workshop. Tell me the basics you need and I'll put in an order for it.' He looked around. 'Hmm. They *really* stripped this one.' Walking through into the kitchen, he tutted. 'Needs plaster and paint, then a complete kitchen set, table and chairs, pots, a stove if we can find one. Beds' – he glanced over his shoulder – 'for three of you.' Walking to the back, he stared through the grimy window into the yard. 'Chamber pots. Let's check the outhouse.'

Outside in the sunlight, Kara spoke quietly. 'I know we're refugees, dependent on the generosity of strangers. But Helena can't be the first like this . . . ?'

Heyne glanced back at the terraced house and shook his head. 'No, she isn't. Most people go through something like it, sooner or later; but they get over it eventually.' He looked back at the outhouse. 'Good, they left the toilet seat. My lady, I know this accommodation is not up to your normal standards, but the fact is, we're beginning again from scratch, with barely any resources. We're lucky enough that Her Majesty negotiated a settlement with the revolutionaries that gives us this compound, and resources to . . . well, I'm not sure I can talk about that yet. But we're welcome here for now, anyway, and we're not going to starve.' He turned and headed back through the kitchen door, glanced through into the front room – where Helena was sitting on the trunk, rocking slowly from side to side – and then climbed the creaking staircase to the top floor and the two cramped bedrooms below the attic.

The young boy was still crawling around the empty south-facing bedroom, jumping up and down and making believe in some exciting adventure. Heyne tested the windows. 'The glass is all here and the windows open. Good.'

'How long will we be here?' Kara asked bluntly.

'As long as they want to keep us.' He shrugged. 'You don't want to go back home, my lady.' His eyes lingered a moment too long on her stomach. 'Not now, maybe not ever.'

'But my husband – '

'He'll follow us over here.' Heyne's tone brooked no argument, even though his words were spoken with the voice of optimism rather than out of any genuine certainty. 'Don't ever doubt it.'

'But if we can't go back' – she frowned – 'what use are we to them?'

Heyne shook his head. 'Nobody's told me yet. But you can be sure Her Majesty has something in mind.'

*

Stumbling through workdays like nothing he'd ever seen before, walking in a numb haze of dread, Steve Schroeder had spent the weeks since 7/16 waiting for the other shoe to fall.

There was the horror of the day's events, of course, and then the following momentous changes. Agent Judt sitting in one corner of the office for the first week, a personal and very pointed reminder that he'd accidentally turned down the kind of scoop that came along once in a lifetime – a chance to interview Osama bin Laden on September the twelfth – and then the consequences as the scale of the atrocity grew clearer. Then the surreal speech by the new president, preposterous claims that had no place in a real-world briefing; he'd thought Mr. Cheney was mad for half an hour, until the chairman of the Joint Chiefs came on-screen on CNN, gloomily confirming that the rabbit hole the new president had jumped down was in fact not a rabbit hole at all, but a giant looming cypher like an alien black monolith suddenly arrived in the middle of the national landscape –

And then the India–Pakistan war, and its attendant horrors, and the other lesser reality excursions – the Israeli nuclear strike on Bushehr, the riots and massacres in Iraq, China's ballistic nuclear submarine putting to sea with warheads loaded and the tense stand-off in the Formosa Strait – and then the looking-glass world had shattered, breaking out of its frame: the PAPUA Act, arrests of radicals and cells of suspected parallel-universe sympathizers, slower initiatives to bring forward a national biometric identity database, frightening rumors about the military tribunals at Guantánamo that had so abruptly dropped out of the headlines –

One day, after a couple of apocalyptic weeks, Agent Judt wasn't there anymore. And when a couple of days later the president had his third and fatal heart attack and there was a *new* president, one who spoke of *known unknowns* and *unknown unknowns* and seemed to think Dr. Strangelove was an aspirational role model, there was a new reality on the ground. The country had gone mad, Steve thought, traumatized and whiplashed by meaningless attacks: 9/11 and strange religious fanatics in the Middle East had been bad enough, but what was coming next? Flying saucers on the White House lawn? Not that there was any White House lawn for them to land on, anymore. (President Cheney had promised to rebuild, once the radiation died down, but that would take months or years.)

Two weeks after the attack, Steve went to see his HMO and came away with a prescription for Seroxat. It helped, a bit; which was why, on his way home from a day shift one evening, he was alert enough to realize he was being followed.

Downtown Boston was no place to commute on wheels. Like most locals, Steve relied on the T to get him in and out, leaving his truck in a car park beside a station. He didn't usually pay much attention to his fellow passengers – no more than enough to spot a seat and keep a weather eye open for rare-to-nonexistent muggers – but as he got off a Green Line streetcar at Kenmore to change lines something drew his attention to a man stepping off the carriage behind him. Something familiar about the figure, glimpsed briefly through the crowd of bodies, triggered a rush of unease. Steve shivered despite the muggy heat and hurried across the tracks behind the streetcar, heading for his own platform. *It can't be him,* he told himself. *He spooked and ran.* He looked around behind him, but the half-recognized man wasn't there anymore.

What to do? Steve shook his head and hunkered down, waiting for the C Line train to North Station.

He knew something was wrong about five seconds after his train began to squeal and shudder away from the platform; knew it from the hairs on the back of his neck and the slight dip of his seat as the man behind him leaned forward, putting his weight on the seat back. 'Hello, Steve.'

He tensed. 'What do you want?' It was hot in the streetcar, but the skin in the small of his back felt icy cold.

'I'm getting off at the next stop; don't try to follow me. I think you

536

might like to have a look at these files. There's an e-mail address; mail me when you want to talk again.' A cheap plastic folder bulging with papers thrust over the seat back beside him like an accusing affidavit. He caught it before it spilled to the floor.

'What if I don't want to talk to you?' he asked.

The man behind him laughed quietly. 'Give it to your FBI handler. He'll shit a brick.'

The streetcar slowed; Steve, too frightened to look round as the man behind him stood up, clutched the folio to his chest. *Jesus, I can't just let him get away –*

The doors opened with a hiss of compressed air. Steve began to turn, caution chiding him – *He might be armed* – but he was too late. Mike Fleming, Beckstein's friend, had disappeared again. Steve subsided with another shudder. *Fleming knows too damn much,* he thought. He'd known about 7/16 before it happened. *What if he was telling the truth? What if it's an inside job?* The prospect was unutterably terrifying. The looking-glass world news nightmare that had engulfed everything around him a month ago was bad enough; the idea that there really was a conspiracy behind it, and his own government shared responsibility for it, left Steve feeling sick. This was a job for Woodward and Bernstein, not him. But Bob Woodward was dead – one of the casualties of 7/16 – and as for the rest of it, there was no one else to do whatever needed doing. *I could phone Agent Judt,* he told himself. *I could.*

A week or two ago, before the latest wave of chaos, he'd probably have done so immediately. But the end-times chaos of the past month had unhinged his reflexive loyalty to authority just as surely as it had reinforced that of millions of others. He unzipped the folio and glanced inside quickly. There was a cover sheet, laser-printed; he began reading.

It is a little-known fact that, contrary to public mythology, the president of the United States of America lacks the authority to order a strategic nuclear attack. Ever since the dog days of the Nixon administration, when the drunken president periodically phoned his diminishing circle of friends at 3:00 A.M. to rail incoherently about the urgent need to nuke North Vietnam, the executive branch has made every effort to ensure that any such decision can only be made stone-cold sober and after a lengthy period of soul-searching contemplation. An elaborate protocol exists: A series of cabinet meetings, consultations with the Joint Chiefs, discussions with the Senate Armed Services Committee, and quite possibly divine intervention, a UN Security Council Resolution, and the sacrifice of a black goat in the Oval Office at midnight are required before such a grave step can even be placed on the table for discussion.

However . . .

Retaliation after an attack is *much* easier.

If the former vice president put the plan in motion, diverted superblack off-budget funds to the Family Trade Organization, jogged Mr. Bush's elbow to sign the presidential orders setting in motion the research program to build machines around slivers of vivisected neural tissue extracted from the brains of captured Clan world-walkers, then perhaps the blame might be laid at his door. But it was his successor in the undisclosed location, former mentor and then vice president by appointment, who organized the details of the strike and bullied the Joint Chiefs into drafting new orders for USSTRATCOM tasking them with a mission enabled by the new ARMBAND technology. And it was the Office of the White House Counsel who drafted legal opinions approving the use of nuclear weapons in strict retaliation against an extradimensional threat, confirming that domestic law did not apply to parallel instances of North American geography, and that the two still-missing SADM demolition devices were necessary and sufficient justification: that such an operation constituted a due and proportionate response in accordance with international law, and that the Geneva Conventions did not apply beyond the ends of the Earth.

Complicity spread like a brown, stinking cloud through the traumatized rump of a Congress and Senate who were themselves the survivors of a lethal attack on the Capitol. President Cheney had ensured that the opposition would vote the way they were told; the PAPUA bill was as efficient an enabling act as had been seen anywhere in the world since 1933. A few dissenters – pacifists and peaceniks mostly – spoke out against the far-reaching surveillance and monitoring regime, but the press and the public were in no mood to put up with their rubbish about the First, Second, and Fourth Amendments; with the nation clearly under attack, who cared if a few whining hippie rejects talked themselves into a holiday in Club Fed? Better that than risk them giving aid and comfort to enemy infiltrators with stolen nukes. Rolling out the new identity-card system and national DNA database would take a couple of years, and until it was in place there'd always be the risk that the person walking past you in the street was a soldier of the invisible enemy. An eager Congress voted an ever-increasing laundry list of surveillance and control orders through with unanimous consent, each representative terrified of being seen to be weak on security.

And when the president went before the House Armed Services Committee in secret session to present certain legal opinions and request their imprimatur upon his war plans – the full House having already voted to declare war on whoever had attacked the capital city – nobody dared argue that they were excessive.

*

Midmorning in Gloucestershire, England. It was a bright day at Fairford, and behind the high barbed-wire-topped fence the air base was a seething hive of activity. Officially a British Royal Air Force base,

Fairford had for decades now provided a secure forward operating base for USAF aircraft staging out to the Arabian Gulf. Newly upgraded to provide a jumping-off point for operations in Iraq, boasting recently improved fuel bunkers and a runway so long that it was designated as a Space Shuttle transatlantic abort landing strip, for three weeks Fairford had been playing host to the B-52s of the Fifth Bomb Wing, USAF.

The Clan couldn't reach them in England, ran the official thinking. Not without international travel on forged documents.

Now they were queueing up on the taxiways: The aircraft of the Fifth Bomb Wing had been ordered to fly home. But first they were going to make a little detour.

For the past week, C-17s had been flying in nightly from Stateside, carrying anonymous-looking low-loaders, which were driven to the bomb storage cells and unloaded under the guns of twitchy guards. And for the past two days technicians had been double- and triple-checking the weapons, nervously working through the ringbound manuals. Yesterday there'd been a hiatus; but in the evening the ordnance crews had turned out again, and this time they were moving the bombs out to the dispersal bays, under guard. Finally, around midnight, a last C-17 arrived, carrying a group of specialists and a trailer that, over the following hours, made the rounds of the readying air wing.

Nobody outside the base saw a thing. The British authorities could take a hint; the small and dispirited huddle of protesters, camped by the front gate to denounce the carpet-bombers of Baghdad, had been rounded up in a midnight raid and hauled off to police cells under the Terrorism Act, to be held for weeks without counsel or charge. The village nearby was cowed by a military police presence that hadn't been seen since the height of the Troubles: Newspaper editors received discreet visits from senior police officers that left them tight-lipped and shaken. Fairford, to all intents and purposes, had vanished from the map.

At 11:00 A.M. Zulu time, the first of thirty-six B-52H Stratofortresses ran its engines up to full throttle and began its takeoff roll.

It was a hot day, and the huge plane's wing tanks were gravid with jet fuel; it climbed slowly away, shaking the ground with a bellowing thunder like the onrushing end of the world.

*

The Atlantic Ocean was wide, and the jet streams blowing west-to-east over Ireland slowed the bombers as they climbed towards their cruising altitude of forty-eight thousand feet, miles above the air corridors used by the regular midmorning stream of airliners heading west from the major European and Asian hubs. The operations planners had seen no reason to warn or divert those airliners; when CARTHAGE was complete they would, if anything, be safer.

Over the next seven hours the BUFFs shadowed the daily commuter herd, tracking along the great circle route that took them just south of Greenland's icy hinterlands before turning south towards Newfoundland and then on towards Maine. As they neared the coast, the bombers diverged briefly from the civil aviation corridor, skirting around Canadian airspace and then flying parallel to the regular traffic, but farther east, staying over deep water for as long as possible. It was more than just the diplomatic nicety of keeping aircraft engaged on this mission out of foreign airspace: If anything should go catastrophically wrong, better that the cargo should ditch in the Atlantic waters than come down over land.

As they passed the southernmost end of Nova Scotia, the bombers finally turned west. The final encrypted transmission came in: Meteorological conditions over the target were perfect. Downstairs from the pilot and copilot, the defensive-systems operators were busy at last, running the activation checklist on their ARMBAND units – gray boxes, bolted hastily to the equipment racks lining the dark cave of the bomber's lower deck – and the differential GPS receivers to which they were connected by raw, hand-soldered wiring looms. Meanwhile, their offensive systems operators were running checklists of their own; checklists that required the pilot and copilot's cooperation, reading out numbers from sealed envelopes held in a safe on the flight deck.

*

A hundred miles due east of Portland, the bomber crews completed their checklists. It was nearing three o'clock in the afternoon on the eastern seaboard when they lined up. At a range of fifty miles, the largest city in Maine was spread out before them, glittering beneath the cloudless summer sky. An observer on the ground who knew what they were looking at – one with very sharp eyes, or a pair of binoculars – would have seen a loosely spaced queue of aircraft, cruising in echelon far higher than normal airliners. But there were no such observers. Nor did the civilian air traffic control have anything to say in the presence of the FBI agents who had dropped in on them an hour ago.

Overhead, without any fuss, the bombers were going out.

*

Another day, another world.

In the marcher kingdoms of the North American eastern seaboard, life went on. A frontal system moving in from the north was bringing cooler, denser air southeast from Lake Ontario, and a scattering of high cloud cover warned of rainfall by evening. The daily U-2 reconnaissance overflight had reported a strong offshore breeze blowing, carrying dust and smoke out to sea; it was expected to continue for at least twenty-four hours.

The wheat harvest was all but over, and rye, too; the peasants were still laboring with sickle and adze in their strip fields, and the granaries were filling, but an end to toil was in sight. Their lords and masters busied themselves with the summer hunt, wild boar and deer fat and heavy; the season of late-summer parties was in swing, as eligible daughters were paraded around before their fathers' friends' sons, and barons and dukes sought surcease from the stink of the cities by touring their estates and the houses of their vassals.

There was quiet unrest too. Among the hedge-lords, whispered rumor spoke of the upstart tinker families becoming absent neighbors. Houses were mysteriously empty, houses that had weathered the campaign by the late pretender and survived the subsequent wave of murders that had engulfed the Clan. Some spoke of strangeness; families with children sent away, the parents' bright-eyed cheer

542

covering some grim foreboding. Rumors of tinker Clansmen in their cups maundering about the *end of the world*, grumbling about absent cousins trying to run before the storm surge while they, the heroic drunk, chose to stand firm against the boiling wave crests –

And the queen, Prince Creon's widowed pregnant wife, had not been seen in public for nearly two months.

The queen's absence was not in and of itself remarkable – she was pregnant, and a retreat from court engagements was not unexpected – but the totality of it attracted notice. She hadn't been seen by *anyone* except, it appeared, her mother. The dowager duchess (herself mysteriously absent for a period of decades) was in residence in Niejwein in one of the Clan's less badly damaged great houses, busying herself with the restoration of the Summer Palace (or rather, with commencing its reconstruction from the ground up, for its charred beams and shattered stones would not be fit for habitation anytime soon). And *she* had seen her daughter the queen-widow, and loudly testified to that effect – to her bouts of morning sickness and desire for seclusion. But. The queen hadn't been seen in public for weeks now, and people were asking questions. Where was she?

Now, high above the thin mares' tails, a curious thing can be seen in the heavens.

A row of strange straight clouds are rushing across the vault of the sky, quite unlike anything anyone remembers seeing in times gone by. True, for the past month or so the witch-clouds have been glimpsed from time to time, racing crisscross from east to west – but only one at a time.

Today, two rows of knife-straight clouds are ploughing southwest, as if an invisible god has drawn two eighteen-toothed combs across the horizon, one comb flying two thousand feet above the other. They cover the dome of the sky from side to side, for they are not close together; a knowledgeable observer would count twelve miles between teeth.

Flying just ahead of each tine is a B-52H Stratofortress of Fifth Bomb Wing, Eighth Air Force, Air Combat Command. Thirty-five out of thirty-six aircraft carry in each of their two bomb bays a rotary dispenser containing six B83 free-fall hydrogen bombs. The remaining bomber is gravid with a single device, a monstrous B53-Y1, a bloated cylinder that weighs over four tons and fills the BUFF's central bomb bay completely. This aircraft flies near the eastern edge of the upper group. It is intended to deliver the president's signature message to the enemy capital: shock and awe.

*

The track from Kirschford down to the Linden Valley was clear of tinker-lord traffic this afternoon. The flow of refugees had slackened to a trickle, for those who wanted to evacuate had for the most part already left. Helena voh Wu and her infants and sister-in-law had come this way a week before; while Gyorg was still occupied with the corvée, shuttling supplies between anonymous storage lockups in Boston and wine cellars in the Gruinmarkt, his dependents had achieved the tenuous sanctuary of a refugee camp in New Britain.

So none of them paused to look up, slack-jawed, as the first wave of bombers commenced their laydown.

A B83 hydrogen bomb isn't very large; it weighs about a ton, and looks exactly like most other air-dropped bombs. The weapons the Fifth Bomb Wing were delivering were equipped with parachutes which retarded their descent from altitude, so that it would take each bomb more than three minutes to descend to its detonation altitude of twenty thousand feet. Flying parallel courses twelve miles apart, the aircraft began to drop their payload at one-minute intervals, seeding a furrow of hells at twelve mile intervals. The distance between bombs was important; any closer, and the heat flash might ignite the Kevlar ribbon 'chutes of the other weapons.

Three minutes and twenty seconds. The trails arrowed south across the sky of the Gruinmarkt, a faint rumble of distant thunder disturbing the afternoon quiet; and then the sky lit up as the first row of eighteen hydrogen bombs, spanning the kingdom from sea to inland frontier, detonated at an altitude of just under four miles.

The flash of a single one-megaton hydrogen bomb is followed by a fireball which dims over a period of nearly a minute. It is visible in good weather at a range of hundreds of miles – light from the flash is scattered by particles in the upper atmosphere, reflected around the curve of the earth. To an observer in Niejwein, the capital city located nearly two hundred miles south of the first row, the northern horizon would have begun to flicker and brighten as if a gigantic match had been held to the edge of the map. There was no sound; there would be no sound for many minutes, for even though the shock waves from the detonations overtook the bombers, it would take a long time for the attenuated noise to reach the capital.

To an observer located closer to the bombing line, it would have been the end of the world.

The heat flash from a B83 detonating at twenty thousand feet is sufficient, in good weather, to ignite cardboard or cotton sheeting, heat damp pine needles to smoldering tinder, and char wood and flesh six miles from ground zero. The leading row of eighteen bombers were spaced close enough that over open ground no spot could remain unseared; only in the lee slope of a steep valley, or the depths of a cellar or cave, was there any hope of survival.

Peasants working in the fields might have glanced up as the sky flashed white above them; it would have been the last thing they saw through rapidly clouding eyes. Their skin reddened and crisped as the grain stubble and trees around them began to smoke; screaming and stumbling for cover, they blundered towards their houses or the tree line, limned in the flaring red burn of a billion leaves igniting simultaneously. There were some survivors of the initial flash: women spinning thread or weaving cloth indoors, millers tending their wheels, even a lucky few sitting behind dry-stone walls or swimming in cool water pools. But as they looked up in confusion they saw the same thing in every direction around them: trees, plants, buildings, even cattle and people smoking and flaming.

And then the hammer-blast of red-hot wind arrived from above, slamming into hedges and walls alike and splintering all before them.

The aircrew saw nothing of this. They flew on instruments, insulated blackout screens drawn across the cockpit windows to prevent reflected light from blinding them. Perhaps they glanced at one another as shock waves buffeted the tail surfaces of the bombers, bumping and dropping them before the pilots regained full control authority; but if they did so, it was with no sympathy for the unseen carnage below. A president had been killed, tens of thousands murdered by emissaries from this world; their word for the task they were engaged in was *payback*.

Seventy seconds later, the second row of H-bombs reached their preset altitude and began to detonate, flashbulbs popping erratically on a wire two hundred and fifty miles wide. And seventy seconds after that, the process continued, weeping tears of incandescence across the burning coastline.

There were a lot of flashes.

*

It took the aircraft nearly twelve minutes to reach Niejwein, two-thirds of the way through their carpet-bombing run. And here, there were witnesses. Niejwein, with a population of nearly sixty thousand souls, was the biggest city within four hundred miles; proud palaces and high-roofed temples rose above a sprawling urban metropolis, home to dozens of trades and no fewer than four markets. And the people of Niejwein had due notice. The flickering brightness on the horizon had been growing for almost a quarter hour; and lately there had been a rumbling in the ground, an uneasy shuddering as if Lightning Child himself was shifting, uneasy in his bed of clay. A strange hot wind had set the bells of the temple of Sky Father clanging, bringing the priests stumbling from their sanctuary to squint at the northern lights in disbelief and shock.

In the Thorold Palace, some of the residents realized what was happening.

At midafternoon, the Dowager Duchess Patricia was holding court, sitting in formal session in the east wing of the palace to hear petitions on behalf of her daughter. A merchant, Freeman Riss of Somewhere-Bridge, was bringing a complaint about the lord of his nearest market town, who, either in a fit of pique or for some reason Freeman Riss was reticent about disclosing, had banned said merchant from selling his wares in the weekly market.

At another time, this complaint might well have interested Dame Patricia as much for its value as leverage against the earl in question as for its merit as a case. But it was a hot afternoon, and sitting in the stiff robes of state beneath a row of stained-glass windows which dammed the air and cast flickering multicolored shadows across the bench before her, she was prone to distraction.

Riss was reciting, in a scratchy voice as if from memory, 'And I deponeth thus, that on the third feastday of Sister Corn, the laird did send his armsmen to stand before my drover and his oxen and say – '

Patricia raised a shaky hand. 'Stop,' she said. Freeman Riss paused, his mouth open. 'Surcease, we pray you.' She squinted up at the windows. They were flickering. 'We declare a recess. Your indulgence is requested, for we are feeling unwell.' She closed her eyes briefly. *I hope it isn't another attack,* she worried; the MS hadn't affected her vision so far, but her legs had been largely numb all week, and the prickling in her hands was worsening. 'Sergeant-at-arms – '

There was a banging and clattering from outside the room. The courtiers and plaintiffs began to talk, just as the door burst open. It was Helmut ven Rindt, lord-lieutenant and commander of the second troop of the Clan's security force, accompanied by six soldiers. Their camouflage surcoats sat uneasy above machine-woven titanium mail. 'Your grace? I regret the need to interrupt you, but you are urgently required elsewhere.'

'Really?' Iris stared at Helmut. *Not you, too?* The clenching in her gut was bad.

'Yes, your grace. If I may approach' – she nodded; Helmut stepped towards her raised seat, then continued to speak, quietly, in English – 'we lost all radio access nine minutes ago. There's nothing but static, and there are very bright lights on the northern horizon. Counting them and checking the decay curves, it's megaton-range and getting closer. With your permission, we're going to evacuate *right now.*'

'Yes, you go on.' She nodded approvingly, then did a slow double take as one of Helmut's troops marched forward. 'Hey – '

The soldier bent to lift her from her throne in a fireman's carry.

Instant uproar among the assembled courtiers, nobles, and tradesmasters assembled in the room. 'Stop him!' cried one unfortunate, a young earl from somewhere out to the northwest. 'He laid hands on her grace!'

That did it. As the soldier lifted Patricia, she saw a flurry of bodies moving towards the throne, past the open floor of the chamber, which by custom was not entered without the chair's consent. 'Hey!' she repeated.

Helmut grimaced: 'Earl-Major Riordan's orders, your grace, you and any other family we set eyes on. We are to leave none alive behind, and you'll not make a family-killer of me.' Louder: 'To the evac cellar, lads! Double time!'

The young earl, perhaps alarmed at the unfamiliar sound of Anglischprache, moved a hand to his hip. 'For queen and country!' he shouted, and drew, lunging towards Helmut. Four more nobles were scarcely a step behind, all of them armed.

For palace guard duty, in the wake of the recent civil disorder, Earl-Major Riordan had begun to reequip his men with FN P90s. A stubby, melted-looking device little larger than a flintlock pistol, the P90 was an ultracompact submachine gun, designed for special forces and armored vehicle crews. Helmut's men were so equipped, and as the misguided young blood ran at them they opened fire. Unlike a traditional submachine gun, the P90 fired low-caliber armor-piercing rounds at a prodigious rate from a large magazine. In the stone-walled hall, the detonations merged into a continuous concussive rasp. They fired for three seconds: sufficient to spray nearly two hundred rounds into the crowd from less than thirty feet.

As the sudden silence rang in Patricia's numb and aching ears her abductor shuffled forward, carefully managing his footing as he slid across blood-slick flagstones. The wounded and dying were moaning and screaming distantly in her ears, behind the thick cotton-wool wadding that seemed to fill her head. The light began to flicker beyond the windows again, this time brightening the daylight perceptibly. Helmut led the way to the door, raising his own weapon as his guards discarded their empty magazines and reloaded; then he ducked through into the next reception room. Patricia looked down from the shoulder of her bearer, into the staring eyes of a dead master of stonemasons. He sprawled beside a lady-in-waiting, or the wife of a baron's younger son. *My people,* she thought distantly. *Mother dearest wanted me to look after them.*

They stumbled out of the cloister around the palace into the sunlit afternoon of a summer's day, onto the tidily manicured lawn within the walled grounds. Something was wrong with the shadows, she noticed, watching Helmut's feet: There were too many suns in the sky. 'Don't look up,' he shouted, loudly enough that she couldn't help but hear him and raise her eyes briefly. *Too many suns.*

The northern wall of the palace grounds was silhouetted with the deepest black, long shadows etched across the grass towards her, flickering and brightening and dimming. A moment of icy terror twisted at her guts as she saw that Helmut and his guard were hurrying towards one of the smaller outbuildings ahead. Its doorway gaped open on darkness. 'What's that?' she asked.

'Gatehouse. There's a cellar, doppelgängered.'

She saw other figures crawling antlike across the too-bright lawn. *Nukes*, she realized. *They must be using* all *the nukes.* For a moment she felt every second of her sixty-two years. 'Put me down,' she called.

'No.' The response came from Helmut. Her bearer was panting hard, all but jogging. Her weight on his back was shoving him down: He had no more breath to reply than any other servant might.

They were nearly at the building. Helmut hung back, gestured at her rescuer. '*Now*,' he snarled. 'Drop her and *go*.'

The man let Patricia slide to the ground, twisting to lay her down, then without pause rose and dashed forward to the entrance. Helmut knelt beside her. 'Do you want to die?' he asked, politely enough.

Behind him the sky cracked open again. Getting closer. She licked dry lips. 'No,' she admitted. 'But I deserve to.'

'Lots of people do. It has nothing to do with their fate.' He slid an arm beneath her and, grunting, levered her up off the ground and into his arms. 'Arms round my neck.' He stumbled forward, into the darkness, following his men – who hadn't bothered to wait.

'I failed them,' she confessed as Helmut's boots thudded on the steps down into the cellar. 'We drew this down on them.'

'They're not our people. They never were.' He grunted again, reaching the bottom. 'We're not part of them, any more than we were part of the Anglischprache who're coming to kill us. And if you reached your age without learning that, you're a fool.'

'But we had a duty – ' She stopped, a stab of grim amusement penetrating the oppressive miasma of guilt. It was the same old argument, liberal versus conservative by any other name. 'Let's finish this later.'

'*Now* she talks sense.' There was an overhead electric light at the bottom, dangling from the top of the vaulted arch of the ceiling. The stonework grumbled faintly, dislodging a shower of plaster and whitewash dust; shadows rippled as the bulb shivered on the end of its cord. Someone had nailed a poster-sized sheet of laminated paper against the wall, bearing an intricate knotwork design that made her eyes hurt. Helmut stepped forward onto the empty circle chalked on the floor. The guards had already crossed over. 'I'll carry your grace,' he told her. Then he turned to face the family sigil and focus.

'I'm not your grace anymore,' Iris tried to say; but neither of them were there anymore when she finished the sentence.

*

Sixty miles north of Niejwein, the first wave of B-52s finished unloading their rotary dispensers. Their crews breathed a sigh of relief as they threw the levers to close their bomb-bay doors, and the DSOs began the checklist to reactivate their ARMBAND devices for the second and final time. Behind them, the second wave of bombers smoothly took their place in the bomb line.

One of them, the plane with the single device in its front bay, flew straight toward the enemy city. With the target confirmed in visual range, her DSO keyed a radio transmitter – a crude, high-powered low-bandwidth signal that would punch through the static hash across the line of sight to the other aircraft in the force. To either side, the formation split, the neighboring aircraft following prearranged courses to give it a wide berth. Twelve miles was an acceptable safety margin for a one-megaton weapon, but not for the device this aircraft carried.

('I'm going to send them a message,' the president had said. 'Who?' his chief of staff replied, an ironic tilt to his eyebrow. 'The Russians.' The president smirked. 'Who did you think I meant?')

The single huge bomb crammed into the special bomber's bay was a B53; at nine megatons, the largest H-bomb ever fielded by the US military: a stubby cylinder the size of a pickup truck. The bomber rose sharply as the B53 fell away from the bomb bay. A sequence of parachutes burst from its tail, finally expanding into three huge canopies as its carrier aircraft closed its bay doors and the flight crew ran the engines up to full thrust, determined to clear the area as fast as possible.

To either side of the heavyweight, the megaton bursts continued – a raster burn of blowtorch flames chewing away at the edge of the world. Behind the racing bomber force the sky was a wall of darkness pitted with blazing rage, domed clouds expanding and rising and flaring and dimming with monotonous precision every few seconds. The ground behind the nuclear frontal system was blackened and charred, thousands of square miles of forest and field caught in a single vast firestorm as the separate waves of incineration fanning out from each bomb intersected and reinforced each other. The winds rushing into the zone were already strengthening towards hurricane force; the bombers struggled against an unexpected sixty-knot jet stream building from the south.

Beneath its parachutes, the bulbous B53 slowly descended towards the city. The strobing flare of distant apocalypses flashed ruby highlights across its burnished shell as it twisted in the wind, drifting towards the roof of a well-to-do carpenter's house on the Sheepmarket Street to the south of the city. The carpenter and his wife and apprentices were standing outside, staring at the horizon in gape-jawed dismay. 'If it be a thunderstorm it's an unseasonal huge one,' he told his wife. 'Better fetch in your washing – ' He whirled at the crashing and crunching from the roof. 'Who did that!' Instant rage caught him as he saw the deflating dome of a white parachute descend across the yard. 'If that be your idea of a prank, Pitr – '

Niejwein, population just under sixty thousand, two and a half miles by one and a quarter, Niejwein, capital of the Gruinmarkt – all gone.

Wiped away as if a bullet had slammed through a map pasted across a target.

Niejwein: home to just under sixty thousand artisans and trades-men and their families, and almost two hundred aristocrats and their servants and hangers-on, and previously home to as many as ninety members of the Clan – of whom only eleven remained at this point – all brought to a laser-bright end by a flash of light from the heart of a star.

The boiling, turbulent fireball resulting from the surface laydown expanded in a fraction of a second until it was over a mile in diam-eter. At its periphery, the temperature was over a hundred thousand degrees: Stone-boiled, the bodies of man and animal flashed into vapor. A short distance beyond it – out to five miles – the heat was enough to melt iron structures. Castles and palaces only a mile or two beyond the fireball, be their walls made of stone and never so thick as a man's body, slumped and then shattered on the shock wave like houses of cards before a hand grenade.

There would be no survivors in Niejwein. Indeed, there could have been no survivors in the open within fifteen miles, had not the other bombers of the strike force continued to plow their fields with the fires of hell.

It was not the intention of the planners who designed Operation CARTHAGE to leave *any* survivors, even in subsurface cellars.

The firestorm raged steadily down the coast, marching at the pace of a speeding jet bomber. Behind it, the clouds boiled up into the stratosphere, taking with them tens of millions of tons of radioactive ash and dust. Already the sun was paling behind the funeral pyre.

In the aftermath, the people of the Gruinmarkt might well be the luckiest of all. It was their fate to be gone in a flash or burned in a fire: a brief agony, compared with the chill and starvation that were to follow all around their world.

*

Huw was in the shed near the far end of the vegetable garden, tight-ening the straps on his pressure suit, when Brilliana found him.

'What in Sky Father's name do you think you're doing?' she demanded.

She was, Huw realized abstractedly, even more pretty when she

552

was angry: the brilliant beauty of a lightning-edged thundercloud. Not even the weird local fashions she wore in this place could change that. He straightened up. 'What does it look like I'm doing?'

Yul chipped in: 'He's getting ready to – '

Brill turned on him. 'Shut up and get out,' she said flatly, her voice dangerously overcontrolled.

'But he needs me to – '

'*Out!*' She waved her fist at him.

'Give us some space, bro,' Huw added. 'Don't worry, she won't shoot me without a trial.'

'You think so?' She waited, fists on hips, until Hulius vacated the shed and the door scraped shut behind him. 'You're not going to do this, Huw. I forbid it.'

'*Someone* has to do it,' he pointed out. 'I've got the equipment and, more importantly, the experience to go into an uncharted world.'

'It's *not* an uncharted world, it's *our* world. And you're not going. You don't need to go. That's an order.'

'You're not supposed to give me orders – '

'Then it's an order from Helge – '

' – Isn't she busy visiting her special friend in New London right now?'

Brill glared at him. 'It *will* be one, as soon as I tell her. Don't think I won't!'

'But if the Americans – '

'*Listen* to me!' She stepped in front of him, standing on her toes until he couldn't help but see eye-to-eye with her. 'We got a report.'

'Oh?' Huw backed down. Heroic reconnaissance into the unknown was one thing, but wasting resources was something else. 'Who from? What's happened?'

'Patricia's guards came across. They wired us a report and Brionne's only just decrypted it. They were in the palace when the sky lit up, the entire horizon north of Niejwein. Helmut reported at least thirty thermonuclear detonations lighting up over the horizon, probably many more of them, getting progressively closer over the ten minutes before he issued the order to evacuate. They were carpet-bombing with H-bombs. *Now* do you understand why you're not crossing over?'

Huw looked puzzled. 'How do you know they were H-bombs?'

'Hello?' Brill's nostrils flared as she squinted at him. 'They lit up the sky from over the horizon *in clear daylight* and they took a minute to fade! What else do you think they might be?'

'Oh.' After a moment, Huw unbuckled the fastener on his left glove. 'More than thirty of them? Coming towards Niejwein?'

Brill nodded mutely.

'Oh.' He sat down heavily on the stool he'd been using while Yul helped him into the explorer's pressure suit. 'Oh shit.' He paused. 'We'll have to go back eventually.'

'Yes. But not in the middle of a firestorm. It was only a couple of hours ago.'

'There's a firestorm?'

'What do *you* think?'

'We're stranded here.'

'Full marks, my pretty one.'

Huw looked up at her. 'My parents were going to evacuate; I should find out if they made it in time. What about your – '

She avoided his eyes. 'What do you think?'

'I'm sorry – '

'Don't be.' She made a cutting gesture, but her eyes seemed to glisten in the afternoon light filtered through the hazy window glass. 'I burned my bridges with my father years ago. And my mother would never think to stand up to him. *He* told her to stop writing to me. I've been dead to them for years.'

'But if they're – '

'Shut up and think about your brother, Huw. At least you've got Yul. How do you think he feels?'

'He – ' Huw worked at the chin strap of his helmet. 'Damn. Where's Elena? Is she – '

'Turn your head. This way.' She knelt and worked the strap loose, then unclipped it. Huw lifted the helmet off. 'Better.' She straightened up. A moment later Huw rose to his feet. He stood uncertainly before her. 'I last saw Elena half an hour ago.'

'Sky Father be praised.'

'That's one way of putting it.' She watched him uncertainly. 'Do you understand what's happening to us?'

Huw took a breath. 'No,' he admitted. 'You're sure they were hydrogen bombs – '

'Denial and half a shilling will get you a cup of coffee, Huw.'

'Then we're all orphans. Even those of us whose parents came along.'

'Yes.' Brill choked back an ugly laugh. 'Those of us who haven't been orphaned all along.'

'But you haven't been – ' He stopped. 'Uh. I was going to ask you to, uh, but this is the wrong time.'

'Huw.' She was, she realized, standing exactly the wrong distance away from him: not close enough, not far enough. 'I didn't hear that. If you were going to say what I think you meant to say. Yes, it's the wrong time for that.'

He swallowed, then looked at her. A moment later she was in his arms, hugging him fiercely.

'If we're orphans there's nobody to force us together or hold us apart,' he whispered in her ear. 'No braids, no arranged marriages, no pressure. We can do what we want.'

'Maybe,' she said, resting her chin on his shoulder. 'But don't underestimate the power of ghosts. And external threats.'

'There are no ghosts strong enough to scare me away from you.'

His sincerity scared her at the same time as it enthralled her. She twisted away from his embrace. 'I need some time to myself,' she said. 'Time to mourn. Time to grow.'

He nodded. A shadow crossed his face. 'Yes.'

'We don't know what we're getting into,' she warned.

'True.' He nodded, then looked away and began to work at the fasteners on his pressure suit.

She paused, one hand on the doorknob. 'You didn't ask me your question,' she said, wondering if it was the right thing to do.

'I didn't?' He looked up, confused, then closed his mouth. 'Oh. But it's the wrong time. Your parents – '

'They're dead. Ask me anyway.' She forced a smile. 'Assuming we're not talking at cross-purposes.'

'Oh! All right.' He took a deep breath. 'My lady. Will you marry me?' Not the normal turn of phrase, which was more along the lines of *May I take your daughter's hand in marriage?*

'I thought you'd never ask,' she said.

'But I thought you – ' He shook his head. 'Forgive me, I'm slow.'

'I'm an orphan, over the age of majority,' she reminded him. 'No estates, no guardians, no braids, no dowry. You know I don't come with so much as a clipped groat or a peasant's plot?'

'Do I look like I care?'

She walked back towards him; they met halfway across the floor of the hut. 'No. But I wasn't certain.'

'For you, my lady' – they leaned together – 'I'd willingly go over the wall.' To defect from the Clan, to voluntarily accept outlawry and exile: It was not a trivial offer.

'You don't need to,' she murmured. She kissed him, hard, on the mouth: not for the first time, but for the first time on these new terms, with no thought of concealment. 'Nobody now alive in this world will gainsay us.' Her knees felt weak at the thought. 'Not my father, nor your mother.' Even if his mother had lived to enter this exile, she was unlikely to reject any Clan maid her son brought before her, however impoverished; they were, indeed, all orphans, all destitute. 'No need to fear a blood feud anymore. All the Clan's chains are rusted half away.'

'I wonder how long it'll take the others to realize? And what will they all do when they work it out . . . ?'

EPILOGUE

BEGIN RECORDING

'My fellow Americans, good evening.

'It is two months since the cowardly and evil attack on our great
nation. Two months since the murder of the president along
with eighteen thousand more of our fellow citizens. Two months
since my predecessor and friend stood here with tears in his eyes
and iron determination in his soul, to promise you that we
would bring prompt and utter annihilation to the enemies who
struck at us without warning.

'Many of you doubted my predecessor's word when he spoke of
other worlds. He spoke of things that have been unknown –
indeed, of unknown unknowns – threats to the very existence of
our nation that we knew absolutely nothing of, threats so serious
that the instability of the Middle East, or the bellicosity of Russia,
dwindle into insignificance in comparison. The horrific tragedy
that unfolded between India and Pakistan last month – and our
hearts go out to all the survivors of that extraordinary spasm of
international madness – demonstrates what is at stake here; as
long as hostile powers exist in other timelines that overlap our
geographical borders, we face the gravest of existential threats.

'But I am speaking to you tonight to tell you that one such
existential threat has been removed: Mr. Cheney's promise has
been carried out, and we shall all sleep safer in our beds tonight.

'At half past two this afternoon, aircraft of the Fifth Bomb Wing
overflew the land of the enemy who attacked us so savagely on
July the sixteenth. And I assure you that our enemies have just
reaped the crop that they sowed that day. Those that attacked us
with stolen nuclear weapons have received, in return, a just and

557

proportional measure of retribution. And they have learned what happens to assassins and murderers who attack this great nation. Gruinmarkt, the nest of world-walking thieves and narcoterrorists, is home to them no longer. We have taken the brand of cleansing fire and cauterized this lesion within our geographic borders. And they will not attack us again.

'This does not mean that the threat is over. We have learned that there exists a multiplicity of worlds in parallel to our own. Most of them are harmless, uninhabited and resource-rich. Some of them are inhabited; of these, a few may threaten our security. I have today issued an executive order to put in place institutions to seek out and monitor other worlds, to assess them for usefulness and threat – and to ensure that never again does an unseen enemy take us by surprise in this way. Over the coming weeks and months, I will work with Congress to establish funding for these agencies and to create a legislative framework to defend us from these threats.

'Good night, and God bless America.'

END RECORDING